STEPHEN JONES lives in London, England. He is the winner of three World Fantasy Awards, four Horror Writers Association Bram Stoker Awards, three International Horror Guild Awards and twenty-one British Fantasy Awards, as well as being a recipient of the HWA Lifetime Achievement Award and a Hugo Award nominee. A former television producer/director and genre movie publicist and consultant (the first three *Hellraiser* movies, *Nightbreed*, *Split Second*, etc.), he has written and edited more than 130 books, including *Coraline: A Visual Companion*, *Necronomicon: The Best Weird Tales of H. P. Lovecraft*, *The Essential Monster Movie Guide*, *Horror: 100 Best Books* and *Horror: Another 100 Best Books* (both with Kim Newman) and the *Dark Terrors*, *Dark Voices* and *The Mammoth Book of Best New Horror* series. A Guest of Honour at the 2002 World Fantasy Convention in Minneapolis, Minnesota, and the 2004 World Horror Convention in Phoenix, Arizona, he has been a guest lecturer at UCLA in California and London's Kingston University and St. Mary's University College. You can visit his website at *www.stephenjoneseditor.com*

PRAISE FOR *BEST NEW HORROR*

"*Best New Horror* is a darkly shining beacon of hope in an unimaginative world." **Neil Gaiman**

"From its inception, the *Best New Horror* series has been an invaluable resource for all of us who believe in the genre." **Clive Barker**

"An essential record, invaluable and irreplaceable, of modern horror fiction in all its range and variousness." **Ramsey Campbell**

"No self-respecting relisher of the macabre should ever deny him- or herself a copy." **Gahan Wilson**

"Anyone who is interested in the contemporary horror scene should buy a copy of this book and devour it." *The Times* (**London**)

"Jones' comprehensive coverage has become the horror genre's most important journalistic effort." *Locus*

"The best horror anthologist in the business is, of course, Stephen Jones." *Time Out*

"A worthy reflection of the diversity and high quality of contemporary horror and dark fantasy, this annual volume remains an absolute necessity." *Publishers Weekly* (starred review)

"The most valuable horror book of the year." *Kirkus Reviews*

Best New Horror 25

BEST NEW HORROR

VOLUME 25

Edited and with an Introduction by

STEPHEN JONES

A Herman Graf Book
Skyhorse Publishing

First published in the UK as The Mammoth Book
of Best New Horror 25 by Robinson, 2014

This edition published by Skyhorse Publishing, 2014

Collection and editorial material
Copyright © Stephen Jones, 2014

Skyhorse publishing books may be purchased in bulk at
special discounts for sales promotion, corporate gifts,
fund-raising, or educational purposes. Special editions
can also be created to specifications. For details, contact
the Special Sales Department, Skyhorse Publishing,
307 West 36th Street, 11th Floor, New York, New
York 10018 or info@skyhorsepublishing.com

www.skyhorsepublishing.com

10 9 8 7 6 5 4 3 2 1

ISBN: 978-1-62873-818-6

Printed and bound by CPI Group (UK) Ltd, Croydon, CR0 4YY

US Library of Congress Control Number is available on file

CONTENTS

xi
Acknowledgements

1
Introduction: Horror in 2013

91
Who Dares Wins: Anno Dracula 1980
KIM NEWMAN

108
Click-clack the Rattlebag
NEIL GAIMAN

113
Dead End
NICHOLAS ROYLE

124
Isaac's Room
DANIEL MILLS

139
The Burning Circus
ANGELA SLATTER

149
Holes for Faces
RAMSEY CAMPBELL

171
By Night He Could Not See
JOEL LANE

182
Come Into My Parlour
REGGIE OLIVER

201
The Middle Park
MICHAEL CHISLETT

213
Into the Water
SIMON KURT UNSWORTH

234
The Burned House
LYNDA E. RUCKER

246
What Do We Talk About When We Talk About Z—
LAVIE TIDHAR

251
Fishfly Season
HALLI VILLEGAS

263
Doll Re Mi
TANITH LEE

284
A Night's Work
CLIVE BARKER

287
The Sixteenth Step
ROBERT SHEARMAN

307
Stemming the Tide
SIMON STRANTZAS

315
The Gist
MICHAEL MARSHALL SMITH

351
Guinea Pig Girl
THANA NIVEAU

365
Miss Baltimore Crabs: Anno Dracula 1990
KIM NEWMAN

394
Whitstable
STEPHEN VOLK

507
Necrology: 2013
STEPHEN JONES & KIM NEWMAN

580
Useful Addresses

ACKNOWLEDGEMENTS

I would like to thank Kim Newman, Vincent Chong, Rodger Turner and Wayne MacLaurin (*sfsite.com*), Peter Crowther and Nicky Crowther, Ray Russell and Rosalie Parker, Gordon Van Gelder, Merrilee Heifetz and Sarah Nagel of Writers House, Mark Miller, Titan Books, Nicholas Royle, Andy Cox, Michael Kelly, David Longhorn, David Barraclough, Johnny Mains, Amanda Foubister, Andrew I. Porter, Mandy Slater and, especially, Duncan Proudfoot, Emily Byron, Clive Hebard, Una McGovern and Max Burnell for all their help and support. Special thanks are also due to *Locus*, *Ansible*, *Classic Images*, *Entertainment Weekly* and all the other sources that were used for reference in the Introduction and the Necrology.

published in *Nightmare: Horror & Dark Fantasy*, Issue 8, May 2013. Reprinted by permission of the author.

A NIGHT'S WORK copyright © Clive Barker 2013. Originally published in *The Bram Stoker Awards Weekend 2013 Incorporating World Horror Convention, New Orleans, LA, Souvenir Book*. Reprinted by permission of the author.

THE SIXTEENTH STEP copyright © Robert Shearman 2013. Originally published in *The Burning Circus: BFS Horror 1: An Anthology for British Fantasy Society Members*. Reprinted by permission of the author.

STEMMING THE TIDE copyright © Simon Strantzas 2013. Originally published in *Dead North: The Exile Book of Anthology Series, Number Eight: Canadian Zombie Fiction*. Reprinted by permission of the author.

THE GIST copyright © Michael Marshall Smith 2013. Originally published in *The Gist*. Reprinted by permission of the author.

GUINEA PIG GIRL copyright © Thana Niveau 2013. Originally published in *The Tenth Black Book of Horror*. Reprinted by permission of the author.

MISS BALTIMORE CRABS: ANNO DRACULA 1990 copyright © Kim Newman 2013. Originally published in *Anno Dracula 1976–1991: Johnny Alucard*. Reprinted by permission of the author.

WHITSTABLE copyright © Stephen Volk 2013. Originally published in *Whitstable*. Reprinted by permission of the author.

NECROLOGY: 2013 copyright © Stephen Jones and Kim Newman 2014.

USEFUL ADDRESSES copyright © Stephen Jones 2014.

For everyone who has appeared in Best New Horror
*over the past quarter of a century – and especially
in memory of those who are no longer with us.*

INTRODUCTION

Horror in 2013

IN EARLY 2013, the US Department of Justice approved the merger of mega-publishers Penguin/Pearson and Random House/Bertelsmann. Australia, New Zealand and the European Union followed and, in early July, Penguin Random House became the largest publishing company in the world.

Meanwhile, Hachette Book Group purchased most of the Hyperion adult backlist from Disney, including the imprint's name. The media-related and children's imprints were not included in the sale.

Independent American imprint Night Shade Books, which had been struggling for several years, was sold to print publisher Skyhorse Publishing and digital publisher Start Publishing in June after some authors agreed to give up additional rights in return for the payment of all outstanding advances and late royalties. Night Shade immediately cancelled its electronic magazine *Eclipse Online*, edited by Jonathan Strahan.

After working on the transition with the new owners for a couple of months, Night Shade founder Jason Williams left the company in August.

Skyhorse and Start were also set to acquire independent publisher Underland Press, founded in 2007 by Victoria Blake. However, the deal was not completed and the imprint was instead purchased by Mark Teppo's new publishing company, Resurrection House.

After being announced as an acquiring editor for Resurrection House, Jason Williams soon left that company as well.

In Britain, Tesco supermarkets were forced to withdraw a sixteen-page colouring book from their website after complaints that *Colour Me Good Arrggghhhh!!* by Mel Elliott featured images from, amongst other films, *Hellraiser*, *Psycho*, *The Silence of the Lambs*, *A Nightmare on Elm Street*, *Jaws*, *An American Werewolf in London*, *The Shining* and *A Clockwork Orange*. The book was being marketed online to children aged from five to eight.

Later in the year Tesco had to apologize again, when it was forced to remove an orange "psycho ward" Hallowe'en costume off its shelves after it was denounced as "staggeringly offensive" by mental-health charities. Rival supermarket chain Asda was also compelled to remove a similar fancy dress costume.

As a result of these complaints, London's famous Angels Fancy Dress shop decided to insist that any customers wanting to buy their "Apron of Souls" *Texas Chainsaw Massacre* Hallowe'en costume would have to show ID to prove that they were eighteen years old or over. The company also set an age restriction on their bloody intestines costume.

It is estimated that the Hallowe'en market in the UK is now worth around £300 million, up from just £12 million in 2001.

Fifty years after his death, writer C. S. Lewis was honoured with a memorial stone in Westminster Abbey in London. The stone was set in the floor of Poet's Corner, alongside such other renowned literary figures as Geoffrey Chaucer and Charles Dickens.

In July, the Providence, Rhode Island, City Council agreed to rename the intersection of Prospect Street and Angell Street "H. P. Lovecraft Square".

* * *

To paraphrase William Goldman's famous quote about Hollywood, apparently nobody knows anything in publishing after it was revealed in July that a "debut" crime novel, *The Cuckoo's Calling* by "former military man" Robert Galbraith, was actually written by J. K. Rowling.

After having been turned down by a number of publishers, including Orion, the book was published in April by Sphere to generally good reviews. However, it had sold just 1,500 copies (including ebooks) before the *Sunday Times* newspaper mounted a textual analysis investigation into the identity of the supposedly first-time author (following a mysterious tweeted tip-off), and the novel became a bestseller literally overnight.

Rowling subsequently accepted a donation to charity from the law firm that revealed her pseudonym.

Stephen King's first novel of the year, *Joyland*, was published as a trade paperback original by Hard Case Crime. Despite the volume's almost pulp-crime cover, the book concerned college student Devin Jones, who took a job at an independent amusement park in 1973 that featured, amongst other things, a haunted funhouse that was actually haunted. The author encouraged readers to buy print editions over ebooks when he announced that *Joyland* would only be available in printed form.

King was back later in the year with *Doctor Sleep*, which was a continuation of his 1977 best-seller *The Shining*. A grown-up Dan Torrance, still haunted by what happened to him as a child at The Overlook hotel, set out to save a girl who shared his psychic powers from a "family" of psychopathic travellers who wanted to feed off their remarkable gifts.

In Britain, there were exclusive slipcased "Special Editions" released separately to the WHSmith and Waterstones bookstore chains.

Joe Hill's *NOS4A2* (get it?) was about a woman who had the power to find "lost" objects and her encounter with a legendary bogeyman, who spirited his child victims away in his car to a magical realm where he drained their souls. Subterranean Press published a signed edition limited to 750 copies ($125.00) and twenty-six traycased lettered copies ($1,000.00).

Dean Koontz's *Deeply Odd* was the sixth book in the "Odd Thomas" series, while the same author's *Innocence* was about two people who lived in seclusion who found each other.

Dan Brown's *Inferno* was the fourth novel concerning Robert Langdon, who investigated the secrets surrounding Dante's "Inferno". It sold one million copies in North America during the book's first five days of release. The second printing was 2.3 million copies.

An unnamed narrator literally returned to his childhood memories, only to discover something evil waiting for his seven-year-old self in Neil Gaiman's masterful novel *The Ocean at the End of the Lane*. In America, William Morrow issued a beautifully produced deluxe slipcased edition, illustrated in full colour by Dave McKean and limited to 2,000 signed and numbered copies ($150.00).

Dan Simmons' *The Abominable* was set around a 1925 attempt to climb Mount Everest.

Billed simply as "a ghost story", Graham Joyce's *The Year of the Ladybird* was inspired by actual events. Set in the summer of 1976, a student took a job at a rundown holiday camp in Skegness and learned more about his past than he wanted to.

A surburban housewife house-sitting a high-rise apartment found herself drawn into a nightmare conspiracy involving an impossible murder in Christopher Fowler's *Plastic*.

In *The Heavens Rise* by Christopher Rice, a group of Louisiana teens faced an ancient evil, while his mother, Anne Rice, published *The Wolves of Midwinter*, the second book in the "Wolf Gift Chronicles" werewolf series.

A complex conspiracy was at the heart of *We Are Here*, the latest thriller from Michael Marshall (Smith), while a retired policewoman inherited a house in a too-good-to-be-true town in Robert Jackson Bennett's *American Elsewhere*.

In Carsten Stroud's Southern Gothic *Niceville*, children kept disappearing from the eponymous town. It was followed by the even more offbeat *The Homecoming*, which combined time travel with the Mob.

Lauren Beukes' *The Shining Girls* was about a survivor's hunt for a time-travelling serial killer who used a condemned house in Chicago as his means of transportation. Reprints of the UK edition contained research photographs and an interview with the author.

A lecturer in creative writing scanned photos of famous writers' studies to see if he could spot his only published book on their shelves in Nicholas Royle's psychological thriller *First Novel*.

A drunken criminologist and an intrepid journalist teamed up to solve a mystery involving mad science and monsters in an alternate London of 1864 in T. Aaron Payton's debut steampunk "Pimm & Skye Adventure", *The Constantine Affliction*.

A second serial killer was at work in the streets of Jack the Ripper's London in Sarah Pinborough's *Mayhem*, while a young girl ventured into an alternate London to rescue her abducted mirror-sister in Tom Pollock's *The Glass Republic*.

Patients were kept asleep for months as part of a new psychiatric therapy in F. R. Tallis' *The Sleep Room*, and a university professor had to study John Milton's *Paradise Lost* to save his daughter from a demon in *The Demonologist* by Andrew Pyper.

A woman investigated her uncle's death in his apparently haunted house in Simone St. James' *An Inquiry Into Love and Death*, while a couple inherited a house with a dark secret in Ronald Malfi's *Cradle Lake*.

During the London Blitz, a brother and sister were evacuated to a house in the Lake District where the girl began to hear the voices of dead children in *The Silence of Ghosts* by Jonathan Aycliffe (aka Daniel Easterman). The author's classic 1991 ghost story, *Naomi's Room*, was reissued at the same time.

A new governess discovered something was very wrong in John Boyne's Victorian ghost story, *This House is*

Haunted, and a woman searched for her missing parents who helped haunted souls find peace in John Searles' *Help for the Haunted*.

Dark secrets were revealed in the home of a taxidermist/puppeteer in *House of Small Shadows* by Adam Nevill, and an amnesiac boy brought terror to a family home in *The Orphan* by Christopher Ransom.

A boy was possessed by his father's spirit in *The Waking That Kills* by Stephen Gregory, while *Storm Demon* was Gregory Lamberson's fifth book featuring detective Jake Helman.

Melvin Burgess' *Hunger* was published under the Hammer imprint, as was *Fire*, the second volume in the "Engelsfors" trilogy by Sara Elfgren and Mats Strandberg. Sophie Hannah's *The Orphan Choir* and Julie Myerson's *The Quickening* were also both Hammer titles.

A serial killer was inspired by fairy tales in Alison Littlewood's *Path of Needles*, and a warlock was stalked by a monster from Russian folklore in Christopher Buehlman's *The Necromancer's House*.

Girls were going missing on both sides of the Mexican–American border in Adam Mansbach's supernatural thriller *The Dead Run*.

In the near future, a Hollywood studio used bio-engineered monsters to attack the inhabitants of a rural town in *Assault on Sunrise*, a sequel to *The Extra*, by Michael Shea.

James P. Blaylock's steampunk romp *The Aylesford Skull* was set in 1883 and pitted eccentric scientist and explorer Professor Langdon St. Ives against his old nemesis, Dr. Ignacio Narbondo.

The Romanov Cross by Robert Masello involved victims of the 1918 flu epidemic frozen in the Alaskan ice, while in Justin Richards' alternate reality thriller *The Suicide Exhibition: The Never War*, in 1940 the German war machine awakened an ancient civilization, the alien Vril, whose involvement could result in the Nazi's ultimate victory in the war for Europe.

Weston Ochse's *Age of Blood* was the second volume in the "Triple Six"/"SEAL Team 666" series, while James

Swain's *Shadow People* was a sequel to the author's *Dark Magic*.

Piper Maitland's *Hunting Daylight* was a sequel to *Acquainted with the Night*, Chuck Palahniuk's *Doomed* was a sequel to *Damned*, and *The Last Grave* was the second in the "Witch Hunt" series by Debbie Viguié.

David Wong's humorous *This Book is Full of Spiders* was a sequel to his *John Dies at the End*.

Watcher of the Dark was the third book in the "Jeremiah Hunt" series by Joseph Nassise, and *The Lost Soul* was the third and final instalment in Gabriella Pierce's packaged "666 Park Avenue" series and a tie-in to the TV series.

Inspired by H. P. Lovecraft, Peter Rawlik's novel *Reanimators* was about the rivalry between Dr. Stuart Hartwell and Herbert West, and their attempts to conquer death itself, while Jeremy Robinson's *Island 731* involved the monstrous results of Japanese experiments during World War II and was inspired by H. G. Wells' *The Island of Doctor Moreau*.

With *Blood Oranges*, Caitlín R. Kiernan "writing as Kathleen Tierney" had some fun with the paranormal romance genre as her junkie monster-hunter protagonist became infected by *both* a werewolf and a vampire.

Dead Ever After was the thirteenth and final "Sookie Stackhouse" novel from Charlaine Harris, as the series ended with Sookie's friends uniting to battle her enemies in a final showdown. A 2,500-copy linen-bound signed edition ($125.00) was also available.

Harris' *After Dead: What Came Next in the World of Sookie Stackhouse* was an alphabetically arranged non-fiction companion to the series.

Fourteen years after the previous volume first appeared, Kim Newman's long-awaited fourth book in his alternate world vampire series, *Anno Dracula 1976–1991: Johnny Alucard*, was finally published. It contained a number of loosely linked novellas and stories, several of which were original to the book.

The vampire novel *Blood of the Lamb* by Sam Cabot (Carlos Dews and S. J. Rozan) involved the search for a secret document stolen from the Vatican.

The Lair was a sequel to *The Farm* by Emily McKay, and *Blood Bond* was the ninth book in the "Anna Strong, Vampire" series by Jeanne C. Stein.

Appalachian Overthrow was the tenth volume in E. E. Knight's "The Vampire Earth" series and marked the beginning of a new story arc, while *The Dog in the Dark* was the eleventh volume in the "Noble Dead" vampire series by Barb Hendee and J. C. Hendee.

The vampire Count Saint-Germain found a new companion in 13th-century Africa in *Night Pilgrims*, the twenty-sixth volume in the series by Chelsea Quinn Yarbro.

Benjamin Percy's epic werewolf/alternate history novel *Red Moon*, set in an alternate world where "lycans" co-existed amongst humans, was heavily promoted as belonging to the new "literary horror" movement – thus basically dismissing the rest of the genre as something less worthy.

John Ringo's *Under a Graveyard Sky* was set during the zombie apocalypse, as a family tried to find safe haven from an infected humanity. A limited, signed edition was also available from Baen Books.

Jamie McGuire's *Red Hill* was about a man-made zombie outbreak, while Joe McKinney's *The Savage Dead* was about a zombie outbreak on a cruise ship.

Rise Again: Below Zero, set in a small Californian mountain community during the zombie apocalypse, was Ben Tripp's sequel to his 2010 novel.

David Towsey's debut novel *Your Brother's Blood* was set after the zombie apocalypse and was the first volume in "The Walkin'" series.

A meth addict and his friends found themselves facing a zombie outbreak in Peter Stenson's first book, *Fiend: A Novel*, while in Seth Patrick's debut novel *The Reviver*, the recently dead were brought back to testify to their own demise. It was the first in a trilogy.

R. S. Belcher's weird Western novel, *The Six-Gun Tarot* was set in the cursed cattle town of Golgotha, which was invaded by the undead, and a boy's mother and sister disappeared during a storm in John Mantooth's *The Year of the Storm*.

Set in 1751 London, *The Tale of Raw Head & Bloody Bones* by Jack Wolf was based on a fairy tale, while a teenager was transported back to 1888 and Jack the Ripper's London in Shelly Dickson Carr's debut novel *Ripped*.

Guillermo del Toro "curated" and supplied new introductions to Penguin Horror's stylish hardcover collector's editions of *Haunted Castles* by Ray Russell, *The Raven* by Edgar Allan Poe, *American Supernatural Tales*, *The Haunting of Hill House* by Shirley Jackson, *Frankenstein* by Mary Shelley and *The Thing on the Doorstep and Other Weird Stories* by H. P. Lovecraft.

Edited with an Introduction by Roger Luckhurst for Oxford University Press, *The Classic Horror Stories* collected nine tales by Lovecraft, along with the author's introduction to his essay "Supernatural Horror in Literature".

The Complete Cthulhu Mythos Tales from Barnes & Noble/Fall River Press, edited with an Introduction by S. T. Joshi, collected twenty-three stories and "revisions" by H. P. Lovecraft.

Also from Barnes & Noble, *Dracula and Other Horror Classics*, collected Bram Stoker's 1897 title novel, *The Jewel of Seven Stars* (1903) and *The Lair of the White Worm* (1911), along with the collection *Dracula's Guest and Other Stories* (1914).

A new edition of William Hope Hodgson's 1912 novel *The Night Land* from HiLoBooks included notes by Erik Davis.

Mike Ashley supplied the Introduction to *Ten Minute Stories/Day and Night Stories*, an omnibus reprinting of two previous collections by Algernon Blackwood from Stark House, which also included a previously uncollected ghost story.

The Complete Tales of Doctor Satan from Altus Press collected Paul Ernst's series of eight stories about the eponymous super-villain from *Weird Tales* (1935–36) with an Introduction by John Pelan.

From Haffner Press, *The Complete John Thunstone* collected all the stories about Manly Wade Wellman's pulp hero, along with the novels *What Dreams May Come* (1983) and *The School of Darkness* (1985). Ramsey Campbell supplied the Introduction and George Evans the illustrations.

Valancourt Books reissued Basil Copper's novels *The Great White Space* and *Necropolis* as attractive print-on-demand paperbacks, along with a welcome reissue of R. Chetwynd-Hayes' *The Monster Club*. All came with new Introductions by Stephen Jones.

Other reissues from Valancourt included *Nightshade and Damnations* by Gerald Kersh, *The Philosopher's Stone* by Colin Wilson and *Bury Him Darkly* by John Blackburn.

Kim Newman's already hefty 1991 novel about a cursed English village, *Jago*, was reissued in a new edition by Titan Books with three additional stories that featured characters and settings from the book.

Tempting the Gods, a collection of twelve stories, was the first volume in "The Selected Stories of Tanith Lee" from Wildside Press and included a profile of the author by the late Donald A. Wolheim.

Graham Masterton's 2003 novel *A Terrible Beauty* was reissued as *White Bones*, while Phil Rickman's 1993 novel *Crybbe* was republished under the title *Curfew*.

Britain's new Waterstone's Children's Laureate, Malorie Blackman, attacked "snobby attitudes" towards books in June, and defended the *Twilight* series against disparaging remarks made by Education Secretary Michael Gove. "The point is that they are reading," said Ms Blackman.

Harry Potter film director Chris Columbus collaborated with Ned Vizzini on the young adult novel *House of Secrets*, in which three siblings were banished by a witch to a mythical land where they had to track down a mysterious tome.

A children's game turned into something darker as three youngsters set out to bury a doll in the grave where it was supposed to be in Holly Black's creepy *Doll Bones*, while childish games conjured up something nasty in the woods in *The Haunting of Gabriel Ashe* by Dan Poblocki.

Having apparently killed her boyfriend in self-defence, a teenager was shipped off to boarding school where something monstrous awaited her in Megan Miranda's *Hysteria*.

A boy discovered that his new high school was haunted in *The Unquiet* by Jeannine Garsee, and a girl haunted her school to discover why she supposedly committed suicide in Katie Williams' *Absent*.

A girl woke up in a hotel for the dead and had to solve her own murder in *The Dead Girls Detective Agency*, the first in a new series by Suzy Cox.

The new girl in town found a boyfriend in the local graveyard in *The Lost Boys* by Lilian Carmine.

Somebody in the town of Milton Lake was using a fabled Ghost Machine to call back the spirits of the dead in *Haunted* by William Hussey, while a young girl searching for her missing grandfather in a sleepy seaside village made friends with a mysterious local girl in Liz Kessler's *North of Nowhere*.

A sea voyage turned to hell in *The Dead Men Stood Together* by Chris Priestley.

When Satan decided to retire, a group of teenagers had to undertake a series of deadly trials to decide who would become his replacement in *The Devil's Apprentice* by Jan Siegel (Amanda Hemingway).

Students discovered that their summer camp dorm used to be an asylum for the criminally insane in Madeleine Roux's *Asylum*, and a girl's school trip to Paris involved ghosts and murder in Katie Alender's *Marie Antoinette, Serial Killer*.

Shadowlands and *Hereafter* were the first two volumes in a new serial-killer trilogy by Kate Brian.

Teenagers became involved with Victorian spiritualists in Sonia Gensler's *The Dark Between*, and a plague of murderous ghosts in London caused chaos in Jonathan Stroud's *Lockwood and Co.: The Screaming Staircase*, the first in a new series.

Something was making the inhabitants of a small Kansas town commit murder/suicide in *The Waking Dark* by Robin Wasserman.

Teenagers used witchcraft to get revenge in Mariah Fredericks' *Season of the Witch*, while Rebecca Alexander's *The Secrets of Life and Death* featured alchemist Edward Kelley and the infamous Countess Bathory.

In Jon Skovron's *Man Made Boy*, the son of the Frankenstein Monster and the Bride lived under Times Square in New York.

When a teenager questioned the beliefs of a doomsday cult, she found her own life in danger in Amy Christine Parker's psychological thriller, *Gated*.

Dark City was the second book in the "Repairman Jack: The Early Years" series by F. Paul Wilson.

The Madness Underneath was the second volume in the "Shades of London" series by Maureen Johnson, and *Belladonna* was the second in the "Secrets of the Eternal Rose" series by Fiona Paul.

Monster High: Ghoulfriends Just Want to Have Fun by Gitty Daneshvari was the second novella based on a series of dolls, while Charles Gilman's *Tales from Lovecraft Middle School #2: The Slither Sisters*, *#3: Teacher's Pest* and *#4: Substitute Creature* were illustrated by Eugene Smith and came with lenticular covers.

The Creeps was the third book in the "Samuel Johnson" series by John Connolly, in which the teen hero and his faithful dachshund investigated a mysterious toyshop and were menaced by Christmas elves.

Andrew Hammond's *CRYPT: Blood Eagle Tortures* was the fourth in the series featuring the Covert Response Youth Paranormal Team, while *Witch & Wizard: The Kiss* was the fourth in the series by James Patterson and Jill Dembowski.

With All My Soul was the seventh and final volume in Rachel Vincent's "Soul Screamers" series, and *Lover at Last* was the eleventh title in the "Black Dagger Brotherhood" series by J. R. Ward.

As an American TV network once said – if you haven't seen it before, then it's new to you. This seems to be particularly true when it comes to young adult fiction these days:

Mary Lindsey's *Ashes on the Waves* was a "dark retelling" of Edgar Allan Poe's poem "Annabel Lee", while *Dance of the Red Death* was the second book in a post-apocalyptic series by Bethany Griffin, based on a story by Poe.

The Ruining by Anna Collomore was inspired by Charlotte Perkins Gilman's "The Yellow Wallpaper", and Jane Nickerson's *Strands of Bronze and Gold* was based on the "Bluebeard" story.

Adam Gidwitz's *In a Glass Grimmly* was a sequel to *A Tale Dark and Grimm*, based on the fairy tales of the Brothers Grimm, and *Black Spring* by Alison Croggon was inspired by *Wuthering Heights*.

A. E. Rought's *Broken* and *Tainted* were inspired by Mary Shelley's *Frankenstein*, Mandy Hubbard's *Dangerous Boy* was a contemporary YA reworking of *Dr. Jekyll and Mr. Hyde*, and *The Madman's Daughter* was the first volume in a new trilogy by Megan Shepherd inspired by H. G. Wells' *The Island of Doctor Moreau*.

Holly Black's second young adult novel of the year, *The Coldest Girl in Coldtown*, was expanded from a short story of the same title by the author and involved a teenage girl trying to survive in a world infected with vampires.

Although credited in big type to L. J. Smith, Aubrey Clark actually wrote *The Vampire Diaries: The Salvation: Unspoken*, the second book in the spin-off series.

Department 19: The Rising and *Department 19: Battle Lines* were the second and third books in Will Hill's series about a secret government agency that hunted vampires.

Richelle Mead's *The Indigo Spell* and *The Fiery Heart* were the third and fourth titles in the "Bloodlines" series, a spin-off from the "Vampire Academy" series.

Christopher Pike returned to his "Last Vampire" series with *Thirst No.5: The Sacred Veil*.

Blood Prophecy by Alyxandra Harvey included a bonus story and was the sixth and final book in the "Drake Chronicles" series, while *Gates of Paradise* was the seventh and final book in the "Blue Bloods" series by Melissa de la Cruz.

Revealed was the eleventh title in the YA "House of Night" vampire series by P. C. Cast and Kristin Cast, while *Neferet's Curse* was a novella set in the series.

Fall of Night was book fourteen in "The Morganville Vampires" series by Rachel Caine (Roxanne Longstreet Conrad). The series concluded with the next volume, *Daylighters*, which included a bonus novelette "for UK readers".

A trio of children dealt with an outbreak of the walking dead in their hometown in Paolo Bacigalupi's humorous novel, *Zombie Baseball Beatdown*, which also featured zombie cows.

Teens were trapped in their high school by a zombie epidemic in Tom Leveen's *Sick*.

Deadlands and *Death of a Saint* were the first two books in a teen series by Lily Herne (mother-and-daughter writing team Sarah and Savannah Lotz) set in a South Africa over-run by zombies, while *Zombies Don't Cry* and *Zombies Don't Forgive* were the first two titles in the "Living Dead Love Story" series by Rusty Fischer.

Through the Zombie Glass was the second book in "The White Rabbit Chronicles" by Gena Showalter, and *Monsters* was the third and final book in the post-apocalyptic zombie "Ashes" series by Ilsa J. Bick.

Zom-B Underground, *Zom-B City*, *Zom-B Angels* and *Zom-B Baby* were the second, third, fourth and fifth novellas in the YA series written by Darren Shan (Darren O'Shaughnessy) and illustrated by Warren Pleece.

A group of young survivors had to cross a zombie-infected London to find a cure in *The Fallen*, the fifth in "The Enemy" series by Charlie Higson.

Aubrey Clark's *The Secret Circle: The Temptation* was a spin-off of the YA witchcraft series created by L. J. Smith.

* * *

Vampires in the Lemon Grove collected eight literary and surreal stories by Pulitzer Prize finalist Karen Russell, and *Evil Eye* collected four Gothic novellas by Joyce Carol Oates.

The Beautiful Thing That Awaits Us All and Other Stories was a hardcover collection from Skyhorse Publishing/ Night Shade Books that contained nine stories (one original) by Laird Barron, with an Introduction by Norman Partridge.

Published by Jo Fletcher Books in an edition illustrated by Alan Lee, *Fearie Tales: Stories of the Grimm and Gruesome*, edited and with an Introduction by Stephen Jones, featured fifteen original stories interspersed with the original Brothers Grimm tales that inspired them by Ramsey Campbell, Neil Gaiman, Tanith Lee, Garth Nix, Robert Shearman, Michael Marshall Smith, Markus Heitz, Christopher Fowler, Brian Lumley, Reggie Oliver, Angela Slatter, Brian Hodge, Peter Crowther, Joanne Harris and John Ajvide Lindqvist.

Psycho-Mania! also edited by Jones contained thirty-four horror/crime tales (nineteen original), along with an original linking sequence by John Llewellyn Probert and a previously unpublished Introduction by Robert Bloch. Contributors included Joe R. Lansdale, Reggie Oliver, Basil Copper, Robert Silverberg, Lisa Morton, Lawrence Block, Robert Shearman, Ramsey Campbell, Christopher Fowler, Harlan Ellison, Neil Gaiman, Michael Marshall Smith and Kim Newman.

Paula Guran edited *The Mammoth Book of Angels and Demons*, featuring twenty-seven stories by Neil Gaiman, George R. R. Martin, Joyce Carol Oates and others. From veteran editor Mike Ashley came a reissue of the 2004 anthology *The Mammoth Book of Sorcerer's Tales* retitled *The Mammoth Book of Dark Magic* in Britain and *The Mammoth Book of Black Magic* in America. It collected twenty-three tales of wizardry and witchcraft from, amongst others, Ursula K. Le Guin, Michael Moorcock, Peter Crowther, Tim Lebbon and Steve Rasnic Tem.

Editor John Joseph Adams' *The Mad Scientist's Guide to World Domination: Original Short Fiction for the Modern*

Evil Genius was a hardcover anthology of twenty-two stories with a Foreword by Chris Claremont. Contributors included Harry Turtledove, L. A. Banks, Alan Dean Foster, Carrie Vaughn, Laird Barron, L. E. Modesitt Jr and Jeffrey Ford, amongst others.

Oz Reimagined: New Tales from the Emerald City and Beyond edited and introduced by Adams and Douglas Cohen featured fifteen stories inspired by L. Frank Baum's children's classic by, amongst others, Tad Williams, Simon R. Green, Jane Yolen, Dale Bailey, Orson Scott Card and Jeffrey Ford, with a Foreword by Gregory Maguire.

Beyond Rue Morgue: Further Tales of Edgar Allan Poe's 1st Detective edited with an Introduction by Paul Kane and Charles Prepolec contained ten stories (two reprints) featuring French investigator Le Chevalier C. Auguste Dupin by Poe, Mike Carey, Joe R. Lansdale, Lisa Tuttle, Stephen Volk, Clive Barker and others.

Edited by the late Martin H. Greenberg, *Ghouls, Ghosts, and Ninja Rats* brought together eighteen paranormal crime stories by such authors as Norman Partridge, Nina Kiriki Hoffman and Mike Resnick.

Stories of Terror and the Supernatural edited by Herman Graf featured twenty-two classic tales by Edgar Allan Poe, Washington Irving, Henry James and others.

Edited by Hank Davis, *In Space No One Can Hear You Scream* contained thirteen scary SF stories by authors including Arthur C. Clarke, Robert Sheckley, Theodore Sturgeon, Clark Ashton Smith and George R. R. Martin.

The fifth volume of editor Ellen Datlow's *The Best Horror of the Year* series from Skyhorse's Night Shade Books imprint contained twenty-six stories and two poems, along with the editor's summation of the year and a list of "Honorable Mentions".

The Year's Best Dark Fantasy and Horror: 2013, edited by Paula Guran for Prime Books, showcased thirty-five authors, while *The Mammoth Book of Best New Horror Volume 24* edited by Stephen Jones featured twenty-one stories and a poem.

Once again, no one story appeared in all three "Year's Best" horror compilations. Datlow and Jones used the same Ramsey Campbell story, Datlow and Guran used the same Jeffrey Ford story, and Guran and Jones used the same Terry Dowling and Alison Littlewood tales.

Laird Barron, Terry Dowling and Priya Sharma all turned up in the Datlow and Guran anthologies with different stories; Gemma Files and Claire Massey were both featured with different works in the Datlow and Jones books, and Guran and Jones shared contributors Neil Gaiman, Joe R. Lansdale, Helen Marshall and Robert Shearman.

Macmillan was the last publisher to settle with the US Department of Justice over allegations of conspiring to fix ebook pricing. Only Apple continued to contest the charges, and in July they were found guilty in a federal court of playing "a central role in facilitating and executing that conspiracy". The company subsequently filed an appeal against the judge's decision.

Founded in 2007 and with around 16 million active members, "social cataloguing" online site Goodreads was purchased for an undisclosed sum by Amazon.com. Amazon also has its own cataloguing site Shelfari and a minority ownership in Library Thing.

Meanwhile, the company announced the creation of a new platform, Kindle Worlds, to publish fan fiction. With licensing deals done with a number of book, TV, movie and game properties, writers' works were sold as ebooks after being vetted, with royalties being split between the fanfic author and the rights holder.

In August, Amazon announced that it would allow sellers to set their own prices on the Marketplace platform after an anti-competition investigation by the Office of Fair Trading. The company originally insisted on a "price parity" policy that prevented traders from selling their products for less than the website price. The change only applied in the European Union.

Controversy surrounded the announcement that DC Comics had hired anti-gay marriage campaigner Orson

Scott Card for the digital comic *Adventures of Superman*. While the company sought to distance itself from Card's views, there were online calls for a boycott by various fans and organizations.

Print-on-demand titles and ebook originals continued to flourish as the mainstream publishers consolidated imprints and mostly continued to ignore the horror genre:

Ramsey Campbell's *Holes for Faces* from Dark Regions Press collected fourteen stories (including the original title story) from the first decade of this century. It was available as a PoD trade paperback, a premium leatherette-bound signed edition limited to 300 copies, and a deluxe leather-bound slipcased edition of fifty-two copies ($199.00) signed by both the author and artist Santiago Caruso.

Editor Paula Guran continued to put out value-for-money reprint anthologies for Prime Books with *Weird Detectives: Recent Investigations*, containing twenty-three tales by Neil Gaiman, Charlaine Harris and Simon R. Green, amongst others. *Once Upon a Time: New Fairy Tales* contained eighteen stories by Jane Yolen, Tanith Lee, Caitlín R. Kiernan and Angela Slatter, amongst others, and *After the End: Recent Apocalypses* featured twenty non-zombie stories by authors including Cory Doctorow and Paolo Bacigalupi.

From the same editor and publisher, *Halloween: Magic, Mystery, and the Macabre* collected eighteen tales celebrating October 31 by, amongst others, Norman Partridge, Carrie Vaughn, Laird Barron, Caitlín R. Kiernan, Chelsea Quinn Yarbro, Brian Hodge and Nancy Kilpatrick.

In *Bad Seeds: Evil Progeny* for Prime Books, editor Steve Berman brought together twenty-seven stories (five original) about bad children by, amongst others, Stephen King, Peter Straub, Joe R. Lansdale, Gemma Files, Michael Kelly and Lisa Tuttle. Berman also edited *Zombies: Shambling Through the Ages* for the same imprint, containing thirty-three stories (eight reprints), and *Shadows of Blue and Gray: Ghosts of the Civil War*, collecting twenty-two stories (eight reprints).

For Lethe Press, the busy Mr Berman put together the PoD anthology *Where Thy Dark Eye Glances: Queering Edgar Allan Poe*, an original anthology of twenty-one stories and five poems that put a gay twist on the life and works of the author. Contributors included Nick Mamatas and Christopher Barzak.

Also from Lethe, *Before and Afterlives* was a retrospective collection of supernatural stories by Barzak.

Animate Objects from Immanion Press collected eight stories (four previously unpublished) and an original poem by Tanith Lee. A special signed edition, with an illustration by the author, was limited to just thirty numbered hardcover copies.

From PoD imprint Altus Press, Will Murray's *Doc Savage: Skull Island* was a mash-up between the pulp hero and King Kong.

The Whispering Horror from Shadow Publishing collected fourteen stories (one original) by German-born author Eddy C. Bertin with an Introduction by David A. Sutton and story notes by the author.

The Lurkers in the Abyss and Other Tales of Terror was an impressive, career-spanning collection of seventeen stories (one original) by David A. Riley. It featured another Introduction by Sutton, who performed the same function for *Worse Things Than Spiders*, which contained twelve stories (one previously unpublished) and a poem by Samantha Lee.

Twenty-three stories from the two volumes of David A. Sutton's own superior 1970s anthologies *New Writings in Horror and the Supernatural* were reissued by Shadow Publishing in an omnibus edition entitled *Horror! Under the Tombstone: Stories from the Deathly Realm*, with a new Foreword by the editor.

Available from Hippocampus Press, *The Wide Carnivorous Sky & Other Monstrous Geographies* collected ten stories (two original) by John Langan, with an Introduction by Jeffrey Ford and an Afterword by Laird Barron.

Lovecraft's Pillow and Other Strange Stories contained thirteen stories by Kenneth W. Faig, Jr, while *SimulAcrum and Other Possible Realities* brought together twenty-nine stories and poems (twelve original) by Jason V. Brock, along with a Foreword by William F. Nolan and an Introduction by James Robert Smith.

The Condemned, the sixth volume in Gray Friar Press' "Gray Matter" showcase series, collected six novellas by Simon Bestwick.

From the same imprint, *Terror Tales of London* was the fourth volume in editor Paul Finch's excellent series of PoD anthologies. It contained thirteen stories (three reprints) by, amongst others, Nina Allan, Roger Johnson, Nicholas Royle, Adam Nevill, Mark Morris, Christopher Fowler and Marie O'Regan, along with historical vignettes about the city.

Simon Strantzas edited *Shadows Edge*, an original anthology based around where worlds meet. It contained fifteen stories by Joel Lane, Richard Gavin, Gary McMahon, Lisa L. Hannett, R. B. Russell, Michael Kelly, Steve Rasnic Tem and John Langan, with a Prologue story and Afterword by the editor.

A man's memories were subtly altered by his past in John Llewellyn Probert's novella *Differently There*, also from Gray Friar Press.

Selected as usual by publisher Charles Black for his Mortbury Press imprint, *The Tenth Black Book of Horror* featured fifteen often gruesome tales in the *Pan Book of Horror Stories* tradition by David A. Sutton, Paul Finch, Ian Hunter, John Llewellyn Probert, Mike Chinn, Thana Niveau and others. From the same imprint, *For Those Who Dream Monsters* collected seventeen stories (two original) by Anna Taborska, along with an Introduction and impressive interior illustrations by Reggie Oliver.

Editor Mark West's *Anatomy of Death (in Five Sleazy Pieces)* was the third volume in Hersham Horror Books' "PentAnth" series of 1970s-style PoD anthologies, featuring five original stories by Stephen Bacon, Johnny Mains, John

Llewellyn Probert, Stephen Volk and the editor. It was followed by *Demons & Devilry*, which collected material by Probert, Peter Mark May, Thana Niveau, David Williamson and editor Stuart Young.

Rachel Aukes' *100 Days in Deadland* re-imagined Dante's "Inferno" as a print-on-demand novel of the zombie apocalypse.

From Ramble House/Dancing Tuatara Press, *The Devil of Pei-Ling* was a reprint of Herbert Asbury's 1927 novel, while *When the Bat Man Thirsts and Other Stories* collected eight tales from the 1930s by Frederick C. Davis.

The Finger of Destiny and Other Stories contained thirteen stories by Edmund Snell, and *Mark of the Laughing Death and Other Stories* brought together eight stories by Francis James (James A. Goldthwaite) published in the pulps during the 1930s and '40s.

All four books included introductions from publisher/editor John Pelan, who also edited *Tales of Terror & Torment Vol.1*, which contained eleven pulp stories from the 1930s by Hugh B. Cave, Norvell Page, Arthur Leo Zagat and others.

Edited by webmaster Jeani Rector, *Shadow Masters: An Anthology from the Horror Zine* was published under the Imajin Books imprint and included thirty-seven stories by Bentley Little, Yvonne Navarro, Scott Nicholson, Melanie Tem, Elizabeth Massie, Simon Clark, Lisa Morton and others, including two written by the editor. Joe R. Lansdale supplied a Foreword.

Published by the HorrorSociety website, *Horror Society Stories Volume 1*, edited by Michael DeFellipo and Mitchell D. Wells featured eleven new stories.

Florida's Miskatonic River Press published two tribute anthologies: *Deepest, Darkest Eden: New Tales of Hyperborea* edited and introduced by Cody Goodfellow included eighteen stories (two reprints) and two poems set in Clark Ashton Smith's prehistoric land by Darrell Schweitzer, Lisa Morton, Brian Stableford, Don Webb, Marc Laidlaw, Robert M. Price, John Shirley and the editor.

Edited and Introduced by Joseph S. Pulver, Sr., *The Grimscribe's Puppets* was a tribute to the work of Thomas Ligotti with twenty-two stories (one reprint) by, amongst others, Michael Cisco, Joel Lane, Darrell Schweitzer, Michael Kelly, Robert M. Price, Richard Gavin, Simon Strantzas, John Langan, Gemma Files and Cody Goodfellow.

Published by Joe Morey's Dark Renaissance Books imprint, *Sherlock Holmes: The Quality of Mercy and Other Stories* collected eleven fantastical stories (four reprints) about Holmes and Watson by William Meikle. Jeffrey Thomas' *Worship the Night* from the same imprint featured eight stories (two original), while *The Universal and Other Terrors* brought together twelve stories (three original) by Tony Richards.

All Dark Renaissance titles were available in deluxe hardcover, signed and numbered hardcover, trade paperback and ebook editions.

Mike Robinson's *The Prince of Earth* from Curiosity Quills Press was about an American woman whose life was threatened by an inexplicable event that happened to her in Scotland twenty years earlier.

From Karōshi Books, *The Moon Will Look Strange* was a welcome debut collection from Lynda E. Rucker containing eleven tales (three previously unpublished), along with an Introduction by Steve Rasnic Tem and story notes by the author.

Edited by S. P. Miskowski and Kate Jonez for Omnium Gatherum, *Little Visible Delight* contained eleven original stories about writerly obsessions by Lynda E. Rucker, Michael Kelley, Steve Duffy and others, including the editors. From the same publisher, Miskowski's novella *Astoria* was about a woman who discovered she could not outrun her demons.

Edited and introduced by Jan Edwards and Jenny Barber, *The Alchemy Press Book of Urban Mythic* contained fourteen stories (two reprints) by Mike Resnick, Christopher Golden, Jonathan Oliver, Alison Littlewood and others. Allen Ashley edited and introduced *Astrologica: Stories of the Zodiac*, which featured fourteen (oddly not twelve) stories by Stuart Young, Joel Lane, Storm Constantine, Megan Kerr and others.

Published only as ebooks by Alchemy Press were Chico Kidd's *The Komarovs*, a new "Captain da Silva" novella involving vampires, zombies, ghosts and doppelgängers, and Cate Gardner's *In the Broken Birdcage of Kathleen Fair*.

Edited with an Introduction by Alex Davis for KnightWatch Press, *X7: A Seven Deadly Sins Anthology* collected seven original stories by Nicholas Royle, Simon Clark, Simon Bestwick and others.

Published under the Megazanthus Press imprint, *Horror Without Victims: A Story Anthology Edited by D. F. Lewis* (that's what the title page says) included twenty-five stories by John Howard, Gary McMahon, Mark Valentine and others.

Anthony Rivera and Sharon Lawson edited *Dark Visions: Volume One* for PoD imprint Grey Matter Press. It contained thirteen stories (one original) by Ray Garton, Jay Caselberg and others.

Crystal Lake Publishing produced a revised edition of Gary McMahon's 2012 collection *Where You Live*, containing nineteen stories (five original) and a new Introduction by the author. From the same imprint, Paul Kane's *Sleeper(s)* was a John Wyndham-style novel in which a sleepy English village became the centre of a mysterious outbreak. David Moody contributed the Introduction.

From PoD imprint Dark Moon Books, *The Spaces Between* collected eight longer stories and novelettes (three original) by Kane with an Introduction by Kelley Armstrong. The cover was by *The Walking Dead* artist Charlie Adlard.

After Death . . . edited with an Introduction by Eric J. Guignard and illustrated by Audra Phillips was a trade paperback anthology from Dark Moon featuring thirty-four stories that examined what may occur after death. The list of contributors included Steve Rasnic Tem, Lisa Morton, James S. Dorr, Ray Cluley, Bentley Little, William Meikle, Simon Clark, Kelly Dunn, Joe McKinney and John Langan.

Tony Richards' supernatural novel *Tropic of Darkness* was published only as an ebook by Pocket Star.

Available from Wildside Press imprint The Borgo Press, *The Chaos of Chung-Fu: Weird Mystery Tales* and *The Ash Murders: Supernatural Mystery Stories* each featured five stories by Edmund Glasby, the son of weird fiction writer John S. Glasby.

Indiana Horror Review 2013 was a self-published PoD volume from editor James Ward Kirk that featured twenty short stories and ten poems while, from the same eponymous imprint and editor, *Cellar Door II* contained twenty-two stories, two pieces of flash fiction, and ten poems. The two titles shared a number of the same contributors.

Canada's Dale L. Sproule self-published his collection *Psychedelia Gothique* under the Arctic Mage Press imprint. It contained sixteen stories (five original), along with a Foreword by David Nickle and an Introduction by the author.

From Australia's Ticonderoga Publications, *The Bride Price* was the debut collection from Cat Sparks, containing thirteen stories (one original), along with an Introduction by Sean Wallace and an Afterword by the author, while Kim Wilkins' *The Year of Ancient Ghosts* collected five novellas (two original) along with an Introduction by Kate Forsyth and an Afterword by the author.

Robert Hood introduced *Everything is a Graveyard*, Jason Fischer's collection of fourteen offbeat stories (three original), and the author supplied the Afterword. Juliet Marillier's *Prickle Moon* contained sixteen pieces of fiction (five original), along with an Introduction by Sophie Masson and Author's Notes.

Edited by Liz Grzyb for Ticonderoga, *Dreaming of Djinn* contained eighteen new Arabian Nights stories, and Grzyb and Talie Helene compiled *The Year's Best Australian Fantasy & Horror 2012*. This third annual volume collected thirty-four stories and poems by Cat Sparks, Angela Slatter, Margo Lanagan, Anna Tambour, Stephen Dedman, Jay Caselberg, Kyla Ward, Terry Dowling and others.

Australia's FableCroft Publishing issued *The Bone Chime Song and Other Stories* by Joanne Anderton, containing thirteen stories (two original) with an Introduction by Kaaron Warren, along with *One Small Step: An Anthology of Discoveries*, the first all-female Australian speculative fiction anthology since the mid-1990s, edited by Tehani Wessely.

Compiled by Tom Roberts and published by Black Dog Books to tie-in to the Chicago pulp and paperback convention, *Windy City Pulp Stories #13* celebrated the 100th Anniversary of Fu Manchu and the 90th Anniversary of the Science Fiction and Fantasy Magazines with fascinating articles and other pieces by E. Hoffman Price, Charles D. Hornig, Leigh Brackett, Doug Ellis, Robert Weinberg and others.

From PS Publishing, a special 30th Anniversary edition of Stephen King's *Christine* included a new Introduction by Michael Marshall Smith and a new Afterword by Richard Chizmar. It was limited to 750 slipcased copies signed by Smith, Chizmar and artists Jill Bauman and Tomislav Tikulin.

Christopher Golden's 2004 novel of paranormal suspense, *The Boys Are Back in Town*, was reprinted in a special signed edition of 200 copies with a new Introduction by Don Murphy.

PS also reissued Joanne Harris' early supernatural novel *Sleep, Pale Sister* in a special signed edition of 200 copies with a new Introduction by Christopher Fowler.

Introduced by Stephen Gallager, *Rabbit Pie & Other Tales of Intrigue* collected fifteen original stories by Brian Clemens, best known for creating TV's *The Avengers*.

Shades of Nothingness contained seventeen stories (five original) by Gary Fry, while *The Moment of Panic* collected twelve stories (five apparently original) along with notes on each by author Steve Duffy.

Stardust: The Ruby Castle Stories collected seven linked stories (one reprint) by Nina Allan, with an Introduction by Robert Shearman.

Brian W. Aldiss' *The Invention of Happiness* was a slim collection of thirty-four original short-short stories written over consecutive days and illustrated by the author.

Exotic Gothic 5 edited by Danel Olson was published as a two-volume slipcased set. It contained twenty-six original stories by Simon Clark, Nancy A. Collins, Joyce Carol Oates, Terry Dowling, John Llewellyn Probert, Thana Niveau, Reggie Oliver, Paul Park, Lucy Taylor and others.

Edited with an Introduction by Lois H. Gresh, *Dark Fusions: Where Monsters Lurk!* included eighteen original tales by, amongst others, Darrell Schweitzer, Michael Marano, Lisa Morton, Nancy Kilpatrick, Yvonne Navarro and Robert M. Price.

Four for Fantasy: A Quartet of Fantastical Stories Collected for World FantasyCon 2013 was a slim hardcover featuring reprints by Brian Aldiss, Joanne Harris, Joe Hill and Richard Christian Matheson, edited by Peter Crowther.

As usual, Crowther also co-edited *Postscripts 30/31: Memoryville Blues* with Nick Gevers. The hardcover anthology contained twenty-five original stories by Alastair Reynolds, Mike Resnick, Lavie Tidhar, Lynda E. Rucker, Darrell Schweitzer, Ramsey Campbell, Scott Edelman and others. A signed edition was also available.

PS Publishing's series of hardcover novellas continued with *The Last Revelation of Gla'aki* and *The Pretence* by Ramsey Campbell, *The Ritual of Illusion* by Richard Christian Matheson, *The Réparateur of Strasbourg* by Ian R. MacLeod, and *We Three Kids*, a Christmas tale by Margo Lanagan. All were available in signed hardcover editions of varying print runs.

The two-volume collection *Darkness, Mist & Shadow: The Collected Macabre Tales of Basil Copper* was reissued in three matching paperback editions from the PS imprint Drugstore Indian Press, adding a new Introduction by Christopher Fowler to those by Kim Newman and editor Stephen Jones.

Under the Stanza Press imprint, PS reissued Brian Lumley's 1982/1999 poetry collection *Ghoul Warning and*

Other Omens with illustrations by Dave Carson and an Afterword by David Sutton.

The secret of a poem with supposedly eldritch powers led a San Francisco bookseller back in time to the Beat-era of 1957 in Tim Powers' *Salvage and Demolition* from Subterranean Press.

From the same publisher, Brian Lumley's short novel *Necroscope: The Möbius Murders* was another adventure about speaking with the dead, Harry Keough, illustrated as usual by Bob Eggleton. A 250-copy signed leatherbound edition was also available.

Robert McCammon's 19th-century-set vampire novella *I Travel by Night* was also available from Subterranean in both slipcased and traycased editions. The author's 1980 novel *The Night Boat* was reissued by the publisher in a signed edition limited to 750 copies, along with a lettered edition of twenty-six.

The Ape's Wife and Other Stories contained thirteen stories with notes on each by Caitlín R. Kiernan. It was also available in a signed, leatherbound edition of 600 copies that included a bonus hardcover novella.

Jewels in the Dust was a collection of thirteen previously published stories by Peter Crowther, with story notes by the author. The book was limited to a special signed and numbered edition of 750 copies.

Bleeding Shadows contained twenty-one stories and nine poems by Joe R. Lansdale, with notes by the author, and Lansdale's daughter Kasey edited *Impossible Monsters*, which featured twelve stories by David J. Schow, Neil Gaiman, Charlaine Harris, Chet Williamson, Al Sarrantonio and the editor's dad, amongst others.

Beautifully produced as a slim hardcover designed to evoke the American Arts & Crafts Movement, *The Gist* featured the title story by Michael Marshall Smith, plus the same story translated into French by Benoît Domis and then translated back into English by Nicholas Royle. A 300-copy signed and leatherbound edition was also available.

Dan Simmons' 1993 collection *Lovedeath* was reissued by Subterranean Press in a signed edition of 250 copies ($125.00) and a lettered edition ($250.00).

The residents of a quiet neighbourhood discovered strange things kept happening in Bentley Little's *The Circle* from Cemetery Dance Publications, while *The Influence* from the same author was about an Arizona community menaced by a creeping evil that came out of the desert.

Also from CD, *Undead* was an omnibus of John Russo's novels *Night of the Living Dead* and *Return of the Living Dead* with an Introduction by the author. It was published in a signed edition limited to 750 copies.

Turnaround was a novella by Craig Spector, about a man writing a life-changing screenplay, while *Sick Chick Flicks* contained three screenplays by Spector's old writing partner John Skipp, with commentary by the author and an interview conducted by Cody Goodfellow.

The Dark Man contained a reprint poem by Stephen King, illustrated by Glenn Chadbourne. It was published in a regular trade edition and a slipcased edition ($40.95).

Cemetery Dance celebrated twenty-five years as a publisher with *Turn Down the Lights* edited with an introduction by Richard Chizmar and featuring stories by some of their biggest authors, including Stephen King, Clive Barker and Peter Straub, while Thomas F. Monteleone supplied an Afterword. There were also special artist editions signed by the editor and artists, the most expensive being $750.00.

Published under the Edgeworks Abbey imprint, Harlan Ellison's *Honorable Whoredom at a Penny a Word* collected fifteen crime and detective stories from the author's early career, while *Blood's a Rover* contained Ellison's Nebula Award-winning novella "A Boy and His Dog", along with additional new "Vic and Blood" material and a two-hour teleplay pilot.

Harlan Ellison's® Brain Movies: Volume Five included scripts for *The Dark Forces*, an unproduced mid-1970s TV pilot, along with an outline for a *Batman* episode, an unfilmed episode of *The Rat Patrol*, the original outline for the author's episode of *Logan's Run*, and episodes of *Burke's Law* and *Ripcord*.

A schoolboy adventure turned into something much darker when a fourteen-year-old girl wanted a relationship from beyond the grave in Michael Aronovitz's novel *Alice Walks*, published by Centipede Press.

From Pendragon Press, *To Usher, the Dead* was a 200-copy hardcover collection of fourteen stories about psychic investigator Thomas Usher by Gary McMahon, with an Introduction and Story Notes by the author. Gardner Goldsmith's vampire novella *Bite* was available in a slim paperback from the same imprint with two additional reprint stories.

Gary McMahon's short novel *The Bones of You* was the ninth volume in Earthling Publications' annual Halloween Series. A divorced father suspected that the abandoned house next door was haunted by the deeds of a dead serial killer. It was available in a signed edition of 500 copies and a traycased edition of just fifteen copies ($350.00).

A teenager dealing with the death of his mother started experiencing bizarre dreams in Mark Morris' novel *It Sustains*, which came with an Introduction by Sarah Pinborough. It was also available in a 500-copy signed edition and a ten-copy traycased edition ($400.00).

Everything You Need was a welcome new collection by Michael Marshall Smith from Earthling. It featured seventeen stories (five original) along with story notes by the author. It was published in a 1,000-copy signed edition and a twenty-six copy handmade traycased lettered edition.

Limited to just 400 copies from Tartarus Press, *Flowers of the Sea: Thirteen Stories and Two Novellas* was a hefty hardcover collection written and illustrated by Reggie Oliver that included three previously unpublished tales, along with an Introduction by Michael Dirda and story notes by the author.

Also published by Tartarus in a run of 400 copies, *Herald of the Hidden and Other Stories* collected ten adventures of Mark Valentine's psychic detective Ralph Tyler (three original), along with six further tales of the supernatural.

Translated by William Charlton, *Darkscapes* by French author Anne-Sylvie Salzman contained fifteen stories (one original) exploring the horror in life and the beauty in strangeness.

Timothy Parker Russell edited *Dark World: Ghost Stories*, featuring fourteen stories (one reprint) by Reggie Oliver, Christopher Fowler, Mark Valentine, John Gaskin, Steve Rasnic Tem and others. The anthology was limited to just 300 numbered softcover copies from Tartarus, with all profits going to the Amala Children's Home in India.

The Heaven Tree & Other Stories from Sarob Press collected five stories (two original) and an Afterword by Christopher Harman.

Ghosts from Spectral Press contained seventeen stories (three original) by Paul Kane, along with the script for a short film directed by Brad Watson, which was included in the book as a DVD insert.

From the same publisher, *Whitstable* by Stephen Volk was the third title in the "Spectral Visions" series. Published to honour the 2013 Peter Cushing Centenary, this masterful novella pitted the ageing Hammer actor against a very real, contemporary evil.

The next book in the series, *Still Life*, was an original hardcover novella by Tim Lebbon, about humans struggling for survival in a post-apocalyptic world.

All Spectral Press titles were available in paperback, and also as hardcover editions limited to 125 signed and numbered copies.

North American Lake Monsters: Stories was the debut collection from Nathan Ballingrud, from Small Beer Press. It contained nine tales, one original.

She Walks in Darkness from Tachyon Publications was a "lost" 1960s Gothic novel by Evangeline Walton with an Introduction by Paul Di Filippo.

Edited by Ellen Datlow for the same publisher, *Hauntings* featured twenty-four reprint stories about ghosts by Neil Gaiman, Joyce Carol Oates, Peter Straub, Caitlín R. Kiernan, F. Paul Wilson, Kelly Link and others.

Richard Klaw edited the anthology *The Apes of Wrath* for Tachyon. It featured sixteen reprint stories about special simians by, amongst others, James P. Blaylock, Edgar Allan Poe, Edgar Rice Burroughs, Robert E. Howard, Hugh B. Cave, Clark Ashton Smith, Philip José Farmer, Steven Utley, Joe R. Lansdale and Howard Waldrop, along with short articles by Jess Nevins, Scott A. Cupp, Mark Finn and the editor.

Set in 1899, a black rain returned the dead to the lonely village of Hardgrove, Nebraska, in *When They Came Back*, a collaborative novel from writer Christopher Conlon and photographer Roberta Lannes-Sealey from BearManor Media.

Edited by Ross Lockhart, *Tales of Jack the Ripper* from Word Horde contained nineteen stories and poems (three reprints) by Ramsey Campbell, Joe R. Lansdale, Laird Barron and others.

Crimewave 12: Hurts from TTA Press contained fourteen stories by Melanie Tem, Stephen Volk, Joel Lane, Christopher Priest, Kristine Kathryn Rusch and others.

Overlook Connection Press reissued Lucy Taylor's 1990s collections *Close to the Bone*, *The Flesh Artist*, *Painted in Blood* and *Unnatural Acts* in trade paperback and ebook editions, along with a new hardcover compilation, *Fatal Journeys*. Overlook also produced *Fatal: A Lucy Taylor Sampler* for the 2013 World Horror Convention, containing six stories and an Introduction by Dave Hinchberger.

For JournalStone, Christopher Golden edited two volumes of *Mister October: An Anthology in Memory of Rick Hautala*. Along with brief remembrances, the two volumes featured forty-five stories (eight original) by Clive Barker, Neil Gaiman, Graham Joyce, Kim Newman, Michael Marshall Smith, Peter Straub and others. Both books were also available as a slipcased set signed by all the contributors.

Published by Jurassic London in conjunction with the Egypt Exploration Society, *Unearthed* edited by John Johnston and Jared Shurin collected eleven classic mummy stories by, amongst others, Arthur Conan Doyle, Edgar Allan Poe and Louisa May Alcott. Shurin alone edited the companion volume, *The Book of the Dead*, which featured nineteen original tales about mummies, illustrated by Garen Ewing.

Edited by Stephen Jones, *Weirder Shadows Over Innsmouth* was the third volume in the loosely connected Lovecraftian series from Fedogan & Bremer. Illustrated by Randy Broecker, it contained seventeen stories (seven original) and a poem by, amongst others, H. P. Lovecraft, Kim Newman, August Derleth, Reggie Oliver, Adrian Cole, Caitlín R. Kiernan, Angela Slatter, Brian Hodge, Ramsey Campbell, Michael Marshall Smith and Brian Lumley. A signed edition of 100 copies was also available.

Meanwhile, Titan Books issued the previous two volumes, *Shadows Over Innsmouth* and *Weird Shadows Over Innsmouth*, as revised and updated paperbacks.

From Chaosium Publication's Cthulhu Mythos-inspired series, *Undead & Unbound: Unexpected Tales from Beyond the Grave* was edited by Brian M. Sammons and David Conyers. It featured nineteen stories of the undead from Cody Goodfellow, Gary McMahon, Robert M. Price, William Meikle and others, including a collaboration between the editors.

Sammons also teamed up with co-editor Glynn Owen Barrass for *Eldritch Chrome: Unquiet Tales of a Mythos-Haunted Future* from the same imprint. Price, Meikle, Conyers, Tim Curran, Lois Gresh, Jeffrey Thomas and the editors were amongst those who contributed eighteen "Cyberpunk-Cthulhu" tales to the anthology.

Following a thirty-five year hiatus, Spectre Press revived its *Cthulhu: Tales of the Cthulhu Mythos* magazine with a fourth edition edited by Jon M. Harvey and featuring Adrian Cole's "Nick Nightmare" story "Nightmare on Mad Gull Island", illustrated by Jim Pitts. Unfortunately, aside from the change to a slim hardcover format with dust-jacket, the design and typography were firmly stuck in the past.

Chandler Klang Smith's *Goldenland Past Dark* from Canada's ChiZine Publications was about a travelling circus in the 1960s.

Terrible secrets and a malignant darkness awaited the new owner of the eponymous haunted summerhouse in *Wild Fell (A Ghost Story)* by Michael Rowe. A woman haunted by her poltergeist met a man with strange sexual predilections in David Nickle's *The 'Geisters*, and two dead people watched each other's pasts through mirrors in Melia McClure's *The Delphi Room*.

Joey Comeau's gory *The Summer is Ended and We Are Not Yet Saved* dealt with the relationship between a mother and son. *The Mona Lisa Sacrifice* was the first book in "The Book of the Cross" series by Peter Roman, and the humorous *Zombie versus Fairy Featuring Albinos* was a sequel to *Ninja versus Pirate Featuring Zombies* by James Marshall.

Celestial Inventories from ChiZine collected twenty-two stories (one original) by Steve Rasnic Tem, while *Tell My Sorrows to the Stones* contained twelve stories by Christopher Golden, one in collaboration with Mike Mignola. Cherie Priest supplied the Introduction.

Canada's Edge Science Fiction and Fantasy Publishing published *Chilling Tales: In Words, Alas, Drown I*, the second volume in a series of original horror anthologies edited with an Introduction by Michael Kelly. It contained twenty stories by David Nickle, Lisa L. Hannett, Ian Rogers, Helen Marshall, Edo van Belkom, Douglas Smith, Simon Strantzas, Sandra Kasturi, Rio Youers, Gemma Files, Bev Vincent and others.

Jennifer Brozek edited *Coins of Chaos*, an anthology of seventeen original stories from Edge about mysterious money. Contributors included Gary A. Braunbeck and Seanan McGuire.

From Canada's Exile Editions, *Dead North: Canadian Zombie Fiction* edited with an Introduction by Silvia Moreno-Garcia was the eighth volume in the "Exile Book of" anthology series. It featured twenty stories (five reprints) by Gemma Files, Simon Strantzas, Claude Lalumière and others.

From the same publisher, *This Strange Way of Dying: Stories of Magic, Desire and the Fantastic* was a debut collection by the Mexican-born Moreno-Garcia, containing fifteen original short stories.

Nicholas Royle's Nightjar Press added to its series of chapbooks with *The Jungle* by Conrad Williams and *Touch Me with Your Cold, Hard Fingers* by Elizabeth Stott. Both were limited to 200 copies.

The Spectral Press chapbook series continued with *Soul Masque* by Terry Grimwood and *Creakers* by Paul Kane, which came with an Introduction by Sarah Pinborough. Both titles were limited to 125 signed and numbered copies.

Scenes Along the Zombie Highway from Dark Regions Press collected forty-two poems (nine reprints) about the walking dead by G. O. Clark, and explorers discovered a strange island in Jason V. Brock's novella *Milton's Children*, available from Bad Moon Books.

The Rolling Darkness Revue 2013: The Impostor's Monocle was performed at The Missing Piece Theatre in Burbank, California, on October 18 and 19, 2013. As usual, Earthling Publications produced a tie-in chapbook containing stories by Peter Atkins, Glen Hirshberg and the elusive Thomas St. John Bartlett, limited to seventy-five signed copies.

Spider Web Castle was a slim, 100-copy chapbook from Ferret Fantasy reprinting a facsimile of Australian writer James Francis Dwyer's story from the December 1926 edition of *Pearson's Magazine*, along with the beautiful two-colour illustrations by Charles Robinson. George Locke supplied a tantalizing historical Afterword.

Gordon Van Gelder's bi-monthly *The Magazine of Fantasy & Science Fiction* entered its 65th year of publication with a wide variety of short stories and novelettes by, amongst many others, David Gerrold, Dale Bailey, Albert E. Cowdrey, Michael Reaves, Steven Utley, Joe Haldeman, Ted White, Tim Sullivan, Rachel Pollack, Susan Palwick,

Marc Laidlaw, James Morrow, Geoff Ryman, Michael Blumlein and James Patrick Kelly.

There were the usual reviews and commentary by Charles de Lint, Elizabeth Hand, Michelle West, James Sallis, Chris Moriarty, Paul Di Filippo, Lucius Shepard, Kathi Maio and others, along with the "Curiosities" columns by Stefan Dziemianowicz, Richard A. Lupoff, Anatoly Belilovsky, Mark Esping and Douglas A. Anderson.

The six issues of *Black Static* from TTA Press featured fiction from Ray Cluley, Lavie Tidhar, Steve Rasnic Tem, Andrew Hook, Gary McMahon, Michael Kelly, Nina Allan, Joel Lane, Daniel Mills, Tim Waggoner and others. Peter Tennant's excellent book review section included interviews with Tem, Allan, S. P. Miskowski and Mark Morris; Mike O'Driscoll looked at TV; and Tony Lee discussed the latest DVD releases. Stephen Volk continued his opinion column while, from issue #34 onwards, the busy Lynda E. Rucker took over Christopher Fowler's commentary spot, due to the latter's work commitments.

It would seem that the new *Weird Tales* team only managed to get a single issue out in 2013. The themed "Fairy Tales" edition included stories by Peter S. Beagle, Tanith Lee, Morgan Llywelyn, Jane Yolen and others. Darrell Schweitzer contributed an article on "Ninety Years of *Weird Tales*", while Tessa Farmer was interviewed about her fairy-tale photos and J. David Spurlock was interviewed about his book on *WT* artist Margaret Brundage. Ramsey Campbell, Jessica Amanda Salmonson, Elizabeth Bear and Orrin Grey all contributed short interviews about the issue's theme.

The January issue of *Fortean Times* (#296) included a feature on the unusual life and career of Robert E. Howard, while the March issue looked at the work of Badger Books author Lionel Fanthorpe.

The May/June issue of *Famous Monsters of Filmland* (#267) featured articles on "The Creation of Cthulhu" and "The New Mythos Writers" by S. T. Joshi, "Lovecraft's Acolytes" by Robert M. Price, and "The Eldritch Providence" by Bob Eggleton, who not only painted the cover for that edition, but also for #269, which was another Japanese *kaijū* special.

Canada's glossy *Rue Morgue* magazine included features on Arthur Machen (with commentary by John Carpenter, Ramsey Campbell and S. T. Joshi), British Horror Movies, 50 Years of Gore and the 40th anniversary of *The Exorcist*. There were interviews with John Connolly, Brian Clemens, Don Coscarelli, Robin Hardy, Sir Christopher Lee, Elijah Wood, Claire Bloom, James Wan, Guillermo del Toro, Philip Kaufman, Herschell Gordon Lewis, Dario Argento, Tom Savini, David Cronenberg, William Friedkin and Wes Craven, along with numerous reviews.

There were more reviews in the special *Rue Morgue Magazine's 200 Alternative Horror Films You Need to See* edited by Rodrigo Gudiño and Dave Alexander.

Quentin Tarantino chose his "Top 50 Best Sequels" for *Video WatcHDog*. There was also a feature on Universal Classic Monsters and tributes to Gerry Anderson, Ray Harryhausen and Jesús Franco, along with the usual reviews, columns and letters.

The September 13 issue of *Entertainment Weekly* included an excerpt from Stephen King's *Doctor Sleep*.

Locus featured interviews with Lavie Tidhar, Tim Powers, Tanya Huff and the inevitable Neil Gaiman, and there was a shorter "Spotlight" conversation with artist Caniglia. Amongst the special features was a welcome look at the small and independent genre presses.

The British Fantasy Society's *BFS Journal* continued to play musical chairs with its editorial team as the two trade paperback editions included opinion pieces by Ramsey Campbell, Mark Morris, Lou Morgan, Stephen Volk and Jonathan Oliver, along with fiction and poetry from, amongst others, Gary McMahon, Megan Kerr, Lavie Tidhar, Ian Whates and Allen Ashley. There were features on writing historical fantasy, the rise of weird Westerns, the state of role-playing games, inventing monsters, justifying fan fiction, the importance of cover art, and the role of "grimdark" fiction. Paul Finch, Ben Baldwin, Tom Fletcher, Tom Brown and Tommy Donbavand were all interviewed.

The BFS also published two hardcover anthologies only available to members of the Society. For an organization dedicated to the literary aspect of the genre, it was unfortunate that the typography and design of *The Burning Circus: BFS Horror 1* was so disappointing. At least editor Johnny Mains managed to attract an impressive line-up that featured Adam Nevill, Thana Niveau, Angela Slatter, Alex Hamilton, Lynda E. Rucker, Stephen Volk, Muriel Gray and Rob *(sic)* Shearman, along with an Introduction by outgoing BFS President Ramsey Campbell.

Juliet E. McKenna edited and Introduced a companion BFS anthology entitled *Unexpected Journeys*, which contained eight stories (one reprint) by, amongst others, Gail Z. Martin, Adrian Tchaikovsky, Liz Williams and Chaz Brenchley.

The fifth issue of *Shadows & Tall Trees* included stories by Gary Fry, Claire Massey, Richard Gavin, Ray Cluley and Lynda E. Rucker. Editor Michael Kelly announced that, with future editions, the format would change to an annual trade paperback and ebook.

Another small magazine with continuing concerns over its frequency and format, David Longhorn's superior small magazine *Supernatural Tales* reached its 25th print issue with three editions published in 2013. Amongst those authors featured were Iain Rowan, Tina Rath, Lynda E. Rucker, John Llewellyn Probert, Christopher Harman, Brian J. Showers, Michael Chislett and Peter Bell. The title also included eclectic reviews by the editor.

James R. Beach's *Dark Discoveries* magazine published issues themed around "Horror and Rock" and "Dark Fantasy". They featured fiction by F. Paul Wilson, Robert E. Howard and Ramsey Campbell, Angeline Hawkes, Weston Ochse, Joe McKinney and Steve Rasnic Tem, along with interviews with Rob Zombie, John Skipp, Jonathan Maberry, Boris Vallejo, Chris Morey of Dark Regions Press,

Dark Horse Comics' Scott Allie, and the return of Robert Morrish's "What the Hell Ever Happened To . . .?" column, spotlighting Sean Costello. Articles included, amongst other topics, Alice Cooper's *Welcome 2 My Nightmare* album, Stephen King's connection to rock 'n' roll, Thomas Ligotti and music group Current 93, the sword & sorcery legacy of Robert E. Howard and an introduction to author Karl Edward Wagner.

The two issues of Ireland's *Albedo*, edited by Bob Neilson and others, featured fiction, interviews and reviews covering all aspects of the genre. Issue #43 included a piece in which David Gerrold, David Morrell, Mike Resnick, Jane Yolen, Ellen Datlow, Eileen Gunn, Steve Rasnic Tem, Jack Womack, Raymond E. Feist, Amber Benson, Gary Wolfe and other luminaries put forward their opinions about "The Most Important Issue Facing Writers Today".

Hildy Silverman's *Space and Time: The Magazine of Fantasy, Horror, and Science Fiction* published its usual two editions featuring fiction and poetry, along with a tribute to Josepha Sherman in issue #118. Subscribers to the cancelled *Realms of Fantasy* magazine received complimentary print and electronic versions of *S&T*.

The four issues of *Morpheus Tales* featured fiction and poetry in a much-improved format with glossy colour covers.

The 25th issue of Justin Marriott's *Paperback Fanatic* was a perfect-bound "*Weird Tales* Special". Along with numerous full-colour cover reproductions, the magazine included a reminiscence by Ramsey Campbell, plus pieces on *Avon Fantasy Reader*, the British editions of *Weird Tales*, Frank Belknap Long, Leo Margulies, C. L. Moore, Clark Ashton Smith, Seabury Quinn and Christine Campbell Thomson's "Not at Night" anthologies.

Along with fiction and reviews, the second volume of Jason V. Brock's multi-coloured and perfect-bound *[Nameless]*, billed as "a bi-annual journal of the macabre, esoteric and intellectual . . .", offered some interesting articles on the history of television animation in America, the story behind August Derleth's "Stephen Grendon" pseudonym, and horror themes in *Space: 1999*, along with interviews with George A. Romero and Rod Serling, the latter conducted by William F. Nolan back in 1963.

Brock was also one of a number of contributors to the fourth volume of Centipede Press' annual paperback magazine *Weird Fiction Review*, edited by S. T. Joshi. The *Famous Monsters*-inspired edition featured short fiction and poetry by Lynne Jamneck, Michael Kelly, Leigh Blackmore and others, along with some interesting articles on H. P. Lovecraft's discovery of William Hope Hodgson, Rod Serling's *The Twilight Zone*, Dennis Etchison's *The Dark Country*, monster magazines, Henry S. Whitehead, Jack Davis, Algernon Blackwood, Forrest J Ackerman, an interview with Patrick McGrath, and a colour portfolio of Bob Eggleton's paintings.

As usual, the two issues of Rosemary Pardoe's excellent *The Ghosts & Scholars M. R. James Newsletter* were filled with fascinating news, reviews, articles and letters about the ghost story author, along with fiction by Chico Kidd, Mark Valentine, Peter Bell and others.

Dedicated to the memory of Arthur Machen, a special issue of Gwilym Games' *Machenalia* from The Friends of Arthur Machen celebrated the author's centenary-and-a-half commemoration at the World Fantasy Convention in Brighton with a number of non-fiction pieces by Machen, R. B. Russell and the late Roger Dobson.

After taking a hiatus in 2012, the two issues of *Lady Churchill's Rosebud Wristlet* from Gavin J. Grant, Kelly Link and others, contained stories and poetry by Helen Marshall, Nina Allan and others.

Canada's Ex Hubris Imprints published issues #3 and #4 of *Postscripts to Darkness*, edited by Sean Moreland and Aalya Ahmad and featuring fiction and poetry by Michael Kelly, Albert Choi and others, along with interviews with Gemma Files, Helen Marshall and Tony Burgess.

Doors to Elsewhere from The Alchemy Press collected seventeen of Mike Barrett's terrific essays (one original), from *The New York Review of Science Fiction*, *Wormwood*, *Dark Horizons* and elsewhere, about authors who were mostly published by Arkham House and *Weird Tales*. Following a new Introduction by Ramsey Campbell, Barrett's concise profiles included Arkham House itself, Greye La Spina, Fritz Leiber, Marjorie Bowen, Ernest Bramah, C. Hall Thompson, Clifford Ball, C. L. Moore, G. G. Pendarves and Lord Dunsany, amongst others.

Andrew Lycett's biography *Wilkie Collins: A Life of Sensation*, ran to more than 500 pages.

From Hippocampus Press, *Nolan on Bradbury: Sixty Years of Writing About the Master of Science Fiction* collected twenty-one articles and eight stories by William F. Nolan, along with a piece on Nolan by his subject, tributes to Bradbury by Jason V. Brock, John C. Tibbetts and editor S. T. Joshi, and an Afterword by Greg Bear.

From the same PoD publisher, David Goudsward's *H. P. Lovecraft in the Merrimack Valley* explored the writer's links with the Massachusetts and New Hampshire area. Kenneth W. Faig, Jr supplied the Foreword.

McFarland & Company, Inc. published *H. P. Lovecraft's Dark Arcadia: The Satire, Symbology and Contradiction* by Gavin Callaghan, which was an attempt to objectively re-assess the works and life of the horror writer by ignoring secondary accounts, while *Conan Meets the Academy: Multidisciplinary Essays on the Enduring Barbarian* edited by Jonas Prida contained ten articles about Robert E. Howard's character in popular culture.

In the snappily-titled *The Modern Literary Werewolf: A Critical Study of the Mutable Motif* from the same publisher, college instructor Brent A. Stypczynski looked at were-wolves as representations of a proposed shape-shifter arche-type. It took in not just Jack Williamson's seminal *Darker Than You Think*, but also books by J. K. Rowling, Terry Pratchett and Charlaine Harris, and came with a useful Bibliography.

The Lady and Her Monsters: A Tale of Dissections, Real-Life Dr. Frankensteins, and the Creation of Mary Shelley's

Masterpiece was a biography of the author by Roseanne Montillo.

Compiled by Brian Freeman, Hans Ake Lilja and Kevin Quigley, *The Illustrated Stephen King Movie Trivia Book* from Cemetery Dance Publications included an Introduction by Mick Garris, artwork by Glenn Chadbourne and more than 1,000 questions. It was available in various editions, including a deluxe traycased edition of fifty-two lettered copies containing an original illustration by Chadbourne ($300.00).

From the same imprint, *The Illustrated Stephen King Trivia Book: Revised and Updated Second Edition* edited by Freeman and Bev Vincent added more than 100 new questions to the 2005 volume.

In *The Alluring Art of Margaret Brundage: Queen of Pulp Pin-up Art* from Vanguard Productions, Stephen D. Korshak and J. David Spurlock did their utmost to uncover the background behind the somewhat enigmatic artist, best known for her sexy/bondage pastel paintings that graced the covers of *Weird Tales* in the 1930s. Artist Rowena Morrill supplied the Foreword, and there were essays by Robert Weinberg and Melvin Korshak.

Also from Vanguard, *Frazetta Sketchbook* was the first in a series of art books reproducing sketches and preliminaries by Frank Frazetta, with a Foreword by J. David Spurlock. It was also available in a deluxe hardcover edition with an extra folio.

Hermes Press published *Frank Frazetta: Art and Remembrances*, which featured text by the artist's son, Frank Frazetta, Jr, a Foreword by Kirk Hammett and an Afterword by Jerry Lawler.

Spectrum 20: The Best in Contemporary Fantastic Art, edited as usual by Cathy and Arnie Fenner for Underwood Books, contained more than 500 images from over 300 artists, along with a profile of Grand Master Award-winner Brom.

PS ArtBooks continued to turn out beautiful full-colour volumes of pre-code comic books in a bewildering variety of editions. The "Harvey Horrors Collected Works" series was expanded with further volumes of *Tomb of Terror* and *Witches Tales* with new Forewords by Jeff Gelb, Joe R. Lansdale and James Lovegrove.

The "American Comics Group Collected Works" from PS continued with more volumes of *Forbidden Worlds* and *Adventures Into the Unknown*, including Forewords by Mark Chadbourn and Paul Di Filippo. The second volume in the "Roy Thomas Presents" reprints of *The Heap* featured Forewords by both Herb Rogoff and series editor Thomas, while Lawrence Watt-Evans contributed a comprehensive Foreword to the second volume of *The Thing!* in the "Pre-Code Classics" series.

Based around an old library copy of a fictitious fantasy novel, *The Ship of Theseus* by the mysterious V. M. Straka, *S* by J. J. Abrams and Doug Dorst featured hand-written comments by two students, along with inserted letters, newspaper clippings, etc., contained within a slipcase.

David Britton's *Eduardo Paolozzi at New Worlds* from Savoy Books was an illustrated look at the art of the 1960s artist whose work is most associated with the groundbreaking British SF magazine edited by Michael Moorcock. Design historian Rick Poynor supplied an Introduction, and there was commentary from Michael Butterworth, John Clute and J. G. Ballard.

Lord Horror: Reverbstorm was a huge hardcover graphic novel from Savoy, written by David Britton and illustrated in black and white by John Coulthart, originally published across seven issues of *David Britton's Lord Horror* comic.

Gris Grimly's Frankenstein was an illustrated adaptation of an edited version of Mary Shelley's text, with a Foreword by Bernie Wrightson and an Afterword by artist Grimly.

I. N. J. Culbard adapted and illustrated a graphic novel of H. P. Lovecraft's, *The Shadow Out of Time*.

Richard Corben's adaptation of *The Fall of the House of Usher* for Dark Horse comics also incorporated Edgar Allan Poe's story "The Oval Portrait", while Corben's *The Raven and the Red Death* featured separate adaptations of two other Poe stories.

In Roberto Aguirre-Sacasa's series *Afterlife with Archie* for Archie Comic Publications, Archie, Jughead and the other loveable inhabitants of Riverdale were transformed into the walking dead when Sabrina the Teenage Witch cast a spell that went wrong.

Writers Clive Barker and Mark Miller teamed up with artist Haemi Jang for the twelve-issue series *New Genesis*, a reinterpretation of Biblical horrors from comics imprint Boom! Barker was also credited on one of the two stories that comprised the *Hellraiser Annual 2013* from the same imprint.

No doubt inspired by the success of *Game of Thrones*, Avatar's *George R. R. Martin's Skin Trade* was based on the author's 1988 werewolf novella.

For the first time in a decade, Neil Gaiman returned to the *Sandman* title for *Overture*, an expansive prequel illustrated by J. H. Williams III.

A ghostly female serial killer who called herself "The Light" was murdering New Yorkers at random in Dynamite's *The Shadow*, based on the 1930s pulp character.

IDW's *Classics Obliterated: Mars Attacks* was a spoof on the old *Classics Illustrated* title, with the trading card alien invaders reimagined in stories based on *Moby Dick*, *Robinson Crusoe* and *Dr. Jekyll and Mr. Hyde*. Meanwhile, a hardcover edition of *Classics Illustrated* from Papercutz was devoted to Edgar Allan Poe and featured adaptations of "Murders in the Rue Morgue", "The Gold-Bug" and "The Mystery of Marie Roget".

Although the Showtime TV series may have finally come to an end, Marvel revived sympathetic serial killer *Dexter* in his own eponymous comic, written by creator Jeff Lindsay.

To celebrate the TV show's 20th anniversary, *The X Files* finally got its tenth season in a monthly comic book series from IDW, written by Joe Harris and set in the present day. Series creator Chris Carter executive produced and consulted.

* * *

Peter David's tie-in novel to *After Earth* also included three "After Earth: Ghost Stories", one by Robert Greenberger and two from Michael Jan Friedman, previously published separately as e-stories. *After Earth: A Perfect Beast* was a prequel to the movie featuring work by the same three authors.

The year's other original movie tie-ins included *47 Ronin* by Joan D. Vinge, *The Lords of Salem* by Rob Zombie and B. K. (Brian) Evenson, *Man of Steel* by Greg Cox, *Pacific Rim* by Alex Irvine and *Star Trek: Into Darkness* by Alan Dean Foster.

Published under the Hammer imprint, Guy Adams' *Countess Dracula* reimagined the events of the 1971 movie as happening in 1930s Hollywood, while Shaun Hutson's *The Revenge of Frankenstein* was a new novelization of the 1958 Hammer film.

Ian Doescher's *William Shakespeare's Star Wars* told the story of the original movie entirely in iambic pentameter. Use the Force, Luke, verily.

The Walking Dead: The Fall of the Governor Part One by Robert Kirkman and Jay Bonansinga was the third volume based on the AMC TV series.

Other TV tie-ins included *Grimm: The Icy Touch* by John Shirley, *Once Upon a Time: Reawakened* by Odette Beane, *Supernatural: Fresh Meat* by Alice Henderson and *Supernatural: Carved in Flesh* by Tim Waggoner, while Christa Faust's *Fringe: The Zodiac Paradox* and *Fringe: The Burning Man* were the first two volumes in a new series based on the now-cancelled show.

Lara Parker's *Dark Shadows: Wolf Moon Rising* was based on the 1960s TV show, and *Torchwood: Exodus Code* was co-credited to series star John Barrowman and his sister Carole E. Barrowman.

It was an important year for new *Doctor Who* books. These included the novelizations *The Dalek Generation* by Nicholas Briggs, *Shroud of Sorrow* by Tommy Donbavand, *Harvest of Time* by Alastair Reynolds and *Plague of the Cybermen* by Justin Richards.

Doctor Who: Summer Falls and Other Stories collected three novellas by Justin Richards that were originally published as ebooks, while *Doctor Who: 11 Doctors, 11 Stories* contained tales originally published as monthly ebooks throughout the year. Mike Tucker's novella *Doctor Who: The Silurian Gift* was published at just £1.00 by BBC Books for World Book Day.

Doctor Who: The Doctor – His Life and Times was a fictional biography of the Time Lord by James Goss and Steve Tribe, told through interviews, letters, etc.

Barry Forshaw's *British Gothic Cinema* was an insightful guide to an often-neglected sub-genre of UK cinema. It included some fascinating chapters on films of the 1930s and '40s, Hammer's rivals, and one-shots and short-run series. An Appendix of brief interviews featured pithy insights from, amongst others, Ingrid Pitt, Ramsey Campbell, Christopher Fowler, Kim Newman, Christopher Wicking, Peter James and Stephen Volk.

For Auteur Publishing's "Devil's Rejects" series, Forshaw wrote an incisive examination of Jonathan Demme's *The Silence of the Lambs*, which also managed to take in Dr Lecter's other appearances.

Guillermo del Toro: Cabinet of Curiosities not only looked behind the scenes at the writer-director's movies, but also allowed a sneak peek at his wonderful home of horrors.

From PS Publishing, editor Johnny Mains compiled *The Sorcerers* by John Burke, a fascinating look at the controversy surrounding the true authorship of the 1967 British film starring Boris Karloff. The handsome hardcover not only included Burke's original screenplay (entitled "Terror for Kicks"), but also commentary by Mains, Matthew Sweet, Benjamin Halligan, Kim Newman and Tony Earnshaw, along with a selection of Burke's correspondence from the period.

David Miller's updated biography *Peter Cushing: A Life in Film* was published to coincide with the centenary of the actor's birth in May. It contained previously unpublished correspondence by Cushing himself.

Crab Monsters, Teenage Cavemen, and Candy Stripe Nurses: Roger Corman: King of the B Movie by Chris Nashawaty included reminiscences from the influential director's many discoveries, who looked back over his six-decade career.

In *Chain Saw Confidential*, actor Gunnar Hansen explained what it was like to play "Leatherface" in the original *Texas Chainsaw* movie.

Christopher Wayne Curry's *Film Alchemy: The Independent Cinema of Ted V. Mikels* from McFarland & Company, Inc. looked at the career of the American exploitation director, while Robert Michael "Bobb" Cotter's *The Women of Hammer Horror: A Biographical Dictionary and Filmography* listed the hundreds of women who worked both in front of and behind the camera.

In *Fang Fan Fiction: Variations on Twilight, True Blood and The Vampire Diaries* from the same publisher, Maria Lindgren Leavenworth and Malin Isaksson compared the original book series with the filmed adaptations and the fan fiction based upon them.

The subtitles helpfully told you everything you needed to know about Bryan Senn's *The Most Dangerous Cinema: People Hunting People on Film* and Rob Craig's *It Came from 1957: A Critical Guide to the Year's Science Fiction, Fantasy and Horror Films*.

Editors James Aston and John Walliss collected articles around the impact of the popular movie franchise in *To See the Saw Movies: Essays on Torture Porn and Post-9/11 Horror*, while Aalya Ahmad and Sean Moreland edited *Fear and Learning: Essays on the Pedagogy of Horror*.

Remaking Horror: Hollywood's New Reliance on Scares of Old by James Francis, Jr took its cue from Gus Van Sant's 1998 remake of *Psycho*.

Editor Gillian I. Leitch's *Doctor Who in Time and Space* collected a number of new essays about the BBC series, and Mark Campbell's *Doctor Who: The Complete Guide* was a fully revised and updated guide to every TV episode, along with radio, cinema, stage and Internet spin-offs, plus novels, audio adventures and missing episodes. It also included a website listing and a comprehensive bibliography.

Song of Spider-Man: The Inside Story of the Most Controversial Musical in Broadway History was an insider's view written by Glen Berger, the scriptwriter of the $65-million stage production that debuted in June 2011.

Marc Forster's sprawling $170-million 3-D zombie epic, *World War Z*, may not have had much to do with Max Brooks' original novel, but producer Brad Pitt's UN investigator travelled all over the globe attempting to find a cure for the resurrection virus, as those around him met grisly fates, usually due to their own incompetence. The extended director's cut filled in some of the gaps.

Chloë Grace Moretz was the blood-covered teen with psychic powers and Julianne Moore her fundamentalist-crazy mother in Kimberly Peirce's unnecessary remake of Stephen King's *Carrie*.

Fede Alvarez's extremely gory *Evil Dead*, starring Jane Levy and Shiloh Fernandez, was a perfectly reasonable – if derivative – remake we didn't need, despite being produced by original creators Sam Raimi and Bruce Campbell.

Alexandre Aja's *Maniac* was a remake of the 1980 slasher movie, filmed from the point-of-view of the deranged killer and scalper (Elijah Wood).

Based on Moira Buffini's play *A Vampire Story*, Neil Jordan directed *Byzantium*, about the relationship between a 200-year-old undead prostitute (Gemma Arterton) and her vampire daughter (Saoirse Ronan). Meanwhile, Xan Cassavetes' *Kiss of the Damned* explored the connection between a beautiful vampire (Joséphine de La Baume) and her new screenwriter lover (Milo Ventimiglia).

Creepy family secrets were revealed in Korean director Park Chan-wook's English-language debut *Stoker* which, despite the title, had nothing to do with vampires. Mia Wasikowska, Matthew Goode and Nicole Kidman starred.

January is now established as the month when studios release trashy, low-budget horror movies such as Andrés Muschietti's *Mama*, "presented" by executive producer Guillermo del Toro. When a couple (Nokolai Coster-Waldau and Jessica Chastain) took in two orphaned sisters (Megan Charpentier and Isabelle Nélisse), a malevolent spirit accompanied them.

That same month, Dan Yeager was the latest chainsaw-wielding psycho behind the human-faced mask in director John Luessenhop's pointless reboot/sequel *Texas Chainsaw 3D*. At least it featured cameos by actors from the original film, Marilyn Burns, John Dugan and Gunnar Hansen, along with Bill Moseley from the 1986 sequel.

James Wan's overrated *The Conjuring* starred Patrick Wilson and Vera Farmiga as real-life paranormal experts Ed and Lorraine Warren (*The Amityville Horror*) investigating a farmhouse haunting centred around a creepy doll, while the same director's *Insidious: Chapter 2* also featured Wilson and was a sequel to the 2011 movie. Depressingly, both were huge box-office hits in the US.

One night a year Americans were allowed to go crazy in an otherwise crime-free future in *The Purge*, which starred Ethan Hawke and was made by the people behind the *Paranormal Activity* franchise.

Ashley Bell returned as a woman possessed by a demon in *The Last Exorcism Part II*, which dropped the "found footage" narrative of the first movie, and the family of a suburban Arizona couple (Keri Russell and Josh Hamilton) were plagued by alien "greys" in Scott Stewart's *Dark Skies*.

In Jeremy Lovering's impressive debut feature *In Fear*, a couple (Iain De Caestecker and Alice Englert) found themselves lost on the Irish back roads at night.

Although he was playing Professor Van Helsing on TV, Thomas Kretschmann switched sides to portray the blood-thirsty Count himself in (Dario) *Argento's Dracula 3-D*. In another role reversal, former Dracula actor Rutger Hauer turned up as Van Helsing.

A radio disc jockey (Sheri Moon Zombie) received a record album that literally unleashed Hell in Rob Zombie's *The Lords of Salem*.

Barry Levinson's *The Bay* used "found footage" to make its point about ecological pollution, as a flesh-eating bacteria transferred itself from fish to humans.

In writer/director Elliot Goldner's feature debut *The Borderlands*, Gordon Kennedy and Robin Hill starred in yet another example of "found footage", as two Vatican investigators were sent to a remote church in Britain's West Country to investigate paranormal activity.

Michael Axelgaard's *Hollow* was a micro-budget British *Blair Witch Project*, and a couple expecting twins moved into a haunted house from Hell in the zany comedy *Hell Baby*.

Nobody really needed the "found footage" comedy *Scary Movie V* featuring Heather Locklear, Jerry O'Connell, Snoop Dogg, Charlie Sheen and Lindsay Lohan, but at least it was an improvement over the haunted house spoof *A Haunted House*, which starred the annoying Marlon Wayans.

Twenty-six international directors, including Jorge Michel Grau, Noboru Iguchi, Jake West, Ti West and Ben Wheatley, were invited to make a short film about death based on a different letter of the alphabet in *The ABCs of Death*, while *V/H/S/2* was a "found footage" anthology with multiple directors featuring zombies, demons and aliens.

After a delay of seven years due to distribution problems, *All the Boys Love Mandy Lane* starred Amber Heard as a high school student caught up in a series of killings on a remote Texas cattle ranch. *You're Next*, Adam Wingard's tale of a family fighting back against a gang of animal-masked psychos, had also spent a couple of years sitting on the shelf.

While camping in rural Maine, Katie Aselton (who also directed), Lake Bell and Kate Bosworth were menaced by psycho hunters in *Black Rock*, which was apparently supposed to be a feminist version of *Deliverance*.

Sean Pertwee was the militia leader who took over a Balkans brothel in Paul Hyett's directing debut *The Seasoning House*, and a father had to save his baby daughter from a gang of feral children by taking a stand in an abandoned tower block in the Irish-made *Citadel*.

Nicholas Hoult's nice teen zombie ate the brain of a victim and fell in love with the dead man's girlfriend (Teresa Palmer) in Jonathan Levine's romzomcom *Warm Bodies*, which also featured John Malkovich.

British stand-up comedian Ross Noble played a homicidal zombie clown in *Stitches*, while director Dominic Brunt and his real-life wife Joanne Mitchell travelled to the Yorkshire Moors to renew their marriage and ended up battling zombies in *Before Dawn*.

An exterminator (Greg Grunberg) and a hospital handyman (Lombardo "Bardo" Boyar) tried to stop a giant arachnid destroying Los Angeles in the comedy *Big Ass Spider!*

Ben Wheatley's £300,000 supernatural drama *A Field in England* premiered in Britain on cinema screens, Freeview television, Blu-ray, DVD and Video on Demand, all on the same day. It featured Reece Shearsmith in a story of dark magick set during the English Civil War.

Indie horror movie *Escape from Tomorrow*, about a man traumatized by his visits to theme parks, was secretly filmed inside Disney World and Disneyland by first-time writer-director Randy Moore.

Aleksandr Sokurov's art-house *Faust* updated the story to the 19th century. A suicidal doorman (Luis Tosar) stalked a woman in her Barcelona apartment in Jaume Balagueró's psychological thriller *Sleep Tight*, and *We Are What We Are* was a remake of a 2010 Mexican movie about a family of cannibals.

In Peter Jackson's *The Hobbit: The Desolation of Smaug*, the second film in the extended trilogy, Bilbo Baggins (Martin Freeman) found himself up against giant spiders and the titular gold-hoarding dragon (voiced by Benedict Cumberbatch).

James Franco made a likeable younger version of the character in Sam Raimi's colourful 3-D prequel *Oz the*

Great and Powerful from Disney, which featured Michelle Williams, Mila Kunis and Rachel Weisz as a trio of beautiful witches, and Bruce Campbell as a Winkie guard.

Leather-clad brother and sister Jeremy Renner and Gemma Arterton were celebrity witch assassins during medieval times in Tommy Wirkola's long-delayed *Hansel & Gretel Witch Hunters* in 3-D.

After being pushed back from the previous summer, Jack (Nicholas Hoult) and his companions eventually climbed the giant beanstalk and disappeared at the box-office in Bryan Singer's $185-million *Jack the Giant Slayer*, also released in 3-D. The impressive supporting cast included Ewan McGregor, Bill Nighy, Eddie Marsan, Ian McShane, Stanley Tucci and John Kassir.

Based on Japanese folklore, the $175-million *47 Ronin* was another flop that starred Keanu Reeves as an 18th-century samurai warrior who joined the travelling swordsmen on a quest for revenge and their battles against supernatural enemies.

Robert Downey Jr was back as the smart-mouthed Tony Stark in Shane Black's action-packed 3-D sequel *Iron Man 3*, the best in the Marvel series so far. Ben Kingsley was hilarious as terrorist villain The Mandarin, who turned out to not be quite what everyone expected. Costing $200 million, it had the second-biggest opening weekend in America ever, after *Avengers Assemble*. A revised version of the film, featuring different footage and an appearance by actress Fan Bingbing, was released in China.

Marvel's *Thor: The Dark World* was a totally serviceable sequel in which the Norse god (Chris Hemsworth) teamed up with his scheming stepbrother Loki (Tom Hiddleston) to save London from the Dark Elves, led by the evil Malekith (Christopher Eccleston). Despite a sometimes dull plot, the $170-million movie still managed to surpass what the first movie grossed in 2011.

In his second solo outing in the unexcitingly titled *The Wolverine*, Hugh Jackman's razor-clawed crusader travelled to modern-day Japan in a story based on the 1980s

Marvel Comics mini-series by Chris Claremont and Frank Miller. There he rescued a woman (Tao Okamoto) from ninja assassins and was betrayed by an old friend seeking to steal his powers.

The latest "Marvel One-Shot" short, *Agent Carter*, starred Hayley Atwell reprising her role as British operative Peggy Carter from the *Captain America* films. As an analyst for the nascent S.H.I.E.L.D. organization, she was looking for the mysterious "Zodiac" key.

Zack Snyder's $225-million *Man of Steel* was the second Superman reboot that failed to fly in the past seven years. British actor Henry Cavill donned the cape and boots, while Kevin Costner and Russell Crowe played the hero's adoptive and alien birth fathers. Michael Shannon portrayed Kryptonian villain General Zod, Laurence Fishburne turned up as Perry White and Amy Adams was sidelined as Lois Lane.

After Cobra killed off most of the G. I. Joes, it was up to Dwayne Johnson, Channing Tatum and Bruce Willis to take the evil organization down in the action-packed reboot *G. I. Joe: Retaliation*.

Based on the Dark Horse comic, *R.I.P.D.* in 3-D starred Ryan Reynolds as a murdered Boston detective who joined the Rest in Peace Department and teamed up with Jeff Bridges' deceased Old West lawman to track down the crooked partner (Kevin Bacon) who killed him.

Told via an evocative Ray Bradbury-style wraparound story, Disney's $250-million *The Lone Ranger* starred Armie Hammer as the masked avenger and executive producer Johnny Depp as his eccentric Native American companion, Tonto. It was a lot of fun but flopped at the box office, despite being made by the same team behind the *Pirates of the Caribbean* franchise.

Aaron Taylor-Johnson and Chloë Grace Moretz reprised their roles as teenage crime-fighters in *Kick-Ass 2*, based on the comic by Mark Millar. However, co-star Jim Carrey refused to publicize the film after he objected to the excessive on-screen violence.

With super-warrior Katniss Everdeen (Jennifer Lawrence) now a dangerously iconic figure, the fascist President (Donald Sutherland) forced her to compete again in Francis Lawrence's highly anticipated YA sequel *The Hunger Games: Catching Fire*, based on the books by Suzanne Collins. The film not only broke the five-day Thanksgiving weekend record, but went on to surpass *Iron Man 3* to become the highest-grossing film released in America in 2013.

Along similar lines, *The Mortal Instruments: City of Bones* was based on the popular YA book series by Cassandra Clare and starred Lily Collins as a tough demon-slayer and role-model for young girls.

An alien took over the body of a seventeen-year-old girl (Saoirse Ronan) and nothing much else happened in *The Host*, based on the novel by Stephenie Meyer. It failed to match even the minimal sophistication of the author's *Twilight* series.

Ronan also starred in *How I Live Now*, based on the dystopian YA novel by Meg Rosoff, in which a nuclear attack on London interrupted a forbidden love affair with her cousin (George MacKay).

Beautiful Creatures, based on the popular series of YA novels by Kami Garcia and Margaret Stohl, didn't do well at the box office, as feuding family elders Jeremy Irons and Emma Thompson argued over whether teen witch Lena's (Alice Englert) powers should be used for good of evil.

Logan Lerman was back as the teen Greek demi-god searching the Bermuda Triangle for the Golden Fleece in the belated 3-D sequel *Percy Jackson: Sea of Monsters*, based on the popular YA book series by Rick Riordan. It included zombie pirates, a giant cyclops, the monstrous Kronos and the Furies recast as blind taxi drivers.

Astronauts George Clooney and Sandra Bullock got lost in space in Alfonso Cuarón's technically impressive 3-D *Gravity*, which enjoyed the biggest October weekend opening in the US of all time.

Meanwhile, Harrison Ford and Ben Kingsley brought some much-needed *gravitas* to *Ender's Game*, based on the

militaristic SF novel by Orson Scott Card. A group called
Geeks OUT called for a boycott of the movie due to Card's
anti-gay marriage stance, although that probably had nothing to do with the $110-million movie's drop of sixty-two
per cent in its second week at the US box office.

J. J. Abrams' superior 3-D sequel, *Star Trek: Into
Darkness*, featured Benedict Cumberbatch as an alternate
version of genetically enhanced terrorist Khan Noonien,
played by Ricardo Montalban in the original movie series.

Matt Damon's oppressed everyman just wanted to take
down Jodie Foster's elite satellite society before he died of
radiation poisoning in Neill Blomkamp's perfunctory
Elysium.

Based on a graphic novel by director Joseph Kosinski,
Tom Cruise was beside himself as a technician monitoring a
post-apocalyptic Earth following an alien invasion in
Oblivion, which took most of its ideas from other, better
films. Morgan Freeman turned up as the leader of the human
resistance movement.

Despite waiting for a final twist, there wasn't one in M.
Night Shyamalan's $130-million *After Earth*, in which Will
Smith's unsympathetic military ranger sent his in-training
son (a truly annoying Jaden Smith) on a trek across a post-
apocalyptic Earth filled with dangerous creatures.

Idris Elba was the leader of a team of giant robots that
battled monsters invading from another dimension in
Guillermo del Toro's disappointing $190-million *Pacific
Rim*, a 3-D tribute to the *kaijū* genre. It was a huge box-
office hit in China.

Vin Diesel returned for his third outing as the eponymous
intergalactic criminal stuck on yet another hostile planet in
David Twohy's *Riddick*, which the actor's company
produced and financed.

Based on Sydney J. Bounds' story "The Animators", the
creepy *The Last Days on Mars* featured Liev Schreiber and
a terrific Olivia Williams as members of a space crew trying
not to be turned into dehydrated zombies by an alien
life-form.

Directed by Lana and Andy Wachowski and Tom Tykwer, *Cloud Atlas* was a sprawling adaptation of David Mitchell's centuries-spanning novel. Tom Hanks, Halle Berry, Jim Broadbent, Hugo Weaving, Susan Sarandon, Hugh Grant and other actors played multiple roles, with the most interesting of the interconnected stories being set in a post-apocalypse Hawaii.

Chris Hemsworth couldn't fill Patrick Swayze's shoes as North Korean troops invaded a sleepy American town in an unnecessary remake of the 1984 movie *Red Dawn*.

David Cronenberg's son Brandon directed *Antiviral*, a none-too-subtle comment on celebrity obsession, in which people were injected with viruses from the famous so that they could feel closer to their idols.

Joaquin Phoenix fell in love with his computer operating system (voiced by Scarlett Johansson) in Spike Jones' near-future romance *Her*, while Kirsten Dunst and Jim Sturgess shared space between two planets with their own inverted gravities in Juan Solanas' equally baffling *Upside Down*.

Slacker Gary King (Simon Pegg) convinced his reluctant school friends (Nick Frost, Paddy Considine, Martin Freeman and Eddie Marsan, along with token female Rosamund Pike) to reunite for a pub crawl they failed to complete twenty years earlier in Edgar Wright's enjoyable SF comedy *The World's End*. When they arrived in their hometown, they discovered that aliens were replacing everyone with Stepford-like robot duplicates.

Meanwhile, Seth Rogen, James Franco, Jonah Hill and their mates played self-absorbed versions of themselves as The Rapture engulfed Hollywood in the meta-comedy *This is the End*. Michael Cera, Emma Watson, Rihanna, Paul Rudd, Channing Tatum and the Backstreet Boys all had cameos.

The War of the Worlds Alive on Stage was a filmed record of Jeff Wayne's musical version of H. G. Wells' Martian invasion novel, featuring Jason Donovan, Marti Pellow and a holographic version of Liam Neeson.

Ben Stiller starred in and directed *The Secret Life of Walter Mitty*, a pointless remake of the 1947 movie starring

Danny Kaye and Boris Karloff, based on the 1939 story by James Thurber.

A cross between *Sliding Doors* and *Groundhog Day*, Richard Curtis' time-travelling romcom *About Time* – about a man who could revisit any moment in his life to try things differently – starred Domhnall Gleeson, Rachel McAdams and Bill Nighy.

An exasperated Walt Disney (Tom Hanks) attempted to persuade grumpy author P. L. Travers (Emma Thompson) to sell him the rights to Mary Poppins in the fact-based *Saving Mr. Banks*.

Disney's $150 million CGI fairy-tale musical *Frozen* was the animated hit of 2013, grossing more than $760 million world-wide and easily passing *The Hunger Games* sequel during its second week of release.

Free Birds featured two time-travelling turkeys, the CGI *Walking with Dinosaurs* in 3-D was narrated by a prehistoric bird, and *The Croods* was an animated 3-D comedy about an embarrassing prehistoric family.

The year's other animated releases included the sequels *Despicable Me 2*, *Cloudy with a Chance of Meatballs 2*, *The Smurfs 2* and *Monsters University*, along with *Escape from Planet Earth*, *Justin and the Knights of Valour* and *Epic*.

Robin Hardy's classic 1973 film *The Wicker Man* was re-released in cinemas to celebrate its 40th anniversary in the most complete version ever screened in Britain, and it reportedly took a year and cost Universal $10 million to convert *Jurassic Park* to 3-D for the 20th anniversary of Steven Spielberg's dinosaur epic.

Rob Kuhns' *Birth of the Living Dead* looked at the making of George A. Romero's *Night of the Living Dead* (1968) and its influence on popular media, while Daniel Lutz talked about his childhood experiences living in the most famous haunted house of all time in the documentary *My Amityville Horror*.

On October 19, Johnny Depp presented ninety-one-year-old Sir Christopher Lee with a BFI Fellowship – the highest accolade given by the organization – at the 57th London Film Festival Awards.

Starting that same month and running until January 2014, the British Film Institute hosted live events and screenings at London's BFI Southbank and across the UK as part of its "Gothic: The Dark Heart of Film" retrospective. This included outdoor screenings at the British Museum of *Night of the Demon* and Hammer's *Dracula* and *The Mummy*.

In November, the DVD and game rental chain Blockbuster went into administration in Britain for the second time in 2013, and it finally closed all its 264 stores by the end of the year, with the loss of around 2,000 jobs. Competition from supermarkets, online rentals and streaming were blamed. In America, the chain shut down 300 outlets in October, leaving just fifty franchised stores still open.

Towards the end of World War II, Nazi scientists used Dr Frankenstein's journal to create an army of super-soldiers stitched together from body parts in the direct-to-DVD *Frankenstein's Army*, while Dolph Lundgren led an army of robots against a world filled with zombies in *Battle of the Damned*.

Based on the 2007 novel by David Wong, Don Coscarelli's *John Dies at the End* featured two slackers (Chase Williamson and Rob Mayes) who discovered a street drug that could transport them to different dimensions. Clancy Brown co-starred, and Angus Scrimm turned up as a priest.

Written and directed by J. T. Petty and based on his graphic novel, *Hellbenders* also featured Brown, this time as a member of a team of debauched demon-hunters.

The Cloth starred Danny Trejo and Eric Roberts and was about a secret organization which battled the Devil and his army of lost souls, while the busy Trejo was back as "Father Jesús" in another direct-to-DVD release, *Zombie Hunter*.

Laurence Fishburne and Bill Paxton were amongst the last survivors of a frozen-over Earth who found themselves menaced by cannibals in *The Colony*.

Jaime Murray's art-history professor turned out to be Elizabeth Bathory in *Fright Night 2: New Blood*, an unnecessary DVD sequel to the 2011 remake, while father and daughter Brad Dourif and Fiona Dourif starred in *Curse of Chucky*, the evil doll's sixth outing, written and directed by series creator Don Mancini.

Anne Heche starred in *Nothing Left to Fear*, a slice of religious horror that was produced by former Guns N' Roses guitarist Slash.

Malcolm McDowell was a long way from working with Stanley Kubrick and Lindsay Anderson in *The Employer*, in which his mysterious CEO put prospective employees through a series of murderous tests.

After *Cliffhanger* and *Die Hard 2*, director Renny Harlin's career was also on the skids as his "found footage" movie *Devil's Pass* (aka *The Dyatlov Pass Incident*) was released directly to DVD. It was loosely based on the true-life mystery of nine Russian skiers who were found dead in 1959.

The Collection was a sequel to *The Collector* and featured the same masked killer chopping up his victims with a giant lawnmower.

While it had nothing to do with *Psycho*, *The Bates Haunting* (aka *The Haunting of Bates Hotel*) was set at The Bates Motel & Haunted Hayride, a real-life Halloween attraction in Pennsylvania.

Produced by Marvel Animation Studio, *Iron Man & Hulk: Heroes United* featured Iron Man (voiced by Adrian Pasdar) and the Hulk (voiced by Fred Tatasciore) battling an energy being called Zzzax, who could absorb human minds. The movie combined computer animation with hand-drawn art.

Criterion issued new restorations of the classic ghost movie *The Uninvited* (1944), starring Ray Milland and Ruth Hussey, along with René Clair's comedy *I Married a Witch* (1942) with Fredric March and Veronica Lake.

Scream Factory's *The Vincent Price Collection* brought together *The Fall of the House of Usher*, *Pit and the*

Pendulum, *The Haunted Palace*, *The Masque of the Red Death*, *Witchfinder General* and *The Abominable Dr. Phibes*, while the extras included a commentary with late *Phibes* director Robert Fuest.

The Exorcist was reissued on Blu-ray in a special 40th Anniversary edition and, after showing a 3-D version in US movie theatres for a week in September, Warner Bros. released *The Wizard of Oz 75th Anniversary Collector's Edition* as a five-disc set ($105.00). It included Blu-ray, DVD and 3-D versions of the classic 1939 film, along with a new "making-of" documentary.

The BBC/BFI six-disc set *Ghost Stories for Christmas* featured both versions of M. R. James' *Whistle and I'll Come to You* (1968 and 2010) and an adaptation of Charles Dickens' *The Signalman*. *Schalcken the Painter* from the same distributors was a welcome rediscovery of Leslie Megahey's chilling 1979 *Omnibus* drama, based on the story by J. Sheridan Le Fanu. It came with an illustrated book of essays.

The six-disc set *Doctor Who: Regeneration* contained every regeneration story from William Hartnell to David Tennant. Animation was used to fill-in for the missing fourth episode from "The Tenth Planet" (1966).

Meanwhile, it was confirmed that nine lost episodes of the show from the 1960s had been found in a Nigerian TV station storeroom. They all starred second Doctor Patrick Troughton in the stories "The Enemy of the World" and "The Web of Fear", neither of which had been seen for forty-six years. The BBC subsequently made them available to download on iTunes.

The spirit of Forrest J Ackerman – figuratively, if not literally as writer/director Paul Davids would have you believe – hung over *The Life After Death Project*, which featured Richard Matheson and Whitley Strieber.

The Syfy channel continued to produce low-budget genre movies of varying quality (usually poor), often giving work to actors whose movie or TV careers were all but over.

Shirley Jones' zombified mother attacked her daughter, played by Daryl Hannah, in director John Gulager's *Zombie Night*.

A group of teens had to protect their town from an urban legend in *Scarecrow*, while an American college student studying in Japan tried to save her dead mother's soul in *Grave Halloween*.

Craig Sheffer's Major Hoffman attempted to find a cure for a werewolf virus that had ravaged New York City, while Dennis Haysbert's Lt. General Monning just wanted to create a lycanthropic army in *Battledogs*.

A pair of siblings (Cassie Scerbo and Jonathan Lipnicki) dredging for gold came face-to-face with a horde of horrific sea vampire monsters in *Beast of the Bering Sea*.

Corin Nemec travelled to the Belizean jungle and encountered a mysterious guerrilla warlord and giant insects in *Dragon Wasps*, and the busy actor was back when a rocket carrying nano-technology crashed into a zoo and created *Robocroc*.

A moonshine brew created mutated alligators that began attacking families in the Louisiana bayous in *Alligator Alley* (aka *Ragin Cajun Redneck Gators*).

A freak storm dropped a hoard of unconvincing sharks onto Los Angeles in the absolutely awful *Sharknado*, which featured Tara Reid and John Heard, who should have known better.

Richard Moll played a crotchety lighthouse keeper who knew the secret of a translucent great white shark that was attacking a small coastal community with a dark history in *Ghost Shark*.

Treat Williams and Ronny Cox tried to stop Los Angeles from being overrun by biotech-created prehistoric creatures in *Age of Dinosaurs*, and a group of American base-jumpers discovered a hungry breed of marsupials was stalking them through the Australian backwoods in *Tasmanian Devils*.

Erik Estrada's DEA agent investigated corpses with their throats ripped out and drained of blood in *Chupacabra vs. the Alamo* (aka *Beast of the Alamo*).

A group of apocalypse fanatics (including Brad Dourif) used their knowledge of SF films to save the Earth from a devastating solar flare in *End of the World*, while Greg Evigan and Denise Crosby battled aliens in Syfy's *Invasion Roswell* (aka *The Exterminators*), which marked the 66th anniversary of the famous UFO crash in New Mexico.

Six high school students were attacked by man-eating fish in Larry Fessenden's *Beneath* on the Chiller cable network.

Based on a short story, ITV's *Agatha Christie's Marple: Greenshaw's Folly* found the spinster sleuth (Julia McKenzie) staying at the eponymous country pile that was supposedly haunted by a hooded spectral figure. The cast included Fiona Shaw, Jim Moir (aka comedian Vic Reeves), Judy Parfitt, Julia Sawalha and John Gordon Sinclair.

Jessica Brown Findlay, Vanessa Kirby, John Hurt and Janet Suzman starred in the two-part *Labyrinth*, a German/South African co-production based on the best-selling novel by Kate Mosse, in which the lives of two women were linked centuries apart in a search for the Holy Grail.

Based on the best-selling novel by Diane Setterfield, Christopher Hampton's overwrought adaptation of *The Thirteenth Tale* for the BBC starred Vanessa Redgrave and Olivia Coleman in a story about a dying writer haunted by the actions of her murderous twin.

Narrated by Mark Strong, *The Great Martian War 1913–1917* on the History Channel was a feature-length docudrama mash-up between an uncredited H. G. Wells' *The War of the Worlds* and events surrounding the First World War, with impressive CGI Martian war machines.

Matt Smith's eleventh Doctor and new companion Clara Oswald (Jenna-Louise Coleman) were belatedly back in March with eight new episodes of the seventh season of the revived *Doctor Who*. The slightly disappointing stories included Neil Cross' resurrection of a mummified god on a distant planet and a ghost hunt in an abandoned mansion on the moors; Mark Gatiss' regeneration of a Martian Ice Warrior on a Russian submarine and the discovery of bright-red corpses near a Victorian factory in Yorkshire; and Neil Gaiman's revival of the Cybermen in an intergalactic theme park.

Steven Moffat's over-ambitious season finale saw the return of the Great Intelligence and his funereal Whisper Men, along with archival footage of all the earlier Doctors and the surprise revelation of a previously unknown incarnation.

Guest stars over the eight episodes included Alex Kingston, Celia Imrie, Liam Cunningham, David Warner, Dougray Scott, Diana Rigg and daughter Rachael Stirling, Warwick Davis, Tamzin Outhwaite and Richard E. Grant.

Tactfully ignoring the show's enforced hiatus between 1989–2005, the BBC celebrated the 50th anniversary of *Doctor Who* in a big way.

In March, Royal Mail issued a set of sixteen special postage stamps featuring all eleven Doctors, along with various monsters and the Tardis printed in a miniature sheet. That same month, BBC Books reissued eleven *Doctor Who* novels in matching retro covers, and Eoin Colfer wrote *A Big Hand for the Doctor*, the first of eleven ebooks for Puffin.

Doctor Who: The Companions was a 164-page special edition of *Radio Times* magazine, while a pair of lenticular posters depicted the eleventh Doctor and the Daleks.

AudioGO and Big Finish teamed up to release eleven talking books featuring each of the Doctor's incarnations, read by an actor who played one of his companions, and every month London's British Film Institute showed a vintage episode on the big screen (including "The Mind of Evil" with Jon Pertwee, which only existed in black and white until it was colourized), along with Q&As with special guests.

Made for BBC America, *Doctor Who: The Doctors Revisited* was a half-hour documentary series that focused on one Doctor per episode. Steven Moffat, Neil Gaiman and Matt Smith were among the talking heads. Along similar lines, *The Ultimate Guide to Doctor Who* was a two-hour special in which an amnesiac Doctor (Matt Smith) and Clara

(Jenna Coleman) looked back over all the previous incarnations of the character.

In early August, host Zoë Ball revealed on *Doctor Who Live: The Next Doctor* that Peter Capaldi would be taking over the role. In 1974, a fifteen-year-old Capaldi had a letter published in *Radio Times* congratulating the magazine on its "excellent *Dr Who Special*".

There were several other TV specials – such as *The Science of Doctor Who* with Professor Brian Cox, *Doctor Who: Greatest Monsters and Villains*, and *Me, You and Doctor Who: A Culture Show Special* hosted by Matthew Sweet – before a seven-minute mini-episode, *Doctor Who: The Night of the Doctor*, was released online by the BBC in early November. A dying eighth Doctor (a surprise re-appearance by Paul McGann after the 1996 movie) was regenerated – with the help of Clare Higgins' Priestess of Karn – into the hitherto unknown "War Doctor" (John Hurt).

This led directly into the highly anticipated 50th anniversary show, *Doctor Who: The Day of the Doctor*, which was broadcast around the world on November 23 – the same date that the very first episode was shown back in 1963. Steven Moffat's exciting seventy-five minute special teamed up three incarnations of the Doctor (played by Matt Smith, David Tennant and John Hurt) to battle a triple threat across time and space. Not only was there archive footage of all the previous Doctors, but also guest appearances by Billie Piper and a surprise Tom Baker.

Simulcast in ninety-four countries and shown in cinemas in 3-D to more than half a million people, the show set a world record according to Guinness World Records. More than ten million people watched the special in Britain.

Much more fun was *The Five(ish) Doctors Reboot*, a hilarious half-hour film in which former Doctors Peter Davison, Colin Baker and Sylvester McCoy attempted to get themselves into the 50th anniversary episode. Written and directed by Davison, it featured a host of guest cameos by, amongst others, Sean Pertwee, Olivia Colman, Jenna

Coleman, Matt Smith, Steven Moffat, Katy Manning, Louise Jameson, Carole Ann Ford, Deborah Watling, Sophie Aldred, Sarah Sutton, K-9 (voiced by John Leeson), Paul McGann, John Barrowman, David Tennant, Russell T. Davies, Peter Jackson and Sir Ian McKellan.

Unfortunately, the Christmas special, *The Time of the Doctor*, was a return to the usual incomprehensible mess from writer Moffat, as Matt Smith bowed out after four years as a dying Doctor defending an alien town against such old enemies as Daleks, Cybermen, Weeping Angels, Sontarans and others. At the end of this 800th episode, Smith's Time Lord regenerated as Peter Capaldi's manic new incarnation, and there was a guest appearance by Karen Gillan as former companion Amy Pond.

Broadcast on BBC2 in November, writer Mark Gatiss' ninety-minute drama *An Adventure in Space and Time* chronicled the trials and tribulations of getting the first episode of *Doctor Who* on screen in 1963. David Bradley made a terrific William Hartnell, and he was ably supported by Brian Cox, Jessica Raine and Sacha Dhawan, but the whole production lacked any empathy for its subject matter. William Russell, who played one of the very first companions, had a blink-and-you'll-miss-him cameo, Reece Shearsmith portrayed Patrick Troughton, and the busy Matt Smith also made an appearance.

Writer, director and co-executive producer Mark Gatiss attempt to revive the BBC's classic *A Ghost Story for Christmas* resulted in a stupefyingly dull adaptation of *The Tractate Middoth* which was re-set in the 1950s and featured Sacha Dhawan, Louise Jameson, John Castle, Eleanor Bron and Una Stubbs.

As scriptwriter and presenter, Gatiss also followed in the bicycle tracks of the author for John Das' hour-long documentary *M. R. James: Ghost Writer*, which added nothing new to our knowledge of James beyond an unnecessary attempt to make a case for "Monty" being a closet gay. At least the programme included interviews with film-makers Jonathan Miller and Lawrence Gordon Clark, clips from some earlier BBC adaptations of James' work, and the wonderful Robert Lloyd Parry portraying the author on screen.

Following our first glimpse of the zombie White Walkers at the end of the second season, Diana Rigg joined HBO's *Game of Thrones* as the scheming Tyrell matriarch Lady Olenna, and three major characters were brutally massacred after being betrayed at the now-infamous "Red Wedding" during Season Three's penultimate episode.

Despite not crediting Bram Stoker anywhere on screen, NBC's sexy, steampunk *Dracula* starred Jonathan Rhys Meyers as the seductive vampire posing as an American entrepreneur. He teamed up with Professor Van Helsing (Thomas Kretschmann) to invent a new form of electrical power and get revenge on a secret society known as the Order of the Dragon. Unfortunately, he also fell in love with Mina Murray (Jessica De Gouw), a woman who looked just like his dead wife.

HBO's increasingly complicated *True Blood* returned for its sixth and penultimate season, as humans declared war against all vampires. While Bill (Stephen Moyer) became a vampire demi-god and Eric (Alexander Skarsgård) battled against the new Louisiana governor, so Sookie (Anna Paquin) had her own problems with a powerful vampire-faerie hybrid (Robert Kazinsky) and Rutger Hauer turned up as a wild-haired faerie king.

Season Eight of The CW's long-running *Supernatural* continued with Sam (Jared Padalecki) learning from the angel tablet that he had to undertake three tasks so that he could close the Gates of Hell. Felicia Day returned for a couple of episodes as Charlie Bradbury, and Curtis Armstrong and Amanda Tapping joined the cast as very different angels. In the season finale, Castiel (Misha Collins) once again lost his angel powers, and the ninth series continued the whole war between the angels story arc instead of concentrating on what this show once did best – feature interesting monsters. The Halloween episode was based around *The Wizard of Oz* and in another episode Dean

(Jensen Ackles) ended up talking to the dogs, which is where *Supernatural* was unfortunately heading . . . especially after killing off a major character during the mid-season finale.

In the Fox Network's enjoyable thirteen-episode *Sleepy Hollow*, Revolutionary War spy Ichabod Crane (a likeable fish-out-of-water performance by Tom Mison) awakened after two-and-a-half centuries in the present-day. Helped by police Lieutenant Abbie Mills (Nicole Beharie), he continued his battle against the Headless Horseman, attempted to rescue his witchy wife (Katia Winter) from Purgatory, and began to solve a mystery that dated back to America's founding fathers. Washington Irving wasn't even credited.

The second season of NBC's *Grimm* ended with a two-part episode in which a voodoo Baron (Reg E. Cathey) raised an army of zombies to confront Nick (David Giuntoli) and his friends, while Wesen royal Eric (James Frain) tried to get to Adalind's (Claire Coffee) unborn baby. Season Three began with Nick infected by the zombie virus and Eric being assassinated. Alexis Denisof joined the cast as Prince Viktor, and the Christmas episode featured an evil Santa who did very bad things to children who had been naughty.

There were more than a few shades of the *Da Vinci Code* as Anthony Edwards' sceptical magazine publisher had to find his kidnapped wife and save the world from an evil Nazi-mad scientist in ABC-TV's thirteen-part series *Zero Hour*.

Created by David S. Goyer, Starz's *Da Vinci's Demons* was an alternate history of Renaissance Florence's greatest inventor and his quest for the mystic *Book of Leaves*. Amongst the sex and intrigue, Leonardo (a likeable Tom Riley) had to deal with an apparent outbreak of demonic possession at a convent and travel to the castle of Vlad Dracula (Paul Rhys).

Atlantis, the BBC's follow-up to *Merlin*, quickly forgot about its time-travel opening and concentrated on the Ancient Greece-style adventures of friends Jason (Jack Donnelly), Pythagoras (Robert Emms) and Hercules (Mark

Addy). Together they battled the Minotaur, faced fanatical Maenads, fought vengeful Furies, took a trip to Hades and attempted to assassinate the wicked Queen Pasiphae (Sarah Parish). Jemima Rooper turned up as a cursed Medusa, Juliet Stevenson was a mysterious Oracle and Alexander Siddig played a nïave King Minos, while the final two-part episode featured a nice tribute to the late Ray Harryhausen's *Jason and the Argonauts*.

As Season Two of ABC-TV's *Once Upon a Time* continued, Captain Hook (Colin O'Donoghue) and Cora (Barbara Hershey) arrived in Storybrooke with a crew of zombies to plot their revenge, and waitress Ruby (Meghan Ory) returned to her werewolf form. Meanwhile, back in fairy-tale land, Dr Frankenstein (David Anders) embarked upon his greatest experiment. The third series featured new villain Peter Pan (Jared Gilmore), who tried to put another curse on the town.

ABC's spin-off series, *Once Upon a Time in Wonderland*, starred Sophie Lowe as a Victorian Alice who escaped from a mental institution and fell down a rabbit hole. John Lithgow was The White Rabbit and Iggy Pop played The Caterpillar.

Evil alchemist Paracelsus (Anthony Stewart Head) escaped the bronzing chamber and planned to change history at the conclusion of Season Four of Syfy's *Warehouse 13*.

ITV's overwrought five-part drama *Lightfields* was a follow-up to *Marchlands* (2011) and, as with that show, was set in a haunted house over three generations. Sophie Thompson and Kris Marshall headed the ensemble cast.

The BBC's fifth and final six-part series of *Being Human* set new flatmates – ghost Alex (Katie Bracken), werewolf Tom (Michael Socha) and vampire Hal (Damien Molony) – against Devil incarnate pensioner Captain Hatch (Phil Davis), who attempted to foster a war between vampires and werewolves. Toby Whitehouse's always-engaging series was brought to a satisfying, if bittersweet conclusion that appeared to owe its inspiration to *Blade Runner*.

The third and penultimate series of the very different American version of *Being Human* on Syfy found Aidan (Sam Witwer) returning to find that the vampire community had greatly changed, while Kenny (Connor Price) had turned into an abomination by the season's end.

Although AMC's increasingly tedious *The Walking Dead* concluded Season Three with a face-off between Rick (Andrew Lincoln) and The Governor (David Morrissey), they were back at it again in the fourth series as a flu epidemic broke out amongst the survivors and Carol (Melissa McBride) was banished from the prison. A lot of characters also died.

It were also grim up North for *In the Flesh*, Dominic Mitchell's angst-ridden three-part mini-series for the BBC. Following an apocalyptic "Returning" of the dead, rehabilitated "Rotters" were reintroduced back into society as suffering from reclassified "Partially Deceased Syndrome". When suicide victim Kieren (Luke Newberry) was returned to his home village, it exposed the divisions and intolerance of many of the locals. Supporting an excellent cast of mostly newcomers were Kenneth Cranham and Ricky Tomlinson.

Much the same theme was explored in the far darker eight-part French series *The Returned* (*Les revenants*), which saw increasing numbers of dead people returning to a quiet Alpine village looking no older and with no memory of what had happened to them. As water levels in a nearby reservoir began to drop without any explanation and it appeared that a cannibal serial killer from the past had returned, creepy child Victor (Swann Nambotin) seemed to be the only person who knew what was going on.

The increasingly ridiculous *American Horror Story: Asylum* finally came to an end with the closing down of Briarcliff. The third season, *American Horror Story: Coven*, was a huge improvement over the previous two as the formerly misogynistic show featured a strong cast of female characters led by regulars Jessica Lange, Sarah Paulson, Taissa Farmiga and Lily Rabe, but with the addition this time of Kathy Bates and Angela Bassett. The thirteen-part series, which centred around Miss Robichaux's Academy for Exceptional Young Ladies, a school in New Orleans for budding Salem witches, also featured a reanimated corpse, a talking severed head, a serial-killer ghost and an army of zombies.

Meanwhile, Lifetime's *Witches of East End* – which felt like a re-tread of ABC's cancelled *Eastwick* (which shared a same executive producer) and The WB's *Charmed* – featured a family of witches that included matriarch Julia Ormond and Mädchen Amick, who could turn into a black cat.

In Sally Wainwright's hour-long *Drama Matters: The Last Witch* for Sky Living, a woman (Katherine Kelly) mysteriously turned up on the doorstep of a pensioner (Anne Reid) and revealed more than she should know.

The second season of *Black Mirror*, Charlie Brooker's trilogy of satirical hour-long dramas on Channel 4, featured a widow who was given the opportunity to create a double of her late husband from his social media profiles, a signal that turned people into apathetic onlookers, and a foul-mouthed cartoon bear who stood as a by-election candidate.

Primeval New World, the dull Canadian spin-off from the British TV series, ended its first and only season with a two-part time-travel episode that saw the return of Andrew Lee Potts' Connor Temple from the original show.

After changing the dystopian future, Fox's *Fringe* ended its fifth and final season on a surprisingly positive note.

ABC-TV's *666 Park Avenue* was abruptly cancelled after just thirteen episodes, as Jane (Rachael Taylor) and Henry (Dave Annable) finally discovered the price they had to pay for what they wanted most in life.

The third season of Syfy's *Lost Girl* began three weeks after the defeat of the Garuda, while Season Four kicked off with her friends having no memory whatsoever of Bo (Anna Silk).

Charlotte Rampling joined the cast as the sinister Dr Vogel for the eighth and final season of HBO's *Dexter*, set sixth months after his sister Deb (Jennifer Carpenter) witnessed Dexter (Michael C. Hall) killing Captain LaGuerta. Dexter took on a murderous protégé (Sam Underwood) and, after being reunited with fellow serial killer Hannah (Yvonne Strahovski), the odd couple went after a serial-killer known as the "Brain Surgeon".

Created by Kevin Williamson, Fox's *The Following* starred Kevin Bacon as alcoholic FBI agent Ryan Hardy, who was convinced that Edgar Allan Poe-obsessed serial killer Joe Carroll (James Purefoy) was controlling an army of psychotic "Followers".

When troubled FBI criminal profiler Will Graham (Hugh Dancy) teamed up with secret cannibal psychiatrist Dr Hannibal Lecter (Mads Mikkelsen) to solve gruesome murders, he ended up being framed for Lecter's own crimes in *Hannibal*, a prequel series created by Bryan Fuller. The cast also featured Laurence Fishburne, Gillian Anderson, Eddie Izzard, Gina Torres and Anna Chlumsky. NBC pulled an episode involving children after the Newton school shooting.

A&E's *Bates Motel* was another modern-day prequel show, detailing the somewhat twisted relationship between a teenage Norman Bates (Freddie Highmore) and his widowed mother (Vera Farmiga) when they moved into a certain motel on the edge of town. The first season concluded with Norman's sexy schoolteacher (Keegan Connor Tracy) ending up dead.

After Audrey (Emily Rose) disappeared in the barn at the end of Series Three, she returned six months later with an apparently new identity at the beginning of the fourth season of Syfy's *Haven*, loosely based on *The Colorado Kid* by Stephen King. As Audrey and Nathan (Lucas Bryant) attempted to discover the identity of the Bolt Gun Killer, Colin Ferguson joined the cast as the mysterious William, who knew more about Audrey and the town's Troubles than he was initially letting on.

The rest of CBS-TV's thirteen-episode *Under the Dome*, based on the 2009 best-seller by Stephen King and co-executive produced by Steven Spielberg, could not live up to the opening episode, in which the town of Chester's Mill, Maine, was mysteriously cut off from the world by an invisible force-field.

As it was with genre literature and movies, so the proliferation of young adult fiction also continued on TV with The CW's *Beauty & the Beast*, featuring Kristin Kreuk's simpering New York detective and Jay Ryan's hunky but tormented genetically mutated vigilante. Cat learned the truth about her family's secrets and, after Vincent was kidnapped at the end of Season One, he returned in the second season with new powers and a secret mission.

Following the appearance of ghosts in Mystic Falls, the fourth season of *The Vampire Diaries* ended with the sulky Elena's (Nina Dobrev) graduation ceremony. In the even more ludicrous Season Five, she returned from spending the summer with Damon (Ian Somerhalder), and together they uncovered the true intentions of Dr Wes Maxfield (Rick Cosnett) and the dark history of Whitmore College.

The CW's spin-off series *The Originals* was set in New Orleans, where vampire-werewolf Klaus (Joseph Morgan) battled his former protégé (Charles Michael Davis) for control of the city while they kept control of the local witch population.

ABC Family's *Ravenswood* was a spin-off from *Pretty Little Liars*, as Rosewood's rebellious Caleb Rivers (Tyler Blackburn) moved to the show's eponymous cursed town filled with ghosts and long-hidden family secrets.

Based on the 2012 werewolf-vampire novel by Brian McGreevy, Famke Janssen and Dougray Scott starred in Netflix's thirteen-episode *Hemlock Grove* from co-executive producer Eli Roth, about a creepy Pennsylvania town where everyone also had a secret.

Following the death of a major character, Scott McCall (Tyler Posey) and his friends were forced to use an ancient ritual to save the ones they loved in the much darker third season of MTV's *Teen Wolf*.

In the second series of the BBC's half-hour *Wolfblood*, teenager Maddy Smith (Aimee Kelly) and her family tried to hide their inner wolf powers from Dr Whitewood (Effie Woods).

For teens who found *Game of Thrones* too complicated, The CW's *Reign* concerned the romantic entanglements of a fifteen-year-old Mary, Queen of Scots (Adelaide Kane), along with a woodland cult that practised human sacrifice, a possible ghost, and Rossif Sutherland as a young Nostradamus.

In a terrible teen re-imagining of the British 1970's show *The Tomorrow People* from The CW, Stephen Jacobson (Robbie Amell) discovered that his uncle (Mark Pellegrino) intended to wipe out everyone with mutant powers like his own.

In the fifth and final eight-part series of E4's *Misfits*, the super-powered young offenders encountered a group of Satanists and a childhood bogeyman before their community service was over.

BBC America's *Orphan Black* starred Tatiana Maslany in multiple roles as clones being hunted down by their creators.

Tom (Scott Haran) and Benny (Percelle Ascott) continued their fight against the magic-stealing Nekross in the second series of the BBC's *Wizards vs. Aliens*, and a sixteen-year-old boy (Aaron Sauter) attempted to find his missing astronaut father from clues left in an unfinished graphic novel in *Alien Dawn* (aka *Black Dawn*).

The second series of the BBC's *The Sparticle Mystery* was again set in a world where anyone over the age of fifteen had vanished into a parallel universe, while a group of adults wanted to sacrifice students to the evil underground Egyptian god Ammut in the third season of Nickelodeon's *House of Anubis*. The show bowed out with a ninety-minute special, "Touchstone of Ra".

In Sky's eight-part family comedy *Yonderland*, Martha Howe-Douglas played a bored housewife who stepped through a portal in her larder and found herself a reluctant "Chosen One" in another realm populated by puppet monsters.

Fifteen years after a permanent global blackout, Rachel (Elizabeth Mitchell) and her rebel friends arrived at the tower at the end of the first season of NBC-TV's *Revolution* and prepared to turn the power back on. Following the nuking of the American East Coast, in an unexpected Season Two Aaron (Zak Orth) started having strange visions involving the nano-technology.

Kiefer Sutherland was also back in an unexpected second series of Fox's tedious *Touch*.

The spirits of the dead haunted the corridors of Hope Zion Hospital in the second season of NBC's *Saving Hope*, while a brilliant neurosurgeon (Steven Pasquale) had to battle his own Jekyll-like alter-ego in the same network's *Do No Harm*.

TNT's *Falling Skies* returned for a much more action-orientated ten-episode third season. It started out with Tom Mason (Noah Wyle) now elected president, and concluded with betrayals, both alien and human.

In Syfy's *Defiance*, set on Earth in the year 2046, humans and aliens were forced to co-exist after a long war. The show was developed consecutively as an interactive game.

After receiving a disturbing message from his future self, Alec (Erik Knudsen) soon teamed up again with Vancouver time-travel detective Kiera (Rachel Nichols) in the second season of Syfy's complicated *Continuum*, where they investigated bodies being stolen from the morgue.

Fox's *Almost Human* could almost have been an update of the 1976 show *Holmes and Yo-Yo*, as Karl Urban's android-hating cop was teamed up with Michael Ealy's blue-eyed synthetic partner in a *Blade Runner*-styled 2048. Co-executive producer J. J. Abrams' refreshingly adult SF series was cancelled after just fourteen episodes.

Co-creator Joss Whedon's much-anticipated movie spin-off series for ABC-TV, Marvel's *Agents of S.H.I.E.L.D.*, started off as a dull affair as agent Phil Coulson (the excellent Clark Gregg) apparently returned from the dead after being killed in *Avengers Assemble* to put a select team together to battle a secret organzation known as Centipede and their reluctant super-soldier (J. August Richards). Even a crossover episode with *Thor: The Dark World* and guest appearances by Samuel L. Jackson's Nick Fury and Cobie Smulders' Maria Hill couldn't lift this show out of the doldrums.

In the first season finale of The CW's *Arrow*, Oliver McQueen (Stephen Amell) failed to prevent Malcolm Merlyn's (John Barrowman) earthquake machine from destroying The Glades, and Tommy (Colin Donnell) was killed as a result of his father's insane plans. In Season Two, Moira Queen (Susanna Thompson) was put on trial for her part in Merlyn's plot, we learned the origins of Black Canary (Caity Lotz) and The Flash (Grant Gustin), and there were references to various other characters in the DC Comics universe. If only the tedious flashbacks to Oliver's time on the island hadn't slowed the action down so much.

The first season of CBS-TV's *Elementary* concluded with a twitchy Holmes (Jonny Lee Miller) discovering that Moriarty was in fact Irene Adler (Natalie Dormer), the one woman he had truly loved. The opening episode of Season Two was set in London, as the detective and Joan Watson (Lucy Liu) encountered Holmes' estranged brother Mycroft (Rhys Ifans) and an incompetent Gareth Lestrade (Sean Pertwee), who were both hiding their own secrets.

With writer Richard Castle (Nathan Fillion) and detective Kate Beckett (Stana Katic) now a couple, the fifth season of ABC's *Castle* passed its 100th episode and included *Ring* and *Rear Window*-inspired shows, as well as another featuring a possible "Bigfoot" killer. Even Wes Craven popped up as himself in an episode.

When a local author writing a book about two British B-movie stars of the 1960s was found dead with two puncture marks in her neck, an episode of ITV's *Midsomer Murders* turned into a tribute to Hammer Films. It even managed to include cameos by two actors – Caroline Munro (as an evil Egyptian priestess) and John Carson – who had worked for the studio.

The fourth series of ITV's *Whitechapel* found police detectives Joseph Chandler (Rupert Penry-Jones) and Ray Miles (Phil Davis) investigating a series of murders conducted in the manner of 17th-century "Witchfinder General" Matthew Hopkins, tracking down an apparent witch who flayed the faces off her victims, and investigating a gang of cannibalistic killers living in the sewers under London.

In the penultimate season of USA Network's *Psych*, Shaun (James Roday) and Gus (Dulé Hill) became involved in a "found footage" hunt for a Bigfoot-type creature in the woods, and Juliet (Maggie Lawson) finally discovered that Shaun's psychic powers were fake. Meanwhile, an episode in homage to the 1985 movie *Clue* guest-starred original stars Christopher Lloyd, Lesley Ann Warren and Martin Mull and was dedicated to the memory of Madeline Kahn. In America, viewers on the East and West coasts were able to vote on which ending they wanted to watch.

During the sixth season of *Murdoch Mysteries*, the 1890s Toronto detective (Yannick Bisson) encountered a suspect claiming to be the real Sherlock Holmes, a murder supposedly committed by a vengeful ghost, a man who may have been turned into a Haitian zombie and a woman apparently killed by a lake monster.

In the penultimate episode of the thirteenth season of CBS-TV's *CSI: Crime Scene Investigation*, the death of a ghost-hunter was linked to the legend of a serial killer who murdered eight pre-teen boys, forcing Greg (Eric Szmanda) to use his own suppressed paragnostic powers. Meanwhile, Ozzy Osbourne guest-starred as himself in a two-part episode in which the team hunted for a serial killer inspired by Dante's "Inferno".

Guillermo del Toro created the terrific animated opening sequence for *The Simpsons Treehouse of Horror XXIV*, which featured numerous references to horror icons such as Cthulhu, Godzilla and the Universal Monsters, along with tributes to Ray Harryhausen, Ray Bradbury and Richard Matheson. Other authors featured included Stephen King, H. P. Lovecraft, Edgar Allan Poe and Rod

Serling. It was a shame that the rest of the episode didn't
live up to the titles.

Comedy Central's *Futurama* finally ended its resurrected
run with a *Groundhog Day*-style glitch on the day that Fry
decided to propose to Leena.

An impassive therapist listened to "Mary Shelley" explain
the plot of her novel *Frankenstein* and "Mrs Alfred
Hitchcock" complain about her marriage in Jeremy Dyson's
not-very-funny Sky Arts comedy sketch series *Playhouse
Presents: Psychobitches*.

Iain Banks: Raw Spirit – A Review Show Special on BBC
Scotland featured an exclusive interview that the late author
gave to Kirsty Wark about facing up to the inevitability of death.

In *C. S. Lewis: The Secret Lives and Loves* on BBC4,
biographer A. N. Wilson examined the children's author's
colourful private life.

Actor David Hasselhoff looked at such films as *The Shining*,
The Omen, *Scream* and *Saw* with the help of plenty of talking
heads in the BBC's *The Hoff's Best Horror Film Ever!*

TNT's "Star of the Month" for October was appropri-
ately Vincent Price, with the channel screening *House of
Wax*, *The Mad Magician*, *House on Haunted Hill*, *The Bat*,
The Tingler, *The Fall of the House of Usher*, *Pit and the
Pendulum*, *Twice-Told Tales*, *Diary of a Madman*, *Tower
of London*, *The Raven*, *The Haunted Palace*, *The Masque
of the Red Death*, *The Tomb of Ligeia*, *The Conqueror
Worm* (aka *Witchfinder General*), *The Abominable Dr.
Phibes*, *Theatre of Blood* and other movies featuring the
actor, including his many non-genre roles.

As TNT fully embraced the Halloween month, other
mini-seasons included "Zombie Attacks", "Mad Doctors",
"Vampires", "Spooky Houses", "Bewitching Wives",
"Satan Worshippers", "Maniac Criminals", "Scary Sisters",
"Monsters Need Love Too", "Christopher Lee Horror"
and "Directed by Tod Browning".

BBC Radio 4's *Friday Drama: Vincent Price and the Horror
of the English Bloodbeast* was Matthew Broughton's

hour-long drama about the making of the 1967 film *Witchfinder General*. Nickolas Grace played Price, Blake Ritson was director Michael Reeves and Kenneth Cranham portrayed producer Tony Tenser.

Paul Evans' *Afternoon Drama: Chapel of Souls*, also on Radio 4, was about a ghostly meeting of pathways that led three lost souls to an ancient chapel that had to be reached before midnight. The play was recorded in the Shropshire hills of the Welsh Marches and featured special wildlife recordings by the BBC's natural-history unit.

Listening to the Dead consisted of five separate dramas written by playwright Katie Hims about different generations of a family, each featuring the same ghost of a drowned teenage girl in a blue dress.

In Mike Walker's *The Edison Cylinders*, a physicist (Clare McCarron) listened to some old Victorian wax cylinder recordings and discovered that they contained a malevolent message, while Michael Stewart's supernatural comedy *Dead Man's Suit* featured a loser whose life was transformed after he bought a bespoke suit in a charity shop.

Alastair Jessiman's down-at-heel psychic detective Thomas Soutar (Robin Laing) was on the trail of a missing journalist in *The Sensitive: Terma*, and then he became involved with a celebrated actor while on holiday in *The Sensitive: Black Island*.

In Ed Hime's radio mockumentary *Obey the Wave*, a cult SF writer (Justin Salinger) investigated the 1973 disappearance of the members of a religious movement, including his own parents.

A soundtrack ranging from Dvorak and Bernard Herrmann to Cumbrian folk music and David Bowie accompanied Sarah Hall and Dominic Power's ninety-minute contemporary ghost story *The Stranger's Will* on BBC Radio 3 in February.

Christopher Eccleston was Winston Smith and Tim Pigott-Smith portrayed O'Brien in Jonathan Holloway's two-part dramatization of *Nineteen Eighty-Four*, broadcast as part of Radio 4's "The Real George Orwell" strand early in the year.

Inspired by the works of J. G. Ballard, a week of programmes on BBC Radio in June on the themes of "Dangerous Visions" and "Very British Dystopias" included hour-long adaptations of the author's *The Drowned World* and *Concrete Island*, along with a 1989 interview with Ballard himself.

As part of the first theme, Michael Symmons' hour-long *The Sleeper* was about a teenage girl (Sarah Churm) with the ability to fall asleep in a futuristic Britain suffering from twenty-four hour wakefulness, while in Ed Harris' *Billions* a man (Blake Ritson) discovered that his wife had been replaced by a near-perfect replica supplied by her insurance company.

Set in a future London divided into a crime-free North and a lawless South, a police detective (Justin Salinger) crossed the river to investigate the death of a teenager in Nick Perry's *London Bridge*, and there were shades of Shirley Jackson in Michael Butt's *Death Duty*, in which a weekly lottery system decided a sacrificial victim in a drought-stricken city.

Also in June, BBC Radio 4 broadcast an hour-long adaptation of Clive Barker's short story "The Forbidden" (the inspiration for the *Candyman* movie series) starring Nadine Marshall.

Two months later, Joy Williamson adapted Agatha Christie's classic old dark house mystery *And Then There Were None* into a ninety-minute drama.

In early October, Radio 4's *Book at Bedtime: Algernon Blackwood's Ghost Stories* presented fifteen-minute readings by Matthew Marsh of such unfamiliar stories as "Keeping His Promise", "The Land of Green Ginger", "The Transfer", "The Man Who Lived Backwards" and "The Kit Bag".

During the run-up to Hallowe'en, *Edinburgh Haunts* presented readings of three specially commissioned ghost stories, set in the Scottish city, while with Radio 4's *Pilgrim*, Sebastian Baczkiewicz's doomed immortal wanderer William Palmer (Paul Hilton) returned for eight more adventures during the year.

In Gerard Foster's half-hour comedy *Little Monster*, a couple discovered that their new baby had horns, fangs and a tail.

Terry Pratchett's Eric was a four-part adaptation on Radio 4 of the author's Faustian "Discworld" novel that featured Mark Heap as the voice of minor wizard Rincewind.

Dirk Maggs' production of Neil Gaiman's 1996 novel *Neverwhere*, set in a parallel London Below, launched on Radio 4 in March and then continued over five consecutive nights on Radio 4 Extra. The all-star cast included James McAvoy, Benedict Cumberbatch, Andrew Sachs, Sophie Okonedo, Anthony Head, Bernard Cribbins, Johnny Vegas, Gaiman himself, and Christopher Lee as the Earl of Earl's Court.

Meanwhile, Gaiman's original novel was "temporarily removed" from a New Mexico high school library after complaints from a parent who objected to an "inappropriate" sex scene.

Although commercially available for a few years, five hour-long *Doctor Who* audio dramas, featuring Paul McGann's Time Lord and Sheridan Smith as his companion Lucie Miller, made their radio debut on BBC Radio 4 Extra in January.

In the lead-up to the 50th anniversary, former script editor David Whitaker's 1964 novel *Doctor Who and the Daleks* was read by original companion William Russell as narrator Ian Chesterton. It was followed by the actor's readings of Jonathan Morris' *Doctor Who: Protect and Survive* (with Sylvester McCoy), Eddie Robson's *Doctor Who: 1963: Fanfare for the Common Men* (with Peter Davison) and *Doctor Who: Human Resources* (with Paul McGann), Andy Lane's *Doctor Who: A Thousand Tiny Wings* (with McCoy again), Moris Farhi's *Doctor Who: Farewell Great Macedon*, and Terrance Dicks' *The Dalek Invasion of Earth*.

Presented by Russell Tovey, *Who is the Doctor?* on BBC Radio 2 was a ninety-minute celebration that explored the legacy and lasting appeal of the show through interviews and archive material.

However, Doctor Who was not the only person celebrating an anniversary, as 2013 also marked fifty years since the death of C. S. Lewis. Robin Brooks' *Afternoon Drama: Lewis and Tolkien – The Lost Road* on Radio 4 explored the friendship between the two writers, while Brian Sibley's *The Northern Irish Man in C. S. Lewis* over on Radio 4 Extra starred Geoffrey Palmer as the author of the "Narnia" series.

Through the Wardrobe presented readings of three short stories in tribute to Lewis.

Barnaby Edwards' four-part adaptation of Gaston Leroux's *The Phantom of the Opera* starred Anna Massey, Peter Guinness, James D'Arcy and Alexander Siddig.

Radio 4 Extra's *Haunted* brought together half-hour readings of short stories by, amongst others, Rosemary Timperley, Wilkie Collins, Bram Stoker, H. G. Wells, John Keir Cross, Ray Bradbury, Agatha Christie, R. Chetwynd-Hayes and J. B. Priestley.

A Short History of Gothic included readings of Angela Carter's "The Lady of the House of Love" and Laurell K. Hamilton's "Those Who Seek Forgiveness", and *The Female Ghost* offered a half-hour dramatization of "The Cold Embrace" by Mary Braddon.

A Night with a Vampire featured David Tennant reading extracts from Antoine Calmet's *Dead Persons in Hungary*, Alexei Tolstoy's "The Family of the Vourdalak", Guy de Maupassant's "The Horla", Mary E. Wilkins Freeman's "Luella Miller", Théophile Gautier's "Clarimonde", Angela Carter's "The Lady of the House of Love", Fritz Leiber's "The Girl With the Hungry Eyes", Edith Wharton's "Bewitched", Richard Matheson's "Drink My Red Blood" and Robert Swindell's "A Lot of Mince Pies".

Other short story readings on Radio 4 Extra were grouped under such series titles as *Midnight Tales* (all by Bram Stoker), *Ghost Stories of E. Nesbit*, *Ghost Stories of Walter de la Mare*, *Weird Tales*, *A Short History of Vampires* and *Fear on Four*. *Summer Ghosts* featured readings of three supernatural stories set in daylight.

Repeats of *The Man in Black* were introduced by Mark Gatiss, and Vincent Price introduced *The Price of Fear*. Christopher Lee read both *Christopher Lee's Fireside Chats* (featuring stories by Edgar Allan Poe, Jerome K. Jerome, E. Nesbit, Ambrose Bierce and W. W. Jacobs) and *The Ghost Stories of M. R. James*.

Scottish horror was explored in *The Darker Side of the Border* with half-hour dramatizations of Robert Louis Stevenson's "Olalla" and James Hogg's "Brownie of the Black Haggs".

Four episodes of *Blakes 7 – The Early Years* featured Zoë Tapper, Jason Merrells and James Swallow.

Originally written for *Doctor Who* in the late 1960s, *Aliens in the Mind* finally became a six-part BBC radio drama in 1977. Re-broadcast by Radio 4 Extra in June, horror veterans Vincent Price and Peter Cushing co-starred as two respected medical investigators who discovered that a remote Scottish island was an experimental site for the creation of a race of telepathic mutants.

The radio station also revived *Before the Screaming Begins*, a three-part drama about a wedding anniversary celebration interrupted by an alien invasion starring Jennifer Piercy, James Laurenson and Patrick Troughton. Although the original master-tape had been lost following the initial broadcast in 1979, the show's writer, Wally K. Daly, had made an off-air cassette recording at the time. It was followed by the three-part *The Silent Scream* and *With a Whimper to the Grave*, both also scripted and recorded by Daly.

In *Arthur in the Underworld* on Radio 4, journalist Horatio Clare looked at the life and work of Welsh author and mystic Arthur Machen, while Christopher Frayling investigated the consequences of the infamous 1938 radio broadcast in *Archive on 4: Orson Welles and The War of the Worlds – Myth or Legend?*, with the suggestion that it could have been inspired by a similar BBC production from 1926.

In an episode recorded at the British Film Institute, BBC Radio 3's *Night Waves: Sound of Cinema* featured Matthew Sweet and guests discussing the classic 1961 horror movie *The Innocents*. In another episode, Sweet looked at music that evoked the sinister side of British rural life, including Paul Giovanni's score for *The Wicker Man* (1973) and James Barnard's score for Hammer's *The Hound of the Baskervilles* (1959), while in *Between the Ears: Sound of Cinema: Return of the Monster from the Id*, writer Ken Hollings celebrated the electronic score created by Louis and Bebe Barron for the 1956 SF film *Forbidden Planet*.

In the first episode of Radio 4's *The Reunion*, presenter Sue MacGregor brought together five people who created and starred in the first series of *Doctor Who* fifty years earlier, including original director Waris Hussein and actors Carole Ann Ford, William Russell, Jeremy Young and Peter Purves.

When the global audience of *World Book Club* was asked to vote for the writer who they would most like to be interviewed for the first time, the overwhelming response was for Neil Gaiman. So in September, the BBC World Service broadcast an interview with the writer, based around his novel *American Gods*, with questions put to him by the listeners themselves.

Novelist Naomi Alderman investigated the attraction and influence of fanfic in Radio 4's *When Harry Potter Met Frodo: The Strange World of Fan Fiction*.

With a libretto by Stephen King, music and songs by John Mellencamp and musical direction by T. Bone Burnett, *Ghost Brothers of Darkland County*, released in a boxed CD/DVD set by Concord Music Group, was the result of a creative collaboration that dated back to the mid-1990s.

A ghost story based on events that reportedly occurred at the haunted cottage owned by Mellencamp, the cast of singers included Elvis Costello, Kris Kristofferson, Rosanne Cash and Sheryl Crow, while Samantha Mathis, Matthew McConaughey and Meg Ryan were among the actors involved in the concept album.

Pseudopod, the free weekly podcast of horror stories, featured fiction by Joe R. Lansdale, Thomas Ligotti, Norman Partridge, Algernon Blackwood, Walter De La Mare, Rudyard Kipling and Clark Ashton Smith, amongst many others.

The Woman in Black, which opened at London's Fortune Theatre in 1989 and featured Joseph Fiennes and Frank Finlay amongst its casts, clocked up its 10,000th performance in 2013.

Rebecca Lenkiewicz's adaptation of Henry James' ghostly novella *The Turn of the Screw* at London's Almeida theatre starred Anna Madeley as the possibly unstable governess and Laurence Belcher as her sexually precocious young charge. Illusionist Scott Penrose created the on-stage special effects.

Sebastian Armesto and Dudley Hinton's production of *The Cabinet of Dr Caligari* was performed by young ensemble cast Simple8 at the Arcola theatre in East London. Oliver Birch played the sinister mesmerist and Christopher Doyle was his hypnotized somnambulist Cesare.

Sam Mendes' big-budget musical *Charlie and the Chocolate Factory* opened at London's Theatre Royal, Drury Lane, in June. Based on Roald Dahl's classic 1964 children's story, Douglas Hodge portrayed a creepy Willy Wonka, Nigel Planer was Grandpa Joe, and Marc Shaiman and Scott Wittman wrote the score.

Dancer Jonathan Goddard portrayed the undead Count in the Mark Bruce Company's version of *Dracula*, which toured the UK in the autumn.

Ian Talbot's *Afraid of the Dark*, set in 1950s Hollywood, had its premiere at the Charing Cross Theatre in London in September. The playwright chose to remain anonymous, which was probably for the best given the poor reviews it received.

Performed by the BBC National Orchestra of Wales at London's Royal Albert Hall on July 13, the golden anniversary Doctor Who Prom presented Murray Gold's incidental music, along with pieces by Bizet, Bach and Debussy used in the show. Matt Smith was also involved, along with Jenna Coleman, Carole Ann Ford, Peter Davison and a host of classic monsters. The event was broadcast live on BBC Radio 3.

Danny Elfman and the BBC Concert Orchestra played music from *Batman*, *Edward Scissorhands*, *The Nightmare Before Christmas*, *Alice in Wonderland* and other movies at the world premiere of *Danny Elfman's Music from the Films of Tim Burton*, performed at London's Royal Albert Hall on October 7.

Ben Frost's minimalist opera, *The Wasp Factory*, based on the novel by Iain Banks, premiered in Australia in August before moving to London's Linbury Studio in Covent Garden two months later.

In a closing announcement in November, the much-troubled and hugely expensive *Spider-Man: Turn off the Dark* Broadway musical was projected to make a $60-million loss when it closed its doors after a three-year run in early January 2014. This followed a sharp decline in ticket sales during 2013. Original director Julie Taymor was fired following creative differences and her subsequent lawsuit was settled out of court.

Chicago's Wildclaw Theatre presented Scott T. Barsotti's stage adaptation of *H. P. Lovecraft's The Shadow Over Innsmouth* at the Athenaeum Theatre in December.

That same month a musical version of Bret Easton Ellis' 1991 novel *American Psycho* opened at the Almeida theatre, starring former Doctor Who Matt Smith as yuppie serial killer Patrick Bateman, while the National Theatre of Scotland's production of *Let the Right One In* at the Royal Court was based on the novel by John Ajvide Lindqvist and featured Rebecca Benson as the child-vampire Eli.

Six months after buying LucasFilm for just over $4 billion, The Walt Disney Company announced that it was closing down LucasArts, founded in 1982, and moving the games developer to a licensing model. LucasArts was working on the *Star Wars 1313* game when the closure was announced.

After nearly seventeen years, the ninth instalment of *Tomb Raider* was a reboot of the popular games franchise, detailing how the young Lara Croft was shipwrecked on a deadly tropical island and became the woman we know today.

A fourteen-year-old girl and a ruthless smuggler crossed a post-epidemic America together, battling a fascist government, cannibals and zombie-like creatures in Naughty Dog's acclaimed *The Last of Us*.

The Walking Dead: Survival Instinct was a first-person shooter that served as a prequel to the TV series. Norman Reedus narrated as Daryl Dixon, trying to find his brother. *The Walking Dead*, however, was a storytelling game with minimal action based on the original comic book series. It collected five episodic downloads and put them on disc for the first time.

There were complaints that the horror had been toned down for *Dead Space 3*, in which alien organisms continued to reanimate the dead, and there were more zombies in *Dead Island: Riptide*, as survivors from the first game had to contend with "Drowners" that lurked beneath the water.

Ellen Page voiced the character of Jodie, who had a poltergeist-like companion called Aiden that followed her commands, in the interactive movie *Beyond: Two Souls*, which was billed as "the most cinematic videogame ever released".

The player was a vampire in the near-future set *Dark*, while *The Wolf Among Us* was based on Vertigo Comics' *Fables* series and concerned the folklore characters hidden away in the New York borough of Fabletown.

A rescue mission was sent to discover what happened to Ripley and others in the disappointing first-person shooter *Aliens: Colonial Marines*, based on the movie series, and *R.I.P.D. Rest in Peace Department* was a tie-in to the movie about a pair of dead lawmen.

Warner in Canada's *Batman: Arkham Origins* was a prequel game, set five years before 2009's *Batman: Arkham Asylum*, that featured a younger Dark Knight being pursued by the world's greatest assassins, including the Joker, Black Mask and Firefly. *Batman: Arkham Origins Blackgate* was a portable spin-off game.

In an irony possibly lost on its makers, "A Nightmare on Elm Street Toaster" cooked Freddy Krueger's fire-ravaged features into your slice of bread.

Limited to just fifty individually numbered pieces each, Distinctive Dummies Production's "Vampires of the 70s" series featured nicely detailed one-eighth scale collectible figures of the undead bloodsuckers from *Salem's Lot*, *Night Stalker*, *Count Yorga Vampire* and *Blacula*.

From Dark Horse, a thirteen-inch tall "Forrest J Ackerman Statue" paid tribute to the late editor of *Famous Monsters of Filmland*. It was limited to just 1,000 pieces.

Robert E. Howard's original typed manuscript for the Conan story "A Witch Shall Be Born", inscribed and signed by the author on the first page, was offered for sale in April by Heritage Auctions. It sold for $22,500, a little below the $25,000 estimate.

A rare first edition of *Harry Potter and the Philosopher's Stone*, complete with annotations and drawings by J. K. Rowling, sold for £150,000 in May, which set a new record for the author's work.

A one-of-a-kind phaser rifle used by William Shatner in the second pilot episode of the original *Star Trek*, sold for $231,000 – the second highest price paid at auction for a prop from the 1960s TV series.

Curated by Turner Classic Movies, the inaugural "What Dreams Are Made Of: A Century of Movie Magic at Auction" was held at Bonhams Auction House, New York, on November 25. Showcasing 100 years of props, scripts, costumes and posters, the sale raised almost $6 million.

Amongst the many notable items were a pair of replica ruby slippers from *The Wizard of Oz*, which sold for

$35,000, while a rare pre-production draft of Noel Langley's screenplay for the same film went for $10,000. A whip from *Indiana Jones and the Last Crusade* sold for $10,000, and a diver's helmet from Disney's *20000 Leagues Under the Sea* realized $81,250.

However, the highlight of the auction was undoubtedly the lead statuette from *The Maltese Falcon*, which set a world record for a movie prop at auction, selling for $4.085 million (including premium).

The Bram Stoker Awards Weekend 2013, incorporating World Horror Convention, was held in New Orleans over June 13–16. Author Guests of Honour were Ramsey Campbell, Caitlín R. Kiernan and Jonathan Maberry. Artist Guest was Glenn Chadbourne, Editor Guest was John Joseph Adams, Media Guest was Amber Benson, and Poet Guest was Bruce Boston. Jeff Strand was Toastmaster.

The *Souvenir Book* was a hefty PoD paperback edited by Norman Rubenstein and limited to 600 copies containing fiction, articles and a number of memorial pieces.

At the Bram Stoker Awards Banquet held on the Saturday evening, the Screenplay award went to the movie *Cabin in the Woods*, Graphic Novel to *Witch Hunts: A Graphic History of the Burning Times* by Rocky Wood and Lisa Morton, and Poetry Collection to Marge Simon's *Vampires Zombies & Wanton Souls*.

Lisa Morton also won Non-Fiction for *Trick or Treat: A History of Halloween*, the Collection award was a tie between Mort Castle's *New Moon on the Water* and Joyce Carol Oates' *Black Dahlia and White Rose: Stories*, and Mort Castle and Sam Weller won the Anthology award for *Shadow Show*. The Short Fiction award went to "Magdala Amygdala" by Lucy Snyder (from *Dark Faith: Invocations*) and Gene O'Neill's *The Blue Heron* won for Long Fiction.

Jonathan Maberry's *Flesh & Bone* was presented with the YA Novel award, L. L. Soares' *Life Rage* picked up the First Novel award, and the superior achievement in a Novel award went to Caitlín R. Kiernan's *The Drowning Girl*.

The previously announced Specialty Press Award went to Jerad Walters of Centipede Press, and both Clive Barker and Robert R. McCammon were the recipients of HWA Life Achievement Awards.

For only the third time in its history, the World Fantasy Convention was held outside North America. Celebrating the themes "World Fantasy Convention: The Next Generation" and "Arthur Machen @ 150", the event ran from October 31 to November 3 in Brighton, on England's south-east coast.

Although Guest of Honour Richard Matheson died earlier in the year and Artist Guest of Honour Alan Lee was unable to attend due to work commitments in New Zealand, there was no shortage of guests as the convention welcomed Joanne Harris, Joe Hill, Richard Christian Matheson, Brian W. Aldiss, Tessa Farmer and Robert Lloyd Parry (as "M. R. James"). Life Achievement Award recipients Susan Cooper and Tanith Lee also both attended, and there was a special appearance by Sir Terry Pratchett. When original Master of Ceremonies China Miéville unexpectedly pulled out at the last minute, Neil Gaiman graciously stepped into the breach.

The World Fantasy Awards were presented on the Sunday afternoon. There were Special Convention Awards for Brian Aldiss and William F. Nolan. The Special Award, Non-Professional went to S. T. Joshi for his two volumes of *Unutterable Horror: A History of Supernatural Fiction*, and the Special Award, Professional went to Lucia Graves for her translation of Carlos Ruiz Zafón's *The Prisoner of Heaven*.

Vincent Chong received the Artist award, Collection went to Joel Lane's *Where Furnaces Burn*, and editor Danel Olson's *PostScripts #28-29: Exotic Gothic 4* won for Anthology. Gregory Norman Bossert's "The Telling" (from *Beneath Ceaseless Skies*) won Short Fiction, and "Let Maps to Other" by K. J. Parker (from *Subterranean*) won Novella. The Novel award was presented to *Alif the Unseen* by G. Willow Wilson.

With the World Fantasy Convention being held in Britain, there was, as usual, no separate FantasyCon in 2013. Instead, the British Fantasy Awards were presented alongside the World Fantasy Awards.

The Sydney J. Bounds Award for Best Newcomer went to Helen Marshall for her collection *Hair Side, Flesh Side*. *The Cabin in the Woods* received Best Screenplay, *Saga* by Brian K. Vaughan and Fiona Staples was voted Best Comic/ Graphic Novel, and Sean Phillips won Best Artist.

Interzone picked up the Best Magazine/Periodical, *Pornokitsch* edited by Anne C. Perry and Jared Shurin was Best Non-Fiction, and ChiZine Publications was awarded Best Small Press. *Magic: An Anthology of the Esoteric and Arcane* edited by Jonathan Oliver collected Best Anthology, while Robert Shearman's *Remember Why You Fear Me* was the winner of Best Collection.

Best Short Story went to "Shark! Shark!" by Ray Cluley (from *Black Static*), and John Llewellyn Probert's *The Nine Deaths of Dr. Valentine* was Best Novella. The August Derleth Award for Best Horror Novel was presented to *Last Days* by Adam Nevill, and The Robert Holdstock Award for Best Fantasy Novel went to *Some Kind of Fairy Tale* by Graham Joyce. The British Fantasy Special Award was presented posthumously to Iain M. Banks.

As I am sure you are aware, this is the 25th Anniversary edition of *Best New Horror*.

A quarter of a century is a very long time in publishing and, in the horror genre, the venerable *Pan Book of Horror Stories* is the only anthology series to have a longer run with the same publisher in the UK (and, even then, it changed editors).

These days there are far too many "Year's Best" anthologies out there competing with each other (in all genres), while the number of books, movies, TV shows and other related media has increased enormously over the past decade.

However, although each annual volume takes an inordinate amount of work and time to compile, it has been an exhilarating and rewarding experience ever since Nick Robinson, Ramsey Campbell and I embarked upon this venture twenty-five years ago.

I would like to thank all of the in-house editors who have collaborated with me on these books over the years – not least, my current editor Duncan Proudfoot, who has done everything in his power to support and nurture this title during the time we have worked together – and all the contributors, publishers and, most importantly, readers, who have kept us going for a remarkable twenty-five volumes.

Publishing has never been more uncertain than it is today, and with new technologies and multiple platforms squeezing out print editions, and bricks-and-mortar bookstores closing down almost every week, we face an unpredictable future when it comes to books – and I'm not just talking about horror.

I am extraordinarily proud of what I have done with *Best New Horror* and the remarkable body of work that I have been privileged to showcase within these pages – I truly hope that this series stands as an indispensable record of contemporary horror for every year it has been published. And perhaps more than anybody, I am excited to see where the next few years will take us.

So I just want to thank you all – authors, publishers, booksellers, reviewers and readers alike – for your continued support. For me, horror fiction remains the most vibrant and exciting genre I can imagine working in, and I fervently hope that you will stick with us to see what the future holds.

For now, more than anything, I urge you to *just keep reading*!

The Editor
June, 2014

KIM NEWMAN

Who Dares Wins
Anno Dracula 1980

KIM NEWMAN IS a novelist, critic and broadcaster. His fiction includes *The Night Mayor*, *Bad Dreams*, *Jago*, the *Anno Dracula* novels and stories, *The Quorum*, *The Original Dr. Shade and Other Stories*, *Life's Lottery*, *Back in the USSA* (with Eugene Byrne), *The Man From the Diogenes Club*, *Professor Moriarty: The Hound of the d'Urbervilles* and *An English Ghost Story* under his own name, and *The Vampire Genevieve* and *Orgy of the Blood Parasites* as "Jack Yeovil".

His non-fiction books include *Nightmare Movies*, *Ghastly Beyond Belief* (with Neil Gaiman), *Horror: 100 Best Books* and *Horror: Another 100 Best Books* (both with Stephen Jones), *Wild West Movies*, *The BFI Companion to Horror*, *Millennium Movies*, and the BFI Classics studies of *Cat People*, *Doctor Who* and *Quatermass and the Pit*.

Newman is also a contributing editor to *Sight & Sound* and *Empire* magazines (writing *Empire*'s popular "Video Dungeon" column), has written and broadcast widely, and scripted radio and television documentaries. His stories "Week Woman" and "Ubermensch" have been adapted into an episode of the TV series *The Hunger* and an Australian short film, respectively. He has directed and written the tiny film *Missing Girl*, and he co-wrote the West End play *The Hallowe'en Sessions*. Following his Radio 4 play "Cry Babies", he scripted episodes for Radio 7's series *The Man in Black* ("Phish Phood") and Glass Eye Pix's *Tales From Beyond the Pale* ("Sarah Minds the Dog").

The author's two contributions to this volume of *Best New Horror* are reasonably self-contained selections from the long-in-progress fourth *Anno Dracula* novel, *Johnny Alucard*. There will eventually be a fifth book in the series, and a comic book is also in the works. Fans of the series may also like to note that the following story features the *Anno Dracula* version of occult detective Richard Jeperson, who features in the collection *The Man from the Diogenes Club*.

Previously ... in Anno Dracula: *Dracula is gone, but vampirism has spread across the globe and his former lieutenants – like the Baron Meinster, from Hammer's* The Brides of Dracula *– contest the position of King of the Cats, the monarch of the undead. A movement has arisen to claim Transylvania as a vampire homeland. In London, vampire journalist Kate Reed covers an embassy siege ...*

PALACE GREEN WAS blocked, an armoured car emphasising a point she would have thought established sufficiently well by police vans. Uniformed coppers – the Special Patrol Group, of recent ill reputation – and camo-clad squaddies were kitted up for riot, and locals kept out of their homes and offices muttered themselves towards a resentful shade of disgruntled. To Kate Reed, this patch of Kensington felt too much like Belfast for comfort, though passing trade on Embassy Row – veiled woman-shapes with Harrods bags, indignant diplomats of all nations, captains of endangered industries – was of a different quality from the bottle-throwers and -dodgers of the Garvachy Road.

TV crews penned beyond the perimeter had to make do with stories about the crowds rather than the siege. Kate saw the TV reporter Anne Diamond, collar turned up and microphone thrust out, sorting through anxious faces at the barrier, thirsty for someone with a husband or girlfriend trapped inside the Embassy or, better yet, among the terrorists.

"Evenin' Miss Reed," said a vampire bobby she remembered from the Met's old B Division, which used to handle vampire-related crime.

"It's been a funny old week at Palace Green . . ."

Sensing the imminence of an anecdote with a moral, Kate showed Sergeant Dixon her NUJ card and was let through.

"We've been waiting for you," said the sergeant, with fatherly concern, lifting a plank from the barrier. "This is a rum old do and no mistake."

Anne Diamond and a dozen other broadcast and print hopefuls were furious that one of the least significant of their number had a free ticket to the big carnival. It wasn't even as if Kate were the only vampire hack on the street. She'd spotted Paxman, drifting incorporeally in mist-form through the crowds. She was, however, the only journo Baron Meinster would talk with.

For two years, she had been waiting for the Transylvanian to call in the favour he'd granted by spiriting her out of Romania via his underground railway. She knew he'd helped her to spite the Ceauşescus, with whom he had a long-standing personal feud, but his intervention still saved her life. This was not what she had expected, but the development didn't surprise her either. Since Teheran, embassy sieges had become a preferred means of the powerless lording it over the powerful. Not that the Baron, *soi-disant* First Elder of the Transylvania Movement, would consider himself powerless.

A tall, moustached vampire in police uniform took a firm grip on Kate's upper arm. Dixon retreated without offering the traditional cup of tea.

"Daniel Dravot," she said, "it has been a long time."

"Yes, Miss Reed," said the vampire, unsmiling.

"Still *Sergeant* Dravot, I see. Though not truly of the Metropolitan Police, I'll wager."

"All in the service of the Queen, Miss Reed."

"Indeed."

Dravot had been in the shadows as long as she could remember – in Whitechapel in 1888, in France in 1918. Last she'd heard, he'd been training and turning new generations of vampire secret agents. He was back in the field, apparently.

She was walked over to the command post, a large orange workman's hut erected over a hole in the pavement. Dravot lifted a flap-door and ushered her inside.

She found herself among uncomfortable men of power.

A plain-clothes copper sat on a stool, hunched over a field telephone whose wires were crocodile-clamped into an exposed circuit box. Down in the pit, ear-phones worn like a stethoscope under long hair, was a thin warm man of undetermined age. He wore New Romantic finery – full-skirted sky-blue highwayman's coat, knee-boots and puffy mauve britches, three-cornered hat with a feather – and jotted notes on a pad in violet ink. Above them, literally and figuratively, hovered three vampires: a death-faced *éminence grise* in a gravemould-grubby Ganex mac, a human weapon in a black jumpsuit and balaclava, and a willowy youth in elegant grey.

She recognized all of these people.

The policeman was Inspector Cherry, who often wound up with the cases involving vampires. A solid, if somewhat whimsical plod, he was an old B Division hand, trained by Bellaver. The dandy in the ditch was Richard Jeperson, chairman of the Ruling Cabal of the Diogenes Club, long-est-lived and most independent branch of British Intelligence. He had inherited Dravot, not to mention Kate, from his late predecessors, both of whom she had been close to, Charles Beauregard and Edwin Winthrop. It had been some time since she had last been called to Pall Mall and asked to look into something, but you were never dropped from the Club's lists. The vampires were: Caleb Croft, high up in whatever the United Kingdom called its Secret Police these days;

Hamish Bond, a spy whose obituaries she never took seriously; and Lord Ruthven, the Home Secretary.

"Katie Reed, good evening," said Ruthven. "How charming to see you again, though under somewhat trying circumstances. Very nice piece in the *Grauniad* about the royal fiancée. Gave us all the giggles."

Ruthven, once a fixture as Prime Minister, was back in the cabinet after a generation out of government. Rumoured to be Margaret Thatcher's favourite vampire, he was horribly likely to succeed her in Number 10 by the next ice age, reclaiming his old job. He brought a century of political experience to the ministerial post and a considerably longer lifetime of survival against the odds.

As Ruthven rose, so did Croft. The grey man had resigned his teaching position to return to secret public service. Kate's skin crawled in his presence. He affected not to remember her. Among monsters, there were monsters – and Croft was the worst she knew. He had a high opinion of her, too . . . "Kate Reed was – is – a terrorist, space kidettes," he'd said when he last set eyes on her. Then, he was just an academic, though he'd used her to clear up one of his messes. Soon, he'd be in a position to tidy her away and no questions asked.

"She's here," said Cherry, into the phone.

The policeman passed her the set, hand over the mouthpiece.

"Try to find out how many of them there are," said Jeperson in a stage-whisper. "But don't be obvious about it."

"I don't think we need teach Katie Reed anything," said the Home Secretary. "She has a wealth of varied experience."

Unaccountably, that verdict made her self-conscious. She knew about all these men, but they also knew quite a bit about her. Like them all, she had wound in and out of the century, as often covered in blood as glory. Ever since her turning, she had been close to the Great Game of power and intelligence.

Kate put the phone to her ear and said, "Hello".

"Katharine," purred Baron Meinster. His unretractable fangs gave him a vaguely slushy voice, as if he were speaking through a mouthful of blood.

"I'm here, Baron."

"Excellent. I'm glad to hear it. Is Ruthven there?"

"I'm fine, thank you, and how are you?"

"He is. How delicious. Ten years of dignified petitions and protests, when all I needed to do to get attention was take over a single building. How do you like the banners? Do you think He would appreciate them?"

She knew who Meinster meant when he said "He".

The flags of the Socialist Republic had been torn down, and two three-storey banners unfurled from the upper windows of the Embassy. They were blazoned with a tall black dragon, red-eyed and fanged.

"It's time to revive the Order of the Dragon," said Meinster. "It's how He got His name."

She knew that, of course.

"People here want to know what you want, Baron."

"People there know what I want. I've been telling them for years. I want what is ours. I want a homeland for the undead. I want Transylvania."

"I think they mean immediately. Blankets? Food?"

"I want Transylvania, immediately."

She covered the mouthpiece and spoke.

"He wants Transylvania, Home Secretary."

"Not in our gift, more's the pity. Would he take, say, Wales? I'm sure I can swing Margaret on that. The taffs are all bloody Labour voters anyway, so we'd be glad to turn them over to that drac-head dandy. Or, I don't know, what about the Falkland Islands? They're far distant enough to get shot of without much squawking at home. The Baron could spend his declining years nipping sheep. That's all they ever do up in the Carpathians, anyway."

"There might be a counter-offer, Baron," she told him. "In the South Atlantic."

"Good God, woman, I'm not serious," said Ruthven. "Tell him to be a nice little bat and give up. We'll slap his wrist and condemn him for inconveniencing our old mucka Ceauşescu and his darling Elena, then let him do an hour-long interview with Michael Parkinson on the BBC, just before *Match of the Day*. He should know we like him a lot more than the bloody Reds."

"Is that an official offer?"

"Not in my lifetime, Miss Reed. Will he talk to me?"

"Would you talk with the Home Secretary?"

A pause. "Don't think so. He's an upstart. Not of the Dracula line."

"I heard that," said Ruthven. "I've been a vampire far longer than Vladdy-Come-Lately Meinster. He was turned in the 1870s and he's basically little more than a Bucharest bum boy. I was already an elder when he was sucking off his first smelly barmaid."

They might be of different bloodlines, but Ruthven and Meinster were of a similar type. Turned in their golden youth, they remained petulant boys forever, even as they amassed power and wealth. To them, the world would always be a giant train set. Engineering crashes was great fun.

"Katharine," said Meinster, "you had better come visit."

She really wasn't keen. "He wants me to go inside."

"Out of the question," said Croft.

"Not wise, Kate," said the spy. "Meinster's a mad dog. A killer."

"Commander Bond, your concern is most touching. Are you with the SAS now? Or is everybody dressed up in the wrong uniform these days? What do they call it, 'deniability'?"

"Aren't you supposed to be a *secret* agent, Bond," sniped the Home Secretary. "Does *everybody* know who you are?"

"I met Miss Reed on an earlier mission, sir."

"That's one way of putting it, Hamish Bond."

"Rome, 1959," said Jeperson, from the pit. "Not one of the Club's notable successes. The Crimson Executioner business. And the death of Dracula."

Lord Ruthven ummed. "You were mixed up in that too, weren't you? How you do show up, Katie. Literally all over the map. A person might think you did it on purpose."

"Not really."

"We can't let a civilian – an Irish national at that – compromise the situation," said Croft. "Give the word, and I'll send in Bond and settle Meinster's hash. Set-ups like this are why we have people like him."

Bond stood at attention, ready to kill for England.

"Margaret would have our heads on poles, Croft. And I'm not ready to become an ornament just yet. Katie Reed, do you solemnly promise not to succumb to the Stockholm Syndrome? Meinster's a fearful rotter, you know. Good clothes and a boyish charm are no guarantee of good character."

"I've met him before. I was not entirely captivated."

"Good enough for me. Any other opinions?" Everyone looked as if they were about to say something, but the Home Secretary cut them all off. "I thought so. Katie, our hearts go with you."

"Wouldn't you rather have a gun?" asked Jeperson.

"Ugh. No. Nasty things."

"A shadow? I can have Nezumi here in fifteen minutes. You've worked with her before."

Kate remembered the Japanese vampire girl who used to live in the flat upstairs from hers. An elder, and an instrument of the Diogenes Club.

"Isn't it a school night?"

Meinster would have someone who'd notice even a shadow as mouse-like as Nezumi. It was safer to go into the Embassy alone.

Safer, but still stupid.

She was marched again, with Dravot taking hold of her arm in exactly the same place, to the front line, the pavement outside the Embassy. Power was cut off to the street lamps as well as the building, but large floodlights illuminated the dragon banners, projecting human silhouettes against the walls. It must be very dramatic on television, though she overheard Paxman arguing down the line with a BBC controller who wanted, if no one was being murdered just now, to cut back to the snooker finals. As she approached the Embassy, there was some excitement among the crowd, mostly from people asking who the hell she was.

Kate saw no faces at the windows. SAS snipers with silver bullets in their rifles were presumably concealed on the nearest rooftops. Men like Hamish Bond were trained to use crossbows with silver-tipped quarrels. There were even English longbowmen schooled in Agincourt skills, eager to skewer an undead with a length of sharpened willow.

On one side, Jeperson suavely ran down what they knew about the situation inside the Embassy. On the other, Croft brutally gave bullet points about the things they'd like to know.

So far as they understood, there were about twenty-five hostages, including the Romanian Ambassador, whom no one would really miss since he was a faceless *apparatchik*, and Patricia Rice, a pretty upper-middle-class student who had been visiting in order to arrange a tour of collective farms by her Marxist Student Group. As a bled-dry corpse, Rice would be a public relations nightmare: her great-great uncle or someone had once been a famous comedian, and news stories were already homing in on her. The viewers were following the siege just to see if the posh bird made it through the night. Besides Meinster, there were perhaps five vampire terrorists. It was imperative she confirm the numbers, and find out what kind of ordnance they were packing besides teeth and claws. From what she remembered of Meinster's kids up in the Carpathians, they didn't need that much more.

As they reached the front doorstep, Dravot let her go.

Everyone backed away from her in a semi-circle, skinny shadows growing on the Embassy frontage.

In theory, Kate could be arrested if she crossed the threshold. The Embassy was legally Romanian turf and she remained a fugitive from state justice. It occurred to her that this would be a needlessly elaborate way of whisking her back to the prison she had clawed her way out of. Which didn't mean the *Securitate*, besides whom the SPG were lollipop men, weren't up to it.

She thought of pressing the bell-button, but remembered the power was off. She rapped smartly on the door.

The report was surprisingly loud. Weapons were rattled, and she turned to hiss reassurance. If anything would be worse than being bound in a diplomatic pouch and sunk in a Bucharest dungeon, it would be getting shot dead by some jittery squaddie.

The door opened and she was pulled inside.

In the dark lobby, her eyes adjusted instantly. Candles had been stuck up all around and lit.

She had been grabbed by two vampires. A rat-faced fright who scuttled like an insect, his unnaturally elongated torso tightly confined by a long musty jacket with dozens of bright little buttons like spider-eyes. And a new-born girl with a headscarf, bloody smears on her chin, a man's pinstripe jacket, Dr Martens boots and a sub-machine gun. The girl's red eyes told Kate exactly how she felt about her: hatred, mistrust, envy and fear.

"Patricia Rice?" Kate asked.

The new-born hissed. She had been turned recently, in the four days since the siege began.

No one had told her Meinster was making vampires of the hostages. It was the surest way of triggering the Stockholm Syndrome, she supposed. Rice had given up Marxism and pledged herself to a new cause.

She remembered Meinster in the mountains, explaining why the Transylvania Movement would win. "We can make more of us," he had said. "We can drown them."

Rice took her hand and tugged. Kate stood her ground.

She had been a vampire for nearly a century. This fresh immortal needed a lesson in seniority. Meinster was a fanatic for bloodline, pecking order and respect for elders. It was one reason he was wrong about long-term strategy: he could easily make more vampires, but not more like him. As

Ruthven said, he was a *parvenu* anyway, a pretend-elder barely older than Kate. If Dracula was still King of the Cats, Meinster would never be taken seriously by anyone.

She broke Rice's hold.

"Just take me to your leader," she said.

The rat-*nosferatu* led the way. He moved jerkily, like a wrong-speed silent movie. He was one of the very old ones, far beyond the human norm. Kate had met creatures like him before and knew they were among the most dangerous of vampirekind. They were all red thirst, and no pretence about civilization.

She was taken upstairs to a high-ceilinged conference room. Free-standing candelabra threw active shadows on the walls. Hostages were tied up, huddled against the walls: their arms were striped with scabs, but not their necks. Meinster was conserving his resources.

The Baron stood in one corner with his lieutenants. They were vampire kids, child-shaped but old-eyed. These were his favoured troops, not least because he wasn't himself very tall or broad. On *Not the Nine O'Clock News*, he was impersonated (very well) by Pamela Stephenson.

Meinster wore a very smart grey cloak over a slightly darker grey frock coat and riding boots. His ruffled shirt would have looked better on Adam Ant. His hair was improbably gold, gelled into a fixed wave. His smile was widened by his fangs.

One of his lieutenants had a gun to match Rice's; the other held Meinster's two poodles. In the forest, Kate had seen Meinster kill another vampire for ridiculing his beloved dogs. They were vampire pets, little canine monsters with sharpened fangs, fattened on drops of baby's blood. They must have been smuggled into the country despite quarantine regulations designed to keep undead animals like them out – a more serious crime than terrorism in the opinion of many Home Counties pet owners.

"Katharine, well met."

"Baron," she acknowledged.

"She was insolent," hissed Rice. "I hate her already."

"Shush up, Patty-Pat," said Meinster.

"We don't need her. We only need me. You said so, when you turned me. You said you only needed me. Me."

"Am I beginning to detect a theme tune?" suggested Kate. "'The Me Song'?"

Rice raised a hand to slap but Kate snatched her wrist out of the air and bent her arm around her back. She got snarled up on the strap of her gun.

"You turned this girl, Baron?"

Meinster smiled artfully, a boy caught out.

"Things must be desperate."

She let Rice go. The new-born sulked, face transforming into a bloated mask of resentment and self-pity. She should watch that tendency to shapeshift, or her scowl might really stick. She only had to look at Mr Rat-features to see a dire example of the syndrome.

"May I offer you someone to drink, Katharine? We've a fine selection of fusty old bureaucrats. Oh, and three cultural attachés who admit that they're spies."

"Only three?"

"So far. We can offer Ruthven some interesting documents from the secret files. Nicolae and Elena tell the world about modernisation and harmony with the West, but we both know they play a different hand at home. My old comrade has much to hide. I'd be most willing to share it with your lovely Mrs Thatcher."

"She's not mine. I'm Irish, remember."

"Of course, Katharine. Potato famines, Guinness, Dana. I am well up on the West. As a coming man, I have to learn all these things. Just as He did, a century ago."

When he so much as hinted at the name, his eyes were radiant. She thought she saw tiny twin bats flapping in his pupils.

"You so want to be him, Baron. How well did you know him?"

"He was more a father to me than any human family. More a mother. More anything."

On the subject, Meinster was blind. To him, Dracula was

the King of the Cats, the fount of wisdom and destiny, a God and a champion. Kate knew too many vampires like the Baron, forcing themselves to be what they imagined Dracula had been, hoping to become everything he was but not knowing the whole story.

"At the end, he wanted to die," she said. "I saw that."

"You saw what you wanted to see, Katharine. You are not of his direct bloodline."

"I wish that were true."

"Heresy," shouted Rice, raising her gun and fiddling with anything that might be a safety catch. "She defiles the name of the Father-in-Darkness."

Meinster nodded, snake-swift. The old *nosferatu*, rodent-ears twitching, took the new-born's gun away from her.

"Thank you, Orlok," acknowledged Meinster.

Kate looked again at the reeking thing. She knew who Graf von Orlok was. During the Terror, when London rose against the rule of Dracula, he had been in command of the Tower where the "traitors" were kept. If she had been less fortunate during her underground period, she might have met Orlok before. Several of her friends had, and not survived.

Sometimes, she forgot to be afraid of vampires. After all, she was a bloodsucking leech too and no one was ever afraid of her. Sometimes, she remembered.

Now, looking at the spark in Orlok's grubby eyes, she remembered the first vampires she had seen, when she was a warm girl and the dead were rising all around.

In her heart, nightmare spasmed.

"Katharine, I will prevail," said the Baron.

"How? The British Government doesn't negotiate with terrorists."

Meinster laughed.

"What's a terrorist, Katharine? You were a terrorist. And you've just had a conversation with the Home Secretary. Once upon a time, you were a wanted insurrectionist and Orlok was a lawful authority. Once Nicolae Ceaușescu was a terrorist, my partisan comrade, and the Nazis were our enemy."

That was true.

"And, in our homeland, you were unjustly accused of murder, hunted by corrupt police. Then, when you came to me in the mountains, we had common cause. Nothing has really changed. We have been adrift, I'll admit. Since He passed, we have pretended to be humans, to be just another of the many races of mankind, but we are not. You've never lived with your own kind, Katharine. You've spent a century working with *them*, fighting for the cattle. Yet they still fear and loathe you. Here in England, the warm are polite and pretend not to despise us; but in our homeland, you must have seen the truth. Vampires are hated. And we *must* be hated. Our inferiors must hate and fear and respect us. He knew that. His was the vision we must struggle to bring about. We must be the princes of the earth, not the servants of men. Then, believe me, He will rise again. What you saw was an illusion. Dracula does not die and become dust."

Meinster was trembling with excitement, a boy dreaming of Christmas morning.

Kate saw Patricia Rice adoring her father-lover-fiend.

"First, Transylvania . . ."

Meinster let it hang.

"I've seen who's out there," said Kate. "I know what they can do. Having hostages won't help. You had one card, and you've played it badly."

She nodded at Patricia Rice.

"On the contrary, she was my masterstroke. Are you not, dearest Patty-Pat?"

He reached out and touched Rice's face. She squirmed against his hand, like one of his fanged poodles.

"She will be my Elena, when I rule. The first of my Elenas."

The Baron gave orders to Orlok, in rapid Romanian. Kate only picked up a few words. One of them, of course, was *moarte* – "death".

"First, the fire," said the Baron, sweeping over a candelabrum. Flames caught a tablecloth and swarmed over the furniture. The hostages began screaming. "Now, we make a dramatic departure."

He leaped up onto a windowsill and posed against the tall opening. Searchlights outside swung to light him up. He was a swashbuckling figure, cloak swept back over his shoulders.

"To me, my brides."

Rice hopped up to nestle under one arm. He stretched the other out, beckoning to Kate.

"Become a bride of Dracula, my fiery Irish colleen."

"That's far too presumptuous, Baron."

Orlok picked her up and tossed her to Meinster.

"Comfy?" he asked the two. Kate saw Rice almost swoon in delight, but didn't understand it herself.

Apart from all other considerations, she knew Meinster was gay.

He leaned against the windows and smashed through.

For a moment, Kate assumed the Baron, like his supposed father-in-darkness, could grow wings and fly. Then gravity and reality took over.

They plummeted to the pavement.

Meinster sprang up like a cat. Kate, badly shaken, rolled into the gutter. Rice, knees and ankles broken, howled as the bones knit back together.

People rushed forward.

"I have surrendered," Meinster announced, "to these flowers of English and Irish vampire maidenhood."

A black-clad figure swarmed up the front of the Embassy, to the broken window. Flames were already pouring out, blackening the sill.

There was gunfire inside the building.

Richard Jeperson helped her stand and brush herself down, showing real concern. His style was more Charles Beauregard than Edwin Winthrop: she wondered how long he could last under the likes of Ruthven and Croft, not to mention Margaret Thatcher.

Along with the police, TV crews surged forward.

She heard commentators chattering, speculating on the rapid pace of events.

Another vampire was tossed out of the window, turning to a rain of ashes. Hamish Bond was doing his job. Kate thought Orlok might give him a fight, then she saw Dravot, out of his police helmet, signalling a cadre of black ninja-suited men, vampires all, to move in. Britain had been working for a century to create the vampires it needed rather than the ones imposed upon it.

The front door was smashed. Vampires crawled head-down from the flat roof and lizard-swarmed in through upper-storey windows. It was over in moments.

Jeperson and she were separated from the action by a press of people. Between riot shields, she saw Meinster and Ruthven facing each other, warily but without going for the throat. It was as if they were looking in reflecting mirrors for the first time since their turning.

"What was the point?" she asked. "This was all arranged between them. This wasn't a siege, it was a pantomime. It's not about vampires, it's about communism."

Jeperson was sad-eyed.

"You of all people know Romania," he said. "You've seen what happens in the satellite countries. There's no real détente. We have to get rid of the whole shoddy system. Nicolae Ceauşescu is a monster."

"And Meinster is better?"

"He isn't worse."

"Richard, *you* don't know. You weren't there during the Terror. When people like Meinster, and people like Ruthven, are in charge, people like you, and people like me, get shoved into locked boxes. It happens slowly, without a revolution, without fireworks, and the world grows cold and hard. Ruthven's back and you're supporting Meinster. How long will it be before we start praying for Dracula?"

"I'm sorry, Kate. I *do* understand."

"Why was I here?"

"To be a witness. For history. Beauregard said that about you. Someone outside the Great Game has to know. Someone has to judge."

"And approve?"

Jeperson was chilled. "Not necessarily."

Then, he was pulled away too. She was in a crowd.

A cheer rose up. A line of people, hands on heads, bent over, scurried out of the Embassy door. The hostages. Among them was Orlok, with the poodles. She would have bet he'd survive.

She tripped over thick cable, and followed it back out of the press of bodies. A BBC OB van hummed with activity.

This was news. She was a newspaperwoman.

Somewhere near, she would find a phone. It was time to call her editor.

NEIL GAIMAN

Click-clack the Rattlebag

NEIL GAIMAN HAS written lots of books and short stories and comics and things for adults and children and monsters. He is Professor in the Arts at Bard College in New York, is married to Amanda Palmer, and no longer has any idea where he is living.

"I was in Australia, in the house of critic and old friend Peter Nicholls," he recalls, "and I wanted to write something small and scary, for a book with monsters in it. I remembered a house I had been in in Ireland, one that scared me when I had walked through it in the dark, and crafted this story, with no idea whether it worked or not until I read it in Melbourne Public Library the following day.

"I recorded it last year and we put it up on audible.com and audible.co.uk, for Hallowe'en, with Audible donating money to charity for each free download. It raised a lot of money for very good causes. And, according to people on Twitter, caused a few of them to sleep that night with the lights on, just to be on the safe side."

"BEFORE YOU TAKE me up to bed, will you tell me a story?"

"Do you actually need me to take you up to bed?" I asked the boy.

He thought for a moment. Then, with intense seriousness, "Yes, actually I think you do. It's because of, I've finished my homework, and so it's my bedtime, and I am a bit scared. Not very scared. Just a bit. But it is a very big house, and lots of times the lights don't work and it's a sort of dark."

I reached over and tousled his hair.

"I can understand that," I said. "It is a very big old house." He nodded. We were in the kitchen, where it was light and warm. I put down my magazine on the kitchen table. "What kind of story would you like me to tell you?"

"Well," he said, thoughtfully. "I don't think it should be *too* scary, because then when I go up to bed, I will just be thinking about monsters the whole time. But if it isn't just a *little* bit scary then I won't be interested. And you make up scary stories, don't you? I know she says that's what you do."

"She exaggerates. I write stories, yes. Nothing that's been published, yet, though. And I write lots of different kinds of stories."

"But you *do* write scary stories?"

"Yes."

The boy looked up at me from the shadows by the door, where he was waiting. "Do you know any stories about Click-clack the Rattlebag?"

"I don't think so."

"Those are the best sorts of stories."

"Do they tell them at your school?"

He shrugged. "Sometimes."

"What's a Click-clack the Rattlebag story?"

He was a precocious child, and was unimpressed by his sister's boyfriend's ignorance. You could see it on his face. "Everybody knows them."

"I don't," I said, trying not to smile.

He looked at me as if he was trying to decide whether or not I was pulling his leg. He said, "I think maybe you should take me up to my bedroom, and then you can tell me a story before I go to sleep, but a very not-scary story because I'll be up in my bedroom then, and it's actually a bit dark up there, too."

I said, "Shall I leave a note for your sister, telling her where we are?"

"You can. But you'll hear when they get back. The front door is very slammy."

We walked out of the warm and cosy kitchen into the hallway of the big house, where it was chilly and draughty and dark. I flicked the light switch, but nothing happened.

"The bulb's gone," the boy said. "That always happens."

Our eyes adjusted to the shadows. The moon was almost full, and blue-white moonlight shone in through the high windows on the staircase, down into the hall. "We'll be all right," I said.

"Yes," said the boy, soberly. "I am very glad you're here." He seemed less precocious now. His hand found mine, and he held onto my fingers comfortably, trustingly, as if he'd known me all his life. I felt responsible and adult. I did not know if the feeling I had for his sister, who was my girlfriend, was love, not yet, but I liked that the child treated me as one of the family. I felt like his big brother, and I stood taller, and if there was something unsettling about the empty house I would not have admitted it for worlds.

The stairs creaked beneath the threadbare stair carpet.

"Click-clacks," said the boy, "are the best monsters ever."

"Are they from television?"

"I don't think so. I don't think any people know where they come from. Mostly they come from the dark."

"Good place for a monster to come."

"Yes."

We walked along the upper corridor in the shadows, walking from patch of moonlight to patch of moonlight. It really was a big house. I wished I had a flashlight.

"They come from the dark," said the boy, holding onto my hand. "I think probably they're made of dark. And they come in when you don't pay attention. That's when they come in. And then they take you back to their . . . not nests. What's a word that's like *nests*, but not?"

"House?"

"No. It's not a house."

"Lair?"

He was silent. Then, "I think that's the word, yes. Lair." He squeezed my hand. He stopped talking.

"Right. So they take the people who don't pay attention back to their lair. And what do they do then, your monsters? Do they suck all the blood out of you, like vampires?"

He snorted. "Vampires don't suck all the blood out of you. They only drink a little bit. Just to keep them going, and, you know, flying around. Click-clacks are much scarier than vampires."

"I'm not scared of vampires," I told him.

"Me neither. I'm not scared of vampires either. Do you want to know what Click-clacks do? They drink you," said the boy.

"Like a Coke?"

"Coke is very bad for you," said the boy. "If you put a tooth in Coke, in the morning, it will be dissolved into nothing. That's how bad Coke is for you and why you must always clean your teeth, every night."

I'd heard the Coke story as a boy, and had been told, as an adult, that it wasn't true, but was certain that a lie which promoted dental hygiene was a good lie, and I let it pass.

"Click-clacks drink you," said the boy. "First they bite you, and then you go all *ishy* inside, and all your meat and all your brains and everything except your bones and your skin turns into a wet, milk-shakey stuff and then the Click-clack sucks it out through the holes where your eyes used to be."

"That's disgusting," I told him. "Did you make it up?"

We'd reached the last flight of stairs, all the way in to the big house.

"No."

"I can't believe you kids make up stuff like that."

"You didn't ask me about the rattlebag," he said.

"Right. What's the rattlebag?"

"Well," he said, sagely, soberly, a small voice from the darkness beside me, "once you're just bones and skin, they hang you up on a hook, and you rattle in the wind."

"So what do these Click-clacks look like?" Even as I asked him, I wished I could take the question back, and leave it unasked. I thought: *Huge spidery creatures. Like the one in the shower that morning.* I'm afraid of spiders.

I was relieved when the boy said, "They look like what you aren't expecting. What you aren't paying attention to."

We were climbing wooden steps now. I held on to the railing on my left, held his hand with my right, as he walked beside me. It smelled like dust and old wood, that high in the house. The boy's tread was certain, though, even though the moonlight was scarce.

"Do you know what story you're going to tell me, to put me to bed?" he asked. "It doesn't actually have to be scary."

"Not really."

"Maybe you could tell me about this evening. Tell me what you did?"

"That won't make much of a story for you. My girlfriend just moved in to a new place on the edge of town. She inherited it from an aunt or someone. It's very big and very old. I'm going to spend my first night with her, tonight, so I've been waiting for an hour or so for her and her housemates to come back with the wine and an Indian takeaway."

"See?" said the boy. There was that precocious amusement again. But all kids can be insufferable sometimes, when they think they know something you don't. It's probably good for them. "You know all that. But you don't think. You just let your brain fill in the gaps."

He pushed open the door to the attic room. It was perfectly dark, now, but the opening door disturbed the air, and I heard things rattle gently, like dry bones in thin bags, in the slight wind. Click. Clack. Click. Clack. Like that.

I would have pulled away, then, if I could, but small, firm fingers pulled me forward, unrelentingly, into the dark.

NICHOLAS ROYLE

Dead End

NICHOLAS ROYLE IS the author of *First Novel*, as well as six earlier novels including *The Director's Cut*, *Antwerp* and *Regicide*, and a short-story collection, *Mortality*. He has edited sixteen anthologies, from *Darklands*, in 1991, to four volumes of the annual *Best British Short Stories* series, running from 2011 to the present.

A senior lecturer in creative writing at Manchester Metropolitan University, he also runs Nightjar Press and works as an editor for Salt Publishing, where he has been responsible for Alison Moore's Man Booker-shortlisted *The Lighthouse*, Stephen McGeagh's *Habit* and Alice Thompson's *Burnt Island*, amongst other titles.

"I was on holiday in the south-west of France when I learned, via Twitter, that Alison Moore's first novel, *The Lighthouse*, which I had acquired and edited for Salt, had been longlisted for the Man Booker Prize. It was in many ways an idyllic holiday, in glorious surroundings, but it's funny how the darkness is never far away."

A RAGGED SCREAM TEARS through the leaden heat. He sees a fountain of blood erupt from a body torn in half. Hears – or imagines he hears – the nauseating grind of a siren. Flash of a dentist's overhead light. Muscles tensed to snapping point. Then the eyes, in close-up. James Garner's from *Grand Prix*, but they could be anybody's. They could be his.

He half-opens one eye. From under the brim of his straw hat, he watches a brown lizard with an orange stripe. It moves across the pebbly path like an illuminated message on a dot-matrix information board.

Arms and legs tingling in the direct sunlight, he hears footsteps on the pebbles, sees the lizard dart into the grass.

"Hello, my love," Isabel says as she bends down to deposit her book and towel on the sunlounger next to his.

He pushes the brim of the hat up a little. She leans over him, sarong falling open against her thigh. He watches his hand rise, his finger touching the exposed flesh. The weight of her breasts pulls against the elastic material of her tankini top.

"Coming for a swim?" she says, taking half a step back as a bee lumbers between them.

"No," he says, watching the bee. "I'm not much of a swimmer."

"I love swimming." She backs away, unwinds the sarong.

He hears her enter the pool, one careful step at a time, then the sound of her pushing forward into the water, arms outstretched. The physical reaction he'd had to their momentary closeness begins to subside, and then returns as he pictures her body moving through the water.

He pokes at the brim of his hat so that he can watch the movement of the top of her back and pale shoulders as she swims. He can't make them out at this distance, but she has the faintest freckles on her shoulders and back. The first time he saw them, as he and Isabel undressed each other in her bedroom on a weekday afternoon, he had traced his finger over the random patterns.

They hadn't had long; he'd been expected home.

When she reaches the far end and turns around to come back, the kicking of her legs splashes pool water on to a bricked-up doorway in the nearest wall.

He looks at the doorway. At some stage in the past it had, presumably, led somewhere.

After a while, he realizes the noises have stopped.

"It's thirsty work this, darling," he hears her say.

He smiles and gets up from the sunlounger. The garden of the house is criss-crossed by paths, some of which lead only to flower beds. He takes one that he knows leads to the house, passing between two beds of lilac festooned with butterflies and abuzz with bees. He walks under the archway and enters the gîte, which is attached to the side of the main house. He pours a glass of orange juice and returns the carton to the fridge, then looks at the glass he has poured and picks it up. Condensation forms on the outside of the glass as sweat runs down into the small of his back. He lifts the glass to his mouth.

The glass now half-empty, he places it back on the work surface and stares absently at the wall behind the wicker-work sofa in the lounge area of their studio room. There's a watercolour in a gilt frame above the right-hand end of the sofa and a curtain hanging from a rail covering the wall behind the left-hand end. He approaches the sofa and pulls the curtain to one side. Behind it is a glass-panelled door with another curtain on the other side – in the main house.

In his pocket his phone vibrates. He takes it out to find a text from his daughter.

Hi Dad. I swam 10 lengths ☺ *xx*

He smiles as his index finger picks out his reply.

Well done darling. More than I can manage! xx

He stares at the curtain behind the sofa again, his smile fading.

He returns to the garden with a fresh glass of orange juice to find Isabel floating on her back in the pool absolutely still.

"I don't know how you do that," he says, appraising the outline of her body in the water.

"It's easy."

"I couldn't do it."

"Anyone can do it."

"Not me," he says. "Not without moving my arms and legs."

She keeps her legs together and her arms outstretched and lies perfectly still.

He smiles at her as sweat runs from his hairline.

He kneels down, placing the glass of orange juice by the edge of the pool. Isabel turns on to her front and kicks out behind. She approaches the side, her fingers alighting on the tiled rim. He covers her hand with his and she smiles up at him. He looks down at her breasts, wondering if his sunglasses will conceal his wandering eyes, but knowing they won't. He feels a tightening in his shorts.

"I want you," he says.

Her lips part. She grabs his wrist and is about to try to pull him into the water.

"My phone," he says, resisting.

There's a hoarse scream or a cry from somewhere beyond the confines of the garden. It sounds like an animal in sudden, unbearable pain. It sounds like the same scream that he has heard before.

"What *is* that?" he asks.

"A donkey?" she suggests. "Every time I hear it, I think it's being sawn in half."

"I know how it feels," he says.

Her face hardens; she looks down, her grip on his wrist abruptly relaxing. Then she lets go and drops beneath the surface. She twists around under water and when she kicks to propel herself away from the side of the pool, she gives him a good soaking.

He takes his phone from the pocket of his shorts and places it on the nearest sunlounger, then removes his sunglasses and puts them down next to the phone. He checks her position and dives in.

With his eyes closed he reaches for her as he moves under water. She twists away, trying to free herself from his grasp, but he holds on. They surface and he rubs his eyes.

"I'm sorry," he says, gasping for breath. "I'm sorry. Really. It was a silly thing to say and it's not even true."

She struggles a bit more, but he senses the fight has gone out of her.

"I'm sorry," he says again, and he moves her hair out of her face as they tread water. He draws his legs up and encircles her waist, tightening his grip, but she tips forward, taking them both underwater. His protest emerges in a stream of bubbles.

Isabel is lying on her back on a sunlounger. He is standing a few feet away, wondering if it's forgivable to have sex in a swimming pool. The sun has already dried the remaining droplets of water from her legs, and now the dark patches on her tankini – which she has put back on, since they don't know when the owners might reappear – shrink even as he watches. She is breathing regularly and he thinks she might be asleep.

He passes under the archway to the front of the property. Their hire car stands on the gravel drive. To the left, the single-track lane leads back to the road, the only route to Villefranche de Rouergue. To the right, the lane peters out into a cinder track, which runs into a high hedge. He remembers when they came out for a walk the night before, hearing the creatures in the fields and hedgerows. The churring and chirruping of birds, he had said; the chiming of cicadas, Isabel had thought. He wonders who was right.

He looks down the lane, which Isabel had described as a cul-de-sac. He had pointed out that the phrase, although French, was not used by the French. So the phrase itself was a linguistic cul-de-sac, *n'est-ce pas*?

"Not so much cul-de-sac as *mise-en-abîme*, in that case," he remembers her saying.

He stares into the distance, the skin under his right eye twitching.

In his pocket, his phone vibrates for an incoming text message.

They are in Villefranche, walking through streets of grey stone.

"We could be in Yorkshire," he says, taking her hand and enjoying the warm, damp hollow of her palm.

"Except for the sub-tropical conditions," she says.

"And the French graffiti," he adds, pausing by a stencil of a skull signed, apparently, TOMBO. "And the brasseries and patisseries, and the smell of Gauloises, et cetera."

By mutual consent they turn down an alley that looks as if it will offer another way out. It doesn't. They stand and face one another at the end of the alley, each taking the other's hand, and kiss.

Eventually the medieval town surrenders its main square and they wander around the market. He stays by her side, either holding her hand or touching the back of it. Sometimes their legs come into contact and he presses against her hips, whispering into her ear. She smiles and makes faint noises of pleasure and encouragement.

She stops at a stall selling a variety of dry sausages.

"What's '*myrte*'?" he asks, pointing to one labelled AVEC MYRTE.

"Myrtle, I expect. Sounds delicious."

"I know what '*cochon*' is," he says, looking at another label. "What about '*âne*'?"

"Donkey," she says, catching his eye, before they both turn to look at the looped sausage, a deep reddish brown colour speckled with chalky white mould.

"That explains a lot," he says.

They stop in a café for a glass of wine, then walk back slowly to where they had left the car, parked in a line of vehicles overlooking the railway station. There is a languid quality to Isabel's movements that he finds exquisitely erotic and as he lowers himself into the driver's seat he finds that he is aroused. She fans herself as he starts the engine and he buzzes down her window as well as his own.

The houses lining the road soon fall away and he changes down to second as dictated by the gradient, the car traversing the contours, first one way then the other, to reach higher ground. As they turn left on to the narrow lane down to the hamlet he unclips his seat belt and allows it to loop back on to its spool. She looks at him and raises her eyebrow.

"Last time you waited until we were half-way down the lane," she says.

"I'm relaxing," he says with a smile.

Together in the kitchen they prepare ingredients for dinner.

"Is the sun over the yardarm?" she asks.

"Pretty much."

He opens the fridge and takes out a bottle of wine and a beer. He pours a glass of wine and passes it to her.

"Cheers," they both say.

He pours his beer into a glass. He's always done this since reading in a magazine that being able to smell your beer as you drink it enhances your enjoyment.

He tops up Isabel's wine glass and takes the empty bottles outside and stands them with the others that have accumulated by the side of the gîte. At the end of the week, if not before, he will take them into Villefranche and recycle them. As he looks at the line of bottles standing to attention he suddenly has a very clear memory of his son asking him why, when he had swept up a broken wine glass at home, he had dumped the broken glass in the regular bin rather than the recycling bin for glass, metal and plastic. He had told his son that he believed broken glass couldn't go in the recycling, but had to go in the general waste, and his son had asked about bottles breaking when being dropped in the recycling bin. Was that a problem? he had asked. Did those broken bottles then have to be fished out of the recycling? He hadn't answered, he now realizes. Something else had happened, some distraction had intervened, and they had all moved on and the question had remained unanswered, and he now realizes that it's not that the wine glass is broken that's important, but that it's a different kind of glass, and he feels an urgent need to tell his son, to explain, so that when his son eventually finds out one day, perhaps from someone else, the truth about glass, he won't think back and remember how his father misled him. Lied to him, really. He wants to text him now, his son, text him and tell him about the different types of glass, but it further occurs to him that he doesn't really know enough about it. He doesn't know why the fact that it's a different kind of glass is so important. Surely glass is glass. Surely it all gets melted down and remade, doesn't it? What does it matter if some of it is thin and clear while some of it is green or brown and quite a bit thicker? Although not that much thicker – it depends on the type of glass.

He becomes aware of Isabel standing in the doorway of the gîte with an anxious expression on her face.

"Darling, what's wrong?" she says, approaching him now, arms outstretched. "Why are you crying?" She wipes his tears away. "Darling, darling," she murmurs as she holds him.

In the morning they need bread.

"I'll go. You stay in bed," he says.

"No, I want to come with you."

He tries to persuade her to stay, but she refuses.

It's warm but hazy. The haze will have burnt off by the time they get back from Villefranche with the bread.

They park in the same spot overlooking the railway station. Isabel is wearing a white short-sleeved top that gapes at the front when she leans forward. That she appears innocent of intent and oblivious to any effect only makes the effect all the more powerful.

"This is our space," she says.

"I don't like to drive any further in," he says. "Feels like there's no way out. That one-way system."

When they return to the car carrying a baguette and a bag containing two *pains aux raisins*, he fastens his seatbelt but then unclips it almost as soon as they start climbing the hill out of town. Isabel looks at him with that same raised eyebrow.

"Feeling even more relaxed?" she says.

He just smiles.

When they get back, they are standing on the gravel drive when a familiar scream rips open the now vivid blue stillness of the morning.

He turns and looks at her and pulls a sad face, then looks away at the line of empty bottles standing against the wall of the gîte. A bee investigates the neck of one bottle after another, then seems to have a better idea and veers off towards the garden.

He walks around to stand behind her and threads his arms through hers, around her waist, then allows his hands to settle on her wide hips. She leans her head back against his shoulder.

"I think I need a lie down," he says, taking her hand.

He's undressed her before they reach the bed. He kneels down and kisses the gentle swell of her tummy, tasting salt, chlorine, sun cream. He runs his hand down over her leg, almost but not quite making contact. She makes a low sound that tells him she likes what he's doing. He stands up and steps out of his shorts, feeling the weight of his phone in the pocket as he throws them the short distance to the armchair. She lies down on the bed and he goes to lie down next to her and he asks himself if he will be able to lose himself in the moment, or the next series of moments, or if he will be visited by thoughts of his children, if he'll be interrupted by the buzz of his phone's text alert, if he'll be assailed by worries about the hopelessness of the situation in which they find themselves, if he'll be distracted by images, which he realises just at that moment have begun to crowd in on him in the last few days, of dead ends. But, in spite of these thoughts and worries and images, he finds he can actually lose himself in the moment, because, from the first moment he touched her, from the first moment they kissed, he has known there is something unprecedented and different and unique about that touch and that kiss. What he feels for her is overpowering and he senses it's the same for her and she has told him it's the same for her and together they seem to have found something that means something profound to each of them, to both of them, and this meaning appears to be communicable by touch. They want each other, they desire each other, and when he is making love to her – which he is doing right now, right this very moment, and even his being aware of it is not enough to break the spell – it feels, it really feels as if he is doing something, going somewhere, feeling something he has never done before or been before or felt before. He knows it's the oldest feeling in the world, or one of them certainly, but to him, and to her, he thinks, it feels brand new, it feels like nothing they've ever felt before, like something they've never done before, it feels like somewhere neither of them has ever been before. Above all it feels like they are going to this place, performing this act and experiencing this feeling together and at the same time and even as he experiences it he thinks it feels like an out-of-body experience despite the fact it's all about his body and her body and their two bodies coming together and even this awareness does not impinge on the sensation or adulterate his happiness and even that word somehow does not have the undesired effect he so feared, when really you would expect it might, and he thinks to himself that it's a little bit like climbing a mountain, as you keep climbing and you see the summit disappearing ahead of you, a series of false summits, and then you see the real summit just a short way ahead and you know there's no way you're not going to make it and you do make it and you stop and look beyond and the view is the most amazing view you have ever seen and it's the first time you have seen it, this particular view, and it is in no way disappointing or predictable, but is breathtakingly beautiful and bathed in some impossible golden light and even as you think this, even as you think it's the most banal cliché ever to have entered your head, even as you think this, the vision doesn't darken or start to break up or become unstable, but persists, and a new feeling comes over him, one of great calmness, a feeling he can't remember experiencing for a long time, a calmness that fills him like the tide fills an estuary. And while they lie together on the bed and the sweat dries on their skin and they slowly become unstuck, he doesn't worry about his children or even about his wife, he doesn't worry that he and Isabel might be heading down a dead end, he doesn't worry about the screams of the donkey or the

premonitory dream of the siren or the close-up of the terrified driver's eyes in the film he would for some reason
always be reminded of when he went to the dentist as a
child, he doesn't worry about the bee that will return to the
empty bottles lined up outside the gîte and, attracted by the
sticky residue inside one of them, probably one of his empty
beer bottles, stumble inside and perhaps become stuck in
that residue, and he doesn't worry that later when he loads
up the car with the recycling he will fail to notice the bee
inside the bottle and he doesn't think for a moment that
when he releases his seat belt only a short way into the journey into town and Isabel raises her eyebrow at him that he
might be about to need his seatbelt when the bee becomes
unstuck at the bottom of the bottle and bumbles out of the
bottle into the car and barges about, a bee in a car seeming
so much bigger than normal, the size of a bat or a bird, and
the interior of the car seeming so much smaller than normal,
like the interior of a car *after* a horrific accident rather than
before.

DANIEL MILLS

Isaac's Room

DANIEL MILLS IS the author of *Revenants: A Dream of New England* (Chômu Press, 2011) and the short-story collection *The Lord Came at Twilight* (Dark Renaissance Books, 2014). Since 2009, his short fiction has appeared in numerous journals and anthologies, including *Shadows & Tall Trees*, *Black Static*, *The Grimscribe's Puppets* and *The Mammoth Book of Best New Horror Volume 23*.

Recent work is forthcoming in *The Children of Old Leech: A Tribute to the Carnivorous Cosmos of Laird Barron* (Word Horde) and *Mighty in Sorrow: A Tribute to David Tibet & Current 93* (Dunhams Manor Press). Dunhams Manor Press will also publish a novella entitled *Children of Light* as a limited edition chapbook.

The author lives in Vermont and is currently at work on his second novel.

"While much of my fiction derives its inspiration from New England's social and religious history," reveals Mills, "'Isaac's Room' is one of only a few stories I've written that employs a contemporary setting. Of course, the story *is* in some sense a period piece, albeit of a more recent vintage, one in which the Iraq War looms large and AOL Instant Messenger is still a favoured means of communication among college students.

"Falmouth, Vermont, is entirely fictional, as is Falmouth College, though the latter bears some similarity to my own alma mater, the University of Vermont, where I was an undergraduate from 2003 to 2007. And if the story's setting is autobiographical, then its tone is scarcely less so – the narrator's resignation verging on ambivalence as he faces down his past and the ghost of mental illness: 'the places we would haunt forever'.

"'Isaac's Room' was written very quickly in the spring of 2013. Looking back on it now, I can see the influence of J-horror cinema (especially Kiyoshi Kurosawa's films *Kairo* and *Sakebi*) as well as Robert Aickman's 'Your Tiny Hand is Frozen' – though with Instant Messenger standing in for Aickman's telephone."

FALMOUTH, VERMONT. IN my memories, it is always dark there, always winter. The campus of Falmouth College, where I spent my freshman year, appears to me cloaked in the haze of snow and night, lit by sodium lamps and the flash of headlights on drifting powder. The cloud cover is unbroken, grey on black and veined with snowfall, as it was in 2004, when I used to stand on the river-bridge at dawn and watch the light seep into the east.

I was a virgin at eighteen, crippled by shyness and singularly unprepared for the Vermont winter: the chill of it, the isolation. In classes, or in the dining hall, I sat by myself and watched the other students laugh and flirt and make plans for the weekend. When night came, I bundled myself into a sweatshirt and parka and walked the campus with headphones strapped over my ears, filling my head with the roar of black metal: jagged guitars, pulsating beats.

Darkthrone. Burzum. Their howled vocals came to express for me all of the terror and rage I could not admit to anyone, not even myself, and I passed through nightly squalls of sleet and snow before returning to that empty room where I watched hours of amateur porn and punched the walls until my knuckles cracked and split.

My roommate Andrew was from D.C., an ex-sprinter turned full-time drinker. By the spring of 2004, he had lost his place on the track team and his scholarship along with it. Like me, he had no intention of returning to Falmouth for his sophomore year and so abandoned altogether the pretence of studying or attending classes.

His afternoons he spent watching movies or playing X-box, taking occasional breaks to pack a bowl and read *The Lord of the Rings*. At night he went to frat parties and stayed out past daybreak, later shuffling into the room with eyes red and voice hoarse and mumbling good morning. "Morning," I replied, but beyond that, we rarely spoke, and it wasn't long before he dozed off, sprawled sideways on the couch, waiting for night to fall before stirring from his hangover to check his voicemail, his Instant Messenger account.

That was how it started. It was around dinnertime, a Thursday in April. Andrew and I sat back to back at our respective desks, separated by our hand-me-down minifridge with the microwave and TV balanced on top. My headphones were silent. The CD had spun to a finish, and I heard the hum of the radiator behind me, the click of Andrew's fingers on the touchpad. Other sounds too: crackling speakers, a faint patter like rain.

"What are you watching?" I asked without turning around.

No answer.

I asked him again, but he didn't reply, so I stood and crossed the room and leaned in over his shoulder. His laptop screen was cluttered with various chat and browser windows. In one a Quicktime video had just finished playing. He closed the window.

"What was that?"

"Nothing," he said, quickly, and rose from the chair.

He brushed past me, took his coat down from the door.

He wouldn't look at me, but he was clearly unsettled, his features contorted by something like fear. He grabbed the lanyard with his keys and slipped from the room. I didn't ask where he was going or when he would be back.

Alone now, I waited, but he didn't return, and his laptop was open before me. I opened his IM account. Last night, at

3:31 a.m., Andrew had received a message from IM user IsaaC81. The screen name was unfamiliar to me, and he wasn't listed among Andrew's friends either.

Hey, IsaaC81 had written. *U there?*

Andrew was out. *Out*, his auto-reply read.

At 3:33 a.m., IsaaC81 forwarded a link to a Quicktime video file and subsequently logged off. He had not been online since.

I clicked the link. The movie buffered, opened.

It was a webcam video of some kind, shot by a low-res camera and badly pixillated. A desk lamp, angled away from the camera, provided the only illumination, but I was able to make out a small room jumbled with cheap furniture, concrete walls sheathed in white paint

A figure sat the desk. IsaaC81? No, I thought, looking closer. It was a woman.

She was shirtless, shadow-thin, the balls of her shoulders thrusting from snarls of ropy black hair. Her face was shadowed and hidden but for her eyes, which caught the light somehow and shone. She whimpered. Her nostrils flared. Her breath came as a muted scratching.

She stood. The chair scraped on the tiles, and the shadows fell away to reveal her elongated arms, all elbows and joints, her right hand clenched over a glittering edge – a razor, maybe, a shard of broken glass. Her fingers dripped, arms criss-crossed with black lines where the edge had bitten, scraping on bone.

The speakers crackled.

With one swift motion she drove the glass into her belly. The wound blossomed, releasing a torrent of viscous black fluid, like old blood but darker. It poured from her, collecting in her knuckles and dribbling on the floor. A sound like the rain.

She lifted her head. Her eyes burned vividly, nearly white against her dark hair, but I couldn't discern her features before the video ended and Andrew's screen went black. I clicked the link again, but it was dead. *Error 404. Page not found.*

*   *   *

I couldn't sleep. It was after midnight and Andrew hadn't come back to the room. In my mind, a young woman, faceless, carved the flesh from her arms and ribcage. She winced, gasped, and bit her lip to stop from crying out, so that her mouth was smeared and dripping. I switched on the TV, hoping for distraction, but the news was full of footage from Iraq.

A bridge strung with corpses. A man shouting, openmouthed, his hands red and wet.

At 3:00 a.m., I wrapped myself in a hoodie and crossed the hallway to the men's room. The air was moist, sticky, the mirrors misted over. I cupped my hands beneath the faucet and drank from the tap, gulping down water while the showers ran behind me, pouring out whorls of steam. Voices. A man and a woman, their rapid breathing. I shut off the taps.

I went outside. I didn't bring my headphones or walk down to the river-bridge, as I often did, but circled the rain-fogged campus in silence, pushing myself until my legs ached. The college was deserted at that hour, or nearly so, and I had turned back toward the dormitories when I spotted him outside the arts building.

Andrew.

He slouched on a bench in the shadows with his hood pulled up over his head. His face was hidden, but I recognized him by his yellow windbreaker, the way he held his cigarette with the tip turned sideways. Thin trails of smoke rose from it, mingling with the steam of his breath, but I didn't approach him and he didn't seem to notice me.

I went back to the room. I crawled into bed and drifted off as our computers hummed, whirring. The morning skies sparked and faded and Andrew crept into the room. "Are you awake?" he whispered, but I said nothing, and I heard him close his laptop before collapsing on the couch.

The email came the next afternoon. A student had died on campus, a young woman named Annie. The message was evasive in tone, telegraphic in its lack of detail – a suicide, then, and I thought at once of "IsaaC81" and the video he had sent to Andrew. A woman's bone-thin shoulders. A wound gushing black fluid. The email concluded with the date and time of a memorial service to be held later that month, followed by phone numbers for doctors, counsellors.

Andrew was asleep on the couch. His mouth was open, crusted with drool, and I didn't want to wake him. At the library, I bought a cup of coffee from the café and descended two levels to the computer lab: a converted storeroom lit by harsh fluorescent tubes with high windows overlooking the green at ankle-height.

A lone work-study student was on duty. He ignored me as I sat down beneath the windows and logged on to one of the computers. Darkthrone buzzed in my ears, "Transilvanian Hunger", the volume down as I opened up Google and searched for "IsaaC81".

I had to scroll through pages of meaningless results before I found it. The website was called "Isaac's Room", and it appeared to be an online journal of some kind. The page had once belonged to a young man named "Isaac C", who listed the IM screen name IsaaC81 among his contact details. In place of a profile picture, he had uploaded a sepia-tone image of a window in which the photographer was visible in reflection, a knife-thin silhouette – Isaac himself, presumably, though his outlines merged with the room behind him. I looked closer, noting the angled desk lamp, the cheap furniture, the concrete walls.

It was the same room from the video.

My pulse thudded in my throat. I turned off the music, plunging the room into near-silence. I heard the hum of computers in standby, the occasional rustle of paper as the work-study read from his chemistry textbook. I wiped my palms on my jeans and opened Isaac's journal. I began to read.

Some entries described his interests in photography and music: Elliott Smith and Joy Division. In others he discussed his strained relationships with his parents, his longing for a girl named "S" whom he had once dated. *I'm still here*, he wrote. *Alone in that room where we used to sit together. Was it just three months ago? I haven't changed, S, even if you have, and I'm not sure I can believe that. I'm not sure I can believe in anything anymore.*

The most recent post had been made over a year ago. It seemed to consist of a brief message of apology to his parents with references made to Nick Drake and Kafka. At the bottom of this final entry, he had inserted a link to a video file alongside the words *for S*.

I clicked it. The hourglass turned over and over.

Error 404.

I closed the browser, rubbed the sleep from my eyes. My coffee had gone cold while I read and a dozen or more students had entered the lab. Two girls sat together in the corner, whispering, and one of them was crying openly, unashamed.

Dusk. The room swam beneath the glaring tubes. I pressed the play button on my CD player and logged off from the computer. Standing, I donned my coat and hat and glanced up at my reflection on the window, shivering in places like the pieces of a dream: a lamp-lit space, a dripping shadow.

The next day was Saturday. Andrew and I slept in past noon and walked together to the dining hall. Chris was there. Like us, he was a freshman, the son of two New York psychiatrists. Midway through his freshman year, he had enrolled in the environmental programme and subsequently took to sporting tie-dye and twisting his hair into dreadlocks.

He lived down the hall from us in a triple room, where the windows were always open, even in wintertime, a box-fan whirring to vent the pot smoke, the stench of body odour and Nag Champa. Chris had planned a party for later that night and had invited the entire floor but needed Andrew to acquire alcohol for him. Andrew was likewise underage, but he "knew someone", an upperclassman who lived off-campus, and owned a car besides.

Chris passed him an envelope of cash under the table. "Thanks, man," he said, as Andrew took it. "Much appreciated." He stood and made to leave but apparently changed his mind because he paused with his palms flat on the table-top. "And remember," he said. "Grey Goose or Skyy. None of that cheap shit like last time, okay?"

Andrew shrugged. "Whatever you say."

"Good," Chris said, smiling, showing teeth. "I think we all remember what happened the last time." And with that he wandered off, eventually taking a seat at a table of bare-foot girls and rich boys wearing Carhartts.

"Asshole," muttered Andrew.

I thought I'd misheard him. "Sorry?"

"Never mind," he said. "Let's go."

We drove downhill into town and collected Andrew's hook-up from an apartment by the bridge. He was a senior, scarecrow-thin and clad entirely in baggy flannel. He climbed into the back of Andrew's SUV and directed us across the river to a liquor store. We parked outside and waited, the engine running.

Andrew unrolled his window. He lit a cigarette and offered me the pack. I shook my head, and for a while, we were quiet. Andrew smoked thoughtfully, his eyes on the windshield. Cold rain spattered the glass, flattening itself into beads, rivulets.

"Did you know that girl?" he asked. "Annie. The one who died."

The wipers thumped and squealed.

"No."

"I did. Well, I met her once."

"When was this?"

"Last month. It was at one of Chris' parties. He knew her from class, I guess. They hooked up a few times, but she had gotten, well, 'clingy'. That's what he said. So he broke it off."

"But she came to the party."

"She did. She must have been desperate, though, because she drank too much and stayed on even after her friends had left and Chris had hooked up with another girl. In the end, we were the only ones left, the two of us, and his roommates kicked us out."

"What did you do?"

"What do you think? I went home with her."

His cigarette crumbled, shedding flakes of ash. He tapped it against the window and released a mouthful of smoke into the rain. The heat-vents rattled, sounding like the scratch of air over a microphone, the whistle of her breath, black fluid pouring from her veins.

"How did it happen?" I asked him.

He looked at me, features wreathed in smoke, rainwater glinting on his cheeks.

"How did she die, you mean?"

"Yeah."

"Pills. Her roommate found her. It was in the showers. Annie had been there half the night, lying face down and naked with her skin all white and wrinkled."

"Shit," I said. "That's terrible."

"Yeah," he said. "It is."

He stubbed out his cigarette. "And that's not even the worst of it."

He didn't explain. At that moment, our hook-up returned to the car, his arms folded over a soggy cardboard box. Inside were two bottles of Jagermeister, handles of cheap rum and vodka.

"But didn't Chris say . . .?"

Andrew rolled up his window, shifted the car into gear.

"Fuck Chris," he said, and pulled out into traffic.

We were almost to the bridge when we heard the sirens behind us. State troopers. I watched Andrew's eyes in the rear-view as the police approached and overtook us, making for the Interstate. Their blue lights dwindled in the dark, but he didn't blink, not once.

*   *   *

The party started without us. By eight o'clock, when we arrived in Chris' room, a large group of our floor-mates had already assembled. They greeted our arrival with cheers and the rattle of empty Solo cups. Andrew opened the Jager, then the vodka. Chris packed a bowl and handed it around. I didn't smoke, not usually, but tonight I fumbled for the pipe and lighter, thinking of Annie and Isaac's Room, the video Andrew had received: her dark hair, dead eyes white with the light behind them. I breathed deeply, too deeply. I coughed and sputtered, nearly gagging, and closed my eyes as the music washed over me.

Others entered the room. Girls perched themselves on desks and dressers or the protruding arms of furniture and talked loudly to be heard above the music, practically shouting over me where I sat, slumped forward and swaying. The bubbler came round again and I took it, sucking down smoke, so that their voices merged and buzzed in the air above my head. The music was louder now, pulsating, echoed by the rhythm of the blood inside my skull.

Slowly, the room faded, falling from me to join with the dreaming, the darkness of empty rooms. In that place, the ghost of a thin girl hacked fat from muscle, sinew from bone. She whimpered, a beaten dog, and the sound rose like the smoke inside my chest. I tried to speak but I couldn't. Her tongue was my tongue, and her breath was in my mouth.

Andrew's voice.

The sound restored me to the stifling room, the couch with its stink of sweat and spilled beer. He was arguing with Chris, hissing through his teeth, though I couldn't make out the words. The other students were quiet, or mostly so. The stoner girls looked at each other, unbelieving, as Andrew screamed and swore, spittle flying from his lips.

Chris snorted.

"Jesus Christ," he said. "And she hooked up with you? No wonder she killed herself."

Andrew lunged. The punch went wide, and he stumbled forward, off-balance. Chris leapt back, allowing his roommates to seize hold of Andrew's arms. They dragged him to the door and pushed him into the corridor, slamming the door behind him.

Chris just laughed.

I woke up curled around the toilet, lips caked in yellow bile. There was vomit on the seat, streaks down my shirt-front. For a time I didn't know where I was or how I had ended up there but merely lay with my knees tucked into my chest, a foetal position.

Then I heard voices from the showers and recognized my floor-mates' and realized I couldn't have been unconscious for more than an hour or two. I waited until the men's room was empty before creeping from the stall and skulking back to the room.

2:00 a.m.

Andrew's bed was empty, his laptop closed. I sat down at my desk and nudged my computer out of stand-by. The screen flickered, flooding the room with bluish light. I double-clicked Instant Messenger and took down my away message.

A chat window opened, filling the screen.

IsaaC81.

Hey, he typed. *U there?*

I hesitated, still drunk, the taste of bile on my tongue. I closed my eyes to stop the room from spinning and heard the chirp of a received message.

He had sent me a link. A Quicktime file.

Click.

It was the same room, the same dim lighting. Shadows eddied from the desk lamp, spreading in webs to obscure the cheap furniture, the whitewashed walls. A man sat at the desk. In one hand he held a shard of glass, a thin piece hooked like a crescent moon. He was shirtless, his chest matted with coarse dark hairs, and his forearms, too, were bloodied. The bones of his left wrist were visible where the flesh had been stripped away.

He stood. His shadow climbed the wall behind him, doubling his every movement. Darkness dripped from his hands, spattering the floor, but his face was hidden, hooded by its own shadow. He whimpered. The glass flashed, glittering as he drove it into his gut. An oily liquid bubbled up from the wound, spilling free, black and noxious like the depths of loneliness, loathing: his hatred, mine.

He looked at the camera. *Andrew*.

I opened the chat window with IsaaC81.

Yes, I typed, frantic now. *I'm here*.

But he was already offline.

Andrew didn't come back to the room that night. I waited up for him, watched the sky lighten beyond the green blinds. But he never returned, and I fell asleep with Instant Messenger open before me and the blankets wrapped round, my hands twined in the fabric, still shaking.

I woke to an empty room: nauseous, hung-over, temples pounding. I called Andrew's cell, but he didn't answer. I left a voicemail, waited an hour, then walked to the library, where I spent the rest of the evening reading, or trying to read, unable to distract myself from thoughts of Isaac.

Who was he? I knew nothing about him except those few details I had managed to glean from his online journal. There was the girl called S, his obsession with dead musicians, his final note of apology. And the link. *For S*, he wrote.

He was dead, a suicide. He had filmed it with his webcam and posted the video online, forwarding the feed to his ex-girlfriend via IM. It was intended as a final gesture, one last grasping at the light before the darkness hooked him and gathered him to its breast.

But if the Web is a place then he lived and died there and now he haunted it in the same way. I recalled the video he had sent to Andrew and the news of Annie's death that followed. Chris had known her, as had Andrew. "I went home with her," he said, wherever that was, and later, I had seen him in the same room, bloodied and naked and moaning softly.

I walked back to the dorm.

From the footpath I spied the yellow light in our room and assumed that Andrew had returned. But the room was empty. His things were gone: his laptop, his clothes, his bedding. The mattress had been stripped bare, sickly stains visible in the glare of the light overhead. He had taken down his posters as well, and the walls gleamed, white as teeth, a field of snow over which my shadow moved.

I went downstairs. I found the RA in the Rec Room, where he sat watching the eleven o'clock news. He muted the TV and rose from the couch.

"I was looking for you," he said.

"Why?"

"You haven't heard?"

"Heard what?"

He explained.

Saturday night, after leaving the party in Chris' room, Andrew had walked down to the village. He had found a house party and bluffed his way inside. Nobody knew him there, but they all thought he must have taken something, because he was crying when he left, sobbing like a child as he struggled uphill towards the college.

He almost made it. He was nearing the crest of the hill when he passed out by the roadside. He could easily have been killed, of course, but a driver chanced to spot him where he lay and brought him to the hospital.

I swallowed.

The room blurred, retreating rapidly, and I remembered that I had not eaten in days.

"Is he . . .?"

"Oh, sure, he's fine. He's going home, actually. That was what I wanted to tell you. His father flew in this afternoon and helped pack up his things. He was due to be released this afternoon, so he might even be home by now. Try giving him a call, maybe?"

"Thanks," I said. "I'll do that."

The RA scrutinized me closely.

"Are you okay? You look – tired."

"I'm fine."

The RA smiled – a little apologetically, I thought – and wandered off towards the stairwell. After he was gone, the TV continued to play, still muted, unfurling its endless scenes of blackened buildings, ruined streets, smoke standing in plumes above the rubble.

The next Sunday, around dusk, I heard singing from the campus chapel and paused outside to read the announcements. A memorial service was in progress. ALWAYS WITH US, the notice read, accompanied by a grainy photograph of the girl who had died.

Annie. In the photograph, she was smiling, seemingly happy, but her arms were terribly thin and her hair was long and messy. She wore a tank-top, and her shoulders were visible, the bones of them, jutting from the coils of her black hair.

It snowed that night, the last of the season. I walked into town. Sleet raked the sidewalks, showing red then green as the stoplights changed. It swept down the empty roadways, freezing when it struck the concrete, making glass out of the shade trees.

There were no salt trucks or road crews. The whole of Falmouth, it seemed, had retreated indoors to wait out the spring snow. The stillness seeped into me and whirled on my lips, rising on the winds which came, stronger now, shearing limbs from the ice-encrusted trees.

Lines came down. On Canal Street, the lights flickered and fell away. I slunk past darkened houses, a world transformed by silence into silence itself, the same room-less room that Isaac had created: a virtual space in which his shadow persisted, detached from the body he had learned to despise and which he had cut away. *For S.*

Annie, too, had made an offering of herself, first to one man then another and finally to the dark. Andrew had felt responsible and perhaps he was. But I remembered the night that I had seen him outside the arts building when he looked as cold and isolated as I had always felt. "Are you awake?"

he asked me, later, but I didn't answer him, and in the end, he surrendered to it, as Isaac had done, and Annie. He lay down by the roadside and closed his eyes, freezing slowly as he waited – and for what?

I had no idea. Even now, I'm not sure I understand any of it, though I carry the memory of that room inside me: bloodied knuckles, shadows on white walls. I'm older now, and reasonably happy, but I haven't left that place, not really. I transferred from Falmouth and moved away, but a part of me remained behind – the smallest part where others had given everything.

That night, I walked as far as the river. My steps carried me out over the bridge, where the waters plunge to the falls, frothing and white, and I must have stayed there for hours, since it was morning when I turned around. The light came blue-grey through the sleet, a chilling dimness through which I passed, thinking of Isaac and Andrew, their ghosts and mine, unconscious of the rooms we had fashioned for ourselves, the places we would haunt forever.

ANGELA SLATTER

The Burning Circus

SPECIALIZING IN DARK fantasy and horror, Angela Slatter is the author of the Aurealis Award-winning *The Girl with No Hands and Other Tales*, the World Fantasy Award finalist *Sourdough and Other Stories*, and the Aurealis finalist *Midnight and Moonshine* (with Lisa L. Hannett). Recent titles include *The Bitterwood Bible and Other Recountings*, *Black-Winged Angels* and *The Female Factory* (again with Hannett). She is the first Australian to win a British Fantasy Award (for "The Coffin-Maker's Daughter" in *A Book of Horrors*).

In 2013 she was awarded one of the inaugural Queensland Writers Fellowships. She has an MA and a PhD in Creative Writing, and is a graduate of Clarion South 2009 and the Tin House Summer Writer's Workshop 2006. She blogs on her website about shiny things that catch her eye.

"When I was percolating the idea that would eventually become 'The Burning Circus'," recalls the author, "the main image I had in mind was of a woman walking unevenly because only one of her shoes had a heel. I already had the title, but not all the steps the story would take. For a long while all I could imagine was this pair of feet walking along through different landscapes, always off-beat, the rhythm strangely broken, kicking up dust and small pebbles.

"When I got the name in my head of Semiramis (an ancient Armenian queen/goddess) I had my tale – with her name came her history of being ill-used, unjustly punished and determinedly seeking revenge. And the connection of the ancient Semiramis with the doves of Ishtar gave me my weapon of vengeance."

SEMIRAMIS HASN'T BEEN to the circus in such a long time. Other circuses, yes. *The* circus, no.

Above the stand of trees, over to the left where the road curves around to encircle the big park, the striped canvas of the Big Top can be seen, the flame-red pennants waving in the breeze. While she's pinning her eyes there as though it might disappear if not watched, she's not paying attention to her feet, and she stumbles, trips, does a kind of progressive dance but doesn't fall. The heel of her right Mary Jane, though, gives up the ghost – the shoes were old before she got them – and she tries to hammer it back to the sole with nothing but her callused hands. About as effective as using spit for glue. She surrenders, and sets off once again, her gait now the strange staccato roll of a woman with unequal leg lengths.

When she goes up on the left foot it feels, just a little, like flying. Just a little like the old days, that sense of ascending without a tether, then the downswing onto the right, down further than you know you should go, just like that too. Just like wondering if someone was going to catch you. Semiramis knows now only she can catch herself.

The outside still makes her nervous, even though the breeze feels like a kiss. All that space, no confines. *Silly*, she thinks; it wasn't always so. Only she'd gotten so used to being inside, so used to the sight of walls and an entrance that didn't open, not in such a long time. And that window, so tiny and up so high, with the bars, up too high for her to see if he was coming; she wondered some days if that was why he didn't come, coz she wasn't able to look out for him. But the sun arrived regularly, spearing in to wake her each morning; sometimes the rain, too. After the first few years, after she got to know every inch of the walls, the ceiling, the floor, she started living inside her skull, only surfacing when they pushed food in through the trap at the bottom of the metal portal. Sometimes not even then.

But then one day, oh one day, the door *opened*; the whole, entire, actual door. Pushed hard to break the rust on the hinges, and two men standing there looking embarrassed as if they'd discovered her crouching over the stinking hole in the corner. That was it. No fanfare, no shining light, no great revelation, just a couple of fat deputies staring at her like she was something they were surprised to find.

Truth be told, she didn't recognize them; then again, she'd never been able to keep faces straight in her head from the time she walked into the Sheriff's Office. The only ones that stayed were from *before*. The folk she'd known and thought of as her family. And she remembered how the world looked each time she flew; she remembered the scenes from every time she let go mid-air and was ever so briefly weightless. Those were the things she remembered. The *before* things.

"Semiramis Baxter?" One of them asked, his voice weak to match his chin. She paused. Recalled. Yes. Someone had called her that once. Someone had breathed it in her ear like it was the most precious thing to cross his lips. Yes, that was her.

As she walks, she says it, says her own name, just to hear it hang in the air, just to know it's real. That she's real and so is this, *this* freedom. This terrifying freedom to do whatever she wants.

"Semiramis Baxter, you've served your time." But she didn't think she had. Because there hadn't been a trial, she was very sure; there hadn't been anything. Just talking to a man with a big hat and a star pinned to his shirt; talking to him and saying "I saw the one who did it, he had red hair, and a brown suit, a moustache and his teeth were all crooked." And he nodded, nodded and called a grieving woman into the room, a woman who looked at Semiramis blankly but stared ever so hard at the brooch she wore. Stared and stared and stared. *Yes*, the woman said, *yes, that was the piece of jewellery her husband had given her*. And next there was a lock being turned. Turning on Semiramis Baxter and she vanished for such a very long time.

Then those men at the door, and her standing, trying hard to stretch her calves, her thighs, tripping in her haste to get to the exit, fearful that this offer of liberty, of *air*, would be rescinded. They handed her over to a nun, a penguin of a woman who seemed not to sweat in spite of the heat. The nun took her to a chapter house outside of the town – what was the town called? All this time and she couldn't bring it to mind. The other sisters took care of her, gave her a bath, washed and cut her hair (turned white far too soon), gave her two dresses, neither new. Washed myriad times till they were pale and thin, but she didn't care. They were hers. And the shoes, the battered, brown leather Mary Janes with the wobbly heels. An equally battered suitcase and some plain underwear, a cloche hat that hadn't really had a shape for long years before it came to her. They gave her some money, dry paper dollars and coppery coins; they took her to the station and put a note in her hand with the name and address of a woman in Chicago who was expecting her to come and be the help.

She thanked them and smiled and got on the bus. She woke from a dream of his face as he gave *her* the brooch; she heard him saying "I'll come get you, my honey, my little peach, my one special girl. Only do this little thing for me – I can't help you if I'm locked up, can I?" She didn't say, "If I *don't* do this little thing I won't need your help." She was a good girl. She walked right into the Sheriff's Office, just like Gabe asked, told the man exactly what he told her to say, wearing that damned brooch, the one that she knew too late Gabe had pulled from the woman's collar while she'd hunched over her husband as he bled out. Semiramis should have known it all along, when she found that scrap of green silk stuck to the pin when she unclipped it to put it on.

She'd opened her eyes, stared through the dirty windows, out at the wheat fields and the silos for a while, then got off the bus well before Chicago.

She kept moving, making money when she needed, not fussy about how she did it. Moving, moving, moving, always moving. Looking for them, looking for the troupe to which she'd once belonged; looking for *him*. So many states, so many cities, so many tiny, tiny little townships. It was so easy to disappear in this land, even a circus could find places to hide. Even one as queer as the Burning Circus.

She found other things along the way, other people who could and did help. The kindness of strangers was the strangest thing she'd ever encountered. And in New Orleans there'd been a woman with soft lips, gentle hands and dangerous knowledge; a woman who'd showed her tastes she hadn't even known she had. This was the one who suggested what Semiramis might need, how she might get the amends due to her. This woman was the one who'd conceived them, such small things, so simple, not at all voracious; just needing some blood now and then, a bitty bit of meat. The soft part of Semiramis' upper arms, the inner flesh, was scarred over many times. And they took in a little of her pain, a little of her bitterness, a little of her righteous need for an accounting, each time they fed.

Then, having given Semiramis what she'd come for, having handed her the weapon of her requirement, the woman begged her not to leave – but she did anyway. Semiramis had wandered, here and there, following old posters and rumours, stories and lies and wishes. And she spent so much time thinking about how the circus had fled. How not a one of them had come to see her. Not a one had warned her. Not a one had stepped up in her defence. They were happiest attracting just enough attention to entertain people and encourage them to part with their coin for it. But anything more than that? Anything that might make someone take a hard look at Gable Brandt? Gabe who was gold to them all, coz he brought the crowds.

Didn't matter to Gabe that he pulled down the largest income of them all. It didn't stop him supplementing his income with creative acquisition. *That* night wasn't the first time he'd followed some fool woman to a dark corner and scared the gems off her – although it was the first time he'd left a corpse behind – and it wouldn't have been the last, Semiramis was sure. So she sat in diners, listened to gossip, followed whispers of theft, sometimes asking questions but not too many.

Then one day, there it was – the poster. Not old, either, not yellowed by wind and months past, not blurred by rain and sun; not looking so worn that she knew she'd missed it. Them. Him.

This poster was *fresh*. And there they were, or some of them anyway: Timo the Dwarf, Lucia the Bearded Lady, Ferdi and Helenca the Siamese Twins, Veronese the Ring Master, Berto and Atla, the Lizard Woman, the singing bears, the deformed horse they passed off as a unicorn. Yet others she didn't know, new blood come along after she'd been left behind. And *him*, the finest looking man she ever did see; oh, Gabe was older, she could tell, but he remained so muscular, his jaw so defined, his moustache waxed to such sharp points! Still the main act – the Lord of the Air.

She rounds the bend and walks to the ticket booth, pays out a few of her last coins, smiles at Billy-J, whose voice was just breaking last time she saw him. Now he's a doughy-looking young man. He doesn't recognize her; no one would. She no longer resembles the bird-boned beauty with ebony hair and ruby lips; and she's heavier too – not so much physically, but the time inside, the enforced ground-ing, it's made her seem more affected by gravity.

Semiramis joins the flow of bodies heading towards the Big Top, her old suitcase, holes poked in the sides, thumping rhythmically against her legs. Sometimes it bumps other people but she ignores them, doesn't see their looks or hear their grumbling. She hears the noises from the case, though, and she hushes the creatures, tender as a mother. She's moving forward, forward, forward into the faded canvas palace that smells of sawdust and sweat, grease paint and stale perfume. She finds a seat, planting herself determinedly at the end of the row and refusing to shuffle along; others must climb over her. She pushes her case beneath the seat and promptly forgets it. The show begins and she is riveted.

The older clowns are slower in their japes, less nimble than they were; the new ones have clever quick tricks and trips, pratfalls and practical jokes. Then the flea-bitten lions, and the tigers with toothache, their fur coming out in tufts every time they jump. Next the ill-tempered elephant, she recognizes; its trainer is wary, someone she doesn't know. Jugglers, acrobats, the girl with the *unicorn* are a passing, glittering parade.

Then there's Berto as he takes centre ring. Berto wearing his tiny shorts with all his hair waxed off so there's nothing for the fire to take hold of; his lack of eyebrows makes him look perpetually surprised. Every night, Semiramis remembers, he's rubbed down with a secret mix (the shorts, too, are soaked in it), the stuff that will burn, burn, burn without touching him. She can see how deeply the wrinkles have cut into his face, how dry his skin is after years of this treatment. *He's decrepit*, she thinks, and puts a hand to her cheeks as if for reassurance.

As she watches, his wife Atla takes a lit brand, promenades about, showing it to the audience so they can all see it, hear the *crackle* as it swallows oxygen. Then Atla circles back and gently touches the torch to her husband, nightly living out many a woman's fantasy. And Berto, he goes up like a Roman candle, turning slowly in a circle, untouched by the flames, if not the heat. Semiramis looks away, examining the crowd, unnoticed; all *their* eyes are glued to the human torch as he makes a slow circuit of the ring, displaying himself like a saint proud of martyrdom.

Semiramis doesn't care.

They don't matter.

This isn't what she came for.

You might think Berto's what they all come to see, night after night, a man set alight, but no. *Now's* the time for the grand finale. Flying beats burning hands down.

As Berto's inferno dies down and Atla helps him shuffle away, the Ring Master directs the spectators' attention upwards.

There *he* is, fine as fine can be, Gabe dressed in his long leotard, arms and chest bare. Even from here she can see the way his eyes sparkle, how they pass over the crowd, resting on all the pretty girls in their summer dresses, resting on their pearl necklaces and brooches, their bracelets and rings, assessing value and what he might get for them in the next town – and who might be the easiest mark. She wonders if he's killed anyone else in the time they've been apart, if anymore heroic and unexpected husbands rounded corners as Gabe robbed a woman he thought was alone.

Beside him on the high platform is a girl, tiny, hollow-looking; staring at him like he's god, like he's life and death, and he is, with no net below. A man can burn on the ground to mild interest, but those who defy gravity? All the risk, all the glory. Oh yes, a catcher is gold. A flyer is replaceable as breath. That girl up there, easy to substitute one for another as the sequins on her costume.

Semiramis remembers flying – the sensation of letting go, the moment before gravity realized you were hers, and then the strong hands at your wrists, the feeling that you'd defied everything and were still *alive*. All things have their time, though, she knows that now. All things, all scenes, all acts. No flyer stays aloft forever.

She imagines Gabe turning to flame, imagines the rope ladder disappearing in a twist of orange and red and gold. She imagines him up there, trying to get down fast enough to escape, leaving the girl behind in his haste. She imagines the burning debris falling, falling, falling onto all those pretty summer dresses, turning their wearers into so much pulled pork. She imagines him anointed with a crown of fire.

Semiramis shakes herself. These thoughts are pointless, weightless like so much expelled air. Beneath her seat, vibrating against the back of her heels she can feel the suit-case, its contents reacting to her turmoil, linked to her as they are by blood, her tiny minions, her lovely light little demons. As inside, so it is without.

She finds she has lost time and realizes that – if he hasn't changed the act – the girl's part is coming to an end. Gabe always was a creature of habit and he'd not do anything that distracted a gaze from himself. The girl flies towards him and he helps her up onto the platform, gestures vaguely to indicate the crowd should clap her efforts. Before the applause has died down, he launches into his finale, taking the attention as he executes a slow swing away from the platform, just as he always did in the old days.

How many? wonders Semiramis. *How many between this girl and me? How many did he fail to catch? How many got too spooked and ran? How many got left behind? How many, how many?*

He waits for the swinging to stop, for the bar to steady and become static, then Gabe performs his masterstrokes, all his movements effortless. A casual clowning that has the audience laughing and gasping; he is an aerial drunk, standing, swaying, falling, catching himself at the last moment, looping himself gracefully back around the bar, refusing gravity's demands. He dances, grandstands, feints, makes the hearts below seem to consolidate into one organ, beating in time, pounding and swooping and diving in time with his death-defying acts. Oh, Gabe is worth the money all right.

And Gabe, oh Gabe never falls. Semiramis believes this implicitly, because this is what Gabe taught her. In all their time together, he never once even slipped. He never once used a net. *His concentration*, he'd told her, *was absolute*. It might look like he's mugging for the watchers below, but no, that's just part of the trick. Up there nothing can distract him. Not one thing. Never. Gabe has absolute faith that he will never fall.

Semiramis pulls the suitcase out from under her seat.

She places it on her lap and sets her fingers on the tarnished brash clasps. Hunching forward, she curls her body over the battered rectangle, and sighs *Fly*. Two light touches, two whispered *snaps*, and she lifts the lid as she straightens.

The dirty-white, barely fleshed doves burst upwards, red eyes burning, wings flapping, flapping, flapping as they rise unerringly. Gabe is making his last turn, his final faux-forgetful misstep, hands reaching pretending to miss the bar, the ropes, everything. The birds catch him off-guard, hitting him in the chest, the face, the eyes, unbalancing him, blinding him, defeating him utterly.

And he falls, he falls as surely as a duck shot out of the sky. He meets the ground with an astonishing sound, a sound Semiramis never thought to hear. All around her people scream and shout, cover their eyes, hold their children close as if they might protect them from the sight of poor old Gable with his bones all askew and his brain coming out his ears.

Semiramis ignores them.

They don't matter.

It was him she came to see.

RAMSEY CAMPBELL

Holes for Faces

RAMSEY CAMPBELL CELEBRATES fifty years in horror this year with the publication from PS of his latest novel, *Think Yourself Lucky*, along with a volume of all the author's correspondence with August Derleth, edited by S. T. Joshi. Meanwhile, he's currently working on the next novel, *Thirteen Days at Sunset Beach*.

"'Holes for Faces' was one of those ideas that clamour to be written and seem to come with an almost ready-made development," explains Campbell. "Some years ago we visited Naples for a few days. I think it was on the first full day that we found the catacombs of San Gaudioso under the church of Santa Maria della Sanità, which is located as described in the tale. The corpses are indeed displayed in that fashion. Need I say more?

"I was writing notes as soon as we left the tombs. Pretty well all the excursions we made in and around Naples appear in the story, macabrely transformed. The restaurant is based on our favourite, the Osteria da Antonio on Via Depretis. Writing all this makes me want to book us the next flight back."

As CHARLIE TURNED away from the breakfast buffet his mother gave a frown like the first line of a sketch of disapproval. "Don't take more than you can eat, please."

He didn't know how much this was meant to be. He put back one of the boiled eggs that chilled his fingers and used the tongs to replace a bread roll in its linen nest, but had to give up several round slices of meat before her look relented. "Come and sit down now, Charles," she said as though it had been his idea to loiter.

His father met him with a grin that might have been the promise of a joke or an apology for not venturing to make one. "Who wants to go to church today, Charlie?"

It wasn't even Sunday. Perhaps in Italy it didn't have to be. "At least we won't be robbed in there," his father said.

"You're safe in Naples, son," the man at the next table contributed. "We've always been."

"How old will you be?" his equally bulky wife said.

"I'm nearly eight." Since the frown looked imminent, Charlie had to say "I'm seven and nine months."

"That's three quarters, isn't it," the man said as if Charlie needed to be told.

"Just you stay close to your mummy and daddy and mind what they say," said his wife, "and you'll come to no harm."

It was Charlie's mother who was fearful of the streets. When they'd arrived last night after dark she'd refused to leave the hotel, even though it didn't serve dinner. His father had brought Charlie a sandwich in the room, and the adults had made do with some in the bar. He'd been too nervous to finish the sandwich, instead throwing it out of the window and hoping birds would carry off the evidence. Going back to the buffet might betray what he'd done, and he did his best to take his time over his plate while the adults introduced themselves. "Don't miss the catacombs," Bobby said as he pushed his chair back.

"Unless anything's going to be too much for someone," his wife Bobbie said.

"Nobody we know," said Charlie's father.

"Teeth," his mother said to send Charlie up to the room, where she inspected herself in the mirror. She'd plaited her long reddish hair in a loop on either side of her face, which was almost as small and sharp as his. His father's hair reminded Charlie of black filings drawn up by a magnet that had tugged his father's face close to rectangular. His mother gave Charlie's unruly curls a further thorough brush and insisted on zipping his cumbersome jacket up, all of which struck him as the last of her excuses to stay in the hotel.

The street was just as wide as it had seemed last night, and many of the buildings were as black, but shops at ground level had brought most of them to life. While the broad pavements were crowded Charlie couldn't see any criminals, unless any if not all of the people chattering on phones were arranging a crime, since even the women sounded like gangsters in cartoons to him. Reaching the opposite pavement was akin to dodging across a racetrack – no traffic lights were to be seen. Charlie's mother tried to hold his father back, but she was already clutching the boy's hand with one of hers and her handbag with the other. "It's how the locals do it," Charlie's father said. "We won't get anywhere if we don't show a bit of pluck."

There were bus stops around the corner near the harbour, and gusts of April wind that made Charlie's mother zip up the last inch of his jacket. On the bus she clung to her bag with both hands and sat against him. At least he was by the window, and had fun noticing how many cars were damaged in some way, bumpers crumpled, wings scraped, side mirrors splintered or wrenched off. His father looked up from consulting the Frugoguide to say "Underworld next stop."

Wasn't that where gangsters lived? A pedestrian crossing proved to lead across the road to a lift beside the pavement. A face peered through the little window as they reached the lift, and Charlie's mother didn't quite recoil. "We'll be fine down there, won't we?" Charlie's father asked the attendant. "You wouldn't be taking us otherwise."

The man waved his hands extravagantly. "No problem."

When the lift came to rest at the foot of the shaft the doors opened on a view like a secret the city was sharing with the visitors – a street of shops and tenements hidden from the road above. Between the tenements clothes on lines strung across the alleys flapped like pennants. "Come on, Maur," Charlie's father urged. "It doesn't get any better than this."

Charlie didn't know if she was frowning at the prospect or at disliking the version of her name. As they followed his father out of the lift she took a firmer grip on Charlie's hand. "Is that the church you brought us to see, Edward?"

Charlie thought his father was trying not to sound let down by her response. "I expect so."

The stone porch under a tower that poked at the pale grey sky was at least as tall as their house. Beyond the lumbering door a marble silence held the flames of dozens of candles still. At the far end of the high wide space a staircase with carved babies perched on the ends of the banisters framed the altar. The floor looked like a puzzle someone must have taken ages to complete, and Charlie wondered what a puzzle was supposed to have to do with God. His mother released his hand and seemed content to stroll through the church, lingering over items he couldn't see much point in. As he tried to keep his footsteps quiet his father came back from consulting a timetable. "We need to go down now," he murmured.

A pointer that didn't quite say CATACOMBS sent the family along a corridor. An old woman with a face like a string bag of wrinkles was sitting by a door. "No English," she declared and shook her head at Charlie, who thought she was barring him and perhaps his parents too until he realised she meant they didn't have to pay for him and couldn't expect her to speak their language. As his father counted out some European coins a man rather more than called "Don't go without us."

"Well, look who it never is," his wife Bobbie cried. "We thought we'd take our own advice."

As soon as Bobby handed the guide the notes he was brandishing she stumped to open the door. At the bottom of a gloomy flight of steps a corridor led into darkness. "Will you look after me, son?" Bobbie said. "Don't know if I can trust him."

Charlie wasn't sure whether this was one of those jokes adults made. While the corridor wasn't as dark as it had looked from above – the round arches supporting the brick roof were lit the amber of a traffic light – the illumination didn't reach all the way into the alcoves on both sides of the passage. "You could play hide and seek if nobody was watching," Bobby told him.

Hiding in an alcove didn't appeal much to Charlie. Suppose you found somebody already was? Dead people must be kept down here even if he couldn't see them, and who did Bobby think was watching? Charlie stayed close to his parents as the old woman shuffled along the corridor, jabbing a knuckly finger at plaques and mosaics while she uttered phrases that might have been names or descriptions. The movements in the alcoves were only overlapping shadows, even if they shifted like restless limbs. "You've not seen the best yet, son," Bobby said.

This sounded less like an adventure than some kind of threat, and Charlie was about to ask whether it was in the guidebook when Bobby whispered "Look for the people in the walls." As though the words had brought it to a kind of life, Charlie saw a thin figure beyond the next arch.

It was standing up straight with its hands near its sides. He thought it was squashed like a huge insect and surrounded by a stain until he made out that it seemed to be a human fossil embedded in the plaster. There was more or rather less to it than that, and once he'd peered at the ill-defined round-ish blotch above the emaciated neck he had to blurt "Where's its head?"

The old woman emitted a dry wordless stutter, possibly expressing mirth. "Maybe it's hiding in the hole," Bobby said. "Maybe it's waiting for someone to look."

The skeletal shape implanted in the wall had indeed been deprived of its skull. Perched on the scrawny neck was a hole deep enough for a man's head to fit in. "Don't," Bobbie said as if she was both delighted and appalled.

Charlie had to follow his parents under the arch as the old woman poked a finger at the gaping hole and let out a stream of words he might have taken for a curse or an equally fervent prayer. Now he saw bodies in both walls of the passage, and wished he didn't need to ask "Who took all their heads?"

"Maybe it was someone after souvenirs," Bobby said. "I don't suppose this lot were too tickled with losing their noggins. Watch out they don't think we're the ones that did it."

"They can't think. They've got no brains left."

"You tell him, son," Bobbie enthused just as his mother said "Charles."

He'd felt as if his words had robbed the figures in the walls of power until her rebuke gave it back to them. He could imagine the headless bodies peeling themselves loose from their corpse-shaped indentations and the stains that must have been part of them once, to jerk and stagger rapidly towards him. Far too soon some of them were at his back while others surrounded him, and there were surreptitious movements in the holes they had for heads – glimpses like animals retreating into their burrows to hide until people had gone by. Surely those were just the shadows of the visitors, and Charlie was making himself look closer when Bobby said "Don't stick your hand in, son. You never know what's waiting."

"Don't touch, Charles," his mother said at once.

"I wasn't going to."

"And," she said, "please don't speak to your mother in that fashion."

"Take no notice, son," Bobbie advised. "He was just having a joke."

"I'd like us to leave now, please," Charlie's mother said. "I think everyone's seen enough."

When Charlie turned to follow her he caught sight of a movement above the neck of the embedded body beside him, as if a face like a featureless stain had swung to watch. She must be causing it, there and in the cavities the other fleshless bodies had in place of heads. He tried not to look, especially back, while he trotted after her. It was only his father who was close behind him. The church was meant to be a refuge, and no footsteps other than the family's were clattering across the stone floor to the exit, however many echoes there might be. Outside all the clothes on the lines might have been miming agitation that his mother was trying to conceal. "I think we've been down here long enough," she said.

Long enough for what? Rather than ask, Charlie hurried after her to the lift, where the sight of a face peering through the small window had lost some of its appeal. As the lift creaked upwards his father consulted the guidebook. "They took the heads somewhere for safety," he said.

As Charlie wondered who was being kept safe and from what, his mother said "I'd like to put them behind us, thank you, Edward."

"How far?" Charlie blurted.

"I've been surprised at you today, Charles. I hope you won't let us down any more."

She strode to poke the button for the traffic lights, and his father hung back to murmur "They thought something might be catching, Charlie. That's why they took the heads off, to protect people."

Who might something catch, and why? As Charlie made to ask, his mother doubled her frown at them. "Come on, Charlie," his father muttered. "We don't want you ending up in more trouble."

Once they'd joined the queue at the bus stop Charlie's mother grasped her handbag every time a moped raced through the increasingly gridlocked traffic. The bicycles buzzing like wasps didn't bother Charlie, but he could have done without the face that kept looming at the window of the lift across the road. Very eventually a bus appeared in the distance, and less than ten minutes later it arrived at the stop.

From the bus he watched cars inch past one another, their drivers reaching to pull side mirrors inwards. The ruse would have amused him more if he hadn't seen one reflected face swell up like a worm emerging from a hole as the driver hauled at the mirror. Having leafed through the guidebook, his father said "Who'd like to go up to a park?"

"Let's," Charlie's mother said at once.

The picture in the book showed a railway platform made of steps alongside an equally steep train. When the bus came to an official stop at last and his father led the way to the station, however, Charlie saw an ordinary horizontal platform leading to a tunnel, where he tried to enjoy the sight of a blank-faced train worming its way towards him out of the dark. At first there wasn't much to see when the train moved off, though a toddler in the next carriage kept poking her head up to peer at him. Her breath on the window between the carriages blurred her face and turned it grey. He tried to focus his attention on the tunnel, where he couldn't see any holes in the walls – nowhere that anything could creep or struggle or bulge out from.

A wind boarded the train when, having escaped into the open, it reached the top of a hill, and Charlie's mother tugged his zip under his chin. At a restaurant between the station and a park they had a pizza big enough for the three of them. Plastic sheets around the dining area didn't just obscure the view but made the face of anybody who came near seem to take shape only gradually and not quite enough.

There were views from all sides of the park. The guidebook fluttered like a captured bird while Charlie's father named buildings and piazzas and streets. The boy was more taken with Vesuvius, a hump the colour of its own dark smoke across the bay. "Would you like to use the telescope, Charles?" his mother said, but the notion of looking through a hole that brought things closer didn't tempt him. As she pocketed the coin for the slot machine he saw a face struggling through a gap in a mass of foliage behind her. Only the leaves were active, and the statue was on the far side of the bush.

"We can take a ferry tomorrow," Charlie's father said on the way back to the hotel, "to somewhere your mother should like." Charlie thought she'd heard more than was intended – perhaps a rebuke. Nobody spoke much until they were up in their room. As soon as his father started looking in the Frugoguide she said "I'd like to eat wherever's nearest."

"I hope that won't be its only merit," said his father.

"I hope some things mean more to you than your stomach." Her glance at Charlie made it plain what should. "Time for a rest before we go out," she said to bring all discussion to an end.

Charlie tried to lie still on his bed while his parents did on theirs beside him. He might have liked to see their faces, which were turned away from him. His father's hand lay slack on top of the side of his mother's waist, and Charlie had a sense that it was inhibited from moving, just like him. He struggled not to think this might be how it would feel to be embedded in a wall. You'd have to move eventually, however you could. He strained to keep his restlessness discreet, but once his bed had creaked several times his mother said wearily "We may as well go for dinner."

The nearest restaurant was just two doors away from the hotel. It was an osteria, which sounded too much like a word for panic. Two mirrors the length of the side walls multiplied the room full of small tables. A waiter set about befriending Charlie, calling him signor and pouring him a sip of lemonade to taste as Charlie's father sampled the wine. He told Charlie that his choice of spaghetti Bolognese was the best dish on the menu, so that the boy felt obliged to finish it, though it wasn't much like his mother's recipe. As his parents drank the liqueur that came with the bill she said "I'll be happy to come here every night."

"Seconded," Charlie's father said, though Charlie didn't think she had been inviting a vote.

The boy might have shared their enthusiasm except for the word for the restaurant. It was engraved on the frosted window, and the O was a transparent oval like a hole a face would have to squash itself through. From the table at the back of the restaurant the letter resembled a hollow full of the darkness outside, and Charlie had glimpsed more than one face in it during the meal. Perhaps they'd belonged to people with an eye to dining, though they hadn't come in. "And I'm sure you'll want to see your friend again, Charles," his mother said.

She hurried him back to the hotel and up to the room, where she said "Face and teeth." Once he'd washed the one and brushed the others she dealt him a kiss so terse it was barely perceptible, and his father squeezed his shoulder. As Charlie lay under the quilt with his eyes shut he heard his mother say "I'm quite tired. You go down to the bar if you want, of course."

"No need for that," his father said before the low voices moved to the bathroom, where Charlie heard him murmur "Don't keep making that face." He imagined putting a face together like a jigsaw, a fancy preferable to the dreams he felt threatened by having. Eventually his parents finished muttering and went to bed. They weren't with him as he tried to find his way home through the town, where all the signs were as incomprehensible as the answers people gave him. In any case he didn't like speaking to anyone he met, however expensively dressed they were; they looked too thin inside their elegant costumes, and he couldn't make much of their faces. Perhaps there were none to be seen – not yet, at any rate. When they began to squirm up from the holes in the collars he stuffed the quilt into his mouth to mute his cries. Having to explain to his parents would be even worse than the dream.

At breakfast the English couple came over. "Bobby has something to say to you," Bobbie said.

"I'm sorry if I caused any upset down below."

"Don't be saying things like that at breakfast. In the catacombs, he means," Bobbie said as though apologising for a child. "Did he go too far, son?"

"He was joking. You said."

"So long as you don't forget," Bobbie said and turned to Charlie's mother. "We've been putting you down for a teacher."

"We both are," his father said.

At least all this helped distract them from how little the boy ate. After breakfast the family walked down to the harbour, to find the sea had grown so boisterous that the ferries had been cancelled. Now that Charlie saw all the windows in the boats he was happy to stay on land, even though he hadn't noticed any faces at them. "There's always Pompeii," his father said.

Opposite the main railway terminal was a kind of market, men hoping to sell shabby items that cluttered the pavement. One peddler had a dog, presumably not for sale. Its bony piebald face poked out of a discoloured plastic cone around its neck, and it bared uneven yellow teeth in a silent snarl. On the train Charlie tried to forget it and anything it brought to mind. The clocks on the stations were some help, since every one showed a different incorrect time. "They've stopped time," his father said as Charlie imagined he might have told the delinquents he taught creative writing in the unit at the school. Perhaps because modern history was her job, his mother didn't seem to think much of the idea. Charlie wasn't sure how to feel about the notion, but then this was true of much in his life.

Beyond the gates to Pompeii, where a woman's face nodded forward in the ticket booth, was an entire ruined town. Sightseers clustered like flies around the nearest buildings, where the open fronts were covered with wire mesh as if to cage the occupants – figures that Charlie wished he could mistake for statues lying on shelves. "Not more mummies," his mother protested.

"They aren't, Charlie. They're just casts."

Weren't those the husks worms left behind where they crawled out of the earth? "What does that mean?" Charlie had to ask.

"They're plaster." This seemed reassuring until his father added "They're the shape of whoever was there when the volcano caught them. All that was left were hollows where they'd been, and that's what the plaster was put in."

Too many if not all of the contorted figures looked about to writhe and creep towards their audience, and the idea of dead shapes that had grown in holes didn't appeal to Charlie either. He followed his parents into the town, where the streets were the colour of bone – of the shapes in the cages. The face that poked out of an unglazed window belonged to a girl somebody was photographing. After that Charlie kept alert for cameras, which often brought faces out of holes in the walls. He was glad his parents had forgotten to bring their cameras because of disagreeing over what to pack.

Lunch was no excuse to leave, since they'd bought sandwiches and drinks on the way from the station. They picnicked in the amphitheatre, where Charlie's father attempted to entertain him with a speech about someone called Spartacus who'd lived in Vesuvius and set people free. The passing spectators seemed more amused than Charlie's mother did, and Charlie didn't know which of his parents to side with. "Sorry if that was too much like school," his father eventually said.

"Perhaps Charles thinks it hasn't anything to do with him."

"All history does, Charlie. It isn't just behind us, it's part of us."

Charlie didn't care for either of his father's notions, which stayed with him as he trudged through the crumbling skeleton of a town. His father wanted to show him and especially his mother frescoes and mosaics recommended by the Frugoguide, but the boy was distracted by more faces at windows than there were amateur photographers. He wished he'd thought sooner to unzip his jacket, since as soon as he did his mother said "I think that's the best of the day."

He hoped that didn't mean worse was to come. He felt as if the clocks on the stations were holding time back. He couldn't see the dog in the market opposite the terminal, but if it was about, what else might he have overlooked? Despite the gathering dusk, his father made a detour on the way to the hotel.

The inside of this church was high and pallid, with pillars like polished bones. As the twilight blurred the figures outlined in the windows, their blotchy faces seemed poised to nod forward. Did he glimpse a face beyond the door of a confessional? The box made him think of an upright coffin in one of the kinds of film he wasn't allowed to watch. When he peered towards it the face was snatched into the gloom, and he heard a bony rattle. "Have you had enough for one day, Charlie?" his father said.

In a number of ways the boy had, but he confined himself to admitting "I'm a bit tired."

In the hotel room he felt as if his parents were waiting to catch him not just being tired, and he turned his back so that they couldn't see his face. At the restaurant the waiter gave them the same table and asked if the signor wanted his favourite. Charlie thought it safest to say yes, along with please when his mother's frown began to gather. A different dish might have been even harder to finish while he was aware of the O on the window. He kept thinking a face was about to peer in at him, and far too often faces did, retreating into the dark before he could distinguish any features they might have. When he tried to ignore the gaping oval he began to fancy that one face too many was hidden in the repetitive reflections on both sides of him.

"Face and teeth," his mother said upstairs with a toothy grin as a demonstration if not a joke. As well as the mirror on the bathroom wall a round one stood on a shelf above the sink. It magnified Charlie's reflection, and when he lurched to turn it away he saw his face swell up like a balloon, baring its teeth. He couldn't help taking the sight to bed, where he was visited by faces that grew bloated, parts of them bulging out of proportion as the heads struggled to emerge from their lairs. Each time he woke he had to jam the quilt into his mouth.

He might have left his plate at breakfast empty if his parents wouldn't have wanted to know why. When he returned to the table four people were watching him. "Were you disappointed you couldn't go on your boat?" Bobbie said.

He wasn't sure how much of a lie to tell. "A bit," he said.

"It's your last day, Charles." Perhaps his mother didn't mean this to sound ominous, because she added "Would you rather not spend five hours on a ferry? Tell the truth."

"Don't mind."

It was rather that he couldn't think what he would prefer. When his mother raised her hands like a weary victim of a hold-up his father said "Would you like a surprise for your last day, Charlie?"

The boy wished they wouldn't keep using the phrase. "If you like," he couldn't avoid saying.

"Aren't I allowed to know either, Edward?"

"We don't want to give it away, do we, Maur?" Charlie's father covered the side of his face while he mouthed at her, and Charlie hoped she'd winced only at his dropping half of her name. "That'll be a thrill for him," Bobbie said.

Surely the surprise wasn't more of Pompeii, though the family boarded that train. The clocks on the stations made Charlie feel as if time had abandoned him. His father stood up when the train reached Herculaneum. Weren't there supposed to be mummies there too? It was only when his father bought bus tickets from a bar outside the station that Charlie realised his treat was Vesuvius.

As the bus climbed out of the town he saw a fair beside the road and felt guilty for wanting to be there instead. The nearer the volcano came, the less of an adventure it seemed likely to be. It loomed above the road like a storm rendered solid while his father read out from the guidebook that the Romans used to believe volcanoes were entrances to Hell. Why would he take Charlie anywhere like that? Did the boy deserve it somehow?

Beyond a ticket booth a man was handing out sticks at the foot of the route to the crater. Much of the track consisted of loose flat stones, which made footsteps sound bony and thin, especially all those at Charlie's back. The path kept promising and failing to grow less steep, and whenever he tried to take more of a breath the wind assailed him with the stench of the volcano. It smelled as if the earth were farting, and if he'd been with other boys he might have been able to laugh.

Near the summit the path led between souvenir stalls. Among the trinkets Charlie noticed skulls, which gave him the unwelcome notion that someone might have brought the heads up from the catacomb to sell. The crater wasn't reassuring – a vast hollow in which fumes crept out of the black earth, he couldn't see exactly where, to crawl about as though groping for their own shapes. Charlie didn't like to wonder what kind of creature Spartacus had been to live here, never mind what he'd set free.

He did his utmost to look pleased with the treat for his father's sake and to give his parents one less reason to disagree. At last his father asked if he'd seen enough. As they passed between the stalls again a cloud like an emanation of the crater massed overhead. Charlie felt walled in by skulls, which were no less ominous for being plainly manufactured. When a wind followed him down from the summit he could have thought more than the stench of rot was after him. Some of the people toiling uphill had tugged hoods around their faces against the wind, which yanked at the material so that their features thrust up at Charlie. More than one of them bared their teeth, surely only at the wind.

The bus had almost reached the station when Charlie's father turned to him. "I know something else you'll like."

He meant the fair. It had a roundabout Charlie went on twice, and a dog with a ruff around its neck, prancing on two legs while its front legs clawed at the air. There was a target gallery where neither Charlie nor his parents could shoot quite straight enough, and a stall where you flung wooden balls to knock grinning faces backwards, leaving dark holes. He didn't want to try that, and he hurried past to an attraction screened by trees. At once he wished he hadn't seen it, but his parents already had.

Two life-size figures were painted on a board taller than his father. No doubt they were meant to be comical. The man sported a clownish costume so baggy it made him look puffed up by gas, while his partner wore a spangled dress that bared her bony hirsute legs. They had no faces, only holes for them, filled just now by the dark swollen sky. Charlie was about to thank his parents for the treat and flee towards the road when a man bustled over, gesticulating with a camera. "Go on, Charles," his mother said. "Put your head through, then at least we'll have one photograph."

The surge of dread was worse for being undefinable. The prospect of causing an argument between his parents dismayed him as well. "You and dad first," he said in desperation.

As soon as they stepped behind the board he felt he'd risked them to save himself. They seemed unconcerned when they put their faces through; they even produced grins, though his mother's resembled her habitual patient expression, while his father's looked hopeful. The boy was able to respond, having thought of an excuse not to go near. "I won't reach."

"Of course you will," his mother said, letting her grin subside now that the camera had whirred twice. "Lift him up, Edward."

She pulled her face out of the hole to watch until he had to venture behind the board, to see only his parents and its unadorned back. His father took Charlie's waist in both hands and raised him like an offering to the hole in front of them. "Gosh, there isn't much of you," he murmured. "We'll have to feed you up."

Charlie saw his mother give them both a resentful look. He kept his head back until the photographer motioned vigorously for him to bring it forward. As the edges of the skull-sized orifice loomed around his face he saw the blurred misshapen body he'd acquired. The camera whirred and whirred again, and he thought the ordeal was over until his mother said "I'll take him, Edward. You deserve a turn."

He couldn't let her see him hesitate to go to her. "You aren't so skinny," she said as she hoisted him with her arms under his armpits, so that he wondered if she'd just wanted an excuse to weigh him. When his head came level with the hole she said "Don't do what you did with your face."

Had she noticed his reluctance? He jerked his head forward and did his best to grin. As he realised that his body had become the scrawny thing in a dress, the camera went off. He struggled to hold his face still while the shutter sounded once more, and then he made himself heavy so that his mother put him down. The photographer beckoned them all to a caravan, where he indicated a printer and moved his hands apart to specify the size of photograph. The machine quivered and rattled and eventually disgorged six large prints. Only the pictures of Charlie's parents were clear. In the rest, presumably because nervousness had made him move without realising, the boy's face was an indistinct bulge with a bony slit for a mouth.

"I think that's quite enough expense," his mother said when the photographer flourished the camera. His father paid and was handed the pictures in an envelope. The way out of the fair led past the painted board, and Charlie almost managed not to look, but couldn't resist glancing over his shoulder. Although nobody had been behind or even near the board, two swollen blotchy faces were dangling through the holes. They looked as if the process of emerging had come close to pulling them apart, given how much of them drooped over the edge of the holes. In the instant before he succeeded in wrenching his gaze away, Charlie saw that the effort had bared not just their teeth.

He clutched both his parents by the hands, apparently to their surprise, and dragged them towards the road. On the train he sat next to his father, away from the window, and couldn't tell where it was safe to look. The walk to the hotel felt like an omen of worse – the pavement market where the dog with its head in a hole might be lurking, the church with the box for faces to peer from, the restaurant where a head ducked towards the O of the engraved sign to grin out at him. He just managed to suppress his cry, having recognised the waiter who'd befriended him.

As his father unlocked the room Bobbie looked out of the one across the corridor. "Having a good last day?"

"I'd say so," Charlie's father said.

"We've an early start tomorrow. If you two want some time to yourselves after dinner we'll be in our room."

"You can ring us if there's any problem, son," Bobby said.

"You don't mind, do you, Charlie?" said his father.

Admitting his fears out loud seemed likely to make them more real. Perhaps only his silence about them was keeping them away. Besides, he felt responsible for the tension between his parents, especially since they couldn't discuss it in front of him. "I'll be all right," he prayed aloud.

"He'll behave himself, don't worry." He gathered Bobbie meant her husband. To Charlie's parents she said "We'll keep an eye."

He was unwillingly reminded that the faces in the holes hadn't been too good at keeping theirs. Once he was in the room he knew he wouldn't be able to lie still; trying would only make him shiver. "Can I read?" he pleaded.

"I said he ought to have brought some of his books, Edward."

"Can't I read the one about here?"

"I certainly don't see why not," his father said not even mainly to him, and passed him the guidebook.

Charlie was looking for reassurance, but there wasn't much. Spartacus had been a rebel slave who'd set up camp on Vesuvius six years before it erupted. Lot's wife in the Bible had probably been turned into a kind of mummy by a volcano. Charlie could have lived without learning this, never mind that some of the headless remains in the cata-comb had been painted on the walls where the bodies used to be. Even if this explained the uneven outlines he'd mistaken for stains, it made the figures far too reminiscent of the ones at the fair, and what had happened to the bodies? The guidebook left that out as if it would do people no good to know. He was gazing at the page rather than read on when his father said "Too much for you, Charlie? Time for a feed."

In the restaurant the task of grinning at the waiter made the boy's face feel as constricted as it had by the board at the fair. He managed to avoid looking whenever anything loomed at the oval in the window. He took all the time he could over the meal the waiter assumed was his favourite, and succeeded in eating some of it as long as he forgot how the mirrors could be hiding an intruder. Eventually his mother said "Time to say goodbye, Charles."

The other couple must have heard them come upstairs, because Bobby called "Ready" as if he were playing hide and seek. Charlie hurried to the bathroom, hoping to outdistance his mother's night-time phrase, but she called through the door "Face and teeth." At the sink he shut his eyes so as not to see his bulbous face in the magnifying mirror. His parents delivered their signs of affection and waited for him to climb into bed. "We won't be any longer than we need to be," his mother said.

As soon as he couldn't hear their footsteps Charlie lurched out of bed to switch on the nearest light and then the rest of them. He tried watching television with the sound turned low, but he couldn't find any programmes in English, which made him feel as if the people on the screen were saying things it was vital for him to understand. They reminded him of his parents and the secrets he suspected were about him. He didn't want to read the guidebook in case it contained more information he wouldn't want to be alone with, and the sight of the photographs from the fair would be worse. He read every word in the folder about the hotel and tried to avoid looking at the spyhole in the door; every glance at it felt too much like inviting a response. He'd lost count of how often he'd read through the folder by the time he heard a fumbling at the door.

Was it one of his parents? Whenever they drank a lot they seemed to have trouble climbing the stairs at home – but the noise was too shapeless, almost not there and yet more present than he liked. With more reluctance than he'd ever previously experienced Charlie tiptoed to the door and stretched up to peer through the spyhole. When he glimpsed a shape so ill-defined it looked incomplete, vanishing from sight like a worm withdrawing into the earth, he managed to stay at the door long enough to jam the end of the chain into the socket. Once he'd shot the bolt as well he retreated to his bed and dragged the quilt over the whole of himself.

He was in a nervous fitful doze when he heard the fumbling again. He pressed the quilt against his ears so hard that he didn't hear the voices and the rapping on the door until they must have gone on for some minutes. He floundered off the bed and ran to let his parents in. Bobbie and her husband were watching from across the corridor. "Who on earth do you think you are, Charles?" his mother demanded. "This is our room."

He thought of an answer he hoped would placate her. "I didn't want any robbers to get in."

She only shook her head as if she had an insect in her hair and gestured him into the room, not even glancing at the other couple as his father murmured to them. From his bed Charlie heard his parents muttering at length in the bathroom. If they'd resolved their differences while they were without him, he'd spoiled that now. He heard his father declare "I'm not saying what I think has made him like this."

Eventually his parents went to bed. Their silence felt as ominous as the cloud above Vesuvius, and weighed on the dark. Charlie listened for signs that they'd fallen asleep, which might relieve at least some of the foreboding even if it left him by himself, but he didn't know whether they'd drifted off by the time he did. He dreamed they were at the door again, although when he managed to unchain it and open all the bolts and locks, the faces that poked at him out of his parents' heads weren't theirs. He clutched at the pillow to blot out his screams as his jolt awake almost flung him off the bed. The quilt dragged the pillowcase back so that the pillow bulged into his face. The pillow was lumpier than he remembered, and the irregular padding that covered the lumps was unhelpfully thin. Feathers must be spilling out of the pillow to make it feel as though fragments were flaking off. Charlie was pulling his head back, disliking the dry sour taste, when his thumbs dug into the contents of the linen sack – into something hinged, where an object stirred like a worm. In the faint light from the corridor he saw that his bed-mate had widened its withered eyes and bared its mottled teeth.

His shrieks brought Bobby to pound on the door while Bobbie blinked across the corridor. "Just a nightmare," Charlie's father said, perhaps with desperate optimism. Charlie's mother rubbed the boy's shoulders with more vigour than affection, not looking at his face. There was nothing in his bed or under it, which only made him wonder where the extra guest had gone. His mother shook the pillow when it was clear that she thought it was time he lay down. He almost hoped some unexpected contents would appear for his parents to see.

Even when he held the end of the pillowcase shut with both hands under the quilt he was afraid something would wriggle forth if he slept. Whenever he jerked awake from a few seconds' forgetful doze he clutched the pillowcase harder. At last it was time for breakfast, where he felt as if Bobby and Bobbie had left early because of him. He took as little from the buffet as he thought he could get away with taking while everyone in the room seemed to be aware of him, but he couldn't even eat that much. "I expect you're eager to be home," his father said, not really as if he believed it himself.

The day was so sunlit Charlie might have thought it was celebrating his departure. The light was pretending there was nowhere anything he dreaded could hide. In the taxi to the airport a face spied on him through the mirror. Knowing that it was the driver didn't comfort him, any more than the way the women at the check-in desk and the boarding gate scrutinised him. Very eventually he and his parents were allowed to shuffle onto the plane, where he stared at every-body seated further down the cabin until his mother said "Sit down, Charles. That isn't how you've been taught to behave."

He watched people filing along the aisle to sit behind him and in front of him. The procession was slow enough for a funeral, and made him feel breathlessly trapped. The face that had followed him out of the catacombs could hide anywhere – wherever his parents wouldn't believe it was. He craned around to peer between the seats at his mother, hoping she'd forgiven him for causing last night's scene, but she met him with a frown. "Turn round, Charles, please. You've shown us up enough."

"Look out of the window," his father urged, and Charlie couldn't let them sense his fear. As he ducked towards the cramped pane a blotch of a face swelled up to meet him – his own. At once he understood everything. His mother kept telling the truth about him, about the face and teeth, and his father didn't want to say what had made him how he was. The past was indeed part of him. The ground began to move before his eyes as the plane headed for the runway, and when he sat back the blurred face retreated into hiding – into him. He closed his eyes in the hope his father wouldn't make him look again, but it didn't help him forget. He couldn't leave behind the horror his parents were bringing home.

JOEL LANE

By Night He Could Not See

JOEL LANE'S FINAL collection of short fiction, *Where Furnaces Burn* from PS Publishing – a book of supernatural crime stories set in the West Midlands – won the World Fantasy Award in October 2013. Less than a month later, the author died in his sleep. He was just fifty years old.

His stories appeared in numerous magazines and anthologies including *Black Static*, *Weird Tales*, *Cemetery Dance*, *Crimewave*, *Gutshot*, *Psycho-Mania!*, *Evermore*, *Gathering the Bones*, *The Mammoth Book of Best British Crime* and no fewer than five previous volumes of *The Mammoth Book of Best New Horror*. His other publications include the short-story collections *The Earth Wire*, *The Lost District*, *The Terrible Changes* and *Do Not Pass Go*, along with the acclaimed novella, *The Witnesses Are Gone*.

Joel Lane was one of a new generation of British horror writers that included Nicholas Royle, Michael Marshall Smith, Mark Morris and Conrad Williams, who began their careers in Margaret Thatcher's 1980s and came to dominate the field with stories that combined traditional horror themes with the social, sexual and political upheavals of the time. Perhaps more than any of his contemporaries, Joel's fiction continued to rally against the system and prick our conscience beneath a deceptive veneer of genre fiction.

It is with great pride, tinged with obvious sadness, that I am able to present here what will probably be his final contribution to this series . . .

THE FIRST JASON knew about it was a story in the *Express & Star*. A forty-six-year-old woman had been found dead on a train between Walsall and Aldridge. Cause of death unknown. The only sign of violence was the paint on her face and hands, which might have been daubed on before or after her death. The police wondered if it was linked to cult activity. They gave her name: Gail Warner. There was no photo. At the end of the brief report, the journalist noted that in the last year, two other dead people in the UK had been found smeared with paint in the same way.

It wasn't such an unusual name. He wasn't even sure the age was right, though it was close. If it was the same person, did Mark know about it? They probably hadn't stayed in touch – teenage lovers never did. Jason might have stood a chance with Gail if she hadn't been wrapped around Mark like a pale ribbon. A few times they'd turned up late for a meeting of the Yardbirds, looking flushed and gratified. Jason had bitten through his lip thinking about it, still had the scar. But then Clare had come along and it had ceased to matter.

The gang's name came from Yardley, where they'd all lived. It seemed very distant now, like a film he'd seen in his teens. The Swan Centre, their main stamping ground, had recently been knocked down. The knot of reeking subways in front of it had been replaced by a concrete walkway over the Coventry Road that trembled from all the cars passing through. Yardley felt more like an airport than a district now. You couldn't stand still without getting vertigo.

Jason felt restless. Being reminded of the past wasn't good for him. But it was too cold to go out for a walk, and he had work tomorrow so the pub wasn't a good idea. He walked around the house, mentally listing the repair tasks that needed his attention, knowing they wouldn't happen any time soon. What you can't sort out, you have to walk away from. But why had he stayed here? The posters he'd put up to cover the damp in the hallway were looking bruised.

The gang hadn't been that bad. Clapton's Yardbirds were probably guilty of worse crimes. At least on record. Most of it was running: handling stuff for the big boys, passing on messages, occasionally breathing down some unwashed neck or helping some no-mark to have a small accident. Nothing to give Richard Allen sleepless nights. Like the Krays, they'd only hurt their own. The hurting had got out of hand. It always did.

Four cigarettes later, he phoned his old mate Darren in Walsall. They'd worked together in a security firm back in the nineties, driving cash and prisoners across the region. Then Darren had joined the police force. He knew about the Yardbirds – at least, he'd heard the radio edit – but he wasn't the type to moralize. It was all just work to him.

Darren took the call on his mobile. They swapped greetings. As usual, Jason had no recent news. Darren had got divorced, and something bad had happened in Aldridge that he couldn't talk about. Then Jason asked him if he'd heard about the dead woman on the train. "I think I used to know her. Was she blonde?"

"Not when our pathologist saw her. Someone had smeared green paint on her hair and forehead. There was more paint on her hands, but it was different – a kind of blue, like she was cold. Pastel colours. Skin paint, like they use on stage, not industrial paint. What kind of nutter puts make-up on a dead wench?"

"The paper said it might be a weird cult of some kind. Apparently there were two more deaths like that last year."

"Not around here, there weren't. But it could be a cult. Some Internet thing maybe. Too few and far between to be connected any other way."

"This dead woman. What did she look like?"

"Skinny and pale. Her hair was grey. Might have been blonde once."

"Thanks. It's not the girl I knew." He wondered if Darren could tell he was lying. "I'll see you around, mate. Take care."

"Stay out of trouble, you." Jason snapped his hinged phone together. The living-room door was closed, but the house felt colder than before. The faint ringing in his head might be a distant siren, an echo of static on the phone, or just a headache coming on.

After several failed attempts, his virus-ridden computer let him access the web. He searched for the combination of "dead", "head and hands" and "paint". Most of the links were to academic websites on religious art, but one led him to a story in the *South Wales Evening Post*. A body washed up in Swansea Bay last autumn had been identified as that of Mark Page, a businessman in his forties who'd lived in the city for nine years after leaving Birmingham. Police were unable to explain the traces of paint on his head and hands. They suggested it had to do with cult activity or gang warfare. Either way, drugs were behind it.

Jason switched off his computer and sat in the dark for a few minutes. The phone rang, jarring his skull. He stumbled downstairs and picked up the receiver without speaking. It was Darren. "Just spoke to a colleague, Theresa, who knows about one of the other cases. The body of a middle-aged man was found on an industrial estate in Manchester, half-eaten by rats, with green paint in his hair and blue paint on what was left of his hands. About nine months ago. They never did identify him. Don't suppose you've got any idea who it was?"

"How would I know?" *Tony Matthews.*

"Course not. Silly of me."

Jason flipped his middle finger violently at the damp-stained wall. "Well, see you around."

His head was aching so badly he thought he was going to throw up. A few minutes' kneeling over the toilet bowl, the chemical odour of the blue disinfectant scouring his nostrils, produced no offering but a trickle of colourless fluid from his mouth. *Mark, Gail, Tony and me.* But something was missing. He'd locked away the memories and they'd rotted in the dark. He needed a key.

No, he needed a drink. There was nothing in the house. Jason locked his front door with trembling fingers, stared up and down the narrow road. He didn't know what for – but if it knew him then surely he would know it.

The pub on the corner was packed, but he managed to struggle to the bar just before eleven. Some pubs had late opening now, but not this one. He ordered a double Scotch and a double vodka, and took them carefully away from the bar before pouring one into the other and gulping the mixture like wine. A cold fire spread through his gut, lighting him inside but making the pub seem darker. An old drunk stumbled into him and backed away, raising his hands in apology. Jason stared at the ruined face, the swollen red nose.

Too few and far between to be connected any other way.

Back at the house, he unlocked the door to the boxroom. Dust was smeared over the cases and boxes he'd shut away here. The grey carpet was littered with mouse turds like tiny black commas, punctuating a story he didn't want to read. Any suitcase he opened might release blind memories on tattered wings, flying around his head. Just as the fear reached a point where he'd have to curl up and hide his face, the light glinted on the rusty lock of a black briefcase.

He'd long since lost the key, but his claw hammer ripped away the leather flap easily. With the hammer still in one hand, he reached inside and took out the small gun and the clip of bullets. Never used – at least, not on something alive. He lifted it to his mouth, kissed the side of the barrel.

That night, he slept with the loaded gun on the bedside table. He'd find a quiet place to test it. As sleep wove its cobwebs against his face, pulling him down into a stillness where no memory could find him, Jason whispered an old verse silently to himself. He had no idea what it meant. But then, it had never been anything but nonsense:

Far and few, far and few
Are the lands where the Jumblies live
Their heads are green and their hands are blue
And they went to sea in a sieve

Near midnight, the canal was deserted. The moonlight glinted from broken factory windows and outlined shapeless masses of weed and dead leaves on the water surface. There was no colour anywhere. Jason made his way cautiously down the slope from the trees opposite the Yardley cemetery, then followed the barely visible towpath towards Digbeth and the city centre. Across the dull water, the backs of derelict factories were coated with mould. The night air was so cold you had to breathe it in before it released the smell of decay.

The last time he'd been down here, there'd been narrow-boats on the water and lights in the factory windows. A generation ago – but he'd made no children to grow up, and neither had Clare. They'd walked this way together, as far as the old church at Bordesley Green. Where the fencing gave way to a cluster of workshops and brickyards, easy to break into from the canal side.

Ahead of him, the city lights hung like a dripping constellation. He thought he could see a faint red light among them, making its way towards him. The gun was a hard weight against his ribs. It had to be Danny Vail – but why had he waited so long? Like water in a barrel, accumulating worms and decay before it finally overflowed. He'd always been mad. A little pale-faced Jewish boy with a hook-nose they'd teased him about, called him "Dong" after the Edward Lear poem they'd read in the first year. The Dong with the luminous nose. But Clare had liked him, and had relieved him of his virginity before deciding she needed something harder. He'd broken up with her when she joined the Yardbirds.

Jason had made a play for her, of course, and she'd gone as far as slow kissing with him in the cinema on the Coventry Road. But that was it. Tony hadn't got much further, and

Mark wouldn't have dared try anything with Gail around. But Jason had got more and more obsessed with Clare. She was the boldest of the gang: the one who stole for the challenge of it, ran the most dangerous errands, got out of trouble with an innocent smile and a clean pair of heels.

He'd come to believe that the thrill of petty crime was the only kind of sex Clare was interested in. But he'd still taken every opportunity to watch her at a distance, eavesdrop on her conversations. And one night he'd seen her emerging from a garage with Terry Joiner – who was a grown-up criminal, one of a serious local gang called the Finish. When they'd gone, Jason had slipped into the unlit garage and seen the evidence. Picked up the used condom and sniffed it, jealousy pulsing through his brain like sheet lightning.

A few days later, the Yardbirds' main capital – a stash of banknotes and speed wraps worth nearly five hundred pounds – went missing. Only they knew where it had been hidden, in a builder's yard off the Grand Union Canal. Jason went to Mark and Gail, told them he'd overheard Clare talking about it with Terry. "She said she wants to join the Finish. That was the price of her getting in. That and . . . whatever else she was giving him. I saw them come out of a garage."

The five of them walked out from the Swan Centre, on a winter night like this one. Maybe a little colder. There was ice on the black water. Clare wasn't keen to go, said she was feeling sick. Had she guessed what was coming? Jason avoided looking at her, when usually he couldn't look at anything else. They reached the unlit yard, crawled through the gap in the chain-link fence. Mark took a torch out of his shoulder bag, as usual. Then he brought out a coil of rope and a kitchen knife. Clare just stared at him.

She wouldn't talk. Denied there was anything between her and Terry. Said the Yardbirds was the only gang she'd ever wanted to belong to. Stared hard at everyone else, one by one, when Gail started talking about the missing speed and cash. "Tie her up," Gail said. And then the beating started. Jason felt sick and excited at the same time. It went too far, they were too young to stay in control. The knife was used. Then Clare broke and confessed to everything. How she was already in the Finish. How she'd handed Terry the stolen stuff. How she'd give the Yardbirds anything they wanted, any way they wanted, if they'd let her go.

And all the exhilaration of victory drained from them, leaving only chill and darkness, when Gail said "We can't."

It was Tony who knocked her out, using one of the bricks that littered the yard. They half-filled a canvas bag with bricks and tried to put her in, but she wouldn't fit. So they tied the bag around her waist and lowered her into the canal. There was no moon that night, and Jason hadn't seen her face in the water. That hadn't stopped him seeing it since.

A few weeks later, most of the body came to the surface. The police talked to the Yardbirds – he suspected Danny was responsible for that – but there was no evidence. How could sixteen-year-olds possibly be involved in that? More suspicion fell on the Finish, who had to clear out of the region for good. The secret broke up the Yardbirds, of course, and Jason lost touch with the others before he'd even finished school. Thirty years of nothing. And now this.

Where the chain-link fence had been, a rusty sheet of corrugated iron was lying flat on the gravel. Beyond it, he could make out a few bags of rubbish and a loose coil of razor wire. A grey rat crept out of the shadows towards Jason, then stopped. Jason pulled out the gun and fired, missing the rat. The sound echoed from the blank factory walls.

He'd bought the gun with the money from his first job, cleaning old car parts in a garage so they could be sold as scrap. It had taken him a long time to raise the money. He'd never used the cash, or sold the powder, that he'd taken from the builder's yard and hidden in the misshapen stone bridge further along the canal. For all he knew, that package was still there. That was the first real lesson he'd learned: you can never pay back.

*   *   *

The house was in Sparkbrook, near the ruins of the Angel pub. Nearly ten years since the tornado had blown a tree into its roof, but no sign of any repair work. Even after midnight, some of the Asian groceries on the Stratford Road were open for business. Jason had parked half-a-mile away to avoid being noticed. He approached the house warily, but there was no light in the windows. The front yard was heavily overgrown with brambles and shrubs. The door needed a new coat of paint. All the curtains were open.

Looking for Danny Vail on the Internet had been a long shot – and finding his name in the *Birmingham Mail* online had been a shock. He was the contact for an educational theatre company that went to schools in the Midlands. It had to be the same guy – Jason remembered he'd been keen on drama. So he hadn't been able to leave either. They'd lived within five miles of each other all this time, but Jason didn't remember seeing him since they'd left school. If he could find Danny, then Danny could find him. It was time to act.

His breaking and entering skills were rusty, but he was well prepared. Down the side alley and through the fence, smashing a few rain-blackened planks. Over the chaotic back garden to a window that hadn't been cleaned in years. Glue sprayed on the window, a bin bag stuck over the glass. A few gentle taps with a rock hammer and the glass came away like burnt skin. No sound anywhere in the house. The smell of damp and bleach. He drew the gun and walked slowly up the unlit stairs.

In the bedroom, a crumpled single bed with no occupant. There were two flattened cans on a low table. Jason twisted the catch on one. Some kind of paint, was it face-paint? There was more in the other can: one blue, the other green. Narrow fingers had left grooves in the paint.

The next room was a kind of study, with bookshelves and an old wooden desk that even had an inkwell. The walls were covered with sheets of paper. Jason moved his torch-beam over a few of them. They were photocopies of pages from old books – Edward Lear, Lewis Carroll, others he didn't recognize. Nonsense poems with grotesque Victorian illustrations. The books on the shelves were all children's books, fifty or more years old. They smelt faintly of decay.

One book was lying on the desk, face down. An antique copy of Lear's collected poems. Jason sat down and put the loaded gun by his right hand. Then he opened the book. A thin scrap of paper fell out. A cigarette paper, with something written on it in tiny old-fashioned script. He had to hold it against the back cover of the book to make out the words:

> *There was a young lady named Clare*
> *Who died with green weed in her hair*
> *And her hands that were still*
> *Turned blue from the chill*
> *Alas, there was no one to care*

Was that someone moving downstairs, or just the sounds of an old house settling in the night? Jason switched off his torch. There was no light on the staircase. He was still holding the old book. A faint scratching sound – probably mice. Then the door swung open silently. He glimpsed a tiny skull-like face with a red light attached to it. With a dreamlike slowness, he lifted the gun. It was only as his finger curled on the trigger that he realized the barrel was pointing at his own head.

The shot echoed in the still house. Danny thought the whole district had blown up. The intruder's face tore off like a mask, exposing the ruin behind it. The desk was coated with blood. Danny stood for a while, shaking. He'd got to phone the police. But there was something he needed to understand first. Why had the burglar been sitting in the dark? He'd known there was someone here from the shattered living-room window. But the power cut had stopped him putting the light on. Instead, he'd found the face-torch that he wore for cycling after dark.

He didn't know why the intruder had shot himself. Nor could he explain the green paint in the dead man's hair or the blue paint on his hands. It looked rather like the make-up he'd been using for the new children's show. Could this be one of his colleagues? He couldn't recognize what was left of the face. And despite the horror of the situation, he was conscious of real anger. The madman had got blood all over his book. His special book – the one he'd read aloud from every night for thirty years, as if it were a book of prayers or spells.

REGGIE OLIVER

Come Into My Parlour

REGGIE OLIVER HAS been a professional playwright, actor and theatre director since 1975. Besides plays, his publications include the authorized biography of Stella Gibbons, *Out of the Woodshed*, published by Bloomsbury in 1998, and six collections of stories of supernatural terror, of which the fifth, *Mrs Midnight* (Tartarus, 2011) won the Children of the Night Award for Best Work of Supernatural Fiction in 2011 and was nominated for two other awards.

Tartarus Press has also reissued his first and second collections, *The Dreams of Cardinal Vittorini* and *The Complete Symphonies of Adolf Hitler*, in new editions with new illustrations by the author, as well as his sixth collection *Flowers of the Sea* (2013). The author's novels include *The Dracula Papers I – The Scholar's Tale* (Chômu, 2011), *Virtue in Danger* (Zagava Books, 2013) and *The Boke of the Divill* (Dark Renaissance, 2014). An omnibus edition of his stories entitled *Dramas from the Depths* is published by Centipede Press, as part of its "Masters of the Weird Tale" series. His stories have appeared in more than fifty anthologies, including five previous volumes of *The Mammoth Book of Best New Horror* series.

"Some of my first childhood memories are of books," Oliver recalls, "mostly old ones which had been passed down through my family for generations. There was one in particular which both fascinated and terrified me. It was a Victorian book of children's verse which contained Mary Howitt's poem, 'The Spider and the Fly'.

"But it was not so much the poem itself as one of its illustrations that gave me nightmares – so much so that my mother destroyed the offending page in the book. She later told me that both she and her father before her had, as children, been given the creeps by the same picture.

"The image stayed with me over the years and formed the nucleus of this story. After I had written the tale I found the illustration in question on the Internet. It was not quite the grotesque horror that my childhood imagination had made of it, but it was still distinctly troubling."

> "*Will you walk into my parlour?*" *said the Spider to*
>   *the Fly,*
> "'*Tis the prettiest little parlour that ever you did spy;*
> *The way into my parlour is up a winding stair,*
> *And I've a many curious things to shew when you are*
>   *there.*"

—"The Spider and the Fly"
by Mary Howitt (1799–1888)

SOMEHOW I ALWAYS knew that there was a problem with Aunt Harriet.

She was my father's only sister – step-sister, as it happens – and older than he was by eleven years. She was unmarried and her work was something to do with libraries; that much was clear, but the rest was rather a mystery. She lived in a small flat near Victoria Station in London, which we heard about but never saw, but she often used to come to stay with us – rather *too* often for my mother's taste. In fact, the only time I ever remember my parents "having words", as we used to say, was over Aunt Harriet yet again coming down for the weekend.

"Yes, I know, I know, dear," I heard my father say. "But I can't exactly refuse her. She is my sister."

"Exactly," said my mother. "She's only your sister. You *can* say no to her occasionally."

But apparently my father couldn't. Fortunately she did only stay for weekends, that is, apart from Christmas, but I'll come to that later.

At that time we lived in Kent and my father commuted into London by train every weekday morning. Where we lived was semi-rural; there were places to walk and wander – there were woods and fields nearby. I like to think that my younger sister and I had a rather wonderful childhood; if it were not for Aunt Harriet.

Am I exaggerating her importance? It is a long time ago now, but I rather think I'm not. I suspect that she loomed even larger then than she does in my memory.

She was a big, shapeless woman who always seemed to be wearing several layers of clothing whatever the weather. She dyed her hair a sort of reddish colour and rattled a little from the various bits of jewellery she had about her. (She was particularly fond of amber.) Her nose was beaky and she carried with her everywhere an enormous handbag, the contents of which remained unknown.

When she came she brought with her an atmosphere of unease and discontent. She never allowed herself to fit in with us. If we wanted to go for a walk, she would stay behind. If we decided to stay indoors, she would feel like going out. She rarely took part in any game or expedition we had planned, and when she did there was always a fault to find with the arrangements. On the other hand, almost invariably she wanted, often at the most inconvenient times, to "have a talk" as she put it, with my father. He never refused her demands and so they would go into his study, often for several hours, to have their talk.

I once asked my mother what it was all about.

"They're probably discussing the Trust," she said.

I never really understood this Trust. I once asked my father about it but he refused to reveal anything. Many years later, after my father's death, I searched among his papers for evidence of it and could find nothing. The little I knew came at second-hand from my mother. She said that some distant relation had left a sum of money jointly to my father and Aunt Harriet, and Aunt Harriet was always trying to get more income from it, or do something mysterious called "breaking the Trust" so that she could extract a lump sum for her personal use.

I don't think my aunt ever really cared about my sister and me as people, but she would ask us the kind of questions that grown-ups tend to ask – questions that are almost impossible to answer. "How are you getting on at school?" "Have you made any nice friends there?" I don't think she would have been interested in our answers even if they had been less boring and evasive than the ones we gave her.

Mealtimes were especially grim. In the first place Aunt Harriet was a vegetarian and my mother, out of courtesy I suppose, insisted that we were also vegetarian during her stays. That meant doing without a Sunday Roast which we resented. My mother was not a great cook at the best of times, but she was particularly uninspired in her meatless dishes. Then, during the meal, Aunt Harriet would either be silent in such a way as to discourage conversation from us, or indulge in long monologues about office politics in the library service. This always struck us – that is, my sister and me, and probably my parents too – as horribly boring. We gathered from her talk that work colleagues were always trying, as she said, "to put one over" on her, and she was always defeating them.

In spite of this, you may be surprised to know, I came to be fascinated by her. I suppose it was because she was, at the same time, such a big part of our lives, and yet so remote. Her life in London, apart from those dreary office politics, was a closed book. She never talked about going to theatres or concerts or exhibitions or watching sport. She didn't even really talk about books. She never mentioned any friends. It was this mystery about her that started all the trouble.

It began, I suppose, one Sunday in September when I was nine, and Aunt Harriet was then approaching sixty. We had just finished lunch and the meal had not pleased Aunt

Harriet. It had been, if I remember rightly, Cauliflower Cheese, not one of my mother's cooking triumphs admittedly, but perfectly edible. My aunt's complaint had been that my mother should have made an effort to supply something more original from the vegetarian repertoire.

She began, "I'm not complaining, but—" a disclaimer which, paradoxically, often prefaced her complaints "—I'm just saying. You might occasionally like to take a look in a vegetarian cookbook for your own benefit. Of course *I* don't mind; *I'm* just your sister-in-law, but if you were to have guests here, important guests – of course I know *I'm* not important – and *they* happened to be vegetarian—"

At this point my father, usually the most patient of men, exploded. He could put up with a lot of things but this was not to be borne, especially as it involved my mother whom he adored. Even so, it was a brief explosion, and fairly reasonably expressed.

"Oh, for heaven's sake, stop talking nonsense, Harriet!" He said, not in his usual quiet voice.

My aunt sniffed, rose from the table and announced that she had never been so insulted in her life and was going for a walk. She then quitted the dining room and a few seconds later we heard the door bang. We ate the rest of the meal in virtual silence.

After lunch my curiosity got the better of me. It was a damp dull sort of day, so the prospect of going out was not inviting even without the possibility of meeting Aunt Harriet, sullen faced, tramping about the countryside. I decided that this was my moment for exploring her room and seeing if I could find any clues to her bizarre behaviour.

There was one spare bedroom in the house for guests, and because few occupied it but she, it was known as "Harriet's Room". She stayed there most weekends in the year and, though the furnishings of the room were very impersonal, she had somehow made the place her own.

First of all, there was the smell. It wasn't an unpleasant smell in itself, but because it was from the perfume she wore it had dark associations. It was musky, spicy, not exactly unclean but somehow not fresh. The atmosphere was heavy with it because, with typical disregard for my parents' heating bills, she had left the bar of an electric fire on in her room.

The dressing table was crowded with an assortment of bottles of unguents and medicines. Aunt Harriet was, in her quiet way, a hypochondriac, always suffering from some kind of affliction from heart palpitations to boils.

On the dressing table were also a number of black lacquer boxes, some rather beautiful, either painted or decorated with inlaid mother-of-pearl. Tentatively, and knowing that now I was somehow crossing a line, I opened one box, then another, then another.

They all contained jewellery or trinkets, the stones semiprecious and mostly made out of her beloved amber. Many were in the shape of animals or strange beasts of mythical origin. One in particular intrigued me. It sat on a bed of cotton wool in a small box of its own. The box was black like the others with a scene painted in gold on the top in the Japanese style of cranes flying over a lake bordered by waving reeds. The thing inside this box was carved out of amber, a dark, translucent reddish brown, smooth and polished to perfection. It appeared to be an insect of some kind, perhaps a beetle or spider, with a bloated body and eight strange little stumpy legs of the kind you see on caterpillars. The workmanship was extremely fine and, as I now think, Japanese, like the box. Its head was round and dome-like, with two protruding eyes almost complete spheres emerging from the middle of the head. Into these amber eyes the carver had managed to insert two tiny black dots which gave them a kind of life and, somehow, malignity. He (or she?) had carved the mouth-parts to give an impression of sharp, predatory teeth – or whatever it is that insects have instead of teeth. It was beautifully made, and horrible. I shut the box quickly.

I turned my attention to the bedside table. It was piled high with books, mostly old and somewhat battered, but some finely bound. I noticed that many of the bindings had little square discolourations as if a label had been removed from their surfaces. I wondered if my aunt had brought them here to read because they were an odd selection. There was an early 19th-century treatise on metallurgy, a volume on alpine plants by a Victorian clergyman with some fine colour plates, a few modern novels in their original dust-jackets and several children's books. Besides these volumes, I noticed a small plain wooden box, this time not containing trinkets but a neat set of small brushes, a needle-sharp scalpel knife, two pairs of tweezers and small square glass bottles containing fluids such as ink eradicator. I was puzzling over this mysterious collection when I heard someone behind me.

"What are you doing in my room, little man?"

I think I jumped several feet into the air in my fright. I had been sitting on the bed facing away from the door and Aunt Harriet had crept in unnoticed. The next moment she had me by the ear.

"I asked you what you were doing. Well . . .?"

It was some moments before I was sufficiently in control to reply.

"Just looking."

"Looking? Looking for what?"

"I don't know."

"Do you make a habit of snooping around the rooms of your parents' guests?"

"No!"

"Oh, so you think it's all right to snoop around in *my* room. Is that it?"

"No! Let me go!" She had not released my ear.

"What do you think your father would say if I said I found you in my room trying to steal my things? Mmm?"

"I wasn't stealing anything! You won't tell him, will you?" I was not afraid of my father as such – he was not a fierce man – but I was afraid of disappointing him. At last Aunt Harriet began to relax her grip on my ear, but she had left it throbbing and painful, full of the blood of embarrassment.

"We shall have to see about that. I *may* not have to tell him," said Aunt Harriet in a softer, almost caressing voice which was, however, no more reassuring. "It all depends on whether you're going to be a helpful boy to me. Are you going to be a helpful boy, or a nasty, spiteful, sneaking boy?"

"Helpful," I said, instantly dreading the menial task she would almost certainly set me.

"So I should think. All I'm going to ask is something really quite simple—" Suddenly she looked alarmed and turned around. My six-year-old sister Louise had wandered in and was standing in the doorway, her wide blue eyes staring at us in amazement. She had pale golden curls in those days and looked the picture of innocence, but evidently not to my aunt.

"Run away, little munchkin," she said. "Can't you see I'm talking to your grown-up brother?" Louise had never been called a "munchkin" before. She probably didn't know what it meant – neither did I, for that matter – but it sounded cruel from my aunt's lips so she burst into tears. Aunt Harriet stared at her in astonishment. She obviously had no idea why she had provoked such a reaction. After Louise had run off, still wailing, to find my mother, my aunt said, "That child has been dreadfully spoilt."

I felt that it was my turn to leave so I started to shuffle towards the door. Aunt Harriet hauled me back by the ear again.

"Hold hard, young Lochinvar. Where do you think you're going? I haven't told you what I want you to do, yet, have I?"

"You can do it later, Aunt Harriet."

"Later won't do. Later will never do." Then she told me what she wanted. At some time during the week I was to go into my father's study and from the second drawer down on the left-hand side of my father's kneehole desk I was to extract a blue folder labelled FAMILY TRUST. I was then to place it under the mattress in my aunt's room so that when she came the following weekend she might study it at her leisure.

It was a simple task, but it terrified me. I didn't know which was worse – to defy my aunt or to betray the trust of my father. I was going back to school shortly so I decided to postpone any decision and hope that Aunt Harriet would have forgotten all about it by the time she came next. That, of course, was a vain hope.

When she came the following weekend I avoided her as much as I could until finally she caught me early on Sunday morning as I was passing her door on the way to the bathroom. She dragged me inside and closed the door. She was strong for her age and build.

"Where is it?" she hissed into my face. She wore a Chinese silk dressing gown covered in dragons over a red flannel nightdress.

"Where's what?"

"Don't you play games with me, little man. You know perfectly well what I wanted. Why didn't you get it for me?"

"I couldn't," I extemporized. "The drawer was locked."

"Little liar!" she said. "I've seen your father open that drawer a thousand times and never once has he used a key. Dear God, can't you do just one simple little thing for me?"

"Why can't you get it yourself?"

"Because I can't. Never you mind. Because I need you to prove to me that you're not a nasty sneaking little boy, but someone who is loyal and will do his aunt a small favour. I am very disappointed with you. As a matter of fact, I was planning a little treat for you if you had succeeded. I was going to invite you up to London like a proper grown-up guest, and I would have given you tea in the Victoria Hotel with toasted tea cakes covered in butter and taken you to see a pantomime, and the Victoria and Albert Museum, and shown you the beautiful and valuable things in my home. You'd have liked that. You like nosing into other people's property, don't you? But now you'll never have any of that because you won't do a simple thing for your poor old aunt." She paused for breath and studied me closely. She could see I was unimpressed.

"Do you know what is going to happen to you if you don't do as I say?" she said, putting her face so close to mine our noses almost touched.

"No," I said. Then, suddenly feeling that she was engaged in a game of bluff, I added, "And I don't care."

"Don't care, eh?" she said withdrawing her face and studying me intently. "Don't care was made to care. I want to see that file by Christmas, or else . . ."

"Or else what?"

Aunt Harriet once again put her huge old face very close to mine. I was almost overwhelmed by her musky perfume. In a loud croaking whisper, she said, "'I can show you fear in a handful of dust'. Do you know who said that?"

I shook my head.

"A very famous poet called Tom Eliot. I knew him once – rather well, actually. He was very much in love with me at one time. A great many famous men were in love with me in those days, you know."

I found this impossible to believe then, but years later when I was going through my late father's things I found a single photograph of Aunt Harriet as a young woman in the mid-1930s. It was a studio portrait and she was posed, rather artificially, elbow on knee, face cupped in her palm, staring at the camera. She wore a long double rope of pearls knotted in the middle as was the fashion and a loose rather "arty" dress. Her dark shiny hair was cut in a page-boy bob which framed a perfectly oval face, like one of Modigliani's women. Below the fringe of hair her big dark eyes had allure. You might well have described her as attractive; you might also have said that the hungry look in her eyes and the sulky, sensual mouth signalled danger.

"I can show you fear in a spider's web," she said. "Do you know who said that?"

Again I shook my head.

"I did. And I can too. So beware, my young friend. Beware!"

With that I was dismissed. I was inclined to regard her threats as empty, or rather that is what I wanted to believe. In the months running up to Christmas she came, much to our relief, less frequently at weekends, but when she did she always found an opportunity to get me on my own. Then she would ask one question: "Have you got it yet?" I would shake my head and that would be that, or so I thought. She seemed strangely untroubled by my refusal to co-operate. Then came Christmas.

She always spent several days with us over Christmas, arriving on Christmas Eve and occasionally lingering until New Year's Day. Her presence was not so annoying as it might have been because my parents were hospitable during the season. In the company of people other than family Aunt Harriet would occasionally make an effort to be pleasant, provided that she felt that the guests were not beneath her notice socially. It was the one time too when my mother would not make any concessions to my aunt's vegetarian diet, simply feeding her with the vegetables that dressed the turkey.

Aunt Harriet came that Christmas Eve, as usual with great fuss and circumstance. She did not drive, so my father had to fetch her from the station in the car. It was dark when she arrived at our house and a light snow was falling, the little specks of white dancing in the wind. I remember looking out of the window of our house as her vast black bulk squeezed itself out of our car and onto the drive. She seemed to regard the snow as a personal annoyance, and flapped her hand in front of her face to brush away the flakes, as if they were stinging insects. As she lumbered towards the front door my father was busy getting her suit-cases and parcels out of the boot.

I knew about these parcels from previous Christmases. They were all very grandly wrapped and decked out with tinsel and fancy ribbons, but they never contained anything anyone really wanted. To my father she gave cigars which he very rarely smoked; and to my mother, almost invari-ably, a poinsettia plant with its piercingly red and green foliage.

I once heard my mother say to my father: "Doesn't she know I hate poinsettias? Nasty gaudy plants. They look like cheap Christmas decorations. Ugh!"

"Why don't you tell her?" said my father smiling.

"Good grief, no! Can you imagine the scene she'd make?" And they both laughed.

Louise and I always got books, but they were hardly ever new ones, and never what we actually wanted. Some of them, I now think, were probably quite valuable, but even that was a cheat, as I'll explain later.

My mother, Louise and I were lined up in the hall, as usual, to greet her. When she got to me she murmured, "Have you got it?" I shook my head. She sort of smiled and pinched my cheek in a would-be friendly manner, but she pinched so hard that my face was red and sore for quite some time afterwards. I had a feeling that there was worse to come.

Christmas passed off much as usual. Aunt Harriet refused to come to church, saying that she worshipped God in her own way, whatever that meant, and that anyway the whole business of Christmas was just a debased and commercialized pagan ceremony. When the turkey was being carved she insisted on referring to it loudly as "the bird corpse". It was no better and no worse than usual. Then, after the dinner, came the present giving.

My father got his usual cigars and my mother her hated poinsettia. I forget what Louise received, but I certainly remember my present. It felt heavy inside its red and gold Christmas paper.

When I unwrapped it I found, not much to my surprise, that it was a book. Of its kind it was rather a sumptuous volume, bound in green artificial leather, heavily embossed with gold. It was in astonishingly good condition considering that the date on its title page was 1866. The pages were thick and creamy, their edges gilded. I noted that the book was illustrated throughout – *drawn*, as the title page announced, *by eminent artists and engraved by the brothers Dalziel*. All this might have attracted me, but for the title of the book itself: *A Child's Treasury of Instructive and Improving Verse*.

I did not like that at all. Now, I was nine at the time, but I already considered myself a young adult, not a child. Louise, at six, was still a child, not me. I read quite grown-up books like Sherlock Holmes, and *Treasure Island*, and *The Lord of the Rings*. Moreover, I did not want to be instructed and improved – I got quite enough of that at school, thank you. I felt the first sting of Aunt Harriet's revenge for my failure to do as she had told me. Then I looked at the flyleaf.

It was not quite as smooth as the other pages. It was slightly buckled and looked as if it had been treated with some kind of bleach. On it Aunt Harriet had written in purple ink: *To Robert. Happy Christmas from Aunt Harriet.* Then, in smaller writing a little further down the page she had written: *p256*.

When I thanked Aunt Harriet for her present with a rather obvious lack of enthusiasm, she merely smiled and tried to pinch my cheek again, but I avoided her. "It's a very precious book," she said, "I think you'll find it interesting."

"Oh, it's beautiful," said my mother, for once backing up my aunt. "Those wonderful Dalziel engravings. They were the best, weren't they? And such perfect condition! Where did you find it, Harriet?"

Aunt Harriet gave my mother a dark look, as if she suspected some kind of insinuation in her question. Then, seeing that my mother was, as always, being innocently straightforward, she smiled. "I have my methods," she said.

Later that night when I was in bed I began to ponder over Aunt Harriet's present and that cryptic little note, so I got the book and turned to page 256. It was a poem entitled "The Spider and the Fly" by someone called Mary Howitt.

*"Will you walk into my parlour?" said the Spider to
     the Fly,*
"'Tis the prettiest little parlour that ever you did spy;

The way into my parlour is up a winding stair,
And I've a many curious things to shew when you are
*   there."*
"Oh no, no," said the little Fly, "to ask me is in vain,
For who goes up your winding stair can ne'er come
*   down again."*

At the time I wasn't much into poetry and this was really not my thing at all, but the verse had an oddly compelling quality. I somehow had to read on. There was this ridiculous conversation going on between a spider and a fly – as if two insects could talk! – and the spider was enticing the fly into her den and the fly was, so far, refusing. It was so strange, this weird blend of insect and human life, like a dream, that I was held. I turned the page.

It was then that I got a shock. I was confronted with a black and white engraving. It showed a creature standing in front of a cleft in a rock with the winding stair within going up into the darkness. I say "a creature" because it was half-human, half-spider, and it appeared to me to be a "she", mainly because the head bore a quite shocking resemblance to Aunt Harriet. There was the same longish nose and wide shapeless mouth; above all the bulging eyes had the same predatory stare. The head was fixed, without a neck, onto a great bloated, bulbous body, again rather like Aunt Harriet's. From the base of this sprang two long, thin legs that sagged at the knee joints as if the great body was too heavy to be held upright. From the body – or thorax, I suppose – came four almost equally thin arms, two from each side. The muscles on the arms were as tight and wiry as whipcord, and what passed for hands at their extremities were more like crabs' pincers and looked as if they could inflict terrible pain.

Standing in front of this monstrous creature, its back to the viewer, was what I assumed was the fly, though it barely resembled one. It looked more like a very tall thin young Victorian dandy. Its wings were folded to form a swallow-tailed coat, one thin arm rested on a tasselled cane and a top hat was set at a jaunty angle on top of its small head. It looked a feeble, doomed creature.

The picture and the poem seemed to me all of a piece, at once surreal and yet frighteningly vivid, inhabiting a world of its own, full of savage, predatory monsters and enfeebled victims. I read on until the inevitable ending.

> *With buzzing wings he hung aloft, then near and*
> *   nearer drew,*
> *Thinking only of his brilliant eyes, and green and*
> *   purple hue –*
> *Thinking only of his crested head – poor foolish*
> *   thing! At last,*
> *Up jumped the cunning Spider, and fiercely held him*
> *   fast.*
> *She dragged him up her winding stair, into her dismal*
> *   den,*
> *Within her little parlour – but he ne'er came out again!*

There were some moralising lines after that, something about *to idle, silly flattering words, I pray you ne'er give heed*. But that was just a piece of nonsense put in to give the poem respectability. It was the image that remained, and the torturing fear of being seized and carried up a winding stair into the darkness.

I barely slept that night, and when I did it was worse than being awake. Waking or sleeping there was the sense that something was in one corner of my room. I saw it – if I saw it at all – only on the edge of my vision, and not when I looked at it directly: a bloated thing with a head but no neck, and with several arms or legs that waved at me in a slow way, like a creature at the bottom of the sea. This torment lasted until the frosty dawn when light began to filter through my thin window curtains. At last I managed some untroubled sleep until, hardly two hours later, I was summoned down to breakfast.

On Boxing Day afternoon my parents had a party for neighbours and their children. Aunt Harriet was less than enthusiastic about the affair and went out for a walk immediately after lunch so as not to involve herself in the preparations. On her return, just as a cold, sallow sun was setting, the party had begun. She sat amongst the guests in the sitting room sipping tea and smiling on the proceedings as if she were a specially honoured guest. Occasionally she would condescend to talk to some of our older friends. Various games were organized for the children who came, including Hide and Seek. When this was proposed, Aunt Harriet beckoned me over and said, "I give you permission to hide in my room. They'll never find you there."

The idea did not appeal to me at all, but it stayed in my head. Those of us who were to hide began to disperse about the house and I remember finding myself in the passage outside my aunt's room. It was a moment when the temptation to enter her room seemed unconquerable as I heard the numbers being counted inexorably down to one in the hallway below. I entered her room.

I did not turn the light on. The room was warm and had that familiar musky smell. In the dim light I felt my way across to a walk-in cupboard which I entered and then shut behind me. I was now in utter darkness and silence. The noise and bustle of the house had vanished and the only sensation to which I was alive was that of touch. As I sat down on the floor of the cupboard, my face was brushed by the soft cool tickle of my Aunt Harriet's fur coat. How did she reconcile the possession of this article with her vegetarianism? That was a question that only occurred to me long years later.

At first I felt a curious exhilaration. I was alone, unseen and quiet. I had myself to myself and no one would break in on my solitude for a long while. I was free of the importunings of my little sister or the more serious demands of my parents. Moreover, the house, heated generously for once by central heating, Christmas candles and company, had become a little stuffy. In here it was exquisitely cool. I allowed my undistracted thoughts to slow to a standstill; I may even have fallen asleep.

Darkness is a strange thing – it is both infinite and confining; it holds you tight in its grasp, but it holds you suspended in a void. Silence operates in a similar way. Slowly the two combine to become a threat. I had no idea how much time had passed before I began to feel that it was time that someone found me, but how could they? I was so well hidden. It was then that I decided to open the cupboard door and let myself out. But it would not open.

My heart's thumping was suddenly the loudest noise in the universe. I was trapped forever in darkness and silence. I banged and kicked at the cupboard door, but to no effect. It seemed to have the strange unyielding hardness of a wall rather than a piece of wood. I shouted as loud as I could, but my voice was curiously close and dead as if I had entered a soundproof studio at midnight.

It was then that I became aware that the space I was in was not entirely dark. Yet I was confused because, though I knew the cupboard I was in to be about three feet by six feet square, the light that I saw seemed to be coming from a great distance. It was an indeterminate blue-green in colour, a rather drab hue, I thought. I stretched out my hand towards it in the hope of touching the back of the cupboard, but I felt nothing but the faintest brush of cold air, as if someone were blowing on my hand from beyond my reach.

By this time I had no sense of where the front, or the back, or the sides of the cupboard were. All appeared to be beyond my reach, and when I felt upwards I could not even sense the cold softness of my aunt's fur coat. Moreover the floor began to feel icy and damp. I stood up. Nothing now existed but the distant blue-green light.

The next thing that happened was that the light began to grow. The difficulty was that I could not be sure whether I was moving towards it or it towards me. All I knew was that with each move, the atmosphere became more icy, as if I had been transported out of doors into an Arctic void.

The light began to assume shape, and I started to sense that it was a luminous object that was moving towards me. It came not steadily, but in little fits or scuttlings. The thing had six legs or arms and a bulbous body that glowed. The head, smaller but equally round, was darker, though the eyes shone. Their colour was reddish, like amber. It came on and my own body became paralysed with fear, so that I could not retreat from it.

The eyes fixed themselves on me. I tried to raise my hands and found them confined by some fibrous substance, heavy and sticky. In an imitation of my movement, the creature stopped and raised two of its forelimbs in the air and began to wave them in front of its face. It appeared to be in the act of communicating with someone or something, but not with me. Then, with a sudden leap, it was on me and its sinewy, fibrous legs were pawing at my face. I cried out and fell, and when I opened my eyes again I found that I had fallen out of the cupboard into my aunt's room. I was covered in cobwebs.

When I emerged from her room the house was quiet, and for a moment I thought it was deserted, but a faint sound from below reassured me. When I came downstairs, I found that my parents, Aunt Harriet, and Louise were there, but all our guests had gone. I was chided for having fallen asleep in my hiding place. My Aunt Harriet smiled, but my mother was looking anxiously at me.

"You're shivering," she said. "You must be sickening for something. Come along. Off to bed with you."

I was told later that it was flu of some sort and quite serious, but I remember virtually nothing about the next few days. Fortunately none of the others in the house caught my influenza and Aunt Harriet went home early to avoid infection. When I had recovered some sort of consciousness and was beginning to convalesce I asked for some books to read. I noticed that the ones provided did not include *A Child's Treasury of Instructive and Improving Verse*. I asked after it, but was told by my mother that she had burned it in the garden. In the delirium of my fever I had talked about it endlessly, and with apparent terror. "And when I looked in it, I could see why. There were the most beastly illustrations in it. Beautifully done, but beastly."

"What sort of things?"

"I don't know . . . Hobgoblins and demons, and . . . All sorts of horrid things."

"But why did you have to burn it?"

"Oh, I had a book like that when I was a girl. It caused no end of trouble," she said, and that was all she would say.

Some weeks later news reached us that Aunt Harriet had died. She had been crossing a busy road near her flat in Victoria late at night, and a car had hit her and she had had some sort of heart seizure from which she never recovered. The details are vague in my mind, and I have never sought clarity by looking at her death certificate. It is enough to say that in death she was as much trouble as she was in life. It transpired that shortly before that Christmas when she last came to us, she had been dismissed from her job in the library service. There were allegations about missing books which were never fully resolved, and my parents had to satisfy the authorities that we did not have any stolen books in our possession, nor had we profited from their illegal sale.

With the exception of a small bequest to an obscure animal charity, Aunt Harriet had left all her property to my father. There came a time when both my parents had to go up for a few days to deal with the sale of my aunt's flat and its contents. I begged to be allowed to come with them and help, but they firmly refused, so Louise and I were left at home in the care of a neighbour. On their return my parents looked exhausted and somehow haunted. It was only a few months later that my father began to show signs of the illness that later took his life.

Deprived of a sight of it myself, I begged my father and mother for details of what they had found in Aunt Harriet's flat, but they were not forthcoming. My father simply would not discuss it, and all my mother said was:

"You wouldn't have liked it. It's a horrible place. There were cobwebs everywhere."

MICHAEL CHISLETT

The Middle Park

MICHAEL CHISLETT LISTS Arthur Machen, Fritz Leiber, Robert Aickman and Clark Ashton Smith amongst his influences, and he takes as his literary maxim these words of Edward Gorey: "If a story is only what it seems to be about, then somehow the author has failed".

He has had fiction published in numerous magazines and anthologies for more than twenty years, including two previous appearances in *The Mammoth Book of Best New Horror*. His novella, "The Badlands", appeared in David Longhorn's *Supernatural Tales* last year as a special issue. Look out for more stories forthcoming in that periodical and elsewhere.

As the author explains: "I was walking with my girlfriend Maria on a Sunday afternoon through Pepys Park at New Cross. As we crossed over the road at the park's end, I noticed an alleyway with a sign indicating that another park was above us, further up the hill. I used to live a few minutes' away from there and never knew of its existence; passed it dozens of times in fact, without seeing.

"This park was much higher than the other. Not really like that described in the story, except for the view over South London, which, blessed by a rainbow, becomes a deep, green forest.

"I began thinking of the difference between what we think is there and what might actually be. In relationships as well as geography. I came across this quote from Paul Eluard: 'There is another world, but, it is in this one'. That seemed apposite to the story."

"I DIDN'T KNOW THAT there were other parks," admitted Tom to Mina, as they crossed over. "You would have thought that he'd have said, when we were shown the flat."

Tom and Mina had moved into their new home a few days before, and were now spending a Sunday afternoon exploring what was, to them, an almost unknown region. The local park had been a selling point with the estate agent; a *pleasaunce*. The word, in his trade's cant, magically transformed a London suburb, mostly of Victorian houses, into one "leafy". It was indeed a well-tended garden, set on a hill's gentle slope, with London spread below and washed bright after morning showers. The glass-and-steel city shone – tower, pyramid, and ziggurat rose, brave and erect in shards of reflected light. It gave the view (so Mina said) an enchanted aspect.

Above them a multicoloured arc shimmered in the clear blue sky. A rainbow blessed the metropolis, terminated in a haze further up the hill and beyond the park. Mina waved a hand, greeting the rainbow with delight. She exclaimed: "We have to find the end of it. Because of the pot of gold there, which will help pay the mortgage."

Tom smiled in agreement as, hand in hand, they walked up the path towards the park gate, past a children's playground. It was empty, he noted, though a roundabout whirled as if its riders had just left. He speculated as to why, apart from he and Mina, the park was empty on a sunny Sunday afternoon. For London it was a singularly quiet suburb. Sleepy, dreaming, one might say . . . but for a sound of voices that could be heard, soft at first but becoming gradually louder. The voices seemed to be coming from uphill. Were they singing?

"How many sides has a hill?"

Mina delighted in asking such questions. His little conundrum, Tom liked to call her.

"Two. A top and a bottom. An under and an over."

"That's almost exactly it. An upside and a downside."
Mina then sang the catch of an old song. "Jack and Jill went
out to play, over the hill and far away . . ."

Without finishing the lyric (her memory for them was
never good) she pointed across the road as they reached the
park gate.

"The rainbow's end is over there, down that little lane.
Shall we go over?"

Immediately opposite, in a continuation of the path
they'd walked, an alley ran between high walls. At the
narrow way's end a gate could be seen. A post, topped by
two hands with pointing fingers, gave directions. One indicated that across the road Middle and Upper Park could be
found, while the other pointed to Lower Park, where Tom
and Mina stood.

The walls continued along the other side of the street.
Tom wondered what they enclosed. The voices could still be
heard from the other side of the hill, beyond the wall. He
realized that they were singing the song that Mina had
started. Life was full of such coincidences, though.

"Odd that there are separate parks. They were probably
one big park, once upon a time."

"Three parks are thrice as nice. The rainbow's end must
be in the park above this one."

Hand in hand they crossed over. At the alley's mouth a
sign – another quaintly old-fashioned hand-and-finger –
pointed to a gate. The close way was barely wide enough for
the couple to walk abreast along its short length. Ivy clung
to the stone walls, and the metal gate, though unlocked, was
covered by nets of spiderweb. This gave the entrance a
neglected feel, as though it had only recently been opened
after a long period of closure.

By the gate was another hand sign, but this one pointed
straight down, as though it were broken, and two fingers
were open in an inverted "V". It bore the legend MIDDLE
PARK.

"Someone's idea of a joke," hazarded Tom.

"There should be a main entrance to them all ... somewhere."

"On the other side, probably. Is this Middle or Upper Park? The sign's confusing."

"We shall find out. The gate's been unlocked for us, Tom!"

Curiosity aroused, they pushed open the gate and walked through. They found themselves on a prominence, surprisingly higher than the garden below and facing the city's southern purlieus. They stood and admired the prospect.

"What will be the view from the third park?" wondered Mina. "We've seen north, south, east, and west. So it must be a fifth direction."

Like the lower park, this one had bright flowerbeds and a keepers' brown hut. A path meandered down a hill that was much steeper on this side than on its northern aspect. A wooden, green-painted pagoda crowned the rise. On this exotic structure they found a notice board that gave details of various flora and fauna. Tom remarked on the unusual lack of graffiti on the building. In the grass before them mushrooms, thriving in an unusually wet summer, grew in a speckled troop.

"Do you think they might be edible?" asked Mina as, letting go of Tom's hand, she bent down to examine the fungi. "They're like Chinese ones, with the different shapes."

"They must come with the pagoda. We could have them for tea," Tom joked as he studied the crop. "Best not to, though, not with coloured ones. Unless we're sure."

"What's there to be sure of? We are in the Orient, with the pagoda and the mushwumps. There ought to be a Chinese garden here." Mina spoke lightly as, ignoring Tom's warning, she reached out her hand to pluck a mushroom. At her touch the red and yellow dappled fungi unexpectedly exploded in a cloud and she jumped, sneezing and waving her hand in front of her face. Motes hung the air for a moment before drifting away on the balmy afternoon breeze.

"I don't think they were actual mushrooms." As Tom spoke some lingering spores caused him to sneeze as well. It was so violent a sneeze that his vision blurred.

"My eyes are watering. Are they red?" asked Mina, dabbing at her face with a tissue. "I hope they're not toxic. You hear scary things about fungi."

She presented her face to Tom, looking up at him. His vision clearing, he examined her blue eyes. As his own eyes adjusted something appeared just at the edge of his field of vision, vanished when he glanced after it. He turned his gaze back to Mina's eyes.

"No, they're okay," he reassured her. "Don't worry. The park keepers wouldn't let anything poisonous grow here. Health and safety."

He took the opportunity to kiss her and stroke her blonde hair. She responded with a hug. But that floater was back at the corner of his eye . . .

"Oh look! The rainbow is going. We've sneezed it away."

Even as they embraced, the arch of colour began to fade. The mushrooms, too, now seemed drained of colour. Their hues, as if borrowed from the rainbow, became a uniform, shrivelled grey.

"You have to be careful with sneezes," said Mina, disengaging from Tom and blowing her nose again. "They can let the devil in."

"The velocity of a sneeze is incredible," added Tom. His nose still tickled as he studied the mushrooms. He looked down the hill, then, his eyes following the serpentine path to where it entered a grove of trees at the foot of the slope. Black things were on the grass. Crows! Still and watchful rags of old night on the greensward. Few buildings could be seen, and he thought of how verdant London really was when one took the time to notice. Some steeples rose amid the greenery, along with the metal pylon at Crystal Palace and the tower of the Horniman Museum. Other wooded hills dotted the skyline. The ancient forest reclaiming its own? Perhaps. It had never been too far away, really. A hidden world, lain dormant for a while within a landscape we had thought to know . . .

As though she had read his thoughts, Mina said: "The Great North Wood."

Tom nodded. He had the feeling that here, in this place, they could glimpse the ancient arboreal world, despite their immediate surroundings bearing the stamp of Man – the path, the pagoda, the neatly cut grass and bedded flowers, the parkie's brown hut. There was something other, something to which he could not give a name.

Mina spoke again. "This was the very edge of the Great North Wood. It ran from the Weald right up to London. It was not all that long ago, really, that it was cut down. Most of it, anyway. A hundred and fifty years." As she spoke she stared into the distance, like one entranced. "They still remain, bits of the wood, between the streets and houses, overlooked. I think that people don't want to see what's there, at the edge-land, if you know what I mean?"

Then she added: "Gypsies lived in the Great North Wood. It was famous for them."

"I know what you mean," Tom said, although he was not quite sure.

Apart from Tom and Mina and the still, dark birds the park appeared deserted. Not a soul was visible on its high green slope and empty benches. (Did the keeper take Sunday off?) Tom slid an opportunistic hand down her waist to squeeze a buttock through tight jeans and whisper (as though someone nearby might hear?): "We could go into the bushes."

"Don't even think about it," she told him. But, smiling, she didn't remove his hand.

At the margins of the park, its wild edges, bushes and trees grew in lush abundance – enough to conceal any goings-on from prying eyes. The park covered only a few acres but, perhaps thanks to the twisting path, gave an Escher-like impression of a much larger territory. The effect of the enclosing wall of verdure was to camouflage the actual dimensions of a landscape that rejected the tyranny of fixed perspective. And if the separate parks were united, without roads and houses and walls to divide them, a considerable domain would be encompassed.

Where, in relation to its sisters, lay the Upper Park? Tom thought of them as female, it seemed right. In this district there was Mabbs Hill and Annis Hill – one named for the queen of the fairies, the other bearing an old, out-of-fashion English name.

"Shall we go down the path, to see what's there?"

"I'd rather try the bushes," Tom grinned, giving her another squeeze.

"The last time we tried that it was me who got their bum stung by nettles! I want to find the other park, explore a bit. There's another funny signpost with the fingers."

Indeed there was, just where the path down the hill began. Tom hadn't noticed it before. He studied it dubiously. It bore three hands with fingers pointing in various directions, but there were no words to name routes or places. One indicated the way they had just come, another pointed down the hill along the path. And the third – again with two open fingers – pointed at the ground where Tom and Mina stood. It had probably come loose.

Tom became convinced that the signpost hadn't been there before. Which was silly. *You just didn't notice it.* Then the hands began to revolve on the post as the singing came again.

It came from nearby – not exactly in the park, but just outside, disturbing the still afternoon. There was no sound of traffic, Tom suddenly realized, and no birdsong. The latter was strange, given the abundance of foliage. The singing grew louder, voices rising and falling. It was a choir, almost chanting the old song about somewhere over the hill and far away, repeating the words. As in a religious rite, he thought. There were a number of old churches in the area. Some offered an exotic, exuberant form of worship. Was it from them that this song came? Or perhaps from another, more local tradition?

The hands stopped turning, their fingers now pointing at them as Mina slipped from Tom's grasp. Seeming to forget him, she walked away down the path.

"Wait for me!" he called. He looked over his shoulder, seeking another exit from the park, but couldn't find one. If his geography was correct going down the hill would take them well away from home. And home was a place he had the sudden inclination to return to. He could be alone with Mina, for one thing, but there was also a niggling uncertainty at the back of his mind. He was beginning to feel disorientated, perplexed by the park's capricious bounds. Even the signposts couldn't agree on location or direction.

As he followed Mina down the path he saw she was looking attentively to one side, as if listening to a companion speak. She stopped suddenly, seeming confused. In a moment Tom had caught up and took her hand again. Staring at him she shook her head, then laughed.

"That was funny! I thought you were walking beside me."

"I was left behind. You walked off."

"I could have sworn . . ."

She shook her head again and they continued down the winding path. She took another look at Tom, as though (he thought) she were not quite sure of who he was, or why he was there with her.

Then he realized that they were not alone in the park. A man was walking ahead of them, well down the hill. Tom had not seen him before. Perhaps he'd been in the bushes with the woman? Because there was a woman, or at least a blonde feminine figure, walking some way ahead of the man. At first the man seemed to be following her, but then he hurried past, the two seemingly oblivious of one another.

"I want to find the other park. If this is the middle one, then the upper will be much higher. On another plane." She pointed to the two figures further down the hill. "We can follow those two up there. That must be where they are going."

"They are down," said Tom. "We are up. Let's go home. We can find it another day."

Surprisingly she responded in a sing-song voice, like a child reciting doggerel.

"Given is the time and given the place, when the upper and lower come to embrace." Then she spoke normally. "We don't want to miss that, do we? I don't, anyway. It's so rare that it happens."

"What on earth are you on about, Mina?"

"I'm not sure myself! The words of songs just keep coming into my head. But I would like to see the place, find it. Not many do. We're privileged, actually."

On occasion, Mina would go into what might be called a fey mood. Tom had always indulged them, and he decided to humour her now.

"We'll have a look for it then. It can't be too far away."

"You know what, Tom?" She paused and pointed down the hill. "I think that the rainbow has something to do with it. See! It's come back, to show us where it lies."

Indeed, the shining arc had returned, further down the slope, beyond the stand of trees at the end of the path. It bathed the spot in a peculiar greenish-gold haze. It was somehow logical that the other park, either middle or upper, should be there.

Below them the man entered the grove, to be followed a few moments later by the blonde woman. Tom and Mina followed. She began to sing, not very well, but with some commitment:

"Somewhere, over the rainbow, bluebirds fly, there's a land that I heard of once in a lullaby . . ."

Forgetting the rest of the words, she repeated the verse before stopping.

Tom turned to look at the bow of light and saw that behind them two new figures were descending the path – a man and a woman. The latter seemed familiar. Did the park attract blondes? But, before Tom could get a proper look, Mina had let go of his hand and was forging ahead. He increased his pace and caught her hand again. And again she looked at him with some surprise before pulling him along in sudden haste.

"Come on, we don't want to miss it."

"It can't be far," he replied. "No rush."

But again she let go of his hand and began to run down the path, never looking back.

"Mina!" he cried after her, "Why so urgent?"

She called something in response which Tom couldn't make out. Then, with a shrug, he followed after.

Mina had slowed to a brisk walking pace but somehow Tom couldn't quite catch up with her. He didn't care to run, but a fast walk should have him overtaking her. Perhaps it was down to the gradient of the hill, which seemed steeper than it had looked from the crest of the hill. Then there was the meandering path, so sinuous that if a walker kept to it they could not but turn left or right after every few steps.

"This is hardly the old straight track!" he called to Mina. "This is the right road to the . . ."

Mina had again spoken without looking back at him, and Tom didn't catch her last word. They were quite close, now, and he tried to grab her by the arm, but grasped only air. His vision must be at fault, because now she was some yards ahead, striding determinedly on.

Tom stopped for a moment in perplexity. Why was the path so much longer and steeper than it had first appeared? It was, he realized, more than a question of perspective. He looked back up the hill to see that the path apparently formed a circle. *The lie of the land.* The land was indeed lying to him, and Tom was shocked at the deceit. If he walked straight up the hill, leaving the path, it would take only a couple of minutes to reach the green pagoda. There were others standing by it now, quite a crowd looking down at him. Where had they come from? Had they been there all the time, and he had somehow not noticed them?

That must be it, for they were the singers, though calling or chanting might better describe the sound. Were they a congregation, participants in some outdoor religious service?

Tom turned, intending to call Mina. She was now at the very bottom of the hill, and not alone. The man who had been on the path now had her hand in his, as though leading her into the stand of trees.

"Mina!" he called, and ran down the hill as fast as he could. He left the pathway, thinking to follow a direct route. But somehow the earth gently tilted, forcing him back onto the winding way. He tried again to run across the grass, but to no avail. More insistently this time, he was pushed back onto the path. And another signpost had appeared, this one bearing a familiar notice:

KEEP OFF THE GRASS

The post was topped by three fingers again. One pointed uphill, the second level with his head, the third straight down. The middle finger span around then and stopped, pointing directly at him. Tom watched it for a moment, then began to feel a distinct sensation of dizziness, vertigo even. Closing his eyes, he rested a hand on the post to steady himself. When he opened his eyes again all three digits had turned to point to the foot of the hill where Mina stood, deep in animated conversation with her new companion.

The man looked vaguely familiar, but at this distance Tom couldn't be sure if it was someone they knew. But that was beside the point. The man was taking a liberty with his girlfriend. He would see to that.

As Tom hastened down the path, keeping well clear of the grass on either side, he had the feeling he was being followed. One of the crowd on the hill, perhaps? He turned to look, but as he did so the follower passed him on the other side. Tom did what's often called a double take, for the person who'd just passed him was Mina. Or her double. Doublers! It was said everyone had them. Even he possessed one, he realized, in the form of the fellow at the foot of the hill with . . . whoever it was.

The Mina who walked just ahead of him took his hand, which was reassuring. The pair below were gesturing for them to follow, into the trees.

"Amazing!" he cried. "They are . . . they might be us. Even their clothes."

Mina said nothing, just smiled and pointed to where the rainbow painted the land below in a kaleidoscopic glitter. They walked quickly downhill and passed through the trees, coming to a small bridge over a stream. There was another signpost with pointing digit, indicating the crossing. It read MIDDLE PARK. They had found it at last. The other couple had disappeared but, given the uncertainty of the landscape, were surely somewhere about.

By the near-end of the bridge there stood a board with a notice attached, which they stopped to read. Instead of the expected by-laws, there was a hand-written message in bold capitals. Mina read aloud:

"See what is there, not what you are told is there." Her voice was breathless with excitement. "I know that I have been here before. Seen it. Dreamt . . ."

Then she ran across the bridge, into the enchanting at the rainbow's end. Mina, Tom realized, was to be the treasure there. He paused, uncertain, and called her name, which was not enough, for the girl had already been translated.

And in the blink of an eye all had changed again, and he stood alone by the gate of the park, where the road ran. Not the yellow-brick one, either. He looked up to see brightness fade in the air. It might have been his name that was called from it, just once. But it might not, and by then it was too late to follow, anyway.

SIMON KURT UNSWORTH

Into the Water

SIMON KURT UNSWORTH lives in an old farmhouse miles from anywhere in the Lake District, where his neighbours are mostly sheep and his office is an old cheese store in which he writes horror fiction (for which pursuit he was nominated for a 2008 World Fantasy Award for Best Short Story).

His latest collection, *Strange Gateways*, was recently released by PS Publishing, following the critically acclaimed *Quiet Houses* (from Dark Continents Publishing) and *Lost Places* (from Ash Tree Press).

His stories have been published in a large number of anthologies including *Exotic Gothic 4*, *Terror Tales of the Cotswolds*, *Terror Tales of the Seaside*, *Where the Heart Is*, *At Ease with the Dead*, *Shades of Darkness*, *Haunts: Reliquaries of the Dead*, *Hauntings*, *Lovecraft Unbound* and *Year's Best Fantasy 2013*. This is his sixth appearance in *The Mammoth Book of Best New Horror*, and he was also in *The Very Best of Best New Horror*.

A forthcoming collection will launch the Spectral Press "Spectral Signature Editions" imprint, while his novel *The Devil's Detective* is due from Doubleday in the US and Del Rey in the UK early in 2015.

Unsworth reveals: "'Into the Water' was dragged out of me during a single weekend's intensive writing, holed up in a log cabin in the Lake District in the middle of a bitterly cold winter. Its initial inspiration was something I'd seen during a swim in Salford Quays in Manchester a couple of summers earlier.

"I'd swum over a picnic table, standing feet in the mud and face upwards, at the bottom of the Quay, and had an immediate image of four of Lovecraft's Innsmouth-tainted denizens seated around it, one lazily reaching out to take hold of some morsel of food drifting along in the currents above him. I'd never known quite what to do with the image until I was asked to contribute to *Weirder Shadows Over Innsmouth*, in which this tale first appeared. I realized that here was the opportunity I needed to work out precisely why those four were seated there and how they'd got there.

"The thing is, I'm not a big Lovecraft fan. Don't get me wrong – I like the stories (some a great deal), but his stuff isn't particularly what I have in my mind when I write. The stories are sometimes stuffy, a little claustrophobic (and not in a good way) and hysterical, despite a certain elemental power that the best of them contain. They're rarely subtle, and sometimes veer dangerously close to cliché or stereotype. Consequently, I had to try and work out which bits of HPL's mythos I wanted to take and what parts to leave, and how to then marry this to my own interests and concerns and style (assuming I have a style, of course).

"I started to think about the floods that have occurred in recent years (many of which I then managed to reference in the story) and why they might have happened if they weren't merely the result of aberrant weather conditions. I wondered about how the Old Ones might be able to return, subtly at first so that no one realized until it was too late, and about how they might manipulate the world about them to their own ends, and 'Into the Water' was the result.

"I had a huge amount of fun kick-starting the end of the world sitting in that cabin in the Lakes as the world froze outside my window, imagining towns submerged and the land slowly being taken, inch by watery inch. I like things with tentacles and fins and blank, cold eyes, I like aquatic horror and I like the world I created for this story. Wherever he is, I hope that HPL approves."

K APENDA WATCHED THE water, and the water ate the Earth. "Isaac, the high street's finally going under, we need to go and catch it," said Needham from somewhere behind him. Kapenda raised his free hand in acknowledgement but didn't move. Instead, he let his eye rise, up from the new channel of brown and churning floodwater to the bank above. The house's foundations were exposed by the water so that it now teetered precariously on the edge of a gorge. *Fall*, thought Kapenda, *fall, please*. The house didn't fall but it would, soon, and he hoped to be here when it did.

"Isaac!" Needham again. The talent was already at the high street, waiting. The talent was like a child, got fractious and bored if it wasn't the centre of attention; *Don't keep the talent waiting*, was the motto. *Don't annoy the talent* was the rule. Sighing, Kapenda finally lowered the camera and turned to go.

It had rained for months, on and off. Summer had been a washout, the skies permanently thick with cloud, the sun an infrequent visitor. On the rare occasions the clouds broke and the sun struggled through, grounds steamed but didn't dry out. The water table saturated upwards, the ground remaining sodden until the first of the winter storms came and the rivers rose and the banks broke and the water was suddenly everywhere.

They were less than a mile from the town, but the journey still took several minutes. The roads were swollen with run-off, thick limbs of water flowing down the gutters and pushing up from the drains, washing across the camber and constantly tugging at the vehicle. Kapenda wasn't driving but he felt it, the way they pulled across the centre line and then back as Needham compensated. It had been like this for days now all across the south of England. Kapenda leaned against the window, peering at the rain and submerged land beyond the glass.

There were figures in the field.

Even at their reduced speed, they passed the little tableau too quickly for Kapenda to see what the figures were doing, and he had to crane back around to try and keep them in view. There were four of them, and they appeared to be crouching so that only their shoulders and heads emerged from the flooded pasture. One was holding its arms to the sky. There was something off about the shape of the figures – the arms held to the clouds were too long, the heads too bulbous. Were they moving? Still? Perhaps they were one of those odd art installations you sometimes came across, like Gormley's standing figures on Crosby beach. Kapenda had filmed a segment on them not long after they had been put in place, and watching as the tide receded to reveal a series of bronze, motionless watching figures had been quite wonderful and slightly unnerving. Had they done something similar here?

The rain thickened, and the figures were lost to its grey embrace.

The talent, a weasel of a man called Plumb whose only discernible value was a smoothly good-looking face and a reassuring yet stentorian voice, was angry with Needham and Kapenda. As Kapenda framed him in shot so that the new river flowing down Grovehill's main street and the sandbagged shops behind it could be seen over Plumb's shoulder, Plumb was moaning.

"We've missed all the dramatic stuff," he said.

"We've not," said Needham. "Just trust in Isaac, he'll make you look good."

"It's not about me looking good," said Plumb, bristling, brushing the cowlick of hair that was drooping over his forehead. "It's about the story."

"Of course it is," said Needham. "Now, have you got your script?"

They didn't get the lead item on the news, but they did get the second-string item, a cut to Plumb after the main story so that he could intone his description of Grovehill's failed flood defences. Kapenda had used the natural light to make Plumb seem larger and the water behind darker, more ominous. He was happy with the effect, especially the last tracking shot away from the talent to look up the street, lost under a caul of fast-moving flood whose surface rippled and glittered. The water looked alive, depthless and hungry, something inexorable and unknowable.

Now that, thought Kapenda, *is how to tell a story*, and only spotted the shape moving through the water when he was reviewing the footage a couple of hours after it had gone out. It was a dark blur just below the waves, moving against the current and it vanished after perhaps half a minute. Something tumbling through the flow, Kapenda thought, and wished it had broken the surface – it would have made a nice image to finish the film on.

Plumb had found an audience.

They were in the bar of the pub where they were staying: the tiny, cramped rooms the only place available. The flood had done the hospitality industry a world of good, Kapenda thought; every room in the area was taken with television and print reporters.

"Of course, it's all global warming's fault," Plumb said.

"Is it?" said the man he was talking to. The man's voice was deep and rich, accented in a way Kapenda always thought of as old-fashioned. It was the voice of the BBC in the 1950s, of the Pathé newsreels. He punctuated everything he said with little coughs, as though he had something caught in his throat.

"Of course," said Plumb, drawing on all the knowledge he had gained from reading one- and two-minute sound-bite pieces for local and, more latterly, national news. "The world's heating up, so it rains more. It's obvious."

"It's as simple as that," said the man, and caught Kapenda's eye over Plumb's shoulder. One of his eyes was milky and blind, Kapenda saw, and then the man, disconcertingly, winked his dead eye and smiled.

"He really is an insufferable fool, isn't he?" the man said later to Kapenda, nodding at Plumb, who was now holding court in the middle of a group of other talents. What's the collective noun for the talent, thought Kapenda? A show-off? A blandness? A stupidity? He moved a forefinger through a puddle of spilled beer on the table, swirling it out to make a circle. The man, whose name was David, dipped his own fingers in the puddle and made an intricate pattern on the wood with the liquid before wiping it away.

"He thinks he understands it," said David, and gave one of his little coughs. "But he doesn't."

"What is there to understand?" asked Needham. "It's rain. It comes down, it floods, we film it and he talks about it and tries to look dramatic and knowledgeable whilst wearing an anorak that the viewers can see and wellingtons that they can't."

"This," said David, waving a hand at the windows and the rain beyond. He was drunk; Needham was drunker. "It's not so simple as he wants to believe. There are forces at work more complex than mere global warming." He coughed again, a polite rumble.

"Pollution?" said Needham. Kapenda thought of his camera, of the eye he held to his shoulder to see the world, about how he'd frame this discussion. One at each edge of the screen, he decided, in tight close-up, David's opaque eye peering into the lens as Needham's head bobbed back and forth, up and down, like a bird. Needham was a good producer and director because he stressed over the little details, but a bad drinking companion because he got like a terrier over tiny fragments of information.

"Pollution? Possibly, but no answer about the Earth is that simple. Why is the water rising so fast? So far? Mere geography, or something more? My point is that we look to the wrong places for answers, because the real answers have faces too terrible to contemplate," said David and then stood. He was tall and solid, not fat exactly but well built, his waistcoat straining under the pressure from his ample belly.

"You're looking in the wrong place, all of you." And with that, nodding his thanks for the company, David turned and walked away. Kapenda grinned at the look of confusion on Needham's face, saw that Plumb was heading back their way and quickly rose himself.

"I need a walk," he said.

"A swim, surely?" said Needham, and he and Plumb laughed. Kapenda did not reply.

The pub was on a hill – it was why it remained mostly unaffected by the storms and the rising floodwater. The rain was coming in near-horizontal sweeps now, gusting along in cold breaths that made Kapenda shiver. Lightning crackled somewhere over the fields, followed by thunder that reminded him of David's voice and cough. The forecasters were saying that this storm would burn itself out in the next day or so, but they'd said that before and been wrong. The previous week, the rains had continued through the period they'd confidently predicted would be dry, and the groundwater rose and rose. What had he come outside for? Not air, not even to be away from Needham and Plumb, not really.

Kapenda went down towards the lights that were strung out along Grovehill's main street. Generators, housed in the nearby community hall, powered the lamps and rope barriers and prevented him from getting to the water. Even at this time of night, news crews were clustered along the ropes, each filming or preparing for filming. He tried to look at the scene as though he was holding his camera – was there something here not about the floods but about the press response to it? No, that had been done.

There had to be something new, some fresh angle. As the rain pattered down around him, Kapenda thought. What was the weirdest thing he'd seen since this all started? He'd been in the tiny town of Chew Stoke a few weeks earlier, filming the remains of a vehicle that had been washed into a culvert and whose driver had died. In Grovehill, no one had died yet but there were abandoned cars strewn along the streets and surrounding tracks, hulking shapes that the water broke around and flowed over in fractured, churning flurries.

That was old. Every television station had those shots. He'd been there the year before when the police had excavated a mud-filled railway tunnel and uncovered the remains of two people who had been crushed in a landslide. What they needed was something like that here, something that showed how weak man's civilized veneer was when set against nature's uncaring ferocity. He needed something that contrasted human frailty and natural strength, something that Dali might have painted – a boat on a roof, or a shark swimming up the main street. He needed that bloody house to collapse.

What about the figures in the field?

Actually, the fields were a good starting point. They had flooded heavily and most were under at least four or five feet of water, but due to some quirk of meteorology or geography the water on them was sitting calm. Somewhere, he thought, somewhere there's an image in that smooth expanse that I can use.

Kapenda waited until morning, and such light as came with sunrise, before investigating. He left a note for Needham, who likely wouldn't be up until mid-morning anyway, and drove back along the roads towards the field. Through the windscreen, the road ahead of him moved like a snake, constantly surging and writhing.

The dark shape was in the first field he came to, drifting slowly along, spinning. Kapenda saw it through the tangle of hedgerow and stopped, climbing out into knee-high water and lifting his camera to his shoulder. He couldn't see well, was too low, so climbed onto the vehicle's doorsill and then higher, onto its roof. Was this the field where he had seen the figures? He thought it was, although there was no sign of them now. From his raised vantage point, he saw what the shape was, and started filming.

It was a dead cow. It was already bloating, its belly swelling from the gases trapped within, and its eye peered at him with baleful solemnity. Its tongue trailed from its open mouth, leached to a pale grey by the water. Its tail drifted after it like an eel. There was another beyond it, he saw, and more beyond that. A herd, or flock, or whatever a group of cows was called, trapped by the water and drowned.

Drowned? Well, probably, but one of the further animals looked odd. Kapenda zoomed in, focusing as he did so. The dead creature's side was a ragged mess, with strips of peeled flesh and hide along its flank exposing the muscles below. Here and there, flashes of white bone were visible. Its neck was similarly torn, the vertebrae visible through the damaged flesh. As he filmed, the creature span more violently as a current caught it, slamming it into a tree trunk; the collision left scraps of meat clinging to the bark. Kapenda carried on filming as the cow whirled away, watching as it caught on something under the water, jerked and then suddenly submerged, bobbing back up before vanishing again. A great bubble of air, so noxious Kapenda could smell it from his distant perch, emerged from where the cow had gone down.

It was as Kapenda climbed down from the roof that he saw the thing in the hedgerow.

It was jammed, glinting, into the tangle of branches and leaves about four feet from the ground. From the surface of the water, he amended. Leaving his camera in the jeep, he moved cautiously towards the glint, feeling ahead with his feet. The ground dropped away as he stepped off the solid surface of the road, the water rising against him. It came to his thighs and then his waist; he took his wallet and phone from his jeans and zipped them into his jacket's inner pocket; they were already in plastic bank bags, sealed against the damp. Carefully, not wanting to slip, lose his footing and be washed away like the cows, he leaned into the hedgerow and pushed his arm into it. The thing was tantalisingly out of reach. He pushed in harder, felt his feet shift along the submerged earth and then he was over, falling into the water and going under.

It was cold, clenching his head in its taut embrace and squeezing. Kapenda kicked but his feet tangled into some-thing – branches or roots – and were held fast. Something large and dark, darker than the water around him, banged into him, began to roll over him and force him further under the water. He wanted to breathe, knew if he opened his mouth he'd take in water and drown, and clenched his jaw. The thing on him was heavy, clamped onto his shoulder and was it biting him, Jesus yes, it was biting him and pushing him down and he was trapped, was under it and couldn't shift it and then something grasped his other shoulder, hard, and he was pulled up from the water.

"No! No! Let him be!" It was David, hauling Kapenda from the water, pulling him back to the jeep. "What were you doing in the water? You could have bloody drowned!"

Kapenda collapsed to his knees, back into the water but held up by the jeep, and vomited. His breakfast came out in a soup of dirty liquid, the sight of it making him retch even more.

"Are you okay? Do you need to go to the doctor? The hospital?" David was calmer now, more concerned than angry.

"No," said Kapenda after a moment. "I think I'm okay. What was it?"

"A dead cow," said David after a moment. "What were you doing, going into the water?"

"I saw something in the hedge," said Kapenda, and it sounded ridiculous even as he said it. He managed to rise to his feet, using the side of the jeep as a support. Water dripped from him.

"Let me see then," said David. The man looked paler in the daylight, as though he was somehow less there, his dead eye bulging from a face that was round and wan. Its milky iris peered at Kapenda. His other eye was dark, the sclera slightly yellowing. Was he a heavier drinker than he'd appeared the night before? He had patches of rough skin, Kapenda saw, dried and peeling.

There was a bike leaning against the back of the jeep and Kapenda was suddenly struck with the image of David cycling down the centre of the road, his front wheel cutting a "V" though the water, his feet submerging and re-emerging with each revolution of the pedals, and it made him smile.

"Now, let's see this thing you were prepared to drown to get," said David, also smiling.

"Oh, I—" started Kapenda, about to say that it was still in the hedge, and then realized it wasn't. He was holding it.

It was a small figure, made from some dull metal. It had a suggestion of legs and arms and a face that was nested in tentacles, its eyes deep-set and its mouth a curved-down arc. Was it an octopus? A squid? A long chain dangled from it, fine-linked and dully golden. More figures were hooked to some of the chain's links, tiny things like toads with swollen genitalia and fish with arms and legs. David held the figure up by the chain, peering at it.

"What is it?" Kapenda asked.

David didn't answer. Instead, he span it, watching as it caught the pallid light. Its surface was smooth, but Kapenda had the impression it was the smoothness of age and wear, that the ghosts of old marks still lay under its skin. Finally, David spoke, muttering under his breath, words that Kapenda didn't catch.

"Do you know what it is?" asked Kapenda. He was starting to shiver, the shock and the cold catching him. He wanted to go back to the hotel and dry off, warm up.

"Yes," said David. "I saw one once, as a child, and I hoped not to see one again so soon. Still, I suppose it explains a lot." He rubbed one of the patches of dry skin on his neck slowly.

"The water's coming, my friend," he said, "and there's nothing we can do to stop it. Its time is here again. Well, if you're sure you're okay to drive, I'll leave you be. Take my advice, stay out of the water."

"I will," said Kapenda, "and thank you."

"Think nothing of it," said David and coughed again, his own private punctuation. He winked his sightless eye once more and then went and mounted his bike, wheeling it around to point back to Grovehill. Moments later all Kapenda could see of him was his back, hunched over the handlebars as he went down the road. Behind him, tiny waves spread out across the water and then broke apart.

It was only when Kapenda got back into the jeep that he remembered the bite – sure enough, his jacket was torn in two semi-circles, to the front and rear of his shoulder, and the skin below bruised but not broken. He got back out of the jeep to try and see the cow but it must have floated off, and the only thing to see was the flood, ever restless and ever hungry.

The house collapsed just after lunch.

They were filming at the rope barrier again, this time framing the talent against a shot down the street to show how the water wasn't retreating. "Forecasters say that, with the recent rainfall, the water levels aren't expected to recede until at least tomorrow, and if more rain comes it could conceivably be several days or more," Plumb intoned. "Great sections of the south-west are now under water, economies ruined and livelihoods and lives destroyed. Even today, we've heard of two more deaths, a woman and child who drowned in their lounge in the village of Arnold, several miles from here. Questions are being asked of the defences that the government installed and why the Environment Agency wasn't better prepared. Here, the people merely wait, and hope."

Kapenda waited until Plumb had done his turn, letting him peer meaningfully down the flooded street, before lowering the camera. One of the other crews had found a flooded farm earlier that day and had proudly showed their footage to everyone, of the oilslick forming across the surface of the water in the barn and around it as the water worked its way into the abandoned vehicles and metal storage canisters, teasing out the oil and red diesel they contained. The rainbow patterns had been pocking and dancing in the rain, and the image had been oddly beautiful; Kapenda had been professionally impressed, and privately jealous.

"Was that good?" asked Plumb, and then stopped and listened as the air filled with a dense rumbling, grinding sound like something heavy being pushed over a stone floor.

"The building's gone," someone shouted, a runner with a phone clamped to his ear, "it's completely collapsed. The flood's surging!"

As the man spoke, a fresh wall of water appeared between the furthest buildings, higher than those that had come before it, driven by the tons of brick and wood and belongings that had suddenly crashed into the flow. The wave was a dirty red colour, curled over like a surfer's dream. Somewhere, it had picked up trees and a car, a table, a bed and other unidentifiable shapes – all of these Kapenda saw even as he was raising the camera. In the viewfinder, he caught the things in the water as they hit the buildings, saw the car crash through the window of a chemist, saw the bed hurtle into and buckle a lamp post, saw bricks bounce and dip like salmon on their way to spawning, and then the wave was upon them.

He moved back, never stopping filming, cursing under his breath that he'd missed the actual collapse. Things churned through the water, dark shadows darting back and forward under the surface, their edges occasionally breaking through to the air only to roll back, splash their way under again.

The water level rose rapidly, submerging the makeshift barriers and eating away at the bottom of the hill. As Kapenda and Needham and the talent moved swiftly back, jostling in amongst the other film crews, cars were lifted out of the side streets and began to jolt through the water. One of the lights exploded as the water reached the electric cables, and the others shorted in a series of rapid pops that left behind ghost spots in Kapenda's eyes and an acrid smell of smoke in the air. Moments later, one of the generators made a series of groaning sounds from inside the community hall and black smoke breathed out from the windows as it, too, shorted out. The police pushed the crowd back, followed all the while by the water.

By nightfall, Grovehill was lost. The rains, which had continued to fall all day, had finally abated as the light faded but the floodwater had continued to rise, submerging most of the houses and shops up to their roofs. In the pub, the conversation was subdued, slightly awed. Most of the crews had worked on weather stories before; Kapenda himself had been at Boscastle in 2004, filming the aftermath of the flash flood, but this was worse – it showed no signs of receding.

Two cameramen had died when the building collapsed. One had been caught in the initial surge of water, swept away like so much flotsam. The other, further down the torrent, had been on the edge of the bank when something turning in the water, the branches of an uprooted tree it was supposed, had reached out and snagged him, lifting him from his feet and carrying him off. His talent, a pretty blonde stringer for a local news programme, had been taken off in shock talking about how the water had eaten the man.

"I saw one of those in Russia," said a voice from behind him.

It was one of the other cameramen – Rice, Kapenda thought he might be called. Rice nodded at the thing Kapenda had pulled from the hedge, sat on the table by his glass of beer.

"Russia?" asked Kapenda

"I was in Krymsk in 2010 and in Krasnodar," said Rice, "back in 2012, when the flash flood killed all those people. We found a few of those around the port in Krymsk and in the fields about Krasnodar. We did a segment about them, but it was never shown." He picked up the figure and dangled it, much like David had done, eyeing it.

"It's almost identical," he said. "Strange."

"What is it?"

"We never found out, not really. I always assumed it was some kind of peasant magic, some idol to keep the floods away. If that's what it was, it didn't work though, the damn things were always where the water was at its highest. I found one hanging from a light fitting in the upper room of a school that was almost completely submerged." He put the thing back on Kapenda's table.

"What happened to your segment?"

"Got archived, I suppose," said Rice. "Pretty much what we expected. I didn't mind, not really. Russia was a nightmare, and I had bigger things to worry about than whether the piece I filmed got shown."

"Really?"

"Really. It was chaos, thousands of people made homeless, streets full of mud and water and corpses. In Krymsk, everything got washed into the Black Sea, and the harbour was blocked with debris for weeks after. The local sea life was well fed, though."

"Jesus," said Kapenda.

"Yeah," said Rice. "You'd see them, dark shapes in the water, and then some floating body would suddenly vanish. The official estimate for Krymsk was one hundred and seventy dead, or thereabouts, but I'll be damned if it wasn't far higher though. I had a friend covered the Pakistan floods, was in Sindh and Balochistan, and he told me there were things like that there as well, hanging from the trees just above the flood line."

"The same things?"

"Yeah," said Rice again. "And I'll tell you one other thing that's odd."

"What?"

"That old woman that died in the flood at St Asaph the other week? That drowned in her home? There was one hanging outside her house, and one outside the house of the mother and child that drowned yesterday."

"What? How do you know?"

Rice merely smiled at Kapenda. *I have my sources*, the smile said, *and I'm keeping them secret*. "Keep it safe," he said as he turned and went back to the bar, "you never know when you might need protection against the water."

Needham was in a bad mood.

It was the next morning, and he had been trying to find someone local to interview. He wanted the talent to do some empathy work, get Plumb to listen sympathetically and nod as some teary bumpkin showed them their drenched possessions and talked about how their pictures of Granny were lost forever, but there wasn't anyone.

"They won't talk to you?" asked Kapenda.

"They've all fucking vanished!" said Needham. "There's no one in the emergency shelters, no one worth mentioning anyway, and they certainly aren't staying at any of the farms, I've checked. Most of them have been abandoned too. The police aren't sure when anyone's gone, or they're not saying if they know."

"They must be somewhere," said Kapenda.

"Must they? Well I don't know where to fucking find them," said Needham.

"Perhaps they all swam away?" said Plumb and laughed. Neither Kapenda nor Needham joined in.

"It'll be dead cows and flooded fucking bushes again, you'll see," said Needham, disconsolate. "Isaac, can't you find me something new?"

"I'll try," said Kapenda.

David was standing in the water in one of the fields a little further out from Grovehill. Kapenda saw his bike first, leaning against the hedge and half under water, and pulled the jeep over to see what the man was doing. There was a stile in the hedge and David was beyond it, out into the field proper. Kapenda waded to the wooden gate and climbed it, perching on the top and calling, "Hello!"

"'For Behold'," said David loudly, his voice rolling across the water, "'I will bring a flood of water upon the earth to destroy all flesh in which is the breath of life under Heaven'. Hello, Isaac. They knew, you see – they understood."

"Who knew? Understood what?"

"We have always waited for the water's call, those of us with the blood, waited for the changes to come, but now? Some of us have called to it, and it has come."

"I don't understand," said Kapenda. He wished he had brought his camera – David looked both lonely and somehow potent, standing up to his chest in the water, his back to Kapenda. It was raining again, the day around them grey and murky.

"What are you doing?"

"It has been brought this far but I worry," said David, his voice lower, harder for Kapenda to hear. "How much further? How much more do we want? And what of what comes after us? The sleeping one whose symbol you found, Isaac? It wants the world, drowned and washed clean, but clean of what? Just of you? Or of everything – of us as well? We should have stayed in the deeps, but no, we have moved into the shallows and we prepare the way as though we were cleaning the feet of the sleeping one, supplicants to it. We might be terrible, Isaac, but after us? Do you have a god? Pray for its mercy, for the thing that comes after us – the thing that we open the way for – will be awful and savage beyond imagining."

"David, what are you talking about?"

"The water, Isaac. It's always about the water." David turned – in the fractured, mazy light, his face was a white shift of moonlike intensity. His eyes were swollen, turning so that they appeared to be looking to opposite sides of his head. His skin looked like old linen, rough and covered in dry and flaking patches. He seemed to have lost his hair and his neck had folded down over itself in thick, quivering ridges. "It would be best for you to leave, Isaac. You have been saved from the water once, but I suspect that once is all."

"David, please, I still don't know what you mean. Tell me what you're talking about."

"I thought we had time, that the calling that cannot be ignored would never come, but it is too late. Others have hastened it, and the water calls to us even as they call to it. I can't stand against it, Isaac. The change is come."

"David—" Kapenda began, but the older man turned and began to move off across the field, bobbing down shoulder deep into the water with each long stride, sweeping his arms around as though swimming.

"David!" Kapenda shouted, but the man didn't turn. Just before he was lost to view, the water around him seemed suddenly full of movement, with things rising to the surface and looking back at him. Kapenda, scared, turned away and returned to the jeep.

"I've found us a boat!" said Needham when Kapenda got back. He didn't seem bothered that Kapenda hadn't found anything new to film.

"Your idea about the fields yesterday, about how smooth they are, it got me thinking," Needham continued. "Now the flow's slowing down, it's safe to go out in a boat, not in the fields but around the houses. They got film of the barns yesterday, didn't they? Well, we'll go one better, we'll get film of the houses, of Grovehill!"

Plumb was already in the boat, bobbing gently at the edge of the flood. It was a small dinghy with barely enough room for the three of them. Kapenda had to keep the camera on his shoulder as Needham steered the boat using the outboard on its back. Why had he come? Kapenda wondered.

Because, he knew, this was where he belonged, recording. Whatever David had meant, whatever this flood and the ones that had come before it were, someone had to catch them, pin them to history. Here, in this drowned and drowning world, he had to be the eyes of everyone who came after him.

Needham piloted the boat away from the centre of Grovehill, down winding lanes among houses that were under water to their eaves. They went slowly – here and there, cars floated past them, and the tops of signs and traffic lights emerged from the flood like the stems of water plants. Kapenda filmed a few short sequences as they drifted, with Plumb making up meaningless but portentous-sounding phrases. Mostly, the imagery did the talking. At one point, they docked against a road emerging from the water that rose up to a hill upon which a cluster of houses sat, relatively safe. Kapenda focussed in, hoping for footage of their occupants, but no one moved. Had they been evacuated already?

Several minutes later, they found themselves drifting over a playing field, the ghostly lines of football pitches just visible through the still, surprisingly clear water. While Plumb and Needham argued a script point, Kapenda had an idea – he fixed the water cover to the lens of the camera and then held it over the side of the boat and into the water. The surprising clarity would hopefully allow him to obtain good images of the submerged world, eerie and silent. Leaning back and getting as comfortable as he could, Kapenda held the camera so that it filmed what was below while he listened as the talent and the director argued.

"Hey!" a voice called, perhaps twenty minutes later. It was distorted, the voice, coming from a loudhailer. Kapenda looked up. Bouncing across the surface towards them was one of the rescue boats, a policeman in its bow waving at them.

"Oh fuck," said Needham.

"What?" asked Plumb.

"I didn't actually ask permission to come out here," said Needham.

"Shit!" said Plumb. "We'll be fucking arrested!"

"We won't. Isaac, have you got enough footage?"

"Yes."

"Then we play innocent. Plumb, charm them if you can."

"You have to go back!" the policeman called. Needham raised an arm at him and as the launch pulled alongside them, the talent began to do his stuff.

By the time they sorted out the police, with many mea culpas from Needham and much oleaginous smiling from Plumb, it was late. The water had continued to rise, its surface now only a few feet down the hill from the pub's door. Plumb made a joke about being able to use the boat to get back to it, but it was almost true and none of them laughed.

Inside, most of the crews were quiet and there was little of the talking and boasting and arguing that Kapenda would have expected. There were less of them as well; some had already left, retreating north to the dry or hunting for other stories. In Middlesbrough and Cumbria, rivers were bursting their banks and Kapenda watched footage on the news of flooded farmland and towns losing their footing to water. In one tracking shot, he was sure he saw something behind the local talent, a tiny figure hanging in a tree, spinning lazily on a chain as the water rose to meet it.

Back in his room, Kapenda started to view the film he had taken that day. The first shots were good, nice framings of Plumb in the prow of their dinghy with Grovehill, drowned, over his shoulder. He edited the shots together and then sent them to Needham, who would work on voiceovers with Plumb.

Then he came to the underwater footage.

They were good shots, the focus correct and imagery startling. The water was clear but full of debris – paper and clothing and unidentifiable things floated past the lens as it passed over cars still parked in driveways, gardens in which plants waved, houses around which fishes swam. At one point the corpse of a cow bounced languidly along the centre of a street, lifting and falling as the gentle current carried it on. The dead animal's eyes were gone, leaving torn holes where they used to be, and one of its legs ended in a ragged stump. It remained in the centre of the shot for several minutes, keeping pace with the boat above, and then it was gone as they shifted direction. Kapenda's last view of it was its hind legs, trailing behind as it jolted slowly out of sight.

They were in a garden.

At first, he thought it was a joke. Someone had set four figures around a picnic table, seated in plastic chairs, some kind of weird garden ornamentation, and then one of the figures moved and Kapenda realized that, whatever they were, they were real.

Three were dark, the fourth paler, all squat and fat and bald. One of them held a hunk of grey meat in its hand, was taking bites from it with a mouth that was wide and lipless. Their eyes, as far as Kapenda could tell, were entirely black, bulging from the sides of their heads. All four were scaly, their backs ridged. As Kapenda watched, one of the figures reached out and caught something floating past and its hand was webbed, the fingers thick and ending in savage, curved claws.

As the figures moved off the side of the screen, the palest looked up. Thick folds of skin in its neck rippled, gill slits opening and closing. Its mouth was wide, open to reveal gums that were bleeding, raw from tiny, newly emerging triangular teeth. It nodded, as though in greeting, and raised a webbed hand to the camera.

One of its eyes was a dead, milky white.

Kapenda turned off the camera and went to stand by the window. He took the little figure from his pocket, turning it, feeling its depth-worn smoothness as the chain moved through his fingers.

He watched as figures swam through the ever-advancing water below him, never quite breaking the surface, forming intricate patterns of ripple and wave. Rice had called the thing from the hedge an idol. Was it simple peasant magic? No, this was nothing simple, nothing innocent. The idol looked nothing like the figures in the flood, was something harsh and alien. What had David said? That it was the thing that came after?

What was coming?

The rain fell, and the water rose to eat the Earth.

LYNDA E. RUCKER

The Burned House

LYNDA E. RUCKER is an American writer living in Dublin, Ireland. This is her fifth appearance in *The Mammoth Book of Best New Horror*, and her fiction has also appeared in such places as *Best Horror of the Year*, *The Magazine of Fantasy & Science Fiction*, *The Year's Best Dark Fantasy and Horror*, *Shadows and Tall Trees*, *Nightmare Magazine* and *Postscripts*.

She is a regular columnist for *Black Static*, and her first collection, *The Moon Will Look Strange*, was released last year from Karōshi Books. She is currently working on a novel, the usual assortment of short stories, and a novella for Remains, the new horror imprint from Salt Books.

"I had the title for this story in my head for years before I started to write it," explains Rucker. "I'd seen a piece on the news about a particularly tragic house fire in which some children had died, and the idea persisted as one about a house that would be a space of such collective sadness it would be shunned to the point of its neighbours almost literally forgetting its existence.

"Later a series of strong images and a desire to write an older protagonist led me back to 'The Burned House', and although it went through a number of revisions, as most of my stories do, much of it arrived fully formed, which is unusual for me."

One you're at the yard . . .

THE BURNED HOUSE stood at the back of a scrubby lot. If a house could be said to glower, then glower it did: rising from the ashes which were all that was left of its south face, sitting back on its haunches, its wooden front porch inexplicably wrapped in chicken wire (to keep out trespassers? to keep something in?), its second floor rearing up and threatening to topple.

The FOR SALE sign had been there forever – whoever had first put it there was probably dead by now – and punctuated the scene like a particularly unfunny joke. Nobody was ever going to buy the burned house.

Agnes Swithin, jogging through the chilly dusk, her breath steaming, slowed and then stopped before it. Her kneecap had begun to throb again. She clutched at the splintery fence with hands that looked older than she felt, the skin translucent over knots of prominent blue veins, and willed the pain to move up through her body and out her fingers. The doctor said running made it worse, but Agnes couldn't bear being sedentary. *Why don't you try swimming or walking*, the doctor had said helpfully, a fresh-faced young woman Agnes might have taught just a few years earlier, who clearly (Agnes imagined) thought that she, Agnes, ought to be engaged in a more geriatric form of exercise. Afternoons in the pool at the Y surrounded by soft fleshy women wearing bathing suits modestly trimmed with skirts. Yoga for the ancient and decrepit. Agnes had never actually been to the senior yoga class, the pool, or even the Y itself, but she felt she could picture it all the same.

She caught her breath, then, not from exertion, nor from the pain in her knee.

A girl in a white dress had emerged from around the south side of the house. The girl was thin – too thin, transparently thin, head and hands and feet like bough-breaking burdens on the ends of twig-like neck and arms and legs. The legs were bare, the dress stark white against tanned skin. Or it might have been a nightgown. She could have been twelve, fifteen, older; her frailty lent her an ageless quality. Agnes, who resolutely did not believe in ghosts, imagined for a bad moment or two that she was looking at precisely that.

Two you're through the gate . . .

The truth about the burned house was that if you thought about it too much, you realized it was an enigma, only nobody thought about it much at all. The house had stood in its dilapidated state for as long as anyone knew, including Agnes, who had just entered her seventh decade. The house had neither been condemned nor selected for restoration; it simply was. Yet over those decades it could not be said to have deteriorated further, not in any significant sense. The roof ought to be gone, the walls collapsed, the house reduced to a pile of boards over its long years of neglect, and it was not. A gutter might have unhinged itself, a pilaster might have crumbled, but overall it aged with an enviable and impossible grace, apparently ticking along in its very own timestream.

People rarely noticed, because they rarely thought about the burned house. Sometimes it was remembered in the manner of a dream that returns moodily and incompletely to consciousness: "Oh! I wonder if the burned house is still there?" Rarely did anyone venture to find out. Just as dreams never make sense as the conscious mind tries to catch hold of them, neither did the burned house.

The lots on either side of it were empty, and an old bungalow sat on the one just behind it, a bungalow perpetually for rent because it never kept its tenants long. A weather-beaten big wheel waited forlornly in the weeds of the neat brick ranch house just across the street.

The dead-end street itself had bad associations: people tended to avoid it, although nobody could really say why. There was little reason to turn down it unless you were unfortunate enough to live there, for however short a time, and if you were tempted to do so – perhaps you had followed confusing and incomplete directions and needed to turn the car around and start over in the opposite direction – well, there was a more agreeable cul-de-sac a block away that would do. Agnes rarely if ever had gone for a run down the street on which the burned house stood. Earlier, as the evening was creeping in, she had been on the phone with her brother, and something he said stirred old memories, and she thought as others had done before her – *oh! the burned house!* – and now she was here, just before the gate, like the old jump-rope rhyme they'd recited as children.

> *Three you're at the window . . .*

The girl raised an arm in greeting, and Agnes raised one back, reassured. It seemed unlikely that a ghost would proffer a friendly hello.

The girl said, "You look cold. Why don't you come in and have some coffee?"

Her voice was not ghostly, either; in fact, a south Georgia twang flattened it, same as most everyone in those parts. She pronounced coffee "cawfee". Agnes, whose curiosity had nearly been her undoing on more than one occasion, said that did sound tempting.

"Come on round the back," said the girl.

Agnes said, "No, I couldn't, really," or maybe it was, "No, I *shouldn't*"; or she intended to. Yet even as she thought to say it she picked her way through the knee-high weeds of the front yard, and heard herself not declining the invitation, but describing the scene to an acquaintance later: *It was like some unseen force had taken hold of me.* That didn't seem quite right. If an unseen force had you in its grip, would you necessarily know what it did or did not compel you to do? Would it move you bodily, or would it nestle in the folds of your brain, induce you to actions even as you continued to believe that you were in charge of yourself? She thought this even as she rounded the corner to a backyard more overgrown than the front, as she observed the broken windows, the scattering of dead leaves across the concrete steps of the back porch, even as she knew when the girl took her hand that she took the hand of a ghost.

Four you're tempting fate . . .

More than fifty years ago, as children, Agnes and her brother and their friends had dared one another to go near the burned house – to pass through its wooden gate, to run and touch its crumbling chicken-wire porch – but Agnes, at least, never got that close. Her brother, an important (by his account) Los Angeles entertainment attorney, had not returned to town since their mother's untimely death from breast cancer thirty years earlier. *Don't know how you do it, Aggie*, he would say with false heartiness over the phone. He never said what he meant by "do it"; staying in one place, she supposed, years of teaching science at the local high school. Her life must have seemed impossibly dull to him.

I dare you; I double dare you; I double double dare you; I double triple dare you! With such linguistic improbabilities they raised the stakes so high that somebody had to give sooner or later. They'd conjured shapes at the window of the burned house, and shadows of the dead lurching through the ash. And when they jumped rope or played hopscotch or wanted to scare their smaller siblings, they had the jump-rope rhyme. Agnes could no longer remember all the words but it was a piece of silly counting doggerel. The words and cadence kept her awake as a child as she invented superstitions to accompany them; if she spoke without errors, she could pass another night safely.

Five you're past the doorway . . .

"Coffee," the girl said again, as if to remind her.

The kitchen was an old-fashioned one, which only made sense, Agnes supposed. The neat gas stove with its quaint cupboard-sized oven bore the name MAGIC CHEF in script-like letters. In the corner stood an icebox, its wooden doors fixed shut with heavy metal clasps. The room stirred a memory of her grandmother's kitchen. But a fine undisturbed ash covered the countertops, the range, the large wooden table flush against the far window, the chairs and the sink. Agnes trailed one finger through the cinders along the counter nearest her. When she looked again at the mark she'd left it was gone. *As if I am the ghost, not her.*

The girl thrust a steaming cup of not-ghostly coffee at her. "Milk? Sugar?"

"Black," said Agnes. She sipped. The coffee tasted eighty years old.

The girl was not drinking any coffee herself. The house was as cold inside as it was outside, but the girl looked flushed. As Agnes watched, little blisters appeared on her upper lip, then the bare skin of her arms, and then, as her lips blackened, she said, "I'm sorry," and fled through the adjoining blue door.

Agnes waited, but the girl did not reappear. She put down the mug of coffee and followed the girl through the door.

Six you're in the hall . . .

Agnes and her brother were not, had never been, close. They did not reminisce fondly about the past. On the rare occasions that they did speak, they talked about nothing: his latest wife, the antics of his spoiled children, which of his hot new clients she might have heard of. (None – he did a lot of work for West Coast hip hop artists, whose names Agnes only recognized through the occasional overheard student conversation.) They never really discussed Agnes' life, and they both preferred it that way; he didn't like to listen and she didn't like to share.

But earlier that evening she'd phoned because she thought she remembered that one of her nieces had a birthday coming up soon. She had a vague, unrequited sense of obligation toward the lot of them, although she had trouble keeping names and numbers straight (having never met them, for one thing). And it turned out she had just missed

Cameron's birthday – a nephew, not a niece – and he was out, anyway, so that left Agnes and her brother exchanging uncomfortable pleasantries.

Her brother was the one who brought it up. "The damndest thing," he said. "One of my client's houses almost burned down the other night, and it got me thinking about that burned house, the one we used to play in. You remember it?"

She remembered it, but they never went inside; she was sure of it.

"No," he said, "no, I did. You weren't there, maybe. I remember I was with some older kids."

She asked what it was like.

He barked out a little laugh. "Scary as hell," he said. "I wonder if kids still play around it. Kids there still play outside anymore? They don't here."

"I can't imagine it's still there any longer," she said, even though she knew better.

"Maybe not." He sounded regretful.

"How's Veronica?" she said. Veronica was his new wife. He told her, but she wasn't listening anymore. He'd unlocked the jump-rope chant in her head, at least a few lines of it, and those lines kept running circles till they ran her right down to the burned house itself.

Seven on the stairway . . .

No one waited in the hallway beyond. No footsteps, no sounds of life at all. For one moment Agnes thought it was snowing inside; then she realized it was fine cinders, swirling and falling all about her. Her footprints vanished as she made them, buried by the ash.

Framed photographs hung along the wall, covered in blackened, melting glass. She wondered then where the light source lay; it could only be glowing embers of the fire itself, but she saw no actual flames. Agnes passed several closed doors on her way to the staircase at the front of the house. She knew that stairs in a derelict house were likely to be dangerous, but she couldn't bring herself to leave after having seen so little. All along the stair runner, a blue carpet woven with gold threads, little burning rings formed and re-formed. She was sorry she hadn't asked the girl her name, so she could call for her.

Top of the stairs, and another corridor. She followed the crackling sound, and the smell of smoke.

Behind her, a child's voice said, "Hello."

The small boy was dressed in blue striped pyjamas.

"Have you come to rescue us?" the boy asked.

Eight you feel the pall . . .

"No," Agnes' mother had said. "No, I don't want you playing around that old place. Wasn't it condemned?" It was not.

"What happened?" Agnes asked her mother. "Do you remember? Who lived there? Did anybody die when it burned?" She was so young that she still believed herself immortal, and thought those capable of dying a different species altogether.

"Oh, it's a terrible story. They couldn't get the children out in time. Some people said it was the mother, that she'd drugged the household so she could run away with a man that night." Her mother paused significantly. "A Negro man," she said. "It happened in the evening, just before nightfall. The husband was out of town on business. Some people said those children weren't even his." Her mother kissed the top of her head. "You shouldn't think about it, Agnes Swithin. It happened a long time ago, before you were born. Even I was just a baby. Who's been filling your head with stories?"

Agnes, wondering who the children could belong to if not their father, said, "No one."

Nine you're walking slowly . . .

Agnes could not say why she felt some time had passed, but she was certain of it. She looked at her watch, the expensive

Garmin she'd bought to train for a 10K before the knee injury, but its face had melted.

"I don't know. Do you need rescuing?"

"My sister says so. Where is she?"

"I don't know," Agnes said. "She asked me and then . . ." She had almost said *she vanished*, but it seemed rude; was it wrong to remind a ghost that it was, in fact, a ghost?

The boy said, matter-of-factly, "No one ever helps us."

Agnes wondered what kind of help she could possibly render. To the south, the corridor was lost in darkness. The burned wing. "What's down there?"

The boy, who had come to stand beside her, replied in the same matter-of-fact voice. "That's where we died."

They walked towards it together. Agnes had begun to shiver with the cold, but as they neared the south wing, although she could still see nothing, she felt the heat of the flames. She hoped the boy would not begin to blacken and char beside her as the girl had done downstairs.

He came to an abrupt stop long before she could see the corridor's end. He said, "You're not a kid." She didn't answer, and he added, "I can't keep going."

But Agnes could. She remembered as she walked that the burned wing was nothing but ash now, and wondered what she must look like to an observer: two stories high and floating on air.

Ten watch where you tread . . .

The child's game said you were "getting warmer" as you approached the source. Agnes never saw the burned south wing until she was in it. One moment the corridor lay dark before her; the next, she stepped into the flames.

Agnes gasped. She walked on flames; they could not touch her but they billowed out before her like a grand cascading carpet. The fire roared in her ears, and beyond that lay only silence. The smoke rose about her but she did not breathe it. She reached out to touch a doorknob licked by fire, and passed her hand through the flames without injury.

The door swung open at her touch. She passed through another doorway, where the room was engulfed, as was the four-poster bed in the centre. As she drew nearer, she saw the boy and his sister there, looking for all the world as though they slept peacefully.

The boy's eyes snapped open. "You're not a kid," he said again. "It's only kids who can come here. Why are you here? Who are you? What's wrong with you?" His face had turned dark, and angry.

Agnes tried to speak, to tell them something, but when she opened her mouth, smoke wafted out instead of words.

Eleven bid goodbye now . . .

Agnes is ten years old. Someone has just told her that after you're dead, your nails and hair keep growing. For some reason, Agnes has understood this to mean that if she removes her nails and hair, she will never, ever die. She trims her nails too close to the quick but cannot yet bring herself to go any further; she has already chopped her hair close against her scalp when her mother comes across her sobbing at her reflection in the bathroom mirror. Later her mother will take her for her first-ever hair appointment at a beauty shop downtown, where a girl will valiantly try and fail to make sense of the butchery Agnes has inflicted upon her own locks.

Agnes is sixty-one years old. Someone has just told her it's always cold where the dead sleep, even the dead who have burned to death. Who would tell her such a thing? Maybe it was a thing she dreamed. In this gloaming, in this dying of the day, the burned house is burning down and the dead are dying all the time. Soon, dying is all the dead know how to do. But this time is different. And time is different here. This time is sirens; someone has seen the flames leaping from the burned house, and called the emergency numbers. But the fire will be fought from the outside. No one will risk themselves racing into the burned house, because they imagine there will be no one inside to save.

Twelve you're here instead . . .

"One thing," said her brother. They had said their goodbyes already. Agnes had one hand on the front doorknob; she was ready to drop the phone on the counter and head out on her run. "One thing," he said again. "Don't go near the burned house. Or the place where it used to be, at least."

Agnes said, "Why on earth would I do that?"

"Just don't."

Thirteen now you're dead . . .

Agnes Swithin dreams in flames. Yellows, oranges blues and reds, blazing, writhing, birthing sparks that flare into new and bigger fires, blackened wood and charred flesh and all transformed, gone to cinder, gone to ash.

She can see shapes of people gathering, lining the sidewalk outside. She will run to them. She is a good runner, and she will join them easily. She leaps to her feet, but something is holding her back. They have her by the arms, the girl and her brother, and when she looks at them their faces are not the smooth unblemished faces of childhood, but burned and ravaged horrors. Surely she can shake them free; she will tear their arms from their sockets if she has to. She staggers forth and she can hear the murmur going up from the crowd. "Someone's in the fire."

She tries to call out to them, to tell them yes, someone *is* in the fire, it's Agnes Swithin, the biology teacher from the high school. They will know her. They will save her. She can even see some of their faces, some she recognizes: students, and parents of students, some of whom she taught as well. And yet the two are still tugging at her, and all of them are weeping. A large burning chunk of the second-story roof plummets before her, throwing up more flames and black, choking smoke and cutting off the rest of the world. The faces, the crowd itself, are lost to her now. Now she clutches the hands that restrain her. They are all she has, and she holds on tight. They whisper as they draw her deeper, telling of a house with a thousand and more rooms, of corridors you could walk forever and a day, telling of things born of fire, born of infernos, born of boredom, born of loss. The house is still burning, they are passing into secret and febrile places, and outside the burned and burning house, the late winter dusk is falling, falling into night.

LAVIE TIDHAR

What Do We Talk About When We Talk About Z—

LAVIE TIDHAR IS the World Fantasy Award-winning author of *Osama* (2011), as well as *The Violent Century* (2013) and *A Man Lies Dreaming* (2014). He also won the 2012 British Fantasy Award for best novella (for "Gorel and the Pot-Bellied God"). He edited the three *Apex Book of World SF* anthologies, and his comics mini-series, *Adler*, is forthcoming from Titan Comics.

"It occurred to me at some point that I wanted to write a zombie story without any zombies," reveals Tidhar. "I've never been sure what they're meant to represent – the breakdown of social order? The evils of consumerism? The end of a relationship? Or maybe they just lurch about for fun. I don't know.

"But I like the idea of Raymond Carver being caught in the middle of a zombie outbreak. I suspect he might have enjoyed himself – more than people in his stories usually do anyway."

"D^{ON'T.}" She turned her head from him and looked away. She looked at the wall. He said, "Lenore . . ."

"And don't call me that no more."

Silence between them. He couldn't break it. She looked at the wall. The white paint was chipping at the bottom. A fly, very slowly, traversed it, like a mountaineer on a sheer wall of ice.

After a while he got up and shuffled to the kitchen. She heard the refrigerator door open and close. She heard the sound of his eating. She looked at the wall.

We were sitting over coffee, watching the crowds. You were having affogato. I was having an Americano. Our choices spoke for themselves. "No point watching your weight any more, is there?" you said. You waved your hand at the hordes outside. "Look at them."

I did. There was nothing else to do but drink coffee and watch them. "Sometimes I think it's the end of the world, or something," you said.

"It *is* the end of the world," I said.

You sighed, and shook your head, and your black hair fell down to your shoulders. "You're so immature," you said.

I could have said a lot of things at that point. I didn't. After a time I put my hand across the table and, after a little while longer, yours met mine and we held hands, briefly.

"I need to pee," you said. "Will you walk me to the bathroom? I'm afraid."

"They don't mean any harm," I said, and you nodded and said, "I know. They're just . . . they're not like us any more. Maybe they never were."

Still, neither of us made to get up. We sat and drank our coffee and watched the crowds outside. After a while you started to hum. I can no longer remember the song. I find it hard to picture your face, I mean, really see it. Only parts – the laughter lines, the way your earlobe curved. The rest of you is gone.

Sometimes I wake up at night and it is dark, and there is no sound outside, and I try to remember the music, but I can't. The notes are all gone.

*　　*　　*

She was going through the kid's things. The kid's room, with its posters on the walls and its small-sized writing desk. Little notes to herself, everywhere. A T-shirt thrown carelessly on the chair with a single giant letter, slashed across the soft material in dark paint: Z.

The room was messy. Weird Japanese cartoon figures on the walls, pale Goth girls in black gazing soulfully from their posters, sci-fi paperbacks with dog-ears and '60s psychedelic art. *You raised a weird kid*, she thought. She felt strangely proud.

Notes the kid left to herself. *Learn to use an Uzi.*

Check expiry date of tinned foods – question mark and a circle outlining it.

How to hot-wire a car – Internet?

Always be alert.

She looked around the room. She sat down on the kid's bed. A photo in a frame, on the desk, the kid and her, smiling for the camera. A note pinned to the frame, too, and she plucked it off and looked at it. In neat but childish handwriting it said, *If Mother becomes one of them, shoot her too. Promise.* A little heart drawn next to it. She put it down again and looked at herself and the kid in the frame, looking happy, even if it was only for that one moment, even if it was only for the camera.

It is raining. It seems to have been raining more and more, and the sky is black with streaks of startling blue. The grave had been dug and the coffin lowered and now it was being covered again, with earth.

"I stopped going to funerals, you know. It felt as if the dead never stayed in the ground, after a while. I'd picture them shambling out in the dead of night, tearing out the coffin, digging their way up to the surface. It used to horrify me, the thought of all that dirt under their nails. They'd follow me home. They'd lay siege to my apartment. I only have a small apartment. Two rooms. I share it with my cat, Mozart. He'd hiss when he'd sense them coming. I guess you could say I'm a hoarder. I keep things. I find it hard to throw anything away. I keep imagining, if it happens, when it happens, I'll be prepared. Don't you get the feeling most people aren't really alive? That inside, deep inside they'd already died, they're just not showing it outwards yet? They walk the streets just like you or I do, they shop, they press the button for the elevator to go up, or down, or to stop. But they're dead.

"I stopped going to funerals. After a while they don't get buried any more, I guess. What's the use? They just shamble around, with dead eyes, and look for food. I never leave my apartment any more. I have everything I need, and Mozart keeps me company. Mainly, I watch. From my window I can see the whole world, at least the only part of it that matters. At night I imagine fires. Everything we have is so perishable. I imagine a big bonfire, a primal bonfire of the sort I imagine Vikings lit up, in the winter, after looting and setting fire to a whole village. I imagine books, postcards, notebooks, tapes, cassettes, chair legs, hair, toenail clippings, newspapers, car wheels, plastic bags, traffic signs, all going, going, going up in smoke and fire and the fire roars, it sings, and I watch it with Mozart by my side, there on the windowsill, and we listen to music. Something soothing, I guess. Classical. Do you think—"

But she only shakes her head, the hint of a smile touching one corner of her mouth, and says, "It's different when there are birds, don't you think? To listen to them, when the sun rises – it reminds you of everything that had gone before."

And he has a mental image when she says that, so strong that it makes him hold on to her; of a small and silent bird, a common sparrow, maybe, or a robin or a finch, and it is still, and cold. It is small enough to fit in his palm, and he holds it, and somehow the feel of it, the stillness of it, fills him with dread. And he leaves his apartment, his cat, his books and records, and he goes down the stairs, counting as he goes, like a child against the dark, one, two, three, four until he reaches the ground. And he walks towards the fire and the cold silent bird is in his hand.

"But you can't kill all the birds," she says, with that hint of a smile, with the confidence of youth. And it makes him wish he could hold her still, could stay, holding on to her, forever. She looks at him, as if puzzled, then pulls gently away. "Will I see you again?" he says.

"I don't know," she says. "It's raining."

A sea of black umbrellas opens, and they walk away from the grave, through the silent tombs, and the rain falls down and turns the ground to mud.

HALLI VILLEGAS

Fishfly Season

HALLI VILLEGAS IS the author of three collections of poetry: *Red Promises*, *In the Silence Absence Makes* and *The Human Cannonball*. Her book of ghost stories, *The Hair Wreath and Other Stories*, was published in 2010 by ChiZine Publications. She was the co-editor of the anthologies *Imaginarium 2012: The Best Canadian Speculative Writing* and *In The Dark: Tales of the Supernatural*.

Her genre work has appeared in anthologies that include *Chilling Tales 2*, *The White Collar Anthology*, *Bad Seed*, *Incubus* and *Girls Who Bite Back*. She has just finished her first novel, which has paranormal investigators, serial killers and mermaids in it.

"This story is a 'love letter' to the town I grew up in," Villegas explains. "A place of façades and falseness that haunts my writing. As a child I had a pathological fear of fishflies, which seem to symbolize everything about my home town – mindless life and death.

"Even though I say I have outgrown my fear of them, I haven't really outgrown my fears of anything."

THE BEDROOM WAS stifling. The ceiling fan's soft sucking sound as it moved through the humid air only intensified her discomfort. Of course he was asleep beside her, not much kept him awake. He hadn't wanted to put the air conditioning on yet, saying it was too expensive, that the nights were still cool enough for sleeping with windows open, that the fan would regulate the temperature. So here she was lying awake in their new home, a perfect centre entrance Georgian, hating him.

They moved in a month ago and Marisol still didn't believe it was real. They had left behind a small bungalow in the city for this gracious home in a beautiful suburb along a lake, twenty minutes away from the city's centre. The place where the rich used to have their summer cottages, where executives from the car companies that drove the city's economy had their mansions on the cul-de-sacs and leafy streets, where the executive's lawyers lived two doors away in mock Tudors and homes with French doors.

It wasn't a new suburb, like those terrible bedroom communities with the tiny yards and every house a replica of the next; this was old money, old Wasp wealth cocooning itself here. Each house different, each lawn perfect, two shopping areas, the Hill and the Village, with coffee shops and dress shops, hardware stores and the Village Market grocery store.

Marisol was drifting now, floating in a sort of heat-induced stupor, watching as the soft black shadows in the corners of the bedroom deepened and shifted, resolving themselves into a woman who walked towards the bed. A wide hairband held her hair back, and she wore a bright pink and green sleeveless shift, a strand of pearls around her neck. She skirted around the end of the bed and glanced once at Marisol whose eyelids were getting heavier, closing almost, and Marisol saw that the woman's blue eyes were nothing but glass beads and that she hated Marisol.

The next morning Marisol woke up to Neil singing in the shower. The white hydrangeas and pink bows on the wallpaper danced in the sunlight, the pale-blue check curtains billowing softly with an early morning breeze. Both had been in the house when they moved in. Marisol had ditched the Guatemalan rugs and mismatching thrift-store finds painted in bright colours that she had decorated their bungalow with and embraced the Sister Parish style of decorating that their new home seemed to expect. The furniture from Neil's parents' estate had helped, their four-poster bed, the sunroom wicker, the chintz-covered sofas all fit perfectly. Like the furniture, Neil belonged here. He had grown up in this suburb, and had always wanted to return.

"Once a Grand Beach man," he had said, "always a Grand Beach man."

Small droplets of water fell on her cheeks. For a moment Marisol wondered if she was crying, but it was Neil, fresh from the shower, shaking his wet blond hair over her like a dog.

She reached out for him but he moved away smiling with his perfect white teeth.

"Get up lazybones, get up. Today we'll run some errands in the Village, and drive by the lake, have lunch in the park. Sound good?"

Marisol smiled and nodded. She got out of bed and walked to the bathroom. On the way there, buried in the soft pile of the rug, something hard bit into the ball of her foot. She bent down and felt for the object. She picked it up holding it on the palm of her hand. It was a small blue glass bead.

The Village was very clean, there was no graffiti, no garbage. Each storefront had period details to make it look like an American colonial town. As Marisol and Neil got out of the car, a chattering group of teen girls, long legs, tan, clean sheets of blonde hair, tiny cut-off shorts and polo shirts, brushed by them. The girls were eating ice cream, their little pink tongues licking and darting, their gleaming teeth nipping at the cones. They stared at Neil for a moment, at his blond handsomeness and then swayed on. Marisol felt very small and dark, a blotch on the bright place they had come to. While she stared after the girls, she felt something land on her arm. She looked down at her arm and saw an insect she had never seen before. It had a mealworm like body, with two beady eyes and transparent wings that stood straight up. Marisol brushed at it with her hand, but it clung to her. She shook her arm, but still the thing hung on, staring at her with its caviar eyes.

"Neil, get this thing off me. It's stuck, it's laying an egg or something." Marisol's voice rose. She never had liked bugs, and though she wanted to be adult about it, this thing unnerved her. "Is it sucking my blood? What the hell is it?"

Neil held her arm still and easily plucked the creature off her by its wings. He tossed it into the air and it fluttered a few feet away and landed on the window of a car.

"Haven't you ever seen a fishfly before Marisol?" Neil asked smiling at her.

"They hatch their eggs on water, so Grand Beach gets a big swarm of them around this time of year. One is nothing. Wait till they all hatch. Some years they are so thick on the ground your car skids, and they cover the windows of the stores until you can't see in."

"Jesus Neil, that's horrible." Marisol rubbed her arm where the fishfly had landed. "'Like some biblical plague.'"

"Actually we're happy to see them that heavy. It means that the lake is healthy." He put his arm around Marisol. "They don't have mouths and they die after one day and one night. They just want to mate, they're not interested in you." He hugged Marisol to him. "Let's go get that drill so I can put up your bookshelves. I'll protect you from the vicious fishflies."

The hardware store had a sickening rubbery smell, oily. But it was very light and open, the front filled with displays of garden ornaments, backyard barbecues, nylon flags with watermelons or baskets of flowers embroidered on them. There were aisles of cooking ware, glasses, ice-tea jugs. It was only at the far back of the store that it started to look like a real hardware store, with displays of tools, coils of garden hose, and boxes of nails and screws.

"Neil, oh my god, how have you been?"

A tall woman with a shiny brown bob and big dark doe eyes was hugging him. Marisol saw her thin arms with long muscles and freckles on the tan skin, and took in her brightly painted toenails in bright-green thong sandals.

"Bunny! It is so fucking great to see you." Neil gave the woman a shoulder shake, "I've moved back into town." Neil stepped away from the woman and pulled Marisol next to him. "This is my wife Marisol."

Bunny looked at Marisol, "Marisol, that's so unusual. Such an exotic name. Where are you from?"

Marisol looked at the silver Tiffany bean necklace glistening on Bunny's collarbone.

"Houston."

Bunny smiled. "Houston. So hot there. But I meant originally, what's your background?"

"My father's Mexican."

Bunny turned to Neil, "Oh my god Neil, you have got to come over for G&Ts sometime soon. Chip is going to flip out that you are here. Do you still talk to any of the Rustic Cabin's gang? Remember that night after your swim meet at Windmill Point?" Neil began to talk, Bunny shifted her weight to one hip and Marisol knew they were going to have a long conversation. She slipped away down the back aisles of the store, looking for the electric drill that had been the original purpose of their trip.

The back aisles of the store with the tools and other bits of hardware were much quieter then the front where people milled about picking up lawn chairs and planters. Here the air was dusty, filled with the smell of sawdust and that silver-black scent Marisol had first noticed when she came in the store. It was heavier here, and she didn't think she could last very long. It was giving her a terrible headache. She trolled up and down the unmarked aisles looking for the drills. There didn't seem to be any sales people in this part of the store, perhaps they were all off helping other customers who were in desperate need of a cement garden goose. On the back wall of the store she found the drills, they were on shelves next to a hanging display of hammers. A heavyset man in madras shorts and a pink polo was standing staring at the hammers. He had the reddened wind-burned complexion of a sailor, his greying hair flopped over one eye but was cut short over the ears, much like Neil's own haircut, what Marisol thought of as standard Wasp man hair.

He didn't look at Marisol who was gazing at the drills in an agony of indecision. For some reason drills always upset her, she imagined them breaking through the soft bone at your temple, or through the eye, the way they used to give lobotomies.

Marisol glanced at the man, secretly hoping he might give her advice. Didn't men like to give advice about the best tools and such, because Marisol thought all the electric drills looked alike.

"Hammer will do the job," Marisol heard the man say. She thought he was talking to her but he was still facing the display of hammers, "Hammer will get it done."

The man reached up and pulled down a hammer with a silver head and a shiny wooden handle. He swung it once as if testing its heft. Marisol flinched despite herself. The man still seemed oblivious to her presence. Then the man turned and looked directly at her. His eyes were blue, glassy as if he were drunk. The corneas were almost perfect circles, *like beads*. The woman from her dream walked through her mind again, staring at her with hatred.

"Hammer will get it done," he said again, slightly slurring his words. He *was* drunk. The man swung the hammer upwards and Marisol cowered, she saw now that the silver head was covered in blood, that the blood was running down the man's tanned forearm, covering the little golden hairs there in a thick wash of gore. His eyes were beads and one fell out at her feet rolling away down the empty aisle of the store and there was nothing behind it but a black hole. Marisol screamed bringing her hands up to cover her face, to protect herself from his blow.

Neil was beside her, "Honey what is it, what's wrong?" Behind him Marisol saw Bunny looking curiously at her.

There were other people there too, a man in a vest that said VILLAGE HARDWARE hurried over. "Is everything all right?"

"A man, swung a hammer at me."

"A man?" The Village Hardware employee glanced around, so did Neil. The others began to talk among themselves and glance down nearby aisles.

"He was drunk, I could see it in his eyes," Marisol said.

Bunny laughed lightly, "A drunken maniac in Grand Beach, how exciting." Marisol looked at the small crowd. Of course the man was gone. Marisol hadn't expected otherwise. Of course now they would think she was crazy. Bunny smiled, and for the first time Marisol noticed what small teeth she had, like a little rodent's, white bits of porcelain filling her mouth.

Bunny put her hand on Neil's arm and said "You must come for drinks some evening, we'll put some steaks on. Call me?" Neil nodded still looking at Marisol with concern. "Goodbye Marisol," Bunny said smiling at her again with absolutely no feeling behind it, "it was great to meet you."

Marisol felt calm but she was tired. She begged off the park for the day, telling Neil "I didn't sleep well last night with the heat. I probably had some sort of narcoleptic episode just now." She laughed and Neil did too.

He dropped her back at home, and went to work with his friend on his boat, helping to ready it to put in the water in a week or two.

"Then we can go for a sail on the lake."

"That would be nice," Marisol said kissing him, "have fun." But she thought again about the fishflies and wondered if they would be even worse on the lake.

She lay in the room with the white hydrangeas and the pink bows, the ceiling fan revolving above her, now sounding to Marisol like the rush of blood through her body that she heard when she pressed her ear to her pillow. She fell asleep and twitched in her sleep like a dog chasing a dream rabbit.

The nights had not gotten any easier. Neil was still against air conditioning, told her to take a cold shower before bed and she would feel cool enough under the ceiling fan's breeze. We are by the lake, he said, it cools down at night. Marisol knew he was echoing the words of his parents, who were echoing the words of their parents in a long lineage of cottages and camping, grand houses run with small economies to hide the old gold groaning behind every warped floorboard and tartan-covered sofa. She had taken to walking the neighbourhood in the heavy evenings, hoping to tire herself out enough so that she could sleep. A good night's sleep was all she needed.

No one in Grand Beach seemed to use curtains on their first-floor windows, so the front rooms were open to anyone who walked by, like dioramas. Night after night as Marisol walked the sidewalks of Grand Beach she looked in the windows. The living rooms and dining rooms painted in the Grand Guignol red they seemed to favour here, the shining brass chandeliers, the baby grand pianos with the silver-plated picture frames ranged across the top, the Ethan Allen dining-room chairs waiting around a table.

Tonight it was particularly still. No dog walkers, no teenagers whispering past on their way to parties in parks and on docks at the lake's edge. Moist air made her scalp itch and feel as if there was a thin layer of cream between her shirt and her back.

Marisol walked and peered in the windows, gazing from the sidewalk into all these other lives and wondering what they were like, how easily did they fit into their skins? Tonight there was a party. The biggest house on their street was lit up.

In the dining room Marisol could see people milling around the table, plates in their hands, eating canapés, holding drinks. In the living room, a man sat at the piano playing. The faint sounds of the Beach Boys' "Help Me Rhonda" drifted out to where she stood. She had to see in, she crept closer to the house.

Yew bushes flanked the front under each of the bay windows. Marisol squeezed in between the bush and the brick wall. She felt the silken brush of a cobweb, but it didn't deter her. Looking just over the window ledge she could see right into the dining room. The crackers and cheeses, the fruit, the half-collapsed cake, *birthday*, *anniversary?* On the sideboard bottles of wine, the inevitable gin and tonic, Pimms. There were fewer people in the room than earlier, they had drifted into the living room to hear the piano. Now Marisol could hear them singing along to "Rock Lobster".

There were two women and a man left in the red dining room. The women – slender, wearing black shift dresses, and low black sling-back pumps. Pearls against the bronze of their backs where the dresses dipped low. One blonde, the other brunette. The man was blond, in khakis and a blue sports coat, his white shirt opened at the neck. He looked like an ad for J.Crew. His feet were sockless in deck shoes. The group was half-turned towards the window and Marisol watched them talk and eat. Their mouths barely moving as they did so, the women throwing back their heads in laughter, and the man twisting his gin and tonic in his hand this way and that. They picked more food from the table, and began to talk more animatedly.

Now their jaws seemed to be swinging loose, unhinging a little and then with a short shake they would clack them back shut. The canapés looked, on closer inspection as Marisol pressed right up against the window, like bits of uncooked meat. The juice dribbled down their chins and they ignored it, smiling and clacking their jaws back into place with each bite. They put their plates down on the table and moved to the living room.

Marisol ran across the front steps in a crouch and squatted down again behind the bushes under the living-room window this time. Motown was playing, and the trio had positioned themselves on a sofa facing the piano. There was no blood on their chins now, and the strange shake of their heads to fix their dangling jaws had stopped. One of the women looked familiar to Marisol but the woman kept looking away, frustrating Marisol with her inability to place her. *What am I doing spying here? Maybe I am asleep.* But the cold of the bricks against her chest and the sharp cat-piss scent of the Yew hedge told her otherwise.

When the room erupted in laughter and clapping, the woman stood up and went over to the man playing the piano and hugged him. Marisol knew now. It was Bunny.

Bunny glanced up for a moment and seemed to look out into the dark and see Marisol there, but her eyes were empty, reflecting back the light in the living room as if they were windows themselves. The man that had been with Bunny in the dining room joined her at the piano, shaking the player's hand and Marisol saw with a sinking feeling that it was Neil. *When did Neil go out?* He had still been sleeping when she left the bedroom. But maybe it wasn't Neil, they all looked alike here, cut from the same cloth.

Still Marisol wanted to go back home and reassure herself that Neil was asleep in their bed, snoring softly in his old crew T-shirt and boxers, the way she had left him. She crawled from behind the bushes and, still staying low, ran to the sidewalk. Then she hurried down the street, away from the house.

Marisol decided to go around a block and head up the parallel street to her road. She didn't want to run into Bunny, although that was unlikely. How would she explain being out alone this late? And what if that *had* been Neil? She wasn't sure she wanted to confront him right now, at night, as if she had been following him like some crazy woman.

The houses on the street that ran right behind her street were slightly larger with wider yards. Each one stood like a bastion of respectability. Their screened-in porches, well-tended lawns, fresh awnings and paint unimpeachable. There was something dark at the foot of a driveway that belonged to a white Dutch colonial house with green striped awnings and a wide porch with geraniums and wicker. *A child's bike?*

But the shape was soft, the shape of the shadows that Marisol had peered into night after night in the corner of her bedroom. She walked slowly, but knew she could not ignore it, could not run away. It would only be waiting in front of another house on another street.

It was a woman in a white eyelet dress that was hitched up past her thighs. Her blonde hair was spread around her like a halo and one of her arms was flung over her head as if she were waving. Her eye socket was crushed in, her mouth hanging open as if in dumb wonder at her own death. Marisol saw that the shoulder of the white dress was stiff with the clotted dark brown of the blood and liquid that had spilled from her eye. The cheekbone caved in, one white tooth glistened on her lower lip where it had been knocked from her head. Scattered around her were blue beads that shone in the light from a street lamp, one of the tasteful swan-necked ones that lined Grand Beach's wide and pleasant streets.

Marisol scooped some of the beads up and put them in her pocket. They made a pleasant glassy sound as they knocked against each other, a rhythm of sorts.

Closer to her house she began to see masses of winged creatures swirling around the street lamps. They flew at the lights in frantic motion, there were so many that it looked as if a black cloud was hanging below each lamp. Marisol felt them tickle along her arm, and then on her neck as they landed on her clothes and tangled in her hair. She pulled at them but they stuck, their long tails quivering with the effort to cling. She brushed at them fiercely, but still they came, on an erratic blind path towards something only they could sense.

It was fishfly season and they were swarming.

Marisol pulled fly after fly off her. She knew they had no mouths but it seemed each one snipped a snippet of her flesh as they fell. She began to run, to try to outpace them, but they flew on in mindless waves. On the lake their egg sacs burst open again and again and they rose in clouds looking for others of their kind to mate and die with.

The porch light of her house was on and they were dense under it. She would have to go through them to get in her door. So she covered her head with her arms and ran up the steps, frantically pulling open the screen where they clung and throwing open the heavy front door, slamming it behind her before they could get in.

She stood in the front hall under the blazing copper light fixture there and pulled off those that still stuck to her clothes and skin. They fluttered around, finally landing on the light. *I'll brush them off in the morning. In the morning when they have all died.* Marisol left the light on in the front hall, so they would not follow her upstairs. She didn't want to feel their bodies brushing up against her in the smothering night.

In the bedroom the fan still moved through the air making no difference, the way she supposed Neil's love would make no difference in the long run.

He was there, asleep, his mouth open wide, his arms and legs sprawled across the bed, into the space she slept, as if she had never existed.

Marisol went into the bathroom and switched on the light. She took one of the blue beads from her pocket and held it up to her eye. It was cool and smooth in her hand, and everything was faint beyond it. She held it closer to her eye, so that she could no longer see her own brown iris in the mirror.

Gently she rested it against her eyelids, just to see. She pushed a little harder.

Just to see, she told herself, *just to see.*

TANITH LEE

Doll Re Mi

TANITH LEE WAS born in London, England, and is married to the writer/artist John Kaiine. In 1975 DAW Books of America, publishing several of her early SF/fantasy novels, liberated her into becoming a professional writer. To date she has written around ninety novels and collections, over 320 short stories, four radio plays and two television scripts (both for the BBC).

Her most recent book releases are *Space is Just a Starry Night*, a SF collection from Aqueduct Press, and *Cruel Pink* and *Turquoiselle*, two dark, speculative novels in the Colouring Books series from Immanion Press. Forthcoming from Immanion is *Ghosteria*, a collection of the author's ghost stories, including several new tales and a recent short novel, not previously published.

"A conversation with an editor friend triggered for me this idea – of a 'doll' that is also Something Else," she explains. "And, too, I hate wanton cruelty, not only to live things (humans, animals), but also to so-called inanimate objects.

"I've always been haunted by a (rather good) movie, seen early in life, where a piano was smashed up for 'fun' and thrown into the sea. I can still hear its death cry."

Folscyvio saw the Thing in a small cramped shop off the Via Silvia. In fact, he almost passed it by.

He had just come from the *Laguna*, climbed the forty mildewy, green-velveted steps to the Ponte Louro and so crossed over to the elevated arcades of the Nuova. Then he glanced down, and spotted Giavetti, who owed him money, creeping by below through the ancient alleys. Having called and not been heard – or been ignored – Folscyvio descended quickly. But on entering the alley he saw Giavetti was gone (or had hidden). Irritated, Folscyvio walked the alley, clicking his teeth together. And something with a rich wild colour slid by his right eye.

At first his attention was not captured. But then, having walked a few more steps, Folscyvio's mind, as he would have put it, tapped him on the shoulder: *Look back, Maestro*! And there behind the flawed and watery window-glass, hung about by old, plum-coloured bannerets and thick cobwebs, was the peculiar Thing. He stood and stared at it for quite five minutes before going into the shop.

He was, Folscyvio, of medium height, but seemed taller due to his extreme leanness. His was a handsome face, aquiline, and reminiscent, as was more genuinely much of the city, of The Past. His hair was very long, very dark and thick and heavily if naturally curled. His eyes, long-lashed and bright, were narrow and of an alluring, or curious – or *repellent* – greyish-mauve.

No one was immediately attendant in the shop. Folscyvio poised for some while inside the open window-space, staring at the Thing. In the end he stepped near and examined a paper that had been pinned directly beneath.

Not many words were on the paper, these written old-fashionedly by hand, and in black ink: *Vio-Sera. A vio-sirenalino. From the Century 17. A rare example. Attributable, perhaps, to the Messers Stradivari.*

Folscyvio scowled. He did not for an instant credit this. Yet the Thing did indeed seem antique. Certainly, it was a *sort* of violin. But – but . . .

The form was that of a woman, from the crown of the head to her hips, the area just between the navel and the feminine pudenda. After which, rather than legs, she possessed the tail of a fish. She was made of glowing auburn wood – he was unsure of its type. All told, the figure, including the tail, was not much more than half a metre in length.

It had a face, quite beautiful in a stark and static kind of way, and huge eyes, each of which had been set with white enamel, and then, at the iris with a definitely fake emerald, having a black enamel pupil. Its mouth was also enamelled, pomegranate red. The image had breasts too, full and proud of themselves, with small strawberry enamel nipples. In the layers of the carved tail had been placed tiny discs of greenish, semi-opaque crystal. Some were missing, inevitably. Even if not a product of the Stradivari, nor quite so mature as the 1600s, this piece had been around for some time.

The two oddest features were firstly, of course, the strings that ran from the finger board of the Piscean tail, across the gilded bridge to the string-clasper, which lay behind a gilded shell at the doll's throat; while the nut and tuning pegs made up part of the tail's finishing fan. Secondly, what was odd was the *hair*, this not carved nor enamelled, but a fluid lank heavy mass, like dead brown silk, that flowed from the wooden scalp and meandered down, ending level, since the doll was currently upright, where, had the tail constituted legs, its knees might have been.

A grotesque and rather awful object. A fright, and a sham too, as it must be incapable of making music. For the third freakish aspect was, obviously, at the moment the doll *was* upright. But when the instrument – if such were even possible – was *played* what then? Aside from the impediment of its slightness yet encumberedness, the welter of hair – perhaps once that of a living woman, now a hundred years at least dead? – would slide, when the doll was upside down, into everything, tangling with the strings and their tuning, the player's hands and fingers – his *throat* even, the bow itself.

Thinking this, Folscyvio abruptly noted there were also omissions from the creature, for she, this unplayable mermaid-violin, this circus-puppet, this con-trick, had herself neither arms nor hands. A mythic cripple. Just as he had thought she might render her player. Another man, he thought, would already loathe her, and be on his way out of the shop.

But it went without saying Folscyvio was of a different sort. Folscyvio was unique.

Just then, a thin stooped fellow came crouching out of some lair at the back of the premises.

"Ah, Signore. How may I help you?"

"That Thing," said Folscyvio, in a flat and slightly sneering tone.

"Thing . . . Ah. The *vio-sera*, Signore?"

"*That*." Folscyvio paused, frowning, yet fastidiously amused. "It's a joke, yes?"

"No, Signore."

"*No*? What else can it be but a joke? Ugly. Malformed. And such a claim! My God. The *Stradivari*. How is it ever to be played?"

The stooped man, who had seemed very old and perhaps was not, necessarily, gazed gently at this handsome un-customer. "At dusk, Signore."

Even Folscyvio was arrested.

"*What*? At dusk – what do you mean?"

"As the fanciful abbreviation has it – *vio-sera* – a violin for evening, to be played when shadows fall. The Silver Hour between the reality of day and the mysterious mask of night. The hour when ghosts are seen."

Folscyvio laughed harshly, mockingly, but his brain was already working the idea over. A concert, one of so many he had given, displaying his genius before the multitude of adoring fanatics – sunset, dusk – the tension honeyed and palpable – *chewable* as rose-petal lakoum . . .

"Oh, then," he said. Generously contemptuous: "Very well. We'll let that go. But surely, whoever botched this rubbish up, it was never the Famiglia Stradivarius."

"I don't know, Signore. The legend has it, it was a son of that family."

"Insanity."

"She was, allegedly, one of three such models, our *vio-sirenalino*. But there is no proof of this, or the maker, you will understand, Signore. Save for one or two secret marks still visible about her, which I might show you. They are in any case, Masonic. You might not recognize them."

"Oh, you think not?"

"Then, perhaps you might."

"Why anyway," said Folscyvio, "would you think me at all seriously interested?"

The stooped old-young man waited mildly. He had whitish, longish hair. His eyes were dark and unreadable.

"Well," said Folscyvio, grinning, "just to entertain me, tell me what price you ask for the Thing? If you do ask one. A curiosity, not an instrument – perhaps it's only some adornment of your shop." And for the very first he glanced about. Something rather bizarre, then. Dusty cobwebs or lack of light seemed to close off much of the emporium from his gaze. He could not be certain of what he now squinted at (with his gelid, grey-mauve eyes). Was it a collection of mere oddities – or of other instruments? Over there, for example, a piano . . . or was it a street-organ? Or *there*, a peculiar vari-coloured railing – or a line of flutes . . .

Folscyvio took half a step forward to investigate. Then stopped. Did this white-haired imbecile know who the caller was? Very likely. Folscyvio was not unfamous, nor his face unknown. A redoubtable musician, a talent far beyond the usual. *Fireworks and falling stars*, as a prestigious publication had, not ten weeks before, described his performance both in concert halls and via *Teleterra*.

Suddenly Folscyvio could not recall what he had said last to the old-young mental deficient. Had he asked a price?

Or – what *was* it?

When confused or thrown out of his depth, Folscyvio could become unreasonable, unpleasant. Several persons had found this out, over the past eighteen years. His prowess as a virtuoso was such that, generally, excuses were made for him and police bribed, or else clever and well-paid lawyers would subtly "usher" things away.

He stared at the ridiculous auburn wood and green glass of the fish-tail, at the pegs of brass and ivory adhering to the glaucous tail-fan.

He said, with a slow, and velvety emphasis, "I'm not saying I want to buy this piece of crap off you. But I'd better warn you, if I *did* want it, I'd get it. And for a – shall I say – very *reasonable* price. Sometimes people even *give* me things, as a present. You see? A diamond the size of my thumb nail – quite recently, that. Or some genuine gold Roman coins, circa Tiberio. Just *given*, as I said. A *gift*. I have to add, my dear old gentleman, that when people upset me, I myself know certain ... *other* people, who really dislike the notion that I'm unhappy. They then, I'm afraid, do these unfortunate things – a broken window – oh, steel-glass doesn't stop them – a little fire somewhere. The occasional, *very* occasional, broken ... bone. Just from care of me, you'll understand. Such kind sympathy. *Do you know who I am?*"

The slightest pause.

"No, Signore."

"Folscyvio."

"Yes, Signore?"

"*Yes.*" Oh, the old dolt was acting, effecting ignorance. Or maybe he was blind and half-deaf as well as stooped. "So. How fucking much?"

"For the *vio-sirenalino*?"

"For what fucking else, in this hell-hall of junk?"

Folscyvio was shouting now. It surprised him slightly. Why did he care? Some itch to try, and to conquer, this stupid toy eyesore. Besides, he could afford millions of libra-eura. (Folscyvio did not know he was a miser of sorts; he did not know he was potentially criminally violent, an abusive and trustless, perhaps an evil man. Talent he had, great talent, but it was the flare and flame of a cunning stage magician. He could play instruments both stringed and keyed, with incredible virtuosity – but also utter emotional dryness. His greatest performances lacked all soul – they were fire and lightning, glamour and glitter, sound and fury. Signifying nothing? No, Folscyvio did not know any of *that* either. Or . . . he thought he did not, for from where, otherwise, the groundless meanness, the lashing out, the rage?)

Unusually, the stooping man did not seem unduly alarmed. "Since the need is so urgent," he said, "naturally, the *vio-sera* is yours. At least," a gentle hesitation, "for now."

"Forget 'for now'," shouted Folscyvio. "You won't get the Thing back. How much?"

"Uno lib'euro."

Everything settled to a titanic silence.

In the silence Folscyvio took the single and insignificant note from his wallet, and let it flutter down, like a pink-green leaf, into the dust of the floor.

The enormous lamp-blazing stadium, fretted by goldleafery and marble pillars, with a roof seemingly hundreds of metres high, and rock-caved with acoustic-enhancing spoons and ridges, roared and rang like a golden bell.

It had been a vast success, the concert. But they always were. The cheapest ticket would have cost two thousand. Probably half a million people, crushed luxuriously onto their velvet perches like bejewelled starlings, during the performance rapt or sometimes crying out in near orgasmic joy, were now exploding in a final release that had less to do with music than . . . frankly, *with* release. One could not sit for three hours in such a temple and before such a god as Folscyvio, and not require, ultimately, some personal eruption.

They were of all ages. The young mingled freely with those of middle years, and those who were quite old. All, of course, were rich, or incredibly rich. One did not afford a Folscyviana unless one was. Otherwise, there were the disks, sound only as a rule, each of which would play for three hours, disgorging the genius pyrotechnics of Folscyvio's hands, all those singing and swirling strings of notes, pearl drops of piano keys.

Sometimes, even included on a disk, since a feature, often, of the show, the closing auction, and the sacrifice. The notes of *that* (though they were *not* notes), faultlessly reproduced: the stream-like ripple, the flicker of a holy awakening, the *other* music, and then the *other* roar, the dissimilar applause, very unlike, if analysed, the bravos and excelsiors that were rendered earlier.

Oddly though, these perfect disk recordings did not ever, completely (for anyone), capture the thrill of being present, of *watching* Folscyvio, as he played. Even the very rare, and authorised, visuals did not. If anything, such records seemed rather . . . flat. Rather . . . soulless. Indeed, only the bargaining and sacrifice that occasionally concluded the proceedings truly came across as fully exciting. Strange. Other artists were capturable. Why not the magnificent Folscyvio? But naturally, his powers were elusive, unique. There was none like him.

For those in the stadium, they were not considering disks, or anything at all. They knew, as the concert was over, there was every likelihood of that *second* show.

Look, see now, Folscyvio was raising his hand to hush them. And in his arm still he held the little *vioncello*, the very last instrument he had performed upon tonight.

Colossal quiet fell like a curtain.

Beyond the golden stadium and its environs, hidden by its windowlessness, the edges of the metropolis lay, and the *Laguna* staring silver at the moonlit sea. But in here, another world. Religious, yet sadistic. Sacred, yet – as some critic had coined it – savage as the most ancient rites of pre-history.

Then the words, so well known. Folscyvio: "Shall we have the auction, my friends?"

And a roiling cheer, unmatched to any noise before, shot high into the acoustic caves.

The *Bidding For* began at two thousand – the cheapest seat-price. The *Bidding Against* sprang immediately to four thousand. After this, the bids flew swift and fierce, carried by the tiny microphones that attended each plushy perch.

For almost half an hour the factions warred. The *Yes* vote rose to a million scuta-euri. The *No* vote flagged. And then the *Maestro* stilled them all again. He told them, with what the journals would describe as his "wicked lilt" of a smile, that after all, he had decided perhaps it should not be tonight. No, no, my friends, my children (as the vociferous and more affluent *Yeses* trumpeted disappointment) not *this* time, not *now*. This time – is out of joint. Perhaps, *next* time. This night we will have a stay of execution.

And then, in a further tempest of frustrated disagreement and adoring hosannas, Folscyvio, still carrying the *vioncello*, left the stage.

"But what are you doing *there*, Folscy-*mio*?"

Uccello the agent's voice was laden with only the softest reproach. He knew well to be careful of his prime client; so many of Folscyvio's best agents had been fired, and one or two, one heard, received coincidental injuries.

Yet Folscyvio seemed in a calm and good-humoured mood.

"I came to the coast, dear Ucci, to learn to play."

"To . . . to *learn*? *You*? The *Maestro* . . . but you know everything there is to—"

"Yes, *yes*." One found Folscyvio could become impatient with compliments, too. One must be careful even there. "I mean the new Thing."

"Ah," said Uccello, racking his brains. Which new thing? Was it a piano? No – some sort of violin, was it not? "The . . . mermaid," he said cautiously.

"Well done, Ucci. Just so. The ugly nasty wrongly sized little upside-down mermaid doll. She is quite difficult, but I find ways to handle her."

Uccello beamed through the communicating connection. Folscyvio, he knew, found ways often to cope with females. (Uccello could not help a fleeting sidelong memory of buying off two young women that Folscyvio had "slapped around", in fact rather severely. Not to mention the brunette who

claimed he had raped her, and who meant to sue him, before
– quite astonishingly – she disappeared.)

"Anyway, Ucci, I must go now. *Ciao alia parte.*"

And the connection was no more.

Well, Uccello told himself, pouring another ultra strong
coffee, whatever Folscyvio did with the weird violin, it
would make them all lots of money. Sometimes he wished
Folscyvio did not make so much money. Then it would be
easier to let go of him, to escape from him. Forever.

He had found the way to deal with her infuriating hair. Of
course he could have cut it off or pulled it out. But it was so
indigenous to her flamboyant grotesquery he had decided to
retain it if at all possible. In the end the coping strategy came
clear.

He drew all the hair up to the top of the wooden scalp,
and there secured it firmly with a narrow titanium ring.
This kept every fibre away from his hands, and the bow,
once he had upended her and tossed the full cascade back
over his left shoulder, well out of his way. Soon others, at
his terse instruction, had covered the titanium in thick
fake gold, smooth and non-irritant. Only then did he have
made for her a bow. It was choice. What else, being for his
use.

As for the contact-point, it had been established thus: her
right shoulder rested between his neck and jaw. Now he
could control her, he might begin.

By then she had been carefully checked, the strings found
to be new and suitable and well-tended, resilient. He himself
tuned them. To his momentary interest they had a sheer and
dulcet sound, a little higher than expected, while from the
inner body a feral resonance might be coaxed. She was so
much better than Folscyvio had anticipated.

After all this, he adapted to his normal routine when
breaking in a novel piece.

He rose early and took a swim in the villa pool, break-
fasted on local delicacies, then set to work alone in the quartet of rooms maintained solely for the purpose. Here he

worked until lunch, and after *siesta* resumed working in the evening.

The house lay close to the sea, shut off from the town, an outpost of the city. In the dusk, as in the past, he would have gone down to the shore and taken a second swim in the water, blue as syrup of cobalt. But now he did not. However pleased with, or aggravated by, the mermaid he might have become, at twilight he would always play her. He had not, it seemed, been entirely immune to the magical idea that she was a *vio-sera*, a violin of the Silver Hour.

It was true. She did have a fascination for him. He *had* known this, he thought, from the moment he glimpsed her in the sordid little shop off the Via Silvia. He had become fascinated by instruments before in this manner, as, very occasionally, by girls. It happened less now, but was exciting, both in rediscovery, and its power. For as with all such affairs of his, involving music, or the romantic lusts of the body, he would be the only Master. And at the finish of the flirtation, the destroyer also.

By night, after a light dinner, he slept consistently soundly.

The *Maestro* dreamed.

He was walking on the pale shore beside the sea, the waves black now and edged only by a thin sickle moon. At spaces along the beach, tall, gas-fired cressets burned, ostensibly to mimic Ancient Roma. Folscyvio was indifferently aware that, due to these things, he moved between the four elements: earth and water, fire and air.

Then he grew conscious of a figure loitering at the sea's border, not far from him.

In waking life, Folscyvio would have kept clear of others on a solitary walk – which anyway, despite his wished-for aloneness, always saw, in a spot like this, one of his bodyguards trailing about twenty metres behind him. Now, however, no guard paced in tow. And an immediate interest in the loiterer made Folscyvio alter course. He idled down to the unravelling fringes of the tideless waves, and when the figure turned to him, it was as if this meeting had been planned for weeks.

No greeting, even so, was exchanged.

Aside from which, Folscyvio could not quite make out who – even, really, *what* – the figure was. Not very tall, either bowed or bundled down into a sort of dark-hooded coat, the face hidden, perhaps even by some kind of webby veil. Most preposterously, none of this unnerved Folscyvio. Rather, it seemed all correct, exactly right, like recognizing, say, a building or tract of land never before visited, though often regarded in a book of pictures.

Then the figure spoke. "Giavetti is dead."

"Ah, good. Yes, I was expecting that. Has the debt been recovered?"

"No," said the figure.

It was a gentle, ashy voice. Neither male nor female, just as the form of it seemed quite asexual.

"Well, it hardly matters," said Folscyvio who, in the waking world, would have been extremely put out.

"But the death," said the figure, "all deaths that have been deliberately caused, they do matter."

"Yes, yes, of course," Folscyvio agreed, unconcerned yet amenable to the logic of it.

"Even," said the figure, "the death of *things*."

Folscyvio was intrigued. "Truly? How diverting. Why?"

"All things are constructed," the figure calmly said, and now, just for a second, there showed the most lucent and mellifluous gleam of eyes, "constructed, that is, from the same universal, partly psychic material. A tree, a man, a lion, a wall – we are all the same, in that way."

"I see," said Folscyvio, nodding. They were walking on together, over the shore, the waves melting in about their feet, and every so often a fiery cresset passing, as if it walked in the other direction, casting out splinters of volcanic tangerine glass on the wrinkles of the water.

"You are an animist," said the figure. "You do not understand this in yourself, but you sense a life-force in every instrument on which you set your hands. And being sufficiently clever to recognize the superior life in them, you are jealous, envious and vengeful." There was no disapproval, no anger in the voice, despite what it had said, or now said. "To a human who is *not* a murderer, the destruction of life is crucially terrible, whether the life of a man, a woman, or a beast. To an animist these events are also terrible, but, too, the slaughter of so-called *objects* is equally a horror, an abomination – a tree, a wall – and especially those objects which can speak or sing. And worse still, which have spoken and sung – for the one who kills them. A piano. A violin."

"A violin," repeated Folscyvio, and a warm and stimulating pleasure surged up in him, reminiscent, though physically unlike, the sparkle of erotic arousal. "A *violin*."

Then he noticed they had reached the end of the shoreline. How strange: nothing lay beyond, only the gigantic sky, scattered with stars, and open as the sea had seemed to be moments before. Although the sea, evidently, had been contained by a horizon. As this was not.

Folscyvio worked with the doll-mermaid-violin, mostly sticking to his routine, where departing from it then compensating with a fuller labour in the day or night which followed. (During this time he discovered no secret marks, Masonic or otherwise, on its surface. But of course, the shopkeeper had lied.)

Three, then four months passed. The weather-control that operated along the coast maintained blissful weather, only permitting some rain now, at the evening hour of the *aperitivo*.

He ordered Uccello to cancel a single concert he had been due to give in the city. Uccello was appalled. "Oh never fear, they'll forgive me. Change the venue of my next one, to make room for those worshippers who missed out." Folscyvio knew he *would* be forgiven. He was a genius. One must allow him room to act as he wished. Only those who hated and despised him ever muttered anything to the contrary. And they – and Folscyvio knew this also well – would be careful what they said, and where. It was well known, Folscyvio's fanatics did not take kindly to his defamation.

* * *

Without a doubt, beyond all question, he had mastered her. It was the beginning of the fifth month. He stood in front of a wide mirror (his habitual act prior to a performance) and put himself, in slow motion, through his various flourishes, emotives, intensities, particularly those that were intrinsic to the new and extraordinary instrument. Already he had formulated the plan for her deployment and display before he should – finally, and after prevarication – take hold of her. She was to preside, to start with, at the off-centre front stage. She would then be upright, that was when the *doll* appearance of her would be the most obvious. Her hair would pour from the gold tiara, carefully arranged about and over her breasts, her face smooth and glowing from preparatory days of polishing, her emerald eyes (also polished), shining and her pomegranate lips inviting. She would be standing on her aquatic tail, in which all the missing scales by now were replaced. The fan-tail base of it would balance on a velvet cushion of the darkest green. Magnetic beams would hold her infallibly in position. (The insurance paid for this, not to mention the threats issued, both legal and otherwise, would make certain all was well.)

After posing and scrutinizing all his moves and postures, Folscyvio played to the mirror the selected pieces on the *viosera*, as he proposed to at the forthcoming concert now only two weeks away. Everything went faultlessly, of course.

Sometimes he would be assisted, during a concert, by an accompanying band, comprising percussion, certain stringed instruments, a small horn section, and so on. All these accoutrements were robotic; he never employed human musicians. The *Maestro* himself always checked the ensemble over, tuned and – as a favourable critic had expressed it – "*exalted*" them for a show. However, on this occasion, when he reached the moment that he accessed the *vio-siren-alino* (the "Mermaid", as she had been billed), the exquisite little robot band would fall quite silent. At which, being non-human, no flicker of envy would disturb any morsel of it.

Then, and only then, at a signal from the *Maestro*, ultra protective rays would spin the mermaid violin, whirling her to her true position, upside down.

Folscyvio, amid the crowd's predicted applause and uproar, would lift her free. Like a heroine in some swooning novel of the 19th, 20th, or early 21st century, she would lie back upon his shoulder, her hair drifting in a single silken, burnt-sienna wing down his back (the hair had been refurbished, too). In this fainting and acquiescent subjection of hers he would hold her, and bring the slender bow to bear upon her uptilted, supine body, stroking, spangling, *making love* to her, breasts to tail.

In the wide mirror he could see now, even if he had already known, the eroticism of this act. How gorgeously perverse. How sublime. How *they* would love it. And oh, the music she could make . . .

For her tones *were* beautiful. They were . . . *unique*. And only he, master of his art, had brought her to this. Even that dolt Uccello, hearing a brief example, a shred of Couperin, a skein of Vivaldi, and of Strarobini, played, recorded and audioed through the speaker, had exclaimed, "But, Folscy-*mio*, never did I hear you play anything with quite this . . . *vividity*. What enchantment. Folscyvio, you have found your true voice at last!" And at this, unseen since the viewer was not switched on, the *Maestro* had scornfully smiled.

The concert was quite sold out. Beyond even the capacity of the concert stadium. Herds had paid, therefore, also to *stand* and listen in the gardens outside, where huge screens and *vocaliani* were to be rigged. It was to be a night of nights, the Night of the Mermaid. And after that night? Well.

She was a doll. A toy. An aberration and a game – which he had played and won.

One night for her, then, the best night of her little wooden life. That would be enough. Live her dream. Who should aim at more?

* * *

The venue for the concert was two miles inland of the city and the *Laguna*, up in the hills. This stadium was modern, a curious sounding-board of glazing, its supporting masonry embedded with acoustic speakers. The half-rings of seats hung gazing down to the hollow stage. They would be packed. Every place taken, the billionaire front rows to the craning upper roosts equipped with magnifying glasses. Amid the pines and cypresses outside, the huge screens clustered. Throughout the city too others would be peering at the *Teleterra*, watching, listening. And beyond the *Laguna*, the city, in many other regions all across the teeming and disassembled self-absorption of the planet, they too, whoever was able and had a mind to, they too glued to the relay of this performance.

Unusually the concert was to begin rather early, the nineteenth hour of that light-enduring mechanically-extended summer night. Sunset would commence just before twenty-one. And the dusk, prolonged by aerial gadgets, would last nearly until the twenty-second hour.

Almost everyone had learned about the new and special instrument – though not its nature. A *mermaid*? They could barely wait. Speculation had been rife in the media for weeks.

So they entered the stadium. And when first they saw – *it* – during that vast in-gathering, startled curses and bouts of laughter ran round the hall. What *was* it? Was it hideous or divine, barbaric or obscene? Unplayable, how not? Some joke.

Eventually the illumination sank and the general noise changed to that wild ovation always given the *Maestro* Folscyvio. And out he came, impeccably clad, his lush dark hair and handsome face, his slender, strong hands, looking at least a third of a metre taller than he was due to his lean elegance, and the lifts in his shoes.

Hushing them benignly, he said only this: "Yes. As you *see*. But you must *wait* to *hear*. And now, we begin."

From the nineteenth almost to the twentieth hour, just as, muted and channelled through the venue's glassy top the sun westered, Folscyvio performed at his full pitch of stunningly brilliant (and heartless) mastery.

As ever, the audience were stirred, shaken, opened out like fans – actual fans, not fanatics – gasping, weeping, tranced slaves caught in the blinding *blitzkrieg* of his glare; they slumped or sat rigid until the interval. And after it, fuelled by drink, legal drugs, and chat, they slunk back nearly bonelessly for another heavenly beating.

And Folscyvio played on, assisted by his little robot orchestra. He took to him a piano, a *mandolino*. But all the while, the mermaid doll stood upright on her green cushion, with her green tail, her green eyes, her *smallness* – dumb. Obscure and . . . waiting.

Some twenty minutes before twenty-one, the sunset swelled, then faded. The ghostly dusk ashed down. It was the Silver Hour, when the shadows fall. And tonight, here, it would *last* an hour.

The penultimate acts of the show were done. The orchestra stopped like a clock. Folscyvio put aside the mandolin. Then, stepping forward quite briskly, he gave the signal, and the mermaid was whirled upside down – whereupon he seized her. And as the crowd faintly mooed in suspense he settled her, in a few well-practised moves, her head upon his shoulder, the hair flowing down his back like a wing. He lifted the bow out of its sword-like sheath, which until then had been hidden in a cleverly-spun chiaroscuro.

Silences had occurred in history. The city knew silences. *This* silence however was thicker than amalgamating concrete. In a solid silver block it cased the concert hall.

Folscyvio played to them, within this case, the mermaid violin.

High and burningly sweet, the tone of the strings. Pelt-deep and throbbing with contralto darkness, the tone of the strings. A vibrato like lava under the earth, a supreme updraught like a flying nightingale. A bitter pulsing, amber. A platinum upper register that pierced – a needle – to conjure an inner note, some sound known only at the dawn of time, or at its ending. Consoling sorrow, aching agony of joy.

Never, never had they heard, nor anyone ever conceivably, such music. Even they could not miss it. Even he – even Folscyvio – could not.

He had not mastered the instrument. *It* had mastered *him*. *It* played *him*. And somehow, far within the clotted blindness and deafness of his costive ego – he *knew*. The *Maestro*, mastered.

Perhaps he had dubiously guessed when practising, when planning out this ultimate scene upon his rostrum of pride.

Or perhaps even, at that watershed, he had managed to conceal the facts from himself. For truth did not always set men free. Truth could imprison, too. Truth could kill.

On and on. Passing from one perfect piece to the next, seamless as cloth-of-Paradise, Folscyvio the faultless instrument, and the violin played him. All through that Silver Hour. Until the shadows had closed together and not a mote of light was left, except where he still poised, the violin gleaming in his grip, the bow fluttering and swooping, a bird of prey, a descending angel.

But all-light melted away and all-quiet came back. The recital was over.

How empty, that place. As though the world had sunk below the horizon as already the sun's orb had done.

The artificial lights returned like fireflies.

There he stood, straight and motionless, frowning as if he did not, for a second or so, grasp where he was, let alone where he had been during the previous hour.

But the audience, trained and dutiful, stumbled to its feet. And then, as if recollecting what *must* come next, began to screech and bellow applause, stamping, hurling jewels down on to the stage. (It had happened before. Folscyvio had even, in the past, graciously kept some of them; the more valuable ones.)

After the bliss of the music, this acclaiming sound was quite disgusting. A stampede of trampling, trumpeting things – that had glimpsed the Infinite, and could neither make head nor tail of it, nor see what should be done to honour it.

Seemingly unceasing, this crescendo. Until it wore itself out upon itself. The hands scalded from clapping, the voices cracked with overuse. Back into their seats they crumbled, abruptly old, even the youngest among them. Drained. Mistaken. Baffled.

Inevitably, afterwards, there would be talk of a drug – illegal and pernicious – infiltrated into the stadium, affecting everyone there. But that rumour was for later, blown in like a dead leaf on the dying sigh of a hurricane.

Probably Folscyvio did suspect he was not quite himself. Some minor ailment, perhaps. A virus, flimsy and unimportant. Nevertheless he felt irritated, dissatisfied, although realising he had played superbly. But then, he always did. Nothing had changed.

Now he would swiftly draw this spectacle to a close. And in the favourite way: theirs. *His*.

He said, very coldly (was he aware how cold?), "We will finish."

No one anymore made a noise. Sobered and puzzled, they hung there before him, all their ridiculous tiers of plush seats, like bits of rubbish, he thought, piled up in rows along gilded and curving shelves, in the godforsaken fucking cupboard of this mindless arena.

He must have hesitated a fraction too long.

Then, only then, a scatter of feeble voices called out for the auction.

Folscyvio smiled, "wintry and fastidious" as it was later described by an hysterical critic. "No. We will not bother with the *auction*. Not tonight. Fate is already decided. We will go directly to the sacrifice." For once some of them – a handful among the masses there – set up loud howls for mercy. But he was adamantine, not even looking towards them. When the wailing left off, he said, "She has had her night. That is enough. Who should aim for more?"

And after this, knowing the cue, the stadium operatives crushed the lights down to a repulsive redness. And on to the stage ran the automatic trolley which, when all this had begun those years ago, had been designed for the *Maestro* by his subordinates.

Again, afterwards, so much would be recalled, accurately or incorrectly, of what came next. All was examined minutely.

But it did no good, of course,

They had, the bulk of this audience, witnessed "The Sacrifice" before. The sacrifice, if unfailingly previously coming *after* an auction, when invariably the majority of the crowd bayed for death, and put in bids for it (the cash from which Folscyvio would later accommodate), was well known. It had been detailed endlessly in journals, on electronic sites, in poems, paintings and recreated photo-imagery. Even those who had never attended a Folscyvio concert, let alone a sacrifice, *knew* the method, its execution and inevitable result. The *Maestro* burned his instruments. Sometimes after years of service. Now and then as on this night, following a single performance.

Pianos and *chitarras*, such larger pieces, would tend to sing, to shriek, to call out in apparent voices, and to *drum* like exploding hearts in the torment of the fires. But the *vio-sirenalino* – what sound could she make, that miniature Thing, that doll-mermaid of glass, enamel and burnished wood and hair?

Despite everything, many of them were on the seats' edges to find out.

She leaned now, again upright in the supporting rays of the magnetic beams. When he poured the gasoline, like a rare and treacly wine, in a broad circle all about her, saturating the green cushion, but not splashing her once, a sort of rumbling rose in the auditorium. Then died away.

Folscyvio moved back to a prudent distance. He looked steadily at the mermaid violin, and offered to her a solitary mockery of a salute. And struck the tinder-trigger on the elongated metal match.

Without a doubt there was a flaw in the apparatus. Either that, or some jealous villain had rigged the heavily security-provided podium. Or else – could it be? – too fast somehow for any of them to work out what he did – did *he*, Folscyvio, somehow reverse the action? As if, maybe, perceiving that never in his life after that hour would he play again in that way, like a god, he wished to vacate the stage forever.

The flame burst out like a crimson ribbon from the end of the mechanical match. But the mermaid violin did not catch fire. No, no. It was Folscyvio who did that. Up in a tower of gold and scarlet, blue and black, taller even than he had been – or seemed – when alive, the *Maestro* flared, and was lost at once to view. He gave no sound either, as perhaps the violin would not have done. Was there just no space for him to scream?

Or was it that, being himself very small, and cramped and hollow and empty, there was no proper crying possible to him?

In a litter of streaming and luminous instants he was obliterated, to dust, a shatter of black bones, a column of stinking smoke. And yet – had any been able to see it? – last of all to be incinerated were his eyes. Narrow, long-lashed, grey-mauve, and – for the final and first time in Folscyvio's existence – full of fire.

CLIVE BARKER

A Night's Work

CLIVE BARKER HAS been described as a visionary, fantasist, poet and painter. As a novelist, director, screenwriter and dramatist, he has left his artistic mark on a range of projects that reflect his influence on contemporary media.

He began his career in the London theatre, scripting original plays for his group The Dog Company, including *The History of the Devil*, *Frankenstein in Love* and *Crazyface*. Soon, Barker began publishing his influential *Books of Blood* short fiction collections; but it was his debut novel, *The Damnation Game*, that widened his already growing audience.

He changed course again in 1987 when he directed the movie *Hellraiser*, based on his novella "The Hellbound Heart", which became a cult classic, spawning a slew of sequels, several lines of comic books, and an array of merchandising. In 1990, he adapted and directed *Nightbreed* from his short story "Cabal". Two years later, Barker executive produced *Candyman*, as well as the 1995 sequel, *Candyman 2: Farewell to the Flesh*, both based on his story "The Forbidden". Also that year, he directed Scott Bakula and Famke Janssen in the *noir*-esque supernatural detective tale, *Lord of Illusions*. *Gods and Monsters*, which Barker executive produced in 1998, garnered three Academy Award nominations and an Oscar for Best Adapted Screenplay.

His literary works include such best-selling fantasies as *Weaveworld*, *Imajica*, and *Everville*, the children's novel *The Thief of Always*, *Sacrament*, *Galilee* and *Coldheart Canyon*. The first of his quintet of children's books, *Abarat*, was published in 2002, followed by *Abarat II: Days of Magic, Nights of War* and *Arabat III: Absolute Midnight*. He is currently working on the fourth in the series.

As an artist, his neo-expressionist paintings have been showcased in two large-format books, *Clive Barker: Illustrator Volumes I* and *II*, and in 1999 he joined the ranks of such illustrious authors as Gabriel Garcia Márquez, Annie Dillard and Aldous Huxley when his collection of literary works was inducted into the Perennial line at HarperCollins, who then published *The Essential Clive Barker*, a 700-page anthology with an introduction by Armistead Maupin.

The following piece of flash fiction was originally published in the *Souvenir Book* of the 2013 Bram Stoker Awards Weekend in New Orleans, where he was a recipient of the Horror Writers Association's Lifetime Achievement Award. It is, perhaps, every writer's nightmare . . .

I RETIRED TO BED a little after one, exhausted. Sleep came readily enough, but it wasn't an easy slumber.

Somewhere in the middle of the night I dreamed a story of great elaboration.

It involved, as far as I remember, a race of miniature men, and a pair of escalators which I was pursued up and down, up and down, for reasons I have now forgotten, but which seemed, in the grip of this dream, essential to the plot.

I was highly excited by my story; so much so that in the midst of it I thought to myself: *When I've dreamed it all, I'll wake up and write it down. This is a best-seller; I'll make millions!*

The story came to a wonderful conclusion, satisfying every question it posed. I woke up, and hurriedly started to write. Oh, I could scarcely believe it! Every idea – every image – was crystal clear. And yes, it was just as riveting now as it had been when I dreamed it. My body ached by the time I'd finished, but I was ecstatic.

I turned off the lamp and lay back in bed. But as sleep seemed to come over me again I realized, with a kind of leaden disappointment, that I had not truly woken; merely dreamed that I'd done so.

The story was still unrecorded.

I fumbled to recollect what had seemed so pungent moments before, so inevitable, while telling myself, *Wake! Wake, damn it! Quickly now before you lose it!*

It seemed to work. Again, I took the pen in my hand and scribbled out the dream I'd had. But this time I didn't get through half of it before I realized that it was delusory.

I let the dreamed pen drop, and struggled to catch hold of what was left of the story. Miniature men, yes! Escalators, yes! A woman in a gold dress, perhaps? Or was that something I'd read before I went to bed? And the dog with the blue tail; where did he belong? Had he been an intrinsic part of my immaculate plot, or had he strayed in from somewhere else?

Oh Lord, it was getting muddier by the moment.

I woke again. And again I picked up the pen. This time I was deeply suspicious of my state. With reason. After just a few words I knew I was still dreaming. And now my previous story was little more than a few senseless wisps. I would never catch it now, I knew.

I despaired of it. And once I relinquished all hope of having my vision intact, I was at last awake.

It's pathetic, I know, to be setting down *these* words, as though the tale of how a glorious thing was lost can be the equal of the thing itself.

And as I write – now, this very *word*, this very *syll ab le* – the suspicion rises in me that even this faint echo is insubstantial, and must be given up if I am ever to open my eyes.

ROBERT SHEARMAN

The Sixteenth Step

ROBERT SHEARMAN HAS written four short-story collections, and between them they have won the World Fantasy Award, the Shirley Jackson Award, the Edge Hill Readers' Prize and three British Fantasy Awards.

His background is in the theatre, as resident dramatist at the Northcott Theatre in Exeter, and regular writer for Alan Ayckbourn at the Stephen Joseph Theatre in Scarborough. His plays have won the *Sunday Times* Playwriting Award, the Sophie Winter Memorial Trust Award, and the Guinness Award in association with the Royal National Theatre. He regularly writes plays and short stories for BBC Radio, and he has won two Sony Awards for his interactive radio series, "The Chain Gang". However, he is probably best known for reintroducing the Daleks to the BAFTA-winning first season of the revived *Doctor Who*, in an episode that was a finalist for the Hugo Award.

The author's latest collection, *They Do the Same Things Different There*, is published by ChiZine.

"I love big hotels," says Shearman. "I love the anonymity of them. I love the fact they're clean and tidy and when I arrive – I haven't yet messed them up with all my rubbish. And that I can imagine the politeness of the staff and the way they clean my bath and leave me fresh soap is because they like me and enjoy my being there, right up to checkout when the bill is paid.

"But bed and breakfasts are another matter altogether. You're invading some family's home. Oh, they're polite enough, but it's a cool politeness – they have *lives*, these people, and they inflict them upon you by putting up photographs of their children, they've got all sorts of personal possessions and they've left them blatantly all over the house where you can see. They resent me. I know it. When they make me a fried breakfast in the morning. When they purse their lips as they spoon on my plate a runny egg. So I resent them right back.

"When I worked in the theatre I stayed in a lot of bed and breakfasts. Sometimes I did it for weeks on end. I'd get to my bedroom and I'd lock the door behind me and I'd keep the family out. And if I had to use the bathroom, I'd run across the corridor as fast as I could so no one could catch me.

"This is a story about all those dreadful nights in one particular seaside hotel, where the seagulls kept me awake."

So, was the house haunted? Probably not; but it certainly had some peculiar quirks, and Mrs Gallagher always felt obliged to tell her guests of them. She'd warn those taking the box room that they might be able to hear weird whispering sounds in the night – but there was no doubt it was simply an effect of the wind coming in off the North Bay, sometimes in the winter the wind off the coast could be pretty fierce. There was a spot in the breakfast room, she said, upon which if you stood for too long you'd get a chill right down to your very marrow; I never found that spot, although I looked hard enough, I might have felt a chill in any number of different places but never anything that touched my marrow even closely.

And there was the staircase, and that was harder to explain. There were fifteen steps leading upwards to the first floor, the first nine straight up, the tenth curving around to the left as you ascended. They were covered with a thin shag carpet, and supported by wooden banisters. Fifteen steps in all – but if you went downstairs in the dark, there, at the bottom, you would find a sixteenth.

It only happened in the dark. If you put the lights on to count, there'd always be the fifteen, looking perfectly ordinary. If you took a candle downstairs with you, the sixteenth couldn't be found, and nor on nights when the moonlight was pouring in neither. But if it were pitch-black, if when you looked down you couldn't see your feet or where they might be leading, then that extra step would be waiting for you. And only as you went downwards, never on the way up.

It was a strange thing, but not especially unnerving. Mrs Gallagher only told her guests of it so they wouldn't stumble, not so they should feel spooked or scared. Especially in the holiday season, she said, when the arcades were open late, and the sea was warm enough for night-time paddling, guests might come back once she'd gone to bed, and she didn't want anyone waking her if they tripped. They'd be fine if they went straight to bed themselves, of course; it would be if they came down afterwards for a glass of water, say, that they might run into problems.

You'd get guests trying it out, of course. Especially the young ones, newly-wed husbands trying to show off to their wives, squaddies on leave egging each other on. We could tell the sort. We could tell that, first chance they'd get, they'd brave it for themselves. We were smart. We'd encourage them to get it out of the way on the first night, we'd do it before anyone had gone to bed so it wouldn't disturb. We'd turn out all the lights and pull the curtains and let them have their fun. Down they'd come, counting off the stairs as they did so, maybe laughing a bit, maybe trying to scare each other. They'd reach the sixteenth step, they'd laugh a bit more, they might even kick at it to make sure it was real. We'd give them a minute or two, and then they'd lose interest, and we could turn the lights back on and get on with more important matters. It wasn't as if the extra step *did* anything once you'd found it; it was just a step, after all.

George and I tried it too, the first night we arrived. Mrs Gallagher asked whether she should turn off the lights so we could check for ourselves, and George smiled in that charming way he sometimes had and said he was quite sure he didn't need to put her out. Even I was fooled, I assumed he wasn't interested. But late that night, once he'd had his business with me, and we were lying in the dark, he said that we should go down the stairs and see what this extra step palaver was all about. I couldn't sleep either, the waves were noisy; in years to come I'd realize there was no more reassuring sound in all this world, but I wasn't used to it yet. I was a bit afraid, and I told George so, but he pooh-poohed that; he said it would all be nonsense anyway.

George was in his pyjamas, I was in my nightie, and I remember neither of us wore slippers. He held on to my hand, and told me to count the stairs off with him. I was frightened, yes, but it wasn't a bad frightened, and I told myself it was like all those things at the funfair on the beach, this was the dodgems and the ghost train, all rolled into one. George was even whispering jokes at me, and he had a nice voice when he whispered. We reached the fifteenth step, and George said, "Shall we go on?" And I was going to say no, let's not, let's turn back and go to bed, but he was only teasing, of course we went on; he took another step downwards, and he pulled me after him. We stood on the impossible step. "It has to be a trick," said George, and he sounded a bit angry, the way he did when he thought the foreman was cheating him. My bare feet were cold. The carpet had run out at the fifteenth step – this one beneath seemed to be made of stone – but then, no, not stone, because it wasn't so hard as all that, and it was getting smoother, like it was old mud breaking under our combined weight or even loosening to our body heat, it was getting softer, even liquid now, and I was sinking into it, and yet it was still so very *cold*.

I tried to pull away, but George was still holding me. So I pulled harder, I wrenched myself out of his grip, and that's when I stumbled. I felt myself beginning to fall and I couldn't stop myself, and all I could see was the black and I didn't know how far away the ground might be.

It was just a few feet, of course, and I was more shocked than hurt. And there was suddenly light, and there was the landlady, holding a candle, and leaning over the banister down at us. "Are you all right?" she asked.

"Yes," I said. "Sorry."

"I did warn you. Please go back to bed."

She stayed on the stairs so she could light our way. As we passed her she didn't bother to hide her disapproval. "Sorry," I said again. George didn't say a word.

George was cross with me that night. I told him about the cold step, but he said he'd felt only carpet, just like on all the other steps, and that I was being stupid.

You asked me for the truth. And this is the truth as I understand it.

George was not a good man, but he was not a bad man either, not entirely. Mrs Gallagher would say I was justifying again. She said I did a lot of justifying, and I suppose she was right. But I know what's fair, and I want to be fair to George. I've known some bad men. There's no tenderness to bad men, and George, he could sometimes be tender.

He said what we did wasn't theft. We'd come into town, and would stay at a little hotel, a bed and breakfast maybe, nothing grand. And then when it was time to move on, we'd sneak away without paying. He said that proper theft would have been if we'd taken the silver with us as we went, but we never did that, George had too much pride. But the idea was there in his head, wasn't it? He'd spoken it out loud. With George, I knew, if it was in his head, if that little seed of an idea was planted, it was the beginning of everything.

But for the time being it wasn't theft, not really – and we would come into a town, and George would spend the days out looking for work. He'd go to the factories, he'd go to the warehouses. He said that as soon as he got a job he'd return to the bed and breakfasts, every single one, and he'd pay them back. I'm sure at the start he even meant that.

George would come back to the hotels and tell me there was no work to be found – but he'd heard talk of work a few miles away, the next town along, just over the hill, just across the moors, wherever. And off we'd go chasing it. I hated it when we had to move on, but George always looked so much happier, he'd suddenly beam with hope, and that made up for it. He might carry my bags as we walked; he might even sing.

One day we reached the coast. And there was nowhere further for us to go, not unless we changed direction.

"I could be a fisherman," George said. "I would enjoy catching fish all day long. Good honest work. It's all going to work out. You'll see." As far as I knew, George hadn't been inside a boat his whole life, but it was wiser not to say anything.

There were lots of bed and breakfasts to choose from. It was a holiday town, but off-season, everything was empty. I don't know what brought us to Mrs Gallagher's. Fate, I suppose. Who knows why things happen, they just do.

George rang the doorbell, and doffed his hat, and gave that smile he was good at. I did my best to look like the respectable housewife on holiday that I always wanted to be.

Most landladies would ask for a deposit. We had to hand over the deposit without appearing to mind, as if there were plenty more where that came from. Sometimes it was the hardest bit of acting I had to do. Mrs Gallagher didn't want a deposit.

"No deposit?" said George. "Well, well." And he smiled wider, but he also frowned, as if suspecting he was being conned.

"No deposit," agreed Mrs Gallagher. "All my guests pay when they leave."

She told us about the whispering in the box room, but the hotel was empty, we could pick any room we wanted, and I was glad George allowed us a room that wouldn't scare me. She told us about the strange chill in the breakfast room. She told us about the step you could only find in the dark.

*   *   *

In the morning she served us breakfast. She didn't mention the night's disturbance, and nor did we. She asked us how we wanted our eggs. "Fried, and runny," said George. I told her I'd like mine poached. She gave a curt nod, then went into the kitchen.

She brought us out plates of sausage and bacon and fried bread. I had a poached egg. "Where's my egg?" George demanded to know. Mrs Gallagher said she only had one egg, and apologized.

George glowered. He managed a few bites of sausage, then pushed his plate away. I knew how hungry he must be, but he had such pride. He lit a cigarette, stared at me through an ever thickening cloud of smoke. I pretended not to notice. I wanted to eat as much of my breakfast as I could. I hoped that, if I ate fast enough, he wouldn't say anything until I'd finished.

"You enjoying that?" he said too soon, softly, dangerously softly.

I knew there was no right answer. I looked at him. I tried to keep my expression as neutral as possible.

He took my plate. He held it up, as if to inspect it closely, as if to ensure it was fit enough for his queen. He spat on it. Then he put the plate back down on the table, and ground out his cigarette in the middle of the food, in the middle of the egg.

"I'll be back later," he muttered, got up, and left.

I was still so hungry. But I didn't want to eat from my plate, even though the spit was only my husband's, and I loved my husband. And I didn't want to eat from his, in case he came back.

Mrs Gallagher took away the plates, and if she was surprised they were still heavy with food, she didn't comment.

I stayed the day in the bedroom.

That evening George came back, and he was all smiles. He said maybe he'd found a job after all – a fisherman had said he would take George out on his boat in the morning, try him out for size. He'd brought back a couple of bottles of beer, I don't know where he'd got them, and he let me have a little bit. When that night he did his business, he was kind and quick.

The next morning he left early. I got to eat my breakfast on my own. It was delicious.

That same night George came back to the hotel angry. The fisherman hadn't waited for him. It had all been some bloody big joke. I asked him where he'd been all day, and that was a mistake. Later that night he apologized. He said the fisherman had waited for him, he'd gone out in the boat. But the waters had been very rough, and he hadn't been well. The fisherman found it funny. He supposed it was funny, come to that. I mean, he'd get used to the sea if he had to, but in the meantime, it was funny. Didn't I think it was funny? It was all right, he said, he didn't mind if I did, we could laugh at it together, like we used to laugh at things. I gave him a kiss, and that made him feel better.

He said he'd try his luck again. Maybe another fisherman would take him out. Maybe the first fisherman wouldn't have told all the others. We had breakfast together. Mrs Gallagher asked how we wanted our eggs. He said he wanted his fried, but runny. I said I'd have mine poached. She brought me a plate of sausage, bacon, and a poached egg. She brought George a plate of fried eggs, and nothing but fried eggs, the yolks all broken and pooling thickly into one another. George stared at the plate, and didn't say a word.

Mrs Gallagher asked me my name. I hesitated, and she saw I hesitated — but then I told her my name anyway, the real one, not the one George liked me to use.

"Mine is Nathalie," she said.

"Natalie?"

"Nathalie. It's French." She didn't look very French. Her arms were big and thick, her face rough like sand; in years to come I'd think that sand must have blown off the beach and got stuck deep in her skin and she hadn't been able to scrub it out. Not my idea of French at all; George's mother had shown me some fashion magazine, back in the days we were allowed to visit, and there were French women inside, and Nathalie Gallagher was nothing like them. "You're in trouble," Nathalie Gallagher said.

"No, I'm all right."

"You're in trouble. I could help you. You could stay here with me. I can run this place alone if I have to do, but I could use an extra pair of hands. I couldn't pay much, but you'd get bed and board."

"And George?" I said.

She didn't say anything to that.

"George wouldn't like it," I said. I knew all he wanted to do was get his own job, and be able to look after me.

"I had a disappointing husband too," said Mrs Gallagher. She told me that her husband had brought her back to England after the war. She didn't say which war, and I presumed it was the last one, but it was so hard to tell how old she might be. I didn't like to ask. "He said he had some property, I thought he must be a duke or something. Turned out he owned a hotel. I had to spend my days learning how to make full English breakfasts. Yes, he was a disappointment."

"Where is your husband?" I asked. "Is he dead?" The words seemed so blunt, I could have bitten my tongue.

Mrs Gallagher didn't seem offended though. Indeed, she gave my question some thought. "No, I don't think so," she said at last. "He's probably still alive."

I kept the job offer in my head, turned it over and gave it a good prod whenever things were bad. Things were bad a lot that week. I thought I would tell George when he was in a good mood, maybe he'd see the value in it, even if it were just short-term, even if it could just tide us over a while and give us some sort of *home* – but George was never in a good mood, there was no work out there, and the mood just got worse and worse, so I decided I'd just have to tell him quickly and get it over with and trust to luck.

He didn't shout, that was good. He turned from me, and lit a cigarette, and stared out of the window down upon the cliffs and the sea, as if in deep thought, as if giving it actual consideration.

"It's time we left," he said.

"So soon?"

"There's nothing for us here. We'll go tonight."

We packed our stuff, waited until it was dark. Past midnight I said to George that we should get going, but he shook his head impatiently, it wasn't time yet, he had a feeling for these things. We sat there on the bed, side by side, in silence, and George listened out for noise. At last he took my hand, and squeezed it, and that was the signal, and I think it was done in affection too.

It was pitch black. George carried the bags, he told me to walk ahead of him. I clung on to the banister rail. I counted the steps downwards, one, two, three, four, and at five the staircase curled around towards the final descent to the front door. Now, we both knew about the extra step that was waiting down there, and neither of us mentioned it, and I dare say we'd both factored it into our calculations, sixteen stops until we reached the bottom. But now I was in the dark I thought of it only with dread – and I mean that, a hard, heavy dread – I didn't want my feet to touch that step – I didn't want any part of my body to come into contact with something so cold and so inexplicable – and here I was, inching further towards it, another step down, then another, then another, as if I were falling somehow, as if I were falling and there was no way to climb back up, I couldn't change my mind, I couldn't turn around, my husband was behind me blocking my way and he would never let me free. And another step, and another – and I wondered if I'd miscounted already, were there two steps to go, or three? Three before . . .? I didn't want to reach that step but I didn't want to get past it either – and it sounds silly but it suddenly seemed to me that step was a dividing line between all of my sorry past and all the future before me – and if I got past the step, then that was it, the future waiting there in the darkness was just more of the same, just more of the same. Two steps. One. I *had* miscounted, but there was no delaying it now, that step in front of me had to be the extra one. And then there was light from up above, and the darkness was spoiled, so there was no extra step at all, and the relief I felt was so overwhelming that it took me a moment to realize we must have been discovered.

The candle didn't give much light, but it was enough. Mrs Gallagher stared down at us.

George said, "We're leaving. We don't want any trouble."

Mrs Gallagher said nothing.

George said, "We're not going to give you any trouble. We'll just leave, and be on our way."

Still nothing.

He said, "When I get a job, I'll come back. I'll pay you then. I'm not thieving."

Mrs Gallagher said, "Just go. But don't you ever come back."

"Well then," said George. "Well! Then I won't. You bet I won't." And he actually grinned at her, and doffed his hat.

I wanted to say I was sorry. I couldn't find the words, as easy as they were. I tried to smile at her, something, but she didn't look at me, not the whole while. That's what hurt.

George opened the front door, and we stepped out into the wind, the night, our future together.

I thought maybe he wouldn't come looking, maybe he just wouldn't care, and would let me be. I thought maybe he might even be relieved, one less mouth to feed, I wouldn't slow him down any more. But still I'd keep checking behind me as I walked on, still I'd keep off the main roads, hide sometimes in bushes – because whether he wanted me or not, of course he'd come looking. He had his pride. That's all he had.

I didn't even know which direction I was headed in. And so I shouldn't have been surprised when I reached the coast, but I was. I thought we'd travelled so much further than that, that the coast was weeks behind us. But there it was, the cliffs at my back, the sea in front, and I trudged my way along the beach squashed between the pair of them.

I certainly hadn't expected to find Mrs Gallagher again. If I had looked for her house I'm sure I wouldn't have found it. But I gazed up, and there it was ahead of me, it was the only place in miles that seem to give off any light, maybe I fancied the only place in the world.

I knocked at the door.

"I'm sorry," I said. "I'm sorry, I'm sorry."

"You're in trouble," said Mrs Gallagher. And at last I understood what she meant. Because I was in trouble, and I hadn't quite dared believe it until then – but of course I've known, that's why I'd run away, wasn't it? Because it was all right, my being trapped with George for the rest of my life. Maybe that's all I deserved. But not my child. Not my child. Never.

"You'd better come in," Mrs Gallagher said.

I arrived just before the holiday season, and there was a lot to learn.

I learned how to make beds, not in the ordinary way, but in the hotel way.

I learned how to clean a room quickly, so that you could give the impression everything was spick-and-span on the surface, and not draw attention to the real dirt underneath.

I learned how to make a proper cooked English breakfast. I got quite good at them, but Mrs Gallagher was always better, so she stayed in charge of the kitchen. "My husband taught me, said he cooked the best fry-ups in Yorkshire," she said. "His only promise that was worth a damn."

I was given a room on the ground floor, and at first I was happy about that, it meant I didn't have to use the staircase at night. But I was never very comfortable there. The little window looked out on to the street, you could hardly tell we were by the sea at all. And sometimes in the night, I could hear noises under the floorboards – like distant footsteps, shuffling about beneath the ground. I told Mrs Gallagher about them, but she just shrugged, said she'd never heard of that before. But she moved me upstairs to the box room. There was that whispering sound in the box room, but it was just the wind and the ocean spray, and I liked it, and soon I found the strange echo it made in the darkness very comforting, like the elements were trying to send me to sleep.

When the hotel packed out, and it did most of July and August, even the box room had to be let. Then I would share a bed with Mrs Gallagher. It was a large bed, and quite comfortable, and there was plenty of room – and I was a little afraid at first that a big woman like Mrs Gallagher would snore, George snored something chronic and he wasn't half her size. But she slept so still, sometimes it was though she was hardly beside me at all.

I want you to know nothing untoward ever happened between me and Mrs Gallagher. And when August was over, somehow I just didn't move out from the room, and I just stayed with her. It meant there was one less bed to make.

And when the pregnancy was full on and I couldn't do much work, Mrs Gallagher never minded. She said I could stay in bed, or sit downstairs, whatever made me most comfortable, and she'd bring me cups of tea, and slices of cake, anything I wanted. "It's nearly time," she said to me one day, and I asked whether I should go to the hospital. "You don't need a hospital," she said, "I can do this. Do you trust me?" And I did trust her, and I was glad, I hadn't wanted to leave.

She fetched hot water and towels, and you came out, and it was easy, I think your birth was the easiest thing I had ever done. You were the simplest, most natural thing in my entire life. "It's a boy," said Mrs Gallagher, and she looked happy, but I think she may have been a little disappointed. She helped me name you. Did you know that? Do you like your name? It was Mrs Gallagher who picked it.

She told me that I shouldn't call her Mrs Gallagher, I should call her Nathalie. And I did so, from time to time, just to make her smile. But I thought of her as Mrs Gallagher, and I liked her that way – not formal, you understand, but protective, and strong, and better than me.

* * *

I started in my sleep, I couldn't breathe. I opened my eyes and saw a figure was standing over the bed, and I was held down, there was a hand tight across my mouth. I couldn't call out.

"Hello," whispered George, genially enough.

I opened my eyes wide, and blinked, in what I hoped he'd take as a fond greeting.

I didn't know how he'd found me, and I never did know. I suppose he might have broken into all the bed and breakfast establishments across the country until he'd got the right one. That seems quite likely.

He said to me, "I've got a job! It's all going to be all right. I've got lots of money, and it's all going to be as it was, and you can come back with me now, and you'll never be hurt again!" That sounded fine, but his hand was still on my mouth, and pressing down hard, and his fingernails had curved round and were digging painfully into my face.

You started to cry. You didn't care about being quiet, I don't know whether you were disturbed by the intruder, or just hungry – I'm guessing it was hungry, you were always hungry. George hadn't even seen the cot, I think; then he whirled around, and he let me go.

"He's yours," I whispered.

"Mine," he said. And he sounded amused, he seemed to like the sound of that.

"You're both mine," he said. And he wasn't bothering to whisper any more, and that was bad, it meant he didn't feel the need to be secret any more.

Mrs Gallagher didn't stir. "Is she dead?" George asked bluntly, and laughed.

"No," I said.

"I want to talk to her."

Mrs Gallagher's eyes opened at that. She was already awake.

"I didn't steal from you," George said. "I didn't steal from *you*."

Mrs Gallagher didn't say anything to that. Neither did I. George considered.

"Get up," he said. "Both of you."

"I'll come with you, George," I said. "But you don't need her, let's just go."

He slapped me around the face then, and it wasn't especially hard, but I hadn't been slapped for a long while and it hurt.

"We're all going outside," he said.

"What are you going to do with her, George?"

"I don't know," said George, "I don't know." And he sounded genuinely worried about that. I thought he was going to cuff me again, but he didn't bother.

Mrs Gallagher got out of bed. She struck a match, and lit a candle. And it was brighter than I expected, too bright, surely; and I saw two things that startled me. One was George himself – his clothes were torn, and he had a ragged beard that seemed in the flickering light like a scar across his face. And I realized he had no pride in anything any more. And the second thing – that was the ugly little knife he was carrying.

"Get moving," he said.

We walked down the stairs ahead of him. Both of us were in our nightdresses, and I thought how cold it would be out there in the dark, and that maybe that was the least of our concerns; the shag carpet was at my bare feet; and you were in my arms, and bless you, you'd gone back to sleep, you weren't scared of anything, you were with mummy and you felt safe.

I asked George once again what he was going to do, and I tried to find the right things to say that had always made him feel better, the ones that calmed his rages – but it'd been too long ago, I couldn't remember any. George didn't reply, and that was just as well, because it meant I heard Mrs Gallagher plainly when she hissed at me: "Jump."

We were in sudden pitch black. She must have blown out the candle.

And I felt her then leap into that black, and I didn't know how far off the ground we were, I couldn't judge it at all – I couldn't tell how many steps there might be, or what was waiting for us at the bottom. And I didn't care, I leaped too.

George gave a cry of – what? Surprise? Anger? Probably a mixture of both, and he started down the stairs after us, and then he shouted out again, and this time it was fear.

Mrs Gallagher struck another match. She lit the candle. The glow seemed to take an agonisingly long time to reveal anything.

George had hit the sixteenth step. And then had carried on going downwards. He had found a seventeenth, maybe an eighteenth too. The floor was up just around his knees. It looked as if his legs had been severed, and he was balancing his body on two unbloodied stumps; no, it looked like the downstairs floor had become a lake, and he had sunk below the surface. And Mrs Gallagher and me, we, we were walking impossibly upon water.

"Help me," he said. The light seemed to give him some courage, he even dared show impatience. "Get me out of this."

He grunted, tried to turn himself about, but there was nowhere for his body to go – nowhere, but onwards. And so doing, he took another step.

For a moment I thought his body was in free fall, but it came to a stop, the line of the floor now was across his chest. He looked so frightened. He grunted again, his face contorted with effort, and he pulled one of his arms free, and waved it at us. At me.

"I'm sorry," he said. "Please. Help me. Please." He reached out to me. And I think I would have gone had it been for my sake alone. I would have pulled him out. Or he would have pulled me in, more likely, in and under, just as he had done over and over for all those years. I loved him. But there was more than my love to think about now.

He saw that I wasn't going to help. And I thought he might threaten me. I thought he'd tell me he'd kill me. I think that would have been better. But his face just fell, that's all, and he looked so very sad.

He tried to pull up his second arm. He couldn't. He put his free hand flat upon the ground, tried to use it to prise himself out. It was no good.

One more step forward. And now only his head was peeking out, and he had to tilt his face toward the ceiling so he could speak. He said, so softly, as if in awed wonder – "The steps are so steep. Oh God. Oh God. They're so *steep*."

Mrs Gallagher stepped out. He looked at her with such hope. He thought she might want to save him, even now, in spite of all. I knew she wouldn't.

She stood right beside his head. If he'd wanted to, he could have bitten her feet. If he'd wanted to. He looked up at her, and she looked down on him, and she didn't gloat.

He opened his mouth to say something, and she shook her head, and he closed it again.

She blew out the candle.

When the guests came, we'd tell them of the noises in the attic, and the cold chill in the breakfast room, and of the extra step the staircase would grow in the dark. We didn't talk of the strange footsteps under the house, the ones you could hear just sometimes, when the sea was quiet and the wind was at lull. They didn't need to know everything.

I said that nothing untoward ever happened between me and Mrs Gallagher, and nor it did. But I wouldn't have minded.

I told her too late. She was dying, and fading so fast – she'd started the holiday season with the same no-nonsense energy as always, but then she'd got so slow, and so tired, and eventually we just asked our guests to leave and closed the doors on them. She lay in the bed, and I gave her all the space I could, I'd have moved to another room, but she told me she wanted me to stay by her in the night. I said that I loved her. I said that I had loved her for so long, and wanted to show her, wanted to do anything to her that would make her happy.

She smiled at me. She said, "That would have been nice."

And I kissed her. I kissed her sand-studded cheeks, her skin was so coarse beneath my lips and there was nothing I could do to make it soft.

Still she never snored, still she slept so peacefully that some nights I woke up thinking she might already be dead. And there was that one night I woke, and she wasn't there beside me. She hadn't moved from the bed for over a week, she hadn't the strength, and I was so frightened, I thought maybe she'd died and her body had simply melted away. I left the bedroom, went out into the darkness of the house, I lit a candle, I called for her. There I found her, down the staircase, on the bottom step, and she was stamping down on it weakly, without stopping, as if she couldn't stop, not until I spoke to her. She turned up to me, up to the light. "I can't get through," she said. "Why won't it let me through?" It was the only time I ever saw her cry.

She died only a few days later. I wasn't there for the very end, but I don't think it would have mattered much to her, she didn't know where she even was by then, and if she called out a name it would be Thomas. Her missing husband, maybe? Even a son? Who knows? At the end of the day there was still so little I knew about her.

We found her body, you and I. You weren't scared at all. You are still so young, and so fearless. You don't even remember, do you?

I know you don't remember Mrs Gallagher. My Nathalie. My own. But she was good to you. I wish you'd ask about her, and not about your father.

You know most of the rest of it.

Mrs Gallagher had left the house to me in her will. I had no idea, she had never discussed it with me. But I was not a blood relative, of course, and certainly could not have been considered a spouse, and after the death duties were paid there was no way I could afford to keep it. I sold it on.

Bed and breakfasts were all I knew now, that and the sea. I didn't want to stay in the town, too many people seemed to know about me and my relationship with Mrs Gallagher, and I had no shame of it, but I wanted nothing to do with them. That's why I moved us to the south coast, so far away, and bought our little hotel here. The sea here is warmer, the wind not as fierce, but I don't mind, I'm getting old too.

I want you to understand this. You are not your father.

Your father was not a good man, though he wasn't a bad man entirely. And you, I know there is good in you. I know you are better than he was. You must try to be better. The path you are treading, it isn't the way. You have been caught stealing once, and we were lucky that charges were not pressed, and I know that if you've been caught once, you've got away with it a dozen times before. And I know your business with the girls down town too, you think I don't hear? Mary Suffolk, and that Annie girl. And I don't judge. But you mustn't be cruel to them. Please, not cruel.

And you despise my hotel, and you despise me, and you want to leave, and I understand that. And all you want to know about is your father.

I have told you what I know.

And in the night sometimes, in the pitch black, I have gone down the stairs, and counted them off. I know you have heard me. I know that you have heard, but don't like to ask. I shall tell you anyway. Because Mrs Gallagher told me. That when all those years ago she lost her husband, Thomas, or whatever his name was, when he found that extra step, and all those steps leading downwards from it, ever on downwards with no bottom most likely. She told me that it wasn't in that house that she'd lost him. She moved away, and bought another hotel, right at the edge of the land, where she felt she could be free of him. And the extra step had followed her. Her husband had followed.

Because maybe we can't just bury our mistakes, and move on. Maybe we carry them around with us, regardless. Maybe I'll never be free of George. That seems right. That seems just. He's had his punishment, I'll take mine.

I go down the stairs. And there are twenty-one steps in the daytime. I can feel a twenty-second in the night.

You're not your father, and you're young, and you need to make your own mistakes. So go make them. But don't make too many. I have come too far, and sacrificed too much. I will not tolerate it.

I want to make sure you never have to join your father.

You've complained about sounds beneath the floorboards in your bedroom. Stamp your feet hard, that'll usually shut the bastard up.

SIMON STRANTZAS

Stemming the Tide

SIMON STRANTZAS IS the author of four collections of short fiction, including the recently published *Burnt Black Suns* from Hippocampus Press. His writing has appeared in *The Mammoth Book of Best New Horror*, *The Best Horror of the Year* and *The Year's Best Dark Fantasy & Horror*; has been translated into other languages; and has been nominated for the British Fantasy Award. He lives in Toronto, Canada, with his wife and an unyielding hunger for the flesh of the living.

"'Stemming the Tide' is set at the Hopewell Rocks in New Brunswick, Canada," reveals the author. "The mechanics of the tide are true, though I must confess the actual landscape differs in many ways from the real setting . . . apart from the walking dead, of course. Still, that landscape isn't what the story was about, but rather the dissolution of relationships and the growing spite that can occur near its end.

"This tale came together in a very short time – only a few days, in fact – which its length no doubt suggests; but unlike much of my work it did its coming together in a blazing heat, burning on its way out."

MARIE AND I sit on the wooden bench overlooking the Hopewell Rocks. In front of us, a hundred feet below, the zombies walk on broken, rocky ground. Clad in their sunhats and plastic sunglasses, carrying cameras around their necks and tripping over open-toed sandals, they gibber and gabber amongst themselves in a language I don't understand. Or, more accurately, a language I don't *want* to understand. It's the language of mindlessness. I detest it so.

Marie begged me for weeks to take her to the Rocks. It's a natural wonder, she said. The tide comes in every six hours and thirteen minutes and covers everything. All the rock formations, all the little arches and passages. It's supposed to be amazing. Amazing, I repeat, curious if she'll hear the slight scoff in my voice, detect how much I loathe the idea. There is only one reason I might want to go to such a needlessly crowded place, and I'm not sure if I'm ready to face it. If she senses my mood, she feigns obliviousness. She pleads with me again to take her. Tries to convince me it can only help her after her loss. Eventually, the crying gets to be too much, and I agree.

But I regret it as soon as I pick her up. She's dressed in a pair of shorts that do nothing to flatter her pale lumpy body. Her hair is parted down the middle and tied to the side in pigtails, as though she believes somehow appropriating the trappings of a child will make her young again. All it does is reveal the greying roots of her dyed black hair. Her blouse . . . I cannot even begin to explain her blouse. This is going to be great! she assures me as soon as she's seated in the car, and I nod and try not to look at her. Instead, I look at the sunbleached road ahead of us. It's going to take an hour to drive from Moncton to the Bay of Fundy. An hour where I have to listen to her awkwardly try and fill the air with words because she cannot bear silence for anything longer than a minute. I, on the other hand, want nothing more than for the world to keep quiet and keep out.

The hour trip lengthens to over two in traffic, and when we arrive the sun is already bearing down as though it has focused all its attention on the vast asphalt parking lot. We pass through the admission gate and, after having our hands stamped, onto the park grounds. Immediately, I see the entire area is lousy with people moving in a daze – children eating dripping ice cream or soggy hot dogs, adults wiping balding brows and adjusting colourful shorts that are already tucked under rolls of fat. I can smell these people. I can smell their sweat and their stink in the humid air. It's suffocating, and I want to retch. My face must betray me; Marie asks me if I'm okay. Of course, I say. Why wouldn't I be? Why wouldn't I be okay in this pigpen of heaving bodies and grunting animals? Why wouldn't I enjoy spending every waking moment in the proximity of people that barely deserve to live, who can barely see more than a few minutes into the future? Why wouldn't I enjoy it? It's like I'm walking through an abattoir, and none of the fattened sows know what's to come. Instead they keep moving forward in their piggy queues, one by one meeting their end. This is what the line of people descending into the dried cove looks like to me. Animals on the way to slaughter. Who wouldn't be okay surrounded by that, Marie? Only I don't say any of that. I want to with all my being, but instead I say I'm fine, dear. Just a little tired is all. Speaking the words only makes me sicker.

The water remains receded throughout the day, keeping a safe distance from the Hopewell Rocks, yet Marie wants to sit and watch the entire six hour span, as though she worries what will happen if we are not there to witness the tide rush in. Nothing will happen, I want to tell her. The waters will still rise. There is nothing we do that helps or hinders inevitability. That is why it is inevitable. There is nothing we can do to stem the tides that come. All we can do is wait and watch and hope that things will be different. But the tides of the future never bring anything to shore we haven't already seen. Nothing washes in but rot. No matter where you sit, you can smell its clamminess in the air.

The sun has moved over us and still the rocky bottom of the cove, and the tall weirdly sculpted mushroom rocks are dry. Some of the tourists still will not climb back up the metal grated steps, eager to spend as much of the dying light wandering along the ocean's floor. A few walk out as far as they can, sinking to their knees in the silt, yet none seem to wonder what might be buried beneath the sand. The teen-ager who acts as the lifeguard maintains his practised, affected look of disinterest, hair covering the left half of his brow, watching the daughters and mothers walking past. He ignores everyone until the laughter of those in the silt grows too loud, the giggles of sand fleas nibbling their flesh unmistakable. He yells at them to get to the stairs. Warns them of how quickly the tide will rush in, the immediate undertow that has sucked even the heaviest of men out into the Atlantic, but even he doesn't seem to believe it. Nevertheless, the pigs climb out one at a time, still laughing. I look around to see if anyone else notices the blood that trickles down their legs.

The sun has moved so close to the horizon that the blue sky has shifted to orange. Many of the tourists have left, and those few that straggle seemed tired to the point of incoher-ence. They stagger around the edge of the Hopewell Rocks, eating the vestiges of the fried food they smuggled in earlier or laying on benches while children sit on the ground in front of them. The tide is imminent, but only Marie and I remain alert. Only Marie and I watch for what we know is coming.

When it arrives, it does so swiftly. Where once rocks cover the ground, a moment later there is only water. And it rises. Water fills the basin, foot after foot, deeper and deeper. The tide rushes in from the ocean. It's the highest tide in the world over. It beckons people from everywhere to witness its power. The inevitable tide coming in.

Marie has kicked off her black sandals, the simple act shaving inches from her height. She has both her arms wrapped around one of mine and is staring out at the stead-ily rising water. She's like an anchor pulling me down. Do you see anything yet? she asks me, and I shake my head, afraid if I open my mouth what might come out. How much longer do you think we'll have to wait? Not long, I assure her, though I don't know. How would I? I've refused to come to this spot all my life, this spot on the edge of a great darkness. That shadowy water continues to lap, the teenage lifeguard finally concerned less with the girls who walk by to stare at his athletic body, and more with checking the gates and fences to make sure the passages to the bottom are locked. The last thing anyone wants is for one to be opened accidentally. The last thing anyone but me wants, that is.

The sun is almost set, and the visitors to the Hopewell Rocks have completely gone. It's a park full only with ghosts, the area surrounding the risen tide. Mushroom rocks look like small islands, floating in the ink just off the shore. The young lifeguard has gone, hurrying as the darkness crept in as fast as the water rose. Before he leaves he shoots the two of us a look that I can't quite make out under his flopping denim hat, but one which I'm certain is fear. He wants to come over to us, wants to warn us that the park has closed and that we should leave. But he doesn't. I like to think it's my expression that keeps him away. My expression, and my glare. I suppose I'll never know which.

Marie is lying on the bench by now, her elbow planted on the wooden slats, her wrist bent to support the weight of her head. She hasn't worn her shoes for hours, and even in the long shadows I can see sand and pebbles stuck to her soles. She looks up at me. It's almost time, she whispers, not out of secrecy – because no one is there to hear her – but of glee. It's almost time. It is, I tell her, and try as I might I can't muster up even a false smile. I'm too nervous. The thought of what's to come jitters inside of me, shakes my bones and flesh, leaves me quivering. If Marie notices, she doesn't mention it, but I'm already prepared with a lie about the chill of day's end. I know it's not true, and that even Marie is smart enough to know how warm it still is, but nevertheless I know she wants nothing more than to believe every word I say. It's not one of her most becoming qualities.

The tide rushes in after six hours and thirteen minutes, and though I'm not wearing a watch I know exactly when the Bay is at its fullest. I know this not by the light or the dark oily colour the water has turned. I know this not because I can see the tide lapping against the nearly submerged mushroom rocks. I know this because, from the rippling ocean water, I can see the first of the heads emerge.

Flesh so pale it is translucent, the bone beneath yellow and cracked. Marie is sitting up, her chin resting on her folded hands. I dare a moment to look at her wide-open face, and wonder if the remaining light that surrounds us is coming from her beaming. The smile I make is unexpected. Genuine. They're here! she squeals, and my smile falters. I can't believe they're here! I nod matter-of-factly.

There are two more heads rising from the water when I look back at the full basin, the first already sprouting an odd number of limbs attached to a decayed body. The thing staggers towards us, the only two living souls for miles around, though how it can see us with its head cocked so far back is a mystery. I can smell it from where we sit. It smells like tomorrow. More of the dead emerge from the water, refugees from the dark ocean, each one a promise of what's to come. They're us, I think. The rich, the poor, the strong, the weak. They are our heroes and our villains. They are our loved ones and most hated enemies. They are me, they are Marie, they are the skinny lifeguard in his idiotic hat. They are our destiny, and they have come to us from the future, from beyond the passage with a message. It's one no one but us will ever hear. It is why Marie and I are there, though each for a different reason – her to finally help her understand the death of her mother, me so I can finally put to rest the haunting terrors of my childhood. Neither of us speaks about why, but we both know the truth. The dead walk to tell us what's to come, their broken mouths moving without sound. The only noise they make is the rap of bone on gravel. It only intensifies as they get closer.

For the first time, I see a thin line of fear crack Marie's reverie. There are nearly fifty corpses shambling toward us, swaying as they try to keep rotted limbs moving. If they lose momentum, I wonder if they'll fall over. If they do, I doubt they'd ever right themselves. Between where we sit and the increasing mass is the metal gate the young lifeguard chained shut. More and more of the waterlogged dead are crowding

it, pushing themselves against it. I can hear the metal screaming from the stress, but it's holding for now. Fingerless arms
reach through the bars, their soundless hungry screams
echoing through my psyche. Marie is no longer sitting. She's
standing. Pacing. Looking at me, waiting for me to speak.
Purposely, I say nothing. I'll let her say what I know she's
been thinking.

There's something wrong, she says. This isn't—

It isn't what?

This isn't what I thought. This, these people. They aren't
right . . .

I snigger. How is it possible to be so naïve?

They are exactly who they are supposed to be, I tell her
with enough sternness I hope it's the last she has to say on
the subject. I don't know why I continue to make the same
mistakes. By now, I'd have thought I would have started
listening. But that's the trouble with talking to your past
self. Nothing, no matter how hard you try, can be stopped.
Especially not the inevitable.

The dead flesh is packed so tight against the iron gates
that it's only a matter of time. It's clear from the way the
metal buckles, the hinges scream. Those of the dead that
first emerged are the first punished, as their putrefying
corpses are pressed by the thong of emerging dead against
the fence that pens them in. I can see upturned faces buck-
ling against the metal bars, hear softened bones pop out of
place as their lifeless bodies are pushed through the narrow
gaps. Marie turns and buries her face in my chest while grip-
ping my shirt tight in her hands. I can't help but watch,
mesmerized.

Hands grab the gate and start shaking, back and forth,
harder and harder. So many hands, pulling and pushing.
The accelerating sound ringing like a church bell across the
lonely Hopewell grounds. I can't take it anymore, Marie
pleads, her face slick with so many tears. It was a mistake. I
didn't know. I never wanted to know. She's heaving as she
begs me, but I pull myself free from her terrified grip and
stand up. It doesn't matter, I tell her. It's too late.

I start walking toward the locked fence.

I can't hear Marie's sobs any longer, not over the ruckus the dead are making. I wonder if she's left, taken the keys and driven off into the night, leaving me without any means of transportation. Then I wonder if instead she's watching me, waiting to see what I'll do without her there. I worry about both these things long enough to realize I don't really care. Let her watch. Let her watch as I lift the latches of the fence the dead are unable to operate on their own. Let me unleash the waves that come from that dark Atlantic ocean onto the tourist attraction of the Hopewell Rocks. Let man's future roll in to greet him, let man's future become his present. Make him his own past. Who we will be will soon replace who we are, and who we might once have been.

The dead, they don't look at me as they stumble into the unchained night. And I smile. In six hours and thirteen minutes, the water will recede as quickly as it came, back out to the dark dead ocean. It will leave nothing behind but wet and desolate rocks the colour of sun-bleached bone.

MICHAEL
MARSHALL SMITH

The Gist

MICHAEL MARSHALL SMITH is a novelist and screenwriter. Under this name he has published eighty short stories and three novels – *Only Forward, Spares* and *One of Us* – winning the Philip K. Dick, International Horror Guild, and August Derleth awards, along with the Prix Bob Morane in France; he has been awarded the British Fantasy Award for Best Short Fiction four times, more than any other author.

Writing as "Michael Marshall", he has also published seven international best-selling thrillers, including *The Straw Men, The Intruders* – recently filmed as a mini-series by BBC America – and *Killer Move*. His most recent novel is *We Are Here*.

"Usually I'm happiest with the stories that have been written quickly," Smith reveals. "I like to have an idea, sit down to write it as soon as possible, and emerge with a first draft at most a day or two later.

"'The Gist' . . . well, I conceived of the basic notion in an instant – along with the idea of then having the story translated via a series of languages, and then back to English again, to see whether 'the gist' survived – but the story then took about seven years to write. A little bit here, a little bit there, a re-write, a fallow period. The translation process then took another three years, before it was finally ready to be published by Subterranean Press, who waited through the process with enormous patience.

"The end result is that I'm a different man to the one who started the project nearly a decade ago. I have no idea whether the gist of me has survived the years . . ."

I

"I'M NOT DOING it," I said.

Portnoy gazed coolly back at me. "Oh? Why?"

"Where do I begin? Ah, I know – let's start with the fact you haven't paid me for the last job . . ."

"That situation could be remedied."

". . . or the one before that."

The man behind the desk in front of me sighed. This made his sleek, moisturised cheeks vibrate in a way that couldn't help but put you in mind of a successful pig, exhaling contentedly in its sty, confident that the fate that stalked its kind was not going to befall *him* tonight, or indeed ever. A pig with friends in high places, a pig with pull. Pork with an exit strategy. The impression was so strong you could almost smell the straw the pig lay in – along with a faint whiff of shit.

"Ditto."

"Great," I said, briskly. "We'll attend to the financial backlog first, shall we? Then I'll get onto the other reason."

"You sadden me, John," Portnoy said, as he reached down to the side and opened the top drawer of his desk. This meant, as the desk was double-sided, that the corresponding drawer-front on my side disappeared. From his end he withdrew a chequebook that was covered in dust. Literally. "Anyone would think you do this only for the money."

"Anyone would be absolutely right."

"I don't believe you." He tilted his head forward and allowed his spectacles to slide down his nose, the better to inspect the means of payment now laid in front of him. After a long pause he flipped it open, and peered bemusedly at the contents.

"Forgotten how to use it?"

He looked at me over the rims of his glasses, as if disappointed. "Surely you can do better, my boy."

"Perplexed by the instructions printed thereon?" I elaborated, "Which must presumably be in Latin, at least, or Indo-European? Perhaps even facsimiles of petroglyphs representing routes to local lunching spots, with crosses indicating wine bars and the nearest cab rank?"

"Better. What manner of total were you expecting? For the two alleged late payments?"

"Seven hundred and fifty quid. Because it's three. *The Diary of Anna Kourilovicz*, remember?"

"Good lord." Portnoy shook his head, evidently wondering what had overcome him to vouchsafe such outlandish sums. I said nothing, however. I'd come this far in a settlement negotiation before to find Portnoy suddenly derailed by a phone call, an ill-advised comment on my part, or some movement of the spheres only he could sense. If that happened the whole process had to start again, at a later date, and so I wasn't going to let it go pear-shaped this time. I needed the money, badly.

He took a pen from his tweed jacket – a pen which had, I entertained, no doubt cost him far more than the sum currently causing him such pain – and wrote in the book, concluding with his ponderous signature. He tore out the cheque with an oddly decisive movement and waved it in the air to dry the ink, before finally laying it on the desk.

I grabbed it and stuffed it in my wallet with a thick wash of relief. The rent was paid. Say what you like about Portnoy – and people did say many things, on the quiet – but his cheques never bounced.

"You're a gent."

He grunted, and sat looking at me while re-igniting the fat and noxious cigar which had been idling in a saucer at his elbow. I watched, and waited, casting half an eye over a page of Shakespeare's *A Midsummer Night's Dream*, purporting to be from the original folio edition, that Portnoy had framed on the wall behind his desk.

Those who knew Portnoy only slightly suspected the page of being fake, there to impress the naïve. People who knew him a little better, as I did, were prone to believe it was genuine – and that he'd started the rumour of it being fake just to mess with people's heads. Along with many other aspects of Portnoy's life and business, it was unlikely the real truth would ever be known.

As always, his basement office was murky, lit only by a small, old lamp on the corner of the desk, and thin slats of light striking down from a high, pavement-level window on the far wall, enlivened by turning motes of dust. The effect was so subdued that you couldn't see what lined all four walls, or stood in haphazard-seeming piles over most of the floor, to almost shoulder height.

You could smell them, though, even through the permanent fug of cigar smoke.

Books. Thousands of them.

"Well?" he said, eventually.

"Well what?"

"We're square. So what was the other reason?"

"Simple." I picked up the object that had been the initial focus of our conversation. "It's a fake. Or nonsense. Or both."

"I don't believe so. The gentleman I obtained it from has an immaculate record in providing me with titbits."

Titbits. An interesting word for volumes that routinely fetched Portnoy upwards of ten, twenty or even a hundred thousand pounds. "He's let you down this time. What's the provenance?"

For a moment the dealer looked shifty. This intrigued me. Despite being roguishly dishevelled, and somewhere in that indefinable age (amongst the portly and ruddy-faced) between late-forties and mid-sixties, there was a word I always applied to Portnoy in my head. *Sleek*.

But now, for a period of time perhaps equal to that required for a hummingbird to flap its wings (once), he didn't look sleek.

"You needn't concern yourself with that," he muttered. "I already have. I'm satisfied."

"Well, that's okay then," I said, standing. I had a mind to celebrate payday with a visit to the pub, starting immediately. "You don't need me to—"

"A thousand," Portnoy said.

I sat back down. I realized immediately how very like him this was – not merely doubling my usual fee, but going straight for the financial jugular. He had the measure of me, and knew it. So did I.

"Maurice," I said.

He winced. Apparently I always said it wrong, making it sound either too much or not enough like "Morris", I'd never been clear which.

"I honestly think it's a fake, or a joke."

"It's neither."

"In which case I'm still not the man for the job."

"You are."

I laughed. This was ridiculous. "How can I translate something out of a tongue I've never seen before? Which I don't even think is a real language?"

"I'm confident you'll uncover the gist."

"Look . . ."

"For twelve hundred pounds."

Twelve hundred meant not just next month's rent, but a replacement laptop (second hand, naturally, and scuffed after its most recent descent from the back of a lorry), of which I was in dire need. It meant a small gift for Cass (assuming I could track her down), in which case she might consent to being my sort-of girlfriend again, or at least going through the motions once or twice.

It meant a *very* long evening in the pub.

Portnoy reached into his jacket and pulled out his wallet. From this he drew a wad of notes, and slowly sorted the wheat from the chaff. I read them from where I sat. Six hundred quid. He coughed, a long, wet-sounding eruption bedded deep in his lungs.

"Half now, half when you come back," he said, when he'd finished.

My head was spinning. Portnoy *never* paid except on completion – and this was nearly as much as the sum I'd just levered out of him, much of which had been owed for nearly two months.

"Just do what you can, my boy," he said. "Hmm?"

I picked up the book and the cash and left before he could change his mind.

II

In a break from my usual practice, I'd bothered to pop home to stow Portnoy's book there before going to the pub. It was, therefore, lying safely on the table when I jack-knifed to a sitting position on the sofa, at three o'clock the following afternoon.

A quick fumble through my wallet confirmed what I'd suspected immediately upon waking. The bulk of the six hundred quid was gone. Three hundred on an over-specced and under-the-counter laptop, to be fair – but where was the rest of it? Some of it in my stomach, a portion of it up my nose, plus I seemed to have a new and much groovier mobile phone that I didn't remember acquiring via the usual high-street channels – but that couldn't account for *all* of it, surely?

I was exceedingly glad I'd brought the book home first, or it would have become Schrödinger's Tome, equally likely to be at any random point in London – or at least the subset of those points which lay within easy lurching distance of The Southampton Arms.

Christ.

Being me is not a fate everyone would enjoy. There are risks, and frequent disappointments. I'm not all that keen on the arrangement myself, to be honest.

I braced myself by drinking a huge amount of coffee and going through the process of transferring my files from the old laptop, feeling like a military policeman supervising the last desperate airlift from Saigon. The screen flashed at regular intervals, staying blank for up to five seconds at a time. The hard disk was far too audible, and smelled alarming, like a digital grave.

When everything was safely transferred to the new one I shut the old machine with relief, and lobbed it into the corner of the room which holds things broken, empty, or otherwise held in disdain. Like the other three corners of the room, in fact. My flat is a craphole, or so I've been told. I don't see it myself. It's a single-room studio with a tiny bathroom off the far end, and a laughable kitchenette which I've never used. The place is certainly untidy, but that's not my fault. I've tried tidying it and within hours it's untidy again, far more quickly than can be accounted for by any normal means. Evidently that's simply its natural state, and there's nothing I can do about it.

Three walls are lined with bookshelves which sag under the weight of dictionaries, grammars, other reference and theoretical texts. Actually, the fourth wall is too, now. This has a pair of windows in it, but I don't like a lot of sunlight because it makes it harder to read a computer screen (not to mention it's bad for old books and manuscripts, and hangovers), and so the blinds are permanently down and the piles of extra dictionaries, grammars, reference and theoretical texts have gradually grown to block most of their span.

I have a couch/bed thing, a big table, and a useful collection of pub ashtrays and pint glasses. What else do you need? I don't think it's a craphole.

Eventually I left off tinkering with the new laptop (whose own hard drive had a disconcertingly choppy whine, but at least the screen worked properly) and pulled Portnoy's book toward me.

It was time to start earning the rest of the money.

III

What I do for Portnoy, as you may have gathered, is translate. I can read nine languages fluently, another eight or ten given a bit of warning, and pick my way through fragments of quite a few more. It's just something I can do, and doesn't betoken any great intelligence in other spheres, more's the pity.

The annoying thing is that I can't actually *speak* any of them. Give me a tattered document in medieval High German or Welsh or even Basque – which is as near a Stone-Age remnant as you'll find, and really *hard* – and I'll be able to tell you what it says. The gist, at the very least. Put me in a café in Paris, however, and while I can understand perfectly what people are saying, I can't seem to say much in reply. It's like there's a barrier in my head, a glass wall that the words get trapped behind. I have the vocabulary, I know the grammar so well it's as if I *don't* know it – which is exactly how it should be – but the words just won't come out of my head and dance on my tongue. I went to Calais for a boozy weekend with Cass once, and she did far better than I with the waiters just by bellowing English nouns.

The upside, almost as if it's there to compensate, is that I'm unusually good at the written or printed word – which is why Maurice Portnoy pays me (when he remembers).

The core of the antiquarian book trade naturally lies in providing clients with books they're actually *looking* for. Through an immense and spidery network of contacts, Portnoy keeps his eye out for works on customers' wish lists, or those he knows he can find a home for: first editions, modern and ancient; short-run autobiographies or privately produced ephemera; seminal illustrated volumes of botany, alchemy or alarmingly frank (and to modern tastes, downright illegal) pornography – whatever these men have set their foetid collectors' hearts on (and the majority of them *are* men, members of our obsessive and fetish-friendly sex). In this regard Portnoy is much the same as other dealers, and plies an unexceptional trade.

His real business, however, is in the books that people *don't* know about. The books that got lost.

I got talking to this bloke once in the pub, a novelist. He told me he'd just discovered there was a Romanian edition of one of his novels. An acquaintance happened to be on holiday in the region, recognized the writer's name on the spine of a battered paperback on a second-hand stall in the market of a small town. Otherwise, the author would never have known about it. Granted, that's just a translation, but bear in mind this was only a couple of years ago, too. Think back over the hundreds of years we've been printing books – and the centuries before that, when they were copied by hand. How are you going to know that a book once existed, long after anyone involved with it is dead? If there's a copy somewhere, yes, or a reference to it in another book. Otherwise . . . they've vanished. People didn't keep records like they do now. You printed a book, sold it, and when it was gone, it was gone. Often books were printed privately, in runs of a hundred, twenty, even just five, and proudly so – it's said that Goethe's old man viewed his son's willingness to appeal to a more "mass" market with permanent disdain.

It's different now, of course. Our entire culture has turned obsessive-compulsive, recording everything and storing it on computer servers across the world, the better to information-swamp us into a state of baffled ignorance. But a book hand-copied by unknown scriveners in the twelfth century? It's history. Vanished into the undertow, as if it had never existed.

Until . . . someone finds one.

That's what Portnoy's "titbits" are. Lost books. Not in the sense that no one can find a copy, but because *no one knew there was a copy out there to be found.*

Some are merely volumes by unknown authors, or previously unknown titles by established names. Others turn up in more mysterious states, missing covers or whole chunks and without any indication of who wrote it, or when. Portnoy can fill in the "when" – expertise in bookbinding techniques, the evolution of paper stock and modes of printing or hand-written script will generally give you a date within twenty-five years either way. You have to be on the look-out for fakes, of course, (when someone's tried to make a manuscript look older than it is) or occasions when a genuinely eldritch tome has been rebound at a much later date, an old book now lurking between younger covers. Portnoy has an eagle eye for this kind of thing, too.

Most collectors are searching for the known, naturally. Being known – and merely rare – is precisely what makes something conventionally collectable. That's why Gutenberg Bibles, the first "mass" printing of that venerable fantasy tale, fetch the head-spinning sums they command. Only about fifty copies survive from the original paper edition of one hundred and eighty, and examples of the much smaller vellum edition are even more scarce. Most are in museums, and they're genuine works of art over and above their state of precedence. But what if an unknown rival had done a small trial printing the year before – of which only one copy remained, lost and forgotten in some hidden attic? And what about copies of other, more unknown books, collections of words now vanished from public awareness – like dinosaurs without bones or fossilized tracks to mark their passing?

There are people out there who want this stuff, and want it very much *indeed*.

So Portnoy receives these books, often battered and torn and water-damaged, and makes a judgement on their age. If they're in English, he passes them by people he knows who can make guesses at authorship. These people can further refine the date, too, from clues in the use of language. There's the issue of semantic drift, for example, where words start out meaning one thing and over time morph into something different.

"Henchman" is a mildly interesting English example. In the fourteenth century it was a positive term, literally meaning a "horse attendant" – the squire who walked beside high-ranking men and kept an eye on their boss' steed. It continued to mean this for a few centuries, and appears thus in *A Midsummer Night's Dream*, as a matter of fact, where Oberon says, "I do but beg a little changeling boy/To be my henchman". By the eighteenth century it had side-stepped to designate the chief sidekick of Scottish Highland chiefs, and then by nineteenth century America the word had strayed yet further, to mean a "political supporter" – a fairly short step from its current meaning of "a criminal associate", ha ha. Working out the precise sense in which these shape-shifting words are being used can help nail a text to quite a specific time frame.

Sometimes they're *not* in English, however, and that's where I come in. If it's in one of my fluent languages, I can do it right there in the basement beneath Portnoy's decep-tively bland shop in Cecil Court, one of London's few remaining book alleys. I don't *like* to do it that way, because it makes Portnoy feel he can pay me even less, but he's too wily to fall for any nonsense about me needing reference books, when the thing's obviously in a seventeenth century strand of one of the regional variations that eventually became subsumed into modern-day French.

Whenever I can, however, I take them home, and get to the bottom of them there. Most of the time, the results are mundane. A previously unknown pamphlet on the history of a one-horse town in Umbria in the 1760s remains dull, however few people knew it existed. There are collectors who revel in the purity of simply owning a book no one else knows exists, but that's a precarious thrill. Portnoy knows about it now, of course, as do I . . . and as soon as anyone *else* comes across a reference to it somewhere, the bubble bursts. So there's naturally a higher attraction to books that aren't just unknown, but possess fascination in their own right. That's when the price truly leaps up into the sky.

The Diary of Anna Kourilovicz was a case in point – a bound manuscript in a version of Russian used in the mid-1800s. Ms Kourilovicz had very bad handwriting. She also had an extremely colourful life – or imagination, I was never sure which – that she set down in detail, and that involved varied, frequent and eyebrow-raising couplings with men, women and pets of note in St Petersburg society of the time. There is a *lot* of cash swilling around the former Soviet Union these days, and the kinky stuff always goes for the highest prices. I don't know how much Portnoy made when he sold *The Diary*, but for several weeks his sleekness went up a very significant notch. The next time I was in his office he even gave *me* a cigar, which I tried to enjoy, though it tasted like someone had set fire to a wet dog. It didn't stop him paying me late, of course, but then he hadn't offered me twelve hundred quid to do it, either.

Which made me think whatever I now held in my hands must be something he was hoping would turn out to be very interesting indeed.

IV

At first glance, the book had one obvious thing going for it – it was attractive. It had been laid out in a style between Arts & Crafts and Roycraft (tight and detailed typography, with woodcut-style design ornaments), and was actually a curious blend of the two, putting its publication – even to my graphically untrained eye – somewhere between 1890 to the early 1900s, and most likely in England, Germany or Austria.

So far, so good.

The problem was that it was nonsense.

There *was* text – rather a lot of it, in fact – but it wasn't in any language I'd ever seen.

There used to be a lot more languages than there are now, of course. The Languedoc region of France was so named to distinguish its inhabitants as those who said "*oc*" to mean "yes", rather than "*oui*", as used elsewhere – and when Italy began to standardize its tongue late in the nineteenth century, only three per cent of the population were speaking the dialect which has now come to be known as "Italian".

The lost varieties are generally at least recognizable, however. What was in front of me didn't look like any breed of English, French, Italian, German, Spanish, Scandinavian or Slavic language that I'd ever seen, and the lack of Cyrillic characters help rule out a slew of others.

The obvious answer was that it was a code. If so, then Portnoy was out of luck. One of the many things I have no skill for is working out puzzles. I hate them, actually. I suspected he had reason to believe this *wasn't* a cipher, however, as in that case he'd have given it to someone who possessed those skills. In fact, he'd possibly already done so – ending up with me as a last resort.

So what made him think it was worth twelve hundred notes to work out what it was? It had to be the provenance – where the book had come from. One of his shadowy procurers must have told him the context was very good indeed. After three hours of flicking through the book it still looked like bollocks to me, however.

I photocopied a few random pages on the little printer/ scanner/copier thing I have, and took them with me to the pub. At some point in the evening I lost track of them, a little before I lost track of myself.

V

When I woke in the middle of the following night, it took me a few moments to work out where I was. I'll be honest and admit this is not an unknown phenomenon. What *is* unusual is for the location not to be my own dwelling, however. Once in a while I've regained consciousness in someone else's house – that of a random woman, generally, in whose rumpled waking face I see mirrored my own weary disappointment at our mutual fate – but usually it's my own gaff that I wake to find myself face-down on the carpet of. Not this time.

I sat up, and saw I was in a park.

Not a very large one – only about seventy meters square – but with quite a lot of trees, the rest of the space given over to instruments designed to beguile the energies of children of pre-school age.

A roundabout, and a pair of swings. A couple of slides, one in the manner of a pirate ship.

Something in the shape of a horse, on which I could have rocked hectically back and forth, had I been much smaller and determined to make myself very sick.

Inspection of a metal waste bin a few yards away suggested I was in something called Dalmeny Park. This was promising, as I was pretty sure there was a Dalmeny Road not *too* far away from where I lived. The park in general looked very vaguely familiar, in fact, though it was hard to understand why. It was surrounded by houses and gardens except at the gate, which was accessed down an alley between a couple of unremarkable dwellings. It would be hard to even know of its existence, unless you were already inside, and I could imagine no circumstances in which I would have been in the park before.

Less positive was the fact that when I got to the gate, I found it was locked. This was not some small and easy-to-vault-over affair, either, but a ten feet high job, evidently designed to stop the place being used as an alfresco drugs den and/or informal homeless shelter. A sign on the gate alleged the place shut at dusk. As I hadn't left the pub until well after closing time – the Southampton operates a generous lock-in policy – it didn't seem likely that I'd entered the park this way.

I turned around and saw that much of the perimeter of the park gave onto people's back gardens, the walls to which varied from five to eight feet in height. So it was more likely I'd come in via that route.

But . . . How had I got into someone's garden, and then over the back of their wall and into here? And why, more to the point? What on earth had possessed me?

And how was I going to get out?

I lurched around the edge of the park, pushing behind the tall shrubs which lined most of it. I was relieved to find that in the far corner was another gate, which – though it didn't give onto public space – at least looked like it might lead by the side of a mansion block, beyond which the road presumably lay.

This gate was only about eight feet high. I stared up at it, feeling drunk, bilious and far from confident.

"What the hell are you doing?"

At first I couldn't work out where the voice was coming from. Then I saw that someone was approaching the gate from the other side, occluded behind a hellishly bright torch beam.

"I don't know," I said.

"What do you mean you don't know? What are you *doing* in there?"

It was a man's voice, and had an odd rhythm to it.

"I don't know that either," I said.

"You're drunk."

"Yes," I agreed, quickly, eager to be helpful. "I think that's a big part of the problem."

He lowered his torch enough to allow me to glimpse a man in late middle age, wearing a dressing gown.

"I'm really sorry," I said.

He unlocked the gate, giving me a comprehensive ticking off in the process, rehearsing a number of things he should be doing – calling the police, the council, my mother – but I found it hard to make out the individual words, or to form a more comprehensive apology.

Instead I thanked him and hurried up the path past the side of the block. It occurred to me as I made it to the road that I'd only solved part one of the problem, as I still didn't actually know where I was. But I didn't want to push my luck.

It took forty minutes of wandering the streets to find my road, which – had I not been travelling in shambling circles for most of it – was actually only about half a mile from the park. I let myself into the house and climbed up the stairs on hands and knees, as if undertaking the final desperate assault on a very high and idiosyncratically carpeted mountainside.

Only when I was safely inside my flat did I realize I could still hear the rhythm of the voice of the man with the torch, beating inside my head.

VI

When I woke again late the next morning, my location was more explicable. I was exactly where I had been when I'd fallen back to sleep. Face-down on my own sofa. I was sufficiently relieved by this that I didn't even much mind when rolling over sent me over the edge, to land with a crash on the floor.

I drank a lot of water while sitting at the table. I still didn't understand what had happened. Sure, I'd drunk a lot of beer. But I've done that before (the previous night, for example, and the one before that). How I'd got from drunk-in-the-Southampton-Arms to being unconscious-inside-Dalmeny-Park remained a mystery.

As I'd scurried away under the torch-wielding man's scrutiny, I'd had time to note that the side of the building didn't look even remotely familiar. I suspected this meant it hadn't been the way I'd gained access to the park. Climbing over even that lower gate would have been a major undertaking, one which you'd have thought should have stuck in my beer-addled brain.

So how *had* I got in there? Via someone's garden?

In which case, had I also gone via someone's *house*?

It suddenly seemed horribly possible that I'd met someone in the pub, gone back to their house with them, and then – for one reason or another – left by a rear exit, making it as far as the park before crashing out.

Not ideal, obviously. Not the outline of a classy evening, a soirée of distinction and restraint. Oh bloody hell. Why did I have to be me? Wasn't it someone else's turn yet? Wasn't there *anyone* else who fancied taking on the job for a while, so I could have a rest?

In the end I decided to just forget about it. I find that's the best approach to events in your past which you'd prefer not to bring into your present or future. Just pretend they didn't happen.

In the meantime distract yourself.

To aid this I reached once more for Portnoy's tome. I dimly remembered having spent a fairly diligent hour or so in the pub the previous evening, trying to make sense of the photocopied pages I'd taken with me – even swapping words back to front, in the hope it was some simple code which Portnoy's other sages might have missed through lack of familiarity with foreign or obsolete languages.

Nothing had come out of it, and at first glance the text looked no more explicable this morning than it had the day before. After a few minutes of flipping back and forth through the pages, however, I noticed something was tugging at my brain, trying to bring itself to my attention. It wasn't until I tried saying some of the words out loud that I understood what it was.

The words remained nonsensical, but there was a *rhythm* to them.

I never paid much attention in class during the parts where they explained iambic pentameters and all that jazz (nor during quite a lot of the other bits, to be honest) so I couldn't put an actual name to the rhythm, but as I turned to other pages at random and read out further chunks, I became convinced I'd finally spotted something. The ratio of long and short words, the way in which the blocks of text were organized and contained by commas and full stops, seemed to have a kind of pattern.

It wasn't universal – it's not like the whole thing went ti-tum-ti-tum ti-tum-titum – but each section *did* seem to have a kind of aural organising principle, when you said the words aloud. By chance I happened to come across one of the passages I'd photocopied the night before, and as I read through it, I realized something else. It was this rhythm I'd heard in the voice of the man with the torch, who'd let me out of the park I'd found myself in.

It hadn't been in his words, but in my mind – put there through reading and re-reading this section while pouring beer into my head. Which was kind of weird.

VII

Portnoy took a long puff on his cigar and looked at me.

"Yes?" he said. "And?"

"Well, that's it," I said.

My head was splitting, and it was becoming clear that the hope that this insight would do – and be worth the other six hundred quid – had been overly optimistic. "I still can't make anything of the actual words – and I've tried everything I know. But these rhythms can't be unintentional. It must be what the thing is about."

"A book of rhythms."

"Yeah."

Portnoy just looked at me some more.

"I mean, that must be pretty unusual, right? Very rare?" I could sense this wasn't at all what Portnoy had been hoping for, but ploughed on regardless. "Maybe it's a manual of poetic meter, or something."

"Oh, that's wonderful news," he snorted. "Those go for simply *enormous* sums, as I'm sure you can imagine."

He thought for a while in silence, staring down at the surface of his desk, gently biting his lip.

"No," he said eventually. "I'm not convinced. You're not there yet. You need to keep on trying."

"Christ," I said, "Look, it's *something*. And I honestly don't think there's anything else there to be found. I spent all yesterday evening in the pub with this bloody thing, trying everything I could—"

"You took this book *to the pub*?" Portnoy said, sharply.

"No," I said, hurriedly. "Obviously not. I photocopied some pages, and—"

"Which pub?"

"Um, the Southampton Arms," I said. "On Junction Road. You won't know—"

"Of course I know it," he snapped. "I had the misfortune to grow up in that very area."

"Oh," I said, surprised.

"Don't *ever* do that again," he said. "Do you have any *idea* what would happen to the value of this book, if it got out that it existed?"

"Trust me, I don't think there are any antiquarian book dealers working undercover in my local boozer."

"Your fellow sops probably don't imagine that amongst their number is someone who can sight-read medieval Dutch," he bellowed, semi-reasonably. "And yet there you are, getting merrily shit-faced and falling off stools."

"Sorry," I said, chastened. "I just didn't think that . . . well, sorry. Sorry."

For the second time in three days, Portnoy wasn't looking sleek. In fact, he was looking the closest I've ever seen to angry. And a little scary, too.

"Where are the photocopies now?"

"Um," I said.

VIII

Even to someone well acquainted with the practice of drinking in the afternoon, pubs look different during the day. Natural light is friendly to neither their interiors nor denizens, and since the Nazi health bastards stopped us smoking inside, they smell bad too. Stale alcohol, a waft of disinfectant from the toilets, whatever vile gunk they use to clean out the pumps – all overlaid with the background tang of dust in ancient carpets. Now this olfactory assault is no longer hidden below the welcoming fug of fag smoke, walking into a pub of a late morning can make you wonder why on earth you spent the whole of the previous evening there. Luckily, a quick pint can usually remind you.

I got half of one down me before asking what I'd come to ask.

"Ron?" I said, addressing the slab-faced landlord. It would be romantic to imagine he'd once been a boxer, a plucky local hopeful gone spectacularly to seed – and Ron wasn't adverse to that rumour being spread around – but it's more likely he merely spent his youth and post-youth engaged in the kind of villainous pursuits that come hand in hand with outbursts of spirited violence. Even in his sixties he remains an extremely handy-looking geezer, and I definitely wouldn't want to wind up on the wrong end of either of his ham-sized fists.

"John," he replied, in his courtly fashion.

"Your rubbish. What happens to it?"

Ron cast a droll eye around the bar, but the only other person sitting at it was already too drunk to provide much of an audience.

"We throw it away," Ron said. "Is that . . . wrong?"

"But, I meant, at what time? First thing, or . . .?"

"Nah. We like to save it. The bloke comes round to collect, and we say 'No, you're all right mate, we'll keep it until next week.'"

"And what time *does* he come round?"

Ron abruptly dropped the show, realising I was going to be dogged about it. "It's still out the back. Why? You lost something?"

"Few bits of paper I had with me last night. Forgot them when I left."

"Not surprised," he said. "You was bladdered. Muttering to yourself like a twat, you were. Almost thought about not serving you the last four or five pints."

"Muttering?"

"Yeah. Same thing, over and over. Couldn't make it out. Sounded like a sodding poem, or something."

That sounded weird, but I didn't want to risk being diverted from what I was driving at.

I opened my mouth to ask the next question, but had to pause while I underwent a long coughing fit. Ron watched the process with some satisfaction.

"Sounds nasty," he said, when I'd finished.

"Yeah," I said. "It feels it." The cough was harsh and glassy – a legacy, no doubt, of having spent a portion of a cold night crashed out on damp grass in a park. "Look, Ron – thing is, has your rubbish been taken, or not? I need those pages, is what it is."

He jerked his head toward the side door. "Help yourself."

I swallowed the rest of my pint, indicated I'd like another, and spent twenty minutes in the alley that ran down the side of the pub, sifting through bin bags. Cass used to call bin bags – especially when stacked in a black pile by the side of a building – "house poo". I always liked that, and trust me, the bin bags of pubs deserve the term more than most. I wouldn't have been rummaging through them at all, had Portnoy's response to the pages being lost not been as strong as it was. He really was not happy about it *at all*, which made me all the more intrigued as to what the hell the story was behind this book.

I found the photocopies, eventually, in about the eighth bag. I remembered bringing approximately six pages with me, and that's how many I managed to dredge up. I'm not sure what most of them were covered in, but I hope to Christ it wasn't on the pub menu – or, at least, that no one had eaten it. Especially me.

I wiped the pages off as best I could, and in doing so saw that the second sheet contained the passage that had taken me to Portnoy's that morning. The liquid in the gloop smeared over it had done something strange to the laser print, making it look as though it was standing off the page a little. I still thought I could determine some kind of consistent rhythm in the collections of letters, and it still meant nothing.

In the end I folded the pages in half, and half again, and stuffed them in my pocket. I had a well-earned cigarette and then went back in the pub, where – after washing my hands in the gents – I took my place back at the bar.

I didn't know what to do next. I wanted (*needed*) the rest of the cash Portnoy had promised. I had no idea what else to try, however, and the combination of a hangover and whatever bug I'd picked up wasn't making my head a place of clarity. Neither was the new beer entering my system, most likely, though it was at least making me feel slightly better. I decided I'd have one more pint then go back to the flat and . . . dunno. Try looking through the book some more.

"You're doing it again."

I raised my head to see both Ron and the nearly-comatose other bloke at the bar looking at me.

"Doing what?"

"The muttering."

I frowned. "Really?"

Ron turned to the bloke. "Was he muttering?"

"You was . . . *muttering*," the man said, laboriously.

I realized that I had been, and was again, that my lips were soundlessly shaping the same phrase over and over. It was as if, suddenly and after all this time, I could vocalize a foreign language after all. It just wasn't one that I knew.

I got off the stool without ordering another beer, and walked quickly home.

IX

Portnoy wasn't in when I called, and he cleaved to the incredibly annoying habit of not having an answerphone. He'd been extremely insistent that I let him know immediately about the fate of the pages, however, so I remained where I was and waited to call him again.

In the meantime I sat at the table, putting the book in front of me. After a moment I opened it, somewhat more cautiously than on previous occasions.

It was just a book. Of course.

But things get under your skin.

I remembered the first time I'd met Cass, for example. It was in a pub, obviously. She'd been there with a couple of mates, as had I, and somehow over the course of many drinks the two groups wound up mingling. At the end of the evening, two new – and very temporary – couples disappeared off into the night. Cass and I were not one of them, though we did talk for hours and swap phone numbers.

The next morning I woke with her in my head.

I was alone on what serves for my bed, but bang in the centre of a head seared with hangover was this petite, red-haired girl. Not saying anything. Just there. She remained in vision for the whole of the day – sometimes right in front of me, sometimes glimpsed out of the corner of my internal eye. When I woke up the next morning and found that she was again my first waking thought, I bit the bullet and called her.

I'm not sure we ever quite "went out with each other", as such, though we did spend quite a lot of time together in pubs for a while, and took that one day-trip to France; and on days when I feel scratchy and crap, and put at least some of this down to the vague sensation of missing someone, I suspect it's her that I miss.

Portnoy's book, or its contents, had started to feel the same way. Not as if I wanted to snog it, obviously. As if it had climbed into my head. This could just be for self-evident reasons: having pissed away the first half of the money, I needed the other six hundred even more urgently, and he clearly wasn't going to give it up without due cause – which meant me getting to the bottom of this sodding tome. The cold, flu or whatever I had was getting worse too, making my head muddy and unclear. My cough had by now reached epic proportions. I was trying to unleash it as seldom as possible, on the grounds that it stirred reserves of phlegm so deep it felt like it was endangering the foundations of the house.

I called Portnoy's office again. He still wasn't there. Then, maybe because she was in my head from remembering her being in my head, I called Cass' mobile.

"You've got a bloody nerve," she said, before I'd even had time to say hello.

"Have I?"

"You don't remember?" she said.

X

Two hours later I was back in the Southampton, sitting fretfully at a table and waiting for her. In the meantime I'd managed to get hold of Portnoy and reassure him about the missing pages. He sounded less scary afterwards, and listened to me wheeze and cough with something like paternal concern.

"If I might make an observation," he said, when I'd finished, "you're bottling it up, my boy. Let it all go. Release it. Will you try doing that, John?"

I said I would. I then spent a few minutes trying to position my lack of further ideas about his book as being an analysis worth six hundred quid. He heard me out with good grace, appeared to even think about it for a nanosecond, but then said he was confident I would have made more progress soon – and that he'd look forward to an update in his office on Monday . . . which was days and days away, so at least I didn't have to sort it out right now.

On the way to the pub I took his advice, however, and (when no one else was around) treated myself to a good old cough, a third-hangover-in-a-row and let-yourself-go-red-in-the-face and double-up-and-really-go-for-it job.

It felt like something important was coming loose inside, but then – *bam*: it was over, and I felt fine. Well, better, anyway. Head still fuzzy, but chest suddenly absolutely back to normal.

I'd been in the pub half an hour, and was on my second pint, when I noticed that someone was standing in front of my table. I glanced up to find Cass looking down at me. You have to be sitting down for her to do that – she's pretty tiny.

I've always liked skinny, petite girls. There's such a weird contrast between the amount of space they appear to take up, and their actual weight, both physical and psychic. It's as if they extend beyond the range of their bodies. Because they look so small, it's surprising, too, how much mass they actually contain. Someone so light on the planet still weighs in at over a hundred pounds, which is a lot to have in your arms, or on top of you – and the difference between the sight of them and their unexpected physical heft has a great attraction, not least because of the surprise and shock of them actually *being* there, voluntarily that close to you. This density also means that once encountered, the attraction continues, as a matter of their gravitational pull.

This, I knew even as I was thinking it, was not the kind of thought that usually ran through my mind. It sounded rather grown-up and brainy, in fact. I wondered about telling Cass some of it, but then realized she was frowning at me pretty severely.

"What?" I asked.

"Was all that supposed to *mean* something?"

"Christ – was I talking out loud?"

"You was saying *something*, but God knows what it was. Are you calling me fat?"

As she sat down I saw she'd already got herself a drink, which made me feel a bit rubbish, because I knew she'd have done this on the assumption I might not have the cash to buy one for her, and that I might actually be intending to let her buy all mine.

I realized suddenly that I was thirty-four and not making a very good job of it. "Thanks for coming."

"Haven't got long," she said, businesslike. "Me and Lisa is going clubbing."

"On a Wednesday?"

"It's Friday, you nutter."

"*Really*?" That explained why the pub was so full. It also meant that I had less time than I'd thought to come up with something sensible about Portnoy's book. Christ.

Cass sipped her bucket of chardonnay and looked at me pretty seriously. "You alright, babe?"

"I think so," I said. "Got flu, or something. Head's a bit ropey, that's all."

"Still hung-over, I should think."

"Look – what actually *happened* the other night?"

"You was in here," she said, briskly, as if reading back dictation. Do people still do dictation these days, sit there writing down the gist and rhythm of what people say? No idea. "You'd had a few already. You called me, said come over and have a beer. I wasn't doing nothing, so I said okay. Got here about an hour later, which time you was three sheets and scribbling all over some bits of paper you had with you – but we had a laugh and I'm thinking, 'Okay, he's pissed as a fart but I do like him', so, you know. We stayed for the lock-in, gave it some welly, an' all. Then you said you'd walk me home."

"That doesn't sound so bad," I said, relieved. I mean, by my standards, that's like a week working for a charity in Rwanda.

"But you *didn't*, see."

"Oh."

"We got halfway there, and you suddenly said you wanted to show me something. I said 'Yeah, right, and I bet I know what it is, an' all,' but you said no, it wasn't that, and be honest I was so pissed by then I thought sod it, why not, even if it is a shag he's after. So you start leading me down these side roads and it didn't look like you knew where you were going, but then there's this alleyway and at the end there's a kiddie's park or something. Locked up. And you said you used to play there when you was little, and why don't we climb the fence and go have a look around."

"Right," I said, feeling cold. Maybe Cass remembered that I'd grown up out in Essex, and had never even been to London before I was eighteen. Maybe she didn't.

"Nearly killed yourself getting over that fence. Nearly killed me, an' all. But we get inside, and it's cold enough that I'm feeling even *more* pissed, and I'm thinking, 'Well, this is one to tell the grandchildren anyway,' though not if we actually *do* shag, leave that bit out, obviously, but then . . ."

She stopped talking. Her face went hard.

"What?"

"You went funny."

"Funny how?"

"You'd been doing this muttering thing half the way there, saying something over and over really quietly. But now you're standing in the middle of the park, and you don't even look like yourself. You was . . . you was being really odd."

"What do you mean?"

"Dunno. You just didn't look like yourself. And you was saying things, but it didn't sound like you."

"Then what happened?"

"I sat on a bench, had a ciggy. Thought 'let him get on with it'. Then just as I've put out me fag, suddenly you make this weird sound, and fall down."

"What, just keeled over?"

"Flat on your back. I laughed my head off until I realized you was out cold."

"So what did you do?"

"I pissed off home, didn't I. Checked you was breathing and everything, but you know, bloody hell, babe, it was sodding freezing and I'd had enough."

I didn't know what to say. I sat looking at her.

She rolled her eyes. "You know you're doing it again, don't you?"

"Doing what?"

"Saying things, under your breath."

"Yeah, of course," I lied. "It's, uh, I'm memorising something. For work."

"You're barmy, you are."

She drained the rest of her glass in a swallow, and stood up. "Got to go. If I don't get to Lisa's before she opens the second bottle then we won't be going nowhere, and I really fancy a boogie tonight."

She gave me a quick peck on the cheek, and then she was off, cutting through the crowds at the bar like a fish through reeds it had known all its life.

I honestly didn't mean to have another pint. I was just sitting there, looking at all the people, trying to gather the strength to leave, and to find some distraction from the fact I was a bit freaked out by what Cass had just told me. Ron caught my eye from behind the bar, and I gave him a quick upwards nod, just meaning "hello" – one of those things you can say without saying, a physical utterance – but he mistranslated my intentions and starting pulling me another Stella instead.

And so it went.

XI

I don't know how many hours later it is, but I'm standing outside somewhere and it's very cold. My hands hurt and I look down and I see I've cut the back of one. How?

Climbing the fence, presumably.

Because I'm back there again. In the park.

I turn around and recognize the things in it. The big slide, the small one. The pirate ship. The swings and the little wooden house.

But when it comes to this last item, I'm not recognising it in the right way.

It's drizzling a bit and so I walk over to the wooden house. It's small and battered, about four feet by three feet, open at both ends and with a roof over it, painted yellow some time ago. I go in the front end and perch on the tiny bench inside, and I know I've been there before; that though all the rest of the childrens' stuff in the park is fairly recent, this house has been here a long time, as long as the park itself.

I get out a cigarette, and try to sort through my memories of the other night, the one Cass told me about. She didn't say anything about me sitting in a little house, and she would have mentioned it, if I had. I didn't sit in there after I woke up, either – I just tried to find a way out. So why do I think I've been in there before?

I put my head in my hands. I don't feel right. My mind is full of beer and I can't think straight. Having my eyes shut isn't helping either, and so I raise my head and open them again, and as I do I'm suddenly overcome by a memory, so sharp and vivid that for a split second it's more real than anything else.

In the memory I'm sitting exactly where I am now, on this bench in this little wooden house. I'm not here because I'm drunk and sheltering from the rain, however. I'm here because it's a wooden house and I always sit in here for a while when we come to the park.

I do not feel cramped. There's plenty of room.

And then I turn toward the little door at the front, and . . .

Suddenly I jerk up, banging my head on the roof, and lunge outside.

But he isn't there.

I know who I'm expecting to . . . no, not "expecting" to see, because I know now that what I've just experienced was a memory, and not happening in real time. I know who I was *remembering* looking up to see, on some unimportant Saturday morning a long time ago.

I look around, still convinced he's going to be here somewhere, maybe over at the bench, or looking vaguely at the houses, or slipping behind a tree.

It's my dad.

This is our park, the one we come to together.

And when I find I can't see him, and the memory suddenly starts to fade, I feel miserable, because it has been so long since I've seen my father's face, so many years since he died, and I miss him.

Then it's gone, whatever long-ago morning I'm remembering, and I'm just a very pissed man standing in the middle of a park, in the rain and the dark, and feeling alone and pretty scared.

I lurch over to the main gate and very slowly, very laboriously and very carefully, clamber back out – on only three or four occasions coming close to tumbling off and smashing my skull to smithereens.

I trudge up the alley and find a street I think I recognize. I walk along it, and keep going, and by the time I get back to the house in which I live, I've remembered both that my dad isn't actually dead, and that the bastard never took me to a park in his life.

XII

Saturday and Sunday blurred into one. I spent some of it in the pub, some in the park, some of it walking the streets, but most of it in my flat. Whenever I was at home, I found myself reading from the book.

Not "reading" from it in a literal sense, I suppose, but letting it sit in front of my eyes. The conscious extraction of meaning from a procession of words is not, after all, the only way of interacting with a text, or with anything else in the world.

By now I had become sufficiently familiar with the book's contents that I'd realized there was more than one rhythm to the words, that in the beginning they fell into one loose pattern – the one I thought I'd heard in the voice of the man who'd let me out of the park – but that by the end it had changed. No matter how much time I spent looking at the middle sections, however, I couldn't put my finger on where the transition occurred.

I found that I was intrigued rather than bothered by this. I cannot, after all, recall the point where I became the person who lives in this flat and exists how I do, after being the person who was so far in advance of the other students at university that the lecturers just let me do my own thing, convinced I would amount to a great deal. I cannot recall when the four-year marriage I abandoned, toward the end of my twenties, started to be something I no longer wished to be involved in – nor at what point I stopped bothering to send birthday and Christmas cards to the daughter that I'd gained from it. I cannot remember when I became exhausted instead of merely tired.

Things rarely stop and start at easily identifiable points, after all. If they did, then it would be much easier to know when to hold up your hand and say "Wait, hang on, hang on, *stop* – I'm not sure I like where this is going". Life tends to shade from one state to the next, to evolve, or devolve, to grow and develop, or fade and fall apart.

Books and sentences and words hide this, with their quantized approach to reality, their pretence that meanings and events and emotions stop and start – that you can be in one state and then another that is different and that the whole of life is not one long, continual flux. Whole languages collude too, especially the European ones, setting object against subject and giving precedence to the latter over the former: only rare exceptions like certain Amerind dialects structuring themselves to say "a forest, a clearing, and me in it", instead of the individual-as-god delivery of "I am in a clearing in a forest".

I think of these things as I sit. I find other things changing, too, aspects of the world becoming different. In the local corner store, for example, I discover myself chatting fluently to the strikingly beautiful Polish girl behind the counter, in her own language. I find myself walking away with her phone number, too, which is not the kind of thing that usually happens in my life.

I begin to feel hopeful that change is still perhaps possible in life, and that it is happening to me.

XIII

I arrived at Portnoy's shop at midday on Monday, as requested. I'd made no further progress, but had stopped worrying about it. He wanted to meet, so we'd meet. I'd tell him I didn't know what the book was supposed to be about, and he wouldn't give me the remaining six hundred pounds, and that was that. Life would go on.

When I got to Cecil Court I saw through the window that Portnoy was with a customer, so I lurked outside and had a cigarette. Though the cough hadn't come back, the smoke felt weird in my lungs, and so mostly I just held it in my mouth instead. Portnoy's book was in a carrier bag in my hand. There had been times over the weekend where I'd found it difficult to imagine handing it back to him, so much a part of my life had it become. At some point in the night that had changed. I was tired of it now, tired of its music and transitions, tired of not knowing what it was about. Ignorance isn't always bliss. Sometimes it's just a huge pain in the arse, especially when it's about to cost you six hundred quid.

The customer eventually left, clutching something in a neat brown paper bag. An early Wodehouse first, most likely, one of Portnoy's minor stocks in trade. I entered the shop to the sound of him coughing.

"Sounds like you've got what I had," I said.

He nodded. "Could be, my boy, could be."

Clear grey light was coming through the shop window, and it struck me how seldom I'd seen him lit by anything other than his subterranean lair's murky glow. Today his skin looked very pale, and waxy.

I held the carrier bag up toward him and started to speak, but he shook his head.

"Downstairs," he said, and reached over to flip the sign on the door to CLOSED.

I followed him down the narrow and abruptly turning staircase that led to the basement office. The gloom down there seemed even more sepulchral than normal, so much so that I was halfway across the floor before I spotted that something was different: even then it was the smell that gave it away first, or the lack of it.

I stopped, looked around. "What happened to all the books?"

"Moved them on," he said.

"What, *all* of them?" The room was entirely empty. Aside from the desk and its two chairs, everything was gone. Even the framed page of *The Dream* on the wall. All that remained was dust.

"Some were sold, others put in storage."

He sat at his side of the desk, and I sat at the other.

"Are you shutting up shop?"

"Good lord, no," he said, lighting one of his cigars. "Well, in a way, I suppose. I'm moving on."

"Moving on? Why?" I felt panicky.

"The cost of living where I do has simply become too high, especially as the fabric is falling apart. The lease is up."

"But you don't actually *live* here, do you? In this building?"

He smiled. "I meant it figuratively."

I had no idea what he was talking about, and didn't really care. I put the bag with the book in it on the desk. He looked at it, then back up at me.

"What's that?"

"The book," I said. "I'm giving it back. I can't do what you asked."

"And what did I ask you to do?"

"Translate it. Tell you what the book was about."

"No. All I asked for was the gist."

"How could I give you that without translating it?"

He smiled again, kindly. "A good question. But you have. Can't you feel it?"

I was distracted by the smell of his cigar. It smelled good. It made me wonder, in fact, why I smoked cigarettes.

He evidently noticed me looking at the object in his hand, and held it out to me.

"Want to try?"

I took it, put it in between my lips. Drew some of the smoke into my mouth, and let it lie there a while.

"Nice," I said, putting the cigar back in the ashtray.

"I have to be elsewhere in an hour," Portnoy said, "so I suggest we get down to business right away."

"Business?" My head felt fuzzy, as if I'd drunk far too much coffee. The cigar smoke, perhaps. But I allowed myself to hope that – as he appeared to be claiming that I had done what he asked – he might actually be intending to pay me the other six hundred pounds. "What business?"

He reached into his jacket pocket, and took out a small set of keys and a piece of paper with an address written on it. He put them on the table.

"There are six months left on this building," he said, indicating two of the keys. "I'm afraid that will be more than sufficient, given your condition."

"What are you talking about?"

"The address on that piece of paper is where you live. A *pied-à-terre* in Fitzroy Square. Not overly large, but extremely comfortable. I have left a fairly substantial sum of money in a suitcase under the bed."

I stared at the young man opposite me. "Portnoy, what the hell are you talking about?"

"I'm not a bad person," he said. "I'd like you to be at ease in the time that's left. The money should see to that. I've left a note in the drawer of the bedside table, too, should you decide to, ah, self-medicate. The phone number on the note is that of an extremely reliable and discrete gentleman who can supply morphine at short notice."

"Morphine?"

"The pain can be very bad," he said, apologetically. "It's only going to get worse, I'm afraid."

Only then did I realize that, instead of having my back to the room, the wall was behind me. That I was sitting on the opposite side of the desk to normal. And then that the man I was facing was not Portnoy.

It was me.

I tried to say something about this, but was derailed by a cough. It went on for a long time, and hurt a very great deal. When I finally pulled my hand away from my mouth, I stared at it. It was Portnoy's hand.

"What have you done to me?"

"Not so much," the other man said. "Think of it as somatic drift, if you need a word. It's never a book's cover that matters, after all, but what's inside. The gist. You found him in the end."

"'Him'? Don't you mean 'it'?"

"No," he said, standing. "Good luck. And remember that gentleman I mentioned." He picked up the bag from the desk, and replaced it with something in a frame. "A leaving present."

I reached out for it, feeling tired and old and unwell. I tilted it toward me, and saw it was what had always hung on the wall behind him, that single page from the first folio of *A Midsummer Night's Dream*. Seeing it close up for the first time, I noticed that three words had been lightly underlined, in pencil.

Thou art translated.

"I don't understand."

"From the Latin '*translatus*'," Portnoy said, "serving as a past participle of '*transferre*' – to bring over."

He picked up the cigar from the ashtray, and stuck it in his mouth.

Around it he said "Goodbye, dear boy," and left.

XIV

In a month the deterioration has already become marked. From notes left in Portnoy's flat I learned that my new body has lung cancer, of a belligerently terminal variety. Nothing that can be done about it – except, I suppose, what he did.

I wouldn't know how to even embark upon such a course, even if I still had the book, which I do not. It is with him, wherever he is, in whichever quarter of the world he is starting upon his new life. Or a new chapter of it, at least. I wonder how many times he has done it before, how many younger men, like me, have allowed his meaning to be substituted between their covers. A great many, I suspect.

My days are comfortable, in any event. I sit in the large leather chair in his sitting room and look through the books he left behind, or out of the window at the trees in the square. If the pain gets very bad, I avail myself of the substance I now obtain from the gentleman Portnoy recommended. It beats knocking back pints of Stella, that's for sure.

On afternoons when I don't feel too dreadful I go for walks, watching the leaves turn, feeling the weight of the city around me, appreciating these things while I still have time.

Last week I even took the tube a few stops north, early one evening, and sat at a table in the corner of the Southampton for a while. Yes, naturally I was hoping that Cass might come in, and wonderously, she did. Her eyes skated over me, not recognising the portly, grey-skinned edition in which I now find myself bound. She had a few raucous glasses of wine with some guy I didn't recognize, but took herself off into the night alone. I wish her well, wherever she is.

After she left I walked slowly around to Dalmeny Park, and down the alleyway, and looked through the closed gates. There's no way I could climb them now, and it's not really my place, after all. My body knows it, however. It remembers being there as a child, with its father, and so I let it stand there for a while, before wheezing my way back up the road and waiting until a cab came to take me back to my nest.

Where I continue to die.

The odd thing is that I don't mind too much.

Some stories, some people, deserve their length and span. They merit a novel-length treatment, have things to tell and other lives to illuminate. The real Portnoy – whoever or whatever he was – is one of those, and I'm sure he's already making far better use of my body than I ever did. There are others, people like the man I was, who should aspire only to being a novella, or perhaps not even that.

Short stories have their place in the world, after all. The tale remains afterwards, beyond death, and perhaps one day someone will read mine and understand what I amounted to.

A few events and mistakes, several hang-overs and a kiss, and then a final line.

THANA NIVEAU

Guinea Pig Girl

THANA NIVEAU IS a Halloween bride who lives in the Victorian seaside town of Clevedon, where she shares her life with fellow writer John Llewellyn Probert, in a Gothic library filled with arcane books and curiosities.

She is the author of *From Hell to Eternity*, which was short-listed for the British Fantasy Award for Best Collection 2013. Several of her stories have been reprinted in *The Mammoth Book of Best New Horror* previously, and other tales appear or are forthcoming in *Exotic Gothic 5; The Burning Circus*, *The Black Book of Horror* (Volumes 7–10), *Whispers in the Dark*, *Sorcery and Sanctity: A Homage to Arthur Machen*, *Demons and Devilry*, *Night Schools*, *The 13 Ghosts of Christmas*, *Magic: an Anthology of the Esoteric and Arcane*, *Terror Tales of Wales*, *Terror Tales of the Cotswolds*, *Steampunk Cthulhu*, *Sword & Mythos*, *Love, Lust & Zombies*, *Best British Horror*, *Bite-Sized Horror 2*, *Death Rattles* and *Delicate Toxins*.

"'Guinea Pig Girl' is my twisted little Valentine to Japanese horror films," admits the author. "It's easily the most gruesome story I've ever written, although in a way it's actually kind of sweet and romantic. I love J-horror, but I've never seen any of the notorious 'guinea pig' films (I suspect they're a bit much, even for me). I'm also fascinated by the mindset of people who love pure torture porn.

"The second guinea pig film, the evocatively titled *Flower of Flesh and Blood*, was famously mistaken by Charlie Sheen for a snuff film and reported to the FBI. It isn't, of course, but I couldn't help but wonder what he felt while watching it and genuinely believing he was seeing a snuff film. Did he watch it all the way through? Or was he freaked out at the first inkling that it might be real and turn it off? How many others have watched films like it thinking what they were seeing was real? And what if that blurred line made the watcher vulnerable? What if it could weave a sort of spell?

"I wanted to write about someone who loved gory horror but felt conflicted about it and I really liked the thought of a male voyeur being more of a victim than the female ostensibly being tortured."

S HE WAS BEAUTIFUL. Quite the most beautiful woman Alex had ever seen. But it wasn't just her beauty. What he loved most about her was the way she suffered.

He had been horrified the first time. He'd felt the stirring in his loins and then the growing hardness in his trousers. A sidelong glance at his mate Josh, whose film it was, then some uncomfortable shifting.

"Holy shit," Josh said with a laugh as the freak in the lab coat cut off one of Yuki's fingers.

She screamed, her beautiful mouth stretched open, her slanted eyes as wide as they would go. She screamed. Josh laughed. Alex got hard.

"Yeah," he said, to say something. Then he squirmed as Yuki's torture continued and his erection grew.

Oh, how she suffered.

That night he'd wanked himself silly over the image of her terrified, pleading face. He didn't dare go as far as imagining himself pinning her down on the filthy mattress in the basement room, fisting a hand in her long black hair and telling her how he would take her to bits, piece by piece. No, he didn't dare. The image flickered in the background of his thoughts but he shied away from it. Pictured himself instead as the guy who came to tend her wounds, give her water and a bit of food, hold her and reassure her that he would help her escape if he could, honest, but they were watching him too . . .

It was sick.

He felt ashamed and disgusted once the last throbs of pleasure had faded and he'd cleaned himself up and thrown the handful of tissues in the bin, wishing he could incinerate them. He felt as filthy as the room she'd been imprisoned in throughout the film. He'd let himself go this time but that was it. He didn't get off on stuff like that, no way. In junior school some bullies had once tried to make him join in with torturing old Mrs Webber's cat and he hadn't been able to do it. *He'd* suffered then, suffered their ridicule and taunting, them calling him a pussy. But he wasn't like them, couldn't bring himself to hurt something else, something helpless.

So why did Yuki make him feel like this?

Days later he still couldn't get some of the imagery out of his head. It was just some dodgy Japanese torture porn film he couldn't even remember the name of but he remembered every moment of every scene Yuki was in. She was tiny and fragile, the way so many Japanese girls were. Sexy and girl-ish, slutty and innocent all at the same time. An intoxicating package in any context, but seeing her so helpless and vulnerable had done something to Alex. That wounded expression, her eyes streaming with tears, her hands clasped as she pleaded in words he couldn't understand . . . It got under his skin.

He'd wanted to dive into the film and save her, protect her, and yet that wasn't where his fantasies steered him afterwards. On the way to work his hands had clenched on the steering wheel as he sat in traffic and he imagined them wrapped around Yuki's slender throat. If he closed his eyes he could hear her gasping for breath. He could smell her urine as she pissed herself in terror.

Sick.

And yet every night his hand slipped down between his legs and all it took was the thought of her wide eyes and high-pitched cries to make him unbearably aroused. He couldn't banish the images. All he could do was let them wash over him as he came so hard his ears rang. Again and again.

Yuki Hayashi. Actress. Born 13 April 1989 in Hokkaido, Japan. Filmography: *Victim Factory 1 & 2*, *Love Hotel of the Damned* and *Aesthetic Paranoia* (filming).

Alex clicked on each film and read the synopses. They were all low-budget rip-offs of the notorious "guinea pig" films from the '80s. Girls got kidnapped and tortured and that was basically it. Sometimes they also got raped.

The fourth one in the filmography wasn't finished yet and *Love Hotel of the Damned* didn't seem to be available anywhere, not even on Josh's pirate site. But Alex ordered the others.

Like all rip-offs, *Victim Factory* aspired to take things a step further than its inspiration. The gore was over the top, even by Alex's standards, and it was made worse by the homemade feel of the production. They looked like snuff films shot on someone's home-video camera.

Yuki's debut was as "2nd victim" in an unpleasant scene where she was grabbed off the street and taken to an abandoned asylum. There she was stripped naked and thrown into a room stained with the blood of previous victims. To wait. After listening in terror to the screams and cries of another girl, Yuki was dragged off to the torture chamber next door for her turn. The killer bound her wrists tightly with rope and looped them over a large hook. He turned a crank that noisily hoisted her off the ground while she screamed and wept and kicked her pretty legs. Even her slight weight looked as though it was dislocating her shoulders and Alex winced. How could you fake that?

Finally, in a bizarre moment of artistry, the killer carved a series of Japanese characters into Yuki's skin with the jagged edge of a broken samurai sword. The subtitles only translated the spoken dialogue so Alex had no idea what the words inscribed on her flesh meant.

It drove him mad.

The exotic swashes and flourishes streamed with blood that looked disturbingly real, a striking contrast to Yuki's pale skin. Alex could almost believe that the mutilation had actually happened but for the fact that in the second film, the one Josh had shown him, she was unmarked. Pristine and ready for more. Ready to have her fingers and toes snipped off one by one, her mouth forced open with a metal dentist's gag and her tongue cut out.

He searched the Net for more information, but the films didn't appear to be widely known. There was the occasional mention on a message board, but Alex couldn't find any translation for the characters in the carving scene. Nor was there much information about Yuki. He found one screen grab from the first film, which he immediately stored on his phone. Her eyes pleaded with him through the image and he felt obscurely guilty, as though he'd imprisoned her in a tiny digital cage. But he didn't delete the picture.

The films made him feel uncomfortable, almost sick at times. And truthfully, he didn't enjoy the violence. When he played the DVDs again he only watched the scenes with Yuki and even then he felt funny afterwards. But he couldn't get her out of his head. The very thought of her was enough to make him hard and even though he tried to picture her whole and undamaged, the images of torture would quickly take over. He tried to imagine her voice, cheerful and sweet as she chattered on her phone before being abducted in each film, but the musical sounds always devolved into screams of pain and madness.

Her anguish was so excruciatingly real. He couldn't tune it out, couldn't un-see it. And he couldn't help the effect it had on him.

She was there behind his eyes every night, pleading with him to stop, her tiny body struggling helplessly against ropes and rusty chains. And no matter how much he tried to transform the images in his head, he always saw himself wielding the blades, the needles, the bolt-cutters. Her blood ran like wine over his hands and he was drunk on the taste of her.

"Hey, mate, you know that DVD you were after?"

Alex froze, staring at his phone with apprehension. Then he took a deep breath before forcing himself to ask calmly, "Which one?"

"*Love Hotel of the Damned*. I found it."

"Oh, cool," he replied, as nonchalantly as he could manage.

"Yeah, some guy up in Leeds has it and he said he'd burn me a copy for a tenner."

"Thanks, mate. I'll pay you back."

"No problem!" Josh sounded pleased, no doubt proud of himself for tracking down the obscure film. If he had any suspicions about Alex's obsession it wasn't obvious. "I'll drop it by your place next week."

Next week. Alex felt his insides churn hungrily at the thought of seeing Yuki again, seeing her suffer and die in new and terrible ways.

The synopsis of *Love Hotel* made it sound like the worst of the lot. Same "guinea pig" concept but this time set in one of those weird Japanese hotels he'd read about online. The kind where you could fuck a *manga* character on a spaceship or grope a schoolgirl in a room designed like a train carriage. He'd found the trailer for the film on a J-horror fan site and it looked seriously reprehensible. Even some of the hardcore gorehounds said the level of sexual violence was too much for them.

Alex slid down in his chair as his cock began to stir.

The film was even worse than he'd anticipated. Murky and grainy, as though someone had simply held up a cheap camera and filmed it playing on a TV. The poor quality actually made the gore seem more realistic.

Yuki didn't appear until halfway through and Alex almost didn't recognize her. She was thinner and paler and she seemed even more fragile. But she was still beautiful. She wore an elaborate Gothic Lolita dress with frilly petticoats and a lacy apron and mop cap. But not for long. Her "customer" cut the flimsy costume away with a pair of shears. From the way Yuki yelped and twisted, it was clear he was cutting her too. Blood trickled down one arm and over her belly and she stared straight into the camera for one heart-stopping moment. Alex had the uncomfortable sense that he was watching a genuine victim this time and not an actress.

His thumb hovered over the STOP button for a few seconds before he reminded himself that there was a fourth film on the list. *Aesthetic Paranoia*, which she was apparently still shooting. If this was real, surely she wouldn't have made another such film. Surely she'd be shouting "Police!" or "Help!" He was sure he'd recognize that level of distress even in a language he couldn't speak. No, it was just that weird sense of authenticity you sometimes got with ultra low-budget films.

Yuki cried and begged in plaintive Japanese while the man stripped the mattress off the bed and threw her onto the bare springs. He bound her, spread-eagled, with wire that Alex could see biting into her delicate wrists and ankles. Then he threw a bucket of water over her and she screamed again and again, writhing on the springs.

The man lifted the head of the bed and propped it against the wall so that it rested at an angle. The camera zoomed in and around Yuki's naked, shivering body, shooting from underneath the bed to show the mesh pressing painfully into her back, the wires cutting into her skin. In close-up the springs looked rusty and Yuki was bleeding in several places. The detail was too subtle not to be real and Alex began to feel light-headed again. But he couldn't tear his eyes away.

The man held up a series of huge fish hooks with what looked like electrodes attached and Yuki screamed herself hoarse as the hooks were threaded through her skin one by one in a scene that went on for nearly ten minutes. When he was done, the man connected the trailing wires to a machine at his feet. He pressed a button and there was a terrible buzzing sound, followed by another piercing scream. Yuki leapt and bucked against the springs for what felt like an eternity before the current stopped. Wisps of smoke began to rise from the contact points and Alex thought he could smell something burning. Blood ran from Yuki's eyes like tears as she gasped and panted, too breathless to scream. The camera zoomed in on her face and she stared directly out of the screen again, as though she were looking through a window right at Alex.

When the buzzing sound began again Yuki tensed and started to plead frantically, this time with whoever was behind the camera. Alex closed his eyes against her screams and the metallic rattle of the springs and the zap of electricity. He held his breath as it went on and on, wishing it would end.

At last there was silence. Silence and the smell of scorched meat. He shut the film off and ran for the bathroom. He almost made it.

It was several days before Yuki came back.

Alex had put the three DVDs in a carrier bag, knotted it and pushed it to the back of the bathroom cupboard. When Josh had asked how he liked the film he'd forced a laugh and said it was rubbish, with crappy effects. And if his voice had trembled when he'd said it, Josh didn't seem to notice. Yuki's picture was gone from his phone and the J-horror sites he'd bookmarked were erased from his browsing history.

As disturbing as it had been, he knew it was fake. That was part of the point of films like that – to trick the viewer into thinking it was real. Actual snuff films were an urban legend. None had ever been found and they certainly wouldn't be readily available online in any case. People had been fooled by special effects before. And while it was a compliment to the makers of Yuki's films, Alex had seen enough.

He was in bed, almost asleep, when he first heard the sound. A soft rustle, as though someone were reading a newspaper in the next room. He froze. He had the mad urge to call out "Who's there?" even though there was no one else in the flat. Unless someone had broken in. It was that kind of neighbourhood, but the flat was too small for a burglar to hide in without Alex knowing. A rat, then? It would have to be an awfully big one.

His heart hammered in his chest, drowning out any sounds that might be coming from the other room. Seconds passed like hours as he sat staring towards the open doorway, feeling like a child who'd woken from a nightmare. He should get up and switch on all the lights but the thought of putting his feet on the floor, exposing them to the empty space under the bed, was too frightening.

"Get a grip," he mouthed, trying to spur himself into action. But still he didn't move.

There was another sound. A soft slap, like a bare foot on the hard floor. Then another. And another.

His blood turned to ice-water as the footsteps came closer and closer. A thin shape was emerging from the darkness of the corridor. Then he heard the dripping. He could almost believe it was some girl he'd brought home from a club and forgotten about. She'd just got out of the shower without drying off and now . . .

Except it wasn't. It was Yuki.

When she reached the bedroom Alex bit back a scream. She stood in the doorway, naked and dripping with blood. Her arms hung loose at her sides and Alex's stomach clenched as he saw the symbols carved into her body. The calligraphy was more extensive than he remembered from the scene in the film. The cuts ran from the base of her throat, across her small breasts and down her torso.

A strangled sound escaped his throat and Yuki's head turned towards him. It was a careful, deliberate movement, as though she had only located him by the sound and was trying to fix his exact position. She turned and took a step into the room. Alex stared at her in horror, desperate to run but unable to move.

It wasn't real. It couldn't be real. It was a dream or a hallucination, just like the images in his head he hadn't been able to get rid of. But worst of all, he felt himself responding as he always had. Hot desire pulsed in his groin even as bile rose in his throat.

Each step she took opened the cuts further. Blood flowed over her body like water, pooling on the floor. What was almost worse was the residual grace in her movements. She didn't shuffle or sway drunkenly. Rather, she moved with the precision of a dancer, each movement full of purpose. Blood gleamed in the light from the window, shining on her mutilated skin like a wet carapace, and Alex shuddered as he felt himself growing hard.

"No," he managed to whisper. "No, please."

Yuki responded to his voice, reaching out for him. Her eyes were empty pools of black but her lips seemed to be forming a smile.

It took all his courage to shut his eyes and wish the sight away.

He counted to three before his eyes flew open again in fright. Yuki was gone.

It was some time before he was able to get up off the bed and even then his legs threatened to buckle with each step he took towards the doorway. There was no blood on the floor, no evidence that anything had ever been there.

It was the middle of the night but Alex got dressed and drove all the way to work to throw the DVDs away. He snapped the disks in half and scattered them, along with the packaging, into the three large industrial bins behind the office building. He wondered if he ought to say something, but what? A prayer? He wasn't religious so he didn't imagine it would do any good. But surely it couldn't do any harm.

"Goodbye, Yuki," he whispered, and her name felt like an obscenity on his lips. "Please don't come back."

But she did.

It was four nights later and Alex was asleep. He was deep inside a pleasant childhood dream when his eyes fluttered open with a start and there she was, standing over him.

He screamed and scrambled away until he was cowering on the floor against the wall. Yuki cocked her head as if in confusion, her eyes streaming with black, bloody tears, her temples scorched and pierced by fish hooks. She looked thinner, more wasted.

Yuki raised one pale arm and reached for him. He could see the gleam of bone through the cuts on her chest. The wounds gaped like tiny mouths with each movement, as though trying to speak the words they represented. Alex shuddered with revulsion as Yuki drew her hand down over his torso. Her touch was gentle as she took hold of his cock. He stiffened in her grasp, unable to move, unable to resist as she stroked him like a lover. She pressed her blackened lips to his and he closed his eyes with a sickened moan as he came.

Then he crumpled to his knees on the floor, crying.

"Mate, you look like hell."

Alex had been tempted not to answer the door but Josh had kept pounding, shouting that he knew Alex was home.

"Yeah," he mumbled. "Got some bloody bug."

"I've been ringing you for days. The guys at work thought you'd died or something. You didn't even call in sick."

Alex managed a rueful smile. "Too sick to."

"Well, is there anything I can do for you? You need food? Booze? Drugs?"

"No, I'm fine."

But his assurances didn't get rid of Josh. His friend muttered about how stuffy it was in the flat before planting himself on the battered sofa where they'd watched so many DVDs together. He shrugged out of his leather jacket, revealing a black *Faces of Death* T-shirt. Alex stared at the grinning skull and spiky red lettering for several seconds before looking away. Josh didn't seem to notice his uneasiness.

An awkward silence stretched between them but Alex couldn't think of anything to say. He couldn't tell Josh he was seeing ghosts, much less the specifics of the encounters. But Yuki's presence hung in the air in spite of his silence. He could still smell her blood and burnt flesh, still feel the slick touch of her fingers on his skin.

He'd scrubbed himself raw in the shower after the first time, but it hadn't changed anything. She'd returned the next night, and the next. She looked worse with each visit but each time Alex's own body had betrayed him, succumbing to her touch even as he choked back the sickness welling in his throat. He couldn't resist or escape, and each violation only seemed to excite him more.

He was pretty sure he understood what the symbols were now. Hours of online searching had led him to a website about curses. He didn't need to read Japanese to know that one of the characters represented "desire" and another "obsession". He hadn't dared to search further to see if "love" was also among them.

Josh was talking, telling him about some new film he'd just seen, one his girlfriend hadn't been able to stomach.

Alex felt his own stomach churn queasily.

"Anyway," Josh continued, oblivious to his friend's discomfort, "pretty weird about that actress, huh?"

Alex blinked. "What are you talking about?"

"Didn't you get my email?"

"What email?"

"The one I sent you last week. About that Japanese girl. The one in the film you had me track down?"

Alex felt a crawling sensation in his guts. So his fixation on Yuki hadn't been lost on Josh after all. "What about her?"

"She's dead."

The words seemed to come from a long way away, like a transmission he'd already heard. He couldn't speak. The skull on Josh's shirt seemed to be laughing now.

"Alex? You okay?"

He nodded weakly. "Yeah, I think so." Some part of him had already known, of course.

Josh went on. "I figured you liked her since you wanted all her films and I was trying to find a copy of that last one for you – *Aesthetic Paranoia*. She died on the set. Some kind of freak accident."

"When?" Alex managed to ask.

"That's what's so weird, mate. It was only a few weeks ago, before I even showed you *Victim Factory 2*. She was dead the whole time we've been watching her films. Hey, are you sure you're okay? You're white as a fucking sheet."

That night Alex lay in bed listening for the familiar sticky wet slap of her feet. There was no point in trying to resist. Yuki would come for him, would keep coming for him, until there was nothing left of either of them. He'd met her eyes through the screen and she had chosen him. He was special.

He hadn't liked the way Josh had said "we". *We've* been watching her films. He didn't like the thought of Josh seeing Yuki the way he did.

She was no longer able to stand upright, but she could crawl. Her hair hung in matted clumps around her face as she pushed herself towards him on rotting hands and knees. Her skin was peeling away from the bone in places, hanging like strips of charred, wet paper.

"I'm here," Alex said softly, tapping the floor to guide her.

Before she could reach the source of the sound, she stopped. A heavy obstacle was in the way. She reached out a tentative bony hand to touch it. Her fingers moved over the grinning skull and the red letters that were smeared with blood, then found the tear in the material. She prodded the gaping wound in Josh's chest, gingerly touching the bloody edge of the kitchen knife while Josh stared vacantly up at the ceiling.

Yuki frowned, looking lost for a moment before recoiling from the unfamiliar body. Hurt by the deception, she raised her head and a feeble sound emerged from what remained of her throat. Alex could see the glistening strings of muscle trying to work to form words. His heart twisted.

"I'm sorry," he said. "But I had to know I was the only one."

She responded to his voice, turning her head towards him and then making her way to the bed with painful care. Too weak to climb up, she raised her thin arms like a child. Alex ignored the crunch of disintegrating bone as he lifted her up and sat her in his lap, his cock already swelling hungrily. Her lips hung in bloody tatters and he smoothed them into the semblance of a pout as he kissed her.

"I love you too," he whispered. Then he slid his hand between her ruined legs.

KIM NEWMAN

Miss Baltimore Crabs
Anno Dracula 1990

KIM NEWMAN HAS recently scripted (with Maura McHugh) the comic book mini-series *Witchfinder: The Mysteries of Unland* (Dark Horse); a spin-off from Mike Mignola's *Hellboy* series, it is illustrated by Tyler Crook. His forthcoming fiction includes the novels *Kentish Glory: The Secrets of Drearcliff Grange* and *Angels of Music*.

Newman's second fiction contribution to this volume is also taken from the fourth *Anno Dracula* novel, *Johnny Alucard*, allowing the author to play with favourite characters from the movie *Scream, Blacula Scream* and the TV series *Homicide: Life on the Street*.

Previously ... in Anno Dracula: *Geneviève Dieudonné, elder vampire, has been run out of Los Angeles by rising power Johnny Alucard, a vampire movie mogul, and is working as a medical examiner in crime-ridden Baltimore ...*

I

TWO HOMICIDE DETECTIVES stood over a body. Number One Male, late teens/early twenties, five-nine. Black cloak with red trim, jeans, serious running shoes. Face down on the street. Scarlet spiderweb radiating along cracks in the asphalt. The rank tang of dead blood at dawn. Cause of death: multiple GSW.

Murder? Yes – obviously. Yet, not her bailiwick ... except technically.

At first lookover, Geneviève diagnosed a characteristic East Baltimore disagreement-over-the-sale-of-illicit-substances slaying. The crime scene: a come-down-in-the-world neighbourhood. Boarded-up row-houses. Sturdy Victorian homes for the well off, sub-divided a few Depressions back for the struggling poor. Now, shells for skells. Gang graffiti. Junked cars. A violently orange couch upended next to a dumpster. Thin crowd of kept-back-beyond-the-yellow-tape citizens. They'd have seen nothing.

Her blue windbreaker had OCME on the back in over-sized yellow letters, in imitation of those FBI jackets worn to help limit the number of times when federal agents got accidentally shot by fellow law enforcement professionals. She went through a pair of Nike knock-off trainers a month. This gig regularly took her into alleys carpeted with bottle shrapnel and across floors sticky with undrinkable body fluids. She toted her forensic kit in a Gladstone bag she'd had since Gladstone was alive.

She had parked her cherry-red Plymouth Fury just behind the white van from the morgue. The car had been with her longer than most men in her life, and given her less grief. Blake and Grimes, her morgue attendants, were on the scene already, breakfasting on Pop-Tarts.

Walking from her car, she passed a lounger who eyeballed her from under a cowboy hat. Big white guy, out of state. Creepy. Then again, this was Creep Town.

Docs and cops were like aliens here. Real vamps were scarce on the drac corners. Plenty of dhamps hereabouts, though. That's what rattled her cobweb. Folks thinking hard about what she had in her veins, what it could do for them.

She bet Dracula hadn't seen that coming when he made his damn Declaration.

The cops looked up from the body.

"Gené Dee, Gené Dee, what have you got to say to me," sung-chanted the light-skinned African-American detective who always wore a hat.

"*Ou se trouve l'assassin diabolique?*" asked the underfed Jewish detective who always attempted French *avec l'accent diabolique* when talking with her. He lowered his hipster shades to show her soulful comedy eyes.

There had to be something she'd not been told.

"What troubles the mighty murder police?" she asked.

She'd moved from Toronto to Baltimore at the specific request of the Office of the Chief Medical Examiner for Maryland. For some reason Crab Town got more than its share of gimmick killings. Rare moth cocoons in the gullets of preserved severed heads. Mad poets walling themselves up in tribute to Edgar Allan Poe. Giant crustacean attacks. Lately, there'd been a rash of vampire-related freak crimes. A hundred years after the Dracula Declaration, there were still few specialists in vampire medicine, let alone vampire forensics. Despite what had gone down in Los Angeles, she'd been headhunted back to the USA.

. . . but not to work routine drug shootings.

"True you busted Jack the Ripper?" asked the black detective.

"There was no Jack the Ripper," said his partner. "It was a Masonic conspiracy . . ."

"You don't know the half of it," she said.

Sometimes – like now – she felt it was still 1888 and she was stuck in Whitechapel. This was another old, bad district. More open to the skies, less crowded – block after block of empty or seemingly empty houses – but the same stink. City jungle, predators and prey.

Then, she'd lived in the middle of the slum. This time, she was snug across town in a Federal Hill apartment, an easy walk from the morgue on Penn Street. Rents near the harbour were high, so she roomed with two other professional women. Lorie Bryer, an editorial contributor to the *BaltimoreSun*, was intelligent, reasonable and empathetic, which was probably why she got more hate mail than anyone else on the paper. Emma Zoole, an architectural model-maker, specialised in crime-scene reconstructions used in court to walk juries through murders. Neither was a vampire, though Emma was a weekend dhamp. Geneviève was gently trying to persuade Lorie, whom she liked a lot, to ease Emma, a flake with a colourful love life, out of the flat. Geneviève spent enough on-the-job time at crime scenes without coming home to find a doll's-house replica of the Tri-State Hooker Hacker's latest killing room on the kitchen table.

Mr Deceased had six holes in the back of his cloak. An unusual garment, but surely not why Geneviève was here. Dressing like a vampire – rather, like vampires were supposed to dress – didn't make you undead. It was arrant stereotyping, anyway. Unlike Emma Zoole, she didn't sleep in a white coffin and have a wardrobe full of shrouds.

"Meet Alonzo Fortunato," said the black cop. "Honour student. High-school athlete. Once aka "Track" Fortunato. Gave up on gold and started peddling red. Got hisself a new street name. 'Drak' . . ."

"Hence the *un*-fortunate Mr Fortunato's distinctive choice of attire," put in the other detective. "He was a walking billboard for his putrid product. The finest powdered *sang de vampire* in the city, *probablement*."

Geneviève shuddered. The drac craze had followed her from Los Angeles to Toronto to here. It was still spreading. According to DEA reports, the business of selling vampire blood in liquid or powdered form, in various degrees of purity or adulteration, started in New York in the late 1970s, a country away from where she'd been at the time. She still took it personally. Nico, someone she hadn't saved, was one of her personal ghosts. The vampire waif was an early casualty of the drac scene; not of the bleeding process – plenty of vampires bled to nothing to make red powder – but the whole bloody business.

She gave Alonzo Fortunato, today's victim, due consideration.

"Cause of death was a handgun, discharged repeatedly," she said. "You find owner of said gun, you solve case. Drak goes up on the board in black. Commendations all round. Now can I get back to my morgue? I have pressing whodunits . . ."

"Ah ah ah, not so fast, Dr Dee," said the black detective. "Come into the parlour . . ."

When shot, Fortunato had been running from a particular house. She backtracked his likely trail up some steps to an open door. A uniform was stationed on the stoop.

The detectives ushered her inside. The stench was worse here.

Though the windows were boarded, the house was in use. Power was hooked up. Coats on a rack. She was directed into a reception room off the hallway.

Seven more dead people. Four males, two females, one whose sex would have to be determined at autopsy. Predominantly black. Comprehensively shot. Weirdly stretched, as if sculpted from warm wax. A still life with weapons, shell casings, drugs paraphernalia, blood spatter, death. Feathers from murdered cushions still floated like zephyrs on the summer breeze. A free-standing lamp had been felled, casting harsh film-noir shadows.

Too many bodies for Blake and Grimes to get into the van for a single run. They'd need backup. Admin had been on at her about the expense of additional journeys in city vehicles. If they got their way, corpses would be stacked like firewood and moved like furniture.

"Welcome to the war zone," said the Jewish detective. "Savour one of the city's happiest traditions: the yo-on-yo firefight and general massacre . . . Time to sort out who shot who in what order."

"I don't think so," said Geneviève, gingerly moving around the room, trying not to step in or brush against anything that might be mentioned in court. "The limp on-the-couches positions of the bodies indicate a leisurely moment of communal relaxation interrupted by an armed visitor or visitors who unloaded before this krewe could respond. See: all the bullet holes are on that side of the room, away from the hall door. Note firearms still in waistbands, pockets or on side-tables. At a guess, Fortunato was upstairs sleeping or in the can at the time of the surprise visit. He made a vain attempt to use his track skills to get away. Unless they bumped a head on a lintel, your doer or doers probably got in and out without sustaining a scratch. This was a murder raid."

The black detective thumped his partner's arm with a told-you-so grin.

"I still don't understand why you asked for me," Geneviève said.

"Coupla things . . . the teeth, the claws, the eyes."

She had noticed what the detectives meant. She'd need them naked on a table under a good light to be sure, but the corpses all looked dhamp. Sharpened teeth and nails. Bleeding gums and cuticles which weren't yet accustomed to popping fangs or talons. One had an elongated neck, which could have been congenital. Again, this wasn't too surprising. Drac was the drug flavour of the new decade. Cocaine cartels and poppy growers were hurting.

"No, no, no," she said. "A drac angle doesn't make this vampire-related. I'll have Scheiner briefed when these bodies come in . . ."

"These bodies?" said the Jewish detective. "You thought we'd called you to look at *these* bodies? Oh, no no no . . . wrong end of the stick, meet Geneviève Dieudonné. If you'll kindly step this way, through the beaded curtain charmingly redolent of the summer of love, you shall find the reason you and only you are the M.E. for this . . ."

He held the curtain aside.

Geneviève passed through the curtain into the next room – a kitchen.

Only one dead person was here, a very fat man in very tight scarlet underwear. Most of the back of his head missing.

GSW, again. Nothing unusual.

Light was low, but something glittered on the linoleum. An antique carved box lay upside down, lid open. Small white objects scattered.

"Are them what we think them is?" asked the black detective.

Geneviève opened her bag and found the proper implement. She crouched and picked up one of the objects with a large pair of tweezers.

It was a fang. A vampire tooth.

II

There were thirty-eight fangs, presumably not all from one victim – though, since vampire teeth grew back if pulled or broken, it was just conceivable they'd sprouted from the same jaw. Incisors, canines, biters. No molars. A couple were grossly oversized specimens – three-inch tusks. One had a black diamond set in it.

"Another Poe killing?" she asked.

Staging murders in imitation of the tales of Edgar Allan Poe was an odd fad which had caught on lately, especially in Baltimore. In 1849, Poe had died here during a ballot-stuffing bender and been buried (by a nasty irony, prematurely) in a churchyard on West Fayette Street. A headstone still stood and someone's bones lay under it. The poet was supposedly exhumed and reburied in 1875 and Walt Whitman (who attended the ceremony) claimed he recognised Eddy by the distinctive forehead of his skull. Whitman was mistaken. Another unknown egghead lay in the grave. Poe was still around as a vampire, squirming on *Oprah* or *The Jerry Langford Show* whenever another ardent fan sicced an orangutang on his girlfriend's mother or rigged up a basement pendulum to bisect a vacuum-cleaner salesman.

The black detective looked blank.

"'Berenice'," said his partner. "In that *conte cruel*, first published in the *Southern Literary Messenger* in 1835, the perverted perp Egaeus keeps his cataleptic cousin Berenice's gnashers in a box, much like the one these spilled out of."

"And the body outside," said Geneviève. "His name was Fortunato . . ."

"Just like the victim in 'A Cask of Amontillado'. Probable coincidence. Poe killers usually go the whole hop-frog. Wall up their Fortunatos and Madelines . . . hearts under the floorboards . . . plague bacillus spread through the prom. They all have pet ravens or one-eyed cats. I can't recall a Tale of Mystery and Imagination in which a melancholy protagonist muses on the loss of a pale young woman and opens up with an Uzi to ventilate a roomful of sleazoid drac-heads. Of course, I've not kept up with the latterday *oeuvre.*"

"None of the Poe killers count the recent books," she said.

"I like Ed McBain," said the black cop. "No hump ever kills another hump because he read an 87th Precinct paperback."

Geneviève stood. She had an urge to collect the fangs and put them back in the box. The crime scene needed to be undisturbed a while longer.

"Edgar Allan Poe is a special case," she said. "A vampire writer."

She'd seen Poe from across the room a couple of times, when they both had an Italian period. He'd been there in 1959, the night Dracula was killed. They'd not actually met, but she had followed his career.

A few years ago, Alexandra Forrest, a New York editor, sunk her claws into the author and struck a deal for a series of saga-length sequels to his most famous works. *The Usher Syndrome*, *The Dupin Tapes*, *The Valdemar Validation*, *The Pym Particles*. Poe blew the advance on "golden" – high-quality human blood Geneviève could seldom afford on her salary – and a tabloid sensation marriage to a warm groupie who turned out to be thirteen years old, then failed to deliver. Forrest, it was rumoured, did something terrible to Poe's cat. The books eventually came out with Poe's notorious name huge across the covers and tiny footnotes about less-regarded co-authors. Jack Martin, her one-time Hollywood source, was the actual writer of *The*

Mentzengerstein Factor. He was also the "as told to" on the title page of freshly annulled Lydia Deetz Poe's tell-all memoir *Eddy Dearest*, which Geneviève, guiltily, had relished. Now, there was a film out, with a starved-to-a-skeleton Dennis Quaid and black-lace-wreathed Winona Ryder.

Poe was in Hollywood too, working for John Alucard. All monsters together. She had a pang at that, reminded of her exile. It had been ten years. She could probably go back. She was, after all, a government employee now. Still, what was there in Los Angeles for her?

"Who's the tooth-collector?" she asked. "He isn't called anything like Benny Egaeus, is he?"

"No, worse luck," said the well-read detective. "Though his name is a literary reference, intentional or not. The rotund, scatter-brained gent is Wilkie Collins, rising captain in the Barksdale organisation. Risen as far as he can, now. Fallen, too."

"This is a Barksdale house?" she asked.

"Yes, indeed. The Avis of Baltimore drug-dealing concerns. They try harder, because they're number two . . ."

"Which means your prime suspect is Number One . . ."

". . . with a bullet," said the black detective. "Luther Mahoney."

"Charm City's own Kingpin of Krime-with-a-K," said his partner. "The Napoleon of Narcotics . . . the Diocletian of Drac . . . There never was a cat of such deceitfulness and suavity . . ."

"Not that he pulled the trigger. Too busy shooting hoops with the Mayor at a rally for underprivileged youth. This bloodbath is absogoddamnlutely Mahoney, but we ain't gonna put it on Luther. He be the Untouchable Man."

Geneviève understood from Dan Hanson – Lorie's on-off boyfriend, a crime reporter – that the Mahoney organisation was Baltimore's outstanding supplier of drac, crack and smack. Dan said they probably also dealt in horse, whores and s'mores. If Mahoney let competition stay in business, it was because scrabbling for small change was beneath him.

Recently, Barksdale, another family concern, had made aggressive moves into the market, absorbing a succession of Mom and Pop drug dealerships into a loose affiliation. This sort of shift in the city's criminal geopolitics entailed bodies getting dropped. Mahoney was big on endowing community centres, free clinics, playgrounds and cultural events with some of his cash backwash, but he really ought to bestow an additional wing to the city morgue.

Mahoney wasn't a vampire. But he had vampires on his krewe.

If anyone pulled their fangs, he'd be pissed.

Rumour had it that Luther Mahoney was seven feet tall, an African-American albino, an avatar of Baron Samedi. Dan said he was just a smarter-than-average, smugger-than-hell regular gangster. Besides an office building and a palace on the harbour, Mahoney owned a bank on Grand Cayman, a fleet of limousines, a private jet, some major Modiglianis, the bones of Mighty Joe Young and a great deal of Fells Point real estate.

A uniform, Turner, came into the kitchen. She was tall, trim, short-haired – the sort of look seen more often on the cover of work-out videos than at squad room roll-call. Both detectives straightened up in her presence, but she was all work.

"You'll want to see the basement," she announced.

The detectives looked at each other. Turner wasn't saying any more.

While Geneviève had been yakking with homicide, uniforms and CSI had been going through the house. Burke and Grimes were still waiting to get the meat in the wagon and back to the morgue.

"Any more bodies?" she asked.

"Not exactly . . ." said Turner

"Bodes ill. "

There was a classic door-under-the-stairs basement entrance. A set of rickety wooden steps lead into the darkness. She trusted they weren't going to find a mummified Moms Barksdale down there.

Geneviève let the detectives go first. They had to do their job before she could start hers. If she even had a job here.

For some reason she didn't want to think about, her fangs had inched out and were sharp in her mouth.

Of course it smelled bad in the cellar.

Flashlight beams played across coils of rusty wire, old bicycles, bundles of the *Sun*, a shopping trolley full of looted copper pipes. A headless torso provided a momentary scare. It was a wasp-waisted dressmaker's dummy.

Turner showed them a path through the treacherous piles of oddments.

The rear of the basement was where Poe killers liked to put up their new walls. Here, there was a separate room.

"Hello," she said. "Serious security."

The door was open, but it had several locks, some shiny and new.

"A stash?" she ventured.

Turner shrugged.

"Let me guess," ventured the black detective, "the goods is gone . . ."

"So this was more than a murder raid," said Geneviève. "A heist?"

"Look inside and draw conclusions . . ."

The windowless room was lit by fluorescent tubes in wire-mesh cages. Scatter-cushions on the concrete floor, stained with newish and oldish blood. A sink, half-full of rusty water.

She knew from the smell that someone had been living here.

A chain ran from bolts in the wall to a shiny shackle. It had been sheared through. Still-slick blood glistened on the links.

Someone had been *kept* here.

"That silver?" asked the black detective.

"Looks like . . ." said Genevieve.

She touched the metal as lightly as possible with the pad of her little finger, and pulled back as if she'd pressed against a hot stove.

". . . and is, *ouch*. Silver."

A vampire had been imprisoned here.

Silver was too soft and pricey to chain the warm, but handy for anyone who wanted to add a vampire to their collection. Sporting-goods stores sold silver fishnets, barbwire, man-traps and bullets for "home protection". Such transactions were protected under the second amendment. God bless America. Many more wooden pickets were sold than there were picket fences, too.

"Whoever the Barksdales' unwilling anchorite was, they're in the wind now . . ." said the Jewish detective.

"Or someone else has them in another basement," she said.

She looked about the small room for traces of the occupant. Above the sink was a lighter patch of plaster where a mirror had been bolted. A corner still attached showed that it had been smashed. Thumbtacked up were magazine photographs of nude black women with huge afros and defiant stares. A psychedelic astrological chart included unfamiliar houses like Dentalium, Hirudo and Ophiuchus. Hirudo (the leech) was a recent zodiac adoption, the star sign of the vampire.

A Dansette gramophone was plugged in. On the turntable was 'Supernatural Voodoo Woman (Does Her Thing at Night)' by The Originals. A selection of super '70s soul singles was stored in a toast rack.

The detectives found a pile of fifteen-year-old *Playboy* magazines and went straight to the centerfolds. The nudes' necks had been scribbled and scratched . . .

"Perhaps *not* purchased for the enlightening interview with Kurt Vonnegut or the darkly witty cartoons of Gahan Wilson," commented the Jewish detective.

The decor, magazines and music suggested the Barksdales wanted to at least try to keep their captive entertained. The pin-ups implied he was a he. The bloodstains indicated he'd been fed or bled. Probably both.

Geneviève took latex gloves out of her bag. She would have preferred a spacesuit to examine this crime scene.

It wasn't just the filth; it was the concept. This room was a cell, not a lair. She felt the prisoner's rage and despair . . .

. . . presumably alleviated by the rescue or escape, but lingering still.

In the unlikely event of this ever coming to trial, Emma Zoole might have to make a model of this basement, with miniature chain and toy furniture. The space shrank around her, walls closing in like Poe's pit, ceiling lowering. She wanted out of the cell, the basement, the house, but there was more to see.

"Here," said Turner, nudging a cushion aside with a boot.

A pudgy rag doll – brown with scarlet trunks – lay face down, with a rusty nail stuck through the back of its head.

"Remind you of anyone?" Geneviève asked.

III

She didn't get out of the row-house until afternoon.

This was a case where she was required as a vampire rather than for forensic insight. Blake and Grimes had made a start on removing the bodies. At the morgue, others could probe them for usable-in-court bullets. Geneviève had to hang around and give the cops the undead angle.

At interview, OCME had specified this would be part of her remit. She'd been too bemused by the notion of characterising herself as an expert to quibble. She'd lost count of the agencies and institutions – FBI, ATF, CTU, NSA, BPRD, Johns Hopkins, the Baltimore State Hospital for the Criminally Insane – she was theoretically on call for, though only BPRD made regular use of her supposed specialist knowledge. She wondered if the Diogenes Club was still in business. They had used her in a similar fashion, not always happily. Last she'd heard Mrs Thatcher was trying to sell off the building in Pall Mall and shift the Club's functions to paper shufflers in Cardiff. Where once Mycroft Holmes stood in for the British government, there might soon be yuppie flats.

On the whole, vampire crime in the USA was much the same as ordinary crime – just with fangs. Bank robbery, with fangs. Car theft, with fangs. Jaywalking, with fangs. Aside from the specific felony of criminal assault with the intent to consume human blood, which was rarer than the tabloids said, American vampires were statistically less likely to commit most crimes – including murder – than the warm. Courts were handing down 500-year sentences to penalise the long-lived, which threw up new problems for penitentiaries. Lethal injection of a solution of silver sulfate, a ghastly way to go, was the preferred method of vampire execution in death-penalty states.

The factor which threw everything out was drac.

The drug itself was only marginally illegal – how could you legislate against a substance derived from organic matter freely flowing in the veins of law-abiding *nosferatu*? Statutes against organ snatching and private sale of body parts were extended to cover the sale of vampire blood to the warm, though they were seldom invoked if the transaction was the other way around. A tax-paying, Congress-lobbying catering industry, dependent on supplying vampires, wanted no part of this mess.

It was impossible to stay in the drac trade without breaking a dozen state and federal laws a day, but cases against drac lords were even trickier to bring than cases against regular drug cartels. There were task forces all over the place, but few big successes in the War on Drac. Nancy Reagan's "Just Say Yuck" campaign was the punchline of too many red-eyed dhamp stand-up routines.

Geneviève almost missed the innocent days of pale poets quaffing absinthe or hippies tripping on Bowles-Ottery ergot.

It also creeped her out – and she was well aware of the irony – that drac-heads wanted to get into her veins. This wasn't just in the 'hoods, but everywhere. They didn't want to turn, but they wanted to try . . .

She had to worry about what Emma Zoole might do if her dealer didn't come through while Geneviève was helpless in her monthly state of lassitude. If a little cut healed by the time she woke up, would she even know?

A swelling minority argument wanted to legalise, regulate and tax drac.

She couldn't tell the detectives much they hadn't worked out for themselves. But she stood on the stoop, looking down at the body-tape outline that showed where Fortunato had fallen, and ran it through for them, anyway . . .

"Besides whatever kick it is dhamps get out of being vampires for a few hours, the appeal of drac to your traditional drug dealer is ease of supply. It doesn't have to be muled in from Burma or Colombia. You just need a vampire. Either a willing, paid donor or, as the shackle suggests was the case here, a patsy snatched off the street and milked. Drac production isn't quite as simple as squeezing a vein into a baggie. The powdered form common on the street is vampire blood, usually cut with human or animal matter, exposed to sunlight until it granulates. You can leave it out all day to congeal and dry, at the risk of losing a lot of red to evaporation, or you can repurpose the grow lamps you bought when you were raising marijuana to hurry things along."

In a room with polythene sheeting on the walls and floor, trays of drac were processed this way. Here, Barksdale red was measured into foil triangles. That location turned up more dead soldiers – two middle-aged Hispanic women and a pre-*quinceañera* girl, huddled together. For work, they were stripped to bra and panties accessorised with surgeon's masks, shower-caps and disposable gloves. They'd been unsentimentally plugged, execution style. More haulage for Blake and Grimes.

On the street, Barksdale drac was sold as "Fright Night"; the foil wraps had little bat stickers to identify the brand. Mahoney's double-star baggies were known as "Near Dark" in the projects or "Once Bitten" in uptown night-spots. Other common North-Eastern drac varieties were "Vamp", "Monster Squad" and "Lifeforce". Out of New York came "Innocent Blood", "Habit", "Addiction" and "Nadja". Along the Tex-Mex border, a strain called "Cronos" was popular. An especially lethal drac known as "Black Lodge" or "Killer Bob" was spreading from Canada down into Washington State. California had "Hellmouth", "Embraced" and "Lost Boy". Back in Toronto, dhamp-scene murgatroyds snorted or shot "Forever", "Night Inside" and "Amarantha". A lot of crap was talked about bloodlines and purity of sources; it was all the same poison.

Geneviève would never know what a drac hit felt like – it didn't work on vampires. Then again, it didn't need to. Vampires had their own, exclusive high. Every night of the week. The thickness of skin away.

"With demand ever on the increase, drac outfits need multiple vampires in chains or on staff. They get used up rapidly, unless handled with great care. If you want me to take a wild guess at what happened here, I'd say one drac concern had hit on a prime source of red, and another has moved swiftly to acquire the asset. This wasn't a rescue, this was a snatch and grab. The murders were incidental. Or just to leave the trademark. This many dead drac dealers is like a double star on the bag. You know who . . ."

The detectives did.

"What about the voodoo hoodoo?" asked the black cop.

Geneviève had been thinking about the makeshift doll.

"Chalk that up to an uncanny coincidence. You don't really believe shoving a rusty nail through the back of the head of a doll in the likeness of Wilkie Collins could actually cause his brains to burst through a gunshot-like hole in his skull?"

"I believe you can turn into *un chauve-souris enorme*," said the Jewish detective.

"Well, more fool you because I can't."

She tried flapping her arms.

"Any ideas as to the identity of our formerly cooped-up fount of all things *rouge* and rotten? Connoisseur of soul and smut?" he asked.

She shook her head.

"Take a look through the missing persons files and flag the vampires. Though we're a cagey, elusive lot. We disappear frequently and our vanishing acts can easily go unreported. It's as if no one misses us, officers. How can that be?"

The cops shrugged, as one.

Her beeper went off.

"That's me," she said. "Another call on the Medical Examiner signal. So I'm into the ME-mobile and away to fight more dastardly crime. Tell me how this works out, if it works out."

She left them and found her car. The Plymouth still had its hubcaps and was free of gang tags, scratches, bullet holes and piles of human ordure. There was a fresh blood pool in the gutter, though. She unhooked a recently severed human finger from the radiator grille and left it on the sidewalk. If reclaimed, it could probably be reattached.

Like voodoo, her car's self-protection system was something she didn't think about too much.

IV

If this evening was a fair representation of what was on offer through the dating section of the *Sun*'s personal columns, Geneviève would look for another way of meeting eligible men who weren't dead on a table.

Her date was a reasonable-looking, divorced guide-book writer who spoke in a monotone about his ex-wife, his ex-girlfriend and his ex-dog. He dissected his crabs the way she autopsied corpses. She started on golden and moved to pig's blood, remembering they'd agreed to split the bill. Towards the end of the meal, he began fiddling with the button under his tie-knot. A "bite me bite me" tell.

She tuned out when he left off his former dependents to deliver a lecture about "travel-size packets". Normally, when her shift was over, she could forget what she saw on the job ... today, she kept flashing back to the Barksdale basement. She knew her priorities were wrong – by any objective standards, the needless murder of the women in the processing room was the worst horror of the house – but that silver chain and the tiny, strip-lit space haunted her.

Her date didn't notice she'd drifted away.

His top button was undone now. His pulses were strong, but she had a notion that his blood would be milky. The *aperitif* hits of golden had given her a warm glow, which the pig's blood cocktail turned into a savage, needy burn of desire. Not for this man, though.

She'd rather bite his dog.

At that thought, she giggled – inappropriate to his point about favouring shaving gel over foam – and he was offended.

His Adam's apple showed.

She looked at the neatly cracked, sliced and prised-apart crab exoskeleton on his plate.

In her reverie, she found herself in the Ten Bells in Whitechapel in 1888, at a table with Charles. They were talking about the murders.

"It's been nearly a month, Charles," she ventured, "since the 'double event'. Perhaps it's over?"

"No," he said. "Good things come to an end, bad things have to be stopped."

Damn, he was right. Always.

And he was gone, not even a ghost . . .

The present faded back up and her date was talking at her. Like most Americans, he called her Genevieve.

Every time he used her name, which he did unnaturally often, it sounded odder to her, more grating . . .

At a nine-thirty, Lorie – who was responsible for directing Geneviève to the *Sun*'s personals in the first place – would call her beeper. They had agreed on a cut-off point. If the evening was worth pursuing, Geneviève could tell her date it was a wrong number and carry on. If not, she could claim to be summoned to a bloodbath on the other side of town. Door number two was the current favourite.

Her big wristwatch was for work, so she wasn't wearing it. She couldn't see the restaurant clock from where she was sitting.

He was talking about shampoo and conditioner. Time stood still.

Prison was boring. As mind-numbing as this. She'd been imprisoned in her time. In dungeons, convents, an eighteenth-century zoo. In well-appointed apartments and shacks. She had mostly shut down and tried to stay calm, secure that she could outlive confinement, waiting for the walls to fall down or her captors to age and die. She had been forgotten in *oubliettes*. Before the Dracula Declaration, that was easier than it would be now. Then, few had believed what she was.

She didn't know what she'd do if she were captured and held nowadays.

If what went on in the Barksdale basement was now a thing, she must at least work out contingency plans. It could happen to any vampire.

Cut-off time must have come and gone. McCormick & Schmick's Steak and Seafood was emptying out.

Lorie must have got distracted by a deadline, an argument with Dan or one of Emma's loser-guy crises. Geneviève would make her pay for that.

At last, *beep beep beep*.

She didn't even bother with an excuse, just collected her coat and left. She threw down her half of the bill – worked out to the cent in her mind, as an exercise – to avoid any obligation. There would not be a second date.

"I have your number," she said.

When, for convention's sake, she checked her beeper, she didn't recognize the number. Odd. Lorie should have been calling from the apartment. As part of the escape routine, she made a beeline for the restaurant's bank of payphones. She had planned to call Lorie and vent.

A large, rumpled man hogged one of the phones. He was in the habit of eating too much garlic. She took the kiosk furthest from him.

She fished a quarter out of her purse and dialled the number.

It rang for a long time. Then was picked up.

Silence. Except for breathing. Not Lorie's.

"Doctor Dee," she identified herself.

"Listen to me, Doctor Dee," responded a voice she didn't know – male, loud. "I got your gal pal here. A clean snatch. She ain't been puncturated, so far. But things can change, baby. In a flash. You come see me, sister, and we can rap. You don't come, consequences there be, you dig?"

A frightened squeal, curtailed.

"Picture in focus, doll?"

"Yes."

"There's a diner on Reistertown and Rogers. It's open late . . . we be waitin'. I strongly recommend you make good time . . ."

V

She had walked to the restaurant from her apartment and her car was parked at the morgue anyway. So Geneviève took a cab to Northwest Baltimore.

The intersection of Reistertown Road and Rogers Avenue was in Woodmere. Once predominantly Jewish, now middle-class black. Few bodies dropped suspiciously in this neighbourhood, so she hadn't been here often.

The diner was easy to find. It was an Americana postcard, an aluminium-sided '50s relic. The boxcar-shaped building supported a huge orange neon sign which just said DINER.

The windows were steamed up, but she could see people-like shapes inside.

She had the cab cruise by and drop her three blocks up.

For her date, she was wearing her good black dress, heels and one of Lorie's puffy-shouldered jackets.

She took off her shoes and put them in her bag, then put her purse and ID in an inside jacket pocket.

She owned a gun, a habit from her private detective nights. It was locked safely in her desk at the morgue.

Walking the three blocks, cold sidewalk under her soles, she felt her hackles rise. She salivated as her fangs slid from gumsheaths. Her nails elongated and curved.

No one could mistake what she was.

People – not that there were many around – got out of her way.

She hid her bag behind a potted shrub in the diner's parking lot. The only vehicles here were a Cadillac pimpmobile, a beat-up Ford truck and a rusty black van with MONDO TRASHO written on it in lipstick pink. A late-in-the-day punk band? Some freak subculture she'd not come across yet?

She half-expected to be shot with silver as soon as she barged through the Diner door. Instead, she got a slow handclap.

Sat at a table waiting for her was a smiling African-American vampire with a helmet of conked hair like James Brown's, and fur on his cheeks and the backs of his hands. He wore tartan flares over yellow stack-heeled boots, a wide-lapelled jacket with a zigzag pattern in mauve and electric green and matching coat-hanger-shaped tie, plus wraparound mirror shades. His clock had stopped in 1973, which – at a guess – was when he turned. If they didn't go the murgatroyd route with black capes or gauze shrouds, twentieth-century vampires tended to dress the way they had when they died.

She remembered the toast rack of soul records and knew who this was. He seemed to be enjoying his freedom.

The other people in the diner were dhamps, not vamps. A gaggle of flaming creatures: a 400-pound man with a cockatoo mohawk, squeezed into a frilly scarlet ball gown; a mad-eyed old woman, toothless but for temporary fangs, in a ragged nightie; a cadaverous, long-haired white dude with purple moustaches and bullet-holes in his sports jacket; a beehive-do blonde sweater girl with a Sardonicus smile; an emaciated punker, trussed up in bondage trousers and a ripped Ramones T-shirt. This must be the Mondo Trasho gang.

They were mostly crammed into a booth, surrounding a terrified Emma Zoole.

Geneviève was tempted to say "wrong roommate" and leave . . . But she couldn't let Emma take the heat for her and, worse, she had this nagging itch to find out what the hell this was all about.

She could blame Charles for inculcating in her a need to know.

Emma wasn't dhamped. She kept her head down.

"Doctor Dee, Doctor Dee," said the soul vampire.

"You have a name too?"

"Willis, baby. Willis Daniels."

He left a pause for it to sink in.

She had never heard of him, so she couldn't give him the "we meet at last" response he clearly craved.

"Mamuwalde's get," he elucidated.

Prince Mamuwalde was an African vampire. Not a cat to be invoked carelessly. Geneviève had met him and been impressed.

She suspected this son-in-darkness was not a credit to the Prince.

"*Salaam Alaikum*," she said.

Willis tittered, showing a long right fang and a short left one.

"Peace on you too, sister," he said. "Now set your bootie down and let's get to talkin' business . . ."

She slid onto the red-upholstered chair opposite him.

Everything in the diner was cherry-red or silver-chrome, and bolted to the floor. A giant jukebox bore the smiling, faded face of Corny Collins, whose 1960s music show still played late at night or early in the morning on local television. Corny promised "All the teen beat hits to set your toes tappin' and your fingers snappin'!"

The juke played Gene Pitney's "Town Without Pity". A tragic wail of a song.

A blood splatter arced on the wall behind the counter. This krewe had taken out the staff. One of the Mondo Trasho dhampires – a disco punk with roller-skates and an orange crinkly headband – had an unconscious waitress in his lap and was nuzzling her neck with teeth not sharp enough to puncture a vein.

She had no reflection in Willis' shades, but saw the

purple-moustache guy moving to block the door she'd come through. He put up the closed sign. A tall, warm, black woman with angry eyes and a leopard-print outfit sat on a stool at the far end of the diner. She was straight, not flying on drac-wings, and had a Glock 9mm on the counter. Geneviève took the Leopard Lady for the most dangerous person in the room . . .

No, she told herself, *second* most dangerous person in the room. She hadn't lasted since 1416 by being a pussycat.

Emma, the connoisseur of terror, was not enjoying this. She was morbid, but no masochist.

Geneviève tried not to show her fangs.

Willis dipped a long forefinger in a spill of sugar from the table dispenser and drew a smiley face. He licked sugar off his finger.

"I have your missing tooth," she said. "At the morgue."

He shrugged. "It's growin' out, sweet cheeks."

"Don't you want the diamond?"

"Easy to come by."

"For some."

"You an' me, girl. We don't have to try so hard, do we? What do they call it – power of fascination? The oogada-boogada? The Charm."

He made hypnotic gestures.

"Slap the Charm on a person, make 'em do what you want. A trip and a half, Doc. Open up the cash register . . . open up a wrist. Hah, bein' unborn is the best thing ever happened to Mrs Daniels' boy, and that's the truth."

"What *are* you talking about, Willis?" she asked.

He was flustered for a moment, suspicious, prickly. He liked to be taken seriously. He was fundamentally insecure.

In street terms, he was just Blacula's bitch.

Which did not make him any less dangerous.

If it came down to *Die Hard in a Diner*, she could take Willis. She could even deal with the dhamps. But Emma would be killed. The waitress, too. If the Leopard Lady was packing silver bullets, and she had no reason to think she wasn't, Geneviève wouldn't make it either. At her age, she'd go to dust – some dhamps snorted *that*! – which would spare Blake and Grimes the embarrassment of hauling their boss to the morgue.

Emma whimpered. The big Mondo Trasho transvestite stuck a long tongue in her ear. The hag cackled.

"Emma," Geneviève said, "don't worry. They can't hurt you."

"Oh I think they most surely purely can," said Willis.

"Not if you want to keep talking with me."

He held up his be-ringed, hairy hands and made a Stepin Fetchit I's-so-scared face, then chuckled.

"The Charm, you know," he continued. "It come natural to me. Not from bein' a vampire and shit, but from birth. Mrs Daniels was mama-loi from the islands. She never turned, but she had the Charm. S'what voodoo's all about. Makin' puppets of people . . ."

"Puppets of people," Geneviève echoed.

Willis let his grin widen. She intuited he'd practised that so his diamond would glisten. It was wasted now.

"In that basement, someone put you on strings, Willis."

"Mr Wilkie Collins," he said. "Look at him now."

He made a puff gesture at the back of his head. A fraction of an expression crossed the Leopard Lady's face. So Geneviève knew who'd raided the Barksdale house. Looking at her, it seemed possible she'd gone in alone.

"Are you really off the string? Or on another one?"

She indicated the woman with the Glock.

Willis laughed but his cheek-fur bristled. An unusual tell.

"You are misunderstandin' the situation, Doctor Dee. Me an' Georgia Rae's tight."

Georgia Rae Drumgo. Not a name you were likely to forget. Dan Hanson had mentioned her while running through the players in Baltimore's crime organizations. Luther Mahoney's sister. Married to an ex-*Tonton Macoute* Haitian who was currently missing presumed dismembered. Reputed avatar of the avenging, red-eyed spirit Erzulie Ge-Rouge. Executioner and enforcer.

Willis' favourite song came to mind, "Supernatural Voodoo Woman".

"Me an' you could be tight too," said Willis. "What you might call a business opportunity is openin' up . . ."

She knew what was coming but let him continue.

"This drac thing, man, it's huge already. Gonna get bigger. You and me – vampires – we have to be on top of it, or else it be on top of us, you dig?"

He slid his shades down his nose and flashed his eyes at her.

Did he really think his Charm would work on an elder?

"The krewe I was with thought small. Too small."

"Grab a cow, pen a cow, milk a cow?"

He didn't like to be reminded. He would have slice marks on his arms. Drac was the only drug where the dealers got the tracks.

"No longer a feasible business model, Doc."

Eventually, your abducted vampire got used up and went to dust. No more cash flow.

She thought about all those teeth in Wilkie Collins' box. If he only pulled one keepsake from each of his drac-cows that meant Barksdale had been through thirty-eight vampires.

"You don't need a cow, you need a flock . . ."

"Cows come in herds, Willis."

"Whatever . . . do I look like Pa Kettle to you? We're speakin' metaphorically and you started the cow talk."

"Am I to understand that your plan is to turn selected people vampire? The homeless, the lost, stolen children? Then reap the blood harvest . . .?"

"See, you *do* dig, mama."

That was why there'd been no epidemic of vampire disappearances anyone could notice. Barksdale had Willis make vampires out of people who'd already fallen off the map. It was also why they got used up so fast. The stock would be poor in the first place. Then, there was Mamuwalde bloodline. The story went that the Prince was personally turned by Dracula, and so inherited the Dracula rot . . . his get were feeble, and the bloodline thinned with each turning . . .

"You'd *be* the mama."

She felt Georgia Rae Drumgo's eyes on her.

Willis was moving his lips and making a noise, but Georgia Rae was doing the talking. He was still the puppet. She assumed Georgia Rae had a Willis doll somewhere.

If the Mamuwalde bloodline failed to take, Mahoney needed something stronger. Like hers.

So far, Geneviève had refrained from bestowing the Dark Kiss. She'd begged Charles to accept it, but he had refused 'til the end. That was as close as she had come to having get. She wasn't about to break the habit of centuries to keep Luther Mahoney's drac corners hopping with dhamps.

She said nothing.

She could still see Willis' eyes . . . a spark died in them. He had made promises she would not keep.

"Won't come willing; can't be broke," said Georgia Rae, raising her Glock. "Drain her for drac and kill the other bitch."

Geneviève ducked under the table as Georgia Rae fired.

Shots ploughed into the Formica and chrome. Willis yelped as a silver slug punched through his sleeve and the meat of his arm.

"Hey, man, mind my threads!"

The dhamps were on Emma or up and about, bumping into one another, too blitzed to pay attention.

Geneviève lizard-slithered across the tile floor as fast as she could manage.

So much for her good black dress. Lorie's jacket ripped under the arms.

Georgia Rae fired again. Purple-moustache guy got in the way of a bullet and fell.

"Willis, she'll kill you too," Geneviève shouted.

No use. Blacula's bitch wasn't growing any balls tonight.

"You gotta be *reasonable*, girl!" he whined. He was up from the table, hopping in frustration and excitement, like a kid who needs the bathroom.

He must see another basement in his immediate future. Mahoney would keep him going longer than Barksdale, but he'd still be used up . . .

Geneviève back-slid into a booth, using the table as a shield, but there was nowhere else to go.

On the whole, she wished she'd stayed with her date.

No . . . she didn't. She wasn't like that. Georgia Rae, of all people, had seen it straight away. Won't come willing; can't be broke . . .

She saw Georgia Rae's legs – she had leopard-pattern high heels, too – as she marched across the diner. She rapped on the table with the gun.

"Come out," she said.

Geneviève eased herself up from the floor and sat in the booth, fixed table between her and the Leopard Lady. Erzulie Ge-Rouge ascendant. Just now, eyes ablaze, gun smoking, Georgia Rae Drumgo was gunpowder, gelatine, dynamite with a laser beam . . .

There was no use trying to talk with her.

"Blast the bitch, why don't you?" shrieked Willis.

"She ain't goin' nowhere."

Geneviève sensed a moment. Georgia Rae didn't want to draw this out. She'd used her full clip and needed to reload.

The diner door opened and someone wide and whiffy walked in.

"Hey, honkie, can't you see we're closed?" said Willis. "What kind of a jive-ass, mutha-gropin', toad-lickin' . . ."

A very loud noise sounded.

The front of Willis' zigzag eyesore exploded red. His eyes were frozen in surprise.

As Geneviève's ears rang, Willis slowly buckled – threads of scarlet and gristle seeming to float in the smoke around him – and he fell on the floor.

The drac-heads pushed Emma – who was going to need serious therapy if she lived much longer – away and pounced, crawled and leaped across the room, shoving their faces into Willis' wound, snorting and licking, feet turning clawed inside confining shoes, teeth so big they cracked jaws and split cheeks.

The newcomer was a gross warm man with a Stetson and a sawn-off double-barrel shotgun.

Geneviève recognized him. He'd been at the restaurant. And around before then. Outside the Barksdale house this morning. She even remembered him showing up in Canada, sitting in court as she gave evidence against Lucien Lacroix.

Georgia Rae had her gun on the fat cowboy. Stand-off. Except . . . he had one more shell under the hammer and she was empty.

Geneviève slipped out of the booth, quickened by the golden she'd had earlier, and took away Georgia Rae's gun. She put her teeth against the Leopard Lady's jugular and pressed enough to leave dimples, then stepped back.

Georgia Rae looked angry enough to kill with her bare hands.

"Uh uh, honey," said the gunman, finger tight on the other trigger. "Message from on high. Don't mess with the mademoiselle. Nod your head to show you understand."

After a long moment, the Leopard Lady deliberately nodded.

Geneviève spat at Georgia Rae's shoes. A display of French contempt.

"Best take your posse and ride off into the sunrise, I reckon," said the gunman. He had a grating Texan accent.

With a sweet smile, Geneviève gave Georgia Rae back her empty Glock. The Leopard Lady put the gun in a shoulder black and snapped her fingers. The Mondo Trasho dhampires left Willis alone, and came to heel.

Glaring, Georgia Rae moved towards the door.

"On high means *West Coast*, Miz Drumgo," said the man. "Tell Luther . . . tell everyone you know. Change is coming. Get it?"

"Got it."

"Good."

Georgia Rae and the dhampires left. Some of the pack were howling and laughing. They didn't know this was real.

Geneviève checked the waitress. Unconscious, but alive. Behind the counter was a cook with his throat cut. Dead.

Emma Zoole was in shock.

"Where's Lorie?" Geneviève asked.

"At the *Sun*. She left a note to call."

So the roommate she liked was safe. Sweet.

"I'm thinking of moving out," Emma said.

"We can talk about that later."

Geneviève turned to the man with the gun, the man from the West Coast. He was gone. The jukebox whirred, though. He must have dropped a coin in one of the table-top selection machines.

Roy Rogers sang "Happy Trails".

"How about that?" she said, to no one in particular.

She heard sirens from outside. Someone had called the cops.

Uniforms came through the door. And a familiar detective.

"*Sacre bleu, mon brave. C'est un tableau de* splatter *avec jolies filles.*"

STEPHEN VOLK

Whitstable

STEPHEN VOLK IS best known as the writer of the infamous BBC-TV "Hallowe'en hoax" *Ghostwatch* and as creator of the paranormal ITV drama series *Afterlife*, starring Lesley Sharp and Andrew Lincoln. His other screenplays include *The Awakening*, starring Rebecca Hall, Dominic West and Imelda Staunton; Ken Russell's trippy extravaganza *Gothic*, and *The Guardian* (co-written and directed by William [*The Exorcist*] Friedkin). In 1998 he won a BAFTA for *The Deadness of Dad* starring Rhys Ifans, and has contributed to the Channel Four horror series *Shockers*.

For the stage he penned a segment of Kim Newman and Sean Hogan's *The Hallowe'en Sessions*, and his play *The Chapel of Unrest* was performed at London's Bush Theatre in 2013, starring Jim Broadbent and Reece Shearsmith.

Volk's short stories have been selected for *The Mammoth Book of Best New Horror*, *The Year's Best Fantasy and Horror*, *Best British Mysteries* and *Best British Horror*, and he has been a finalist for the Bram Stoker, British Fantasy and Shirley Jackson Awards. His first single-author collection, *Dark Corners*, was published in 2006, and it was followed by *Monsters in the Heart* in 2013, both from Gray Friar Press.

"Sometimes ideas come in one fell swoop, and so it was with 'Whitstable'," explains the author. "I woke up one morning and said to my wife that I had an idea for a story: Peter Cushing is approached by a young boy who mistakenly thinks he is the great vampire-hunter Van Helsing of the Hammer films, and the boy needs his help because he thinks his stepfather is a vampire.

"My wife said, 'And of course, he isn't.' And I immediately thought, 'You're right. He isn't. That is much more interesting!' And so it became about a Cushing who feels sorely inadequate to rise to the challenge of being the kind of hero the boy needs so desperately. Facing monsters when you have a screenplay, he finds, is much easier than facing one who exists in real life.

"From the beginning, I knew instinctively this had to happen at the lowest ebb of Peter's life, after his wife and soulmate Helen died – when he was grief-stricken and turning down all offers of work. In time, as we know, he threw himself back into acting, but I couldn't help wondering what had happened to change his mind, to enable him to go on? That developed and possibly became the most important thematic strand in the story, in the end.

"But if 'Whitstable' is in any way a tribute to the 'Gentle Man of Horror', as some have said, I am more than honoured."

> *Smile for the camera.*
> —Old Saying

H E COULDN'T FACE going outside. He couldn't face placing his bare feet into his cold, hard slippers. He couldn't face sitting up. He couldn't even face opening his eyes. To what? The day. Another day without Helen in it. Another day without the sun shining.

For a moment or two before being fully awake he'd imagined himself married and happy, the luckiest man on earth, then pictured himself seeing her for the first time outside the stage door of the Theatre Royal, Drury Lane: she a shining star who said a platypus looked like "an animal hot-water bottle" – he in his vagabond corduroys, battered suitcase, hands like a Dürer drawing, breath of cigarettes and lavender. Then as sleep receded like the waves outside his window, he felt that dreadful, dreaded knot in his stomach as the awareness of her no longer being there – her non-presence – the awful, sick emptiness, rose up again from the depths. The sun was gone. He might as well lie there with his eyes shut, because when his eyes opened, what was there but darkness?

Habitually he'd rise with the light, drink tea, take in the sea-view from the balcony, listen to the wireless and some-times go for a swim. He did none of these things. They seemed to him to be activities another person undertook in a different lifetime. *Life. Time.* He could no more picture doing them now than he could see himself walking on the moon. The simplest tasks, the very idea of them, seemed mountainous. Impossible.

Yet it was impossible, also, to lie there like a dead person, greatly as it appealed to do so. It was something of which he knew his darling would so disapprove, her reprimand virtu-ally rang in his ears and it was this that roused him to get up rather than any will of his own.

His will was only to . . .

But he didn't even have the strength for that.

She was his strength, and she was gone.

Helen. Oh, Helen . . .

Even as he sat hunched on the edge of the bed, the burden of his loss weighed on his skinny frame. He had no choice but to let the tears flow with the same cruel predictability as his dream. Afterwards, weaker still, he finally rose, wiping his eyes with now-damp knuckles, wrapping his dressing gown over baggy pyjamas and shambling like something lost and misbegotten towards the landing. A thin slat shone between the still-drawn curtains onto the bedroom wall-paper. He left the room with them unopened, not yet ready to let in the light.

A half-full milk bottle sat on the kitchen table and the smell hit him as soon as he entered. The sink was full to the brim, but he poured the rancid liquid in anyway, not caring that it coated a mound of dirty plates, cups, saucers and cutlery with a viscous white scum.

He opened the refrigerator, but it was empty. He hoped the milkman had left a pint on the doorstep: he hated his tea black. Then he remembered why he had no groceries. Joycie did it. Joyce, his secretary, did everything for "Sir". He pictured again the hurt in her eyes when he'd told her on the telephone she would not be needed for the foreseeable future, that she needn't come to check that he was all right because he *was* all right. He'd said he needed to be alone. Knowing that the one thing he didn't want to be was alone, but that was not the way God planned it.

Nasty God.

Nasty, nasty God . . .

He shut the fridge. He didn't want food anyway. What was the point? Food only kept one alive and what was the point of that? Sitting, eating, alone, in silence? What was the point of that?

He put on the kettle. Tea was all he could stomach. The calendar hung facing the wall, the way he'd left it.

The letterbox banged, startling him, shortly followed by a knock on the wood. It was Julian the postman, he thought, probably wanting to give his condolences in person. He held his breath and had an impulse to hide. Instead he kept quite still. Julian was a sweet chap but he didn't want to see him. Much as he knew people's wishes were genuine, and appreciated them, his grief was his own, not public property. And he did not want to feel obliged to perform whenever he met someone from now on. The idea of that was utterly repellent. How he dealt with his inner chasm, his utter pain and helplessness, was his own affair and other people's pity or concern, however well-meaning, did not make one iota of difference to the devastation he felt inside.

He stood furtively by the doorway to the hall and watched as a package squeezed through and fell onto the welcome-mat, and beyond the glass the silhouette of the postman departed.

It had the unmistakable shape of a script.

His heart dropped. He hoped it was not another one from Hammer. He'd told them categorically via his agent he was not reading anything. He knew Michael had newly found himself in the chair as Managing Director, and had a lot on his plate, but could he really be so thoughtless? Jimmy was a businessman, but he also counted him a friend. They all were. More than friends – family. Perhaps it was from another company, then? Amicus? No. Sweet Milton had his funny American ways, but would never be so callous. Other companies were venal, greedy, but not these. They were basically gentlemen. They all knew Helen. They'd enjoyed laughter together. Such laughter, amongst the gibbets and laboratories of make-believe. Now, he wondered if he had the strength in his heart to meet them ever again.

He picked up the package and, without opening it, put it on the pile of other unread manuscripts on the hall-stand. Another bundle sat on the floor, a teetering stack of intrusion and inconvenience. He felt no curiosity about them whatsoever, only harboured a mild and uncharacteristic resentment. There was no small corner of his spirit for wonder. They were offers of work and they represented the future. A future he could not even begin to contemplate. Why could they not see that?

He sighed and looked into the mirror between the hat-hooks and what he saw no longer shocked him.

Lord, the make-up job of a master. Though when he sat in the make-up chair of late he usually had his hairpiece to soften the blow. Never in public, of course: he abhorred that kind of vanity in life. Movies were different. Movies were an illusion. But – fifty-seven? He looked more like *sixty*-seven. What was that film, the part written for him but one of the few he turned down? *The Man Who Could Cheat Death*. But he couldn't cheat death at all, could he? The doctors couldn't, and neither could he. Far from it.

Dear Heavens . . .

The old swashbuckler was gone now. Fencing in *The Man in the Iron Mask*. The Sheriff of Nottingham. Captain Clegg of Romney Marsh . . . He looked more like a Belsen victim. Who was it said in a review he had cheekbones that could cut open letters? He did now. Cheeks sucked in like craters, blue eyes sunk back in deep hollows, scrawny neck, grey skin. He was positively cadaverous. Wishful thinking, he thought. A blessing and a curse, those gaunt looks had been his trademark all these years, playing cold villains and erudite psychopaths, monster-hunters and those who raised people from the dead. Yet now the only person he desperately craved to bring back from the grave he had no power to. It was the one role he couldn't play. Frankenstein had played God and he had played Frankenstein playing God. Perhaps God had had enough.

The kettle whistled and the telephone rang simultaneously, conspiring to pierce his brain. He knew it was Joycie. Dear Joycie, loyal indefatigable Joycie, who arrived between dry toast and correspondence every day, whose concern persisted against all odds, whose emotions he simply couldn't bear to heap on his own. He simply knew he could not speak to her, hear the anguish in her voice, hear the platitudes even if they weren't meant as platitudes (what words could *not* be platitudes?) and, God knows, if he were to hear her sobs at the end of the line, he knew it would tip him over the edge.

Platitude:

An animal that looks like a hot-water bottle.

Hearing Helen's laughter, he shut his eyes tightly until the phone stopped ringing, just as it had the day before. And the day before that.

Quiet loomed, welcome and unwelcome in the mausoleum of his house.

He stared at the inert typewriter in the study, the signed photographs and letter-headed notepaper stacked beside it, the avalanche of mail from fans and well-wishers spilling copiously, unattended, across the floor from the open bureau, littering the carpet. He pulled the door shut, unable to bear looking at it.

Hardly thinking what he was doing, he re-entered the kitchen and spooned two scoops of Typhoo into the teapot and was about to pour in boiling water when he froze.

The sudden idea that Joyce might pop round became horrifically possible, if not probable. She wasn't far away. No more than a short car journey, in fact, and she could be here and he would be trapped. Heavens, he could not face that. That would be unbearable.

Instantly he realized he had to get out. Flee.

Unwillingly, sickeningly, he had no choice but to brave the day.

Upstairs he shook off his slippers, replacing them with a pair of bright-yellow socks. Put on his grey flannel slacks, so terribly loose around the waist. Needing yet another hole in the belt. Shirt. Collar gaping several sizes too big now, too. Tie. No time for tie. Forget tie. Why was he forced to do this? Why was he forced to leave his home when he didn't want to? He realized he was scared. The scaremonger, scared. Of *this*. What if he saw somebody? What if they talked to him? Could he be impolite? Unthinkable. Could he tell them how he really felt? Impossible. What then?

He told himself he was an actor. He would *act*.

Back in the hall he pulled on his winter coat and black woollen hat, the kind fishermen wear, tugging it down over his ears, then looped his scarf around his neck like an over-eager schoolboy. February days could be bright, he told himself, and he found his sunglasses on the mantelpiece in the living room sitting next to a black and white photograph of his dead wife. At first he avoided looking at it, then kissed his trembling fingertips and pressed them gently to her cheek. His fingerprints remained on the glass for a second before fading away.

He walked away from 3 Seaway Cottages, its curtains still drawn, giving it the appearance of a house in slumber. As a married couple they'd bought it in the late 1950s with money he'd earned from *The Hound of the Baskervilles*, because having a place by the sea – especially here, a town they'd been visiting for years – would be good for Helen's breathing. "You have two homes in life," she'd said, "the one you're born in and another you find," and this one they'd found, with its big, tall windows for painting under the heavens and enjoying the estuary views across Shell Ness, clapboard sides like something from a whaling port in New England. They were blissfully happy here, happier than either of them could have dreamed. Now it seemed the house itself was dreaming of that happiness.

He paused and breathed in deeply, tasting brine at the back of his tongue.

Good, clean fresh air for her health.

The mist of his sighs drifted in short puffs as he trudged along the shingle, patchy with errant sprigs of grass, in the direction of the Neptune pub, the wind buffeting his fragile frame and kicking at the ends of his dark, long coat. Above him the sky hung Airfix blue, the sky over a cenotaph on poppy day, chill with brisk respect, and he was small under it.

Automatically he'd found himself taking the path he and Helen had taken – how many times? – arm in arm. Always arm in arm. His, muscular and taut, unerringly protective: hers light as a feather, a spirit in human form, even then. If he had grasped and held her, back then . . . stopped her from . . . *Stupid. Foolish thoughts.* But his thoughts at least kept her with him, if only in his heart. He was afraid to let those thoughts be blown away. As he placed one foot in front of the other he felt that stepping from that path would be some sort of blasphemy. That path was his path now, and his to tread alone.

His heart jumped as he noticed two huddled people coming towards him, chequered green and brown patterns, their scarves fluttering. A man and wife, arm in arm. He felt frightened again. He did not want to see their faces and fixed his eyes past them, on the middle distance, but in his peripheral vision could tell they had already seen him and saw them look at each other as they drew unavoidably closer. His chest tightened with dread.

"Mr Cushing?"

He had no alternative but to stop. He blinked like a lark, feigning surprise. Incomprehensibly, he found himself smiling.

"Sorry." The man had a local accent. "Bob. Bob and Margaret? Nelson Road? I just wanted to say we were really sorry to hear about your wife."

He took Bob's hand in both of his and squeezed it warmly. He had no idea who Bob was, or Margaret for that matter.

"Bless you."

The man and woman went on their way in the direction of West Beach and Seasalter and he walked on towards the Harbour, still smiling. Still wearing the mask.

He was an actor. He would act.

Act as if he were alive.

The sky had turned silver-grey and the wind had begun whipping the surface of the water. After passing the hull of the *Favourite*, that familiar old oyster yawl beached like a whale between Island Wall and the sea, he sat in his usual spot near Keam's Yard facing the wooden groynes that divided the beach, where he was wont to paint his watercolours of the coast. But there was no paint box or easel with him today. No such activity could inspire, activate or relax him and he wondered if that affliction, that restless hopelessness, might pass.

If it meant forgetting Helen, even for an instant, he hoped it would not.

Usually the music of the boats, the flag-rustling and chiming of the rigging, was a comfort. Today it was not. How could it be? How could anything be? When there was nothing left in life but to endure it?

He took off his sunglasses and pulled a white cotton glove from his pocket onto the fingers of his right hand, momentarily resembling a magician, then lit a John Player unfiltered. It had become a habit during filming: he said, often, he didn't want to play some "Nineteenth-Century Professor of the Nicotine Stains". As he smoked he looked down at his bare left hand which rested on his knee, lined with a route-map of pronounced blue veins. He traced them with his finger-tips, not realising that he was enacting the gentle touch of another.

He closed his eyes, resting them from the sun and took into his smoker's lungs the age-old aroma of the sea. Of all the senses, that of smell more than any other is the evoker of memories: and so it was. He remembered with uncanny clarity the last time he and Helen had watched children building "grotters" – sand or mud sculptures embellished imaginatively with myriads of oyster shells – only to see the waves come in and destroy them at the end of a warm and joyful Saint James' Day. Clutching his arm, Helen had said, "Such a shame for the sea to wash away something so beautiful." He'd laughed. His laughter was so distant now. "Don't worry, my dear. They'll make more beautiful ones next year." "But that one was special," she'd said, "I wanted that one to stay."

The fresh salt air smarted in his eyes.

"I know who you are," said a disembodied young voice.

Startled, he looked up and saw a boy about ten years old standing at an inquisitive distance, head tilted to one side with slats of cloud behind him and a book under his arm. He and Helen had no children of their own, or pets for that matter, but felt all the children and animals in the town were their friends. He remembered talking to the twins next door and asking what they wanted to be when they grew up – clergyman, sailor – and them innocently turning the question back at him, albeit that he was already in his fifties: *What do you want to be when you grow up?* Good question, for an actor. But this one, this boy, he didn't recognize at all.

"You're Doctor Van Helsing."

The man's pale-blue eyes did not waver from the sea ahead of him.

"So I am."

The boy threw a quick glance over his shoulder, then took a tentative step nearer. He wore short trousers, had one grey sock held up by elastic and the other at half-mast. Perhaps the other piece of elastic had snapped, or was lost.

"I . . . I saw what you did," he stammered eagerly, tripping over his words, but they nevertheless came ten to the dozen, a fountain. "You . . . you were powerful. He escaped back to his castle and he . . . he leapt up the stairs four, five, six at a time with his big strides but you were right behind him. You were *determined*. And you couldn't find him, then you *could*. And he was about to go down the trapdoor but he saw you and threw something at you and it just missed and made a really big clang, and then he was on top of you squeezing the life out of your throat and it hurt a really lot . . ." The boy hastily put his book between his knees and mimed strangulation with fingers round his own neck. "He had you down on the floor by the fireplace and you couldn't breathe he was so strong and mighty and you went like this—" His eyes flickered and he slumped. "And he was coming right down at you with his pointed teeth and at the last minute you were awake—" The youngster straightened his back. "And you pushed him away and he stood there and you stood there too, rubbing your neck like this. And he was coming towards you and your eyes went like *this*—" He shot a glance to his left. "And you saw the red curtains and you jumped up and ran across the long, long table and tore them down and the sunlight poured in. And his back bent like this when it hit him and his shoe shrank and went all soggy and there was nothing in it. And he tried to crawl out of the sunlight and you wouldn't let him. You grabbed two candlesticks from the table and held them like *this*—" He crossed his forearms, eyes blazing, jaw locked grimly. "You forced him back and his hand crumbled to ashes and became like a skeleton's, and he covered his face with his hand like this, and all that turned grey and dusty too, and his clothes turned baggy because there was nothing inside them. And everything was saved and the sign of the cross faded on the girl's hand. And after you, you – *vanquished* him, you looked out of the coloured window at the sky and put your woolly gloves back on. And the dust blew away on the air."

Indeed.

The man remembered shooting that scene very well. The old "leap and a dash" from the Errol Flynn days. Saying to dear old Terry Fisher: "Dear boy, I seem to be producing crucifixes from every conceivable pocket throughout this movie. Do you think we could possibly do something different here? I'm beginning to feel like a travelling salesman of crosses." He'd come up with the idea himself of improvising using two candlesticks. He remembered the props master had produced a duo at first too ornate to work visually, but the second pair were perfect.

"That was you, wasn't it?"

"I do believe it was," Peter Cushing said.

He did not look at the boy and did not encourage him further in conversation, but the youngster ventured closer as if approaching an unknown animal which he assumed to be friendly but of which he was nevertheless wary, and sat on the wall beside him squarely facing the sea.

The man was now patting his jacket pockets, outside and in.

"What are you looking for?" The boy was curious. "A cross? Only you don't need a cross. I'm not a vampire."

"I'm very glad to hear it. I was looking for a photograph. I usually have some on me . . . I really don't know where I've put them . . ."

"A what?"

"A photograph. A signed one." No response. "Of yours truly." Still no response, puzzlingly. "Isn't that what you'd like?"

"No," the boy said, sounding supremely affronted, as if he was dealing with an idiot.

"Oh . . ."

"I want to ask you something much more important than that. *Much* more important."

"Oh. I see."

Cushing looked around in a vain attempt to spot any parents from whom this child might have strayed, but there were no obvious candidates in evidence. If the boy *had* got lost, he thought, then it might be best for him to keep him quietly here at his side until they found him, rather than let him wander off again on his own. He really didn't want this responsibility, and he certainly didn't want company of any sort, but it seemed he didn't have any choice in the matter.

"I said I'm not a vampire." The boy interrupted his thoughts. "But I know somebody who is. And if they get their own way I'll become one too, sooner or later. Because that's what they do. That's how they create other vampires." The child turned his head sharply and looked the man straight in the eyes. "You said so."

Quite right: he had done. It wasn't hard to recall re-writing on set countless scenes of turgid exposition on vampire lore so that they didn't sound quite so preposterous when the words came out of his mouth.

"Who is this person?" Cushing played along. "I probably need to take care of him, then."

"He's dangerous. But you don't mind danger. You're *heroic*."

Cushing twitched an amused shrug. "I do my best."

"Well it *has* to be your best," the boy said with the most serious sense of conviction. "Or he'll kill you. I mean that."

"Then I'll be as careful as possible. Absolutely."

"Because if he finds out, he'll hurt you, and he'll hurt me." The words were coming in a rapid flow again. "And he'll hurt lots of other people as well, probably. Loads of them." The boy drew up his legs, wrapped his arms round them tightly and tucked his knees under his chin. His eyes fixed on the horizon without blinking.

"Good gracious," Cushing said. "You mustn't take these type of pictures too much to heart, young man."

"Pictures? What's *pictures* got to do with it?" The abruptness was nothing short of accusatory. "I'm talking about *here* and *now* and you're the vampire hunter and you need to *help* me." The boy realized his harsh tone of voice might be unproductive, so quickly added, sheepishly: "Please." Then, more bluntly, with an intense frown: "It's your *job*."

It's your job – Vampire Hunter.
You're heroic.
You're powerful.
Cushing swallowed, his mouth unaccountably dry.

"Where's your mother and father?"

"It doesn't matter about them. It matters about *him*!"

The boy stood up – and for a second Cushing thought he would sprint off, but no: instead he walked to a signpost of the car park and picked at the flaking paint with his fingernail, his back turned and his head lowered, as he spoke.

"My mum's boyfriend. He visits me at night-time. Every night now. He takes my blood while I'm asleep. I know what he's doing. He thinks I'm asleep but I'm not asleep. It feels like a dream and I try to pretend it isn't happening, but afterwards I feel bad, like I'm dead inside. He makes me feel like that. I know it. I can't move. I'm heavy and I've got no life and I don't want to have life anymore." He rubbed his nose. His nose was running. Bells tinkled on masts out of view. "That's what it feels like, every time. And it keeps happening, and if it keeps happening I know what'll happen, I'm going to die and be buried and then I'll rise up out of my coffin and be like him, forever and ever."

Something curdled deep in Cushing's stomach and made him feel nauseous. He obliterated the pictures in his mind's eye – a bed, a shadow sliding up that bed – and what remained was a bleak, dark chasm he didn't want to contemplate. But he knew in his heart what was make-believe and what was all too real and it sickened him and he wanted, selfishly, to escape it and pretend it didn't exist and didn't happen in a world his God created.

He felt a soft, warm hand slipping inside his. *Helen?* But no. It belonged to the little boy.

"So will you?"

"Will I what?" In a breath.

"Will you turn him to dust? Grey dust that blows away like you did with Dracula?"

"Is that what you want?"

The boy nodded.

Oh Lord . . . Oh God in Heaven . . .

Cushing stared down without blinking at the boy's hand in his, and the boy took his expression for some sort of disapproval and removed it, examining his palm as if for a splinter or to divine his own future. The man suddenly found the necessity to slap his bony knees and hoist himself to his feet.

"Gosh. You know what? I'm famished. What time is it?" His fob watch had Helen's wedding ring attached to its chain: a single gold band, bought from Portobello Road market when they were quite broke. The face read almost twenty past eleven. "There's a shellfish stall over there and I think I'm going to go over and get myself a nice bag of cockles." He straightened his back with the aid of his white-gloved hand. "I do like cockles. Do you like cockles?"

The boy, still sitting, did not answer.

"Would you like a bag of cockles? Have you ever tried them?" He took off the glove, finger by finger.

The boy shook his head.

"Do you want to try?"

The boy shook his head again.

"Well, I'm going to get some, and you can try one if you want, and if you don't, don't."

The boy observed the old man closely as he flicked away the tiny cover of the shell with the tip of the cocktail stick and jabbed the soft contents within.

"Will you put a stake through his heart?"

Cushing twirled it, pulled it out and offered the titbit, but the boy squirmed and recoiled.

"You know, long, long ago, people believed in superstitions instead of knowing how the world really worked." He popped the tiny mollusc into his mouth, chewing its rubbery texture before swallowing. "They didn't know why the sun rose and set and what made the weather change, so sometimes they thought witches did it. And because they thought witches might come back and haunt them after they were dead, they'd bury them face down in their graves. That way, when they tried to claw up to the surface they'd claw their way down to Hell instead. But, you know, mostly superstitions are there to hide what people are really afraid of, underneath."

"You know a lot. You're *knowledgeable*," the boy said, happy to have his presumptions entirely confirmed. "But you have to be. For your occupation. Vampire Hunter."

Cushing had had enough of the taste of the cockles. In fact, he hadn't really wanted them anyway. He wrapped the half-empty tub in its brown paper bag, screwed up the top and deposited it in the nearest rubbish bin a few feet away. Whilst doing so, he scanned the car park, again hoping to see the errant parents. "Do you see him in mirrors? Does he come out in daylight? Because that's how I discover whether someone is a vampire or just someone human that's *mistaken* for a vampire, you see."

"He does go out. In the daytime, but . . ."

"Aha. What does that tell you?"

"Different ones have different rules. Sometimes they *can* be seen in daylight like in *Kiss of the Vampire* on TV. You weren't in that one, so you don't know. There are different sorts, like there are different cats and dogs, but you can put a stake through their heart. That *definitely* works, always. And that's what you're brilliant at."

Cushing sat back down next to the boy, put on his single white glove and lit another cigarette. He remembered something that had troubled him in his own childhood. He'd mistakenly thought the Lord's prayer began: *Our Father who* aren't *in Heaven*. But if God *wasn't* in Heaven, where was He? The question, which he dared not share even with his brother, had kept him awake night after night, alone. Where? He rubbed the back of his neck: a gesture not unfamiliar to fans of Van Helsing.

"I know what you're thinking," the boy said. "You're thinking how to trap him."

"No. I'm not."

"What are you thinking then?"

"Do you want me to tell you, truthfully? Very well. I believe if there's something troubling you at home, whatever it is and however bad it is, the best thing to do – the first thing to do – is to tell your mother."

The boy laughed. "She loves him. *She* won't believe me. *Nobody* will. That's why I need *you*."

"Perhaps your mother wants to be happy."

"Of *course* she does! But she doesn't want to be killed and have her blood sucked all out, does she?"

"This man might be a good man trying his best. I don't know him, but why don't you give him time to prove himself to you and I'm sure you'll accept him for what he is."

"I *know* what he is! He won't change. He *won't*! Vampires don't become nice people. They just stay what they are – evil. And they keep coming back and coming back till you stop them!"

"Listen. I'm being very serious . . ."

"I know. You're *always* serious."

"Yes, well. These feelings you have about your mum's new boyfriend . . .?" Peter Cushing felt cowardly and despicable, and even as he was uttering the words disbelieved them almost entirely, but did not know what else to say. "They'll go away, in time. You'll see. They'll pass. Feelings do."

"*Do* they though? Bad feelings? Or do they just *stay* bad?"

Cushing found he could not answer that. Even with a lie.

"My mum wants to marry him. She loves him. He's deceived her because really he doesn't love her at all. He just wants to suck *her* blood, too."

"But you have to understand. I can't stop him."

"Why?"

Cushing stumbled for words. Fumbled for honesty. "I don't know how. You have to talk to somebody else. Somebody . . ."

"Yes you do! You *do*! The villagers are in peril, and *I'm* in peril, and you're Doctor Van Helsing!"

A large seagull landed on the rubbish bin and began jabbing its vile beak indiscriminately at the contents.

"I'm sorry. I'm—"

"Yes, you *can*. Please! *Please* . . .!"

But Cushing could say no more. Dare say no more. The desperation in the boy's voice struck him mute and the rolling eye and the hideous ululating of the seagull made him look away. He felt pathetic and cruel and lost and selfish and small – but he wasn't responsible for this child. Why should he be ashamed? The vast pain of his own grief was heavy enough to bear without the weight of another's. Even a child's. Even a poor, helpless child's. He was an actor, that was all. Van Helsing was a part, nothing more. All he did was mouth the lines. All he did was be photographed and get his angular face blown up onto a thirty-foot-wide screen. Why was the responsibility his? Who asked this of him, and why shouldn't he say no?

Now a second gull, even bigger, had joined the first and added to the cacophony. In a flurry of limbs they squawked and spiked at the bag the cockles were in, then began snapping at each other in full-scale war with the yellow scissors of their horrid, relentless maws.

When their aggression showed no sign of abatement, Cushing crushed out the remains of his cigarette on the stone, hurried over and shooed them away with flailing arms from the debris they were already scattering with their webbed feet and flapping wings. He felt their putrid deadfish breath poisoning his nostrils. They coughed and gurgled defiantly and showed their pink gullet-holes before begrudgingly ascending.

After stuffing the brown paper bag deeper into the bin he turned back, and to his sudden alarm saw the boy walking briskly away.

"Wait."

But the boy did not wait.

Where were the parents? Where were the dashed parents and why were they not—? . . . but all Cushing's thoughts and recriminations hung in the air, incomplete and

impotent. He had denied the boy the help he had craved –
however fantastical, however heartfelt, however absurd –
and now the lad was gone.

"Wait . . ."

Cushing sat back down, alone, and saw that the book
from under the boy's arm was still sitting there.

Movie Monsters by Denis Gifford.

He placed it with its cellophane-wrapped cover on the
desk of the public library. They knew him well there.
They knew him well everywhere, sadly, and he intuited
as he approached that there was an unspoken choreog-
raphy between the two female assistants, vying for who
would serve him and who would be too busy. It was not
callousness that made them do so, he knew – merely the
all-too-British caution that a wrongly placed word might
cause unnecessary hurt. Did they realize their shared eye
contact alone caused hurt anyway? He forced a benign
smile.

"Good afternoon."

"Good afternoon, Mr Cushing." The younger one drew
the short straw. He was still unshaven, had been for days
and he wondered if he looked rather tramp-like. Little he
could do about it now.

"I'm terribly sorry to trouble you, my dear, but I wonder
if you might help me? I found this library book near Sea
Wall today and I wonder if you'd be so kind as to tell me the
name and address of the person it belongs to. They must be
dreadfully worried about losing it. I'd be most awfully
grateful."

"By all means. Just a moment, sir . . ." She checked the
date stamped inside the cover and turned to consult the
chronologically arranged index of book cards behind her.
Her rather thick dark hair fell long and straight across her
shoulder blades. She wore a tight green cardigan and high
heels that made her calves look chunky from behind, and he
pondered whether she was happily married and, if so, for
how long. With how many years ahead of her? "That's fine,

Mr Cushing. We'll make sure he knows his book has been returned."

"No, you see – bless you – it's no trouble for me to return it to him personally. I really am quite grateful for the distraction."

A flicker in her eyes. "Oh. I understand. Of course. In that case . . ." She coughed into her hand and looked at the details a second time. "The name is Carl Drinkwater." She read out in full an address in Rayham Road. "That's one of the new houses over on the other side of the Thanet Way, off South Street. Do you know it?"

"Not at all."

She opened a drawer and produced a small map of the town, unfolded it and marked the street with a circle in red biro as the black one was empty.

"Splendid. Thank you so much." He took her hand and kissed it, as was his habit ("immaculate manners; such a gentleman") before walking to the exit.

"Mr Cushing?" He turned. "Mrs Cushing, sir. I'm so very sorry. She was such a delightful woman."

He nodded. "Thank you so much."

He was astonished to hear the four words come from his throat, because the fifth would have stuck there and choked him. He hoped the woman was married and happy, with children and more happiness ahead of her. He truly did.

He returned home to fetch his bicycle, the Jaguar of more joyful days secreted in the garage these many months: memories preserved in aspic, too painful to be given the light of day. He swapped his woollen fisherman's hat for a flat cap, grabbed a heavier scarf, and, with the library book in his pannier, rode via Belmont Road and Millstrood Road to the boy's house – what appeared to be a two-bedroom bungalow on the far side of the railway track.

The February sun was low by now and the sky scrubbed with tinges of purple and ochre. He chained his cycle to a lamp post opposite and stayed in the protective shadow between an overgrown hedge and a parked white van (FOR ALL YOUR BUILDING NEEDS) as he scrutinized the place from afar.

The garage had a green up-and-over door with a dustbin in front of it on the drive. The lawn grass was thin and yellowing. He could see no garden ornaments and the flatness of the red brick frontage was broken only by a plastic wheel holding a hosepipe fastened to the wall. Two windows matched, a third didn't and the door, frosted glass and flimsy, was off-centre.

He looked at his watch – Helen's ring tinkled against the glass face – and placed it back in his pocket. He blew into his hands, preparing himself for a long wait, hoping he had enough cigarettes left in his packet and, no doubt because of the worry this engendered, lit one, no doubt the first of many. He might of course smoke the lot and find this turned out to be a fruitless enterprise. There was no guarantee the man went out on a Saturday night, though a lot of men normally did. He was not dealing with, perhaps, the most normal of men.

After fifteen minutes or so a dog-walker in a quilted "shortie" jacket passed and Cushing pretended he was mending a puncture with his bicycle pump, never more conscious that his acting had to be as naturalistic as possible. Believability was all. The Labrador sniffed his tyres but the dog-walker, who resembled the sports commentator Frank Bough, yanked the lead and progressed on his way with only the most cursory of nods.

Cushing fixed his bicycle pump back into place and looked over at the house.

Hello. The light was on in the hall now, beyond the frosted glass. Shapes were donning coats. The door opened. He ducked down behind the white van, craning round it to watch a man in a donkey jacket tossing his car keys from hand to hand, a few steps behind him a boy in a football strip following him to a parked Ford Zephyr. Reflections in the windscreen stopped him from getting a good look at the man's face.

Cushing quickly hid in case Carl, whose eyes were on the road ahead, saw him. He listened for the engine to start and waited for it to sufficiently fade away.

As soon as it had, he crossed the road and knocked on the front door. He could hear the television on inside, so rapped again slightly harder. "All right, all right, keep your hair on . . ." A woman approached the glass and he could already make out she wore a red and white striped top, a big buckle on a wide belt and bell-bottomed jeans.

The door opened to reveal someone who, he imagined, thought herself attractive and feminine but who seemed to have endeavoured to make herself anything but. Her hair was drastically pulled back from her forehead in a ponytail, her clothes did nothing to enhance her figure, and there was nothing graceful or pretty in her demeanour or stance. He thought of the quiet perfection of Helen by comparison and had to quickly dismiss it from his mind. He reminded himself of his abiding belief that all women should be respected and accorded good manners at all times.

He took off his flat cap. "Mrs Drinkwater?"

"Yeah."

"You don't know me . . ."

"Yeah, I do."

His eyebrows lifted. "Oh?" Was she a fan of Hammer films, then, like her son?

"Of course I do. I've seen you on the telly."

Fool. He'd been the BBC's Sherlock Holmes over a number of televised adventures alongside Nigel Stock as Dr Watson. Naturally she recognized him. His portrayal of the great detective, after all, had been widely acclaimed.

"Morecambe and Wise," the woman said.

Oh dear, he thought. How the mighty are fallen. Serve him right. The Greeks had a word for it: *hubris*. The sin of pride.

"You live round here," she said.

"That's quite correct. My name's Peter Cushing."

He extended a hand, which the woman saw fit to ignore. "I know."

"May I come in, please? It's about your son Carl."

"What about Carl? What's he done now? I'll kill him."

"Nothing. Absolutely nothing, Mrs Drinkwater. Nothing wrong." He showed her the copy of *Movie Monsters* which he'd tucked under his arm. "I found this library book of his and I'm returning it, you see."

She took the book off him and looked at it but didn't move or speak, even to say thank you.

He said again, equally politely: "May I come in?"

More from being taken unawares than hospitality, the woman stepped back to allow him to enter. He cleaned his shoes on the mat while she walked back into the room with the television on, without asking him to follow her. Though his own manners were faultless, he refused to judge others on their inadequacy in that area. It was often down to their upbringing, he believed, and that could not be their own fault. We are all products of our pasts: none more so than he himself. Some said he was stuck in it. Another, unwanted, era.

But he merely believed politeness and courtesy between human beings was a thing to be valued, in any era. Treasured, actually.

The ironing board was out and she was making her way through a pile of washing, which she resumed, clearly not about to interrupt her workload on his account. She did not offer him a cup of tea or coffee and did not turn down the TV, but simply carried on where she'd left off, half-way through a man's shirt, tan with a white collar, Cliff Richard's variety show the activity's accompaniment. The ceiling was textured with Artex swirls, the fireplace with its marble-effect surround boarded up with a sheet of unpainted hardboard, and a patio door led to a garden enclosed by fencing panels.

He saw a recent edition of the *Radio Times* lying on the arm of the sofa, its cover announcing the introduction of a new villain into the *Doctor Who* pantheon. Dear old Roger Delgado looking as if he'd stepped straight from a Hammer film with his widow's peak and black goatee. He thought of Jon Pertwee's dandyish Doctor compared to his own "mad professor" saving the Earth from the invading hoards of soulless Daleks. He thought how easy it was to save the world, and how hard, in life, to save . . .

"Why d'you want to talk about him?"

"It was Carl who chose to talk to me, in fact. May I?" He noted she seemed confused by the question, so sat himself on the sofa anyway, his voice having to compete with Cliff Richard's. "It was curious, very curious indeed. You see, he approached me earlier today confidently believing I was *actually* Doctor Van Helsing, the character I played in the Dracula films for Hammer several years ago." He chuckled. "Many years ago, actually. How time flies . . ." He noticed a stack of books on the cushion next to him: *The Second Hammer Horror Films Omnibus* with Christopher Lee on its orange cover offering his bare chest to a victim, *The Fifth* and *Seventh Pan Book of Horror Stories*, the Arrow paperback editions of *Dracula* and *The Lair of the White Worm*. "I see he's a fan . . ."

"Monster mad. I wish he wasn't. Not healthy if you ask me. None of it."

He smiled. "Dear lady, that's my bread and butter you're talking about. For my sins."

She didn't match his smile and still didn't turn down the television.

He loosened his scarf. The gas-effect electric fire was cranked up and the skin on his neck was beginning to prickle.

"Carl loves you very much, Mrs Drinkwater." He chose his words carefully. "He cares an awful lot about what happens to you. The more he was talking to me, it was very clear he felt you were in danger. And he was in danger too. Very much so."

She grunted, straightening her back then slamming down the iron and running it back and forth up the sleeve. "He's got an active imagination. Always did, always will. Got his bloody father to thank for that. Telling the kid those stories of his – ghosts, goblins, monsters – scaring him, keeping him awake. What do you expect?"

"I don't think stories hurt people, Mrs Drinkwater. Not really hurt."

"How do you know?" She set the iron on end with a thump. Rearranged the garment roughly. "Have you got children?"

"No. Sadly." He and Helen had not been blessed in that way.

"Then you haven't sat up with them crying and hugging you. Over stories. Or anything else for that matter, have you?"

"That's very true."

"So you don't know anything about it, do you?"

"No, I don't. You're quite right. But . . ." He gazed down at the carpet and noticed he was still, rather ridiculously, wearing his bicycle clips. He reached down and took them off, idly playing with them as he talked, as if they were a cat's cradle or a magic trick. "But what he said concerns me. I'm sorry. You must understand, surely? Children don't say things without reason."

"Don't they? Kids can be cruel. You lead a sheltered life, you do. Kids can get at you in ways you wouldn't even dream of. If they think you deserve it."

"Can they?"

The iron hissed. "You should hear what I get in the ear every day. Dad this, Dad that."

"He idolizes his father."

"Yeah, the father who sneaked him into the cinema to see that *Dracula* you're so proud of when he was eight years old. Oh yeah. Bought a ticket, pushed the bar of the emergency exit, let him in. Like the teddy boys or mods do. To an X film. His *son*. Don't tell me that helped any problems he had in school or anywhere else, because it didn't. He was scared to death of the world before that and, you know what? It made him *more* scared. That's why he's playing silly buggers."

Peter Cushing rubbed his eyes. Dare he ask the question? He was compelled to. He had come here. He would never forgive himself if he didn't.

"Do excuse me for asking this, but has your boyfriend ever . . . ever raised his hand to Carl? Hurt him in any way?"

"No." The woman cut into his last word. "Les loves that boy."

Loves.

"How long have you known him?"

"Long enough." She stiffened. "Why?"

He loves that boy.

"As I say . . . Carl seemed, well, I have to be honest, Mrs Drinkwater . . . troubled."

"Well there's nothing troubling him in this house, I tell you that for nothing. It's all in his bloody mind." The shirt flicked to and fro, the iron hitting it repeatedly like a weapon of violence. She turned her body to face him, hand on hip. "Why do you make those horrible films anyway? Eh?"

"To be truthful I hate the term 'horror film'. Car crashes and the concentration camps and what's happening in Northern Ireland, that's horror. I think of the fantasies I star in as fairy tales or medieval mystery plays for a new generation. If you take the 'O' from Good and add a 'D' to Evil, you get God and the Devil – two of the greatest antagonists in the whole of history. And Van Helsing is important because he shows us Good triumphs. After all, Shakespeare used horrific images in *Titus Andronicus*, and mankind's belief in the supernatural in *Macbeth*, and nobody belittles the fellow for that. I think the best so-called 'horror' shows us our worst fears in symbolic form and tries to tell us in dramatic terms how we can overcome them."

"Yeah, well." Her face, turning back to the ironing board, betrayed an ill-concealed sneer. "I didn't pass enough exams to understand all that. We didn't have books in our house. My dad was too busy working."

He sighed. "Mrs Drinkwater, I'm quite sure you don't want this discussion and neither do I. Please just put my mind at rest, that's all I ask. Truly. Just talk to Carl. Listen to him."

"You've listened to him. Do you believe him?"

"My dear, I'm just an actor. It's his mother he should talk to."

"Or a psychiatrist."

"If that's what you genuinely think."

"It's no business of yours what I think."

"You're quite right, of course." He stood up, putting his bicycle clips in his pocket. "Perhaps I shouldn't have come, but please believe me when I say I did so only out of concern for Carl. I apologize profusely if I've upset you. That wasn't my intention at all."

"You haven't upset me," she said.

"I'm sorry for disturbing you. I'll see myself out."

He thought the conversation was over, but he'd barely reached the door to the hall before she said behind his back: "Why don't you make nice, *decent* films, eh?"

He turned back with sadness, both at the slight and his own ineffectiveness. He knew she felt accused and belittled by his very presence, undermined by his unwanted interference and presumptions and posh voice and good manners and wanted to attack it, all of it.

"Don't you think I've got enough problems with him, without this . . .? Without him talking to strangers . . .? Talking rubbish . . .?"

His blue eyes shone at her.

"I can't believe he's saying what he's saying, honest to God. He's got no business to."

Her cheeks were flushed now, voice quavering on the edge of losing control. "I swear, Les is good as gold with that kid. Better than his real dad, by a mile. You want to know who *really* hurt him? If you want to know the truth, his *father* did. He did that by buggering off. And there isn't a day goes by I don't see that in my son's eyes, so don't come here accusing me or anybody else when the real person isn't here anymore." He could see she fought away demons, the worst kind – and tears.

Instinctively, he walked over and took her hands in his. "I beseech you, my dear. Talk to your son."

Appalled, she backed away from him.

"I don't need to talk to my son."

She reached the wall and couldn't back away any further. His face was close to hers and he looked deeply into her eyes, his own vision misty, almost unable to get out the words he must.

"My dear, dear girl. I've lost someone I loved. Please don't do the same."

She snatched away her hands as if the touch of him was infectious.

"How fucking *dare* you!" She shoved him in the chest. Then shoved him again. "Get out of here." He staggered backwards, feeling it inside the drum of his old, brittle ribs. "Get out of my fucking house! Get *out*!"

Gasping for breath and words, he stumbled to the front door as she berated him with her screams and obscenities and later remembered nothing of getting to his bicycle or getting from Rayham Road to Seaway Cottages except that he had to stop a number of times to wipe the tears from his eyes and by the time he got indoors a thin film of ice had formed covering his cheeks.

A film played in the darkened theatre of his brain. A Hammer film, but not their usual fare. Not set in Eastern Europe in the 19th century, but in Canada in the present, even though it was filmed at Bray. The opening shot of darling Felix Aylmer, who'd played his father in *The Mummy*, ogling two young girls through binoculars. A vile creation. A "dirty old man" in common parlance – hideously inadequate euphemism that it was.

"*He made us play that silly game . . .*"

Square-jawed Patrick Allen as the father. "*If he touched her, I'll kill the swine!*" Gwen Watford, an actress who always appeared to be on the verge of tears. "*You expect me to be objective when a man has corrupted my daughter?*"

Corrupted. Precisely.

He knew many films where the house outside town harboured inconceivable evil, and had starred in quite a few where the villagers marched up to it demanding justice or revenge, but in this picture fear has the upper hand. The family is powerful. The hero, weak. The community knows how old Mr Olderberry "can't keep his eyes off children", but the townsfolk choose to keep their heads firmly in the sand. Even the police think it must be the girls' own fault.

The child's own fault.

The very concept was odious. As odious as the sight of gummy old Felix pursuing the girls through the woods, staggering like Boris Karloff after the one in pigtails, stepping over the overturned bicycle. Wordlessly pulling the rowing boat containing the two children back to shore by its slimy rope . . .

A girl sat up in the tree and it didn't seem at all peculiar but it worried him. It was an oak tree, old and sturdy, with deeply wrinkled bark. The little girl didn't seem distressed but she did seem determined, a strong-willed little soul. She wore a frilled collar like a Victorian child and he thought she was clutching a toy or teddy bear but couldn't make it out clearly through the leaves and branches. "Come down," he called to her. He looked around but there was no one else about. Only him. So it was down to him to do something. "Come down." But the girl wouldn't come down. She just looked down at him, frowning seriously. "Come down. Please," he begged. But still she didn't move. A man came along. A man he didn't know. The man said to him: "What are you doing?" He couldn't answer. He got confused, he didn't know why, but before he could answer anyway, the man stepped closer and went on: "You know exactly what you're doing don't you? Don't you?" Rage and aggression built up in the man's face and his tightly pursed mouth extended to became a vicious-looking yellow beak. And this beak and another beak were prodding and poking at a boy's short trousers, snatching and tearing out gouts of underwear. The underwear was made of paper. Newspaper. And somehow he was upset that what was written was important, the words were important.

He woke to the sound of seagulls snagging and swooping above his roof.

At the best of times, he despaired at their racket. And these were not the best of times. Now the noise was no less than purgatory. As a child in Surrey he'd thought they were angels, but now he held no illusions about the species. The creatures were the very icon of an English seaside town, but they were relentless and without mercy. He'd once seen a large speckled gull going for a toddler's bag of chips, almost taking off its fingers, leaving it bawling and terrified in its mother's embrace. They were motivated by only selfish need and gratification, thought only of their own bellies and their own desires. It seemed almost symbolic that we never ate sea birds, knowing almost instinctively that their insides would be disgusting, inedible, rank, rancid, foul. It seemed to Cushing that their screeching was both a bombastic call to arms and a cry of pain.

He sat up, finding himself on the living-room sofa.

He looked at the clock and saw it was four o'clock. Since it was sunny beyond the drapes, he deduced it must be four o'clock in the afternoon. He was still in his pyjamas and dressing gown and still too tired to care.

He'd hardly slept a wink all night. In fact, the short, shallow period of sleep broken by the dream had been by far the longest. Perhaps an hour. The rest, when he could, had been spent at most in a fitful doze, and that only occasionally, interspersed as it was with shambling wanders round the house or up and down stairs in the dead of night. That darkness inculcated fears was a truism, but such knowledge did nothing to abate it. Fears multiplied as he'd curled up wide-eyed, turning circuitous thoughts over in his mind, multiplying still more while he'd walked aimlessly from room to room, in a futile search for distraction, illumination, resolution or peace of mind. All evaded his grasp.

He had lain in his bed thinking of Carl Drinkwater lying in his. The boy's words, the whole encounter, replayed in his ears. What did he hear? Was he misguided? Did he take it all at face value when he shouldn't have? Was the mother right? All kinds of doubts set in.

Most of all, that he was mentally accusing a man he'd never met of the most despicable act, the vilest *crime* imaginable – based upon what?

He had woken, walked round like a penitent, unable to sleep, as these questions went round and round in his head. Who was he to pronounce? Who was he to judge? Who was right? Who was wrong? Who was good? Who was evil? He wished he could talk to somebody, but who would listen to the silly gibbering of a recently bereaved man whose very job was spinning a preposterous yarn and making it seem true?

It was Sunday but he didn't want to go to church. Too many people. Too many eyes. In fact he hadn't been to church since Helen's funeral. Afterwards the young vicar at St Alphege's had told him: "If you ever want to come and talk, Peter, for any reason, you know where I am." He'd said: "My name's Godfrey. You can call me God." Then he had nudged Peter's arm with his elbow. "I'm joking." Peter didn't want to hear a joke and he didn't want to laugh. He didn't want to go back for a chat with "God" either. "God" could find other people to chat to. He'd rather have a good actor like Peter Sallis or Miles Malleson playing a vicar than that young fake who was acting the part anyway. As Olivier had said, "Be sincere, dear boy, always be sincere – and when you've faked that, you've cracked it."

But if you cannot do good, he thought now, where *is* God? Where?

Unable to turn without a painful reminder confronting him – the furniture was all Helen's choice from her favourite antiques dealer, and every piece of it held a story – he dragged his feet up to his studio, the "playroom", at the top of the house. For five or ten minutes he sat and gazed up through the windows along one wall at the darkening sky above.

The far table was strewn with art supplies, palettes rainbowed with dried paint and uncapped tubes of aquamarine and burnt sienna gone hard as concrete. The miniature theatre sets he'd made to the original Rex Whistler designs sat like frozen moments of time waiting patiently to be awakened. Model aeroplanes dangled on fishing line, Lancaster bomber, Spitfire, Messerschmitt: a veritable Battle of Britain suspended in the air. Frozen in time, like he was in so many ways. A child with his toys. A boy playing at being a man. What was a "play" anyway but "playing"? He thought of Captain Stanhope in *Journey's End*, the part he never got a chance to do. In glass-fronted cabinets the length of the room stood hundreds of model soldiers, the British Army through the ages: the Scots Greys at Waterloo; Desert Rats at El Alamein; Tommies at Normandy. In days gone by he'd get them out and solve international problems on his knees on the carpet. His men were clever, bold, indefatigable, strategic, victorious – always. But they were no use to him now. They'd fought all those battles, but what could they do to fight this one? Now they were as useless and impotent as he himself. He suddenly wanted to give the boy all those toy soldiers. He wanted to give him all the toys in the world.

Helen gazed out at him radiantly from a pastel drawing pinned to the wall.

He slid a record out of its sleeve, placed it on the gramophone and slumped in the threadbare rocking chair letting "Symphony Number One" by Sibelius wash over him. It always had the effect of reminding him of the wonder of human achievements, the humility with which we should revere, in awe, such pinnacles of artistic endeavour, but it struggled to do that now. He cast his mind back to being on set singing Giuseppe's song from *The Gondoliers* to Barbara Shelley, competing with Chris Lee to see who could sing the nightmare song from *Iolanthe* fastest without missing a word. He tried to think of singing and old friends laughing, whilst knowing a child somewhere wept into its pillow.

The doorbell rang.

He opened his eyes. Rather than lift the needle and risk scratching the LP, he let the music play as he went downstairs to answer it.

A figure stood outside in the dark. He could make out the distinctive square shoulders and upturned collar of a donkey jacket. He could see no face, just a man's outline and the collar-length hair covering his ears backlit by the almost iridescent purple of the night sky. He had not replaced the light bulb in the conservatory, which had blown weeks ago, nor had he switched on the hall light in his haste to open the front door. Now he wished he had done both.

"Mr Cushing?" It was a light voice and one he didn't recognize, or had reason to fear, but some part of him tightened.

"Yes?"

Instinctively, Cushing shook the extended hand – calloused, dry as parchment from physical work, not the hand of a poet: an ugly hand – and gazed into the face of a man in his thirties with sand-blond, almost flesh-coloured hair and beard. *Thirty-three*, the older man thought, peculiarly, unbidden. The age Jesus was when he died: *Thirty-three*. The long hair and beard was "hippie"-like, the style of California's so-called "flower children", but now ubiquitous, of course. Under the donkey jacket Cushing saw a red polo-neck jumper and blue jeans, flared, faded in patches from wear – a working man, then. No. He corrected himself from making any such assumption: threadbare jeans were, inexplicably to him, the fashion of the day. Students at Oxford wore jeans. Jeans told him nothing.

"Hello, mate. My name's Les Gledhill . . ."

Les loves that boy.

"First of all, I've got to say I've always been a massive fan of your films. I know, I know probably everyone says that. You probably get bored with hearing it. But I really mean it, sir. I feel quite nervous talking to you, in point of fact . . ." Realising he had not released the actor's hand, the man now did so, laughing and holding his hands aloft, pulling faces at his own crassness and ineptitude.

Les loves that boy.

Cushing didn't ask himself how the long-haired man had found his address. Everyone in town knew where its most famous resident lived – though most conspired in respecting his privacy.

Les loves that boy.

"Sorry. Sorry. Am I disturbing you? Only, it's really important I have a word." The visitor rubbed his hands together vigorously in the night air, hopping from foot to foot. "I, ah, think there's been a misunderstanding. A really, really *big* misunderstanding, mate . . ." he chuckled, "and I really, really want to clear it up before it goes any further." Still laughing, he pointed both index fingers to the sides of his head, twirling them in dumb-show semaphore for the craziness of the situation.

"I'm so sorry to be a bore . . ." Cushing's voice retained its usual mellifluous charm. "It's Sunday evening. This isn't a very good time, to be perfectly honest. In fact, I'm expecting guests any minute . . ." On tip-toes he craned over the other man's shoulder, pretending to be scanning the path beyond.

"This won't take long. I promise to God. Just a minute of your time, mate. If that. Honestly . . ."

"I have food in the oven. I'm most terribly . . ." Blast. The pyjamas and dressing gown were a giveaway that he was lying, and he had to think fast. "I'm, I'm just about to get changed. This really isn't convenient. If you'll excuse me . . ." He did an excellent job also of covering up the fact that his heart was pounding thunderously. *When you can fake that, dear boy . . .*

A hand slapped against the door. "Sorry, mate. Hold on. Hey. *Mate* . . ."

It stopped the door from closing but Gledhill, almost immediately embarrassed by his brisk action, quickly removed it and stuffed it in his jacket pocket, laughing again.

"Listen. Please. I really, *really* want to clear this up, sir. I swear, you have no idea what this is doing to me. You, a respected man in this, this community, I mean, *loved* in this town, let's face it, Christ, thinking . . ." One cheek winced as if in momentary pain. "When she . . . that's why I had to come over, see. I couldn't let . . ."

Cushing wondered why he still felt afraid. Much as he hated to admit it, the man seemed reasonable. Why did he *hate to admit* it? What had he *presumed* the chap would be like? Here he was. Not an ogre. Perplexed, certainly. Bewildered, genuinely. It seemed. And – unless a consummate actor himself – shaken. The voice didn't sound angry or vicious in the least, or beastly. Or *evil* – that was the remarkable thing. It sounded confused, and quite upset. No – *hurt*. Terribly hurt. Devastated, in fact.

"Of course, if you're busy, sir, I understand. Blimey, I have no right to just barge over here, knock on your door, expect you to . . ." Running out of words, the man in the donkey jacket backed away, then turned to go. Then, as he reached the white-painted garden gate, turned back. "Look, the truth is . . . I'd hate you to think I'd done anything to hurt that boy. Or whatever you think. That's just . . . Just not the case. Truly." He made one last, haltering plea. "I . . . I just wanted to explain to you you've got the wrong end of the stick, that's all. That's what concerns me, more than anything. You're a decent man. A perfect gentleman. You don't need this. It's not fair." The front door had not shut and, this being so, he took this for some kind of invitation and walked quickly back into the conservatory.

Peter Cushing's fingers did not move from the latch on the inside of the door. "I'd rather we discuss it here, if we must."

Gledhill stopped, suddenly bowed his shaggy head and plunged his ruddy, working man's hands deep in his jacket pockets, shuffling. "Yes, of course, mate. No problem."

Letting the front door yawn wider in a slight act of contrition, Cushing retraced his steps and switched on the hall light, then returned to stand on the welcome mat whilst the man in the donkey jacket hovered in silhouette at the mercy of the shrill wind cutting in from the sea. It buffeted the door, sending an icy breath through the house, room to room, riffling paperwork like a thief.

Picked out of the darkness by the paltry spill of light from the hall, Gledhill shook a solitary Embassy from its packet.

"Listen." He rubbed one eye. "Carl is a good kid, a great kid. He's quirky, a laugh, in small doses, don't get me wrong. He's a character. But he has problems, that's what you don't realize." The lighter clicked and flashed, giving a splash of illumination from his cupped hand to his chin and upper lip. "He says things. Things that aren't true." A puff of smoke streamed from the corner of his mouth. "All the bloody time. Not just about me. About everybody. The school already has him down as a liar. And a bully. They have problems with him. He hurts other kids. That's what kind of child he is, Mr Cushing. His mother worries about him day and night. So do I. Day and night."

Night.

Cushing remained tight-lipped. The face of a hundred movie stills. Immobile. "You're telling me I shouldn't believe a word that comes out of his mouth."

"Honest to God." The man's next exhale was directed at the moon. The whites of his eyes seemed flesh-coloured too, now. Perhaps it was the ambient yellow glow from within. He dawdled in its penumbra. "You think he's some kind of angel? You don't know him. You don't know any of us." He let that fact, and its obvious truth, bed down in Cushing's mind. "I didn't have to take on this woman with her boy, did I? Let's face it, lots of blokes would run for the hills the minute they know there's a kid in tow. And I haven't, have I? Because I love her. I'm trying to piece this family together. God knows. I'm going to marry her, for Christ's sake. Put everything right for both of them. The boy too. I'm not a bad person." He offered the palms of his hands.

"Then what do you have to fear from me?" Cushing spoke quietly and with precision.

"I don't know." Gledhill shrugged. "I don't know *what* you think."

And he laughed again. And the laugh had a *wrongness*. There was something in it, a grace note, deep down, disingenuous, that the older man detected and didn't like. If pressed, he couldn't have explained it any more than he could have explained why, on meeting his wife he knew instantly they were meant to spend the rest of their lives together: it wasn't even love, it was that he'd met his *soul*. Similarly, the thing embedded in Les Gledhill's laugh was inexplicable, and, inexplicably, *enough*.

"I think you'd better leave now. Good night to you."

He shut the door but found something wedged into the jamb, preventing it from closing. The laughter had stopped. He didn't want to look down and didn't look down, because he knew what he would see there: a foot rammed in between the bottom of the door and the metal footplate.

O, Lord. O, Jesus Christ.

"I'm trying to be reasonable. I'm trying to . . ." Gledhill's teeth were clenched now, tobacco-stained, his face only inches from the other man's. "Why are you doing this?"

"I beg your pardon?"

"Why are you *doing* this?" The Kent accent had become more pronounced, transforming into a Cockney harshness. "I've done nothing to you. I'm a total stranger to you. Have you ever met me before? No. So why are you doing this to me? Going to my house, upsetting my girlfriend. I come home to find her in bits. How d'you think that makes me feel? Before I know it she's firing all kinds of questions at me. Stupid questions. *Ridiculous* questions—"

"Please . . ." The older man's voice was choked with fear. He couldn't disguise it any more. It took all his strength to hold the door in place. "I have nothing more to say."

Gledhill's face jutted closer still, his shoulder firm against the door, holding it fast, and Cushing could detect the strong sweet reek of – *what, blood, decay?* – no, alcohol on the man's breath. But something else too. *Something of death.* "What kind of person are you, eh?"

Cushing stood fast, half-shielded by the door, half-protected, half-vulnerable. "I was going to ask you exactly the same question. Except Carl answered that for me. In his own way."

"How? What did he say?"

"He said you're a vampire."

The laugh came again, this time a mere blow of air through nose and mouth accompanied by a shake of the head, then the bubbling cackle of a smoker's hack. It came unbidden but there was no enjoyment behind it or to be derived from hearing it.

"That kid cracks me up. He really does. Such a joker. You know what? That's hilarious." The turn of a word: "*You're* hilarious." Now Gledhill's expression was deadly serious. "You're being hilarious now."

"That doesn't mean I can't stop you."

"I'm innocent! I've done *nothing* wrong. Haven't you been listening to a bloody *word* I've said? You need to clean your ears out, mate. Get a hearing test, at your age. Pay attention to people. Not just listen to idiots."

"Carl isn't an idiot. I don't consider him an idiot."

"I know you don't." One elbow against a glass panel of the door, Gledhill jerked his other arm, tossing his spent cigarette into a flower bed without even looking where it fell.

"Why do you believe him and not me, eh? What gives *you* the right to cast judgement on *me*, anyway? You, a stupid film star in stupid films for stupid people."

So much for being a lifelong fan. His true colours, at last. "I know evil when I see it."

A grunt. "What? Dracula and Frankenstein and the Wolf Man?"

"No. I'm talking about the true evil that human beings are capable of."

"And what's that, eh? Tell me. Tell me what's going on in your *sick* mind, because I have no bloody idea."

Cushing did not reply. Simply stared at him and with supreme effort refused to break his gaze. He saw for the first time that the monster's eyes were as colourless as the invisibly pale eyebrows that now made an arch of self-pity over them.

"You think I'd hurt him? I wouldn't hurt a hair of his head. Cross my heart and hope to die." With the thumb of one hand, Gledhill made the sign of the cross, horizontally across his chest, then from his chin to his belly.

"It's curious," Cushing said, one hollow cheek pressed to the side of the door. "In vampire mythology, evil has to be invited over the threshold. And she invited you in, didn't she? With open arms."

"Yeah, mate. It's called love."

"Love can be corrupted. I will not be witness to that and let it pass."

"How Biblical." The glistening eyes did not suit the sneer that went with them.

"I have been a Christian all my life. It gives me strength."

"You Bible-thumpers see evil everywhere."

"No, we don't. But to God innocence is precious. It's to be valued above all things. It must be protected. Our children must be safe. It's our duty as human beings."

"Too right. They *do* need to be protected," the creature that was Gledhill said. "From old men talking to young boys on the beach. Boys all alone. What did you say to him, eh? That's what the police are going to ask, don't you think, if you go to them?" His voice fell to a foetid, yet almost romantic, whisper. "That's what people are going to ask. What were they talking about, this old man who lives all alone? This old man who makes horrible, sadistic films about cruelty and sex and torture, someone who's never had any children of his own, they tell me, someone who *adores* other peoples' children? This old man and this innocent little boy?"

His skin prickling with the most immense distaste, Cushing refused to be intimidated, even though the nauseous combination of beer and cigarette breath in the air was quite sickening enough. "I'm quite aware he is innocent, Mr Gledhill. And I'm quite aware what you might say against me."

"Good. And who do you think they'll believe, eh? Me or you?"

"They'll believe the truth."

"Then that's a pity. For you," the mouth said. It wasn't a face any more. Just an ugly, obscene mouth.

Cushing did nothing to back away. He knew that once he did that, physically and mentally, he was lost. But he was backing away in his mind like a frightened rabbit, and he feared that Gledhill could see it in the clear rock pools of his eyes. Frightened eyes.

"I should knock you into next week," Gledhill breathed. "Just the thought of what you were doing, or trying to do, makes me want to puke, d'you know that? But I'm not someone who takes the law into their own hands. I obey the law, me. I'm a law-abiding . . ."

Though he wanted to cry out, Cushing stood his ground. He was resolute, even if he didn't feel it. He felt crushed, battered, clawed, eviscerated. The truth was, he knew, if he gave into impulse and stepped away, then he was afraid that would mean *running* away. And what might follow that? His visitor was clearly big enough and strong enough to barge through a door held by a flimsy old man with no effort whatsoever. Yet he hadn't. Why, the old man dared not contemplate. Sheer *inability*, not bravery, glued him to the spot. But how much of that could the other eyes looking back at him see?

"You need to drop this, I'm telling you," Gledhill said. "For your own good, all right? I'm doing you a favour coming here. You don't get it, do you?"

"Oh, I do. I 'get it' entirely. Thank you for clarifying any doubt in my mind."

Cushing instantly wished he'd kept that thought to himself, but now there was no going back and he knew it.

With all his strength he shoved the door hard in the hope the latch would click and he'd turn the key in the Chubb to double-lock it before Gledhill got a chance to push from his side – but Gledhill had already pushed back, and harder. He was a builder, labourer, something – *heathen*, Cushing didn't know why that word sprang to mind, but he didn't want him in his house, he wasn't a reader he was a destroyer of books, and people. He fell back from the door, panting, a stick man, brittle. Then he did decide to run, the only thing he could do as it flew open, banging against the wall.

He dashed to where the telephone and address book sat on the hall table and snatched up the receiver and put it to his ear, swinging around to face the man in the doorway as his finger found the dial.

To his astonishment Gledhill stopped dead, his feet see-sawing on the threshold, his boots pivoted between toe and heel.

"Sorry! Sorry. Sorry. I'm really sorry, mate! I shouldn't have talked to you like that. Shit! That, that's the booze talking. I don't normally get like that. I don't normally say boo to a fucking goose, me." The swear word pierced Cushing like a blade, deep and hard and repellent. He knew people used it, increasingly, but he hated such foul language. But now he had the measure of the man, and the difference between them, and it gaped wide. In the full glare of the hall light, scarlet sweater radiant, a bloody breast swimming in the older man's vision, Gledhill wiped his long, shiny slug-like lower lip. "But I don't like people making allegations against me, okay? When they're lies. Complete lies, all right? What *normal* man would?"

Les loves that boy.

The low burr on the telephone line change to a single long tone and Cushing tapped the cradle to get a line.

"Please go. Immediately, please. I don't want to continue this conversation."

"Mate, honestly . . ."

"I'm not your 'mate', Mr Gledhill, quite frankly."

His heart thudding in his ears, Cushing dialled with a forefinger he prayed was steady. The wheel turned anti-clockwise with the return mechanism, waiting for the second "9".

The cold had infiltrated and he felt it on his blue-lined skin as he stared at the long-haired man framed in his front doorway against the February night and the other did the same in return. Neither man dared give his adversary the satisfaction of breaking eye contact first. Gledhill hung onto the door-frame, meaty hands left and right. Passingly, Cushing thought of Christopher Lee in his big coat as the creature in *Curse*. But all that monstrousness on the outside, for all to see.

He dialled a second time, straight-backed, not wanting to show the stranger he was afraid, but he *was* afraid. Of course he was afraid. He wasn't a young, athletic man any more, sword-fencing beside Louis Hayward or leaping across tables. Far from it. If this man chose to, cocky, power-ful and threatened, he could stride right in and beat him to a pulp, or worse. There was no guarantee that a man prone to other acts, *despicable* acts, would be pacified by a threat of recrimination at a later date. Or a mere *phone call*. Criminals did not think of consequences. That was one of the things that defined them as criminals. There was noth-ing, literally nothing, to stop his unwelcome guest killing him, if he decided to.

For the third time he placed his index finger in the hole next to the number '9' and took it round the circumference of the dial.

"All right," Gledhill said. "All right. I'll say this, then I'm going. There's nothing going on here, okay? It's as simple as that. Nothing for you to be involved in. *Nothing*. Okay?"

Emergency. Which service do you require?

Cushing stared. Gledhill stared back.

Emergency. Hello?

Gledhill laughed with a combination of utter sadness and utter contempt. "Jesus Christ. You're as loopy as he is. You're losing your *fucking* marbles, old man."

Hello?

Then Gledhill left, slamming the door after him and the hall shook, or seemed to shake, like the walls of a rickety set at Bray, and Cushing did not blink and did not breathe until he was gone, and his after-image – the halo of redness – departed with him. Cut!

Hello?

"I'm most awfully sorry," he whispered into the receiver. "I thought I had an intruder. I can see now that's not the case." He tried to cover the tremor he knew was in his voice, and tried to make it light and chirpy. "I'm perfectly safe. Thank you."

Cushing hung up, re-knotted the cord of his dressing gown, hurried into the sitting room and parted the drawn curtains with his fingers, a few inches only, to see – nobody. Even the last fragment of light and colour had faded from the sky. It was now uniformly black and devoid of stars.

The dryness in Cushing's throat gave him the sudden compulsion to breathe, which he thought a very good idea indeed but strangely an effort. It was as if he had done a ten-mile run, or heavy swim. Not only was his chest still thumping like a kettledrum, he could not get air into his lungs fast enough, and lurched, quite light-headedly, needing to prop himself on the arm of a chair in case he should fall. Sweat broke on his brow. He undid the buttons at his throat but they were already undone. He opened more, but his fingers were frozen and useless, fumbling and befuddled and half-dead.

This man who makes horrible, sadistic films about cruelty and sex and torture ...

Someone who's never had any children of his own, they tell me ... Someone who adores other peoples' children ...

This old man and this innocent little boy ...

Liquid surging up his gullet, he gagged and stumbled from the room to the little lavatory under the stairs, pressing his handkerchief to his mouth, but gagging nonetheless.

After he had vomited on and off for half an hour he half-sat, half-lay in the dark, drained and pathetic, too weak to move. What was the point of moving? He was clean here. He was untouched, though his fingers tingled from the bleach he had thrown liberally down the pan and the acid of it almost made him retch all over again. At least here, huddled on the cold linoleum, he could imagine the Domestos coursing through his veins, ridding him of the foul accusation that had contaminated his home. Here he could bury himself away from vile possibilities, horrid dangers, unspeakable acts and, yes, responsibility to others. What did others *want* of him anyway? He despaired.

What did his *conscience* want of him? To go to the police – with what? The fantasy of a backward child? A child with a vivid imagination, or psychiatric problems, or both? And what would that do but cause trouble, of the most horrifying nature, not least for himself? *An old man talking to a young boy*, he'd been accused of being by the boyfriend. The insinuation turned his stomach anew. What was wrong with that? How dare people misinterpret – but misinterpret they would: they *wanted* to misinterpret, that was the vile thing. Then again, what if he *himself* was misinterpreting? He could see it now, in a flash-forward, a dissolve: FAMOUS ACTOR UNHINGED BY GRIEF. If he stepped forward and spoke up, *he'd* be just as likely the one arrested. Sent to prison. Shamed. *His* picture all over the newspapers. If he was pathetic now, how much *more* pathetic would he be behind bars, or even in the witness box? But what churned in his belly more than all of that was the terrible thought that his failure to act would suit the true offender down to the ground. The creature would be free to continue his cynical, sordid depredations to his heart's content. And that poor boy . . .

God . . .

He shut his eyes. He felt like the terrified Fordyce, the bank manager he played in *Cash on Demand*. Mopping perspiration from his brow. Prissy, emasculated, threatened. Affronted by the taunts of his nemesis. Goaded. His psychological flaws exposed. But that didn't help. What could he *do*? He wanted, wanted so desperately for someone to tell him.

But who was there?

Aching and chilled, he clawed himself to his feet, clambered to the kitchen, poured himself lukewarm water from the tap, and drank. He needed Helen, his bedrock. Now more than ever.

He realized he felt so weak and ineffectual, not just now, but always. He remembered the spectacle of breaking down in tears in front of Laurence Olivier, thinking then, as he thought now: Am I strong enough? Am I strong enough for this?

Yes you are, Helen had reassured him. *If you want to be. You're worth ten of them, Peter. You're strong enough for anything . . .*

Back then, she'd nursed him through a nervous breakdown that had lasted a good six months. Dear Heaven, is that something this odious man could use against him now? His doctor's records of psychological unbalance? He felt the terrifying possibility like another blow to his physical being. The awful likelihood of the dim past regurgitated, raked over in mere spite and venom. It would bring with it dark clouds, as it had done then.

Six months of misery it had been, for him and for Helen too, without a doubt. God only knew how she'd endured it, but she had. And he had endured it too, thanks to her, and her alone. How could it be, he'd wondered, that he, the husband, was supposed to protect her, and there she was, sacrificing everything completely selflessly so that he, this worthless actor, of all things, could pull through?

Then he could hear her voice again, even clearer this time:

Peter, you are completely unaware of your own value. I expect that's why I love you, and so do so many of your friends and colleagues. Can you not see? You must think more of yourself, darling, as we do. You do not need the backbiting and jealousy of the court of King Olivier. Your heart is not suited to it, and I know your enormous talent will out . . . You just need the right opportunity to come along, and it will . . . You must believe that too . . .

Once again he remembered her love and sweetness and once again he felt devastated. He teetered to the living room and collapsed in a chair.

Through the doorway to the hall he could see the pile of unread scripts and it reminded him of the single day of shooting at Elstree, just over a month earlier, on *Blood from the Mummy's Tomb*, the eleventh of January, the day he'd had the phone call to tell him Helen had been rushed to

Kent and Canterbury Hospital. His scenes had been hurriedly rescheduled but Helen had died of emphysema at home on the Thursday. There was no question of him returning to the production. The already filmed scenes with Valerie Leon were scrapped and the role written for him, that of the Egyptologist Professor Fuchs, given to Andrew Keir. Quatermass replacing Van Helsing. The curse of an ancient civilization: it seemed like ancient history now.

Yet clear as a bell was his memory of wandering out alone, all, all alone onto the deserted beach just after Helen had breathed her last from those accursed lungs of hers, the seagulls reeling and swooping and cackling, the gale-force wind hard in his face, the waves that crashed on the shingle sounding to him like a ghastly knell, the thoughtless pulse of the planet. And he'd sung "Twinkle, Twinkle Little Star". He thought he'd gone a little mad that night.

Up above the world so high
Like a diamond in the sky . . .

He'd then found himself, unaware of the passage of inter-vening time, back at 3 Seaway Cottages, running up and down the stairs repetitively, endlessly, far beyond the point of exhaustion. To an impartial observer this might have given the appearance of madness too, but was anything but. In those moments he'd known exactly what he was doing. He'd run up, ran down, ran up again and so on in the vain hope of inducing a heart attack so that he might be reunited with her. He may have cursed God too, a little, that night under the stars. God didn't approve of taking one's own life, but damn God. He'd wanted to be with Helen and that was all he cared about. Then, racing up and down, up and down, he stopped dead as he realized the cruelty of it all. That, if he did commit suicide, he might find himself in purgatory, or in limbo, and separated from Helen forever. The crushing realization had hit him that *that* Hell would be even more unbearable than this, and he crumbled finally, spent.

Helpless, he'd found himself sitting on the stairs gasping for air, wheezing as she had wheezed, his lungs filling like bellows as he wept.

When the blazing sun is gone,
When there's nothing he shines upon,
Then you show your little light,
Twinkle, twinkle, through the night . . .

But God, as they say, moves in mysterious ways. And soon afterwards he had found the letter. Heard her voice as he'd read it:

My Dear Beloved. My life has been the happiest one imaginable . . . Remember we will meet again when the time is right. Of that I have no doubt whatsoever. But promise me you will not pine . . . or, most of all, do not be hasty to leave this world . . .

He had shivered then at the terrible thought that he might have, stupidly, done something so contrary to her wishes. Helen wanted him to go on, and he would go on. He would do what she wanted. He would do anything for her.

Do not be hasty to leave this world . . .

That's what she'd said to him. But the truth is, he thought, I didn't have the courage then, and I don't have it now.

Dear Peter, of course you do. Dying isn't hard. Living without the love of your life is hard. That's the hardest thing of all.

But now I am feeling more lost than ever . . . the child, the boy . . .

You care. That is your greatest strength. People feel it. They see it on the screen.

But this isn't the screen. This is life.

You will know what to do. You make the right choices, Peter. Just believe in yourself. As I do, my darling. Always . . .

He remembered, as if being in the audience watching a scene on stage in a drawing-room play, his father telling him, without any note of malice or cruelty, as if it were a statement of fact like the earth revolving round the sun, that he, Peter, was forty and a failure.

Even the memory of the hurt made him take a quick, sharp breath. But he remembered also the way Helen had stood up to the old man and given him a piece of her mind. His father had never been talked to like that, and certainly not by a woman. The fellow hardly knew what had hit him. And afterwards, when the two of them were alone, what had she said to him?

You have to believe in yourself, Peter . . . Believe in yourself and your abilities and not be brought down by those lesser mortals who for some reason of their own want you not to succeed. God gave you an amazing gift, darling, and God wants it to soar, and so do I. Have faith in your talent. That's all you need, Peter . . . Faith, and love . . .

The stink of bleach burned in his nostrils. It clung to the air and he knew he would not be able to rid the house of it for days. Perversely, he inhaled it deeply, as an act of defiance, determined to breathe in his own house, undaunted.

Faith and love *were* all he needed. Faith in himself, and the love of Helen, which he knew was immortal. That would be enough to get him through. Even this turmoil. Even this pestilence. He suddenly knew it. He was not weak. He was not pathetic.

With her courage, he could soar.

The floor of the interview room was concrete under his feet, the walls whitewashed, the single window set with bars beyond the glass. An old window. A window with tales to tell. *If walls had ears*, the saying goes. Indeed so, he thought. He wondered if it had once been an actual cell and how often names, jibes, scrawls, remarks, obscenities had been eradicated with a new coat of paint. As possible lives had been eradicated, set on this path or that, turned, curtailed, saved, doomed, the guilty punished, the innocent punished come to that.

There was nothing on the table in front of him but his hands, so he stood and paced with them clasped behind his back. They were still dry and cold from the walk. The sea, so often heralded as life-giving, ossified them. Made them into a mummy's hands. Leather-like.

Old man . . .

He closed his eyes. Inside his skull images of the scene from the night before ran though his brain. Multiplied. He saw them again and again. Take after take. Wait a minute, in that one he's quite aggressive. That one, more sympathetic. The clapperboard snapped, making his eyes flicker. Close-up. Take eleven. Man steps from the shadows, his lips open in a horizontal grin . . . No, take twelve, smiling evilly, the hands rubbing together . . .

He always wondered how editors remembered every nuance, every glance or inflection: now, only twenty-four hours later, he had difficulty doing the same. Now he had trouble remembering if the man had said anything to incriminate himself – anything actual, *tangible* – or whether his threat and bluster was born out of sheer panic, a bombastic act of frightened self-defence. What did he know for certain? Just that Gledhill had verbally attacked only the person who'd verbally attacked *him* first, in his absence. Was that inhuman, the behaviour of a cornered animal? Or the all-too-human reaction of an innocent man?

You're losing your fucking *marbles, old man* . . .

He flinched again at the obscenity scrawled on his memory like graffiti on the wall of a public lavatory. Then saw Gledhill's face again, at the gap in the door.

An old man and a little boy . . .

The insidious words' capacity to appal him was undiminished, sickening him to his core. He took a deep breath and dispelled any misgivings. The man was a liar, and had shown his cards. Hadn't he?

Aware of a slump he normally only affected when "old man acting" was required, he pushed his shoulders back, stretched his spine, scratched his chin, the bristles rasping there. While there was nothing on the walls to see himself in, in the mirror at home before setting out he'd seen a salt-and-pepper beard emerging, starting to give him a look like "Dr Terror" from Milton's portmanteau extravaganza, though he knew the particular nastiness in this tale he was living was nothing so comfortably *outré* as ancestral werewolf, voodoo jazz or malignant vine. He wished to goodness it was. He wished he could even be as pragmatic and unflappable as his Inspector Quennell in *The Blood Beast Terror* when luring a gigantic moth to its inevitable flame. But it was all too easy to face monsters with a screenplay in your hand. Even a bad one.

The previous night he had slept in erratic bursts, but not as sporadically as the night before, and did not dream as he had feared he might after his encounter. The framed photograph of Helen had rested on the pillow at his side and the influence of too many third-hand superstitions from bad scripts made him feel it had fended off evil. He'd allowed the thought to comfort him without analyzing it too much. Still sorely sleep-deprived, he had awoken at dawn spiky and brittle but strangely purposeful, and had played Berlioz's "Royal Hunt" from *The Trojans* while he dressed, pausing only to turn it up louder. Twice.

The door opened, the turn of the handle surprisingly sibilant, and a thick-set man entered wearing a brown suit, beige shirt and mustard tie. The shirt had been acquired when he had less of a paunch, and consequently the buttons were under stress and had tugged the ends out above his belt. He ran his index fingers around the rim of his trousers to re-insert them before settling his rump in the chair at the table. His socks and some inches of bare, hairless leg were exposed above slip-ons.

"Peter."

"Derek, dear boy . . ."

"Did you get my card?" The man, in his thirties, had hair slicked back with Brylcreem, and his fluffy growth of incipient sideburns was both ginger and ill-advised.

"Yes." In fact, Cushing knew full well it was with all the other cards, in a pile on the bureau, unopened. He was an actor. He would act. "Thank you so much."

Inspector Derek Wake did not waste time.

"What can I do for you?"

His bluntness bordered on sounding like impatience. Whether the policeman was particularly busy or merely lacking in sensitivity, Cushing didn't want to consider.

Perhaps neither man wanted to indulge in the ritual of feigned sympathy, feigned appreciation. Anyway it was unimportant. That was not why he was here.

He had been to the Inspector before for advice when preparing for a part. Usually he was greeted with a measure of perky, hand-rubbing delight, doubtless providing as it did a welcome diversion from the normal, irksome jobs officers of the law are tasked to perform, many of them unpleasant, many downright dangerous. Advising on a screenplay was many things, however "dangerous" was not one of them. But today Wake was taciturn. Perhaps he had too many things of greater importance on his plate. Cushing didn't imagine meeting a man recently bereaved would make a seasoned copper awkward or restless, given his profession, but perhaps it did. Perhaps this is how he showed it.

He'd brought a few pages of script from *Scream and Scream Again*, the Christopher Wicking draft. He was taking a gamble that Wake hadn't seen the film and didn't know it had already been made and released a year ago. He'd torn off the title page and said the film was called *Monster City* – not a bad title, he thought: he'd been in worse. His role had been Benedek, a Nazi-like cameo with only a couple of scenes, but he told Wake he was lined up to play the Alfred Marks part, Superintendent Bellaver, the Scotland Yard detective given the run around by a spate of vampiric serial murders.

For a full three quarters of an hour he asked the policeman questions about playing Bellaver. How would he address his assistants? How would he talk to a murder suspect? Whether a line seemed plausible. Whether another was properly researched. And when Wake replied, he scribbled notes copiously in the margins, underlining or circling the text, *double-underlining* on occasion, when he received details of special, usable significance. This, he knew, would please Wake as a kind of flattery. These days people's hearts were warmed by an affiliation to Hollywood in the way that past generations were by touching the hem of royalty. But, of course it was all nonsense. He wasn't the slightest bit interested in the Inspector's advice, and was hardly listening to his answers. The important questions – the *vital* questions – were yet to come. He was treading water, if the man but knew it. He had a plan. And it was nothing to do with the neatly formatted pages in front of him.

"Well, thank you. You've been most helpful. I shan't take any more of your time." Cushing rose from the chair. "I'm sure you have better things to do than talk to me." He shook hands in his sincere, country-parsonish way, buttoned up his coat and moved to the door. Whereupon he paused, his fingers fluttering next to his mouth – perhaps too theatrical a gesture? – before turning turned back to the seated detective.

"Yes?"

"Actually there's another script. Not a script, a story treatment I've been sent by a film company. Very intense. Very troubling. I'm not at all sure I shall accept the part, but . . ." He hesitated, tugged his lower lip, waved his hand as if dismissing the idea, criss-crossing his scarf on his chest, showing Wake his back then peeking back over his shoulder. "I feel in my bones the writer hasn't really done his homework. In a legal sense."

"Well, here I am. Run it by me. I'll be able to tell you if it rings true. In a police sense, at least."

"Are you sure? I don't like to—"

"Not at all. I enjoy it. You know I do. It livens up my tea break. Fire away."

"Very well." He sat back down and placed his fingertips together in a steeple. Very Sherlock Holmes. Too Sherlock Holmes? "This is a Canadian production. The lead is a Canadian actress who plays the mother. But they might film it in this country." He didn't like improvising, but in this instance an off-the-cuff quality was essential. The telling details were most important in a barefaced lie. "I play a headmaster. I suppose it's essentially a version of *M*." No flash of recognition. "The Fritz Lang film?" Still nothing. "The Peter Lorre movie? Set in Germany?"

"Oh."

"Have you seen it?"

"Yes, of course." Clearly he hadn't. "Remind me what it was about again."

"Lorre plays a disturbed man. A man who kidnaps and murders children. A child molester who becomes hunted down by society. A horrible character, paradoxically portrayed as sad and lonely and even strangely sympathetic."

"No, I've never seen it." The policeman stood up. "Why would anyone want to see a film about that?"

"These things happen in the world, I suppose."

"All the more reason not to put them in films. I go to the pictures to enjoy myself, I don't know about you." He stood, running his fingers round the rim of his belt yet again. "What did you want to ask me?"

"My, er, character has evidence against the, um, perpetrator . . ." His confidence had wavered. He speeded up his delivery. "In the story, I mean. Incriminating evidence. This is the crux of the plot. Evidence against a family member, not the vagrant who has already been arrested. And I'm curious. What would be the correct police procedure in a case like this?"

Wake shrugged, and having arranged his shirt and trousers to his temporary satisfaction, adjusted the knot of his tie. "We'd have to investigate. Long process. Doctors' reports. Court. It's complex. You'll have to give me the exact details and . . ."

"Everyone would be interrogated."

"Questioned. Yes. Obviously."

"And the boy?"

Another shrug. "Taken into care, straight off, any sniff of evidence. Whoosh. Can't take the risk. Get him out of there." The lick of a lighter on a cigarette tip. Secreted back in the jacket pocket. Smoke directed at the ceiling. "Mum and dad can squabble till the cows come home. Right little cheerful movie this is going to be. Not a comedy, I take it."

"No."

"No. Too right." With his hands on his hips now, the belly jutted unabashed. "Nobody does well out of these cases, I can tell you. Nobody goes home smiling, put it like that. Families get broken up, pieced together again. Except you can't piece them together again, can you? Worst of it is, unless you virtually catch the bloke red-handed, it's one person's word against another, and often as not even the kid won't speak up against their own parent, even if they half-kill them on a daily basis. And the mum sticks up for the feller like he's a bloody angel. So they get off scot-free. Buggered up it is, really buggered up. To be honest, I hate it, more than anything." More smoke, through teeth this time. Breath of a quietly seething dragon. "Sooner string them up and have done with it, ask me. Know the bloody liberals say, what if there's a miscarriage of justice? I say, tell you what. Cut their bloody balls off they won't do it again. I guarantee that."

Which was as much as Cushing needed to hear. He stood up and shook the man's hand generously in both of his.

"Thank you so much."

"Don't do it." The detective flicked ash into a metallic waste paper bin. "You don't want to be associated with that kind of rubbish."

"Perhaps not." One side of his mouth twitched. "I'll consider my various options. Definitely. Thank you, Derek."

Out in the corridor with the sound of a clattering type-writer nearby and garrulous laughter slightly more distant and out of sight, the old man heard from behind him:

"Peter, do you mind if we have a quick word? On an unrelated matter?"

It felt like a cold hand on his shoulder, which was absurd. Two uniformed constables passed him, a man and a woman. They both smiled, as if they recognized him. He touched the rim of his hat.

Smiling, he turned to see Wake leaning against the jamb of the doorway to the interview room, not smiling at all. The policeman switched off the light, closed the door and walked past him up the corridor in the direction of the sergeant's desk, then turned into a glass-sided office and sat behind a desk with several bulging manila files on it which he arranged in piles of roughly equal height.

When Cushing had stepped reluctantly into his office he stood up again, flattened his tie against his shirt-front with the palm of his hand, and crossed the room to shut the door after him. The conversation and clacking of the typewriter became substantially quieter. Wake returned to his swivel chair.

"A man came in this morning and made a complaint about you."

"Oh?" He told himself not to betray anything in his expression. Certainly not shock, though that was what he was feeling. Now the reason for Wake's mood was all too clear.

"May I ask who?"

"I'm not at liberty to say. I told him I'd prefer not to, but if he wanted to make it official, I'd make it official. But he was reluctant."

"I'll bet he was." Under his breath.

Had he heard? Wake's buttons really were straining across his midriff. "He was doing you a favour. He doesn't want to cause any trouble."

"What exactly did he say, Derek? Are you allowed to tell me that? Officially or unofficially?"

"He said you were talking to his little boy."

"That's absolutely correct. I was. I won't deny that. What's wrong with that?"

"Let's just say he doesn't want it." The way he lounged back in the chair was beginning to annoy Cushing. He found it louche, oikish and disrespectful. And the man's fly zip was distressingly taut.

"I chat to all the children. You know that. They chat to me. I'm like the Pied Piper. Helen and I . . ."

"I know. I know." Wake leant forward, elbows on the desk. Pushed the harshness of the angle-poise lamp away. "Listen, it puts me in a very awkward position. When someone comes in with a complaint like this. I don't want it to go any further if I can help it."

"On my part?"

"On anybody's part."

Cushing could feel his lips tight and bloodless with rage and dared not speak for fear of what might come out. So, he's got his retaliation in first, he was thinking. Clever. Before I could make any accusations, he's made his.

Clever man.

Clever monster.

"Look, I know this feller. He's a hell of a nice bloke." Wake raked his hair with his fingers and offered his palms. "We went to school together. I've got drunk with him. He's not a troublemaker, not like some round here. He's got a decent job, down on the boats. My wife knows his family, has done for donkey's years. He visits his mum in the nursing home every Sunday. He helps out at Christmas, with the food and that."

"In other words, you believe him."

"I think things can be misinterpreted, that's all," Wake said. "And he has, probably. I don't mean 'probably'."

Cushing didn't think he could remember such anger building up inside him. It was white hot and it terrified him and he knew if it rose much more he wouldn't be able to control it, and that would be a disaster. He opened the door.

"Thank you so much. I think I'll go now, if you don't mind. Unless you have anything more to say to me."

Wake sighed and rubbed his eyes.

When he looked up to reply, Cushing was gone. Wake sprang up, grabbed the closing door of his office, yanked it back wide and hurried to the sergeant's desk in pursuit of the long dark coat. Remarkably, the older man was outstriding him and he had to break into a run to catch up.

"Peter. Let me drive you home."

"No, Derek. Thank you all the same. I think I'd prefer some nice fresh sea air. Good day to you."

The detective followed him outside, caught up with him a second time and stood in front of him on the pavement, this time blocking his way.

"Look, all I'm suggesting to both of you is keep a wide berth from each other. You, and Gledhill and his family. Both parties. Either that, or sort out your differences without the police getting involved."

"I'm sure we shall," Cushing said, circumnavigating him.

The scenario had changed radically. The script had been rewritten, drastically. Now at least he knew with some certainty that he daren't rely on the police or the legal system. His adversary had prepared the ground, cleverly sown the seeds of doubt in a pre-emptive strike against him. If he made an accusation now it was too risky he would be disbelieved and, worse, far worse, the *boy* would be disbelieved – if the boy even spoke up at all. There was no guarantee he would do so, given his only way of dealing with the situation, it seemed, was through the prism of monsters and monster-hunters. Wasn't it Van Helsing who said "The Devil's best trick is that people don't believe he exists"? In Bram Stoker's novel, he thought, but certainly in the play and Universal film. He remembered the Van Helsing of the book: a little old man who literally talked double Dutch. He remembered asking Jimmy Carreras why he didn't cast a double-Dutchman in the part, and Jimmy saying: "We rather think you should play him as yourself". But the point was, how should he play *this* part, now? He had to stop this man. Alone, if need be. And he needed ammunition. In the words of Inspector Wake, he needed *evidence*.

Without delay he resolved to visit the Fount of All Knowledge.

She was wrapping up a cucumber in newspaper for a customer with whom she was conversing breathlessly. Through a steady stream of clients like this one she gleaned her vital information. A round-faced woman with the general shape of the Willendorf Venus and the given name of Betty, she knew everything to know about everyone in town: even a good deal they didn't know about themselves, he suspected. When Helen and he came to buy fresh vegetables from her and her husband's shop, they invariably came away a little wiser about something of high import, locally. In the woman's opinion, anyway. Which is why Helen had coined her nickname: "The Fount of All Knowledge", and it had stuck. A private joke between Peter and his wife. A private look between them as she twirled a bag of tomatoes at the corners whilst dispensing the latest gossip. A private raised eyebrow. A private hand concealing a wry smile. It seemed so long ago, and only yesterday.

"Lovely morning."

"Hello, Mr C. Yes it is." She wiped the dry earth from her hands to her apron. "The sun's done us proud. For February."

"I should like one of these, please."

The Fount of All Knowledge took the cabbage from his hands and popped it into a brown paper bag tugged from a butcher's hook. The tiny stigma in the corner torn.

"Good to see you out, sir." She looked down at her shuffling feet. "We know how it must be for you. Everyone's been saying."

"Bless you."

"Everybody knows how much you loved each other. I'm sure that's no comfort to you at all." Her cheeks reddened appreciably. "Still . . ."

He held out a handful of coins – the new decimal currency, still a struggle – and allowed her to take the required amount. "I am comforted by the certainty that I will be united with her one day. Of that I have no doubt whatsoever." He smiled. The woman nodded to herself, then rang up the money in a till secluded in the shadows under the awning. "Tell me, my dear. You may be able to help me. Do you by any chance know a woman by the name of Mrs Drinkwater? She has a boy named Carl."

"Annie?"

"Possibly. She lives in a bungalow on Rayham Road."

"That's the one." She picked up a broom and started brushing between the stalls. "Her brother had a hole in the heart. You know, like that footballer."

Cushing nodded but had no idea what she was talking about.

"I wonder, do you know whether she still takes in ironing? I believe her circumstances may have changed recently. I don't want to cause offence by enquiring unnecessarily. Someone tells me she has a new young chap in her life."

The Fount of All Knowledge shook the box of potatoes. "For all the good it'll do her."

"Oh? You sound sceptical."

"I wonder why."

"I've heard nothing but good reports of him. Les, I think his name is. He's excellent with the boy, apparently. Perhaps I've heard wrongly."

"Not got a great track record, has he? Married before. Divorced."

"We don't condemn people for that, do we? Not these days."

"I don't condemn anybody for anything, me." She took a large handful of carrots from a new customer. "I don't repeat what's told to me in confidence. I just wouldn't trust him as far as I could throw that building over there."

This was exactly the kind of information he wanted. But he wanted more. "His first wife? Now, was that Valerie Rodgers, the hairdresser from The Boutique, by any chance?"

"No. Nice girl from Tankerton. Sue something. Blezard, as was. That's it. Works in a tea shop in Canterbury. Pilgrims, I think it's called."

That was all he wanted to know, and the rest of the conversation consisted in a short discussion of who might take in his ironing. He weathered that particular storm until the Fount of All Knowledge ran out of intellectual steam, for which he was abundantly grateful. He touched the rim of his hat. *Bless you. Goodbye.* Which is when *Mr* Fount of All Knowledge appeared from the back of the shop holding aloft a pleat of garlic in two hands, eager to share the joke as if it were the first time he'd thought of it – which it most surely wasn't.

"Garlic, Mr C?"

"Very droll, Mr H," Peter Cushing said, as he always did. "Very droll."

He ran for the bus fearing he'd miss it, and by the time he settled into a seat his lungs were on fire. The pain and breathlessness reminded him of Helen's lungs as the vehicle pulled away from the bus station.

Sadly he realized that he had always kept working to provide for their future together. An old age together without financial worries that was not to be. It made him feel foolish, not that he could have known it would happen like this – never *like this* – but somehow feeling God, a force for good, unaccountably laughed at one's futile plans. Still, the income he had provided from films was able to give Helen a few luxuries, as well as the all-important medical care and attention when her cough got worse and her breathing painful and difficult. He remembered the arrival of the oxygen mask and canister necessary to assist her lungs. Meanwhile he, as Frankenstein, effortlessly transplanted brains and brought back the dead.

Frankenstein always failed because his morality was flawed, because his drive to help humanity was misguided. But in reality doctors failed for much more mundane reasons. When they went to Dr Galewski, the pulmonary specialist, he'd said: "You have left it too late. You should have come to me ten years ago." Frankenstein had never uttered a line so heartless.

He'd taken Helen to France, driving his spanking new blue Mark IX Jaguar to the thermal springs at Le Mont-Dore, spending hours on meditative walks in the hills while his wife rested. Encountering solitary goatherds as he grew a moustache for his next role. Telling her his silly adventures every evening. He remembered how, day by day, her laughter had grown stronger. How she was revitalized by the experience. The doctor from Poland had performed a minor miracle after all. Her cough had disappeared.

But the precious respite was to be hideously short-lived. Her throaty laughter cut short.

The Return of the Cybernauts in *The Avengers*; *Corruption*; *The Blood Beast Terror* . . .

All as her illness worsened.

They decided to sell Hillsleigh, their place in Kensington – Helen had said London "smelled of stale food and smoke" – and move permanently to their beloved holiday home by the sea. He remembered the pitiful sight of her sitting at the bottom of the stairs saying, "Can we go there, please?"

"Of course, my love. Of course."

He had kissed her and held her in his arms. He'd always joked in interviews that they'd married for money: he had £15 and she had seventeen and ten. That came back to him now.

He thought mostly of all the wasted time travelling back and forth to London when he could have been at her side. Fifteen televised hours of the horrid, under-rehearsed BBC *Sherlock Holmes*, an experience he loathed, distracted as he was by Helen's condition, barely able to remember his lines. He remembered the stairlift being installed in 3 Seaway Cottages whilst he was shooting *Frankenstein Must Be Destroyed* – "Hammer's Olivier, impeccably seedy in his spats and raspberry smoking jacket," the *New York Times* said of him in that one. He remembered her reading it aloud to him, delighting in the phrase as she repeated it. And Amicus' Jekyll and Hyde variation, *I, Monster*, catching the milk train to filming because he couldn't bear to spend so much as a night away from her.

After a short, callous period when she'd seemed to recuperate, Helen's respiration had become laboured again. He'd employed dear Maisie Olive to help with the housework because his wife was unable to function any more as the wife she wanted to be. That cut him to the quick, when she'd said it with tears in her eyes. But he didn't want a wife. He wanted *her*.

Her spirits lifted slightly as she decided almost on a whim that breathing exercises were the answer. He'd been buoyed by her sudden optimism but just as quickly her hopes were dashed by a young locum who told her they were a waste of time. He had wanted to strangle the man there and then, just like one of his villains would have done. He'd done it endless times on screen: how difficult could it be in real life? Or take one of those hacksaws of Baron Frankenstein and cut round his skull like a boiled egg, as he did to poor Freddie Jones. Take out that thoughtless brain of his. But the truth was, nothing he could do or think or dream would make the slightest difference to Helen's future, as well he knew.

As it was, that slap in the face by the locum took the heart out of her. He saw it. At that point exactly her spirit crumbled. And he feared his would too, but he dared not let it. He dreaded that her seeing an inner agony written in his features would compound her own. He would act. Act. Act. Act.

He gazed out of the filthy window of the bus. The countryside lay under a gauze of grime and dead insects.

On December the sixteenth, he had his last job before Helen died. Recording *The Morecambe and Wise Special* for transmission on the coming Christmas Day. As scripted, he was required to appear unexpectedly beside Eric and Ernie to complain he hadn't been paid the five pounds for an earlier show. It was a running gag: quite a good one, he thought. People had enjoyed his "corpsing" when he had guest-starred for the first time playing King Arthur, and it was gratifying that the team had asked him back. Helen had said, go on, it would do him good to play against type. To show there was a side of him that was warm and humorous and bright. The side she knew and loved.

Bring me sunshine . . .

He had thought he could get through it, and he had. Now, once again, he could hear the audience laughing through the grime and gauze of the world around him.

Bring me sunshine . . .

Even then, he had known deep down that, while the nation roared with laughter, his wife was at home, dying.

* * *

"Cream tea for two, please." He said it automatically, without thinking. "No, how stupid of me." He smiled. "I mean a pot of tea for one, and a single scone with jam and clotted cream. If you'd be so very kind." He placed the plastic menu back behind the tomato-sauce bottle. "Thank you, my dear."

"Thank you." She finished scribbling on her little pad using a biro with a feather Sellotaped to it in order to resemble a quill pen.

"Excuse me. I'm terribly sorry. Sue?"

"Yes?"

It hadn't been hard to find The Pilgrim Tea Room on Burgate after a short meander through Canterbury's narrow streets. It couldn't have looked more like a tea room if it had tried, with its dark timbers and white-painted plasterwork overhanging a bulging bow window. If not Elizabethan it had a distinctly Dickensian feel about it. He could imagine Scrooge walking by, muffled against the cold in a heavy snowfall, wishing everybody a Merry Christmas and carol singers holding lanterns on sticks. Not a bad role, Scrooge. He would have made a decent fist of it, he thought, had it ever been offered. Standing outside the restaurant, it struck him The Pilgrim was exactly the kind of emporium he and Helen would have gravitated to on one of their day trips. Exactly the kind of place Helen would have chosen. He had almost felt her arm tighten around his, guiding him in.

"Do you mind if I have a quick word? Whilst it's not too busy. I don't want to interrupt your work. It'll only take a moment, I promise."

The woman looked confused and a little frightened. As well she might be. He didn't blame her.

"We're about to close."

"It won't take long, I promise."

She hesitated. "I'll put this order in first, if you don't mind."

"No, of course, my dear. Please do."

He watched her glide to the far end of the shop, collecting empty plates and cups on the way. A Kentish Kim Novak dressed in a black ankle-length dress with a pinny over it, her hair pinned up under a frilly bonnet, the sort Victorian kitchen maids used to wear. It was an illusion dissipated somewhat by white plimsolls that had seen better days, and the lipstick. The overall effect was cheap and, combined with the ridiculously Heath Robinson quill, somewhat absurd. But the whole place was grubbily inauthentic, designed to milk the tourists for a quick bob or two. History was merely its gimmick. She returned with a damp cloth in her hand and wiped down the plastic tablecloth. He lifted his elbows to give her room for her comprehensive sweeps and lunges.

"I've seen your films." She lifted the duo of sauce bottles out of the way one by one. "You're Christopher Lee aren't you?"

He corrected her with consummate politeness, tugging on his white cotton glove.

"No, I'm the other one."

"Vincent Price?"

He kept his smile to himself. "That's right."

He pulled the ashtray towards him and lit one of his cigarettes.

"I'd like to talk to you about Les Gledhill."

The sweeping actions of her arm were energetic but he detected the tremor of a pause which she quickly attempted to hide. The skin on her face seemed to tighten, betraying a tense irritation. Her former relaxed, if busy, manner was suddenly gone. It was as if he had flipped a switch in one of his Frankenstein laboratories and she suddenly looked ten years older.

"You know what? I don't want to know about him. I don't want anything to do with him. He's a nasty piece of work. A sick, nasty piece of work." The swirling motions of the damp cloth on the table became violent, as well as repetitive.

"Did you know he's with another woman now?"

"I hope they'll be very happy together."

"She has a boy."

The woman stopped wiping the table top within an inch of its life and stood up straight. He saw her hand tighten around the dishcloth which she had swapped from one hand to the other. Her knuckles whitened and a few drops of water exuded, hanging like tiny baubles from the joints of her fingers.

"Look, I don't know why you're interested in him and I don't want to know. I don't even want to remember his name. But I have remembered it, thanks to you."

She turned away, but he shifted quickly onto the nearer chair and caught her hand. The one with the damp rag. He felt its wetness seeping through her fingers to his.

"The boy is called Carl. I'm concerned about him, and I'm concerned about his mother." He was looking up into her face but her eyes were darting around the room now, afraid that the scene was drawing attention. "Please. I don't want this man to ruin any more lives. I want to stop him. Is there anything you can tell me? Anything?"

She looked down into the blueness of his eyes. She pulled away her hand, abruptly, to her side, holding it there, then seemed to realize it was an unkindness that was unnecessary to an old man.

"I wish I knew then what I know now, that's all."

"Which is what? Please."

Her voice remained hard, terse with discomfort and something else swimming vast and unpleasant under the surface.

"He fastens onto vulnerable women. He can spot them. He homes in. He uses them. To get what he wants."

He knew she'd already said too much and regretted it. Horribly so. Giving the table a last, cursory wipe, she turned on her heel and walked towards the kitchen with her shoulders back, eyes front. A teenage boy with his head haloed in the fur-trimmed hood of a parka sat at one of the other tables with his shoes, laces undone, planted on a chair. She flicked his shoulder with the back of her hand as she passed by, hardly looking at him.

"Feet. Off."

The youth shot her a fierce look from under a heavy fringe. His mane of dark hair shook as he did so. His nose was long and square with a slight line above the tip from rubbing it too much. His eyebrows had begun to join in the middle. Thick lips, succulent yet dry enough to crack. Slightly crooked teeth. A constellation of pimples on his cheeks, some livid red, others turning yellow with pus. The affliction of the young. Another of God's little cruelties.

"Mum . . ." he complained in a sing-songy way under his breath.

Cushing felt an intense chill and imagined someone had opened and closed the door, but they hadn't.

He looked over at the boy in the parka as the latter played with the sugar dispenser, pouring a measured spoonful onto the table then scooping it, plough-like, with the flat of one hand then the other, prodding it into a perfect square, then making a dot in the centre of the square with the top of his index finger. Then destroying the whole artistic arrangement and starting again. He appeared both to be completely absorbed in the activity and completely bored by it. There was a lazy insouciance in the lad's countenance, something about his very physicality which bordered on barely contained rage.

What had Van Helsing said in *Brides*? That he was studying a sickness. A sickness *part physical, part spiritual* . . .

As if aware of being spied on, the youth looked up. Their eyes met and he knew the old man was staring at him. His features froze, but not with any degree of guilt or foreboding. Without any fraction of self-consciousness or embarrassment. Quite the reverse. He stared back at Cushing with chilling assuredness. Aggression, in fact. A hard gaze, a vicious gaze which would take almost nothing to provoke to violence, and the old man wondered if he had provoked it already, and it scared him to the core to think of what a young man with such a cold gaze might be capable.

"I've said all I'm going to say to you."

It was Sue Blezard's voice again as she placed his cream tea on a tray in front of him.

"I understand."

"No. You don't," she said.

But he feared he did. Very much so.

"Always the one to take the boy to bed . . ." She stood with her back to her son, blocking him out. "Read him a story. Their 'special time', he said . . ." It was as if she didn't even realize she'd said the words. Her anger had said them, spilled them, from some disembodied place, before she'd had a chance to rein them back. Then her back stiffened. That was all. No more. The muscle in her cheek flexed. "Pay at the till when you're ready."

She walked away.

"Thank you," Cushing said, knowing that she had revealed more than she could bear and no less than she was compelled. He respected that. In seeking to end pain, he had caused it, and hated himself for doing so. But it was necessary. So necessary.

The cup and saucer were Wedgwood. He thought it pathetic that he cared about such things.

Some of the pustules on the lad's skin had broken and there were small streaks of blood where they had been picked at. After some minutes his mother brought the youth a hot chocolate and Cushing continued to watch him as he drank it. There were cuts and bruises on his hands as well as nicotine stains, and his fingernails were chewed to the quick. His knee jiggled with the spastic tremor of an old and hopeless alcoholic. It spoke of an inexorable slide into a life Cushing did not want to contemplate. Where was this boy? Not in school, clearly. Then, *where*?

He thought of hurt and anger . . . the road to dissolution, evil, decay.

Their special time . . .

The hurt that prowls.

The scar that infects.

The darkness that perpetuates itself.

He stirred his tea. When he drank it, it was cold.

*   *   *

Afterwards, for a stroll, he visited the Cathedral. It was only yards away and he had not set foot inside for years. He was surprised to find the interior so vast and daunting, more so than he ever remembered feeling before. A massive, over-whelming, empty space. A space in which you could fit several normal-sized cathedrals, certainly. He thought of it now, quite literally. Dozens and dozens of churches, stacked like Lego bricks. He wondered if there was any limit to how large the masons could build an edifice to proclaim their faith? How big does Faith have to be to fill a space the size of this? How much love does God need?

The last tourists of the day moved around the aisles, looking up in awe and wonder, but he was the only one who knelt in the pews and prayed.

With his eyes tightly closed, he heard a baby crying. The sound echoed distinctly in the Cathedral's canyon of stone, but when he stood and looked all round, he could see nobody. No baby. No mother. Nothing. And all was abso-lutely quiet again. Except for the side door creaking gently as it closed to keep out the sun.

He did not know how long he had been sitting in the bath but the water was stone cold and the Imperial Leather had turned it milky and opaque. He felt pins and needles in his bony buttocks so he thought he'd been there a long while, but it worried him he didn't know how long and now his shoulders were shivering and he was sure that under the scummy water his penis had shrunk to nothing. He wanted to pull the towel off the rail but it was slightly out of reach. Then the door of the bathroom opened and Christopher Lee came in, dressed exactly as he had been in the first Hammer *Dracula* in that formidable entrance descending the stair-case. Immaculate hair. Virile. Vulpine. The top of his head almost touched the ceiling as he paced back and forth beside the claw-foot bath in his ankle-length black cloak. He looked terribly upset. "Where's my wife?" he was saying. "Where is she?"

Cushing could do nothing. He felt frozen and invisible.

He woke feeling the millstone presence of death, its crushing inevitability, in a way that he hadn't been so frightened by, or made helpless by, since he was seven years old.

Staring at the ceiling, he thought of the youth in the Pilgrim Tea Rooms, but instead of the pimply, hunched teenager in the parka, the boy sitting there was Carl Drinkwater, his hands wedged between his thighs, staring down at the plastic table-top which his mother was wiping with a wet cloth. Carl looked up and stared, just as the other boy had done. He had tiny smears of blood on his cheeks like the squashed bodies of dead insects.

Like massing vultures they gathered in the sky over the concourse of carrion, an echo of the prehistoric and primal. As the soles of his wellington boots pressed into the shingle with a hushing musicality of their own, their beckoning grew louder, a virulent and unforgiving choir. An announcement, spiteful heralds of his coming. Had he been blind, he thought, he could have purely followed the direction of the cries of the seagulls and found his way to the Harbour, where death was perpetually on the menu.

He carried a shopping basket. Not exactly becoming for a gentlemen, but he didn't care. It was his late wife's, and now it was his. He remembered the two *Harvesters* in the 1950s, when he and Helen had first come here, often used as umpire boats during the regatta. The remains of the railway were still there, the lamp standards still in evidence though the tracks were gone. Two whelk boats still operated on East Quay, commercial ships came in carrying stone and timber, Danish stuff, he was told, and beyond West Quay he often saw grain boats unloading into lorries with a hopper.

Meanwhile fishing boats unloaded their silvery spoils and the gulls were there, hovering, fighting the wind, ready to clash and kill for the pickings they could get from what bloody morsels fell before the trucks loaded up and shipped it out. Old families tended to work the trawlers. Generations. Fathers, sons, grandfathers.

A sheen of blood and seawater striped the concrete. His wellingtons crossed the mirror of it in the direction of the ugly store shed on South Quay, corrugated asbestos on a breeze-block frame, both its barn doors open to the wide "U" of the Harbour, the air punctuated by the tinkling of pulley metal and puttering slaps of wet ropes and lapping water.

It wasn't hard to find out the time of the tides and discover when exactly the boats came in, and he wasn't the only one who gravitated to the Harbour to get the pick of the "stalker" – as they called the odds and sods, small fry not sorted with the prime fish already boxed up and ready on its way to London. If they were regulars, they'd know when a certain boat would berth and they'd be there waiting for the bargains when it returned on the flood tide.

He watched as fishermen in sou'westers and oilskins hurried up and down the ladder on and off the vessel. They weren't hanging around, even with a small crowd present. Business took precedence. A small truck waited, taking the stacked plastic boxes – the catch already sorted during the two-hour steam back from fishing off Margate in Queen's Channel – straight to market.

Les Gledhill was one of them, strands of long wet hair hanging from his hood, cheekbones shiny and doll-like over his damp beard. The stalker was bagged up and marked at the quayside beyond the parked cars, some of it wrapped in newspaper. No airs and graces. 5 DOVER SOLE'S £1. The misappropriated apostrophe was almost obligatory. Others who'd arrived first were helping themselves, and Gledhill was taking their cash in a wet, outstretched palm, skin peeled pink from the scouring weather.

Seeing Cushing out of the corner of his eye, Gledhill at first attempted to ignore him. A transistor radio set on an empty oil drum was playing the recent Christmas hit, "Grandad" by Clive Dunn. Unable to avoid doing so any longer, Gledhill stared at him as he rinsed his hands under a cold-water tap on the quayside and wiped them in a towel. The DJ on the radio switched to the current single at the top of the charts, George Harrison singing "My Sweet Lord".

"What do you have today?" Cushing presented himself as bright-eyed and bushy tailed.

"Depends what you're after."

"Oh, I think I'm open to suggestions." Cushing smiled broadly.

"Well. Got a load of dabs," Gledhill said, forcing a retaliatory smile to match. "Sprats. Herrings. Good winter fish. Dover sole. Skate. Nice skate backbone, if you know what to do with it." His hands looked frozen and painful to the older man as he watched him turn to serve an elderly woman who had the right change. A great deal of nattering was going on between the other customers and the other fisherman – quite sprightly, good-natured banter – and to an onlooker, this conversation would seem no different.

Cushing adjusted his scarf, scratched the side of his chin and pointed at one of the packages lined up before him. "That one will do perfectly."

"Pound."

"Thank you." Cushing happily delved into his purse.

Gledhill picked up the fish in newspaper and handed it to him, and as he did so Cushing saw the blue blur of an old tattoo on the back of his wrist, together with blue dots on his finger joints.

"You know, I was reading the other day . . ." He placed a pound note in the other man's palm. "The fish, it's the old symbol of Christianity. Older even than the cross."

"Fascinating," Gledhill said.

"Yes, it is, rather. Some people say religion has lost its way, but we are all God's children, when all is said and done. Whether we choose to see that or not. Don't you think?"

"You've got a bargain there, squire. I'd go home very happy if I were you."

Turning his back, Gledhill went back to the tap of ice-cold water and washed his red-raw hands with the thoroughness of a surgeon. Cushing had researched surgeon's methods for the Frankenstein films and it was the kind of thing he watched and made a mental note of, habitually. He found it interesting, vital, that there were telltale rituals and practices that made a profession look authentic, or inauthentic if wrong. It was essential to make the audience believe in the part one was playing, however ludicrous the part may be on paper. That was one's job. That was why they called it "make believe". Make. Believe.

Cushing waited.

Believe in yourself, Peter . . .

"Anything else you want, mate?" Gledhill turned his head and stared at the old man. "Apart from the Dover sole?"

Peter Cushing decided he would not be hurried. Why should he be?

"Let me see . . ."

He lingered. And the more he lingered the more he realized he was enjoying the discomfort his lingering engendered.

Les Gledhill did not do anything so obvious as a quick, shifty look towards his colleagues to reveal his unease. He would never have been that blatant. Nor did he become twitchy or self-conscious in any way. In fact his motions became slower and more considered. That, in itself, told a story – that the very presence of the old man in wellington boots made him uneasy. And he didn't like it. A person who got a certain thrill from the control of others seldom enjoyed the feeling that someone else had control of him.

"Have you ever tasted oysters, Mr Cushing?" Gledhill picked up one of the shelled creatures from a plastic bucket in front of him.

"I thought the oysters round here had all succumbed to disease and pollution."

"Not if you know where to look. I think of it as a hobby. Go out on a Sunday. Maybe get a hundred. You haven't answered my question. Sir." His intention was to intimidate, rather than *be* intimidated. That much was clear.

"My preference is towards plain food."

"Then you don't know what you're missing. Marvellous stuff." Gledhill took a knife from a leather satchel. It was a short, stubby one with a curve in the blade. "You break them open." Metal scraped against the shell. He turned the object in his hand and opened it as if it were hinged. "Dab of vinegar if you prefer. Or just as it comes." He ran the knife under the slimy-looking bivalve, cutting its sinewy attachment. It sat in its juices. "Then into the mouth they go." He slid it off the half-shell onto his tongue, savouring it for a second or two, no longer, then swallowed. "One bite. Two at the most. Then down like silk. Nectar. Nothing like it."

"Not for me."

"Not for everybody, that's for sure. Some people find it repulsive. Some can't even bear the idea and run a mile. But to gourmets, those who appreciate the good things in life, well . . . they're a little taste of Heaven." Gledhill's eye was steady again. Unblinking. "Acquired taste, of course . . ."

"If you say so."

"Don't knock it till you try it. As they say."

"Something eaten whilst it is still alive, simply in order to give a person pleasure? I find that rather . . . obscene."

"In a way. In another way, it's the peak of civilized behaviour. The stuff of banquets and kings. Of aristocracy and riches and palaces. The supreme indulgence. The Romans introduced them here two thousand years ago. Long ago as the time of Christ. Makes you think, doesn't it?"

"Perhaps."

"Lot of algae and low in salinity, the Thames Estuary. Knew a thing or two, those Romans." He tossed away the empty shell into a bucket half-full of them, shortly to add to the cultch bed upon which the "spat" of the next generation would settle. "Besides. If we humans don't live for pleasure, what do we live for?"

Cushing thought for a moment.

"Love?" he suggested. But really it was nothing like a question, to his mind.

Gledhill gave a snort, as if it were a bad joke, and wiped his hands in the grubby towel.

"Anything else I can do for you, sir? Or will that be all?"

"Actually there is one thing." Cushing was careful to maintain a matter-of-fact air. "I'm going to a matinee at the Oxford Picture House this afternoon. I rather thought you might like to join me."

Gledhill did not look away. "I don't like going to the cinema as a rule. Not in the daytime."

"Don't tell me you're afraid of the dark?" Cushing's wit fell upon deaf ears. "I'm sure you can make an exception."

"I'm busy."

"I think not. Your working day is evidently over."

"I didn't say I was working, I said I was busy."

"Oh. That's a shame." Cushing feigned disappointment. "It really is a shame. Because I've been to see your ex-wife and son, you see. Yes. Sue and I had a most edifying chat, and I thought you might be interested in what she had to say. It was quite – what can I say? Quite – *special*. I'm being dreadfully presumptuous. I shall go alone." He placed the wrapped Dover sole deep in his shopping basket and walked away a few steps before turning back, as if the next thing he said was a mere afterthought. "I believe the main feature commences at half past two. I do so hate missing the start of a picture, don't you? You can't really enjoy a story unless you see it from the beginning, right through to the bitter end. Don't you find?"

Gledhill was still staring at him. A few foolishly courageous seagulls descended in a flurry on the "stalker" in front of him and took stabs at it, one trying to skewer some fish offal in rolled-up newspaper. Gledhill stamped his feet and clapped his hands, yelling sharply and waving his arms to scare them off. "Go! *Go!* Bloody pests!" Behind him, another fisherman directed a high-powered hose to wash down the flagstones. The gulls took to the skies.

Cushing tapped his shopping basket before walking away.

"Thank you for this. I shall enjoy it."

* * *

Fetching coal to build the fire for that coming evening, he remembered entering the same way from the garden, closing the door with his foot, finding Helen hunched on the divan looking like a frightened child. "I thought you'd left me." "I'm not going anywhere," he'd reassured her. She'd closed her eyes. He'd wrapped a blanket around her and made a fire, as he did now on his knees before the grate. He screwed up sheets of old newspaper in makeshift balls and laid a criss-cross pattern of kindling on top of them.

Maisie Olive had brought tea and said, "She'll be all right, sir."

He'd been smoking a cigarette. "Thank you, yes. She'll be all right."

At nine o'clock the night nurse helped Helen to bed. The last thing she said, clutching his hand, was, "Goodnight, Peter. God bless you."

At three o'clock some instinct he could not explain woke him, and he found her skin cold and clammy to his touch. He switched on the light and the electric blanket and went down to make tea. Her pupils were small dots. He fluffed up pillows and prised them behind her. When he returned with the tea, the night nurse was there saying her breathing was painful and then what breathing there was, painful or not, stopped.

The nurse looked at him and shook her head.

He looked down at Helen and saw all pain and suffering gone from her face. She was serene and at peace. The nurse must have seen his stricken features because she extended her arms, then lowered them.

At that moment Cushing had felt nothing, just a supreme hollowness inside. He'd thought, most strangely of all, if this was in a film I wouldn't be reacting like this at all. I'd be shouting and jumping around and wailing.

"You'd better get dressed now, Mr C," the night nurse said. He was still sitting in the armchair with the tea tray on his lap and it was daylight.

When the undertakers came, they showed him an impressively shiny catalogue of headstones. Many of them reminded him of the ones made out of polystyrene in the property shop at Bray. He'd been in a few graveyards in his time. Most of them taken apart afterwards to be reconstituted as other sets: barn, ballroom, bedroom. If only life could be dismantled, he thought, remade and reconstructed the way sets were, with a fresh lick of paint, good enough for the camera to be fooled. After looking at the brochure, he'd given the undertaker only one absolute specification for the gravestone: that there be a space left beside Helen's name for his own.

In that last year her weight had diminished drastically to under six stone, while he himself lost three. It was as if, unconsciously, he'd been keeping pace with her decline, wanting to go with her every step of the way – and beyond, if necessary.

The previous summer he had dropped out of filming Hammer's *To Love a Vampire*, the follow-up in the Sheridan Le Fanu "Karnstein" saga (even though the part of occultist schoolmaster Giles Barton had been written for him) because Helen had become gravely ill, yet again.

"No more milk train," he'd said.

When she'd been rushed to hospital that last time and he'd been telephoned by Joyce at the studios, he was shocked how tired she looked when he arrived at her bedside. It was immediately clear this was not just a case of a few checkups, as he'd deluded himself into thinking. He'd held her hand tightly and said to her he wasn't on call the next day and he'd bring in a picnic lunch. She smiled and said that'd be lovely. But when he'd arrived with the wicker hamper, like some character from a drawing-room farce, the nurses had told him he was not to be admitted under any circumstances. The doctors said his wife had had a serious relapse and her heart and lungs were terribly weak. He heard very little after that.

He succeeded by sheer persistence in persuading the specialists to let her home. Nobody precisely said that these coming days were her last, but their acquiescence made it obvious. Cushing shook their hands and thanked them profusely. The Polish doctor long ago had said he feared there were no miracles, and this was clearly what he meant, he knew that now. And he knew his wife would need constant medical assistance for the short, precious time she had left.

He arranged day and night care, and rang his agent to cancel his role in the *Mummy* picture they'd started shooting. He was not irreplaceable. Other people in this life were.

Now he remembered the crew sending flowers to the funeral.

As families do, of course.

He remembered, too, sitting at her bedside, tears streaming down his face. "I've made mistakes. I've done things of which I have been entirely ashamed, foolish things . . . Yet through it all, you have been perfect. You forgave . . ."

"I told you so many times, my love," Helen had said. "I never wanted you to feel I possessed you. That was our bargain, remember? What I know doesn't hurt me, so why on earth should it hurt you? It's unimportant. Those things simply didn't happen. You hear?" She'd wiped his cheeks with a corner of the bed sheet. "Not a person in the world could have done for me what you have done . . . But I'm tired, my darling . . . I can't talk now . . ."

In the bedroom now, all alone, he took the crucifix Helen wore from the jewellery box in front of the vanity mirror where she would put on her make-up every morning.

He placed it deep in the hip pocket of the Edwardian tweed suit made for him by Hatchard's, the outfitter on the high street. It was where he bought most of his traditional clothes: caps, cravats, gloves. They knew what he liked there and never let him down. People didn't let him down, that was the remarkable thing in life. He remembered wearing this, his own suit, when filming *I, Monster* with Chris Lee. Now he faced another Jekyll and Hyde, another beast hiding under the mask of normality. A clash with evil in which he could only, as ever, feign expertise. Fake it. But at least with the right tools. And in a costume that felt proper for the fight.

Downstairs, the scripts and letters he had trodden over to get in still lay on the mat inside the front door. He picked them up. Clutched them to his chest. They felt full and heavy. Full of words and ideas and powerful emotions, and his chest empty.

"What if I fail?"

She was as clear in his ear as she'd ever been in life.

You shall not fail, my darling . . . With faith, you cannot fail . . .

"What faith?"

He faced the closed door to the living room.

Your faith that Goodness is stronger than Evil. It's what you believe, isn't it? You always have.

"I know. But is that enough?"

You know it will be. It must be.

He turned the handle and pushed the door ajar.

The room was in darkness as he walked through it. He placed the scripts and cards on the bureau, adding to the pile. He looked at one envelope and held it between his thumb and forefinger. He recognized the handwriting. It was a friend.

So many friends. And yet . . .

Darling, never fear . . . You are the one good thing in a dark world . . . and I am with you . . .

"Helen . . ."

How could he be downhearted when countless individuals led their entire lives without finding a love even a fraction as powerful as the one he had found?

He picked up her photograph and pressed it to his lips.

Square and temple-like, it had gone the way of all flesh. Now mostly a bingo hall, The Oxford in Oxford Street was a piece of faded gentrification, a mere memory of past glory, a vision of empire slowly turning to decay, a senile relative barely cared for and shamefully unloved. All those things. He remembered being told, at some official council function or other, that the original cinema opened in 1912, long before talkies, even before he was born. Rebuilt in 1936 in

Art Deco-style by a local architect, the regenerated Oxford's first film show was Jack Hulbert in *Jack of All Trades*. Extraordinary to contemplate, looking at it now.

He trod out a cigarette on the pavement.

Behind glass, Ingrid Pitt's fearsome, fanged countenance loomed over a tombstone. BEAUTIFUL TEMPTRESS OR BLOODTHIRSTY MONSTER? SHE'S THE NEW HORROR FROM HAMMER! He noticed his own name amongst the other co-stars, George Cole and Kate O'Mara. Inevitably it brought back the letters of condolence he'd received from both of them. And the strangers who had done so, too. He thought it peculiar, yet immensely touching, that those who'd never even met his wife or himself personally would feel moved to make such a gesture. The foibles of the human heart were infinite, it seemed, at times. But that notion did more to give him a chill of apprehension than stiffen his nerves.

Inside, the carpet tiles were disastrously faded and the disinterested girl at the ticket booth barely old enough to be out of school. He did not need to say "upstairs" as he used to, because the seats in the stalls had been removed for bingo tables. Upstairs were the only seats left. With a clunk the ticket poked out and he took it.

"Excuse me for asking. Are you Peter Cushing's father?"

"No, my dear. I'm his grandfather."

In what used to be the circle the house lights were up and he had no difficulty finding his way to a middle seat, half-way back. As yet he was the only one there. He took off his scarf and whipped the dust off it before sitting. It was more threadbare than when he'd come last, but he couldn't blame the owners. Trade was dwindling. The goggle box in the corner was sucking audiences away from cinemas: not that he should complain – there was a time, at the height of his success in that medium, when people joked that a television set was nothing so much as "Peter Cushing with knobs". But now people were becoming inert and frighteningly passive, like the drones predicted in *Nineteen Eighty-Four*, which so horrified when he starred as Winston Smith in the BBC production in the 1950s that it caused a storm of outrage. Questions were raised in Parliament, no less: the remarkable power of drama to jolt and shock from complacency. Some outrage was necessary, he also considered, when picture palaces like this, almost jokily resplendent in Egyptian dynastic glamour, were becoming as decrepit as castle ruins.

He thought again of Orwell's masterpiece and wonderful Helen standing just off camera, her radiant smile giving him a boost of confidence to overcome his chronic nerves. What had been the play's theme? Love. And what was the ghastly phrase of the dictatorship? *Love crime*. Two words that were anathema in juxtaposition. Except, perhaps, in a court of law. Indeed, he wondered if this was his own "Room 101" in which he had to face the very thing he feared most: love, not as something sacred, but as something unspeakably profane.

His stomach curdled – as it often did of late – and he tried to shift his musings elsewhere. To Wally the projectionist, who once proudly showed him his domain, with its two 1930s projectors that used so much oil that, when it came out the other end, he'd use it in his car.

Cushing took his coat from the seat next to him and folded it over the one in front. He was hoping the vacant seat would be occupied. Eventually, if not sooner. For now he had best try to endure the sticky smell of popcorn and Kia-Ora embedded in the surroundings.

He put on his white cotton glove and lit a cigarette. Before he'd finished it Russ Conway's "Donkey Serenade" faded and the house lights went down.

Without the preamble of advertisements, often the case in a matinee, sickly green lettering was cast over the rippling curtains as they creaked begrudgingly open. Mistimed as ever.

AN AMERICAN INTERNATIONAL/HAMMER FILMS PRODUCTION.

Ah yes.

Jimmy ringing him in a panic saying AIP were getting cold feet because they'd cast an unknown in the lead, and a Polish girl at that. They'd already had to defend their decision to the Ministry of Labour, for God's sake: now the Americans had said they'd feel more secure with a "traditional Hammer cast". And so he'd stepped into the breach at the last minute to save Hammer's bacon. He could hardly believe that only a year ago he was filming it all on Stage Two and at Moor Park golf course, with Helen waiting for him at home, alive, when they called it a wrap.

He squinted as colour flecked the dark air and dust motes.

Lugubrious Douglas Wilmer's Baron von Hartog closes the book on his family history. He watches from a high window in the ruined tower of Karnstein castle as an apparition floats around the fog-swathed graveyard below. A phantasm in billowing shroud-cloth, the Evil not yet in human form . . .

The words of the actor in voice-over blended with the words Cushing recalled dimly from the script.

How the creature, driven by its wretched passion, takes a form by which to attract its victims . . .

How, compelled by their lust, they court their prey . . .

"Driven by their inhuman thirst – for blood . . ."

Cushing shifted in his seat. Why were cinema seats so desperately uncomfortable?

The camera tracks in towards a drunk who has staggered out of a tavern and stands urinating against a wall. His stupid face opens in a lascivious grin. Back inside the tavern, his scream chills the air and everyone freezes in horror – the way Hammer does best. The serving wench runs to the door and opens it to find the drunk with twin punctures in his neck. Lifeless, he falls . . .

Peter Cushing looked at his watch. Tricky to see in the dark. The merest glint of glass. Hopeless. Hearing the screech of a sword drawn from its scabbard, he lifted his eyes back to the screen.

Douglas Wilmer waits in the chapel for the apparition to return to its grave. As his eyes widen, the camera pans to a diaphanous shroud more like a sexy Carnaby Street night-gown than anything from the nineteenth century, and the naked, voluptuous figure beneath it. The camera rises to the face of a beautiful blonde. She steps closer and wraps her arms around the frightened, mesmerised Baron. When her cleavage presses against the crucifix hanging around his neck she recoils sharply, her lips pulled back in a feral snarl. Close up: bloody fangs bared in a lustrous, female mouth. With a single swipe of his sword he decapitates her. Moments later, her severed head lies bloody on the castle flagstones at his feet. The lush music of Harry Robinson, as romantic as it is eerie, wells up over the title sequence proper . . .

Still the seat beside Cushing remained empty. He lit a second cigarette. By now he was wondering if he would be sitting through the film alone. Perhaps his attempt to entice the creature hadn't been as clever as he'd thought.

The pastiche Strauss made him cringe every time. He'd never been impressed by the tatty ballroom scene at the General's house. The Hammers were always done cheaply – the ingenuity and commitment of cast and crew papering over inadequate budgets – but now they were starting to *look* cheap. It worried and saddened him. Like seeing a fond acquaintance down on their uppers. Byronic Jon Finch looked heroic enough, he had to admit. He didn't look bad himself as a matter of fact, in that scarlet tunic and medals . . .

Peter Cushing as the General looks on, presiding over his party. He kisses the hand of the delightful Madeline Smith, bidding her and her father, George Cole, goodbye. Or rather: "Auf wiedersehn".

Until we meet again. Obviously. The audience knows he will appear later in the picture. He's one of the stars, after all.

He watched Dawn Addams as the Countess introduce her daughter Mircalla, played with languid hunger by Ingrid Pitt – plucked from her brief appearance in *Where Eagles Dare* after Shirley Eaton (from *Goldfinger*) was deemed too old, even though they were actually the same age. Perhaps Eaton, he thought, simply hadn't given Jimmy Carreras what he wanted, as Ingrid with her European eroticism undoubtedly had. Poor Ingrid, who'd spent time with her family in a concentration camp – ("concentration camp: that's true horror") – and for whom he'd organized a cake and champagne on the anniversary of her father's birth: Helen had wheeled it onto the set and Ingrid had blown out the candles with tears in her eyes.

Peter Cushing asks the Countess if she would like to join in the waltz. "Enchanted," comes her reply.

"The invitation to the dance." A voice in reality: one he recognized all too well.

Without turning his head, he saw the usherette's torch hovering at the end of his row of seats. A silhouette moved closer, given a flickering penumbra by the fidgeting and then departing beam. The donkey jacket seemed almost to be bristly on the shoulders, like the pelt of some large animal, especially with the long, flesh-coloured hair running over its collar. Eyes fixed on the screen, Cushing felt the weight of Les Gledhill settle in the cinema seat beside him. He detected the strong whiff of carbolic soap and Brut aftershave, a multi-pronged attack to cover the daily tang of blood and gutted fish.

Jon Finch is waltzing with the General's niece, Laura, and Ingrid – Mircalla – is looking over at them. Laura thinks she is eyeing up her boyfriend but he says no, it's her she's looking at. A sinister man enters the ballroom dressed in a black top hat and a red-lined cloak. His face is unnaturally pale. He whispers to the Countess, who makes her apologies to the General. She has to go. Someone has died.

Peter Cushing as the General tells her, "It's my pleasure to look after your daughter, if you so wish."

Sitting beside him in the auditorium, Gledhill's face was entirely in darkness.

"Don't tell me you'll tear down the curtains and let in the light. You're not exactly as frisky as you were back in the 1950s, are you?"

"I thought you didn't watch my films."

"Only when there's nothing better on. They're okay for a cheap laugh, I suppose. All they're good for nowadays."

The General says goodbye to the Countess and watches her depart in her coach. Ingrid stares out. The pale, cloaked man on horseback in the woods gives a malevolent grin, showing pointed fangs.

"Things have moved on, haven't you noticed? Blood and gore, all the rest of it. Nobody's scared of bats and castles and bolts through the neck."

Mircalla fondly places a laurel on the General's niece's head. Puts a friendly arm around the young girl's bare shoulders.

"They're just comedy. Nobody's afraid of you anymore."

Cushing chose not to point out that *their* Frankenstein's monster never had bolts through its neck. "I believe I still have a small but devoted following."

"I can see. We can hardly move for your adoring fans." The man he spoke to knew as well as he did that they were the only people in the audience. "They're dying, these old films. Everybody knows it. The last gasp. It's tragic."

"I think you'll find this film has been a box-office hit. Significantly so, in fact. It's rejuvenated the company."

"Really. Look around you."

"You've got to remember it's already been released for five months. And this is a backwater town. And a matinee."

"You're living an illusion, mate."

"Am I?"

"You need to get a grip on reality, old feller. Before you lose it completely. Choc ice?"

Cushing imagined it was not a serious inquiry.

Peter Cushing's beautiful niece is sleeping now. Swooning in some kind of "wet dream" – if that was the expression.

He remembered that this was one of the many scenes that Trevelyan and Audrey Field, who had been campaigning against Hammer for decades, were unhappy about, even with an "X" certificate. The censor had strongly urged the producers to keep the film "within reasonable grounds"

– meaning the combination of blood and nudity, the very thing Carreras was gleeful about now they'd entered the seventies ("The gloves are off! We can show anything!").

In monochrome a hideous creature crawls up the bed. Wolf-like eyes out of blackness become Ingrid Pitt's – Mircalla's.

To Cushing the girl looks as though she has a bearskin rug crawling over her. Nevertheless, the dream orgasm so worrisome to the BBFC is curtailed with her scream.

"You saw the bitch," Gledhill said in the gloom. "What did she say? You know she's a liar."

"There seem to be an extraordinary number of liars in your life, Mr Gledhill."

Peter Cushing and an elderly housekeeper run in and calm Laura down. They say it was a nightmare, that's all. He kisses her forehead and they leave the room. They think of checking on Mircalla, but when they knock there is no answer. They presume she's sleeping. But the bedroom is empty. Ingrid Pitt is outside under moonlight looking up at the window . . .

"I thought she seemed perfectly charming," Cushing said, his eyes not straying from the screen. He pretended that it absorbed his attention. "Another woman with another boy who perhaps doesn't dream of vampires, like Carl, but of another kind of . . . creature of the night."

His companion remained silent. He found it uncommonly difficult to deliver the lines he'd prepared in his head.

"She told me you'd invariably take him off to bed, rather than her. That you'd spend time reading him stories, as a doting father should. Quite rightly. Your, ah, *special time* you called it, I believe . . . I wonder what your son might call it?"

"Now you are starting to bother me, old man."

"I'm rather glad about that."

The Doctor, played by reliable old Ferdy Mayne, tells Peter Cushing that his niece just needs some iron to improve her blood. Cut to Ingrid Pitt at the girl's bedside. Laura tells her she doesn't want her to leave. Ingrid lowers her head and touches her lips to the girl's breast . . .

"What are you going to do? Organize a torchlight parade of peasants to storm up to the Transylvanian castle, beating at the gates?"

Peter Cushing tells a visiting Jon Finch that his niece doesn't want to see anyone but Mircalla.

For a moment Cushing was taken aback by his own close-up. In spite of the make-up he looked tremendously ill. Of course he knew the reason. It was the toll of Helen's illness, even then. He could see the strain in his eyes. But it was a shock to see it now, thirty feet across, vast, on display for the entire public to see. He'd been oblivious to it at the time. He'd had other preoccupations. Now it hit him like a blow and it took a second for him to steady his nerve, as he knew he must.

"You think you're safe because you consider everyone to be as selfish and self-interested as yourself." Cushing did not look at the other man as he lit another cigarette. A scream rang out: the General's niece, after another nocturnal visitation. "You really are unable to contemplate that someone might act totally for the benefit of another human being, even though they themselves might suffer. And that's where you're misguided, and wrong. That's precisely your undoing, you see."

"You obviously know me better than I know myself."

"We shall see if I do."

"Shall we?" Mocking even his language now.

Peter Cushing's niece moans Mircalla's name in her delirium. He holds her hand. When Mircalla is discovered not in her room, he barks angrily at the maid to find her. Ingrid Pitt glides in, non-plussed, saying she couldn't sleep and went to the chapel to pray. She tells him bluntly – cruelly – that his niece is dead.

Cushing blew smoke and watched the horror ravaging his own face on celluloid, vividly reliving playing the scene, having to play it by imagining the devastating loss of one you love, and hating himself afterwards for doing so.

He cries out the name of "Laura! Laura!" Jon Finch rushes into the room with Ferdy Mayne, but no sooner has the stethoscope been pressed to her bare chest than the Doctor sees the tell-tale bite mark, accompanied by a glissando of violins . . .

"Consider this," Cushing said. "If I talk to the police, yes, they might think I'm a crazy old man, they might think I'm guilty – that is a matter of supreme indifference to me, I assure you. But because of my so-called fame as an actor, *your* name will be in the *News of the World*, too, whether you like it or not. Before long the disreputable hacks will be rooting around in *your* past, talking to *your* wife, *your* past girlfriends, *your* other – yes, I'll say it – victims. And if some of them, if only one of them speaks . . . Sue . . . Your son . . . And I think they will. I think they'll *need* to . . . And, irrespective of what happens to me, you'll be seen for what you are."

The General's keening cries echo plaintively through the house, the camera pans across the graveyard of the Karnsteins . . .

"And Carl's mother will know exactly what kind of man she is intending to marry."

A peasant girl walks through the woods. She hears a cry. It's only a bird, but it spooks her. She runs. The camera pursues her like a predator through the trees. She drops her basket of apples.

"Have you thought about what *I'm* going to be saying about *you*?" Gledhill said.

"You're not listening to me. I don't care."

The peasant girl trips, falls – rolls through bracken and thorns – screams, as a woman's body descends over her . . .

"Don't you? What about *your* name? Your good name. Peter Cushing." If Gledhill smiled, the man next to him was happy not to see it. "Up there on a thousand posters. Like the one out in the foyer. Your name, *Peter Cushing*, rolling up at the end of hundreds of movies. *Peter Cushing*, the name you fought for so long to mean something, turned into dirt. Into scum. A name nobody'll speak any more, except in revulsion."

"My name is irrelevant." The old man did not tremble or take his eyes from the images projected by the beam of light passing over his head. He would not be wounded. He would not be harmed.

Gledhill turned his head to him. "Then what about your wife's name, dear boy? Because it's *her* name too, since you married her. *Helen Cushing.* Are you going to be happy to see *her* name dragged through the mud? Because I will. You know I will."

Cushing tried not to make his tension visible.

The gong sounds for dinner and Ingrid – Carmilla now – and Madeline Smith descend the staircase of George Cole's home in striking blue and red, Madeline looking coy and slightly embarrassed about what's just gone on in the bedroom.

"You can't hurt her and you can't hurt me," he said. "It's impossible. You see, she knows I'm here, and she's with me, even now."

"Oh dear . . ." Gledhill laughed in the cinema dark. "I think you're going a little bit mad, Peter Cushing. I think all those horror films have made you see horror everywhere."

The monochrome dream comes again, and this time it is Madeline Smith doing the screaming. Kate O'Mara, the governess, comes in. Another dream of cats. Or a real cat?

"The trouble with this part of the world is they have too many fairy tales."

"Horror isn't everywhere," Cushing said. "But horror is somewhere, every day."

"*You* might believe that."

The man was trying to imply that there would be forces of doubt, powerful forces, to face in the battle ahead. Cushing knew full well there might be – but was undeterred.

"You think you have power. You think you're all-powerful. But you have no power, because you have to feel powerful by attacking little mites who can't fight back. You take their souls for one reason and one reason alone – because you can. And now you're frightened. I can tell. Even in the gloom of this cinema. Good. Excellent." Cushing smiled.

"It's my job to frighten people. You could say I've made a career of it."

A shadow hand creeps along a wall. The peasant-girl's mouth opens for a scream but no scream comes. Cut to the exterior of the hovel – then it does. The mother finds her daughter lolling from her bed with two red holes in her neck. Cut to Carmilla – Ingrid Pitt – floating through the graveyard, her voluptuousness under the Carnaby Street negligée . . .

"Do you want me to suck you off?" Gledhill said.

Cushing could sense his own breathing like a hot whirlwind. Could feel the creaking rise and fall of his chest and hear the beat of his heart, everything about his body telling him to scream, but his brain telling him to remain calm.

"Is that what would make you happy, eh? Or a nice stiff cock up the arse? You look the type. Yeah. Actors. Cravat. Well-dressed. Oh, yeah. I know the type. It's written all over you. *Mate.*"

But this actor found, to his great surprise, he could not be offended. The splenetic assault was as ludicrous as it was desperate, and, strangely, it had the opposite effect than the one intended. The very force of the invective meant his enemy was on the ropes, and it made him feel – empowered.

"Are you trying to disgust me?"

"I *know* I disgust you," Gledhill snarled. "You think you're a wise old *cunt*, I know – but really you just want to *fuck* someone, or something, just like the rest of the human race. You look down on me from on high, but you're in the swamp with the rest of us."

Cushing was astonished that the bad language didn't hurt him any more. He was quite impervious to it.

"I've never judged you," he said. "My only concern is the boy."

Then he felt a coldness in the air and something icy and sharp pressed to his right cheek. He had felt Gledhill's arm snake around his shoulders like that of an eager lover and somehow knew instantly it was the stubby blade of the oyster knife.

"What if I cut off your balls and stuff them in your mouth? Would that shut you up, d'you think? Or is that too much blood? What do you think, even for an 'X'? Never get that past the *fucking* censor, would we, *dear boy*?"

The cold of the knife seemed to spread through Cushing's body. He felt it in his veins. He felt it numbing him inch by inch but remained still and becalmed. "When did you die?" Not even the slightest quaver in his voice. "In your heart, I mean?"

Madeline Smith and Ingrid Pitt are sitting in the shade because Ingrid finds the sunshine hurts her eyes. They see the peasant-girl's funeral moving sedately through the woods, the priest intoning the Agnus Dei. *Full of rage and sadness, Ingrid hisses that she hates funerals. Madeline says the girl was so young. The village has had so much tragedy lately. Ingrid begs her to hold her. They embrace . . .*

"Look, she needs affection." Gledhill nodded towards the characters on the screen. "And the young girl is only too happy to give it."

"The young girl is not herself. She's infected." The knife tip dug a "V" in his skin, rasping against the stubble, loud in his ear.

"What if she's like that deep down in her nature, and the other one has just awakened what she really is? Set her free?"

"That's probably exactly what a vampire might argue. But no one becomes a monster willingly." The knife against his cheek did not move, but he felt it tremble.

Both men's eyes were glued unwillingly to the screen.

That night Madeline begs Ingrid not to leave her room. She never feels tired at night any more, only excited, she says. But so wretched during the day. She hasn't told anyone. Not everything. She can't. How the cat comes onto her bed. How she tries to scream as it stretches across her, warm and heavy. How she feels its fur in her mouth . . .

Both men stared.

Madeline Smith says it's like the life running out of her, blood being drawn, then she wakes, screaming. Ingrid Pitt unties the girl's night dress – poor Madeline told by the producer it was for the Japanese version, but there was no Japanese version – *and Ingrid pushes her back against the plump pillow. Her mouth is on the young girl's throat, then slides down to her young breasts. In close-up, Madeline's pretty eyes* – poor child, Cushing remembered, a virgin, didn't know what lesbians were – *roll wide in simulated rapture . . .*

"How were you bitten? Infected?"

Gledhill pressed the blade harder, making the old man's head shy away. "Life. Life made me like this."

Cushing could not be sure whether he detected glee, sarcasm or resignation. "Others need not be hurt. The very ones who—"

"You think *I* haven't been hurt?" Gledhill spat through locked teeth. "I've been hurt in ways you can't even *fucking* imagine." He wiped spittle from his lips with the back of his free hand.

"That's what made you what you are." Cushing tried not to think of the knife any more, or the threats, or the obscenities. "You know that. And you know deep down the boy must suffer, because you suffered."

"Jesus Christ."

"Who was it?"

"Jesus fucking Christ . . ."

Gledhill snatched the oyster knife away from the old man's cheek, tossing it to his other hand and back, then plunging it dagger-like into the soft upholstery of the seat in front of him, tearing it back and forth, ripping the material, then slicing it across. The dramatic surges of the soundtrack seemed to accompany his action, and when he was finished he hunched forward, the oyster knife gripped in both fists between his knees, his forehead resting on the seat in front, his whole body shaking.

"Who?"

"Leave me. Go."

"I'm not going anywhere."

"You can fuck off."

"I'm quite aware I can."

"Why don't you then?"

Peter Cushing prised open the other man's fingers and gently took the knife from his fingers.

"Who?"

The pale man from the General's party appears. The cadaverous man in the red-lined cape stands in silhouette in the woods as if bearing witness to Gledhill's words.

"Someone who made me think I loved him. Someone who twisted me round his little finger." He sniffed. A mocking musicality came to his voice, lifting it, lightening it: a delusion. "I fell for his charms, you could say." He seemed fearful the bitterness in his words evoked no sympathy. "I have feelings too. Did have. Till he fucking ripped them out of me. Why the fuck am I telling you this?"

Madeline cries out. The house is in darkness. Kate O'Mara, the governess, runs in.

"I know you won't listen to me," Cushing said, "but . . . confess."

A wettish snort, not even a snigger, in reply. "Bless me father for I have sinned. You make a good priest."

"I have done."

Outside the door the two women look at each other knowingly. Kate goes into Carmilla's bedroom and turns down the lamp. In darkness Ingrid slips out of her dress. The moonlight outlines her naked form. Kate moves closer.

"All is not lost. Tell the police. Nothing can be worse than the Hell you're enduring now. Do it. For the sake of your immortal soul."

"Soul?" Now the sound through Gledhill's nose was more weary than dismissive. He sat up straight again in the cinema seat and shook his head. "No. No way. I can't. The boy . . . What would he think of me?"

"Dear God, man." Peter Cushing could not disguise his bewilderment. "What do you imagine he thinks of you *now*?"

The blurry vision of Carmilla enters Madeline's room. The vampire appears to be comforting her in her sickness. The young girl wonders if she'll live until her father comes home . . .

"He loves me," Gledhill said. "I know he does because he shows it. I never have to force him. He never says no. I never force him, ever."

The Doctor arrives saying Mr Morton asked him to look in on his daughter. Kate O'Mara tells him Madeline has been ill, but it's nothing to concern him.

"You know what they do in prison to people like me?"

Garlic flowers. Their antiseptic scent. Village gossip. The Doctor puts a cross round Madeline's neck.

"Sometimes . . ." Gledhill struggled to complete the sentence he had in mind.

"Sometimes I . . ." He failed a second time.

Ingrid returns to the daughter's room. She sees the garlic flowers and crucifix and backs out fearfully.

The two men sat in silence facing the screen.

The Doctor rides through the woods, against unconvincing back-projection. His horse suddenly shies and he is thrown. Carmilla comes around the edge of the lake towards him. In a flurry of autumn leaves she wrestles with him and sinks her fangs into his neck.

Neither Gledhill nor Cushing spoke. It was almost as though they had come to watch a horror film, and nothing more.

George Cole rides for the Doctor, but runs into a coach carrying not only Peter Cushing but also Douglas Wilmer – somewhat aged by make-up since the decapitation prologue – a man The General says he has travelled miles to find. To George Cole's horror the dead body of the Doctor is on the back of the vehicle. Peter Cushing says: "Now I can tell you, and leave us if you wish. Our destination is Karnstein castle."

"What do you want me to do?" Gledhill said.

The great chords crash. The coach pulls up at their destination. Douglas Wilmer holds a lamp aloft.

"Primarily I don't want anything to hurt the boy further, in any way. Bringing in the police and the courts will most surely do that. Horribly. But I shall do that if you leave me no alternative."

"What do you want me to do?" Gledhill repeated.

Cushing said what had been in his heart all along, and begged that some sliver of humanity inside the man still might grasp the simplicity of it:

"Do what is right and good, for once."

"Good?"

Said more in genuine puzzlement than disdain.

"Vampires are intelligent beings, General. They know when the forces of good are arrayed against them."

"Save yourself, in the only way you can. Disappear. Turn to dust."

Carmilla is dragging Madeline down the stairs. She needs to take her with her. Kate O'Mara pleads with Ingrid Pitt to take her too. Ingrid sinks her teeth in Kate's neck. Madeline screams. Jon Finch leaps off his horse and bursts in. Ingrid sweeps his sword out of his hand and grabs him, but he grabs a dagger tucked in his boot and holds it up in the shape of a cross. Ingrid backs away from it. He throws the knife. It passes right through her. Double exposure. She fades and is gone.

In the Karnstein graveyard the vampire hunters see the figure of Carmilla entering the ruins. They follow, led by Douglas Wilmer's lantern. The long cobwebby table is a nod to the first Hammer Dracula, perhaps. One of them finds a necklace on the floor. Peter Cushing looks up. They've found the vampire's resting place.

They lift the stone slab from the floor. Peter Cushing and George Cole carry the coffin into the chapel. Wearing black gloves, Peter Cushing rolls back the shroud. "I will do it." He takes off the gloves. George Cole kneels at the altar and prays. Peter Cushing takes the stake. Raises it in both hands. Thrusts it down into and through her chest. Back at the house, her victim cries out. Ingrid Pitt's eyes flash open, then close, as blood pools on her chest. It is over. But not over.

Peter Cushing says, "There's no other way."

He draws his sword. With it firmly in one hand, he lifts Ingrid Pitt up by the hair in her coffin. Cuts off her head in one swipe.

As George Cole utters a heartfelt prayer that their country is rid of such devils, Peter Cushing's General lowers the severed head into the coffin. And Carmilla's portrait on the castle wall, young and beautiful as she was long ago – in life – turns slowly to that of a decomposed and rotting skull.

Cushing turned his head and found the seat next to him empty.

As the cast list rolled up the screen, he stood and looked around an auditorium lit only by the spill from the projector beam. He shielded his eyes with the flat of his hand but it was clear nobody was present but himself.

He was still standing facing the small, square window of the projection room when the house lights faded up. He found himself even more clearly in a sea of empty seats. The smell of popcorn and Kia-Ora returned. This time he found it almost pleasant.

He walked into the sunlit foyer with one arm in his coat sleeve. A number of young couples were queuing for tickets for the next performance. One person noticed him and smiled. He raised a hand, not too ostentatiously, not wanting to draw attention to himself, then criss-crossed his scarf on his chest and dragged on the rest of his coat. Another few people arrived. Quite a healthy gathering for an early evening showing. He was pleased, in a subdued way, as if one of his children had done well at school, with little help from himself. The film *was* a hit, and as long as the public liked it, he wished it well.

He let the heavy door shut behind him. Even more than usually when he had seen a film in the afternoon, the sunlight came as a shock. It almost blinded him, but he was grateful for the warmth on his skin. He raised his chin and stood with his eyes closed for several minutes, and when he opened them, found it noticeably strange that there was not a single gull in the sky.

Ten minutes later he committed the oyster knife to the sea with a throw worthy of a fielder at the Oval.

When he arrived home at 3 Seaway Cottages he felt Helen's smile in the air immediately, like the most delicate and distinctive fragrance.

"Look." He lifted his hand up in front of his face. "I'm still shaking."

You were wonderful.

"Nonsense."

You are *wonderful, Peter.*

He felt a strange fluttering at the back of his throat and looked at the door to the living room but didn't open it.

"So are you, my love."

Suddenly he found he was ravenously hungry for the first time in he didn't know when.

In the kitchen he took two slices of bread and cooked cheese on toast under the grille, served with a generous dollop of HP sauce. His appetite undiminished, he made two more rounds, slightly burned, just the way he liked it.

That night he slept soundly, and without dreams.

He was woken early the following morning by the telephone ringing as if on a distant shore. He sat up in bed, body lifted as if by a crane, not particularly hurrying to do so. Recent events still had not returned fully to his consciousness. Images drifted. Feelings coagulated, some real, some imagined, all vague and irrepressible. His head was too thick with slumber to sort fact from fiction and he wondered if he was waking up or acting waking up. He needed a minute to think about that, if you'd be so kind. The telephone, impolitely, was still ringing with a persistence normally reserved for insects and small children. He slumped back onto the pillow, hoping to return to the land of Nod. The telephone had other ideas.

When it started to ring the third time he could ignore it no longer. He picked up the receiver, rubbing sleep from his eyes with his other hand. He recited the number, automatically.

"Peter?" A man's voice.

"Yes?"

"Did I wake you?" It was Derek Wake. Appropriately named, in this instance.

"No. Not at all." He was about to add that he'd answered because he thought it was perhaps Joyce ringing, but the Inspector interrupted his thoughts.

"I'm sorry, Peter, but I thought I'd better ring before you hear this on the jungle telegraph. I thought you might want to know. Les Gledhill died in a car accident last night, on the stretch of the M2 between Faversham and the junction with the A249 near Sittingbourne. There doesn't appear to have been any other vehicle involved, and there was no one else in the car at the time." Having said this quickly without pausing, he suddenly stopped.

Cushing felt the silence looming and wished his head was clearer. An element of him wondered if he was still asleep. Meanwhile he heard the detective's voice fill the gap with more words:

"His car left the carriageway. It was a head-on collision. He hit the central reservation, the barrier, span across into the hard shoulder. Complete write-off. As I say, no other vehicle was involved . . . Peter?"

"Yes. I'm here."

He was awake now. Fully. But he did not know what to say.

He wondered if the policeman would ask him next why he was in conflict with Gledhill over some issue concerning his son, and probe more fully why exactly Gledhill had made accusations against him. If he might resurrect the questions he himself had asked during his visit to the station concerning a film story about child molestation. A film which, when examined more closely, would be seen to be a complete fabrication.

But Wake asked none of these things.

"He was dead on arrival at Canterbury Hospital. Died instantly. Appears to have been driving at very high speed, from the tyre marks. No witnesses. Whether he lost control for some reason, or did it on purpose, we don't know. These things happen. You don't often see them coming. Those close to the deceased, I mean . . ."

Disappear. Turn to dust . . .

What he'd meant was, go. Leave town. Go away. Not this. Then he remembered:

What do you want me to do?

Do what is right and good, for once.

Good?

Save yourself, in the only way you can.

Dear Lord . . .

Was Gledhill in his final moments thinking of his immortal soul? Had he simply decided to do something good, for once, as he'd been bidden, for someone other than himself? Or was suicide just what it often was, as Peter Cushing knew all too well, the act of a coward? A weak man's only escape from an unbearable future?

"Peter?"

He rubbed his eyes again. The room wasn't focusing, so he kept them shut. He was aware that the other man could hear his breathing down the telephone and was waiting for him to reply, so he spoke in as steady a voice as he could muster.

"Derek, can I ask you something, please?" he said with his eyes still closed. "I want you to do something. This is very important to me. I can't tell you why, but it is."

The hospital, the car park, the very sight of the building itself inevitably brought back memories of Helen, and he was ready for that. Mercifully, she hadn't passed away there, but during her long illness visits were all too frequent, and each time accompanied by a sense of immense dread, of what might be discovered, of what one, this time, might be told. He was surprised, then, that no such feelings asserted themselves. On the contrary, he felt calm, in fact unusually so. Plainly there was a world of difference between visiting the love of your life and – this.

Naturally Wake had questioned why he wanted to do it, and Cushing wondered how many other questions the policeman kept to himself, and for how long he would continue to do so. But in reply to the man's enquiries – clearly worried at a widower seeing a dead body so recently after the death of his wife – he could only reply honestly that he felt nothing.

"Peter, these places are cold and clinical. They breathe death."

"I assure you, dear boy. I'm perfectly fine."

As they walked along the antiseptic-smelling corridor Wake explained that the sister's expression "Rose Cottage" was the euphemism often used by nursing staff when talking about the hospital mortuary. As they approached it, Cushing thought of the roses he tended in his own garden, around his own front door. The roses Helen loved. He pictured himself snipping one off and handing it to her, as he did, on many an occasion. How she'd invariably reward him with a kiss on the cheek.

They'd done their best to take the curse off the viewing room, of course, but it was still a hospital room badly playing the part of a Chapel of Rest. They almost needn't have bothered. As the door opened it had the feel of a shrunken and poverty-stricken church hall. The floor was the same slightly peeling linoleum as the corridor, the walls insalubrious teak, with cheap beading intended to simulate panelling, and curtains on one wall a deep navy blue, the only colour.

He'd had it explained to him that the post-mortem had been done and the body was now being stored there – presumably in one of those pull-out fridges – until the undertakers collected it. He removed his hat and stepped closer to the bed, bier, table, whatever it was called. He was all too aware that the actions he was going through were normally the province of the close family, even though

Wake had told him Carl's mother had no desire to see the body of her boyfriend. Accordingly, in spite of all he knew about the dead man, he felt he should behave with respect.

At a nod from Wake, who remained at the door, the assistant moved forward and folded down the white sheet covering the face so that the head and shoulders were exposed. Cushing noticed the clean, fastidiously manicured hands before the man stood back.

In death, they say, we are all equal, he thought.

He looked down and saw that a white linen cravat was tucked around the corpse's neck. He reached over and touched its rim with his fingertips. The attendant took a step forward and was about to speak, but Wake raised his hand. The man stepped back.

Tugged down, the elastic of the linen cravat revealed a livid scar running around the circumference of Gledhill's neck, the twine stitches, heavy and harsh, still abundantly visible. Frankenstein stitches. Holes dug deep with thick needles like fish hooks into dead, unfeeling flesh.

"Impact would have killed him outright," Wake said. "The front of the car was like a concertina. Steering column went straight through his chest. No chance."

Cushing pictured himself as General Spielsdorf again, holding the stake over Carmilla's heart and shoving it down with every ounce of his strength. Blood pumping up, filling the cavity as her wild eyes stared in perplexed fury.

"Cigarette?"

Cushing shook his head. Wake lit one of his own and blew smoke. It drifted in front of Gledhill's cadaver like the mist in Karnstein castle graveyard.

"As if that wasn't enough, he was decapitated too. The force of the crash sent him right into the windscreen. They found his head thirty yards down the hard shoulder. Apparently it's not uncommon. Tell you what. I'd never be a motorway cop for all the tea in China."

Cushing saw himself lifting up the body of Ingrid Pitt by the hair. The silvery flash of his sword as it sliced through her throat.

"They've done a decent job."

He wasn't sure what the Inspector meant.

"After a real old mess like that. I mean, he looks at peace."

"Yes," Cushing said, gazing back at the figure on the bed and readjusting the white cravat to its former position. "I think he does."

He didn't know if it was the effect of chemicals used by the pathologist or the fluorescent lighting, but the man seemed years younger, as if, absurdly, all the sins had been lifted off him. His skin unblemished, his hair neatly combed as if by an insistent mother. He wondered what was strange and then realized that, for some mysterious reason, his beard had been shaved off. He seemed, in fact, for all the world, strangely like a child.

Cushing looked at the crucifix on the wall opposite – the room's only concession to decoration – and found himself, in an almost imperceptible gesture, making the sign of the cross over his own heart as he turned away.

As he reached the door he heard Wake's voice behind him.

"Have you got what you want?"

"Mm?"

He turned back. The assistant was covering Gledhill's face with the sheet, and Wake was standing beside him, ash gathering on his cigarette as he sucked it.

"For your research? I presume that's why you wanted to see the body."

"Yes." Cushing tweaked the front of his trilby between thumb and forefinger before placing it on his head. "Yes, I have."

On the way home many thoughts went through his mind, but the one he was left with as he opened the front door was that, earlier, that morning, as his hand had picked up the receiver, he had wanted it to be Joycie at the other end of the line. Much as he feared talking to her, it was a fear he had to face – no, *wanted* to face, and that evening after a supper of Heinz tomato soup he decided to take matters into his own hands, and ring her himself. He was absolutely sure it was what Helen would want him to do. No, what she would *expect* of him. Because it was right.

No sooner had he said her name, "Joycie", than they both wept.

Without hesitation he asked her to come back. Equally without hesitation, she agreed.

"I'm so sorry if I've been rude or inconsiderate . . ."

"No, sir. You've never been that. Never." He could hear her blowing her nose in a tissue. Soon he found himself doing the same.

"What a pair we are," he said. "Dear oh dear. I shall have to get more Kleenex tomorrow, shan't I? I think I need to order a truck-load."

She laughed, but it was tinged with the same kind of enfeebled anguish as his own. He wondered, as he often did, if he would hear his own laughter, proper laughter, that is, ever again.

"You see, Joycie, everywhere I see reminders of her. I can't help it. This room. Every room. Every street I walk. Every person I meet. It's simply unbearable, you see . . ."

"I know, sir."

"Do you forgive me?" he said.

And, before she could form an answer, they wept again, till the tissues ran out.

Facing the sea he heard the tick-tick-tick of the wheels of a pushbike approaching. His was an old black Triumph from Herbert's Cycles tending towards rust, with a shopping basket at the front, tethered to a bollard like an old and recalcitrant mare. The other, soon leaning against it, was one of these Raleigh "Chopper" things (not hard to deduce as the word was emblazoned loudly on the frame) in virulent orange, with handlebars that swept up and back and an "L"-shaped reclining saddle like something out of *Easy Rider*.

The boy, sitting next to him and finishing a sherbet fountain through a glistening shoot of liquorice, said nothing for a while in the accompaniment of sea birds, then, when seemed remotely fitting, pronounced that the vehicle on display was a Mark 1 and had ten speeds. Cushing pointed with a crooked finger and said there was no attachment for a lamp, and the boy said he knew, and they were made like that. He said it was called a Chopper, which Cushing already knew but pretended he didn't and repeated the word, for all the world as if the emblazonment had been invisible. But the object was new and gleaming and admirable, and dispensing some wisdom since he could, he advised the boy to look after it. Possibly the boy looked at the scuffed, worn, weary Triumph and thought that was like an elephant telling a gazelle to lose weight. But he'd been brought up by his mother not to cheek his elders, not that that worried him a great deal when it was called for, but on this occasion he chose to hold his tongue and nodded, meaning he would look after it. Of course he would. He wanted it to look new and gleaming forever.

When the sherbet was finished the boy walked to the rubbish bin and dropped it in. When he sat back down he chewed the remains of the liquorice the way a yokel might chew a straw, moving it from one side of his mouth to the other along slightly blackened lips.

"You look younger."

Cushing had almost forgotten he'd shaved for the first time in weeks. He rubbed his chin. Dr Terror's salt-and-pepper was gone.

"I have a painting in the attic."

"What does that mean?"

"Never mind. You'll find out when you're a bit older."

The boy frowned. "I hate it when grown-ups say that."

"So do I. Very much so. I'm sorry."

He looked at the boy and beckoned him closer. He took out a handkerchief and rolled it round his index finger. "Spit on it." Without considering the consequence, the boy did, trustingly, and Cushing used it to rub the liquorice stains from his lips while the boy's face scrunched up, an echo, the old man thought, of the infant he once was.

"How's your mum?" He folded the handkerchief away.

The reply was a shrug. "She cried a bit. She cried a lot, actually. I didn't." A show of resilience, sometimes stronger in the young. The show of it, anyway. "But I felt sorry for her. She's my mum."

"Naturally."

Cushing did not enquire further. Out at sea beyond the Isle of Sheppey, a cloud of gannets hovered halo-like over a fishing vessel.

"They say it was an accident," the boy said presently, with a secretive excitement in his voice. "But it wasn't an accident, was it? It was you."

"It doesn't matter. It happened. He's gone now. It's over."

"I know you can't say because it's secret, but it *was* you, wasn't it? Acting on my instructions as a Vampire Hunter? I knew you would. I *knew* you wouldn't let me down."

Cushing tugged on his white cotton glove and pulled down each finger in turn, then lit a cigarette and smoked it, eyes slitting.

"How do you feel now? That's the important thing."

The boy wondered about that as if he hadn't wondered about it until that very moment.

"You know what? It's funny. It's really weird. I feel a bit sad. I feel a bit like it's my fault because I asked you to. I know he was evil and that. I know that, and I know he deserved it and everything. I don't know . . ."

"It wasn't your fault, Carl." Would he ever truly believe that? "Look at me, Carl. Please." The boy faced the old man's pale-blue, unblinking eyes and the old man took his hand. "When they choose people as a victim, it's not the victim's fault. It's their fault. You've got to remember that." Peter Cushing knew that now more than ever he needed to keep a steady gaze. "I'm the world expert, remember?"

The boy nodded and took his hand back.

"I know. No need to show off."

Cushing trembled a smile and looked back to sea.

Periodically flicking his ash to be taken by the breeze, he gazed down between the groynes and saw a man in his twenties wearing a cheesecloth shirt and canvas loons rolled up to just under the knee and curly hair bobbing as he ran in and out of the icy surf. A dollishly small girl with a bucket and spade was laughing at him and he chased her and scooped her up in his arms, turning her upside down.

"She doesn't like me saying it, but I keep thinking about my real dad, my old dad," the boy said, prodding a discarded Wrigley's chewing-gum wrapper with his shoe. "I keep thinking perhaps he'll get tired of his new woman in Margate and come back to us. One day, anyway. I know he said he didn't love my mum any more, but he must have loved her once, mustn't he? So he might love her again. You never know. How does love work anyway?"

Cushing could hear no voices, but saw a woman join the man and the toddler on the shingle. The wind tossed the woman's blonde hair over her face and the man combed it back with his fingers and kissed her.

"It's very complicated, as you'll learn, my friend. Very complicated – but in the end so terribly simple." He felt a tiny piece of grit in his eye and rubbed it with a finger. The taste of the tobacco had gone sour and he prodded the cigarette out on the sea wall.

"Do you have bad dreams any more? You see, I have to check the symptoms, just in case. Are you sleeping well?"

The boy nodded, staring at the ground.

"Good. Very good." The old man took off his glove, white finger by white finger. Carl was still staring at the concrete in front of him. "Remember if anything feels bad, if you are hurting, or worried . . . Anything you want to say – anything, you can say to your mother."

"She won't understand," the boy said without looking up, as a simple statement of fact. "She doesn't understand monsters."

The people on the beach were gone and the waves were coming in filling their footsteps. Sometimes it seemed full of footprints, criss-crossing this way and that, people, dogs, all on their little journeys, but if you waited long enough or came back the next day the people were always gone and the only consistent thing was the slope and evenness of the shore.

When Cushing put his single white glove back in his overcoat pocket he discovered something he'd forgotten. Something he'd put there before going to the Oxford to meet Gledhill. He took it out and looked at it in the palm of his hand.

Helen's crucifix.

Opening the thin gold chain into a circle he put it around the boy's neck and tucked the cross behind his scarf and inside his open-topped shirt. The boy did not move as the man did it, and did not move afterwards, imagining some necessity for respect or obedience in the matter, or recognizing some similarity to the procedure of his mum straightening his tie, in addition daunted perhaps by the peculiarity of the tiny coldness of the crucifix against the warmth of his hairless chest.

"I want you to remember what I'm going to say to you. The love of the Lord is quite, quite infinite. In your darkest despair, though you may not think it, He is still looking over you. Never, ever forget that."

The boy thought a moment.

"Is he looking over *you*?"

Cushing had not expected that question, and found himself answering, as something of a surprise:

"Yes. Yes, I believe he is."

Then the boy appeared to remember something, something important, and dug into the pocket of his anorak. He produced a rolled-up magazine, unfurled it and thrust it in front of the man, who had to recoil slightly in order to focus his increasingly ancient eyes on it.

Claude Rains in his masked role as *The Phantom of the Opera* stared back at him. Garish lettering further promised the riches within: films featuring black cats, Ghidorah the three-headed monster, and *Horror of Dracula* – the US title of the first Hammer in the series. What he held in his hands was a lurid American film magazine called, in case of any doubt whatsoever in its remit, *Famous Monsters of Filmland*.

The boy reached over and flicked through until he found a double-page spread of black-and-white stills. He flattened it open and jabbed with his finger.

"Look. It's you."

Indeed it was.

Christopher Lee as the predatory Count, descending upon Melissa Stribling's Mina. Baring his fangs in a mouth covered with blood. Van Helsing – himself – alongside it, dressed in a homburg hat and fur-collared coat.

"I can't read very well," the boy said. "But I like the pictures. The pictures are great. Who's Peter Cushing?"

Cushing looked at the younger man in the image before him.

"He's a person I pretend to be sometimes." He thumbed through the pages, touched immeasurably by the gift. "Is this for me?"

"What? *No*. I want it back. But I want you to sign it, because you're famous."

"Ah. Silly me."

Cushing thought of the close-ups they'd filmed of him so many years before, reacting to the disintegration of the vampire whilst nothing was there in front of him. He thought of Phil Leakey and Syd Pearson, make-up and special effects, labouring away on the last day of shooting to achieve the purifying effect of the dawning sun. He thought of the sun, and of the perpetual darkness he had lived in since Helen had died.

He lay the *Famous Monsters* magazine on the sea wall between them, took out his fountain pen from his inside pocket, shook it, and wrote *Van Helsing* in large sweeping letters across the page, blowing on the blue ink till it was dry.

"Brilliant." The boy held it by his fingertips like a precious parchment and blew on it himself for good measure. "Now I'll be able to show people I met you. When I'm an old man with children of my own." He stood up and held out his hand.

Cushing shook it with a formality the boy clearly desired.

"Enjoy stories, Carl. Enjoy books and films. Enjoy your work. Enjoy life. Find someone to love. Cherish her . . ."

The boy nodded, but looked again at the signed picture in *Famous Monsters* as if he hadn't quite believed it the first time. The evidence confirmed, he pressed it to his chest, zipped it up securely inside his anorak, pulled up the hood and unchained his bike.

"Carl?" Cushing said. "Sometimes you can hide the hurt and pain, but there'll be a day you can talk about it with someone and be free. Perhaps a day when you'll forget what it was you were frightened of, and then you'll have conquered it, forever."

The young face looked back, half-in, half-out of the anorak hood, and nodded. Then he took the antler-sized handlebars and walked his Chopper back in the direction of the road and shops, another imperative on his mind, another game, idea, story, journey, in that way of boys, and of life.

As he tapped another talismanic cigarette against the packet, thinking of his own journey and footsteps filling with water as the tide came in, Cushing heard the tick-tick-tick stop, as if the boy had stopped, and he had. And he heard the cawing of seagulls, his nasty neighbours – The Ubiquitous, he called them – and heard a voice, the boy's voice, for the last time, behind him.

"Will you keep fighting monsters?"

His eyes fixed far off, where the sea met the sky, Peter Cushing had no difficulty saying: "Always."

He sat in the forest dressed in black buckled shoes, cross-legged, a wide-brimmed black hat resting in his lap and the white, starched collar of a Puritan a stark contrast to the abiding blackness of his cape. Over in the clearing the bonfire was being constructed for the burning of the witch. The stake was being erected by Cockney men with sizeable beer bellies wearing jeans and T-shirts. The focus-puller ran his tape measure from the camera lens. Art directors scattered handfuls of ash from buckets to give the surroundings a monochrome, "blasted heath" quality. And so they were all at work, all doing their jobs, a well-oiled machine, while he waited, contemplating the density of the trees and smelling the pine needles. It was March now, and soon shoots of new growth would show in the layer of mulch and dead leaves and the cycle of life would continue.

Work was the only thing left now that made life pass in a faintly bearable fashion. As good old Sherlock Holmes said to Watson in *The Sign of Four*: "Work is the best antidote to sorrow", and the only antidote he himself saw to the devastation of losing Helen was to launch himself back into a gruelling schedule of films. It was the one thing he knew he *could* do, after all. As she kept reminding him. *It's your gift, my darling. Use it.* And the distraction of immersing oneself in other characters was an imperative, he now saw: a welcome refuge from reality.

The third assistant director brought a cup of tea, an apple and a plate of cheese from the catering truck to the chair with Peter Cushing's name on the back.

"Bless you."

Occasionally, very occasionally, that's what he did feel. *Blessed.*

It was a blessing, mainly, to be back working with so many familiar faces. Yes, there were new ones, young and fresh, and of course that was good and healthy too. The young ones, who hadn't met him in person before, possibly didn't notice or remark that he had become sombre, withdrawn, fragile behind his unerring politeness and professionalism – it was the older ones who saw that, all too well. In the make-up mirror he had never looked so terribly gaunt and perhaps they imagined, charitably, it was part of his characterization as the cold, zealous Puritan, Gustav Weil. But it was nothing to do with the dark tone of the film, everything to do with the dark pall cast over his life.

Those who knew him, really knew him, acknowledged that a part of him had died two months ago.

Yet the un-dead lived on.

Here he was at Pinewood and Black Park in the company of vampire twins and a young, dynamic Count Karnstein so seethingly bestial-looking in the shape of Damien Thomas he might well snatch the reins from Christopher Lee and become the *Dracula* for a new generation. The third in the trilogy, this excursion was being trumpeted loudly by the company as Peter Cushing's return to the Hammer fold. Once more written by Tudor Gates, heavily influenced by Vincent Price's *Witchfinder General*, it was the tale of a vampire-hunting posse with Peter Cushing at its head. And with top-billing.

He remembered clearly the lunch a month earlier with his agent, John Redway, and the leather-jacketed young director John Hough at L'Aperitif restaurant in Brown's Hotel, Mayfair.

"You're returning to combat evil, Peter," the director had said. But he wanted a darker tone. He didn't want it to be a fairy tale like other Hammers. He wanted to reinvent the horror genre.

Cushing had said nothing as he listened, but thought the genre didn't need reinventing. The genre was doing very well as it was, thank you very much. He did think the idea was original, however, and the director had convinced him over three courses and wine of his intention to make it as a bleak morality play, manipulating the audience's expectation of good and evil by having them side with the vampires against the pious austerity of Gustav Weil, the twisted, God-fearing witch-hunter, uncle to the vampire twins, Frieda and Maria, played by the pretty Collinson sisters – Maltese girls whose claim to fame was being the first identical twin centrefold for *Playboy*, in the title role. *Twins of Evil* – or was it called *Twins of Dracula* now, the American distributor's illogical and factually incorrect alternative?

"You see, Peter, real evil is not so easy to spot in real life," the director had said. "In real life, evil people look like you and me. We pass them in the street."

"Really?"

"Yes. And that's what I want to capture with this film. The nature of true evil."

Whether it would be a success or not Cushing couldn't know. He would do his best. He always did. He had an inkling how this sort of film worked after all these years and that's what he would bring to the proceedings. That's what they were paying for. That and, of course, his name.

His name.

He remembered the conversation in the dark of the Oxford cinema.

According to the Fount of All Knowledge, Carl's mother moved to Salisbury shortly after Gledhill died, to live with her sister and set up a shop together. He hoped for once the gossip contained some semblance of accuracy. If she sought to rebuild her life afresh, that could only be a good thing. For her, and the boy.

For himself, there were other films on the horizon. He'd told John Redway to turn nothing down. He'd read the script of *Dracula: Chelsea* and it was rather good. He was looking forward to playing not only Lorrimer Van Helsing in the present day, but also his grandfather, in a startling opening flashback, fighting Christopher Lee on the back of a hurtling, out of control stagecoach before impaling him with a broken cartwheel. And if that was a success there were plans for other *Dracula*s. Another treatment by Jimmy Sangster had been commissioned that he knew of, which boded well, and he hoped Michael Carreras would grasp the reins and take Hammer into a new era.

One of the more imminent offers was a role from Milton in his latest portmanteau movie *Tales from the Crypt*, but he didn't care for the part, a variation of "The Monkey's Paw". Instead he'd asked if he could play the lonely, widowed old man, Grimsdyke, who returns from the grave to exact poetic justice on his persecutor. A crucial scene would require Grimsdyke to be talking to his beloved dead wife, and he planned to ask Milton if he'd mind if he used a photograph of Helen on the set. Then he could say, as he'd wished for many a long year, that they'd finally made a film together.

As it was, her photograph was never far away. He kept one above his writing desk at home, and another beside his mirror in his dressing room or make-up truck. At home he always set a place for her at the dinner table, and not a day went by when he didn't talk to her.

Hopefully there'd be other movies in the pipeline. They'd keep the wolf from the door and the dark thoughts at bay – ironic, given their subject matter. Not that he could see his grief becoming any less all-consuming with the passage of time. Time, as far as he could imagine, could do nothing to diminish the pain. The lines by Samuel Beckett often came to mind: "I can't go on, I must go on, I will go on," and he knew that the third AD would be back before too long, to say they were ready for him.

But for the next few minutes, until that happened, he would rest and try to clear his mind as he always did before a take, and picked up his Boots cassette recorder from between his feet, put on the small earphones and closed his eyes. He pressed PLAY. The beauty of Elgar's *Sospiri* gave way to Noel Coward singing "If Love Were All".

One of Helen's favourites, and his own.

He had lost the one thing that made living real and joyful, the person who was his whole life, and without her there was no meaning or point any more. But what had others lost? Yet, they survived.

He pictured the boy on his bicycle riding away, the rolled-up magazine in his pocket. Whilst he was living, he knew, time would move inexorably onward and the attending loneliness would be beyond description, but the one thing that would keep him going was the absolute knowledge that he would be united with Helen again one day.

The spokes of the bicycle wheel turned, gathering speed, blurring.

Life must go on, yes, but in the end – *after* the end – life was not important, just pictures on a screen, absorbing for as long as they lasted, causing us to weep and laugh, perhaps, but when the images are gone we step out blinking into the light.

Until then he was called upon to be the champion of the forces of good. He would spear reanimated mummies through the chest. He would stare into the eyes of the Abominable Snowman. He would seek out the Gorgon. Fire silver bullets at werewolves. He would burn evil at the stake. He would brand them with crucifixes. He would halt windmills from turning. He would bring down a hammer and force a stake through their hearts and watch them disintegrate. He would hold them up by the hair and decapitate them with a single swipe.

He would be a monster hunter.

He would be Van Helsing for all who needed him, and all who loved him.

STEPHEN JONES &
KIM NEWMAN

Necrology: 2013

2013 WAS A truly terrible year. We lost far too many people – from several genre giants to numerous individuals who were far too young and should have had many more creative years ahead of them. (To make matters worse, a lot of names on this year's list were personal friends and colleagues.) So, with heavy hearts, we once again mark the passing of those writers, artists, performers and technicians who, during their lifetimes, made significant contributions to the horror, science fiction and fantasy genres . . .

AUTHORS/ARTISTS/COMPOSERS

British radio producer and scriptwriter **Charles** [Frederick William] **Chilton** MBE died of pneumonia on January 2, aged ninety-five. In 1953 he created the BBC SF radio serial *Journey Into Space*, which was reworked as *Space Force* (1984–85). Chilton wrote three tie-in novels, *Journey Into Space* (1954), *The Red Planet* (1956) and *The World in Peril* (1960), and he later created the anti-war stage musical *Oh! What a Lovely War*.

British film and TV author and researcher **Tise Vahimagi**

was found dead at his flat on January 8, aged sixty-one. He had been undergoing treatment for cancer and suffering from a debilitating virus. His reference books include the *BFI's Illustrated Guide to British Television*, *American Vein: Directors and Directions in Television* (with Christopher Wicking) and *The "Untouchables"*. Vahimagi wrote for *Monster Mag* and *House of Hammer*, and also contributed the "TV Zone" column to *Starburst* magazine for many years.

Keith Armstrong-Bridges, the first elected Chairman of the Tolkien Society (1970–73), died after a long illness on January 11.

American SF writer **Steven [D.] Utley** died of cancer on January 12, aged sixty-four. A couple of weeks earlier he had announced that he had been diagnosed with Type 4 cancer in his intestines, liver and lungs, along with a lesion on his brain. Utley, who had infamously posed nude for Tom Reamy's semi-prozine *Trumpet* in the 1970s, wrote a number of acclaimed short stories, including the Nebula Award-nominated "Custer's Last Jump" and "Black as the Pit, from Pole to Pole", both in collaboration with Howard Waldrop. Utley's short fiction has been collected in *Ghost Seas*, *The Beasts of Love*, *Where and When*, *The 400-Year-Itch* and *Invidible Kingdoms*, and he co-edited the anthologies *Lone Star Universe: Speculative Fiction from Texas* (with George W. Proctor) and *Passing for Human* (with Michael Bishop). He also published poetry under the name "S. Dale".

Italian SF writer and translator **Riccardo [Enzo Luigi] Valla** died of a heart attack on January 14, aged seventy. He worked with publishers Editrice Nord and Arnoldo Mondadori, and translated *The Da Vinci Code* in Italy.

Horror movie collector **Gary D. (Dean) Dorst**, who wrote for *Gore Creatures* and *Photon* magazines, died the same day, aged sixty-five.

French editor and author **Jacques Sadoul**, who was editorial director the successful paperback Science-Fiction J'ai Lu imprint for many years, died on January 18, aged seventy-eight. He edited the "Les Meilleurs Récits" anthology series, and his own novels include *La Passion selon Satan*, *Le Jardin de la licorn* and *Le Miroir de Drusilla*. Sadoul also compiled the art book *2000 A.D.: Illustrations from the Golden Age of Science Fiction Pulps* and the SF study *Histoire de la science-fiction moderne*. He helped found the Prix Apollo Award, given from 1972–99 for the year's best SF novel published in France.

Wargame and role-playing game designer **Lynn Willis**, who worked on the development of such games as *Call of Cthulhu*, *Ghostbusters*, *Elric!*, *Worlds of Wonder*, *Ringworld* and *RuneQuest* at Chaosium Inc., died of Parkinson's disease the same day.

Mexican author and playwright **Carlos Emilio Olvera Avelar**, who wrote the influential SF novel *Mejicanos en la espacio* (Mexicans in Space, 1968) as by "Carlos Olvera", died of pneumonia on January 28, aged seventy-two.

Italian SF translator and critic **Antonio Caronia** died after a long illness on January 30, aged sixty-nine. He wrote and edited a number of books about science fiction, including *Il Cyborg* (1985), along with an encyclopedia about Philip K. Dick. He was also J. G. Ballard's translator.

American folklorist and children's author **Diane Wolkstein** died on January 31, aged seventy. She served as New York's official storyteller from 1968–71.

American writer, editor, poet and reviewer **Anne Jordan** (Anne Devereaux Wilson Jordan Crouse), the former managing editor of *The Magazine of Fantasy and Science Fiction* from 1979–89, died of lung cancer on February 2, aged sixty-nine. A teacher for much of her career, she wrote a number of books and edited the anthologies *The Best Horror Stories from the Magazine of Fantasy and Science Fiction* (with Edward L. Ferman) and *Fires of the Past: Thirteen Contemporary Fantasies About Hometowns*. Jordan founded the Children's Literature Association in 1973, who named an award after her for outstanding contributions in that field.

American art director **James Plumeri**, who worked at New American Library for fifteen years and Bantam Dell for twenty, died the same day, aged seventy-nine. Amongst the mass-market covers he designed were those for Stephen King's *Salem's Lot* and *The Shining*.

Multiple Hugo Award-winning fan-writer, editor and author **Richard "Dick" E. (Erwin) Geis** (aka "Peggy Swenson"/"Alter-Ego") died on February 4, aged eighty-five. Best known for his influential SF fanzine *Science Fiction Review/The Alien Critic*, the reclusive Geis also wrote more than 100 softcore erotic novels, along with four near-future thrillers with Elton T. Elliott.

American TV writer **Ruel Fischmann** died on February 7, aged seventy-three. He scripted episodes of *Salvage 1*, *The Incredible Hulk*, *Fantasy Island*, *The Powers of Matthew Star*, *Silk Stalkings* and *Time Trax*.

Scottish-born author and scriptwriter **Alan Sharp** died of brain cancer in Los Angeles on February 8, aged seventy-nine. He scripted the 1977 film adaptation of Roger Zelazny's *Damnation Alley* and the 2002 version of Ursula K. Le Guin's *Lathe of Heaven*. He also worked on episodes of *The Snoop Sisters* and *Nightmares & Dreamscapes* (Stephen King's "The Fifth Quarter"). One of his former wives was writer Beryl Bainbridge.

American novelist **W. (William) Watts Biggers** (aka "Buck Biggers") died on February 10, aged eighty-five. He created the animated TV series *Underdog* (1964–66), about a canine superhero. It was turned into a live-action movie in 2007.

Blacklisted Hollywood screenwriter and producer **Richard [J.] Collins** died of aspiration pneumonia on February 14, aged ninety-eight. He worked on the scripts of *Cult of the Cobra*, *Invasion of the Body Snatchers* (1956) and an episode of TV's *Planet of the Apes*. A member of the Communist party, after he was called before the House Un-American Activities Committee as an unfriendly witness in 1947 he did not work for four years. As a result, he recanted and named more than twenty colleagues and friends in the industry, thus saving his own career. When actress Dorothy Comingore, Collins' first wife, refused to answer questions, it resulted in the end of her movie career.

American SF writer and professor of creative writing **Daniel Pearlman** died on February 18, aged seventy-seven. Some of his stories are collected in *The Final Dream & Other Fictions*, *The Best-Known Man in the World & Other Misfits* and *A Giant in the House & Other Excesses*. His other books included the novels *Black Flames* and *Memini*, and the novella *Brain and Breakfast*.

Eighty-six-year-old Cuban writer **Angel** [José] **Arango** [Rodriguez] died in Miami, Florida, on February 19. The last survivor of his country's three founding fathers of SF, during the 1960s he published four collections of SF stories which were followed by the series of novels comprising *Transparencia*, *Coyuntura*, *Sider* and *La Columna Bifida*.

American comics artist **Scott Clark**, who worked for WindStorm, Marvel, Aspen and DC Comics, died on February 21, aged forty-three. He started his career in the early 1990s and contributed to such titles as *Brightest Day*, *Batman Inc.*, *Grifter* and *Manhunter*. He also illustrated a number of covers for *Deathstroke*.

American editor, author and fan **Jan Howard Finder** (aka "Wombat") died of complications from prostate cancer on February 25, aged seventy-three. He edited the fanzine *The Spang Blah* and was a Fan Guest of Honor at ConFrancisco, the 1993 World Science Fiction Convention. He also edited the 1982 anthology *Alien Encounters*. An expert on J. R. R. Tolkien, he organized the First Conference on Middle-Earth in 1969 and, later, tours of the *Lord of the Rings* film sites in New Zealand.

Prolific Italian film composer and jazz pianist **Armando Trovajoli** died on February 28, aged ninety-five. His more than 200 credits include *Uncle was a Vampire*, *Atom Age Vampire*, *Mole Men Against the Son of Hercules*, *Hercules and the Captive Women*, *The Giant of Metropolis*, *Werewolf in a Girls' Dormitory* (as "Francis Berman"), Mario Bava's *Hercules in the Haunted World* (featuring Christopher Lee), *Planets Around Us*, *Dr. Jekyll Likes Them Hot* and *Frankenstein 90* amongst many other titles in various genres. The first of his two wives was actress Pier Angeli.

Scottish thriller writer **Campbell Armstrong** (Thomas Campbell Black) died in Dublin, Ireland, on March 1. He was aged sixty-nine. The son of a Glasgow shipyard engineer, his books included the best-selling horror novel *Jig*, and he also wrote novelizations of the movies *Raiders of the Lost Ark* and *Dressed to Kill*.

Canadian comics writer and *manga* translator **Toren Smith** died on March 4, aged fifty-two. He wrote strips for *Epic Illustrated*, *Amazing Heroes* and Eclipse Comics, and in 1986 he moved to Japan to create Studio Proteus, one of the top two companies to translate and sell *manga* to the English-speaking world. Smith was briefly married to SF and fantasy artist Lela Dowling in the early 1980s, and in 1991 he married Japanese illustrator Tomoko Saito.

Belgian comics artist **Didier** [Hermann] **Comès** died on March 7, aged seventy. His best-known graphic novel is *Silence* (1980).

American writer and editor **David B.** (Beecher) **Silva** died in early March, aged sixty-two. From 1982–91 he edited the influential, World Fantasy Award-winning small press magazine *The Horror Show*, which led to the anthology *The Definitive Best of The Horror Show* from Cemetery Dance Publications. Silva's novels include *Child of Darkness*, *Come Thirteen*, *The Presence*, *The Disappeared*, *All the Lonely People*, *The Many* and "The Family" series (in collaboration with Kevin McCarthy). A 1991 winner of the Bram Stoker Award for his story "The Calling", his short fiction is collected in the International Horror Guild Award-winning *Through Shattered Glass*, *Little White Book of Lies* and *The Shadows of Kingston Mills*. With Paul F. Olson, Silva edited the anthologies *Post Mortem: New Tales of Ghostly Horror* and *Dead End: City Limits*, along with the weekly industry newsletter *Hellnotes*, which they co-founded in 1997 and still continues as a website today.

American illustrator **Mitchell Hooks**, whose work includes the cover painting for the original paperback edition of Richard Matheson's *The Shrinking Man*, died on March 18, aged eighty-nine. Besides covers for publishers including Avon, Bantam, Fawcett and Dell, Hooks also contributed to *Cosmopolitan*, *McCall's*, *Redbook* and *The Saturday Evening Post*, as well as designing such movie posters as *Dr. No* and *The Face of Fu Manchu*.

Britain's most successful horror author, **James Herbert** OBE, died in his sleep on March 20. He was sixty-nine. After studying graphic design at Hornsey College of Art, he worked in a London advertising agency, where he wrote his first novel in his spare time. He submitted his manuscript of *The Rats* to six publishers on the same day. Only three replied and just one accepted it. It was published in 1974 in an edition of 100,000 paperback copies, which completely sold out within weeks. It has never been out of print since. Herbert went on to write a string of best-selling novels, including *The Fog*, *The Survivor*, *Fluke*, *The Spear*, *Lair*, *The Dark*, *The Jonah*, *Shrine*, *Domain*, *Moon*, *The Magic Cottage*, *Sepulchre*, *Haunted*, *Creed*, *Portent*, *The Ghosts of Sleath*, *'48*, *Others*, *Once . . .*, *Nobody True*, *The Secret of Crickley Hall* and *Ash*. A number of his books were filmed. *The City* (1994) was a graphic novel in *The Rats* sequence illustrated by Ian Miller, while *James Herbert's Dark Places: Locations and Legends* was a collaboration with photographer Paul Barkshire. Herbert was Guest of Honour at the 1988 World Fantasy Convention in London, and he was presented with the Grand Master Award at the 2010 World Horror Convention in Brighton.

American horror writer **Rick Hautala** (Richard Andrew Hautala) died of a heart attack on March 21, aged sixty-four. He began his career in the 1980s and wrote more than thirty novels, including *Moondeath*, *Moonbog*, *Night Stone*, *Little Brothers*, *Moonwalker*, *Winter Wake*, *Dead Voices*, *Cold Whisper*, *Dark Silence*, *Ghost Light*, *Twilight Time*, *Shades of Night*, *Beyond the Shroud*, *The Mountain King*, *Impulse*, *Cold River*, *The Wildman*, *Reunion*, *Indian Summer*, *The Demon's Wife* and *Mockingbird Bay*. As "A. J. Matthew" he published *The White Room*, *Follow* and *Unbroken*. Hautala co-wrote five novels with Christopher Golden in the "Body of Evidence" series along with a

Poltergeist: The Legacy TV tie-in, and he collaborated with Matthew Costello on *Star Road*. His short stories are collected in *Bedbugs*, *Four Octobers*, *Untcigahunk: Stories and Tales of the Little Brothers*, *Occasional Demons* and *Glimpses: The Best Short Stories of Rick Hautala*. He was a former vice-president and trustee of the Horror Writers Association and a recipient of the HWA's Lifetime Achievement Award in 2012.

American screenwriter and producer **Don Payne** (William Donald Payne) died of bone cancer on March 26, aged forty-eight. A writer and producer on TV's *The Simpsons*, he scripted *My Super Ex-Girlfriend*, *Fantastic 4: Rise of the Silver Surfer* and *Thor*, as well as coming up with the original story for *Thor: The Dark World*.

Forty-five-year-old American writer **Jennifer Schwabach** died the same day after a long illness. She published two novels, *Dark Winter* and *Curse's Captive*, and contributed stories and poems to a number of titles, including *Marion Zimmer Bradley's Fantasy Magazine*.

American editor, author and fan **Paul Williams** died of early-onset Alzheimer's disease in a hospice on March 27. He was sixty-four. Williams likely developed the illness after hitting his head in a bicycling accident in 1995. After moving to California in the late 1960s, he became a friend of Philip K. Dick and was named the author's literary executor after Dick's death in 1982. Four years later he published the biography *Only Apparently Real: The World of Philip K. Dick* and was also responsible for thirteen volumes comprising *The Complete Stories of Theodore Sturgeon*, personally editing eleven of them before he became too ill to continue. Williams was also often described as the first rock critic, founding the influential music magazine *Crawdaddy!* while still a college student in 1966. He wrote a number of books about music and the counter-culture movement, and he managed Timothy Leary's brief bid to become governor of California in 1969.

American illustrator **Bob Clarke** (Robert J. Clarke), whose work appeared in *Mad* magazine during the late

1950s and early '60s, died on March 31, aged eighty-seven. His first professional work, at the age of seventeen, was as an uncredited assistant on the *Ripley's Believe It or Not* newspaper strip.

Prolific Gothic romance writer **Daoma Winston** died on April 1, aged ninety. Her many titles include *Moorhaven*, *Emerald Station*, *The Haversham Legacy*, *The Long and Living Shadow*, *The Inheritance*, *The Wakefield Witches*, *Seminar in Evil*, *Sinister Stone* and *The Vampire Curse*. Many of her books feature supernatural elements.

British author and film collector **Basil Copper** died of complications from Alzheimer's disease on April 3, aged eighty-nine. A former newspaper journalist, he made his fiction debut with "The Spider" in *The Fifth Pan Book of Horror Stories* (1964). His macabre and supernatural short fiction is collected in the Arkham House volumes *From Evil's Pillow* and *And Afterward the Dark: Seven Tales*, along with *Not After Nightfall: Stories of the Strange and the Terrible*, *When Footsteps Echo: Tales of Terror and the Unknown*, *Here Be Daemons: Tales of Horror and the Uneasy*, *Voices of Doom: Tales of Terror and the Uncanny*, *Whispers in the Night: Stories of the Mysterious and Macabre*, *Cold Hand on My Shoulder: Tales of Terror & Suspense*, the self-published *Knife in the Back: Tales of Twilight and Torment*, and the two-volume *Darkness Mist & Shadow*. Copper's novels range from the Cthulhu Mythos-inspired *The Great White Space* and *Into the Silence*, to the Gothics *The Curse of the Fleers*, *Necropolis*, *The House of the Wolf* and *The Black Death*. A former Chairman of the Crime Writers' Association, he also continued the exploits of August Derleth's consulting detective "Solar Pons" in eight overlapping collections and a novel, published fifty-three books featuring Los Angeles private investigator "Mike Faraday", and ghost-wrote two "Phantom" novels under the "Lee Falk" byline. Copper also wrote two non-fiction studies about the vampire and the werewolf, and in 2010 he was presented with the Grand Master Award at the World Horror Convention in Brighton.

American comics writer **George Gladir**, who created *Sabrina the Teenage Witch* with artist Dan DeCarlo, died the same day, aged eighty-seven. He worked on many other titles for Archie Comics and later became the head writer for the satirical magazine *Cracked*. Gladir received the Bill Finger Award for Excellence in Comic Book Writing in 2007.

Legendary comic book artist and editor **Carmine Infantino** died on April 4, aged eighty-seven. He began his career working for Timely Comics (later Marvel) in the early 1940s, but he is best known for his work with DC Comics, starting with such Golden Age titles as *Flash Comics*, *All-Flash*, *Green Lantern* and the *Justice Society of America*. In the late 1950s, editor Julius Schwartz commissioned Infantino to revive The Flash in *Showcase* #4 and the Silver Age of comics was born. During the 1960s, the artist worked on numerous DC characters, including Adam Strange (in *Mystery in Space*), Batman and Robin, Batgirl, Elongated Man and Deadman. Infantino was eventually promoted to art director and, later, editorial director at DC, where he brought Joe Kubert, Neal Adams, Jack Kirby and others into the company. He was publisher of DC from 1971–76, before he returned to freelance drawing on such film and TV adaptations as *Star Wars* and *V*. He was also the artist on the *Batman* newspaper strip from 1990–91.

America's best-known movie critic, **Roger [Joseph] Ebert**, died of cancer the same day, aged seventy. The Pulitzer Prize-winning writer started out as a science fiction fan – editing and publishing his own SF fanzine *Stymie* and contributing to others, such as *Kipple*, *Parsection* and *Psi-Phi* – before going on to script the softcore sex comedies *Beyond the Valley of the Dolls* and *Beneath the Valley of the Ultra-Vixens* (as "R. Hyde") for director Russ Meyer. He published two stories in *Amazing*, and for twenty years, starting in 1986, he co-hosted the syndicated movie review show *Siskel & Ebert* with Gene Siskel (who died in 1999), giving a thumbs up or a thumbs down to the latest releases. Ebert fondly recalled his days in fandom in his Introduction to *The Best of Xero* (2004), edited by Pat and Dick Lupoff.

British writer and critic **Roger** [Alan] **Dobson** died on April 12 of complications from a stomach ulcer. He was fifty-nine. He edited a number of books about Arthur Machen (often in collaboration with Mark Valentine), along with the periodicals *Aklo: The Journal of the Fantastic* (1988–98), *Redondan Cultural Foundation Newsletter* (1994–98) and *The Lost Club Journal* (1999–2004). Dobson also scripted a number of BBC radio programmes, ranging in subject matter from movie Scream Queens and a celebration of *The Eagle* comic to the Caribbean literary realm of Redonda, and he contributed articles to a wide range of magazines, including *Antiquarian Book Monthly*, *Strange Attractor* and *Faunus*.

American writer **Nick Pollotta** (Nicholas Angelo Pollotta, Jr) died of cancer the same day, aged fifty-eight. A former stand-up comedian (as "Nick Smith"), he wrote more than fifty novels under his own name and various pseudonyms, including *Illegal Aliens* (with Phil Foglio), *That Darn Squid God* (with James Clay), *Damned Nation*, *Belle, Book and Candle* and three "Bureau 13" role-playing game tie-ins. He also contributed to other series as "Jack Hopkins" and under the house names "James Axler" and "Don Pendleton".

New Zealand fan and collector **T. G. L. Cockcroft** (Thomas George Cockcroft) also died on April 12, aged eighty-six. He had been in a nursing home for some years following a stroke. In the early 1960s he published a number of seminal indexes, including *The Tales of Clark Ashton Smith*, *Index to the Verse in Weird Tales*, *Index to the Weird Fiction Magazines: Index by Title* and *Index to the Weird Fiction Magazines: Index by Author*, amongst other titles.

American screenwriter **Michael France** died of complications from diabetes the same day, aged fifty-one. He worked on the original stories for the James Bond films *GoldenEye* and (uncredited) *The World is Not Enough*, and scripted the Marvel Comics adaptations *Hulk* (2003), *The Punisher* and *Fantastic Four* (2005). During the early 1970s, France published the short-lived 007 fanzine *Kiss Kiss Bang Bang*.

British occult expert **Rob** (Robert) **Turner** died on April 15, aged sixty. As well as translating many occult texts, he was also a major contributor to *The Necronomicon* (1978) and its sequel, *The R'Lyeh Text*, both edited by George Hay.

American comics writer **Robert Morales**, best known for the 2003 Marvel mini-series *Truth: Red, White & Black* – a Captain America prequel – and *Captain America: Homeland* (2004), died on April 18, aged fifty-five. A graduate of the Clarion Writers Workshop, he was an executive editor at *Reflex* magazine in the early 1990s, where he brought Neil Gaiman on board as a consulting editor. A close friend of Samuel R. Delany, Morales was intended to be the author's literary executor.

American artist **Quinton Hoover**, who contributed many designs to *Magic: The Gathering* and other collectible trading card games and role-playing books, died on April 20, aged forty-nine. Hoover was also co-creator of the comic *Morgana X*.

American fantasy and SF author **Andrew J.** (Jefferson) **Offutt** reportedly died of cirrhosis after a long illness on April 30. He was seventy-eight. After winning a story competition in *If* magazine in 1954, his professional career began six years later with a story in *Galaxy*. He published more than seventy-five books, including *Evil is Live Spelled Backwards*, *The Castle Keeps*, *The Galactic Rejects*, *Messenger of Zhuvastou*, *Genetic Bomb* (with D. Bruce Berry) and *My Lord Barbarian*, along with the "War of the Wizards" trilogy (with Richard K. Lyons) and the "War of the Gods on Earth" series. Offutt continued the adventures of Robert E. Howard's Conan in *Conan and the Sorcerer*, *The Sword of Skelos* and *Conan the Mercenary*, and Cormac Mac Art in six volumes beginning with *The Sword of Gael* (the final two in collaboration with Keith Taylor). He also extended the "Thieves' World" shared universe with *Shadowspawn*, *Deathknight* and *The Shadow of Sorcery*, edited five volumes of the *Swords Against Darkness* anthology series, and wrote erotica as "John Cleve", "J. X. Williams" and "Jeff Douglas". Offutt was twice president of the Science Fiction Writers of America, from 1976–78.

American screenwriter, producer and director **Mike Gray** (Harold Michael Gray) died of heart failure the same day, aged seventy-seven. He began his career filming TV commercials and documentaries in the early 1970s before going on to script *The China Syndrome*, *Wavelength* (which he also directed) and an episode of *Star Trek: The Next Generation* (he produced the 1988–89 season). Gray also produced and developed the 1986–87 TV series *Starman*, based on the movie of the same name.

American comic book artist and illustrator **Dan Adkins** (Danny L. Adkins) died on May 3, aged seventy-six. Beginning his career in such SF fanzines as *Sata*, *Amra*, *Vega* and *Xero*, he joined the Wally Wood Studio in 1964 as Wood's assistant, working on *T.H.U.N.D.E.R. Agents* and Warren's *Creepy* and *Eerie*. Along with work for Marvel (notably *Doctor Strange*), DC Charlton, Dell, Harvey and other comics publishers, Adkins also contributed art to *Amazing Stories*, *Fantastic*, *Galaxy*, *Infinity*, *Science-Fiction Adventures*, *Worlds of If*, *Amra*, *Monster Parade* and *Famous Monsters of Filmland*.

Scottish-born author **Deborah J. Miller** died of cancer on May 6, aged fifty. Her novels include *Swarmthief's Dance*, *Swarmthief's Treason* and (as "Miller Lau") the "Last Clansman" trilogy: *Talisker*, *Dark Thane* and *Lore Bringer*. Miller was also the principal founder of the David Gemmell Awards for Fantasy.

Marion Sturgeon (Marion Teresa McGahan), the third wife of late SF and fantasy author Theodore Sturgeon, died on May 19, aged eighty-three. The couple separated in the mid-1960s after having four children, but they never divorced.

Described by the *New York Times Magazine* as "one of American literature's most distinctive and undervalued voices," SF and fantasy author **Jack Vance** (John Holbrook Vance) died in his sleep on May 26. He was ninety-six. Vance published his first story, "The World-Thinker" in *Thrilling Wonder Stories* (1945), and went on to write some of the most influential books in the genre, including *The Dying Earth*, *Big Planet*, *The Languages of Pao*, *The Eyes* *of the Overworld*, *The Dragon Masters*, the "Demon Princes" quintet, *The Last Castle*, *Madouc*, the "Lyonesse" and "Cadwal Chronicles" trilogies, and many others. He also had eleven mysteries published under his birth name and three as "Ellery Queen". Vance won a World Fantasy Award, a Nebula Award, an Edgar Award, and three Hugo Awards (the third for his 2009 autobiography *This is Me, Jack Vance!*), and he received the World Fantasy Life Achievement Award and the SFWA Grand Master Award. He spent his later years creating jazz music.

Veteran American anthologist and book collector **Victor S. Ghidalia** died on May 28, aged eighty-seven. During the late 1960s and '70s he edited such anthologies as *The Little Monsters* and *More Little Monsters* (both with Roger Elwood), *Beware the Beasts* and *Beware More Beasts*, *The Mummy Walks Among Us*, *Horror Hunters*, *Satan's Pets*, *Young Demons*, *Eight Strange Tales*, *Wizards and Warlocks*, *The Venus Factor*, *Dracula's Guest and Other Stories*, *The Oddballs*, *Androids, Time Machines and Blue Giraffes*, *The Devil's Generation*, *Gooseflesh!*, *Nightmare Garden* and *Feast of Fear*. While working at his day job with ABC-TV, Ghidalia was involved in turning Richard Matheson's story "Mother by Protest" into Lorimar Productions' 1974 ABC Movie of the Week, *The Stranger Within*, starring Barbara Eden and George Grizzard.

American author, sociologist and Catholic priest **Andrew M.** (Moran) **Greeley** died on May 29, aged eighty-five. In 2008 he suffered a skull fracture and serious brain injury when he was thrown into the street after his coat was caught in the door of a departing taxi. Best known for his mystery and detective novels, he also wrote SF and fantasy, including *The Magic Cup*, *God Game*, *The Final Planet*, *Angel Fire* and its sequel *Angel Light*. Greeley also co-edited the anthology *Sacred Visions* with Michael Cassutt.

Publisher, author and editor **Richard Ballantine**, the son of SF publishers Ian and Betty Ballantine, died the same day, aged seventy-two.

American playwright and novelist **David Rogers** died of cardiac arrest on June 5, aged eighty-five. A former actor, his stage adaptations include Aldous Huxley's *Brave New World* and musical versions of J. R. R. Tolkien's *The Hobbit*, William Shakespeare's *A Midsummer Night's Dream*, and Daniel Keyes' *Flowers for Algernon* (as the Tony-nominated *Charlie and Algernon*).

American author **John Boyd** (Boyd Bradfield Upchurch) died on June 8, aged ninety-three. His first novel, *The Last Starship from Earth*, was published in 1968, and he went on to write twelve more books, mostly SF, including *The Rakehells of Heaven*, *Sex and the High Command*, *The Organ Bank*, *The Gorgon Festival*, *The Doomsday Gene* and *The Girl with the Jade Green Eyes*. His one SF story, "The Girl and the Dolphin", appeared in *Galaxy* (1973).

Just two months after publicly announcing his condition was terminal, Scottish author **Iain** [Menzies] **Banks** died of cancer on June 9, aged fifty-nine. In tribute, the city of Edinburgh held a season of events over the summer of 2013 in celebration of his work. Banks' debut novel, *The Wasp Factory* (1984), was a literary best-seller, and he followed it with *Walking on Glass*, *The Bridge*, *A Song of Stone* and *Canal Dreams*, all containing elements of fantasy or horror. Other novels include *Espedair Street*, *The Crow Road* (filmed for TV), *Complicity* and *The Quarry*. He was credited as "Iain M. Banks" on such SF titles as *Consider Phlebas*, *The Player of Games*, *Use of Weapons*, *Feersum Endjinn* and *Inversions*, amongst others. Before his death, Banks was announced as a Guest of Honour at the 2014 World Science Fiction Convention in London, and he had an asteroid named after him on June 23, 2013.

New Zealand-born **Michael Baigent** (Michael Barry Meehan), who co-wrote the speculative history *The Holy Blood and the Holy Grail* with Richard Leigh and Henry Lincoln, died of a brain haemorrhage in Brighton, England, on June 17. He was sixty-five. When Baigent and Leigh sued author Dan Brown for freely using elements of their book in *The Da Vinci Code*, they lost the case and were ordered by the High Court to pay £3 million in legal costs.

American author [Harold] **Parke Godwin** died in a care facility on June 19, aged eighty-four. He made his genre debut in the 1977 anthology *Brother Theodore's Chamber of Horrors*, and some of his short stories were collected in the World Fantasy Award-nominated *The Fire When it Comes*. With Marvin Kaye he collaborated on the novels *The Masters of Solitude*, *Wintermind* and *A Cold Blue Light*, and his other works include *A Memory of Lions*, *A Truce with Time: A Love Story with Occasional Ghosts*, *The Tower of Beowulf*, *Lord of Sunset* and the "Snake Oil Wars", "Firelord" and "Robin Hood" sequences. He published two books as "Kate Hawks" and edited *Invitations to Camelot: An Arthurian Anthology of Short Stories*. Godwin's story "Influencing the Hell Out of Time and Teresa Golowitz" was adapted into a 1985 episode of TV's *The Twilight Zone*, and he was a Guest of Honour at the 2011 World Fantasy Convention.

Danish-born **Kim Thompson**, co-publisher of comics imprint Fantagraphics Books (with Gary Groth), died of lung cancer the same day, aged fifty-six. He was also involved with *The Comics Journal* magazine and edited more than 200 issues of the bi-weekly *Amazing Heroes*. Thompson was instrumental in bringing European comics and graphic novels to America, and he received the Inkpot Award in 2001.

Edgar Vernon McKnight, Jr, the reviews editor for the journal of the Science Fiction Research Association, died of ALS on June 22, aged fifty.

Genre giant **Richard** [Burton] **Matheson** died on June 23, aged eighty-seven. His many novels include such classics as *I am Legend*, *The Shrinking Man*, *A Stir of Echoes*, *Hell House*, *Bid Time Return* and *What Dreams May Come* (all filmed). His short fiction is collected in numerous volumes, including *Born of Man and Woman: Tales of Science Fiction and Fantasy*, *Third from the Sun*, *The Shores of Space*, *Shock!*, *Shock II*, *Shock Waves* and the World Fantasy Award-winning *Richard Matheson: Collected Stories*, amongst many others. His stories "Duel", "Steel", "The Box", "No Such Thing as a Vampire", "First Anniversary" and "Dance of the Dead" were all filmed, and he scripted fourteen episodes of the original *The Twilight Zone* series (including the classic "Nightmare at 20,000 Feet"). Matheson also scripted the movies *The Fall of the House of Usher* (1960), *Master of the World*, *Pit and the Pendulum* (1961), *Tales of Terror*, *Night of the Eagle* (with Charles Beaumont, based on Fritz Leiber's *Conjure Wife*), *The Raven*, *The Comedy of Terrors*, *The Last Man on Earth* (as "Logan Swanson"), Hammer's *Fanatic* and *The Devil Rides Out* (aka *The Devil's Bride*), *De Sade*, *The Night Stalker*, *The Night Strangler*, *Dying Room Only*, *Scream of the Wolf* (based on "The Hunter" by David Case), *Dracula* (1973), *The Stranger Within*, *Trilogy of Terror* and *Trilogy of Terror II* (both with William F. Nolan), *The Strange Possession of Mrs. Oliver*, *Dead of Night*, *The Martian Chronicles* (based on the stories by Ray Bradbury), *Jaws 3-D* (with son Richard Christian Matheson), *The Dreamer of Oz* and *Twilight Zone: Rod Serling's Lost Classics*. He also wrote episodes of TV's *Thriller* (August Derleth's "The Return of Andrew Bentley"), *The Alfred Hitchcock Hour*, *Star Trek* ("The Enemy Within"), *The Girl from U.N.C.L.E.*, *Journey to the Unknown*, *Night Gallery*, *Circle of Fear* and *Amazing Stories*. Matheson received Lifetime Achievement Awards from the World Fantasy Convention and Horror Writers Association, and was named World Horror Grand Master and International Horror Guild Living Legend. Despite his death, he remained an honorary Guest of Honour at the 2013 World Fantasy Convention in Brighton, England.

Len Leone (Leonard P. Leone, Sr), the innovative art director at Bantam Books from 1955–84, died on July 1, aged ninety-two. Leone used top illustrators such as Bob Larkin, Fred Pfeiffer, Boris Vallejo, Lou Feck, Robert Maguire, Dean Cornwall, John Berkely, Vincent DiFate, Ron Lesser and many others on Bantam's paperbacks, and he was responsible for hiring James Bama to illustrate the covers for the *Doc Savage* reprint series, for which Leone designed the distinctive logo and cover lettering.

Italian screenwriter **Vincenzo Cerami** died on July 17, aged seventy-two. He wrote *Pinocchio* (2002) starring Roberto Benigni and was assistant director on the "La Terra vista dalla luna" segment of *The Witches* (1967). Cerami was married to actress Mimsy Farmer from 1970–86.

British artist **David Fairbrother-Roe**, who painted the covers for some of Anne McCaffrey's early "Dragon" books, died of cancer on July 21. He also produced covers for C. J. Cherryh, John Barth and George Macbeth, along with record sleeves for Nazareth and Jon Anderson, amongst others. For the last twenty years of his life, Fairbrother-Roe became a recluse, remaining in his home in the Welsh coastal village of Ferryside.

American Tolkien scholar and specialist in mythology and Finnish folklore, **Anne C. Petty** died of cancer the same day. Her non-fiction books include *One Ring to Bind Them All: Tolkien's Mythology*, *Tolkien and the Land of Heroes* and *Dragons of Fantasy*, and her short story "The Veritas Experience" was published in *The Best Horror, Fantasy & Science Fiction of 2009*. Petty was also the author of the dark fantasy/horror novels *The Thin Line Between*, *Shaman's Blood* and *The Cornerstone*.

British author, journalist and musician **Mick Farren** (Michael Anthony Farren) died of a heart attack on July 27, after collapsing on stage while performing with a new line-up of his anarchistic rock band The Deviants in London. He was sixty-nine. Farren began writing SF in 1973 with *The Texts of Festival*, and his books include *The Quest for the DNA Cowboys*, *The Feelies*, *The Long Orbit*, *Armageddon Crazy*, *Necrom*, *The Time of Feasting*, *Kindling* and *Conflagration*, amongst others. Some of his short fiction is collected in *Zones of Chaos*, and his rock albums include the 1978 release *Vampires Stole My Lunch Money*.

Egyptian-born graphic designer **J. C.** (Jean-Claude) **Suares** died of complications from a bacterial heart infection in New Jersey on July 30, aged seventy-one. As well as working for the *New York Times*, the *New Yorker* and *Publishers Weekly*, Suares redesigned the look of *Variety* in the 1990s. His books include *Rocketship: An Incredible Voyage Through Science Fiction and Science Fact*, *Alien Creatures* and *Fantastic Planets*.

Welsh-born scriptwriter, author and playwright **Jon** [Ewbank] **Manchip White** died in Knoxville, Tennessee, on July 31, aged eighty-nine. After appearing in the 1951 BBC production *A Tomb with a View*, he switched to co-writing such films as Hammer's *The Camp on Blood Island*, *The Day of the Triffids* (uncredited) and *Crack in the World*, along with episodes of *The Avengers*, *Suspense* and *Witch Hunt*. White's play *The Obi* became the basis of the 1966 voodoo movie *Naked Evil*, and he also scripted radio versions of *Journey to the Centre of the Earth* (1949) and *The War of the Worlds* (1950). His sixteen novels include *Nightclimber*, *The Game of Troy* and *The Garden Game*, while some of his short fiction was collected in *Whistling Past the Churchyard: Strange Tales from a Supernatural Welshman*.

The death was reported on August 2 of sixty-six-year-old American SF writer **Patricia** [Marie] **Anthony**. Her idiosyncratic novels include *Cold Allies*, *Brother Termite*, *Conscience of the Beagle*, *Happy Policeman*, *Cradle of Splendor*, *God's Fires* and *Flanders*. Some of Anthony's short fiction is collected in *Eating Memories*.

British author **Douglas R.** (Rankine) **Mason**, who published numerous SF books under the name "John Rankine", died on August 8, aged ninety-four. Best known for his "Dag Fletcher" space opera series, which began in *New Writings in SF 1* (1964), his many other books include *One is One*, *The Plantos Affair*, *The Ring of Garamas* and several *Space: 1999* tie-in novels.

American Egyptologist and author **Barbara Mertz** (Barbara Louise Gross), who also wrote under the names "Elizabeth Peters" and "Barbara Michaels", died the same day, aged eighty-five. Best known for her historical mysteries and the "Amelia Peabody" series about a Victorian Egyptologist, her many novels include *Sons of the Wolf*, *The Crying Child*, *Witch*, *Wait for What Will Come*, *The Walker in Shadows*, *The Wizard's Daughter*, *Someone in the House*, *The Grey Beginning*, *Stitches in Time*, *The Last Camel Died at Noon* and *Devil May Care*. Some of her short fiction is collected in *Other Worlds*.

American writer and editor **Amy** [Deborah] **Wallace**, the daughter of novelists Irving Wallace and Sylvia Wallace (both of whom she collaborated on books with), died of a heart condition on August 10, aged fifty-eight. She wrote the erotic novel *Desire* and co-compiled *The Book of Lists: Horror* (with Del Howison and Scott Bradley). Her affair with Carlos Castaneda was detailed in her 2003 memoir, *Socerer's Apprentice: My Life with Carlos Castaneda*.

Iconic best-selling American author **Elmore** [John] **Leonard** [Jr] died on August 20, three weeks after suffering a stroke. Best known for his crime and Western novels, *Touch* (1987) was about a man with healing powers and *A Coyote's in the House* (2004) was a YA animal fantasy. He was named Grand Master by the Mystery Writers of America, and received a National Book Award Medal for Distinguished Contribution in 2012.

Nick Robinson (Nicholas John Winwood Robinson), the founder and publisher of UK imprint Robinson, died of cancer on August 30, aged fifty-eight. He began his career as an assistant editor at the arts magazine *Apollo* and worked at publishers Chatto & Windus and Breslich and Foss before starting up Robinson Publishing in 1983. Always an innovative publisher and fan of genre fiction, he was soon working with Mike Ashley and Ramsey Campbell, and it goes without saying that *Best New Horror* would not exist without his continued support over the years and the success of his "Mammoth" line. In 1999 he was given the opportunity to merge the company with Britain's oldest independent publisher, Constable & Co., creating Constable & Robinson. The new company thrived thanks to its self-help books and early move into electronic publishing, and it won both Independent Publisher of the Year and the IPG Digital Publishing awards in 2012. From 2009 onwards, Robinson gradually stepped back from his day-to-day duties, becoming Chairman of the company. Following his death, Constable & Robinson was sold to Little, Brown.

Acclaimed Irish poet **Seamus** [Justin] **Heaney**, who published a new translation of *Beowulf* in 1999, died the same day, aged seventy-four. He was awarded the Nobel Prize in Literature in 1995.

SF legend **Frederik** [George] **Pohl** [Jr] died on September 2, aged ninety-three. As a fan, editor and author, he shaped science fiction for more than seven decades. From 1939–43 he edited the pulp magazines *Astonishing Stories* and *Super Science Stories* before becoming a major author in the 1950s. He collaborated with C. M. Kornbluth on *The Space Merchants*, *Search the Sky*, *Gladiator-at-Law* and *Wolfbane*, and Jack Williamson on a number of titles, including the popular "Undersea" and "Starchild" trilogies. Pohl's many other titles include *Slave Ship*, *Drunkard's Walk*, *A Plague of Pythons*, *Man Plus*, the multi-award-winning *Gateway*, *Beyond the Blue Event Horizon*, *Heechee Rendezvous*, *The Gateway Trip*, *JEM* and *The Coming of the Quantum Cats*. His short fiction is collected in more than twenty volumes. During the 1950s he edited Ballantine's original *Star Science Fiction* anthologies and the following decade he was editor of the digest magazines *Galaxy* and *If*. He was also a SF editor at publishers Ace and Bantam. A winner of the Hugo, Nebula, Campbell Memorial and American Book awards, he was president of the SFWA from 1974–76, and named SFWA Grand Master in 1992. Pohl's five wives included Judith Merril and Elizabeth Anne Hull, and his memoir *The Way the Future Was* was published in 1978.

British screenwriter and playwright **Brian Comport**, whose credits include such early 1970s horror films as *Mumsy, Nanny, Sonny & Girly*, *The Fiend* (aka *Beware My Brethren*) and *The Asphyx*, died on September 5, aged seventy-five.

American author **A.** (Ann) **C.** (Carol) **Crispin**, best known for her tie-in books, died of cancer on September 6, aged sixty-three. She collaborated with Andre Norton on the "Witch World" novel *Gryphon's Eyrie* and created the "StarBridge" space opera series, comprising a solo novel and six additional collaborations with other authors. *Storms of Destiny* was supposed to be the first in a new urban fantasy series. Her tie-ins included *Star Trek* and *V* novels, the popular *Stars Wars* "Han Solo Trilogy", and various movie novelizations and spin-offs (including *Pirates of the Caribbean*). Co-founder (with Victoria Strauss) of the watchdog group Writer Beware, she was named Grand Master by The International Association of Media Tie-In Writers in 2013.

Sixty-six-year-old convention organizer, writer and editor **Bob Booth** died of lung cancer in a hospice the same day. As "Robert E. Booth" he published some short stories in the 1980s and '90s, but he will be remembered as one of the founding committee of the World Fantasy Convention in 1975 and co-founder of Necon (the Northeastern Writers' Convention) with his wife Mary in 1980. Booth edited *The Big Book of Necon* in 2009.

American screenwriter and producer **Lou** (Louis) **Morheim** died on September 8, aged ninety-one. He was executive producer on *The Outer Limits* (1964), and his other TV credits include the pilots for *The Unknown* and *The Immortal*. He also produced the TV movies *Madame Sin*, *Scream Pretty Peggy* and *Devil Dog: The Hound of Hell*. Morheim scripted *The Beast from 20,000 Fathoms* and a number of episodes of the 1954–55 TV series *Sherlock Holmes* starring Ronald Howard as Holmes.

American scriptwriter and producer **Don Nelson** (Donald Richard Nelson) died of an aortic aneurysm and complications from Parkinson's disease on September 10, aged eighty-six. He wrote episodes of the TV shows *The Ghost & Mrs. Muir*, *The ABC Saturday Superstar Movie* ("The Mini-Munsters") and *Herbie the Love Bug* (he was also supervising producer), along with Disney's *Herbie Goes to Monte Carlo*, *The Munsters' Revenge* (which he also co-produced) and the animated special *The Jetsons Meet the Flinstones*.

Artist **Joan Hanke-Woods** (Delphyne Joan Woods) was found dead in her Chicago apartment on September 16. She was sixty-seven. Nominated for the Best Fan Artist Hugo Award every year from 1980–86, she won in 1986 and her work appeared in such magazines as *Galaxy*, *Fantastic Films* and *The Comics Journal*. Hanke-Woods was a Guest of Honour at WindyCon in 1984.

Horror author **Gary** [Phil] **Brandner** died of cancer of the oesophagus on September 22, aged eighty. Best known for *The Howling* werewolf trilogy (which was turned into a diminishing movie series for which Brandner co-scripted *Howling II: Stirba – Werewolf Bitch*), he wrote more than thirty novels, including the "Big Brain" trilogy, *Walkers* (aka *Death Walkers*, filmed for TV as *From the Dead of Night*), *Hellborn*, *Tribe of the Dead* (aka *Quintana Roo*), *The Brain Eaters*, *Carrion*, *Doomstalker*, *Mind Grabber* and *Rot*. Brandner also scripted the 1989 movie adaptation of his novel *Cameron's Closet*, and he wrote the novelization of the 1982 film *Cat People*.

Italian screenwriter and script doctor **Luciano Vincenzoni**, best known for his "spaghetti" Westerns such as *For a Few Dollars More* and *The Good, the Bad and the Ugly*, died of lung cancer the same day, aged eighty-seven. His other films include *Mr. Hercules Against Karate*, *Orca* (which he also produced) and Ruggero Deodato's *Cut and Run* (uncredited).

Tom Clancy (Thomas Leo Clancy), the American author of such best-selling military thrillers as the near-future *The Hunt for Red October*, *Patriot Games* and *Clear and Present Danger*, died on October 1, aged sixty-six. A number of his books have been filmed and turned into video games, and his name appears above the title of many technothrillers and military series written by other authors.

American SF fan and bookseller **Elliot K.** (Kay) **Shorter** died of cancer the same day, aged seventy-four. He worked for *Locus* from 1968–70 and opened specialty genre bookstore Merlin's Closet in Providence, Rhode Island, in 1979.

British literary agent, romance author and former publisher's editor **Dorothy** "Dot" **Lumley** (Dorothy Houghton) died of cancer on October 5, aged sixty-four. After leaving Leicester University with an honours degree in psychology and a divorce from her first husband, she worked in various editorial capacities for UK imprints New English Library and Magnum Books (an imprint of Methuen) before founding the Dorian Literary Agency in 1986. A regular attendee at FantasyCon and other conventions, her genre client list included her former second husband Brian Lumley, Stephen Jones, R. Chetwynd-Hayes, Karl Edward Wagner, Dennis Etchison, Peter Atkins and others.

British-born journalist and author **Philip Nutman** died in an Atlanta hospital of acute organ failure after being taken off life support on October 7. He was fifty. While working for the BBC in London during the 1980s he freelanced as a media journalist for such magazines as *Venue*, *Shock Xpress*, *L'Ecran Fantastique*, *Fangoria*, *Twilight Zone Magazine*, *Gorezone*, *Fear*, *Skeleton Crew* and many others. He made his short fiction debut in the zombie anthology *Book of the Dead* edited by John Skipp and Craig Spector, and he expanded that story into his only novel, the Bram Stoker Award-nominated *Wet Work* (1993). Other stories appeared in *Borderlands 2*, *Splatterpunks* and *The Year's Best Horror Stories Series XIX* and *XX*. Nutman also wrote a number of comic books for Chaos! and other publishers, along with low-budget movie scripts – including *The Girl Next Door* (based on the novel by Jack Ketchum), which was filmed in 2007.

Leland Sapiro (Leland Shapiro), who took over the American fanzine formerly known as *Fantasy Advertiser/ Science Fiction Advertiser/Inside Science Fiction/Inside* and renamed it *Riverside Quarterly* in 1964, died on October 8, aged eighty-nine. The academic title was published intermittently until 1993 and was nominated for Hugo Awards in 1967 (despite accusations of ballot-stuffing), 1969 and 1970.

Stanley Kauffmann, who bought Ray Bradbury's novel *Fahrenheit 451* while working as an acquisitions editor at Ballantine Books in 1953, died of pneumonia on October 9, aged ninety-seven. He was also an author and film critic for the *New Republic* and *New York Times*.

Film and TV writer **Mann Rubin** died on October 12, aged eighty-five. He began his career in the early 1950s writing for DC Comics' *Strange Adventures* and *Mystery in Space*. He also published short stories in *Alfred Hitchcock Magazine* and mystery anthologies. Rubin scripted a number of episodes of *Tales of Tomorrow*, along with episodes of

Alfred Hitchcock Presents, *Land of the Giants*, *Circle of Fear*, *The Six Million Dollar Man*, *Matt Helm*, *The Bionic Woman*, *Future Cop*, *Lucan*, *Project U.F.O.*, and the movies *Brainstorm* (1965) and *The Amazing Captain Nemo*.

Japanese writer, poet, illustrator and lyricist **Takashi Yanase**, creator of the popular *manga* and *anime* super-hero "Anpanman", died on October 13, aged ninety-four.

American publisher and anthologist **Martin Greenberg** died on October 20, aged ninety-five. Not to be confused with anthology editor Martin H. Greenberg (who died in 2011), he co-founded independent imprint Gnome Press with David A. Kyle and fellow members of The Hydra Club in 1948. For Gnome, Greenberg edited the anthologies *Men Against the Stars*, *Travelers of Space* (illustrated by Edd Cartier), *Journey to Infinity*, *Five Science Fiction Novels* (aka *The Crucible of Power*), *The Robot and the Man*, *All About the Future* and a collection of non-fiction articles about SF, *Coming Attractions*. Following disputes about payments (Isaac Asimov called Greenberg a "crook"), the press went out of business in 1962. Greenberg later ran an art supply store in Long Island, and he received the First Fandom Hall of Fame Award in 2000.

Frank Dietz (Franklin M. Dietz, Jr), who co-founded (with his first wife Belle and David A. Kyle) the New York Science Fiction Society (aka the Lunarians) in late 1956, died in October. He also helped start the annual Lunacon convention, which he chaired for fourteen years, starting in 1957. Dietz was the convention's Fan Guest of Honour in 2007. He was involved in the publication of a number of fanzines, including *Science Fantasy and Science Fiction*, *Ground Zero* and *Luna Monthly*, and he helped run Luna Publications, which published a collection of interviews, *Speaking of Science Fiction*, in 1978. Dietz was one of the organizers of the Guild of Science Fiction Recordists, who taped events at many conventions, and he had an original tattoo of a mouse on his upper arm, done especially for him by artist Hannes Bok.

Screenwriter **Elinor Karpf** died on October 21, aged seventy-three. With her first husband, Stephen Karpf, she wrote the 1970s TV movies *Sandcastles*, *Gargoyles* and *Devil Dog: The Hound of Hell*.

American author and English professor **William** [Neal] **Harrison**, who adapted his 1973 story "Roller Ball Murder" into the screenplay for the movie *Rollerball* (1975), died on October 22, aged seventy-nine. The film was remade in 2002.

American editor and fan **Andrea M. Dubnick**, who helped run the "Twilight Tales" readings in Chicago's Red Lion Pub for many years, died on October 31, aged sixty-three. Dubnick and Tina Jens were nominated for a Bram Stoker Award for the reading series in 2001, and she co-edited the 2007 anthology *Tales from the Red Lion*.

American comics artist **Nick Cardy** (Nicholas Viscardi, aka "Nick Cardi") died on November 3, aged ninety-three. He began his career in the 1940s working for the Eisner and Iger Studio packaging comics, and in 1950 he started drawing the daily *Tarzan* newspaper strip for Burne Hogarth. However, Cardy is best known for his later work with DC Comics on such titles as *Tomahawk*, *Aquaman*, *Teen Titans*, *House of Mystery*, *House of Secrets* and *Tales of the Unexpected*. During the early 1970s, he became DC's primary cover artist, before leaving comics to work as a commercial illustrator. Along with magazine and advertising art, Cardy also produced movie posters (including *Apocalypse Now*). He returned to some limited comics work in the late 1990s.

Persian-born author **Doris Lessing** (Doris May Tayler) died in London on November 11, aged ninety-four. After moving to Britain from South Africa, she published her first book in 1950. She wrote more than fifty novels, many short-story collections, plays, non-fiction and a book of poetry. A Guest of Honour at the 1987 World Science Fiction Convention in Brighton, a number of her titles are SF, including *Briefing for a Descent Into Hell*, *The Summer Before the Dark*, *Memoirs of a Survivor* (filmed in 1981), *Re: Colonised Planet 5 Shikasta*, *The Fifth Child*, *Ben in the World*, *Mara and Dann: An Adventure* and *The Cleft*. Lessing received the Nobel Prize in Literature in 2007.

Canadian scriptwriter and producer **David Tynan** died of pancreatic cancer the same day, aged sixty-two. He scripted episodes of TV's *War of the Worlds*, *Silk Stalkings*, *Highlander*, *Poltergeist: The Legacy*, *The Lost World*, *First Wave* and *Flash Gordon* (2007–08). He received producing credits on *Highlander*, *Poltergeist: The Legacy* and *First Wave*, and was creative consultant on *Flash Gordon*.

Australian librarian, bibliographer and bookseller **Graham** [Brice] **Stone** died of a stroke on November 16, aged eighty-seven. He had been diagnosed with tubercular encephalitis in January. A leading authority on Australian SF, in 1951 he founded the Australian Science Fiction Society and published the newszine *Science Fiction News* (1953–59). Stone also contributed material to such titles as *Future Science Fiction*, *Popular Science Fiction* and *Science-Fiction Monthly*. In the 1960s he published two editions of his *Australian Science Fiction Index*, which was followed by the *Journal of the Australian Science Fiction Association*, *Index to British Science Fiction Magazines 1934–1953*, *Notes on Australian Science Fiction* and the comprehensive *Australian Science Fiction Bibliography*. Stone received the A. Bertram Chandler Award for Outstanding Achievement in Science Fiction from the Australian SF Foundation in 1999.

Joseph J. Lazzaro, who contributed many articles to *Analog* magazine, died on November 18, aged fifty-six. He also published two collaborative SF short stories.

Japanese-born American writer and publisher **Robert Reginald** (Michael Roy Burgess, aka "C. Everett Cooper"/"M. R. Burgess"/"Boden Clarke") died of heart failure on November 20, aged sixty-five. In the mid-1970s he founded Borgo Press, which later became an imprint of Wildside Press. His many non-fiction works include *Science Fiction and Fantasy Literature: A Checklist 1700–1974* (with Mary A. Burgess and Douglas Menville), *Reginald's Science Fiction and Fantasy Awards* (with Daryl F. Mallett), *A Guide to Science Fiction and Fantasy in the Library of Congress Classification Scheme* and *Futurevisions: The Golden Age of the Science Fiction Film*, along with guides to the work of Jeffrey M. Elliott, Julian May, Charles Beaumont, William F. Nolan, Reginald Bretnor, Colin Wilson, Brian W. Aldiss, Elizabeth Chater, Jack Vance, William F. Temple, S. Fowler Wright, Gary Brandner, George Zebrowski, Stephen King, Pamela Sargent, Ursula K. Le Guin, Katherine Kurtz and himself. Reginald's many anthologies include *Ancestral Voices: An Anthology of Early Science Fiction*, *R.I.P.: Five Stories of the Supernatural*, *The Spectre Bridegroom and Other Horrors*, *Ancient Hauntings*, *Phantasmagoria: Supernatural & Occult Fiction* and *Dreamers of Dreams: An Anthology of Fantasy* (all with Douglas Menville). He was also the author of a number of short stories collected in *Katydid & Other Critters: Tales of Fantasy and Mystery*, *The Elder of Days: Tales of the Elders* and *The Judgment of the Gods and Other Verdicts of History*, while his novels include the "Nova Europa", "Phantom Detective" and "War of Two Worlds" series.

Less than a month after he won the World Fantasy Award for his collection *Where Furnaces Burn*, British writer and editor **Joel Lane** died in his sleep on November 25 from heart failure brought on by sleep apnoea, with diabetes as a contributing factor. He was fifty. His short fiction appeared in the collections *The Earth Wire & Other Stories* (winner of the British Fantasy Award), *The Lost District and Other Stories*, *The Terrible Changes* and *Do Not Pass Go*, and he also published a novella, *The Witnesses Are Gone*. Lane was the author of two mainstream novels, *From Blue to Black* and *The Blue Mask*, he edited the anthologies *Beneath the Ground*, *Birmingham Noir: Urban Tales of Crime and Suspense* (with Steve Bishop) and *Never Again* (with Allyson Bird), and he published two volumes of poetry.

American comics artist **Al Plastino** (Alfred John Plastino) died of complications from prostate cancer the same day, aged ninety-one. He began his career at DC Comics in 1948 and worked extensively on all the *Superman* titles during the 1950s, co-creating "Supergirl", "Brainiac" and the "Legion of Super-Heroes" with writer Otto Binder. Plastino also illustrated the syndicated *Batman with Robin the Boy*

Wonder newspaper strip (1968–72) and he was the uncredited ghost artist on the *Superman* strip from 1960–69.

American author and historian **T.** (Theodore) **R.** (Reed) **Fehrenbach** who, as "T. R. Fehrenbach" published the SF story "Remember the Alamo!" in *Analog* (1961), died on December 1, aged eighty-eight. He also had a story in the anthology *Lone Star Universe* edited by George W. Proctor and Steven Utley.

American SF author **Hilbert** [van Nydeck] **Schenck** [Jr] died on December 2, aged eighty-seven. An engineer and teacher, he published his first fiction in *The Magazine of Fantasy and Science Fiction* in 1953, and his books include the novels *At the Eye of the Ocean*, *A Rose for Armageddon* and *Chronosequence*, along with the collections *Wave Rider* and *Steam Bird*. Several of Schenck's stories and novellas were nominated for Hugo and Nebula Awards in the 1980s.

American publishing attorney, book packager and investor **Richard Gallen**, who worked with various publishers, including Baen Books, Bluejay, Tor and Carroll & Graf, died on December 3, aged eighty.

British author **Colin** [Henry] **Wilson** died on December 5, aged eighty-two. He had suffered a stroke in June that had left him unable to speak. One of literature's "angry young men" of the 1950s, he made his debut with *The Outsider* (1956), a study of outsiders in culture that took its title from an H. P. Lovecraft story. In 1967 Arkham House published Wilson's Lovecraftian novel *The Mind Parasites*, and he followed it with *The Glass Cage*, *The Philosopher's Stone*, *The Space Vampires* (filmed as *Lifeforce*), *The Personality Surgeon* and the four volume "Spider World" series. His other novels include *Ritual in the Dark*, *The God of the Labyrinth* and *The Black Room*, and he also wrote and edited a number of non-fiction books about the occult.

American author and journalist **Hugh Nissenson**, who wrote the near-future SF novel *The Song of the Earth* (2001), died on December 13, aged eighty.

Rosemary F. Wolfe (Rosemary Dietsch), who was married to author Gene Wolfe for fifty-seven years, died of complications from Alzheimer's disease on December 14, aged eighty-two.

Best-selling American young adult author **Ned Vizzini** (Edison Price Vizzini) committed suicide from a fall on December 19, aged thirty-two. He had suffered from depression for many years. The semi-autobiographical *It's Kind of a Funny Story* (2006) was filmed four years later with Zach Galifianakis, and he also wrote the SF novel *Be More Chill* and an alternative fantasy, *The Other Normals. House of Secrets* and *House of Secrets: Battle of the Beast* were both co-written with movie director Chris Columbus, while *Teen Angst? Naaah* . . . was a memoir of his teenage years. Vizzini also wrote for TV's *Teen Wolf* and *The Last Resort*, and he had been working on NBC's *Believe* at the time of his death.

Nancy Kemp, the former wife of American SF publisher Earl Kemp, with whom she co-edited the 1960 Hugo Award-winning fanzine *Who Killed Science Fiction?* (1960), died after a long battle with uterine cancer on December 22.

Polish composer **Wojciech Kilar** died of cancer on December 29, aged eighty-one. He composed the soundtracks to *Dracula* (1992), *Fantôme avec chauffeur* and *The Ninth Gate*, and his music was also used in the first season of TV's *American Horror Story*.

PERFORMERS/PERSONALITIES

American-born actress **Patty Shepard** (Patricia Moran Shepard, aka "Patty Sheppard"/"Patti Sheppard") died of a heart attack in Madrid, Spain, on January 3, aged sixty-eight. A former model, her film credits include *Dracula versus Frankenstein* (aka *Assignment Terror*), *The Werewolf versus the Vampire Woman, Escalofrío diabólico, The Witches Mountain, Hannah Queen of the Vampires* (aka *Crypt of the Living Dead*), *Refuge of Fear, Rest in Pieces, Slugs: The Movie* (based on the novel by Shaun Hutson) and *Edge of the Axe*. Shepard also portrayed a ghost in a 1975 episode of the TV series *El quinto jinete* ("La renta espectral").

Italian actress **Mariangela Melato** died of pancreatic cancer in Rome on January 11, aged seventy-one. She made her debut in Pupi Avati's *Thomas and the Bewitched* (1970) and went on to appear in many films, including the 1980 remake of *Flash Gordon* (as "Kala").

Canadian-born actor **Conrad Bain**, who starred in the 1978–85 TV series *Diff'rent Strokes*, died in California on January 14, aged eighty-nine. He also appeared as Mr Wells, the clerk at the Collinsport Inn, in four episodes of the 1960s *Dark Shadows* TV series.

Bengali-British actress **Sophiya Haque** (Syeda Sophia Haque) died of cancer on January 16, age forty-one. A former music VJ/host, she appeared in episodes of *Fairy Tales* (2008) and *House of Anubis*, and was also in the non-genre Indian film *Hari Puttar: A Comedy of Terrors* (2008).

Adult film actor, producer, writer and director **Fred J. Lincoln** (Fred Perna, aka "Tony Vincent"), who portrayed psychotic killer "Weasel Podowski" in Wes Craven's *The Last House on the Left* (1972), died on January 17, aged seventy-five. He was also in the adult films *The Altar of Lust*, *The Case of the Smiling Stiffs*, *A Touch of Genie*, *The Devil in Miss Jones Part II*, *Friday the 13th: Part II – The Next Generation*, *Edward Penishands 3* and *The Last Whore House on the Left*.

British character actor **Bernard** [Arthur Gordon] **Horsfall** died in Scotland on January 28, aged eighty-two. He appeared in *Cinderella* (1958), *On Her Majesty's Secret Service*, *Mr. Horatio Knibbles*, *Quest for Love* (based on a story by John Wyndham) and *The Hound of the Baskervilles* (1988), along with episodes of *Pathfinders to Mars*, *Out of This World*, *The Avengers*, *Out of the Unknown*, *Doomwatch*, *Doctor Who* ("Planet of the Daleks" etc.), *The Changes*, Nigel Kneale's *Beasts*, *Hammer House of Mystery and Suspense*, *Virtual Murder* and *Murder Rooms: The Dark Beginnings of Sherlock Holmes*. In the 1980s, Horsfall moved with his wife, actress Jane Jordan Rogers, to the Isle of Skye to become a crofter.

Patty (Patricia Marie) **Andrews**, the last surviving member of the singing Andrews Sisters, died on January 30, aged ninety-four. With her elder sisters LaVerne and Maxene, the trio brightened up a number of wartime movies during the 1940s and their many hits included "Don't Sit Under the Apple Tree" and "Boogie Woogie Bugle Boy". The sisters later turned up in the 1947 Bing Crosby and Bob Hope comedy/fantasy *Road to Rio*. Patty's first husband, agent Martin Melcher, left her for Doris Day.

British-born actor **Robin** [David] **Sachs**, the son of actors Leonard Sachs and Eleanor Summerfield, died of heart failure in Los Angeles on February 1, aged sixty-one. His credits include Hammer's *Vampire Circus*, *The Lost World: Jurassic Park*, *Ravager*, *Babylon 5: In the Beginning*, *Galaxy Quest* and the animated *Resident Evil: Damnation*, along with episodes of *Nowhere Man*, *Baywatch Nights*, *F/X: The Series*, *Babylon 5*, *Buffy the Vampire Slayer*, *Star Trek: Voyager*, *Alias* and *Torchwood: Miracle Day*. Sachs was also the voice of the Silver Surfer in the 1994 cartoon TV series *Fantastic Four*.

American leading man **John** [Grinham] **Kerr**, who played the young hero in Roger Corman's *Pit and the Pendulum* (1961), died of congestive heart failure on February 2, aged eighty-one. His other credits include a 1959 TV movie of *Berkeley Square* and episodes of *The Alfred Hitchcock Hour*, *Search Control* and *The Invisible Man* (1975). He all but retired from acting in the late 1970s to become a lawyer.

German-born actor [John] **Peter Gilmore**, who starred in the BBC TV series *The Onedin Line* (1971–80), died in London on February 3, also aged eighty-one. Along with many *Carry On* films, he also appeared in *The Abominable Dr Phibes*, *Warlords of Atlantis*, and episodes of TV's *Dead of Night* and the 1984 *Doctor Who* serial "Frontios". The first of his three wives was actress Una Stubbs.

American drama teacher **Sidney Berger** died on February 15, aged seventy-seven. He appeared in both the 1962 and 1998 versions of *Carnival of Souls*. Berger's acting students included Randy Quaid, Dennis Quaid and Brent Spiner.

British character actor **Richard** [David] **Briers** CBE died of emphysema on February 17, aged seventy-nine. Best known as the star of the BBC sitcom *The Good Life* (1975–78), he also voiced "Fiver" in the animated *Watership Down* (1978), portrayed the blind Grandfather in Kenneth Branagh's *Frankenstein* (1994), and played "Smee" in the 2003 version of *Peter Pan*. His final film role was in *Cockneys vs Zombies* (2012). Briers also appeared in the 1987 *Doctor Who* serial "Paradise Towers" and episodes of *Tales of the Unexpected* and *Torchwood*.

Scottish actress **Elspet Gray** (Elspeth Jean MacGregor-Gray), who was a regular on the 1971 children's TV series *Catweazle*, died in London on February 18, aged eighty-three. She also appeared in episodes of *Strange Experiences* ("Halloween"), *Colonel March of Scotland Yard* (with Boris Karloff) and the *Doctor Who* serial "Arc of Infinity". Gray was married to actor/comedian Lord Brian Rix.

American character actor **Lou Myers** (Lewis Eddy Myers) died of heart failure on February 19, aged seventy-seven. He appeared in *The Passion of Darkly Noon* and *Volcano*.

American leading man **Dale Robertson** (Dayle Lymoine Robertson), who starred in the TV series *Tales of Wells Fargo* (1957–62), died of complications from lung cancer and pneumonia on February 27. He was eighty-nine. Robertson appeared in the movies *The Boy with Green Hair* (uncredited) and *Son of Sinbad* (with Vincent Price), along with an episode of TV's *Fantasy Island*.

American actress and singer **Bonnie [Gail] Franklin**, who starred in the popular sitcom *One Day at a Time* (1975–84), died of pancreatic cancer on March 1, aged sixty-nine. A protégé of tap dancer Donald O'Connor, as a child actress she appeared in a 1954 TV version of *A Christmas Carol* starring Basil Rathbone as Marley's ghost. Later appearances include episodes of *The Man from U.N.C.L.E.*, *The Munsters* and *Touched by an Angel*. Franklin also starred in the title role of a 1973 stage production of *Peter Pan*, and she directed twelve episodes of the revival TV series *The Munsters Today* (1988–90).

American TV character and voice actor **Malachi Throne** died of lung cancer on March 13, aged eighty-four. He appeared in episodes of *The Outer Limits*, *Voyage to the Bottom of the Sea*, *Star Trek* (he had turned down the role of "Dr McCoy"), *The Man from U.N.C.L.E.*, *Batman* (as "False Face"), *Lost in Space*, *The Wild Wild West*, *The Time Tunnel*, *Tarzan*, *Land of the Giants*, *Search Control*, *The Six Million Dollar Man*, *Electra Woman and Dyna Girl*, *Ark II*, *Project U.F.O.*, *Star Trek: The Next Generation*, *M.A.N.T.I.S.*, *Babylon 5* and the 1975 special *It's a Bird . . . It's a Plane . . . It's Superman!* Throne narrated the teaser trailer for *Star Wars*, and he was also in the SF comedy movie *Eat and Run*.

British character actor **Frank Thornton** [Ball], who starred in the BBC sitcoms *Are You Being Served?* (1972–85) and *Last of the Summer Wine* (1997–2010), died on March 16, aged ninety-two. He also appeared in *The Tell-Tale Heart* (1960, uncredited), Roger Corman's *The Tomb of Ligeia* (with Vincent Price), *Gonks Go Beat*, *Carry on Screaming!*, *The Bed Sitting Room*, *The Magic Christian* (uncredited), *The Private Life of Sherlock Holmes*, *Digby the Biggest Dog in the World* and *Vampira* (aka *Old Dracula*), along with episodes of TV's *The Avengers*, *The Champions* and *The New Avengers*.

American adult film actor and director **Harry Reems** (Herbert Streicher, aka "Herb Streicher"/"Peter Long"/ "Stan Freemont"/"Herb Stryker"/"Harry Reams"/"Bob Walters"/"Richard Hurt"/"Peter Straight"/"Tim Long"/ "Hari Rimusu"/"Bruce Gilchrist"), best known for his role as the doctor in the infamous *Deep Throat*, died of organ failure on March 19, aged sixty-five. He had been suffering from pancreatic cancer. Reems' numerous credits include *Dark Dreams* (1971), *Penetration* (aka *So Sweet So Dead/ The Slasher is . . . the Sex Maniac!*), *The Devil in Miss Jones*, *Case of the Full Moon Murders* (aka *The Case of the Smiling Stiffs*), *The Amazing Dr. Jekyll* (as "Dr Charles Jekyll III"), *Sherlick Holmes* (in the title role, 1975), *Demented*, *Whore of the Worlds*, *Ten Little Maidens*, *Love Bites* and *Lust in Space*. A reformed alcoholic, he retired from the screen in 1988 and later became a successful real estate broker.

Derek Watkins, the British trumpet player featured on every James Bond soundtrack from *Dr. No* to *Skyfall*, died on March 22, aged sixty-eight.

American actor and teacher **David Early** died of cancer on March 23, aged seventy-four. He was featured in George A. Romero's *Dawn of the Dead*, *Knightriders*, *Creepshow*, *Monkey Shines* and *The Dark Half*. His other movie credits include *The Silence of the Lambs*, *Innocent Blood* and *Zombie Mutation*.

Rotund British actor **Richard Griffiths** OBE died of complications following heart surgery on March 28, aged sixty-five. Best known for his portrayal of the dastardly Uncle Vernon Dursley in the *Harry Potter* series, he also appeared in *Superman III*, *Britannia Hospital*, *Greystoke: The Legend of Tarzan Lord of the Apes*, *Sleepy Hollow* (1999), *A Muppets Christmas*, *Bedtime Stories*, *Pirates of the Caribbean: On Stranger Tides*, *Hugo* and *About Time* (uncredited), along with TV's *Whoops Apocalypse* and the mini-series *Gormenghast*.

Veteran Irish character actor **Milo O'Shea** (Milo Donal O'Shea) died of complications from Alzheimer's disease in New York City on April 2, aged eighty-five. Best remembered for playing the villainous Durand-Durand in *Barbarella* (1968), he also appeared in *The Angel Levine*, *Theatre of Blood* (with Vincent Price), *Digby the Biggest Dog in the World*, *Professor Popper's Problem*, *Arabian Adventure* (with Christopher Lee and Peter Cushing) and Woody Allen's *The Purple Rose of Cairo*. O'Shea's many TV credits include episodes of *Out of This World*, *Out of the Unknown*, *Journey to the Unknown* (aka *Journey Into Darkness*), *Orson Welles' Great Mysteries*, *Beauty and the Beast* (1988) and *Early Edition*.

Mouseketeer turned musical/comedy actress **Annette** [Joanne] **Funicello** died of complications from multiple sclerosis on April 8 (the same day as former British Prime Minister Margaret Thatcher). She was seventy. Best remembered for co-starring in a string of iconic 1960s AIP teen movies with Frankie Avalon and various veteran actors

– including *Beach Party*, *Muscle Beach Party*, *Bikini Beach*, *Pajama Party*, *Beach Blanket Bingo*, *How to Stuff a Wild Bikini* and *Doctor Goldfoot and the Bikini Machine* – her other movie credits include Disney's *The Shaggy Dog* (1959), *Babes in Toyland* (1961), *The Misadventures of Merlin Jones* and *The Monkey's Uncle*, along with The Monkees' psyche-delic *Head*. Amongst Funicello's TV credits are several episodes of *Fantasy Island*. Her one-time boyfriend, singer Paul Anka, wrote the songs "Puppy Love" and "Put Your Head on My Shoulder" based on their relationship.

Sara Montiel (Maria Antonia Alejandra Vicenta Elpidia Isadora Abad Fernández, aka "Sarita Montiel"), one of Spain's greatest film stars and the first Spanish actress to conquer Hollywood in the 1950s, died the same day, aged eighty-five. She starred in the 1953 Mexican comedy/fantasy *Ella, Lucifer y yo* opposite Abel Salazar. Her first husband was American director Anthony Mann, and she counted Gary Cooper and James Dean amongst her many lovers.

British-born stuntman/actor and TV director **Richard J. Brooker**, who played the mindless psycho behind Jason Voorhees' hockey mask in *Friday the 13th Part III*, died from a heart attack on April 8, aged fifty-eight. He also appeared in the 1983 movie *Deathstalker*, on which he was stunt co-ordinator.

American comedy legend **Jonathan Winters** (Jonathan Harshman Winters, Jr) died on April 11, aged eighty-seven. A prolific voice actor, his movie appearances include *The Loved One*, *More Wild Wild West*, *Alice in Wonderland* (1985), *The Flintstones* and *The Shadow* (1994). A regular on *Mork & Mindy* (1981–82) as "Mearth", Winters' numerous TV credits include episodes of *Shirley Temple's Storybook*, *Twilight Zone* ("A Game of Pool"), *Disneyland* ("Halloween Hall o' Fame") and as the voice of "Coach Cadaver" in *Gravedale High* (1990).

American actress **Christine** [Lamson] **White**, who played William Shatner's wife in the classic *Twilight Zone* episode "Nightmare at 20,000 Feet", died on April 14, aged eighty-six. She also appeared in William Castle's *Macabre* and episodes of *Alfred Hitchcock Presents, One Step Beyond* and *Thriller*. White was James Dean's girlfriend in New York from 1951–54.

Actor **Mike Road,** the voice of "Roger T. 'Race' Bannon" in the cartoon TV series *Jonny Quest* (1964–65) died the same day, aged ninety-five. Road also did voice work for *The Flintstones, Space Ghost, Birdman, The Herculoids, Fantastic 4, The New Scooby-Doo Movies, Valley of the Dinosaurs, The Fantastic Journey, The Fantastic Four* and *Space Stars*. He appeared in the 1966 SF movie *Destination Inner Space*, plus episodes of *I Dream of Jeannie, Bewitched* and *The Wild Wild West*.

American actor **Richard LeParmentier,** who played ill-fated "Admiral Motti" in *Star Wars* (1977), died on April 15, aged sixty-six. His other credits include *Rollerball* (1975), *The People That Time Forgot, Superman II, Octopussy* and *Who Framed Roger Rabbit*, along with episodes of TV's *Space: 1999, Hammer House of Mystery* and *Worlds Beyond*. LeParmentier was married to actress Sarah Douglas from 1981–84.

Radio broadcaster **William Burchinal,** who played a zombie in George A. Romero's *Night of the Living Dead* (1968), died on April 17, aged ninety.

American character actor **Allan** [Franklin] **Arbus** died of congestive heart failure on April 19, aged ninety-five. A semi-regular on TV's *M*A*S*H*, he appeared in episodes of *Wonder Woman, Salvage 1* and *The Amazing Spider-Man*, and his movies include *Scream Pretty Peggy* and *Damien: Omen II*.

British stuntman and actor **Nosher Powell** (George Frederick Bernard Powell) died on April 20, aged eighty-four. A former boxer, he began his film career in the mid-1940s and appeared (often uncredited) in *The Road to Hong Kong*, Hammer's *She, Circus of Fear, The Magic Christian, One More Time, Venom, Krull, Eat the Rich* and *Willow*, along with episodes of TV's *Adam Adamant Lives!, The Avengers, Randall and Hopkirk (Deceased)* and *Blake's 7*. Additionally, Powell did stuntwork in Hammer's *The Quatermass Xperiment* and *Dracula, The Day of the*

Triffids, *Goldfinger*, *Thunderball*, *Casino Royale* (1967), *You Only Live Twice*, *On Her Majesty's Secret Service*, *Diamonds Are Forever*, *Live and Let Die*, *The Man with the Golden Gun*, *Star Wars*, *The Spy Who Loved Me*, *Superman* (1978), *Moonraker*, *Flash Gordon* (1980), *For Your Eyes Only*, *Octopussy* and *A View to a Kill*.

British character actor **Norman Jones** died of a heart attack on April 23, aged eighty. He appeared in fifteen episodes of *Doctor Who* between 1967–76, and his other TV credits include episodes of *Out of This World* (hosted by Boris Karloff), *The Avengers*, *The Champions*, Nigel Kneale's *Beasts* and *The Adventures of Sherlock Holmes*. Jones was also in the films *You Only Live Twice*, *The Mind of Mr. Soames* and *The Abominable Dr. Phibes* (with Vincent Price).

Northern Irish actor **Sean Caffrey**, who appeared in Hammer's *The Viking Queen* and *When Dinosaurs Ruled the Earth*, died on April 25, aged seventy-three. He was also in episodes of TV's *Survivors* (1977), *Doctor Who* and *Galloping Galaxies!*

Actress **Rossella Falk** (Antonia Falzacappa), known as "the Italian Greta Garbo", died in Rome on May 5, aged eighty-six. She appeared in Fellini's *8½*, *Modesty Blaise* (1966), *Run Psycho Run*, *Black Belly of the Tarantula* and *Seven Blood-Stained Orchids*.

British character actor **Aubrey** [Harold] **Woods** died on May 7, aged eighty-five. He appeared in *The Greed of William Hart* (aka *Horror Maniacs*, with Tod Slaughter), *The Queen of Spades* (1949), *Wuthering Heights* (1970), *The Abominable Dr. Phibes* (with Vincent Price), *Willy Wonka & the Chocolate Factory* (1971) and *Z.P.G.*, along with episodes of TV's *Doctor Who* ("Day of the Daleks") and *Blake's 7*. Woods was also a vice-president of the E. F. Benson Society.

American actress **Jeanne Cooper**, the mother of actor Corbin Bernsen, died of chronic obstructive pulmonary disease on May 8, aged eighty-four. Best known for her recurring role in the daytime soap opera *The Young and the Restless* (1973–2013), she also appeared in *Black Zoo* (with

Michael Gough) and *The Boston Strangler*, along with episodes of TV's *Twilight Zone*, *Thriller*, *The Man from U.N.C.L.E.*, *Cimarron Strip* (Harlan Ellison's Jack the Ripper episode "Knife in the Darkness"), *Kolchak: The Night Stalker* and *Touched by Angel*.

American pop psychologist and actress **Dr Joyce Brothers** (Joyce Diane Bauer) died of respiratory failure on May 13, aged eighty-five. She appeared in *More Wild Wild West*, *Embryo*, *Oh God! Book II*, *Love at Stake*, *Spy Hard* and episodes of TV's *Project U.F.O.*, *Hero at Large*, *ALF*, *The Munsters Today* and *Perversions of Science*. In 1955, Brothers became the only woman to win the top prize on the quiz show *The $64,000 Question*. Her subject was "boxing".

Eighty-year-old American actor [Truman] **Linden Chiles** died on May 15 of injuries he sustained after falling off the roof of his home. He was in the movies *The Wizard of Baghdad*, *Shock Treatment*, *Eye of the Cat*, *Forbidden World* and *Doctor Mabuse* (2013), and featured in episodes of TV's *Twilight Zone*, *My Favorite Martian*, *The Munsters*, *The Man from U.N.C.L.E.*, *The Time Tunnel*, *The Green Hornet*, *The Invaders*, *Land of the Giants*, *Shazam!*, *The Six Million Dollar Man*, *The Bionic Woman*, *Logan's Run*, *Buck Rogers in the 25th Century*, *The Incredible Hulk*, *Knight Rider*, *V*, *Alfred Hitchcock Presents* (1985), *Werewolf*, *The New Adventures of Superman* and *Silk Stalkings*.

Hollywood leading man **Steve Forrest** (William Forrest Andrews) died on May 18, aged eighty-seven. One of his earliest film roles was as an uncredited sailor in Val Lewton's *The Ghost Ship* (1943), and he went on to appear in *Phantom of the Rue Morgue*, *The Living Idol*, *Maneaters Are Loose!*, *Captain America* (1979) and *Amazon Women on the Moon*. On TV Forrest starred in such series as *The Baron* (1966–67) and *S.W.A.T.* (1975–76), and he featured in episodes of *Alfred Hitchcock Presents*, *Twilight Zone*, *The Sixth Sense*, *Circle of Fear*, *Rod Serling's Night Gallery*, *The Six Million Dollar Man*, *Fantasy Island* and *Team Knight Rider*. He was the younger brother of actor Dana Andrews.

Prolific British-born character actor **Arthur Malet** (Vivian R. Malet) died in Santa Monica, California, the same day. He was eighty-five. Malet moved to America in the mid-1950s, where he appeared (often playing older than he was) in such films as Disney's *Mary Poppins* and *Bedknobs and Broomsticks*, *Munster Go Home!*, *The Hound of the Baskervilles* (1972), *Young Frankenstein*, *Heaven Can Wait* (1978), *Halloween* (1978), *Oh God! You Devil*, *Dick Tracy* (1990), *Beastmaster 2: Through the Portal of Time*, *The Runestone* and *Hook*. He was also a prolific TV performer, appearing in episodes of *Shirley Temple's Storybook*, *Alfred Hitchcock Presents*, *The Alfred Hitchcock Hour*, *My Favorite Martian*, *Captain Nice*, *Bewitched*, *The Girl from U.N.C.L.E.* ("The Kooky Spook Affair" etc.), *The Man from U.N.C.L.E.*, *The Monkees*, *The Wild Wild West*, *I Dream of Jeannie*, *Night Gallery* and *Wonder Woman*, amongst many others.

French actress **Françoise Blanchard**, who starred in Jean Rollin's *The Living Dead Girl* (*La morte vivante*, 1982), died on May 24, aged fifty-eight. She also appeared in Rollin's *Sidewalks of Bangkok* and *La nuit des horloges*, *Amazons in the Temple of Gold* (co-directed by an uncredited Jesús Franco) and Franco's *Revenge in the House of Usher* (aka *Zombie 5*).

British comedy actor and author **Bill Pertwee** MBE (William Desmond Anthony Pertwee), best known for appearing in the TV series *Dad's Army* (1968–77) and *Carry On* films, died on May 27, aged eighty-six. He also appeared in the 1973 horror movie *Psychomania* (aka *The Death Wheelers*) and episodes of *Worzel Gummidge* and *Woof!* He was the first cousin of actor Jon Pertwee and scriptwriter Michael Pertwee.

American actress **Jean Stapleton** (Jeanne Murray), who starred in the TV sitcom *All in the Family* (1968–79), died on May 31, aged ninety. She also appeared in *Mother Goose Rock 'n' Rhyme*, *Ghost Mum* (aka *Bury Me in Niagara*), and episodes of *Faerie Tale Theatre*, *The Ray Bradbury Theatre* and *Touched by an Angel*. On stage, Stapleton played Abby Brewster in the 1986–87 revival of *Arsenic and Old Lace*.

British-born actress **Kate Woodville** (Katherine Woodville, aka "Catherine Woodville"/"Katharine Woodville") died of cancer in Portland, Oregon, on June 5, aged seventy-five. She starred in the 1960 BBC series of *The Mystery of Edwin Drood* and played the first character to be killed on TV's *The Avengers*, before moving to America and appearing in the TV movie *Fear No Evil* and episodes of *Star Trek*, *Kung Fu*, *Kolchak: The Night Stalker*, *Gemini Man*, *Wonder Woman* and *Salvage 1*. Woodville was married to actors Patrick Macnee from 1965–69 and Edward Albert from 1979 until his death in 2006.

"America's Mermaid", Hollywood swimming star **Esther** [Jane] **Williams**, died on June 6, aged ninety-one. Amongst her movie credits is the 1943 version of *A Guy Named Joe* and she swam with cartoon characters Tom & Jerry in *Dangerous When Wet*. Williams was married to actor Fernando Lamas from 1969 until his death in 1982. She was cremated and her ashes scattered in the Pacific Ocean.

American TV actress **Maxine Stuart** (Maxine Shlivek), who was under the bandages in the classic "Eye of the Beholder" episode of *Twilight Zone*, died the same day, aged ninety-four. She also appeared in episodes of *The Outer Limits* and *Get Smart*, and the 1994 TV movie *The Haunting of Seacliff Inn*. Stuart was featured as the author's sidekick in Helene Hanff's non-fiction books *84 Charing Cross Road* and *Underfoot in Show Business*.

British character actor **Angus MacKay** died on June 8, aged eighty-six. He was in *Morgan: A Suitable Case for Treatment*, *Revenge* (aka *Terror from Under the House*) and *Quest for Love* (based on a story by John Wyndham), plus episodes of *Doomwatch*, *Tales of the Unexpected* and two series of *Doctor Who*.

Hollywood character actor **Harry Lewis** died on June 9, aged ninety-three. His movie credits include *The Body Disappears*, *The Unsuspected*, *Bomba on Panther Island* and *The Astral Factor*. He was also in episodes of *Adventures* *of Superman*, *Alfred Hitchcock Presents* and *The Six Million Dollar Man*. In the late 1940s Lewis opened the Hamburger Hamlet restaurant with his wife Marilyn and it later expanded into a successful chain.

American character actor **Valentin de Vargas** (Albert C. Schubert) died of myelodysplastic syndrome on June 10, aged seventy-eight. He was in *Touch of Evil* (1958) and episodes of TV's *The Alfred Hitchcock Hour* (Ray Bradbury's "The Life Work of Juan Diaz"), *The Wild Wild West*, *The Hardy Boys/Nancy Drew Mysteries* ("The Mystery of King Tut's Tomb"), *Project U.F.O.* and *V*.

American actress **Valerie** [Pamela] **Allen**, who appeared in *I Married a Monster from Outer Space* (1958), died of lung cancer on June 18, aged seventy-seven. Allen was also in *What Ever Happened to Aunt Alice?* and was married to actor Troy Donahue from 1966–68. She retired from the screen at the end of the 1960s and became a soap opera writer and cruise ship social director.

American actor **James** [Joseph] **Gandolfini** [Jr] died of a heart attack while on vacation in Rome on June 19. He was fifty-one. The star of the TV series *The Sopranos* (1999–2007), he made his movie debut in 1987 horror comedy *Shock! Shock! Shock!*, and his other credits include *Crimson Tide*, *Fallen* and *8MM*.

British actress **Diane Clare** (Diane C. O. G. Dirsztay), who starred in Hammer's *The Plague of the Zombies* (1966), died on June 21, aged seventy-four. Although her acting career only spanned a decade, Clare's impressive list of genre credits also includes *The Haunting* (1963), *Witchcraft* (with Lon Chaney, Jr), *The Vulture*, *The Hand of Night* and an episode of TV's *The Avengers*. She was married to author Barry England from 1967 until his death in 2009.

American actor and scriptwriter **Elliott "Ted" Reid** (Edgeworth Blair Reid) died of heart failure the same day, aged ninety-three. He appeared in *A Double Life* (1947), *The Whip Hand*, Disney's *The Absent-Minded Professor*, *Son of Flubber* and *Blackbeard's Ghost*, and *Heaven Can Wait* (1978), along with episodes of TV's *Alfred Hitchcock*

Presents, *The Alfred Hitchcock Hour*, *The Munsters*, *The Wild Wild West* and *Tales of the Unexpected*. Elliott was also a member of Orson Welles' Mercury Theater and a radio performer on such shows as *Suspense*.

Seventy-eight-year-old American voice actor **Jerry Dexter** (Gerald E. Dexter) also died on June 21, of complications from a head injury sustained in a fall at his home. His numerous credits include *Shazzan*, *The Superman/Aquaman Hour of Adventure*, *Aquaman*, *The Adventures of Gulliver*, *Josie and the Pussycats*, *The Funky Phantom*, *The New Scooby-Doo Movies*, *Sealab 2020*, *Josie and the Pussycats in Outer Space*, *Goober and the Ghost Chasers*, *Fangface*, *Scooby-Doo and Scrappy Doo*, *Drak Pack*, *Spider-Man and His Amazing Friends*, *The New Scooby and Scrappy-Doo Show*, *Super Friends* and *Challenge of the GoBots*.

British comedy actress **Pat Ashton** died on June 23, aged eighty-two. She was in *Bloodbath at the House of Death* (with Vincent Price) and an episode of TV's *Metal Mickey*.

Super-cool American martial-arts film star **Jim Kelly** (James Milton Kelly), who starred alongside Bruce Lee in *Enter the Dragon* (1973), died of cancer on June 29, aged sixty-seven. He also appeared in *Golden Needles*, *Death Dimension* and an episode of TV's *Highway to Heaven*. Kelly later became a professional tennis coach.

American actor and singer **Victor Lundin**, who portrayed "Friday" in *Robinson Crusoe on Mars* (1964), died the same day, aged eighty-three. He was also in episodes of TV's *The Time Tunnel*, *Get Smart*, *Star Trek* (as the first Klingon seen on screen), *The Man from U.N.C.L.E.*, *Voyage to the Bottom of the Sea*, *Batman* and *Babylon 5*. Lundin played "Abraham Van Helsing" in the TV movie *Fatal Kiss*, and he also turned up in the horror films *Scarred* and *Revamped*.

Robert "Bob" **Carter**, who portrayed ghoulish TV horror host "Sammy Terry" (get it?) for local Indianapolis station WTTV Channel 4's *Shock Theater* and *Nightmare Theater* during the 1960s and '70s, died on June 30, aged eighty-three. He would appear on the show with his spider sidekick George (voiced by Bob Glaze).

British character actress **Anna Wing** MBE (Anna Eva Lydia Catherine Wing), died on July 7, aged ninety-eight. A regular on the BBC soap opera *EastEnders* in the 1980s, she also appeared in *The Ghost Sonata*, *The Blood on Satan's Claw*, *Full Circle* (aka *The Haunting of Julia*, based on the novel by Peter Straub), *The Hound of the Baskervilles* (1978), *The Godsend*, *Xtro* and *Tooth*, along with episodes of TV's *Doctor Who*, *The Woman in White* (1982), *The Witches and the Grinnygog*, *The Invisible Man* (1984) and *Fungus the Bogeyman*.

Egyptian-born British TV writer and presenter **Alan** [Donald] **Whicker** CBE, died of bronchial pneumonia on Jersey, in the Channel Islands, on July 12. He was eighty-seven. Best known for his jet-setting documentary and travel programmes, he made cameo appearances as himself in *The Magic Christian* and *Whatever Happened to Harold Smith?* In 1957, Whicker attended the World Science Fiction Convention in London to interview fans in costume for the BBC's *Tonight* programme.

Canadian actor **Cory** [Allan Michael] **Monteith**, who starred in the TV series *Kyle XY* and *Glee*, died from an overdose of heroin and alcohol on July 13, aged thirty-one. His body was found in a Vancouver hotel room. Monteith's other credits include *Bloody Mary*, *Final Destination 3*, *Kraken: Tentacles of the Deep*, *Hybrid*, *White Noise: The Light*, *The Invisible*, *Whisper* and episodes of *Stargate: Atlantis*, *Supernatural*, *Smallville*, *Stargate: SG1*, *Flash Gordon* (2007) and *Fear Itself*.

Fifty-six-year-old British actress **Briony McRoberts** committed suicide by jumping in front of a train on July 17. She had been suffering from anorexia. A former child actress (in 1970s sitcom *Bachelor Father*), she appeared in the 1976 TV film *Peter Pan* (as "Wendy"), *The Pink Panther Strikes Again* and *Edge of Sanity*. McRoberts was married to actor David Robb.

British character actor and director **Mel Smith** (Melvyn Kenneth Smith), who co-starred with Griff Rhys Jones in the BBC TV comedy series *Not the Nine O'Clock News* and

Alas Smith & Jones, died of a heart attack on July 19. He was sixty. Smith appeared in a number of films, including *Morons from Outer Space*, *The Princess Bride*, *The Wolves of Willoughby Chase*, *The Riddle* and *My Angel*, and he directed the 1930s whodunnit *Radioland Murders* from a story by George Lucas.

Ceylonese-born British actor **David Spenser** (David De Saram) died in Spain on July 20, aged seventy-nine. A child radio star in the 1940s and '50s, his films include Hammer's *The Stranglers of Bombay*, Disney's *In Search of the Castaways*, *The Earth Dies Screaming* and *Battle Beneath the Earth*. On TV he appeared in *Secret Beneath the Sea* and episodes of *Adam Adamant Lives!* and *Doctor Who* ("The Abominable Snowmen"). Spenser retired from the screen in the early 1970s to become a radio producer and make TV arts documentaries.

Tough-guy American actor **Dennis Farina** died of a pulmonary embolism on July 22, aged sixty-nine. A former Chicago police officer, he appeared in the movie *Manhunter* (based on Thomas Harris' novel *Red Dragon*) and an episode of TV's *Tales from the Crypt* ("Werewolf Concerto").

Scottish-born leading lady **Rona Anderson** died in London on July 23, aged eighty-six. Her film credits include *Scrooge* (1951), *The Black Rider* and *Devils of Darkness*. She was married to actor Gordon Jackson from 1951 until his death in 1990.

French actor, scriptwriter and director **Michel Lemoine** (aka "John Armando"/"Michel Leblanc") died on July 27, aged ninety. He appeared in *Planets Against Us* (aka *Hands of a Killer*), *Hercules Attacks*, *War of the Planets*, Jess Franco's *Succubus*, *Sadist Erotica* and *Kiss Me Monster*, *Castle of the Creeping Flesh*, *Run Psycho Run*, *Seven Women for Satan* (which he also wrote and directed), *Le syndrome d'Edgar Poe* and the 1997 short *Marquis de Slime*.

Oscar-nominated American actress **Eileen Brennan** (Verla Eileen Regina Brennan) died of bladder cancer on July 28, aged eighty. Her many credits include the movies *The Night That Panicked America*, *Murder by Death*,

Pandemonium, Clue, Babes in Toyland (1986), *In Search of Dr. Seuss, Freaky Friday* (1995), *Toothless, Jeepers Creepers* and *The Hollow*, as well as episodes of TV's *The Ghost & Mrs. Muir, McMillan & Wife* ("Night of the Wizard"), *The Ray Bradbury Theatre, Tales from the Crypt, Touched by an Angel* and *The Fearing Mind*. Brennan was hit by a car and critically injured in 1982.

Syrian-born American actor **Michael** [George] **Ansara** died of complications from Alzheimer's disease on July 31, aged ninety-one. His many movies include *Road to Bali, White Witch Doctor, Jupiter's Darling, Abbott and Costello Meet the Mummy, The Ten Commandments* (1956), *Voyage to the Bottom of the Sea, The Destructors, Dear Dead Delilah, The Doll Squad, It's Alive* (1974), *Day of the Animals, The Manitou* (based on the novel by Graham Masterton) and *Johnny Misto: Boy Wizard*. In 1968 he portrayed Klingon commander Kang in the *Star Trek* episode "Day of the Dove", and later recreated the role in both *Star Trek: Deep Space Nine* and *Star Trek: Voyager*. Ansara also appeared in episodes of *Terry and the Pirates, Alfred Hitchcock Presents, The Outer Limits* (Harlan Ellison's "Soldier"), *The Man from U.N.C.L.E., Voyage to the Bottom of the Sea, Lost in Space, The Girl from U.N.C.L.E., Bewitched, The Time Tunnel, Tarzan* (1968), *Land of the Giants, I Dream of Jeannie, Buck Rogers in the 25th Century* (as "Kane"), *Fantasy Island, The Fantastic World of D. C. Collins* and *Babylon 5*. He was the voice of the animated Mister Freeze in *Batman: The Animated Series, The New Adventures of Batman, Batman & Mr. Freeze: SubZero, Batman Beyond: The Movie* and *Batman of the Future*, along with the video game *Batman: Vengeance*. Ansara directed a 1970 episode of *I Dream of Jeannie* starring his second wife, actress Barbara Eden. He was also married to Jean Byron and Beverly Kushida.

American teen model turned actress and TV presenter **Barbara Trentham** died of complications from leukaemia on August 2, aged sixty-eight. In the 1970s she appeared in *The Possession of Joel Delaney, Rollerball* and the TV movie *Deathmoon*, along with an episode of *Star Maidens*. Trentham was married to British comedian John Cleese from 1981–90.

Oscar-nominated Hollywood actress **Karen Black** (Karen Blanche Ziegler) died of ampullary cancer on August 8. She was seventy-four. Her movie credits include *The Pyx*, *Rhinoceros*, *Airport 1975*, *Trilogy of Terror* (scripted by William F. Nolan and based on three stories by Richard Matheson), *The Day of the Locust*, *Burnt Offerings*, Alfred Hitchcock's *Family Plot*, *The Strange Obsession of Mrs. Oliver*, *Capricorn One*, *Killer Fish*, *The Last Horror Film*, *Cut and Run*, *Invaders from Mars* (1986), *It's Alive III: Island of the Alive*, *The Invisible Kid*, *Out of the Dark*, *Zapped Again!*, *Night Angel*, *Haunting Fear*, *Mirror Mirror*, *Evil Spirits*, *Children of the Night*, *Auntie Lee's Meat Pies*, *Plan 10 from Outer Space*, *Children of the Corn: The Gathering*, *Dinosaur Valley Girls*, *Invisible Dad*, *Light Speed*, *Oliver Twisted*, *Soulkeeper*, *Teknolust*, *Curse of the Forty-Niner*, *House of 1000 Corpses*, *Dr. Rage* (aka *Nightmare Hostel*) and *Repo Chick*. On TV Black was in episodes of *The Invaders*, *Circle of Fear*, *Deadly Nightmares*, *Worlds Beyond*, *Faerie Tale Theatre* and *The Hunger*.

Best known for her co-starring role in Russ Meyer's 1965 cult movie *Faster, Pussycat! Kill! Kill!*, Canadian-born **Haji** (Cerlet Catton) died of an apparent heart attack on August 9, aged sixty-seven. A former exotic dancer, her other exploitation film credits include *Motorpsycho!*, *Confessions of a Sexy Supervixen*, *Beyond the Valley of the Dolls*, *Bigfoot* (with John Carradine), *Wham! Bam! Thank You Spaceman!*, *Ilsa Haren Keeper of the Oil Sheiks*, *Demonoid: Messenger of Death*, *The Double-D Avenger* and *Killer Drag Queens on Dope*. She was engaged to actor Frank Gorshin at the time of his death in 2005.

American-born voice actor **Cliff Harrington** died in Japan the same day, aged eighty-one. He served in the US military and was stationed in that country in the early 1960s, where he became involved in the film industry there. He appeared as "Al" in *King Kong vs. Godzilla* before becoming a dubbing artist on such films *Cyborg 009: Legend of the Super Galaxy* and *Space Pirate Captain Harlock: Arcadia of My Youth*.

American model turned actress **Nora Hayden** (Naura Helen Hayden), who starred as "Dr Irish Ryan" in *The Angry Red Planet* (1959), died on August 10, aged eighty-three. She was also an uncredited harem girl in *Son of Sinbad*.

Twenty-nine-year-old model **Gia** [Marie] **Allemand**, who found "fame" as a contestant on reality TV shows *The Bachelor* and *Bachelor Pad*, was declared brain-dead on August 14 and removed from life support in a New Orleans hospital after attempting to hang herself two days earlier. As an actress, she appeared in the shorts *Ghost Trek: The Kinsey Report* and *Ghost Trek: Goomba Body Snatchers Mortuary Lockdown*.

British stuntman **Mark Sutton**, who was the James Bond stunt double during the opening ceremonies of the 2012 Olympic Games in London, was killed the same day when a wing-diving stunt from a helicopter went wrong. He was forty-two.

Forty-three-year-old American actress **Lisa Robin Kelly** died of a drug overdose on August 15, after checking herself into a Californian rehab facility for alcohol addiction. She appeared in *Amityville: Dollhouse* and *The Survivor* (1998), along with episodes of *Silk Stalkings*, *The X Files*, *Poltergeist: The Legacy*, *Fantasy Island* (1998) and *Charmed*.

Canadian character actor **August** [Werner] **Schellenberg** died of lung cancer in Dallas, Texas, the same day, aged seventy-seven. Among his movie credits are *DreamKeeper* and *Tremors 4: The Legend Begins*. Schellenberg also appeared in episodes of TV's *The New Avengers*, *The Hitchhiker* (aka *Deadly Nightmares*), *Friday the 13th: The Series* (aka *Friday's Curse*), *So Weird*, *Mysterious Ways* and *SGU Stargate Universe*.

American actor **Lee Thompson Young**, a regular on the 2009–10 ABC-TV series *FlashForward*, committed suicide by a self-inflicted gunshot on August 19, aged twenty-nine. A coroner's report confirmed he was suffering from bipolar disorder and depression. Young also appeared in *The Hills*

Have Eyes II (2007) and episodes of *Jake 2.0*, *Terminator: The Sarah Connor Chronicles* and *Smallville*.

Oscar-nominated and five-time Tony Award-winning American actress **Julie** [Anne] **Harris** died of congestive heart failure on August 24. She was eighty-seven. Her movies include *The Haunting* (1963), *Hamlet* (1964), *How Awful About Allan*, *Home for the Holidays* and *The Dark Half* (based on the novel by Stephen King). She was also in episodes of TV's *Tarzan*, *Journey to the Unknown* (Robert Bloch's "The Indian Spirit Guide"), *The Evil Touch*, *Tales of the Unexpected* and *The Outer Limits* (1998). In 1955 Harris co-starred with Boris Karloff in the acclaimed Broadway stage production of *The Lark*.

American baseball player turned actor **Larry Pennell** died on August 28, aged eighty-five. He began his career in the mid-1950s, and his movie credits include *The Space Children*, *City Beneath the Sea* (aka *One Hour to Doomsday*), *Superstition*, *Metalstorm: The Destruction of Jared-Syn*, *Ghost Chase*, *The Borrower*, *Prehysteria! 2*, *The Fear: Resurrection* and Joe R. Lansdale's *Bubba Ho-Tep*. Pennell also appeared in episodes of TV's *Thriller*, *The Outer Limits*, *Land of the Giants*, *Salvage 1*, *Quantum Leap* (as "Clark Gable"), *Silk Stalkings* and *Firefly*.

Radio and television disc jocky **David** [Lewis] **Jacobs** CBE died of Parkinson's disease and liver cancer on September 2, aged eighty-seven. Best known for hosting the long-running BBC TV quiz show *Juke Box Jury* (1959–67), he began his career as an actor, starring in the 1953–54 radio drama *Journey Into Space* (aka *Jouney to the Moon/Operation Luna*, in which Jacobs reportedly played twenty-two different roles). It was followed by the sequels *The Red Planet* and *The World in Peril*, which both featured Jacobs as Frank Morgan and various miscellaneous characters. For a 2008 remake of the original show on Radio 4 he finally portrayed the lead role of "Captain Jet Morgan", and he also voiced the title character for a 2009 revival entitled *The Host*. As himself, Jacobs had a cameo in the early Amicus film *It's Trad, Dad!* and he narrated the documentary short *Haunted England*.

American actor **Dante DiPaolo** (aka "Dane D'Paulo") died on September 3, aged eighty-seven. In the early 1960s he worked in Italy on such films as *Atlas in the Land of the Cyclops* (aka *Monster from the Unknown World*), Riccardo Freda's *Samson and the Seven Miracles* (aka *Maciste at the Court of the Great Khan*), *The Son of Hercules vs. Venus*, and Mario Bava's *The Evil Eye* (aka *The Girl Who Knew Too Much*) and *Blood and Black Lace*. DiPaolo was also in an episode of TV's *The Wild Wild West* ("The Night of the Screaming Terror"). He was married to singer Rosemary Clooney from 1997 until her death in 2002.

British character actress **Barbara** [Purser] **Hicks** died on September 6, aged eighty-nine. She was in *Memoirs of a Survivor* (based on the novel by Doris Lessing), *Britannia Hospital*, *Morons from Outer Space*, *Brazil*, *The Witches* (1990), *Orlando*, *FairyTale: A True Story* and episodes of TV's *The Return of the Borrowers* and *The Memoirs of Sherlock Holmes*.

British actor **Bill Wallis**, who played "Mr Prosser" and "Prostetnic Vogon Jeltz" in the original radio production of *The Hitchhiker's Guide to the Galaxy*, died the same day, aged seventy-six. For the last fifteen years of his life he had suffered from multiple myeloma. Wallis also appeared in *The Bed Sitting Room*, *Brazil* and *The Canterville Ghost* (1986), along with episodes of TV's *The Avengers* ("A Touch of Brimstone" etc.), *The Rivals of Sherlock Holmes*, *The Box of Delights*, *Robin of Sherwood*, *The Silver Chair* and *The Young Indiana Jones Chronicles*.

Low-budget leading lady **Louise Currie** died on September 8, aged 100. She was the best thing in 1940s Monogram and PRC movies, playing a wisecracking heroine in *The Ape Man* and *Voodoo Man* (both starring Bela Lugosi), and the Charlie Chan mystery *The Chinese Ring*. She was also in *You'll Find Out*, *The Green Hornet Strikes Again!*, *Adventures of Captain Marvel*, *The Masked Marvel* and *Citizen Kane* (she was reportedly the last surviving cast member), before retiring from the screen in the mid-1950s to become a decorator with her architect husband, former actor John Good. Currie was also briefly married to actor John Whitney in the 1940s. She later appeared in the 1997 documentary *Lugosi: Hollywood's Dracula*.

Former teenage model turned actress **Patricia Blair** (Patsy Lou Blake), who starred opposite the cream of Hollywood horror stars in *The Black Sleep* (aka *Dr. Cadman's Secret*, 1956), died of breast cancer on September 9, aged eighty. She was a regular on the TV series *Daniel Boone* from 1964–70.

Argentinian-born fashion model turned actress **Lyn Peters** (Evelyn Anne Peters), who starred in *Grave of the Vampire* (1972), died in Palm Springs on September 10, aged seventy-two. She also had small roles in *In Like Flint* and the TV movie *Fear No Evil* (based on a story by Guy Endore), along with episodes of *The Girl from U.N.C.L.E.*, *The Man from U.N.C.L.E.*, *Batman* and *Get Smart*. Peters was married to actor Paul Burke until his death in 2009, and after retiring from the screen she became a successful "caterer to the stars", with clients including Bob Hope and Frank Sinatra.

Jerry G. Bishop (Jairus Samuel Ghan), who from 1970–73 was better known as American TV horror host "Svengoolie" on Chicago's WFLD-TV's "Screaming Yellow Theater", died of a heart attack on September 15, aged seventy-seven.

American actress **Kim Hamilton** (Dorothy Mae Aiken) died on September 16, aged eighty-one. She appeared in *The Leech Woman* and *The Wizard of Baghdad*, along with episodes of TV's *Twilight Zone*, *Alfred Hitchcock Presents*, *Future Cop*, *Project U.F.O.*, *Buck Rogers in the 25th Century* and *Star Trek: The Next Generation*. Hamilton was married to actor Werner Klemperer from 1997 until his death in 2000.

American character actor **Jay Robinson**, best known for his distinctive voice, died of congestive heart failure on September 27, aged eighty-three. After making his movie debut as a scene-chewing Caligula in *The Robe* (1953), his acting career was soon derailed when he was arrested for possession of narcotics (methadone) in 1958. Although a one-year sentence was later overturned, he was later jailed for fifteen months after an old warrant was served on him.

Robinson resumed his acting career in the mid-1960s and went on to appear in *Everything You Always Wanted to Know About Sex* *But Were Afraid to Ask*, *Train Ride to Hollywood* (as "Dracula"), *The Bay City Rollers Meet the Saturday Superstars* (as Dracula again), *The Sword and the Sorcerer*, *Big Top Pee-wee*, *Transylvania Twist*, *Dracula* (1992), *Ghost Ship* (1992) and *Skeeter*. He was also in episodes of TV's *The Wild Wild West*, *Star Trek*, *Bewitched*, *Search Control*, *Planet of the Apes*, *Kolchak: The Night Stalker*, *Dr. Shrinker*, *The Bay City Rollers Show*, *Buck Rogers in the 25th Century* and *Voyagers!* In 1997 Robinson hosted the Discovery Channel series *Beyond Bizarre*.

Canadian-born dubbing artist, sound engineer and occasional actor **Ted Rusoff** died in a Rome hospital on September 28, after being hit by a car more than a month earlier. He was seventy-four. The son of film producer Lou Rusoff and the nephew of Samuel Z. Arkoff, his voice can be heard in the English versions of such (mostly Italian) films as *Yongary, Monster from the Deep*, *Destroy All Monsters*, *Buried Alive* (aka *Beyond the Darkness*), *Nightmare City*, *Cannibal Ferox*, *The House by the Cemetery*, *Absurd*, *Piranah II: Flying Killers* (aka *Piranha Part Two: The Spawning*), *Women's Prison Massacre*, *The Final Executioner*, *Rats: Night of Terror*, *Cut and Run*, *Hands of Steel* and *Cyborg – Il guerriero d'acciaio*, along with the animated TV series *Johnny Sokko and His Flying Robot*. Rusoff also had small (often uncredited) roles in *Catacombs*, *Sinbad of the Seven Seas*, *The Eighteenth Angel*, *Nightworld: Lost Souls* and *Eternal*. He was married to veteran voice dubber Carolyn De Fonseca until her death in 2009.

Seventy-five-year-old Italian leading man and sculptor **Giuliano Gemma** (aka "Montgomery Wood") was killed in a car accident near Rome on October 1. A former stuntman in films such as *Ben-Hur* (1959), he appeared in Antonio Margheriti's *Battle of the Worlds* (with Claude Rains), *Goliath and the Sins of Babylon*, *Hercules Against the Sons of the Sun*, *When Women Had Tales*, Dario Argento's *Tenebrae*, and *Tex and the Lord of the Deep*.

American character actress **Virginia Vincent** [Grohosky] died on October 3, aged ninety-five. She appeared in *The Return of Dracula* (aka *The Fantastic Disappearing Man*), *Night Slaves*, *The Baby* and Wes Craven's *The Hills Have Eyes* (1977) and *Invitation to Hell*, along with episodes of TV's *Tales of Tomorrow*, *The Alfred Hitchcock Hour* and *Kolchak: The Night Stalker*.

Tony Award-winning British stage and screen actor **Paul Rogers** died on October 6, aged ninety-six. Best known for his Shakespearean roles, he appeared in the films *Svengali* (1954) and *A Midsummer Night's Dream* (1968), along with a two-part production of *Dr. Faustus* on TV in 1960.

Seventy-nine-year-old British actor and musician **Noel Harrison**, the son of actor Rex Harrison, died of a heart attack after performing in Devon on October 13. He had been suffering from kidney disease. A former Olympic skier, for one season he co-starred as secret agent "Mark Slate" in NBC-TV's *The Girl from U.N.C.L.E.*, and he was also in the movie *Where the Spies Are* and episodes of *The Evil Touch* and *Alfred Hitchcock Presents* (1989). In 1969 Harrison had a UK Top 10 hit with the song "The Windmills of Your Mind", written by Michel Legrand.

Dependable American character actor **Ed Lauter** (Edward Matthew Lauter II) died of mesothelioma on October 16, age seventy-four. Often cast as authority figures, his movie credits include *Satan's Triangle*, Alfred Hitchcock's *Family Plot*, *King Kong* (1976), *The White Buffalo*, *The Clone Master*, *Magic*, *Timerider: The Adventures of Lyle Swann*, *Cujo*, *Rocketeer*, *Digital Man*, *Rattled*, *Under Wraps*, *Python*, *Starship Troopers II: Hero of the Federation*, *The Lost* (based on the novel by Jack Ketchum), *The Frankenstein Syndrome* (aka *The Prometheus Project*) and *The Town That Dreaded Sundown* (2014). A regular on the Stephen King mini-series *Golden Years*, Lauter was also in episodes of *Manimal*, *Automan*, *Monsters*, *Star Trek: The Next Generation*, *The X Files*, *Highlander*, *Millennium* and *Charmed*.

Western actor **Jon Locke** (Joseph Lockey Yon), who portrayed the Sleestack Leader in TV's *Land of the Lost* (1976), died of complications from a stroke on October 19, aged eighty-six. He also portrayed the Abominable Snowman in the same show and appeared in an episode *of The Bionic Woman* and the movies *Years of the Beast* and *Transylvanian Twist*.

Australian-born actor **Bruce Beeby,** who portrayed "Mitch Mitchell" in the BBC radio series *Journey Into Space* and *The Red Planet*, died in England on October 20, aged ninety-one. On TV he appeared in *Stranger from Space, Out of This World, The Champions, Randall and Hopkirk (Deceased)* and *Timeslip*. Beeby was also in Hammer's *The Devil-Ship Pirates* and the 1970 version of *Wuthering Heights*.

Actress and dancer **Larri Thomas** (Lida L. Thomas) died of complications from a fall at her home the same day, aged eighty-one. She made uncredited appearances (often as a dancer) in *Road to Bali, House of Wax, Here Come the Girls, Mary Poppins* and *The Silencers*, and she was also in *Curucu Beast of the Amazon* and *Earth Girls Are Easy*. Thomas was married to actors John Bromfield from 1955–59 and Bruce Hoy from 1963.

Stylish British actor [Arthur] **Nigel Davenport** died on October 25, aged eighty-five. He appeared in the films *Peeping Tom* (uncredited), *Where the Spies Are, The Mind of Mr. Soames, No Blade of Grass, The Picture of Dorian Gray* (1973), Richard Matheson's version of *Dracula* (as "Van Helsing"), *Phase IV, The Island of Dr. Moreau* (1977), *A Midsummer Night's Dream* (1981), *Greystoke: The Legend of Tarzan Lord of the Apes* and *A Christmas Carol* (1984), along with episodes of TV's *The Avengers* and *Woof!* His second wife was actress Maria Aitken from 1972 until their divorce in 1980.

Emmy Award-winning comedy actress and voice artist **Marcia** [Karen] **Wallace,** who voiced "Edna Krabappel" on Fox TV's *The Simpsons*, died the same day, aged seventy. She also appeared in episodes of *Bewitched, Fantasy Island, ALF, What a Dummy, The Munsters Today, Teen Angel* and *Vampire Mob*, and was in the movies *Teen Witch*, *My Mum's a Werewolf* and *Ghoulies III: Ghoulies Go to College*.

British character actor and photographer **Graham [William] Stark**, best remembered for his various roles alongside his friend Peter Sellers in several *Pink Panther* films, died of a stroke on October 29, aged ninety-one. He appeared with the Goons in *Down Among the Z Men*, and his other credits include *The Mouse on the Moon*, *Casino Royale* (1967), *Jules Verne's Rocket to the Moon* (aka *Those Fantastic Flying Fools*), *A Ghost of a Chance*, *The Magic Christian*, *The Picasso Summer* (based on a story by Ray Bradbury), *Cosmo and Thingy*, *Gulliver's Travels* (1977), *Hawk the Slayer*, *Superman III*, *Bloodbath at the House of Death* (with Vincent Price) and *Jane and the Lost City*. Stark was also in episodes of TV's *One Step Beyond*, *Out of the Unknown*, *Moonacre* and *The Incredible Adventures of Marco Polo and His Journeys to the Ends of the Earth*. In 1963 he appeared on the London stage in Spike Milligan and John Antrobus' absurdist SF play *The Bed-Sitting Room*, and in 2003 he published his autobiography, *Stark Naked*.

American character actor **Paul Mantee** (Paul Marianetti), who had a rare starring role in *Robinson Crusoe on Mars* (1964) opposite Victor Lundin (who died earlier in the year), died of non-Hodgkin's lymphoma on November 7, aged eighty-two. His other movie credits include *Helter Skelter* (1976), *Day of the Animals*, *The Manitou* (based on the novel by Graham Masterton), *Death Ray 2000* and *Lurking Fear* (based on the story by H.P. Lovecraft). Mantee was also very busy on TV, appearing in episodes of *Batman*, *The Time Tunnel*, *The Invaders*, *Voyage to the Bottom of the Sea*, *Search Control*, *Gemini Man*, *The Six Million Dollar Man*, *The Fantastic Journey*, *Logan's Run* and *Buck Rogers in the 25th Century*.

Veteran American character actress **Shirley Mitchell** died of heart failure on November 11, aged ninety-four. She appeared in episodes of *The Veil* (hosted by Boris Karloff),

Shirley Temple's Storybook, *Mister Ed* and *The Smothers Brothers Show* ("The Girl from R.A.L.P.H."), along with the movie's *My Blood Runs Cold* (1965) and *Summer Camp Nightmare*. Mitchell was married to composer and lyricist Jay Livingston until his death in 2001.

Busy American TV character actor **Al Ruscio** died on November 12, aged eighty-nine. Often cast as "heavies", he appeared in episodes of *Thriller* (1961), *The Alfred Hitchcock Hour*, *Voyage to the Bottom of the Sea*, *The Six Million Dollar Man*, *The Invisible Man* (1975), *The Incredible Hulk*, *Salvage 1*, *Fantasy Island*, *Highway to Heaven*, *Amazing Stories*, *The Wizard*, *Outlaws*, *Starman* and *The X Files*. Ruscio was also in the 1991 SF film *Future Kick*, *The Silence of the Hams*, *Xtro 3: Watch the Skies* and *The Phantom* (1996). His wife of fifty-nine years, actress Kate Williamson, died less than a month after him.

American actress **Barbara Lawrence** (Barbara Jo Lawrence), who starred opposite Jeff Morrow in the 1957 SF movie *Kronos*, died of kidney failure on November 13, aged eighty-three. She retired from acting in 1962 to sell real estate.

American actress **Sheila Allen** (Sheila Marie Mathews), who was married to producer/director Irwin Allen from 1975–91 and appeared in a number of his productions, died of pulmonary fibrosis on November 15, aged eighty-four. Allen appeared in the movies *Five Weeks in a Balloon* (uncredited), *City Beneath the Sea* (aka *One Hour to Doomsday*), *The Poseidon Adventure* (1972), *The Towering Inferno*, *When Time Ran Out . . .* and *Alice in Wonderland* (1985), as well as episodes of TV's *Voyage to the Bottom of the Sea*, *Lost in Space* and *Land of the Giants*. She is also credited as a producer on the documentaries *The Fantasy Worlds of Irwin Allen* and *Lost in Space Forever*, the 2006 remake *Poseidon*, and an unaired 2006 TV pilot for a reboot of *The Time Tunnel*.

American character actor **Mickey Knox** (Abraham Knox), the former brother-in-law of Norman Mailer, died the same day, aged ninety-one. After being blacklisted for his left-wing politics, he moved to Italy in the 1950s. Knox appeared (sometimes uncredited) in *The Tenth Victim*, *Stagefright*, *Vampire in Venice*, *Ghoulies II*, *Ghosts Can't Do It*, *Frankenstein Unbound* and *Cemetery Man*, along with episodes of *Adventures of Superman* and *The X Files*. He worked on the scripts of the English-language versions of Sergio Leone's *The Good, the Bad and the Ugly* and *Once Upon a Time in the West*, and Woody Harrelson's character in *Natural Born Killers* is named after him.

American actor **Kirk Scott** died of cancer on November 16, aged seventy-seven. He began his career with a small role in *Targets* (1968) starring Boris Karloff, and he went on to appear in *Cinderella* (aka *The Other Cinderella*), *End of the World* (with Christopher Lee), *Starflight One* and on episodes of TV's *V* and *Quantum Leap*.

American jazz drummer **Foreststorm "Chico" Hamilton** died on November 25, aged ninety-two. He began touring with bands in the 1940s, and he not only composed and recorded the soundtrack music for the 1950s *Gerald McBoing-Boing* cartoons, but in 1965 he also composed and conducted the music for Roman Polanski's *Repulsion*.

American actor **Tony Musante** (Anthony Peter Musante, Jr), who starred in Dario Argento's *The Bird with the Crystal Plumage*, died of complications following surgery on November 26. He was seventy-seven. Musante was also in an episode of TV's *The Alfred Hitchcock Hour*.

British leading man **Lewis Collins**, best known for playing tough-guy "Bodie" in TV's *The Professionals* (1977–83), died in Los Angeles after a five-year battle against cancer on November 27. He was sixty-seven. His other credits include episodes of *The New Avengers*, *Robin of Sherwood*, *Jack the Ripper* (1988), *Alfred Hitchcock Presents* (1989) and the 1990s French/Canadian *Tarzán*.

British leading lady **Jean Kent** (Joan Mildred Summerfield) died on November 30, aged ninety-two. She began her film career in the mid-1930s, and her credits include *The Haunter Strangler* (aka *Grip of the Strangler*, with Boris Karloff), *Bluebeard's Ten Honeymoons* and an episode of TV's *Thriller* (1974).

American leading man **Paul Walker** (Paul William Walker IV), the star of the successful *The Fast and the Furious* franchise, was killed the same day when the speeding car he was a passenger in crashed into a light pole and burst into flames in Valencia, California. He was forty. Walker made his movie debut in 1986 in *Monster in the Closet* (with John Carradine), and he also appeared in *Programmed to Kill*, *Tammy and the T-Rex*, *Pleasantville*, *The Skulls*, *Roadkill*, *Timeline* and *Brick Mansions*, along with episodes of TV's *Highway to Heaven*, *What a Dummy* and *Touched by an Angel*.

British character actor **Barry Jackson** (aka "Jack Berry") who played "Dr Bullard" in TV's *Midsomer Murders*, died on December 5, aged seventy-five. He was the fight arranger for *Adam Adamant Lives!* (1966), and his other credits include episodes of *A for Andromeda*, *Doctor Who*, *Doomwatch*, *The Frightners*, *Orson Welles' Great Mysteries*, *The New Avengers*, *Blake's 7* and *Into the Labyrinth*.

Eighty-two-year-old American character actress **Kate Williamson** (Robina Jane Sparks) died just twenty-four days after her husband, actor Al Ruscio, on December 6. She appeared in episodes of TV's *Tabitha*, *Darkroom*, *Highway to Heaven*, *Something is Out There* and *Beauty and the Beast* (1989).

Classy Hollywood leading lady **Eleanor** [Jean] **Parker** died of complications from pneumonia on December 9, aged ninety-one. She made her movie debut in the early 1940s and her credits include *The Mysterious Doctor*, *Between Two Worlds*, *The Woman in White* (1948, based on the novel by Wilkie Collins), *The Naked Jungle*, *Eye of the Cat*, *Home for the Holidays* and *Once Upon a Spy* (with Christopher Lee), along with episodes of TV's *The Man from U.N.C.L.E.*, *Circle of Fear* and *Fantasy Island*.

Libyan-born Italian *femme fatale* **Rossana Podestà** (Carla Podestà) died on December 10, aged seventy-nine. Her film credits include *Ulysses* (1954), *The Golden Arrow*, *Horror Castle* (aka *The Castle of Terror*, with Christopher Lee), *Seven Golden Men*, *Seven Golden Men Strike Again!* and *Hercules* (1983).

Hollywood *noir* actress **Audrey** [Mary] **Totter** died of congestive heart failure on December 12, aged ninety-five. After supplying the voice of the evil "Karen" personality in Arch Oboler's *Bewitched* (1945), she went on to appear in *The Unsuspected* (with Claude Rains) and episodes of TV's *Science Fiction Theatre*, *Alfred Hitchcock Presents* and *Matt Helm*.

Hellraising Irish-born actor **Peter** [Seamus] **O'Toole** died after a long illness in London on December 14. He was eighty-one. Best known for his starring role in *Lawrence of Arabia* (1962), he was also in *The Night of the Generals*, *Casino Royale* (1967), *The Ruling Class*, *Svengali* (1983), *Supergirl*, *Creator*, *High Spirits*, Alejandro Jodorowsky's *The Rainbow Thief* (with Christopher Lee), *Gulliver's Travels* (1996), *FairyTale: A True Story* (as "Sir Arthur Conan Doyle"), *Phantoms* (based on the novel by Dean R. Koontz), *Stardust* (based on the comic by Neil Gaiman), *Eager to Die* and *Eldorado* (aka *Highway to Hell*). In 1983 the actor also voiced Sherlock Holmes in four animated adventures for children: *Sherlock Holmes and the Valley of Fear*, *Sherlock Holmes and the Sign of Four*, *Sherlock Holmes and the Baskerville Curse* and *Sherlock Holmes and a Study in Scarlet*. On TV, O'Toole appeared in an episode of *The Ray Bradbury Theatre* ("Banshee") and the 1989 mini-series *The Dark Angel* (based on J. Sheridan Le Fanu's *Uncle Silas*).

Japanese-born Hollywood star **Joan Fontaine** (Joan de Beauvoir de Havilland), the estranged younger sister of actress Olivia de Havilland, died in her sleep in Carmel, California, on December 15, aged ninety-six. The Oscar-winning actress made her movie debut in the mid-1930s, and her credits include Hitchcock's *Rebecca* (based on the novel by Daphne Du Maurier), *Jane Eyre* (with Orson Welles), *Voyage to the Bottom of the Sea*, Hammer's *The Witches* (aka *The Devil's Own*) and *Dark Mansions*. On TV, she appeared in episodes of TV's *One Step Beyond* and *The Alfred Hitchcock Hour*. Fontaine's four husbands included actor Brian Aherne, producer William Dozier, and writer-producer Collier Young.

Don Mitchell (Donald Michael Mitchell), who co-starred as "Mark Sanger" in NBC-TV's *Ironside* (1967–75), died the same day, aged seventy. He was also in *Scream Blacula Scream* and episodes of *I Dream of Jeannie*, *Bewitched*, *Tarzan* (1967) and *Wonder Woman*.

American actor and exploitation director **Roger Gentry** (James Edgar Rodgers, aka "Jim Gentry"/"Tim Sommers") died on December 16, aged seventy-nine. He appeared in *The Wizard of Mars* (aka *Horrors of the Red Planet*), *Gallery of Horror* (with John Carradine and Lon Chaney, Jr), *Alice in Acidland*, *The Thing with Two Heads*, *The Love Butcher* and *Death Magic*.

Busy American character actor **Joseph Ruskin** (Joseph Richard Schlafman) died on December 28, aged eighty-nine. He appeared in *Dr. Scorpion*, *Captain America* (1979), *The Munster's Revenge*, *The Sword and the Sorcerer*, *Saturday the 14th Strikes Back*, *Cyber Tracker*, *Star Trek: Insurrection*, *King Cobra*, *Wishcraft* and *The Scorpion King*. He was also the voice of "The Horla" in the 1963 Vincent Price movie *Diary of a Madman*. On TV, Ruskin appeared in episodes of *Alfred Hitchcock Presents* (1958 and 1986), *Twilight Zone* ("To Serve Man"), *The Alfred Hitchcock Hour*, *Mister Ed*, *The Outer Limits*, *Voyage to the Bottom of the Sea*, *Get Smart*, *The Time Tunnel*, *The Wild Wild West*, *The Man from U.N.C.L.E.*, *Land of the Giants*, *Rod Serling's Night Gallery*, *Planet of the Apes*, *The Six Million Dollar Man*, *The Bionic Woman*, *Starsky and Hutch* ("Satan's Witches"), *Wonder Woman*, *Project U.F.O.*, *Knight Rider*, *The Wizard*, *Max Headroom*, *Beyond Belief: Fact or Fiction* and *Alias*. He was reportedly the only actor to have appeared in the original *Star Trek* series and three out of the four spin-offs: *Star Trek: Deep Space Nine*, *Star Trek: Voyager* and *Star Trek: Enterprise*.

British comedy actor **John Fortune** (John C. Wood), who appeared in *Bloodbath at the House of Death* (with Vincent Price), died of leukaemia on December 31, aged seventy-nine. He was also in episodes of TV's *Shades of Darkness* ("The Demon Lover" by Elizabeth Bowen) and *Spine Chillers*.

American character actor **James** [La Rue] **Avery**, best known for his role as "Philip Banks" in TV's *The Fresh Prince of Bel-Air* (1990–96), died of complications from open-heart surgery the same day. He was sixty-eight. He was also in episodes of *Amazing Stories, Beauty and the Beast, The Legend of Tarzan, Charmed, Star Trek: Enterprise* and *Eli Stone*, along with the movies *Appointment with Fear, The Eleventh Commandment, Timestalkers, Nightflyers* (based on the novel by George R. R. Martin), *Body Count, Beastmaster 2: Through the Portal of Time, Spirit Lost, Dr. Dolittle 2, Epoch* and *The Third Wish*. Avery was also the Narrator for the R. L. Stine series *The Nightmare Room* (2001–02) and a prolific voice actor on TV cartoon shows, notably playing "Shredder" in *Teenage Mutant Ninja Turtles* (1987–93).

Ninety-year-old Chinese-born actress **Lidiya Vertinskaya** (Lidiya Vladimirovna Tsirgvava) died in Russia on December 31. She appeared as "The Phoenix" in *Sadko* (aka *The Magic Voyage of Sinbad*, 1953).

FILM/TV TECHNICIANS

Former American child actor turned stuntman and director **David R.** [Richard] **Ellis** died in Johannesburg, South Africa, on January 7. He was sixty. Ellis began his movie career in the 1975 Disney film *The Strongest Man in the World*, and he also appeared in *Nightbeast* (1982) and an episode of TV's *Wonder Woman*. Switching to stunts, he worked on *Deathsport, Invasion of the Body Snatchers* (1978), *Megaforce, The Beastmaster, V* and *V: The Final Battle, The Wraith, Remo Williams: The Prophecy, Warlock, Star Trek: The Final Frontier, Phantom of the Mall: Eric's Revenge, Ghost Dad, Misery, The Addams Family* (1991), *Sliver, Warlock: The Armageddon* and the 1994 version of *The Jungle Book*. Ellis also began a career as a second unit director on such films as *Warlock, Sliver, The Jungle Book, Waterworld, Sphere, Soldier, Deep Blue Sea, Just Visiting, Harry Potter and the Philosopher's Stone, The Matrix*

Reloaded, *R.I.P.D.* and *47 Ronin*. His own credits as a director include *Final Destination 2*, *Snakes on a Plane*, *Asylum* (2008), *The Final Destination* and *Shark Night 3D*.

British director and *bon viveur* **Michael** [Robert] **Winner** died on January 21, aged seventy-seven. Best known for his series of reactionary *Death Wish* movies during the 1970s and '80s, he also directed the 1961 documentary short *Haunted England* and the films *The Nightcomers* (a prequel to Henry James' *Turn of the Screw*), *The Sentinel* (with John Carradine) and *Scream for Help*. Winner made a cameo appearance in John Landis' 2010 horror/comedy *Burke and Hare*.

Oscar-winning South African-born Hollywood producer **Lloyd** [B.] **Phillips** died of a heart attack in Los Angeles on January 25. He was sixty-three, and his credits include *Battletruck*, *Twelve Monkeys* and *Man of Steel*.

Polish-born engineer and physicist **Stefan Kudelski** died on January 26, aged eighty-three. Fleeing from the Nazis to Switzerland in the 1940s, he invented the first portable audio tape recorder and, by the early 1950s, his "Nagra" tape recorder was introduced to TV and radio stations. In 1958, Kudelsi worked out how to synchronize his audio recordings to film, thus allowing moviemakers to capture better sound outside the studio. He won three Academy Awards, two Emmy Awards and the Academy of Motion Picture Arts and Sciences' Gordon E. Sawyer Award for his Science and Technical contributions to the film industry.

Stage dancer/actor turned Hollywood set decorator **Garrett Lewis** died on January 29, aged seventy-seven. His credits include *The Star Wars Holiday Special* (1978), *Short Circuit*, *The Monster Squad*, *Misery*, *Hook*, *Dracula* (1992), *The Shadow*, *Face/Off* and *Bedazzled* (2000).

Veteran British make-up artist **Stuart** [W.] **Freeborn** died on February 5, aged ninety-eight. After working uncredited on such productions as *The Thief of Bagdad* (1940), *Green for Danger* and *Oliver Twist* (1948), his other films include *The Hands of Orlac* (1960, with Christopher Lee), *Tarzan Goes to India*, *Dr. Strangelove or: How I Learned to Stop*

Worrying and Love the Bomb, *Seance on a Wet Afternoon*, *2001: A Space Odyssey*, *Toomorrow*, *10 Rillington Place*, *Blind Terror*, *The Fiend* (aka *Beware My Brethren*), *Alice's Adventures in Wonderland* (1972), *The Adventure of Sherlock Holmes' Smarter Brother*, *The Omen* (1976), *Spectre*, *Superman* (1978), *Superman II*, *The Great Muppet Caper*, *Superman III*, *Santa Claus* (1985), *Haunted Honeymoon* and *Superman IV: The Quest for Peace*. Freeborn is perhaps best known for supervising the make-up effects on *Star Wars* (1977) and its sequels, *The Empire Strikes Back* and *Return of the Jedi*, yet he was never nominated for an Academy Award.

British cinematographer **Les Young** died on February 9, aged sixty-six. He started out as a camera operator on such films as *The Oblong Box*, *Scream and Scream Again* and *Cry of the Banshee* (all starring Vincent Price) before moving on to shoot and produce *Satan's Slave* (starring Michael Gough) and *Terror* (which he also wrote the original story for). Young was also lighting cameraman on one episode of TV's *Tales of the Unexpected*.

Petro Vlahos, who received an Academy Award in 1995 for his pioneering blue-screen compositing process, died on February 10, aged ninety-six. Vlahos also received four other Oscars for technical and engineering achievement, and he was credited as "Technical Advisor" on the 1980 SF movie *Battle Beyond the Stars*.

Raymond [Patrick] **Cusick**, the original production designer on BBC TV's *Doctor Who* from 1963–66, died of heart failure on February 21, aged eighty-five. Not only did he famously help create the first versions of the Daleks, but he also worked on episodes of *Out of the Unknown* and *Rentaghost*, and a 1983 TV movie of Edgar Wallace's *The Case of the Frightened Lady*.

American screenwriter/producer/director **Del** (Delbert) **Tenney**, best remembered for his 1964 drive-in double-bill of *The Horror of Party Beach* and *The Curse of the Living Corpse*, died the same day, aged eighty-two. A former movie extra (*The Wild One*), Tenney's other credits include *I Want* to *Eat Your Skin, Do You Wanna Know a Secret* and the Edgar Allan Poe-inspired *Descendant* (co-directed with Kermit Christman).

Australian-born animator **Bob Godfrey** (Roland Frederick Godfrey) also died on February 21, aged ninety-two. The Oscar-winner created the children's TV series *Roobarb* and *Henry's Cat*, along with such acclaimed short films as *Kama Sutra Rides Again*.

Former silent-movie child actor **Micky Moore** (Dennis Michael Sheffield, aka "Michael D. Moore") died of congestive heart failure on March 4, aged ninety-eight. After being mentored by legendary director Cecil B. DeMille, the Canadian-born Moore made the transition to assistant and then second unit director on such films as *When Worlds Collide* (uncredited), *The War of the Worlds, The Ten Commandments, Visit to a Small Planet, The Man Who Would Be King, Damnation Alley, Raiders of the Lost Ark, Never Say Never Again, Indiana Jones and the Temple of Doom, Willow, Indiana Jones and the Last Crusade, Ghostbusters II, Toy Soldiers, Teenage Mutant Ninja Turtles III, 101 Dalmations* (1996), *Flubber* (1997) and *102 Dalmations*.

Italian screenwriter and director **Damiano Damiani** died on March 7, aged ninety. He worked in various genres, but is best remembered for the grim sequel *Amityville 2: The Possession* (1982).

British animation director **Jack Stokes** (John Albert Stokes) died on March 20, aged ninety-two. Best known for his work on *Yellow Submarine* (1968), his other credits include a short of *The Little Mermaid* (1974), *The Water Babies* (1978), *Heavy Metal* (the "Den" segment), *The Princess and the Goblin, Prince Valiant* (1997), *Christmas Carol: The Movie* (2001) and the short-lived animated TV series *The Beatles* (1966–67).

Prolific Spanish writer, producer, actor and director **Jesús Franco** [Manera] (aka "Jess Franco"/"Jess Franck"/"J, Frank Manera"/"Franco Manera"/"Frank Hollman"/"Clifford Brown"/"J.P. Johnson"/"A.M. Frank" etc.) died of complications from a stroke on April 2, aged eighty-two. Hired by

Orson Welles as second unit director on *Chimes at Midnight* (1965), Franco's more than 200 films, often under various pseudonyms, are of variable quality and include *The Blood of Fu Manchu*, *The Castle of Fu Manchu*, *The Bloody Judge*, *Eugenie . . . the Story of Her Journey Into Perversion* and *Count Dracula* (all with Christopher Lee), *The Awful Dr. Orlof* and its sequels, *The Diabolical Dr. Z*, *Vampyros lesbos*, *Dracula contra Frankenstein*, *La fille de Dracula*, *The Erotic Rites of Frankenstein*, *A Virgin Among the Living Dead*, *Female Vampire*, *Jack the Ripper* (1976), *El sádico de Notre-Dame*, *Faceless* and *Zombie 5*. From the mid-1990s onwards, he began churning out shot-on video productions, such as *Lust for Frankenstein* and *Killer Barbys vs. Dracula*, which made his earlier work look like masterpieces. He was married to his long-time partner and muse, actress Lina Romay, from 2008 until her death four years later.

Jane Henson (Jane Anne Nebel), who is credited with co-creating The Muppets with her husband, puppeteer Jim Henson, died of cancer on April 3, aged seventy-eight.

Sixty-seven-year-old Spanish writer, producer and director [Josep Joan] **Bigas Luna,** best known for the fantasy *Reborn* and the horror film *Anguish*, died on April 6.

American special-effects artist **Marcel Vercoutere**, who made Linda Blair's head turn around in *The Exorcist* (1973), died of complications from dementia on April 13, aged eighty-seven.

American TV comedy writer, producer and director **Jack Shea** (John Francis Shea, Jr) died on April 28 of complications from Alzheimer's disease, aged eighty-four. A former President of the Directors Guild of America (1997–2002), Shea's credits include episodes of *The Charmings* and *Shades of LA*, along with the cult 1969 SF movie adaptation of Keith Laumer's *The Monitors* and the Disney TV movie *The Strange Monster of Strawberry Cove*.

Legendary American-born stop-motion pioneer **Ray Harryhausen** (Raymond Frederick Harryhausen) died in London on May 7, aged ninety-two. A life-long friend of Ray Bradbury and Forrest J. Ackerman, after seeing *King*

Kong (1933) at the age of thirteen, Harryhausen was inspired to start making his own amateur short films. He finally got his break in movies assisting his idol Willis H. O'Brien in producing the Oscar-winning special effects for *Mighty Joe Young* (1949). Harryhausen then branched out on his own, creating the "Dynamation" visual effects for (and sometimes also producing) *The Beast from 20,000 Fathoms*, *It Came from Beneath the Sea*, *Earth vs. the Flying Saucers*, *The Animal World*, *20 Million Miles to Earth*, *The 7th Voyage of Sinbad*, *The 3 Worlds of Gulliver*, *Mysterious Island*, *Jason and the Argonauts*, *First Men in the Moon*, Hammer's *One Million B.C.*, *The Valley of Gwangi*, *The Golden Voyage of Sinbad*, *Sinbad and the Eye of the Tiger* and *Clash of the Titans* (1981). He also made a number of cameo appearances in such films as *Spies Like Us*, *Beverly Hills Cop III*, *Mighty Joe* and *Burke and Hare*. Starting with *Film Fantasy Scrapbook* in 1972, he published a number of volumes about his own work, while Giles Penso's feature documentary, *Ray Harryhausen Special Effects Titan* (2011), celebrated his career. Harryhausen received a Hugo Award in 1959 for *The 7th Voyage of Sinbad*, he was the recipient of the special Gordon E. Sawyer Award for Lifetime Achievement at the Academy Awards in 1992, and he won the British Fantasy Society's Karl Edward Wagner Special Award in 2008. His wife, Diana [Livingstone Bruce], died just five months after her husband.

Former British character actor turned writer, producer and director **Bryan Forbes** CBE (John Theobold Clarke), died on May 8, following a long illness. He was eighty-six. After appearing in such films as *Satellite in the Sky* and Hammer's *Quatermass 2* (aka *Enemy from Space*), he moved behind the camera for *Seance on a Wet Afternoon*, *The Stepford Wives* (1975) and *The Slipper and the Rose: The Story of Cinderella*. From 1969–71 he was Head of Production at EMI-MGM Elstree Film Studios. Forbes also worked (uncredited) on the script for *The Man Who Haunted Himself* (1970) starring Roger Moore, and he wrote the shooting script for the unproduced Hammer film *Nessie*, based on a screenplay by Christopher Wicking and John Starr. He was married to actresses Constance Smith from 1951–55 and Nanette Newman from 1955 until his death.

Filipino writer, producer and director **Eddie Romero** (Edgar Sinco Romero, aka "Edgar F. Romero"/"Enrique Moreno") died on May 28 of cardiopulmonary arrest, brought on by complications from prostate cancer and a blood clot on the brain. He was eighty-eight. A well-respected film-maker in his own country, Romero began his career in the late 1940s, but is best known for such exploitation movies of the 1960s and '70s as the "Blood Island" trilogy (*Mad Doctor of Blood Island*, *Brides of Blood* and *Beast of the Yellow Night*), *Blood Devils*, *The Twilight People*, *Beyond Atlantis* and *The Woman Hunt* (yet another version of Richard Connell's story "The Most Dangerous Game"). His producing credits also include *Terror is a Man* and *Apocalypse Now*.

Florida film-maker **Don Barton** (Donald E. Barton), who wrote, produced and directed the cult 1971 horror film *Zaat* (aka *The Blood Waters of Dr. Z*), about a walking catfish monster, died of chronic pulmonary disease on June 8, aged eighty-three.

Prolific British TV and film director **Jim Goddard** (James Dudley Goddard) died on June 17, aged seventy-seven. After starting out as a production designer on such shows as *Out of This World*, *City Beneath the Sea* (1962), *Secret Beneath the Sea* and *The Avengers*, he made the move to directing in the mid-1960s. His numerous credits include episodes of *The Guardians*, *The Rivals of Sherlock Holmes* and *Space Precinct*, along with the 1987 TV movie of Steven Berkoff's adaptation of Kafka's *Metamorphosis* and the widely derided *Shanghai Surprise* starring then-married couple Sean Penn and Madonna.

Pioneering British animator **John David Wilson**, who directed the cartoon feature *Shinbone Alley* (1971), died of an infection on June 20, aged ninety-three. Wilson began his career in the art department at Pinewood Studios, working on such films as *The Thief of Bagdad* (1940), before he moved on to animation, creating the cartoon credits for *Irma La Douce* and *Grease*. He was also involved with Disney's *Peter Pan* and *Lady & the Tramp*, UPA's *The Tell-Tale Heart*, *The Flintstones*, *Journey to the Stars* (a fifteen-minute short seen by seven million visitors to the World's Fair in Seattle), *The Sonny and Cher Comedy Hour*, *Stanley the Ugly Duckling*, *Spacecats* and *Attack of the Killer Tomatoes* (1991). A planned animated film of *Peer Gynt* never got beyond the design and storyboard stage.

British stage designer **Mark Fisher** OBE died on June 25, aged sixty-six. He designed the sets for productions of *The Rocky Horror Show* and the Queen musical *We Will Rock You*, as well as the 1974 SF movie *Zardoz*.

British assistant director and production manager **David C. Anderson** died of lung cancer on August 4, aged seventy-two. He worked as an assistant director on the first two Bond films *Dr. No* and *From Russia with Love*, *Invasion USA*, *The Texas Chainsaw Massacre 2*, *Miracle Mile*, *Brenda Starr*, *Switch*, *20,000 Leagues Under the Sea* (1997) and episodes of TV's *Tales from the Crypt*. As a production manager, Anderson's credits include *The Shuttered Room* (loosely based on the story by H. P. Lovecraft and August Derleth), *Theatre of Blood* (starring Vincent Price), *The Man Who Would Be King* (based on the story by Rudyard Kipling), *Flash Gordon* (1980) and *Strange Behaviour* (aka *Dead Kids*).

Prolific Italian producer, writer and director **Luciano Martino** (aka "Martin Hardy"/"Frank Cook") died of a pulmonary oedema in Kenya, Africa, on August 14. He was seventy-nine. The brother of director Sergio Martino, he produced (sometimes uncredited) *The Demon* (1963), *Giants of Rome*, *Next!*, *The Case of the Scorpion's Tale*, *All the Colors of the Dark*, *The Case of the Bloody Iris*, *Island of Mutations* (aka *Screamers*), *The Great Alligator*, *Eaten Alive!*, *Cannibal Ferox*, *Murder in an Etruscan Cemetery* (aka *Scorpion with Two Tails*), *Ironmaster*, *A Blade in the Dark*, *2019: After the Fall of New York*, *Miami Golem*, *Blastfighter* and *Hands of Steel*. As a writer, Martino worked on *The Colossus of Rhodes*, *Perseus Against the Monsters*, Mario Bava's *The Whip and the Body*, *Ursus in the Land of Fire*, *Hercules and the Masked Rider*, *Maciste contro I Mongoli*, *Hercules Against the Barbarians*, *Hercules and the Tyrants of Babylon*, *Goliath and the Conquest of Damascus* and *The Sweet Body of Deborah*, amongst many other titles. He was married to actress Wandisa Guida.

Oscar-winning British set decorator **Stephenie McMillan** (Stephenie Lesley Gardner), who worked on all eight *Harry Potter* films, died of ovarian cancer on August 19, aged seventy-one. Her other credits include *Santa Claus: The Movie*, *The Secret Garden* (1993), *Shadowlands*, *Mary Reilly*, *The Avengers* (1998) and *Chocolat*.

American director **Ted Post** died on August 20, aged ninety-five. He began his career in TV in the early 1950s, and his movie credits include *Beneath the Planet of the Apes*, *Night Slaves*, *Dr. Crook's Garden*, *Five Desperate Women*, *The Baby* and *Nightkill*, along with episodes of *Thriller*, *Twilight Zone*, *Ark II*, *Future Cop* and *Beyond Westworld*.

Veteran British cinematographer **Gilbert Taylor** (aka "Gil Taylor") died on August 23, aged ninety-nine. After starting out in 1929 as a camera assistant at Gainsborough Studios in London, his credits include *Seven Days to Noon*, *Dr. Strangelove or: How I Learned to Stop Worrying and Love the Bomb*, *The Bedford Incident*, *Cul-de-sac*, *Theatre of Death* (aka *Blood Fiend*), *Macbeth*, Alfred Hitchcock's *Frenzy*, *The Omen* (1976), *Star Wars*, *Dracula* (1979), *Flash Gordon* (1980), *Venom* and *Voyage of the Rock Aliens*. Taylor contributed additional photography to *2001: A Space Odyssey* and *Damien: Omen II*, and he also worked on episodes of TV's *The Avengers* and *Randall and Hopkirk (Deceased)*.

Globe-trotting British TV presenter, writer and producer Sir **David** [Paradine] **Frost** died of a heart attack at sea, travelling between Britain and Portugal, on August 31. He was seventy-four. Frost executive produced the movie *The Slipper and the Rose: The Story of Cinderella* and the 2003 TV documentary *Bloodlines: The Dracula Family Tree*. He was also set to produce the Hammer film *Nessie*, which was announced but never made. Frost was married to actress Lynne Frederick from 1981–82.

Spanish writer and director **José Ramón Larraz** [Gil] (aka "J.R. Larrath"/"Joseph Larraz"/"Joseph Braunstein") died after a short illness on September 3, aged eighty-four. A former comic book writer/illustrator and fashion photographer, he is best known for his psycho-sexual horror films of the 1970s and '80s, often filmed in Britain. Larraz's credits include *Whirlpool*, *Deviation*, *La muerte incierta*, *Vampyres*, *Emma puertas oscuras*, *Symptoms*, *Scream . . . and Die!* (aka *The House That Vanished*), *Stigma*, *The National Mummy*, *Black Candles*, *Rest in Pieces*, *Edge of the Axe* and *Deadly Manor*. He was the subject of the 2011 documentary *On Vampyres and Other Symptoms*.

American TV movie director **William A. Graham** died of complications of pneumonia on September 12, aged eighty-seven. His credits include *Beyond the Bermuda Triangle* plus episodes of *Great Ghost Stories* (1961), *Batman*, *Otherworld*, *The X Files* and *Seven Days*.

American director and actor **Richard C.** (Caspar) **Sarafian** died of complications from pneumonia on September 18, aged 83. Best known for his 1971 existential road movie *Vanishing Point*, he also directed episodes of TV's *Twilight Zone*, *The Wild Wild West*, *Batman* (1966) and *The Girl from U.N.C.L.E.*, along with the troubled 1990 SF film *Solar Crisis* under the industry pseudonym "Alan Smithee". Sarafian provided the voice of a beaver in *Dr. Dolittle 2* (2001).

Hiroshi Yamauchi, who took Nintendo Company Ltd from a maker of playing cards to a global video-games giant, died from pneumonia on September 19, aged eighty-five. He was president of the company from 1949–2002 and was responsible for the development of the Game Boy and for hiring Super Mario Bros. designer Shigeru Miyamoto.

Veteran Hollywood producer **A. C. Lyles** (Andrew Craddock Lyles, Jr) died on September 27, aged ninety-five. A former publicist who was employed by Paramount

Pictures since 1928, he produced the 1972 horror film *Night of the Lepus* and during the 1960s made a string of low-budget Westerns giving work to old-time movie stars, including Lon Chaney Jr, Bruce Cabot, Jane Russell, John Agar, Richard Arlen, Yvonne De Carlo, Brian Donlevy, Kent Taylor, Terry Moore and others. Lyles was married to actress Martha Vickers from 1948–49.

Hugely influential Hammer Films producer and writer **Anthony** [Frank] **Hinds** died of Parkinson's disease on September 30, aged ninety-one. The son of co-founder William Hinds, he started working for the studio in 1946 and produced *Dick Barton Strikes Back, Dr. Morelle: The Case of the Missing Heiress, Man in Black, Room to Let, Stolen Face, The Quatermass Experiment* (aka *The Creeping Unknown*), *X: The Unknown, The Curse of Frankenstein, Quatermass 2* (aka *Enemy from Space*), *The Camp on Blood Island, Dracula* (aka *Horror of Dracula*), *The Revenge of Frankenstein, The Hound of the Baskervilles, The Stranglers of Bombay, The Brides of Dracula, The Curse of the Werewolf, The Phantom of the Opera, Paranoiac, The Damned* (aka *These Are the Damned*), *The Kiss of the Vampire* (aka *Kiss of Evil*), *The Old Dark House, The Evil of Frankenstein, Fanatic, The Lost Continent* and the TV series *Journey Into the Unknown*. Under the alias "John Elder", Tony Hinds worked on the screenplays for *The Brides of Dracula, The Curse of the Werewolf, Captain Clegg* (aka *Night Creatures*), *The Phantom of the Opera, The Kiss of the Vampire, The Evil of Frankenstein, Dracula Prince of Darkness, The Reptile, Rasputin the Mad Monk, The Mummy's Shroud, Frankenstein Created Woman, Dracula Has Risen from the Grave, Taste the Blood of Dracula, Scars of Dracula, Frankenstein and the Monster from Hell, Legend of the Werewolf, The Ghoul* (1975), *The Masks of Death* and an episode of TV's *Hammer House of Horror*. He resigned from the Hammer Board in 1968, when Joan Harrison was brought in above him to oversee the TV series *Journey Into the Unknown*.

Hilton A. Green, assistant director on *Alfred Hitchcock Presents* and *Psycho*, died on October 2, aged eighty-four. Green also produced the sequels *Psycho II*, *Psycho III* and *Psycho IV: The Beginning*, along with *Encino Man*.

Emmy Award-winning TV animation producer and voice actor **Lou** (Louis) **Scheimer,** who co-founded Filmation Studios in 1963, died of Parkinson's disease on October 17, aged eighty-four. Among the series he produced or executive produced are *The New Adventures of Superman*, *The Superman/Aquaman Hour of Adventure*, *Journey to the Centre of the Earth* (1967), *The Batman/Superman Hour*, *Fantastic Voyage* (1968), *Aquaman*, *Sabrina and the Groovie Goolies*, *Sabrina the Teenage Witch* (1971), *My Favorite Martians*, *Star Trek* (1973–74), *The Ghost Busters*, *Shazam!*, *Isis*, *Ark II*, *The New Adventures of Batman*, *Sabrina Super Witch*, *Space Sentinels*, *Space Academy*, *The New Archie/Sabrina Hour*, *The Freedom Force*, *Tarzan and the Super 7*, *Tarzan Lord of the Jungle*, *Jason of Star Command*, *Flash Gordon* (1979–80), *The Tarzan/Lone Ranger/Zorro Adventure Hour*, *The Kid Super Power Hour with Shazam!*, *Hero High*, *Blackstar*, *He-Man and the Masters of the Universe*, *She-Ra: Princess of Power*, *Ghostbusters* and *BraveStarr*, along with the movies *Journey Back to Oz*, *The Fat Albert Halloween Special*, *A Snow White Christmas*, *Flash Gordon: The Greatest Adventure of All*, *Gilligan's Planet*, *Mighty Mouse in the Great Space Chase*, *The Secret of the Sword*, *He-Man and She-Ra: A Christmas Special*, *Pinocchio and the Emperor of the Night*, *BraveStarr: The Legend* and *Happily Ever After*.

British producer and director **Antonia Bird,** who directed the cannibal horror film *Ravenous* (1999), died of anaplastic thyroid cancer on October 24, aged sixty-two.

Hal [Brett] **Needham,** the highest-paid stuntman in the world who later became a successful movie director, died of cancer on October 25, aged eighty-two. Best known for such comedy action films as *Smokey and the Bandit* and *Cannonball Run*, both starring Burt Reynolds, he also directed the TV movie *Death Car on the Freeway* and the SF adventure *Megaforce*. As a stuntman/actor, Needham appeared in *Our Man Flint*, *Escape*, *The Night Stalker* and episodes of *The Wild Wild West*, *Star Trek*, *The Immortal* and *Fantasy Island*. During his career, he broke fifty-six bones, his back twice, punctured a lung and lost a few teeth. Needham was also the first person to test a car airbag.

American choreographer **Marc Breaux**, who worked (with his wife Dee Dee Wood) on Disney's *Mary Poppins*, *Chitty Chitty Bang Bang*, *The Slipper and the Rose: The Story of Cinderella* and *The Paul Lynde Halloween Special*, died in an assisted-living facility on November 19, aged eighty-nine.

British film and TV director **Alan Bridges** died on December 7, aged eighty-six. He began his career at the BBC in the 1960s, directing episodes of *Suspense*, *Out of the Unknown* and many other series. He also directed the low budget SF film *Invasion* (1966), while his 1987 production of Stephen King's *Apt Pupil* was shut down after ten weeks of shooting due to a lack of funds.

French screenwriter and New Wave director **Édouard Molinaro** died the same day, aged eighty-five. In 1976 he made the comedy *Dracula and Son* starring Christopher Lee and Molinaro's wife, actress Marie-Hélène Breillat. His other credits include the TV movie *Tombé du nid* (1999).

The death was announced in December of British animator **Richard Taylor**, who created the *Charley Says* series of public information films featuring the voice of Kenny Everett. He was eighty-four. In the 1980s Taylor also directed the BBC language-teaching series *Muzzy in Gondoland* and *Muzzy Comes Back*, featuring the eponymous big green alien voiced by Jack May. His *Encyclopedia of Animation Techniques* was published in 1994.

USEFUL ADDRESSES

THE FOLLOWING LISTING of organizations, publications, dealers and individuals is designed to present readers and authors with further avenues to explore. Although I can personally recommend many of those listed on the following pages, neither the publisher nor myself can take any responsibility for the services they offer. Please also note that the information below is only a guide and is subject to change without notice.

—The Editor

ORGANIZATIONS

The Australian Horror Writers Association (*www.australianhorror.com*) is a non-profit organization that was formed in 2005 as a way of providing a unified voice and a sense of community for Australian writers of dark fiction, while helping the development and evolution of this genre within Australia. They also publish an excellent magazine, *Midnight Echo*, and offer a mentor programme, critique group and short story competitions. Email: *ahwa@australianhorror.com*

The British Fantasy Society (*www.britishfantasysociety.org/www.fantasycon.co.uk*) was founded in 1971 and publishes the *BFS Journal*, featuring articles, interviews and fiction, along with occasional special books only available to members of the Society. The BFS also enjoys a lively online community – there is an email newsfeed, a Facebook community, a forum with numerous links, and a CyberStore selling various publications. FantasyCon is one of the UK's friendliest conventions and there are social gatherings and meet-the-author events organized around Britain. For yearly membership details, email: *secretary@britishfantasysociety. org*

The Friends of Arthur Machen (*www.arthurmachen.org. uk*) is a literary society whose objectives include encouraging a wider recognition of Machen's work and providing a focus for critical debate. Members get a hardcover journal, *Faunus*, twice a year, and also the informative newsletter *Machenalia*. For membership details, contact Jon Preece, 9 Ridgeway Drive, Newport, South Wales NP20 5AR, UK (*machenfoam@yahoo.co.uk*).

The Friends of the Merril Collection (*www.friendsofmerril.org/*) is a volunteer organization that provides support and assistance to the largest public collection of science fiction, fantasy and horror books in North America. Details about annual membership and donations are available from the website or by contacting The Friends of the Merril Collection, c/o Lillian H. Smith Branch, Toronto Public Library, 239 College Street, 3rd Floor, Toronto, Ontario M5T 1R5, Canada. Email: *ltoolis@tpl.toronto.on.ca*

The Horror Writers Association (*www.horror.org*) is a worldwide organization of writers and publishing professionals dedicated to promoting the interests of writers of Horror and Dark Fantasy. It was formed in the early 1980s. Interested individuals may apply for Active, Affiliate or Associate membership. Active membership is limited to professional writers. HWA publishes a monthly online *Newsletter*, and sponsors the annual Bram Stoker Awards.

World Fantasy Convention (*www.worldfantasy.org*) is an annual convention held in a different (usually American) city each year, oriented particularly towards serious readers and genre professionals.

World Horror Convention (*www.worldhorrorconvention. com*) is a smaller, more relaxed, event. It is aimed specifically at horror fans and professionals, and held in a different city (usually American) each year.

SELECTED SMALL PRESS PUBLISHERS

The Alchemy Press (*www.alchemypress.co.uk*), Cheadle, Staffordshire ST10 1PF, UK.

Arctic Mage Press, 222 Parkview Hill Crescent, Toronto, ON M4B 1R8, Canada.

Bad Moon Books/Eclipse (*www.badmoonbooks.com*), 1854 W. Chateau Avenue, Anaheim, CA 92804-4527, USA.

BearManor Media (*www.bearmanormedia.com*), PO Box 1129, Duncan, OK 73534-1129, USA.

Black Dog Books (*www.blackdogbooks.net*), 1115 Pine Meadows Ct., Normal, IL 61761-5432, USA. Email: *info@ blackdogbooks.net*

The Borgo Press (*www.wildsidebooks.com*).

Cemetery Dance Publications (*www.cemeterydance. com*), 132-B Industry Lane, Unit #7, Forest Hill, MD 21050, USA. Email: *info@cemeterydance.com*

Chaosium, Inc (*www.chaosium.com*).

ChiZine Publications (*www.chizinepub.com*). Email: *info@chizinepub.com*

Chômu Press (*www.chomupress.com*), 70 Hill Street, Richmond, Surrey TW9 1TW, UK. Email: *info@ chomupress.com*

Curiosity Quills Press (*curiosityquills.com*) PO Box 2540, Dulles, VA 20101, USA. Email: *info@curiosityquills. com*

Crystal Lake Publishing (*www.crystallakepub.com*).

Dark Moon Books (*www.darkmoonbooks.com*), 13039 Glen Ct., Chino Hills, CA 91709-1135, USA. Email: *eric. guignard@gmail.com*

Dark Renaissance Books (*www.darkrenaissance.com*), 315 Paige Court, Colusa, CA 95932, USA. Email: *darkrenbook@gmail.com*

Donald M. Grant, Publisher, Inc. (*www.grantbooks. com*), 19 Surrey Lane, PO Box 187, Hampton Falls, NH 03844, USA.

DreamHaven Books (*www.dreamhavenbooks.com*), 2301 East 38th Street, Minneapolis, MN 55406, USA.

Earthling Publications (*www.earthlingpub.com*), PO Box 413, Northborough, MA 01532, USA. Email: *earthlingpub@ yahoo.com*

Edge Science Fiction and Fantasy Publishing/Hades Publications, Inc. (*www.edgewebsite.com*), PO Box 1714, Calgary, Alberta T2P 2L7, Canada. Email: *publisher@hadespublications.com*

Edgeworks Abbey (*www.harlanellisonbooks.com*).

Ex Hubris Imprints (*www.pstdarkness.wordpress.com*). Email: *postscripts2darkness@gmail.com*

Exile Editions Ltd. (*www.ExileEditions.com*), 144483 Southgate Road 14 – GD, Holstein, Ontario, N0G 2A0, Canada.

FableCroft (*www.fablecroft.com.au*).

Fedogan & Bremer Publishing (*www.fedoganandbremer. com*), 3918 Chicago Street, Nampa, Idaho 83686, USA.

47North, PO Box 400818, Las Vegas, NV 89140, USA.

Gauntlet Publications (*www.gauntletpress.com*), 5307 Arroyo Street, Colorado Springs, CO 80922, USA. Email: *info@gauntletpress.com*

Gray Friar Press (*www.grayfriarpress.com*), 9 Abbey Terrace, Whitby, North Yorkshire Y021 3HQ, UK. Email: *gary.fry@virgin.net*

Hippocampus Press (*www.hippocampuspress.com*), PO Box 641, New York, NY 10156, USA. Email: *info@hippocampuspress.com*

IDW Publishing (*www.idwpublishing.com*), 5080 Santa Fe Street, San Diego, CA 92109, USA.

Immanion Press (*www.immanion-press.com*), 8 Rowley Grove, Stafford ST17 9BJ, UK. Email: *info@aimmanion-press. com*

KnightWatch Press/Fringeworks (*www.fringeworks. co.uk*).

Megazanthus Press (*www.nemonymous.com*).

McFarland & Company, Inc., Publishers (*www.mcfarlandpub.com*), Box 611, Jefferson, NC 28640, USA.

Miskatonic River Press (*www.miskatonicriverpress.com*), 944 Reynolds Road, Suite 188, Lakeland, Florida 33801, USA. Email: *keeper@miskatonicriverpress.com*

Mortbury Press (*www.mortburypress.webs.com*), Shiloh, Nantglas, Llandrindod Wells, Powys LD1 6PD, UK. Email: *mortburypress@yahoo.com*

NewCon Press (*www.newconpress.co.uk*).

Noose and Gibbet Publishing/Karōshi Books (*www.nooseandgibbetpublishing.com*). Email: *info@nooseandgibbetpublishing.com*

Nightjar Press (*www.nightjarpress.weebly.com*), 63 Ballbrook Court, Wilmslow Road, Manchester M20 3GT, UK.

Night Shade Books (*www.nightshadebooks.com*), 1661 Tennessee Street, #3H, San Francisco, CA 94107, USA. Email: *night@nightshadebooks.com*

Overlook Connection Press (*www.overlookconnection.com*), PO Box 1934, Hiram, Georgia 30141, USA. Email: *overlookcn@aol.com*

Pendragon Press (*www.pendragonpress.net*), PO Box 12, Maesteg, South Wales, CF34 0XG, UK.

Prime Books (*www.prime-books.com*), PO Box 83464, Gaithersburg, MD 20883, USA. Email: *prime@prime-books.com*

PS Publishing Ltd/Drugstore Indian Press/PS ArtBooks Ltd (*www.pspublishing.co.uk*), Grosvenor House, 1 New Road, Hornsea HU18 1PG, UK. Email: *editor@pspublishing.co.uk*

Salt Publishing (*www.saltpublishing.com*), 12 Norwich Road, Cromer, Norfolk NR27 0AX, UK.

Sarob Press (*sarobpress.blogspot.com*), La Blinière, 53250, Neuilly-le-Vendin, France.

Savoy (*www.savoy.abel.co.uk*), 456 Wilmslow Road, Withington, Manchester M20 3BG, UK. Email: *office@savoy.abel.co.uk*

Shadow Publishing (*www.shadowpublishing.webeasysite.*

co.uk/), 194 Station Road, Kings Heath, Birmingham B14 7TE, UK. Email: *david.sutton986@btinternet.com*

Small Beer Press (*www.weightlessbooks.com*), 150 Pleasant Street #306, Easthampton, MA 01027, USA. Email: *info@smallbeerpress*

Spectral Press (*www.spectralpress.wordpress.com*), 5 Serjeants Green, Neath Hill, Milton Keynes, Bucks MK14 6HA, UK. Email: *spectralpress@gmail.com*

Spectre Press, 56 Mickle Hill, Sandhurst, Berkshire GU47 8QU, UK. Email: *jon.harvey@talktalk.net*

Subterranean Press (*www.subterraneanpress.com*), PO Box 190106, Burton, MI 48519, USA. Email: *subpress@gmail.com*

Tachyon Publications (*www.tachyonpublications.com*), 1459 18th Street #139, San Francisco, CA 94107, USA. Email: *tachyon@tachyonpublications.com*

Tartarus Press (*www.tartaruspress.com*), Coverley House, Carlton-in-Coverdale, Leyburn, North Yorkshire DL8 4AY, UK. Email: *tartarus@pavilion.co.uk*

Ticonderoga Publications (*www.ticonderogapublications.com*), PO Box 29, Greenwood, Western Australia 6924.

Valencourt Books (*www.valancourtbooks.com*).

SELECTED MAGAZINES

Albedo One (*www.albedo1.com*) is Ireland's magazine of science fiction, fantasy and horror. The editorial address is Albedo One, 2 Post Road, Lusk, Co. Dublin, Ireland. Email: *bobn@yellowbrickroad.ie*

Ansible is a highly entertaining monthly SF and fantasy newsletter/gossip column edited by David Langford. It is available free electronically by sending an email to: *ansible-request@dcs.gla.ac.uk* with a subject line reading "subscribe", or you can receive the print version by sending a stamped and addressed envelope to Ansible, 94 London Road, Reading, Berks RG1 5AU, UK. Back issues, links and book lists are also available online.

Black Static (*www.ttapress.com*) is the UK's premier

horror fiction magazine, produced bi-monthly by the publishers of *Interzone*. Six- and twelve-issue subscriptions are available, along with a new lifetime subscription, from TTA Press, 5 Martins Lane, Witcham, Ely, Cambs CB6 2LB, UK, or from the secure TTA website. Email: *blackstatic@ttapress.com*

Dark Discoveries (*www.darkdiscoveries.com*) sets out to unsettle, edify and involve with fiction, interviews and non-fiction and is published irregularly. JournalStone Publications, 199 State Street, San Mateo, CA 94401, USA. Email: *christopherpayne@journelstone.com*

The Ghosts & Scholars M. R. James Newsletter (*www.pardoes.info/roanddarroll/GS.html*) is a scholarly journal published roughly twice a year. It is dedicated to the classic ghost story and, as the title implies, to M. R. James in particular. Two-issue subscriptions are available from Haunted Library Publications, c/o Flat One, 36 Hamilton Street, Hoole, Chester CH2 3JQ, UK. Email: *pardos@globalnet.co.uk*

Horror Society (*www.horrorsociety.com*).

The Horror Zine (*www.thehorrorzine.com*) is a monthly online magazine edited by Jeani Rector that features fiction, poetry, interviews and reviews.

Lady Churchill's Rosebud Wristlet (*www.smallbeerpress.com/lcrw*), Small Beer Press, 150 Pleasant Street, Easthampton, MA 01027, USA. Email: *smallbeerpress@gmail.com*

Locus (*www.locusmag.com*) is the monthly newspaper of the SF/fantasy/horror field. Contact: Locus Publications, PO Box 13305, Oakland, CA 94661, USA. Subscription information with other rates and order forms are also available on the website. Email: *locus@locusmag.com*. You can also now subscribe to a digital edition at: *www.weightlessbooks.com/genre/nonfiction/locus-12-month-subscription*

Locus Online (*www.locusmag.com/news*) is an excellent online source for the latest news and reviews.

The Magazine of Fantasy & Science Fiction (*www.fandsf.com*) has been publishing some of the best imaginative fiction for sixty-five years. Edited by Gordon Van Gelder, and now published bi-monthly, single copies or an annual subscription are available by US cheques or credit card from: Fantasy & Science Fiction, PO Box 3447, Hoboken, NJ 07030, USA, or you can subscribe via the website.

Morpheus Tales (*www.morpheustales.com*) is billed as "the UK's darkest and most controversial fiction magazine" with quarterly print issues and reviews appearing on the website and myspace versions (*www.myspace.com/morpheustales*).

[Nameless]: A Biannual Journal of the Macabre, Esoteric and Intellectual ... (*www.namelessmag.com*) features fiction, articles and reviews in an on-demand paperback format. Cycatrix Press, 16420 SE McGillivary Blvd., Ste. 103-1010, Vancouver, WA 98683, USA. Email: *info@namelessmag.com*

Nightmare: Horror & Dark Fantasy (*www.nightmare-magazine.com*) edited by John Joseph Adams is an excellent online site for fiction (both new and reprint), interviews and podcasts.

The Paperback Fanatic (*www.thepaperbackfanatic.com*) is an attractive full colour magazine devoted to sleaze and exploitation authors, artists and publishers. It is available by subscription only. Email: *thepaperbackfanatic@sky.com*

Rabbit Hole is a semi-regular newsletter about Harlan Ellison® that also offers exclusive signed books by the author. A subscription is available from The Harlan Ellison® Recording Collection, PO Box 55548, Sherman Oaks, CA 91413-0548, USA.

Rue Morgue (*www.rue-morgue.com*), is a glossy monthly magazine edited by Dave Alexander and subtitled "Horror in Culture & Entertainment". Each issue is packed with full colour features and reviews of new films, books, comics, music and game releases. Subscriptions are available from: Marrs Media Inc., 2926 Dundas Street West, Toronto, ON M6P 1Y8, Canada, or by credit card on the website. Email: *info@rue-morgue.com*. *Rue Morgue* also runs the Festival of Fear: Canadian National Horror Expo in Toronto. Every Friday you can log on to a new show at Rue Morgue Radio at *www.ruemorgueradio.com* and your horror shopping online source, The Rue Morgue Marketplace, is at *www. ruemorguemarketplace.com*

Shadows & Tall Trees (*www.undertowbooks.com*) is changing format to an annual trade paperback and ebook. Editor Michael Kelly is open to previously unpublished submissions of quiet, literary horror fiction. Email: *undertowbooks@gmail.com*

Space and Time: The Magazine of Fantasy, Horror, and Science Fiction (*www.spaceandtimemagazine.com*) is published at least twice a year. Single issues and subscriptions are available from the website or from: Space and Time Magazine, 458 Elizabeth Avenue #5348, Somerset, NJ 08873, USA.

Subterranean Press Magazine (*www.supterraneanpress. com/magazine*).

Supernatural Tales (*www.suptales.blogspot.com*) is a fiction magazine edited by David Longhorn, with subscriptions available via PayPal, cheques or non-UK cash. Supernatural Tales, 291 Eastbourne Avenue, Gateshead NE8 4NN, UK. Email: *davidlonghorn@hotmail.com*

Video WatcHDog (*www.videowatchdog.com*) describes itself as "The Perfectionist's Guide to Fantastic Video" and is published bi-monthly from PO Box 5283, Cincinnati, OH 45205-0283, USA. One year (six issues) subscriptions are available from: *orders@videowatchdog.com*

Weird Tales (*www.weirdtalesmagazine.com*) Nth Dimension Media Inc., 105 West 86th Street, Ste 307, New York, NY 10024-3412, USA.

DEALERS

Bookfellows/Mystery and Imagination Books (*www. mysteryandimagination.com*) is owned and operated by Malcolm and Christine Bell, who have been selling fine and rare books since 1975. This clean and neatly organized store includes SF/fantasy/horror/mystery, along with all other areas of popular literature. Many editions are signed, and catalogues are issued regularly. Credit cards accepted. Open seven days a week at 238 N. Brand Blvd., Glendale, California 91203, USA. Tel: (818) 545-0206. Fax: (818) 545-0094. Email: *bookfellows@ gowebway.com*

Borderlands Books (*www.borderlands-books.com*) is a nicely designed store with friendly staff and an impressive stock of new and used books from both sides of the Atlantic. 866 Valencia Street (at 19th), San Francisco, CA 94110, USA. Tel: (415) 824-8203 or (888) 893-4008 (toll free in the US). Credit cards accepted. Worldwide shipping. Email: *office@borderlands-books.com*

Cold Tonnage Books (*www.coldtonnage.com*) offers excellent mail-order new and used SF/fantasy/horror, art, reference, limited editions etc. Write to: Andy & Angela Richards, Cold Tonnage Books, 22 Kings Lane, Windlesham, Surrey GU20 6JQ, UK. Credit cards accepted. Tel: +44 (0)1276-475388. Email: *andy@coldtonnage.com*

Richard Dalby issues an annual Christmas catalogue of used Ghost Stories and other supernatural volumes at very reasonable prices. Write to: Richard Dalby, 4 Westbourne Park, Scarborough, North Yorkshire Y012 4AT. Tel: +44 (0)1723 377049.

Dark Delicacies (*www.darkdel.com*) is a Burbank, California, store specializing in horror books, toys, vampire merchandise and signings. They also do mail order and run money-saving book club and membership discount deals. 3512 W. Magnolia Blvd, Burbank, CA 91505, USA. Tel: (818) 556-6660. Credit cards accepted. Email: *darkdel@ darkdel.com*

DreamHaven Books & Comics (*www.dreamhavenbooks. com*) became an online and mail-order outlet only in early 2012, offering new and used SF/fantasy/horror/art and illustrated etc. with regular catalogues (both print and email). Credit cards accepted. Tel: (612) 823-6070. Email: *dream@ dreamhavenbooks.com*

Fantastic Literature (*www.fantasticliterature.com*) mail order offers the UK's biggest online out-of-print SF/fantasy/horror genre bookshop. Fanzines, pulps and vintage paperbacks as well. Write to: Simon and Laraine Gosden, Fantastic Literature, 35 The Ramparts, Rayleigh, Essex SS6 8PY, UK. Credit cards and Pay Pal accepted. Tel/Fax: +44 (0)1268-747564. Email: *simon@fantasticliterature.com*

Ferret Fantasy, 27 Beechcroft Road, Upper Tooting, London SW17 7BX, UK. Email: *george_locke@hotmail. com*. Tel: +44 (0)208-767-0029.

Horrorbles (*www.horrobles.com*), 6731 West Roosevelt Road, Berwyn, IL 60402, USA. Small, friendly Chicago store selling horror and sci-fi toys, memorabilia and magazines that has monthly specials and in-store signings. Specializes in exclusive "Basil Gogos" and "Svengoolie" items. Tel: (708) 484-7370. Email: *store@horrorbles.com*

Kayo Books (*www.kayobooks.com*) is a bright, clean treasure trove of used SF/fantasy/horror/mystery/pulps spread over two floors. Titles are stacked alphabetically by subject, and there are many bargains to be had. Credit cards accepted. Visit the store (Wednesday–Saturday, 11:00a.m. to 6:00p.m.) at 814 Post Street, San Francisco, CA 94109, USA or order off their website. Tel: (415) 749 0554. Email: *kayo@kayobooks.com*

Iliad Bookshop (*www.iliadbooks.com*), 5400 Cahuenga Blvd., North Hollywood, CA 91601, USA. General used bookstore that has a very impressive genre section, reasonable prices and knowledgeable staff. They have recently expanded their fiction section into an adjacent building. Tel: (818) 509-2665.

Porcupine Books offers regular catalogues and extensive mail-order lists of used fantasy/horror/SF titles via email *brian@porcupine.demon.co.uk* or write to: 37 Coventry Road, Ilford, Essex IG1 4QR, UK. Tel: +44 (0)20 8554-3799.

Reel Art Collectibles (*www.reelart.biz*), 6727 W. Stanley, Berwyn, Illinois 60402, USA. Nicely designed Chicago store selling movie material, classic comics, vintage toys and rare books. They also host celebrity signings and have regular warehouse sales. Tel: 1-708-288-7378. Facebook: *Reel Art, Inc.*

Kirk Ruebotham (*www.biblio.com/bookstore/kirk-ruebotham-bookseller-runcorn-cheshire*) is a mail-order only dealer, who specializes in mainly out-of-print and second-hand horror/SF/fantasy/crime fiction and related non-fiction at very good prices, with regular catalogues. Write to: 16 Beaconsfield Road, Runcorn, Cheshire WA7 4BX, UK. Tel: +44 (0)1928-560540. Email: *kirk.ruebotham@ntlworld.com*

The Talking Dead is run by Bob and Julie Wardzinski and offers reasonably priced paperbacks, rare pulps and hardcovers, with catalogues issued *very* occasionally. They accept wants lists and are also the exclusive supplier of back issues of *Interzone*. Credit cards accepted. Contact them at: 12 Rosamund Avenue, Merley, Wimborne, Dorset BH21 1TE, UK. Tel: +44 (0)1202-849212 (9:00a.m.–9:00p.m.). Email: *books@thetalkingdead.fsnet.co.uk*

Ygor's Books specialises in out-of-print science fiction, fantasy and horror titles, including British, signed, speciality press and limited editions. They also buy books, letters and original art in these fields. Email: *ygorsbooks@gmail.com*

ONLINE

Cast Macabre (*www.castmacabre.org*) is the premium horror fiction podcast that is "bringing fear to your ears", offering a free horror short story every week.

Fantastic Fiction (*www.fantasticfiction.co.uk*) features more than 2,000 best-selling author biographies with all their latest books, covers and descriptions.

FEARnet (*www.fearnet.com*) is a digital cable channel dedicated to all things horror, including news, free movie downloads (sadly not available to those outside North America) and Mick Garris' online talk show *Post Mortem*.

Hellnotes (*www.hellnotes.com*) offers news and reviews of novels, collections, magazines, anthologies, non-fiction

works, and chapbooks. Materials for review should be sent
to editor and publisher David B. Silva, Hellnotes, 5135
Chapel View Court, North Las Vegas, NV 89031, USA.
Email: *news@hellnotes.com* or *dbsilva13@gmail.com*

The Irish Journal of Gothic and Horror Studies (*www.
irishgothichorrorjournal.homestead.com*) features a diverse
range of articles and reviews, along with a regular "Lost
Souls" feature focusing on overlooked individuals in the
genre.

The Monster Channel (*www.monsterchannel.tv*) bills
itself as "the first and only independent interactive horror
channel!" The 24/7 streaming channel includes first run
indie horror movies, retro VHS gore and hosts horror
classics.

Pseudopod (*www.pseudopod.org*), the premier horror
fiction podcast, continues to offer a free-to-download,
weekly reading of a new or classic horror fiction by a variety
of voices. The site remains dedicated to paying their authors
while providing readings for free and offering the widest
variety of audio horror fiction currently available on the net.

SF Site (*www.sfsite.com*) has been posted twice each
month since 1997. Presently, it publishes around thirty to
fifty reviews of SF, fantasy and horror from mass-market
publishers and some small press. They also maintain link
pages for Author and Fan Tribute Sites and other facets
including pages for Interviews, Fiction, Science Fact,
Bookstores, Small Press, Publishers, E-zines and Magazines,
Artists, Audio, Art Galleries, Newsgroups and Writers'
Resources. Periodically, they add features such as author
and publisher reading lists.

Vault of Evil (*www.vaultofevil.wordpress.com*) is a site
dedicated to celebrating the best in British horror with special
emphasis on UK anthologies (they seem to like this series a
bit better now). There is also a lively forum devoted to many
different themes at *www.vaultofevil.proboards.com*